Memoria del silencio

THE *Memory* OF SILENCE

Memoria del silencio

THE Memory OF SILENCE

UVA DE ARAGÓN
TRANSLATED BY JEFFREY C. BARNETT

Cubanabooks

Published in the United States of America by Cubanabooks.

400 W. 1st St., Dept. ILLC, California State University, Chico

Chico, California 95929-0825

Printed in the United States of America

Cover and text design: Kellen Livingston

Cover art: Humberto Calzado "A Painted Memory II"
Acrylic over photograph by Victoria Montoro Zamorano

Back cover photo of author: Alberto Romeu

Cubanabooks logo art: Krista Yamashita

Edited by Paula Sanmartín & Maria DiFranscesco

Editor In-Chief: Sara E. Cooper

First Edition

10 9 8 7 6 5 4 3 2 1

Library of Congress Control Number: 2014947367

ISBN: 978-0-9827860-4-8

CONTENTS / ÍNDICE

For Fernando, because he inspired me to write a novel.
For my sister Lucía, without whom I wouldn't have been able to write it.
For my mother, who only was able to read the first few chapters,
And for my daughters, who I hope will read to the end.

Uva de Aragón

To Hilda Bolet Dunn, whose passion for life was so large
it couldn't fit on one single Island.
She was my bridge to Cuba.

Jeffrey C. Barnett

ACKNOWLEDGEMENTS

To Gloria, Lisandro, Nara, Toni,
Armando, Patricia, Eloísa, Gemma,
Marta, Margarita, Álvaro,
"el gordo," Antonia, Mercy and Pepe,
for their valuable advice.
To Isabel, for all the copies that she made for me.
To those from whom I stole the tatters
of their lives in order to tell of them here.
And to my parents and grandparents
because they passed down to me
their love of Cuba and her literature.

Thanks to Sara E. Cooper and Cubanabooks,
and special thanks to Jeffrey C. Barnett,
translator, friend, and accomplice,
without whose understanding and dedication
to this novel, this new bilingual edition
would not be now a reality.

*To Humberto Calzado, for the use of his painting "A Painted Memory II,"
acrylic over photograph by Victoria Montoro Zamorano for the cover.*

AUTHOR'S NOTE

All words seem insufficient to express my gratitude to Jeffrey C. Barnett for his interest in my work and especially for his time, effort, dedication and love in the translation of my novel *The Memory of Silence*. He has done a masterful job. I also wish to thank Sara E. Cooper and Cubanabooks for their enthusiastic acceptance of the book for publication.

Recently, an adaption of the novel into a play was produced, under the direction of Virginia Aponte, at the Universidad Católica Andrés Bello in Caracas, Venezuela, with an astonishing positive reaction from the media, students and the general public. This experience made me realize that this Cuban story transcends national boundaries. It is a rewarding experience for an author to come face to face with the universal values of one´s work.

It is my hope that this bilingual edition will expand the novel´s reach, and that it will be read by many students and professors in the academic world, as well as others. If it contributes to a better understanding of the contemporary history of Cuba and its diaspora, as well as the sufferings of all the peoples separated by ideologies or displaced by wars and other conflicts, all my efforts in writing it will be more than compensated.

In addition to the original dedication, I wish to offer this new edition to all Cuban-Americans born in the United States or who came to this country very young, and prefer to read in English, their first language. This is the story of their parents and grandparents, and in many ways, also theirs. I especially wish to dedicate this book to my grandsons Zachary, Cristian, Brandon and Nikulas.

Uva de Aragón
Miami, April 10, 2014

TRANSLATOR'S FOREWORD

I came to know of Uva de Aragón in a rather ironic way. Although she has lived most of her adult life in Florida, it was not in the United States that I learned about her works but fittingly while on a trip to Cuba, where I came across the anthology *Estatuas de Sal* (Statues of Salt). Since the volume promised short stories by contemporary Cuban women writers, I logically assumed that De Aragón resided in Cuba. I was wrong, but at the moment I didn't realize the symbolic significance of my mistake. Later on it would become clear: here was a writer who no longer lived on the Island, and yet she wasn't perceived as an outsider. Instead, the anthology counted her among Cuba's contemporary writers. It presented her merely as a Cuban—not a Cuban-American and not an exile, and understandably so. De Aragón is a writer that defies our attempts to segregate Cubans and Cuban-Americans. As you read the volume you have in your hands right now, you will see why that's important to understand. I however wouldn't draw that conclusion for myself for some time. Instead, I read her contribution to the anthology— *"No puedo más"* ("I Can't Do This Any More")—and filed her work away.

Sometime later I was preparing a course on Cuban literature in translation when I came across another short story of hers, this time in English—"Not the Truth, Not a Lie."[1] I was immediately impressed by the dramatic quality of the story in which two young lovers—one black and one white, one poor and the other rich—are unable to fulfill their love due to the socio-political circumstances in which they live. Like a Cuban Romeo and Juliet, their love is more powerful than the constraints others have placed on them. Another story, "Roundtrip," made an interesting companion piece for my students and illustrated the uniqueness of the author's voice and mindset.[2] What became clear in

[1] *Cuba: A Traveler's Literary Companion,* Ann Louise Bardach, ed. (Berkeley: Whereabouts Press, 2002), 176–182.

[2] *Voice of the Turtle,* Peter Bush, ed. (New York: Grove Press, 1977), 209–215.

these particular stories is that De Aragón does not posit reconciliation as a mere ideological compromise or the defeat of one idea over another. Instead, her works lead us back to inevitable re-unification. Finally, when *Memoria del silencio* came out in 2002, I knew that her voice and message deserved a broader audience, and in fact it couldn't or shouldn't be limited to just one language. Translated here for the first time into English, then, *The Memory of Silence* joins her other translated shorter narrative pieces in the hope that her works will find a broader and well deserved readership.

From Process to Product: The Translator's Challenge

Translators have their favorite maxims to cope with the nature of our work. Günter Grass said, "Translation is that which transforms everything so that nothing changes." The fact is that the translator is faced with a dilemma of being faithful to the author's creation and at the same time creating a second work, one that is as lively and meaningful in its new reiteration as it was in the original. Paradoxically, a translation is a new original. At one and the same time, it both creates and re-creates. This explains why every translated work entails its own unique challenges.

In the case of *The Memory of Silence* I faced many challenges. First of all, there's the problem of deciphering vocabulary peculiar to Cuba. In these instances one cannot rely on dictionaries or even Cuban glossaries if the word is taken out of its cultural or historical context. For example, the word *manteca* means "lard" so a literal translation of the phrase "*Fidel, yo no me rindo por la manteca*" would erroneously yield "Fidel, I won't surrender for lard!"—a phrase that clearly requires some more explanation. Lard was one of the first items in 1963 to be rationed under the Cuban food distribution system, commonly known as the *Libreta de Abastecimiento* or "the Supplies booklet." As such, it arguably took on a symbolic notion as one of the first in a long list of items with an inflated value due to its limited supply. Simply put, lard was a prized commodity. Taking into account the historical context, then, I had to adjust the translation more appropriately to something along the lines of "Fidel, I won't give up for all the tea in China."

Likewise, I felt at times that it was better to leave the word in its original in cases where the author used commonly recognized Spanish words or instances in which the meaning was conveyed through the context. For example, the term of endearment "*mija*" sounds much more affectionate and natural than the stilted "my daughter." There are also cases where I left a term in its original and then added a phrase to imply its meaning. Rather than defining or transliterating what is meant by the Cuban notion of "*medianoches,*" for instance, I included the original but then added "...and other sandwiches" so that the reader could infer its meaning. There are more subtle examples of inference as well. When Menchu tells Lauri, "Calm dawn. You're jabbering away like you were Cachucha or something," I needed to explain who Cachucha was. In fact she (Manela Bustamente) was a zany actress who was well-known in the 1950s for her popular TV comedy *Cachucha y Ramón.* Rather than offering a footnote or other explanation, I decided it would be best to add to Lauri's response "I haven't thought about her *and that TV show* in years."

Regionalisms and culturally-bound vocabulary can be tricky in any work, but the translation of *The Memory of Silence* entailed even greater challenges than just word selection. First, unlike short stories, novels require the translator to maintain consistency and to be attentive to nuances that are interwoven throughout an extended narrative. That means that the translator must be consistent with one's own narrative voice and also keep in mind how different characters would naturally speak from one chapter to the next. In this case it was particularly difficult since the two twin sisters are presented in alternating chapters. To remedy this, I actually had to assign them a personality beyond the text and even associate them with real-life individuals to maintain fidelity to the ways they would naturally go about their individual speech habits.

Equally problematic is that in De Aragón's text there aren't just two narrators, rather there are multiple voices, sources, and perspectives. To clarify, in addition to the two narrative voices, the novel is a collage of clippings and excerpts from actual texts that exist outside the novel and that the two sisters have been saving for the other in a scrapbook of sorts. In fact, there are nearly eighty instances of interpolated texts, including lyrical works, such as poems by Nicolás Guillén, Raúl Rivero, Omar Torres, and Pura del Prado, and also folk ballads, songs, and even a lullaby and an aria. Quite the opposite in terms of tone, there are also newspaper articles and editorials from *Bohemia, El Nuevo Herald,* and *Granma* that required me to employ a style and vocabulary more appropriate of a journalist. (The passages from *The Washington Post, The Miami News,* and *Facts on File* are presented here not as my translations but in their original. As a secondary challenge, these passages had been translated into Spanish by the author for the original novel, and we had to search for the original texts in English for this translation.) And then there are the various speeches by Fidel Castro, with their singular cadence and ideological rhetoric, not to mention the difficult task of translating political slogans. In each case— the lyrical, journalistic, and ideological—I found that I had to adjust the tenor of my expression, the lexicon I could draw from, and the range and tone of my own voice. I found that some of my most rewarding moments in fact came from overcoming the challenges posed by the inclusion of a wide array of outside texts. In particular, I was pleased with my rendition of Nicolás Guillén's poem "Execution," which asks the English translator to convey sophistication and at the same time simplicity. The children's lullaby "Señora Santa Ana" also required careful rendering since it serves as a motif in the work. And finally, I feel that I was able to capture and convey in English the demeanor and rhythm of Castro's political speeches. In short, a text like *The Memory of Silence* required me to be various translators in one.

Two Words, One Concept, Many Audiences

Perhaps every work has an implied narratee or audience in mind. In the case of *The Memory of Silence* it is an ample one, not only because of the subject and setting but also how it goes about sharing its message.

Those interested in Latin American history, Cuban-American relations, and international politics will be intrigued by the inserted passages I mention above. Greater still, the non-fictional passages and references to well-known milestone events serve as passing historical markers that will be easily recognized to anyone living in the United States or Cuba during the second half of the twentieth century. Kennedy's assassination, the Cuban missile crisis, the Civil Rights movement, and other momentous events set the stage for the early chapters, whereas the Mariel boatlift, the fall of the Soviet Union, and Cuba's Special Period frame the final chapters. Readers from a variety of backgrounds will likely see themselves in the work and remember where they were when a certain event took place.

The Memory of Silence inarguably then is a historical novel, but it is as much about the future as it is about the past. From this perspective the text will appeal to a much greater audience than the academic interested in the socio-political reality of the Island. Quite the opposite, it is after all a story of two sisters separated and re-joined after an entire life apart, a story of the triumph of family and love over adversity and politics. The essence of the story is revealed in the two motifs of the title: memory and silence. I was reminded of this fact by the students in one of my literature courses when I taught the novel. I asked them what connotations the Spanish title *Memoria del silencio* brought to mind in their interpretation. Their initial attempts led them to consider conceptual phrases, such as "remembering silence," "memories of silence," "silent memories," "recalling silence," "the remembrance of silence." Still others argued that in Spanish "*the memory of...*" suggests "the memory that belongs to Silence," as if Silence were personified and had its own Memory. It took me some time to settle on the obvious phrase—"*the memory of* silence"—especially since the Spanish original doesn't include the article "The..." In the end my students agreed however. The title should evoke the two ever-present dynamics in the work that combine to create one force: to remember and in doing so to break one's silence.

More than just recovering memory, the novel cathartically attempts to uncover silence and to re-endow the characters with a voice. Time, space, and political circumstance have imposed silence on the two sisters, so it is not surprising that it carries multiple connotations throughout the novel. Some references to silence are unremarkable and expected, such as those that come about from teen-age angst, family quarrels, death, and spousal disagreements. In still other moments, silence is surprisingly associated with positive connotations. There's the comforting and intimate silence that Menchu and Lázaro share, as well as the dazed and reverent silence described at Che's vigil. As one might expect, the word silence most often appears as a commentary of despair and disillusionment on the state of Cuban affairs. In response to the overbearing and omnipresent governmental slogans, for example, Menchu lashes out at the noise of the Revolution: "All I am asking for is silence." This last quote even alters the implication of the title. Is it that the "memory of silence" suggests a longing for a time when there was silence, as if she can't recall a time when there wasn't so much ranting? At other times silence comes about for both characters for many reasons, including shame, stoicism, fear of reprisal, or exasperation, among others. The best example is found in Lauri's nostalgic recollection for her youthful games at her grandmother's house: "…all the cousins would play hide-and-seek and freeze-tag… and then all of my memories in my head become motionless, frozen in time, just like when we pretended we were statues…" Their game of freeze tag becomes an iconic metaphor for Cuba, a static image that most readers associate with 1959 automobiles and other retrospective icons frozen in time. But Lauri's metaphor goes a step beyond that. We rightfully associate stasis with a lack of movement, but this particular image of a childhood game conjures up notions of voiceless statues. Her frozen memories lack movement *and* sound. Not only is Havana a frozen snapshot in time; her reality—and the recollection of that reality—has become static and muted.

As the above examples illustrate, silence results from the dynamic of time away from family, distance of space within family, and the political circumstance affected upon family. Exile—for both those who leave and are left behind—means an altered memory of other. In an ironic sense, however, that which exile impedes is ultimately the source of the author's hope. More clearly, if exile is defined by the separation of family, then familial re-unification is the cure that can reunite Cuba. As an historical novel, the text abundantly documents the resultant ills of the Revolution and lamentable reactions on both sides of the Straits. Nevertheless, the message of hope resides with the fact that the sisters' journals have salvaged and archived their collective memories until they can be shared (in the first and last chapter). In the end, *The Memory of Silence* is a book of hope and reconciliation, but a hope that can only be realized once memory has been recovered and once silence has been broken. Only then will both sides begin to rediscover the future.

Few authors available to us today, in either English or Spanish, have produced works with a more calming and reconciliatory tone. In *The Memory of Silence* we quickly learn that Uva de Aragón is not an arbiter, advocate, or politician. She is an artistic mediator and peace-maker whose love for her native Cuba has inspired her to create characters who long to be reunited. For her characters, Cuba is not limited to a geographic Island located south of Florida nor is Cuban an adjective that refers to one's nationality and place of residence. It is a *patria*, a culture, an identity, an entity too complex to be limited by politics. As I said above at the opening of my remarks, she is a writer that defies our attempts to segregate Cubans and Cuban-Americans. I think you'll find too that *The Memory of Silence* attempts to bridge two cultures so that once more, regardless of where one resides, there may only be one community of Cubans.

A Word of Thanks

I am indebted to so many for their assistance and support during this long process. In particular I would like to acknowledge the H. F. Lenfest Endowment for Faculty Summer Support as well as a publishing subvention made possible by the Office of the Provost at Washington and Lee University. I also owe a special thanks to my colleagues at

Washington and Lee who made suggestions and, more gracious still, listened to me patiently as I mused on and on about semantics. To Uva, of course: the project begins and ends with you. I was continually appreciative of your encouragement, advice, and faith in my skills. And finally, most of all, to my family—Kath, Whitney, and Jessie: despite being a translator, I ironically lack the proper words to show how grateful I am for your support, patience, and everything you did for me to make this translation come about.

Jeffrey C. Barnett
Washington and Lee University
2013

THE Memory OF SILENCE

UVA DE ARAGÓN
TRANSLATED BY JEFFREY C. BARNETT

CHAPTER ONE
Reunion in Miami

"IT TOOK YOU A HALF A YEAR TO SAVE FOR THOSE JEANS. If I were you, rather than wearing those, I'd wear something that's in bad shape, the worst thing I had."

"Are you nuts?"

"Of course not, Menchu, but look, I'm sure your sister is going to buy you a ton of stuff. Know what else? If I were you, I'd take an empty suitcase with me."

"*Chica,* you do have a screw loose. Look, I'm not going to Miami just so my sister can buy me stuff."

"So why are you going then? Don't tell me you're thinking of going and staying!"

"For heaven's sake, Maruja! Do you think I am going to abandon Mamá?"

"So, if it weren't for her, you mean you'd stay?"

"No, of course not. I decided a long time ago that I'd never leave Cuba."

"That's more like it, *compañera!* We can't sell out for Yankee dollars. As the saying goes, "Socialism or Death!""

"Come on, it's a little bit too early in the morning for slogans, don't you think? I haven't even had my coffee yet…"

"Don't get upset, you know I'm only kidding. The truth is that it scares me to death that you might leave me too. You're the last friend I have left…"

"Fine, but don't you go and get all emotional on me or I might have second thoughts. If you only knew… Part of me is dying to go, but at the same time I'm so scared. Who knows? Laurita and I might not even get along… We've led such different lives. If someone had told us as kids that we were going to be separated when we were 18 and that we wouldn't see each other for almost forty years…! After being so close growing up! Imagine, being twins and all… Mamá would dress us alike. No one could tell us apart. Only Mamá."

"That's something considering that these days Mariana gets you confused with your sister. Her mind isn't quite as sharp as it was..."

"I'm hoping that I can convince Laurita to come visit her."

"So that's why you're going! Just to ask your sister to come see the old woman? If she only comes back because you ask her to, and not because she really wants to, then she's not that good of a daughter."

"That's not so. She sends us everything she can."

"Yes, just like you say, she sends *things*. But Man does not live by bread alone. What about love?"

"Everyone's different. That's precisely why I'm going. It's high time for Lauri and me to get to where we can embrace each other and at least respect each other's way of thinking."

"You're too good, Menchu."

"No, Maruja, I'm not any better than anyone else. When Robertico took my sister away, it was as if he had taken half of my life. Now the only thing we have left in common is the memories of our childhood. And more than anything else, what I want to do is stay up all night long, and just talk like we used to do when we were teenagers, and to recall everything, to reminisce about our first party with boys when nobody asked us to dance, or when we used to sneak out and go down to the corner to buy chocolate-covered cookies, two pennies apiece, and we'd make origami from the colored aluminum foil that they came in, and those enormous ribbons that Mamá would always put in our hair. You could make a dress with all that material Mamá used for our hair bows..."

"You don't need to worry, Menchu. You and Lauri are going to get along just fine."

"It's just that I've heard so many stories about people who are nothing but a burden to their families up there. Some of them come back even before the time limit on their permits is up, and they're so happy to be back in their own homes..."

"Hey, there's Pedritín with the car to take you to the airport."

I didn't want to take too long to say goodbye because I was afraid that if I thought about it too much I wouldn't go. It was such a hard decision to leave Mamá, even though it was going to be for such a short visit. Pedritín and I didn't say a word on the way to the airport. He didn't like the idea of me going to visit Laurita in Miami. He couldn't understand that there is nothing more important than family ties. For him, everybody who had taken off was a traitor, a pro-Yankee, and the Yankees were our worst enemies, the ones who threatened our country and endangered our national sovereignty. Fine, we had a lot of sovereignty and very little food on the table, and Man doesn't live by sovereignty alone, as they say, but it was pointless to talk about those types of things with my kid brother. He was so young when the Revolution took place... Well, I guess I don't like to admit my mistakes either, that is, except to myself...because doubting hurts, deep down inside, as if you were carrying a dead child within you... It hurts to see all those houses down in the old part of town, all of them in need of paint and repair. Empty store windows with nothing to sell. Cars that go back forty years. Che Guevara billboards that have turned all yellow. And yet it's true that things have started to get better lately, especially if you have dollars. At least there are people in the streets again. They always have some angle...whether it's legal or on the black market... Regardless, everybody has their hands in the tourists' pockets, either with some type of business—or *bisneando* as we say now—or worse still, *jineteando,* the newest way of referring to the oldest profession—what a euphemism, "riding bareback"! Wow, what a change in Old Havana!

It was so hard to bring myself to do it, but I finally decided to sell my aunt's books. Ivan took them to the Plaza de Armas and got $200 for them. Well, maybe they gave him more, and he kept a chunk. Nowadays, you can't even trust your friends. Anyway, with that we've been able to eat a little bit better over the last few months, and I was even able to leave some for Mamá while I'm away. The truth is I needed the money because I didn't want Lauri to see me looking like I do... After all, people have pride. The bad part was how mad Pedritín got. It's not like he cared that much about any of Tía Flor's books since they were just sitting there collecting dust...

I looked out the window as we drove along, taking in the streets...

the houses...the trees...the people. I wonder how the ones who've left must have felt as they took this route, knowing that perhaps they'd never come back. What must have been going through my sister's mind when she made this same trip? Did she know that she'd be gone for so long, maybe forever? I couldn't live in exile. It is comforting to know that I'll be back within a month.

Pedritín came inside with me to check my luggage and to pay the airport taxes. We said our goodbyes in front of the immigration window, and then he gave me a small package:

"Here, give this to Lauri for me. I want her to know that there are still good things in Cuba."

Then he gave me a big hug. I only remember one other time he had ever hugged me that way. It was in the cemetery after we buried Papá... And then he took off, without once turning his head, despite my yelling:

"Pedritín, take good care of Mamá for me."

We waited for over four hours. It turns out they tell you one thing, but the reality is something quite different. Passengers were supposed to arrive at 10:00 o'clock in the morning for a 1:00 o'clock flight which, turns out, was really not scheduled to leave until 2:00. And on top of it all, the flight was delayed beyond that. I was starving, so I decided to head upstairs to the coffee shop. That's when I noticed a group of people gathered on the terrace. From there they could catch a glimpse of their relatives in the distance who were staying behind. They were waving goodbye, many with tears in their eyes. It dawned on me that all of them were leaving for good, and it reminded me of the day Laurita left, and later on Ricardo too, although in his case we weren't able to come to the airport to say goodbye. As much as I tried to control myself, I got all choked up. To get my mind on something else, I tried looking at the rest of the passengers. There were many women in their fifties, like me, or even older, dressed in their Sunday best, trying hard to hide their poverty. You could immediately figure out which ones had only been visiting and were now heading back to Miami. And not only because of their clothes, but because they looked healthier, had better coloring, and because they complained more. I personally didn't say a word. Why should I bother? We'd take off whenever the pilot, or the air traffic controller, or the guy from security, or whoever, had the balls to make a decision.

Oh, if Mamá heard me say that! She never allowed us to say anything vulgar, not even the boys, although of course Ricardo and Pedritín said their share. Tía Flor was the one who taught Lauri and me all types of bad words. I remember the first time I called my cousin Luisito an asshole! I didn't care if Mamá heard me and washed my mouth out with soap. I wonder how old I was then. I bet Lauri remembers. At least nine or so…

We're finally about to take off. My God, the heat! It's been years since I've been on an airplane. Well, I've only flown twice in my life, that time as a girl when Papá took all of us to New York, and when I went to Moscow with Lázaro. Oh, the travels that Lauri and I planned when we were young. One day we were going to go to Rome, Venice, St. Michaels— because of that novel we had read that we liked so much—Greece, Paris. We always dreamed of going to Paris. We imagined ourselves wearing elegant dresses…with exotic perfume…surrounded by men.

Laurita's life probably hasn't been a bed of roses either. I wonder if she ever truly found happiness with Robertico. And has she possibly gotten used to being a widow? It all happened so fast… There's so much that we don't know about each other. We used to write all the time. I think every day even. And then later on…what happened? It's true that both countries cut off communication but still …

Again tears came to my eyes when I looked out the window and saw the Cuban coastline growing smaller and smaller. "The most beautiful land" as Columbus had called it when he first laid eyes on our land. Is it possible that some type of curse has been placed on Cubans because our Island is so beautiful? I don't think it's a false sense of pride. It's just that Cuba has a special magic that's seductive. I wonder what Lauri must think of our country. A few letters, a telephone call now and then, and those have usually been during times of crisis…none of that's enough for two people to really know each other. When you think about it, we're practically strangers.

So many years of being separated, and so far away from each other, but then in only minutes, I can begin to make out Miami. There are more buildings than I expected. I feel my heart pounding in my chest. My legs are shaking as I step off the plane. And what if I can't recognize her among so many people? It's been so long since we've seen each other. I'm such an idiot. How am I not going to recognize my own twin sister?

Lauri spotted me first.

"Menchu...! Menchu...!"

"Laurita!"

I shouldn't have been worried. It was like we sensed each other even before we saw each other. Our embrace was long and tight. Everything that surrounded us—people, noise, lights, voices—all of it disappeared. For a brief instant, even life itself stopped. The only thing that existed was the two of us crying uncontrollably. We had been inseparable through our childhood and adolescence, and here we were meeting to unveil the mystery of everything that lay behind that wall of water and misunderstandings that had separated Cubans. And yet, for some absurd reason, I couldn't stop thinking about that party long ago where no one asked us to dance.

Lauri was the first one to break the ice.

"Where's your bag?"

The airport was swarming with Cubans. We finally made our way out, and she asked me if I wanted to wait while she went and got the car. I don't know why it scared me so much to wait there by myself. I just felt more comfortable sticking together. The parking garage was huge. Who knows how many stories high? As we got on the road, I started to feel a little dizzy and disoriented. There was so much traffic, and the radio, and—although I should be used to it by now—all of that on an empty stomach. I was tempted to ask her if there was still a ways to go, and if so why not stop and get a coffee. But I didn't see any good place along the way, so I decided not to ask her.

When we finally left the expressway, Lauri said to me, "We're almost there. This area is called Westchester. It's mostly Cuban, and it's very close to the university where I teach."

She made several turns until we stopped in front of a house painted cream with dark brown windows. There were coleus, hibiscus, and palms growing in the front yard.

"I planted them," said Lauri showing me some impatiens, "because they reminded me of Cuba…and Mamá Luya's house in *La Sierra.*"

That comment alone was proof enough for me that my sister had never stopped being tied to us emotionally, in spite of all the years that had gone by and in spite of all the attempts by both governments to keep families apart.

As soon as she opened the door and we walked inside the house, she hugged me again:

"I still can't believe you're here… I'll show you the rest of the house later, but first let me take you to your room. It used to be the kids' room, but now I've made it into a guestroom or for when they let me keep my grandson. Just in honor of your visit I bought new bedspreads and matching curtains. So what do you think, Menchu, remind you of anything?"

"Oh, sis, it's exactly like our bedroom when we were little… The bedspreads have the same colors… And even the pictures of Raphael's *Madonna* that were above our beds! How on earth did you find them?"

"They're really not worth anything. They're just copies from the National Gallery of Art in Washington…but when I saw them, I couldn't resist, and I bought them. I've had them in the closet for years, but I got them framed just for your visit. When you go back, if you want to, you should take yours with you."

"Oh, God, no! They look so beautiful right here. And, besides, I still have the old ones."

"I can't believe it! Oh, Menchu, I have a thousand things to ask you and another thousand I want us to remember together. Just this morning I was thinking of Alicia, the woman who watched us during recess in elementary school, and how we would sing to her all the songs that Tía Flor taught us, and how she'd let us get away with everything… Remember?"

"And just this morning I was reminiscing about how as teenagers we'd stay up all night long and babble for hours…"

"Mamá would always call us 'a couple of parrots.' And a Christmas doesn't go by that I don't think about how we'd go with Papá to Casa Suarez to buy sweets… I've never had a tastier *turrón* than that one."

"And how about those chocolate covered egg yolks?"

"I remember the owner was bald, and he had spots on his hands. He'd wrap everything up in brown craft paper from a big roll. I can just picture it…"

"Oh, I can't believe you remember!"

"It's been so hard on me not to have anyone to share these memories with. But there'll be plenty of time for that. Look, I've got a few empty drawers for you in this dresser and some hangers in the closet… I don't know if you want to shower first, or unpack, or rest… It's entirely up to you. Just tell me what you want to do…"

Laurita tried so hard to please me, and I don't know why, but I felt so uncomfortable. I couldn't help but smile nervously. Finally I uttered:

"What I would like is some coffee…"

"I'll make it right away, froth and all. Did they feed you on the plane? Are you hungry?"

"To tell you the truth, I feel a little weak."

"Poor thing. I've already fixed one of your favorite meals for dinner… but for right now, would you like a yogurt? Some fruit? …Look, I have bananas, apples, tangerines, and grapes. Or do you want a Coke with cheese and crackers? Or maybe some juice?"

"Really, anything is fine, Laurita. And calm down. You're jabbering away like you were Cachucha or something."

"Oh my goodness, I haven't thought about her and that TV show in years!"

In the kitchen Laura poured a couple of glasses of tomato juice and even cut some slices of lemon. Then she arranged some Gouda and crackers on a cutting board. With each little gesture and mannerism, I felt like I was looking into a mirror.

"How fancy!"

"Please…this is only because it's the first day. Later on however…"

"Do you remember how much Papá liked his tomato juice?"

"Yes, and we'd have it every Sunday before lunch."

"After we returned from Mass and listened to records by *Los Panchos*…"

"Yeah, those 78s that you'd stack one on top of the other, and then each would fall on the next one…"

"And now even cassettes are outdated. Everything comes on CDs. I have one by *Los Panchos*. I'm going to put it on for you."

"No, Laurita, not now. We'll start crying again. Come here, sit down with me. This cheese is delicious!"

"They try to make it like the one we had in Cuba. I think it was called *Gallo Azul*, wasn't it? But tell me, how's Mamá?"

"Pretty good… She doesn't like me to leave her side, but she was so happy that we were going to be together again that she didn't even complain."

"And Pedritín?"

"He's doing fine. He took me to the airport."

Lauri moved about talking non-stop with a nervous energy that I never recalled before.

"Lauri, relax and come over and sit down already."

"Oh Menchu, I've missed you so much all these years. There are so many things I want to ask you… I want you to tell me every single thing that's happened in your life, day by day, even if we have to stay up all night long like we used to do when we were kids…" she told me as her voice trembled.

"Come on, sis, it'll be all right. It seems like a miracle that we're together. There were times when I was afraid that we'd never see each other again."

"Me too. I've missed you so much over all these years."

I had no more doubts then.

"Where did you put my suitcase?"

I went through my clothes and looked for the only thing I had been able to bring her, and I explained:

"So many times I wanted to ask you for advice and share things with you... When it became difficult to send letters back and forth, I started keeping a diary... I'd sometimes clip things from the newspaper and glue them into the notebook, or I'd copy a poem I particularly liked...I didn't write every day...sometimes years would go by without me touching it...but every single important thing in my life is in there, Lauri. And I wrote it all just for you."

"And you still have the same beautiful penmanship they taught us in school," she said, trying to control her emotions. "Thank you so much... This is the best present possible, just knowing that you kept me in your thoughts," and then she added in a serious and secretive tone:

"You are not going to believe what I am about to tell you. But I've kept a diary of my life too. And I also wrote it for you and, just like yours, it includes newspaper articles and poems that I've copied. It's incredible! The only difference is that mine is typed...in the last few years I wrote it on the computer. Recently I reread it and put it in order for you, but I swear, I haven't changed a comma."

She left the room and came right back in with a binder that she put in my hands.

"Can I read it?"

"Not yet...I'm going to put it on the nightstand so you can have it for later, when you're alone, before going to sleep... I'll do the same with yours... And I hope that one day you will write a chapter about our reunion in Miami..."

"Of course I will. And you'll have to do add one about your return to Cuba..."

"We'll talk about that later...now come on...let me show you the rest of the house."

"Wait. I almost forgot. I've got something else for you." I took out the little gift that my brother had told me to give to her.

"Pedritín sent this for you."

"For me? What is it?"

"I have no idea."

Lauri softly caressed the tissue paper. Finally she dared to open it. It was a necklace made of seashells. She looked at it for a long time. Then she put it to her nose and drew in a deep breath.

"You know, I think it still smells like a Cuban beach… Damn it, Menchu, what a cross we Cubans have had to bear!"

And then she began to cry uncontrollably as if she were trying to let loose a deep pain within her. I hugged her and we cried together until she jumped and ran to the kitchen.

"Oh my God, I nearly burned dinner."

CHAPTER TWO
Cubans, Go Home!

WHAT I WILL ALWAYS REMEMBER ABOUT HAVANA IS THE LIGHT. When I try to play back in my mind that 13th of July of 1959, I close my eyes, and I see a blinding light that hurts my eyes. We're riding in the station wagon. Robertico and I are sitting in the very back. Since the rear seat faces backwards and the window is so wide, we have a good view of the city that we'll leave in a few hours. Papá is driving with Mamá at his side. Menchu and Pedritín ride in the middle seat with our luggage. The midday sun makes the colors turn more vivid, almost as if the buildings and streets, and even the air itself, were illuminated by a blazing fire. Steam—seemingly made up of red, blue, and yellow dots—rises from the pavement.

We were married yesterday. The ceremony took place in the Vedado Parish. I know that it made Robertico sad that his parents weren't there. We had a small reception at home. Everything was very simple. It wasn't the big event that Mamá and Papá would have wanted for the marriage of one of their daughters. It wasn't what I had dreamed of either. But given the circumstances, it was best not to make a big deal of it. Papá even suggested that Robertico shouldn't use both of his surnames on the invitations. Not Fernández-Luaces but just plain Fernández. But he absolutely put his foot down! I love it when he gets mad! I like listening to his voice, so much that sometimes I get lost in it and in the words. I love each one of his gestures, even the way he frowns. Almost all of my classmates came to the wedding. It was hard not being able to tell them that Robertico and I weren't going to go to Varadero the next day on our honeymoon as we had planned but to the United States, and that the trip would probably be for a lot longer than two weeks. I think that we might be back by September and I'll be able to attend the university. Actually, I have asked Menchu to register for me when she fills out her paperwork. She can forge my signature perfectly, just as I can hers.

The wedding night…I don't know…was different than what I had imagined. It felt so good when Robertico took me into his arms and started kissing me…later on, though, well…I don't have anything to compare it to…but needless to say, it wasn't like in the movies… He was probably nervous, and I know that I certainly was! But it never occurred to me that he was going to take my negligee off so quickly, especially given how long it took Mamá, Menchu, and me to pick it out! And in just a few minutes it was lying on the floor, like dirty laundry. On the other hand, I guess I wasn't there to model underwear…but I still wish he hadn't been in such a hurry!

Everything was over so quickly. And I didn't sleep a wink all night long. I'm not used to sleeping with anyone else in the same bed. Even when I was a little girl and I'd get sick, Mamá would bring me into her room and I'd have a hard time falling asleep. The most pleasant moment was the next morning. After we ate breakfast and watched the waves break against the *Malecón,* we went back to bed and made love once again. I liked it better that second time.

We were going to go directly to the airport, but Roberto read my mind:

"If we hurry, we can take a cab to your house so you can see your family and then your father can take us to the airport. They're probably just getting back from Mass. Why don't you call them and tell them we're heading that way?"

When we arrived, I went upstairs and took a long look at every room. I don't know what strange premonition made me think that I'd never see that house again, the house where I was born and had lived all of my eighteen years. At the same time, I scolded myself for being overly dramatic, a silly young girl influenced too much by Hollywood.

I finally go into my room. I look at the twin beds with their matching bedspreads of pink and blue flowers. Lying on these beds, Menchu and I have shared dreams and worries. We've stayed up until all hours reading novels by Louisa May Alcott or Alexander Dumas, poems by Bécquer, the legends of Ricardo Palma and, of course, our beloved Jose Martí. This is where we studied for hours and hours and where we secretly listened to the baseball games on the radio between La Habana and Almendares when Mamá thought we were already asleep.

I see my schoolbooks on top of the nightstand, including the book I used just a few days ago for my last high school exam. It's *The Geography of Cuba* by Levi Marrero. I take it in my hands and leaf through it. I stare at the pages, with passages underlined, the maps of Cuba that I have colored and, on the inside cover, the lyrics of Lucho Gatica's love songs scribbled in Menchu's handwriting. Robertico is yelling that it's time to go. I leave the book on the bed and look for the wide-brimmed hat that I had bought for the trip, and which I had forgotten to take with me yesterday. Women look so pretty in hats! But not me. Either I don't know how to wear them or maybe they just don't fit me right. I hear voices downstairs calling me. I toss the hat on the bed. Just before going out the door, I take one last look at my bedroom, the home of my adolescence, at the French Provençal bedroom set that our parents gave us when we turned fifteen, at the copies of Rafael's *Madonna* on the wall, hanging just above both headboards, and at my flowery bedspread that cradled my youthful dreams, where the Cuban geography book and the white wide-brimmed hat with its big pink bow now lie.

Mamá Luya doesn't want to come to the airport. Papá says that it's better that way. Otherwise we wouldn't all fit in the car. I say goodbye to my grandmother at the top of the stairs. I smell her fragrance of jasmine and feel the softness of her skin against mine. I start down the stairs. Halfway down, I look up and see her, her beautiful white hair and her steel gray eyes. I know that the minute that I'm out of sight she will begin to cry, but for now her eyes meet mine, and she smiles. I blow her a kiss and run down the steps, fearful that if I were to turn were to around to hug her one last time, no one would be able to pry me away from her.

On the way to the airport I focus on taking it all in—the streets, the trees, the houses, the people—as if I wanted to engrave it into my memory forever. I begin to have doubts. We go by the Sports Palace. I know Robertico and I love each other, but the idea of leaving my family and my country breaks my heart. We're almost there. This is my honeymoon…I should be happy… We'll be back soon, I say to myself.

At the airport in Rancho Boyeros I'm stunned to see my brother Ricardo. He hugs me tight but takes off right away. I don't know if it's because he's late for something or because he's trying to hide his emotions. I hardly have any recollection of the final goodbyes. Only the quiet tears, the hugs, the discreet advice, and a great pain in the middle of my chest, as if my heart were breaking in two. Finally when the plane takes off, I keep looking out the window until the distance and my tears no longer allow me to make out the outline of the Island, which eventually dissolves into blue, the blue of the sky and of the sea. Oh, Cuba! Goodbye!

I cry until I can cry no more. I rest my head on my husband's shoulder and close my eyes. But I can't sleep. All I can see is the blinding light of Havana. It's burned onto my retina. It still hurts my eyes.

∽

Cuba. *Fidel Castro announced his resignation as Cuban Premier July 17 in a TV address. He said "moral differences" between himself and President Manuel Urrutia Lleó left him "no alternative but…to resign." He accused Urrutia of an "attitude bordering on treason" in delaying the action of the revolution, land distribution…and in failing to sign regulations providing death penalties for counter-revolutionaries. Urrutia resigned later July 17, taking refuge with his family in Bauta, a village near Havana… Laws-of-the-Revolution Minister, Oswaldo Dorticós Torrado, 40, was appointed by the cabinet as President… Capt. Antonio Nuñez. 36, executive director of Cuba's Land Reform Institute, said at a press conference in New York July 19 that Urrutia had tried to "blackmail" the Cuban government with false charges that it was Communist-dominated… Nuñez denied that he ever had been a Communist… Castro, who had been under constant pressure by the entire cabinet to withdraw his resignation, told 500,000 supporters at a rally on the 6th anniversary of his 26 of July Movement that he was returning to office "by the will of the people."*

(*Facts on File* 19.978, 243)

✑

When we arrived in Miami, we went to live with my in-laws in a pretty big house in the southwest section of the city. Adela and Roberto had the master bedroom. Juancito, my brother-in-law who was about nine years old then, and Vidal, Adela's youngest brother, also lived with us. Juancito shared a bedroom with his uncle. Robertico and I had the third bedroom. The four of us shared a bath.

A few days later, standing in front of our closet, I realized that all of those elegant dresses from my bridal trousseau were going to be useless. My father had given me a few dollars before we left Cuba and although I had no experience administering money, something told me I should spend as little as possible. Nevertheless, one afternoon when my mother-in-law announced she was going downtown, I decided to go along, and I bought myself a couple of casual outfits, cooler and more modest than what I had in the closet. It was the first time that I had shopped for myself without Mamá's advice. Adela was very discreet, making comments such as, "that looks good on you," or, "that's a good price," but without being in a hurry or pressuring me. Once we finished, she invited me to have a Coke at Walgreens before heading back on the bus. There were a lot of Cubans gathered there, exchanging news about Cuba or getting tips on where to find a job. I ran into the father of my friend María Cristina, who said hello very affectionately. I have always remembered that afternoon. It was one of the best moments I can remember during those first few months.

My father-in-law had been a powerful man, an important attorney on retainer for several big corporations, principally for the match industry. When he watched Castro entering Havana on TV he turned to his wife and told her:

"It's time to get out of here. This man is going to destroy everything."

Most of the people who left Cuba at the very outset were tied to the previous regime in some fashion. Roberto however categorically denied ever having been a Batista supporter or having received preferential treatment. Given how poor off they were in exile, I think I believed him. Still, they must have had some money tucked away somewhere because no one in the household was working. The only thing we did was talk about Cuba, the Revolution, Castro, the Americans... And about going back home.

We all lived glued to the radio, and we'd jump every time the telephone rang. Adela, a pretty woman of forty-something, clumsily played the role of housewife. She'd try to clean the house, do the shopping and laundry, cook, but she was really a disaster. When she didn't burn the rice, it would turn out as hard as a rock. She didn't even know how to fry an egg. One time she washed her husband's white underwear with a red shirt of Juancito's, and the underwear turned pink. My father-in-law said pink underwear was for faggots, and she better figure out how to get them back as they were because he wasn't going to wear them like that and there wasn't any money to buy new ones. Adela cried as hard as if there had been a death in the family. It made me think of the time when our dog got lost and Menchu and I were beside ourselves. Papá scolded us and told us that a pet was a pet, and a person was a person. I walked over to Adela, and patting her on the back, said:

"Don't worry, Adela. Underwear is underwear."

But she kept on bawling, and answered me by saying:

"Yes, but Roberto is Roberto."

The one who was always in the best mood was Vidal. Actually, his name wasn't Vidal. It was really Alberto Castaño, but as a youngster he loved to sing, and they had nicknamed him "Vidal" after the character from the operetta *Luisa Fernanda*. Once in Miami, the frustrated baritone took a correspondence course to learn how to fix TVs. He would place his cards on the supermarket bulletin boards: "Vidal fix television for little money." When someone would call him on the phone, he'd get dressed up as if he were going to a party. He'd wait until no one was around and steal some cologne from my father-in-law, and then he'd rub it on his temples and his dark thin mustache. He'd return home sweaty but with $3 in his pocket, which was how much he charged.

Every once in a while he'd have some extra tubes with him when he came back. When Juancito would ask him if those were the ones that had burned out, he'd explain that the tubes were perfectly fine; it was just that when he put the TV back together again, he had leftovers, and couldn't figure out where they were supposed to go. We would all laugh and thought he was exaggerating until one day an older gentleman, who was plump and short of stature, came to the house, claiming that Vidal had stolen the tubes from his TV. Vidal gave them back immediately, all the while trying to explain in his thick accent in English:

"Sorry, I cannot put back, I cannot put back."

Unlike his brother who was always an optimist, Juancito was a sad child. He suffered in school because he couldn't understand what was said. It didn't look like he fit in either. His old fashioned pants and blue shirt—Adela made him wear his old Cuban school uniform—along with his beautiful dark flowing hair looked out of place among his crew cut, blond, and freckled schoolmates. In the evenings I would help him with his homework. When he came home with an "A," he would reward me by giving me a peck on the cheek, and say:

"You're so good to me, Lauri. What would I do without you?"

That would get me thinking about my own brother, who was about his same age, and then about my father—who insisted that every one of us learn English—and then, finally, about everybody in my family. My eyes would fill up with tears, and there wasn't anything I could do about it. I never wanted Juancito to see me crying so I would open my eyes real wide. My only comfort was knowing that Robertico would be home that evening, and I would able to lose myself in his arms. He was my only safe refuge.

Back in those days, I remember Juancito being happy only once, the day Vidal came home ecstatic because he had fixed two television sets at the same home, and they had been given a generous tip. He kept on showing off the $10 bill as if it were a trophy, and then he'd take a quick glance at each one of us, one after the other, as if he were a baseball player getting ready to throw one of us the ball. And then he finally said:

"Come on, Juancito, I am taking you out for a haircut and to buy you a plaid shirt like your classmates."

Adela pointed out that she needed some hair rinse, but Vidal didn't pay any attention to her, and Juancito returned with his hair cut short and straight. The next morning he wore his new plaid shirt to school and when he came back that afternoon he whispered to me:

"I made a friend today in class. He told me that from now on he's going to call me Johnny."

My mother-in-law was becoming more and more moody every day. She would go from shouting at the top of her lungs to absolute silence, from bossing everyone around like a general, to crying like a baby. I started becoming quite attached to my father-in-law though. He was a little homely, heavy, and sentimental. Sometimes he would put both his hands on his head, and just sigh:

"What has happened to Cuba and to Adela?"

Robertico spent most of his time on the streets looking for a job until he finally found one selling burgers at a place called Royal Castle. At the end of the day they would let the employees take home any burgers that hadn't been sold. They weren't very big, and didn't have the crispy potato sticks inside like they did in Cuba, but at least they filled you up. I don't know how my husband managed to do it, but he would bring home a minimum of one burger for each of us, and sometimes there'd even be a couple of extra ones for Vidal and Juancito, who were always the ones with the biggest appetites.

We couldn't wait for the mailman to come by every day. To get a letter from Havana was the greatest pleasure you could have. We'd read out loud any reference to what was going on politically.

When my girlfriends described with such excitement how the people from the countryside had come to Havana to celebrate the anniversary of the '26 de julio' and had stayed in private homes, my father-in-law became livid and scoffed at the naiveté of Cuba's middle class. And when Robertico's friend wrote us about the protest involving the *Social Catholic Action* my husband grumbled:

"I should have been there."

Still, when a friend of Adela's told us about the rumors regarding the closing of all private schools and even about parents losing legal rights over their children, we reminded ourselves of just how fortunate we were:

"Thank God we left when we did!"

News like that invariably made us feel worse—I preferred Menchu's letters and, of course, Mamá's—but, in spite of all, we were always thrilled to receive those envelopes whose familiar handwriting amounted to a comforting smile from a loved one.

One of our favorite pastimes was to go to the airport and watch other Cubans arrive, especially once the number started to increase so drastically after the summer of 1960. I will always remember the girls with their headbands, their flared dresses over a starched underskirt, the patent leather shoes and white bobby socks, always, always clutching a doll, and with a terrible look of uncertainty showing in their young faces. The young mothers often wore pearls and carried a clutch style handbag under their arms. The men all wore suits and dark-rimmed glasses. All the boys reminded me of Pedritín. They all looked like families coming back from Church, wearing their Sunday best. In reality, they were refugees who had no idea how drastically their lives were about to change. Then, children started to arrive by themselves. Some of them had signs with an address and phone number hanging from their necks. We never discussed it, but I'm sure it was the sight of those kids that made us stop going to the airport. It hurt too much.

༄

President Eisenhower…authorized December 2 the spending of up to $1 million for relief and resettlement of 30,000–40,000 anti-Castro Cuban refugees in New Orleans and in Miami and other Florida areas… Congressman Francis E. Walter (D., PA.) told the Intergovernmental Committee on European Migration in Geneva December 1 that approximately

36,000 Cubans had been granted political asylum in the United States and that Cubans were entering the U.S. at a rate of 1,000 a week.

(*Facts on File* 20.1049, 443)

∽

Back then everybody helped everybody else. Front doors were frequently left open. It wasn't a metaphor. There was no fear of intruders or rapists. And we shared whatever we had, from a jar of peanut butter, courtesy of the *Refugio,* to a tin of cookies, a gift from a charitable American.

In spite of me being happy with Robertico, in spite of our beautiful nights of lovemaking, I missed all of my family so badly, and my friends, and everything I had left behind. The first Christmas hadn't been too bad, especially since we were convinced that we would be going back home to Cuba soon. But now that we were coming up on the second Christmas, I was starting to feel a profound sadness that was becoming harder and harder to conceal. One afternoon I found an old edition of *Little Women* in one of the closets. It was one of the first novels that Menchu and I had read. As I started to read it again, I was overtaken by such an overwhelming sense of anguish that I jolted out of the house. I didn't want anybody else to see me like that. In my confusion, I crossed the street without looking and a small truck screeched to a stop. The driver leaned half of his body out of the window, and at the top of his lungs, yelled at me:

"Hey Cuban, go home!"

I wish I could have told him that nothing would have made me happier, but he was already speeding away while I was sitting there on the curb, crying as if the world were coming to an end. I think that right then and there, I understood that I had become a refugee. I had left Cuba as a newlywed, thinking we would return shortly, and that I could start attending the university as I had always dreamed. But my father-in-law was right: Castro was destroying the country. The arrests and executions were horrifying. And to think that so many Cubans were actually calling for the executions. And that the entire world seemed to applaud what was going on. They've already nationalized several industries. María Aurora's father, who was a client of my father-in-law, dropped dead of a massive heart attack while defending the takeover of his match factory by the government.

∾

Cuba. Unionists Get Asylum. A least 12 Electrical Workers Union leaders were granted asylum in the Havana embassies of Argentina, Peru, Ecuador and Brazil December 14. The labor officials fled a few hours before a Havana rally called to approve the "purification" of their union.

Cuban National Bank President Che Guevara and Soviet First Deputy Premier Anastas I. Mikoyan signed in Moscow December 19 an agreement providing for the expansion of Cuba-Soviet Trade to $168 million in 1961.

That same day Prime Minister Fidel Castro announced in Havana that the USSR had promised to buy 2,700,000 tons of sugar from Cuba at 4 cents a ton in 1961. Communist China and other Communist bloc nations, he said, had pledged to buy 1,000,000 and 300,000 tons, respectively, at the same price.

Guevara Dec. 19 signed a declaration pledging Cuban support of Soviet Premier Khrushchev's foreign policy, including backing of "national liberation movements" in Latin America.

(Facts on File, 20.1051, 462)

∾

During the summer of 1960, rumors started going around about how the Americans were preparing an invasion of Cuba. Around Christmastime, the talk reached a crescendo. The exiles didn't talk about anything else. Many of them visited my father-in-law. All of them talked at the same time, and loudly. On New Year's Eve, we sat in front of the TV that showed the huge crowds in Times Square. And at midnight, when the ball fell, we raised our glasses as my father-in-law toasted:

"Next year, in Havana!"

We hugged each other full of hope.

In January, we were hit by a bad cold front, and the house didn't have a heating system. Someone told us that a church nearby was giving out winter clothing, but Roberto threw a fit and yelled at Adela:

"This cold weather won't last. It's not necessary to spend money on winter clothing. And I forbid you to take charity—we're not poor people starving to death."

Adela and I looked at each other like two accomplices. I left for the church with Johnny (now we all called him that) and we returned with four blankets and two sweaters, one for the boy, the other for Robertico. They were the ones who were outside the most and who got the coldest.

That evening, under the warmth of the blanket that smelled a little bit of mothballs, Robertico made love me to me…but in a different way than before. He moved slowly, as if he wanted to savor each and every moment, and with an intensity filled with a fierce sadness. I noticed that he didn't wear a condom as he usually did so I wouldn't get pregnant, but I didn't say anything. When we had finished and we were no longer cold, we lay there for a long time, naked and cuddling each other. I was drifting off to sleep, when he said:

"If there's an invasion of Cuba, my father and I are going. You'll have to be strong."

I nodded.

"I know this isn't the best time, but if I die, I want to leave you with a child."

It had never occurred to me that Roberto wouldn't be with me forever. I shivered. I put my nightgown back on and went back to his arms.

"Don't be silly. You're never going to die."

We never used a condom again. Robertico hated them anyway.

I never knew how or when, but they both signed up for the invasion. One evening my father-in-law turned off the TV, made sure we were all present, and spoke very seriously:

"The men in this family are going to fulfill their sacred duty to Cuba. Very soon, Vidal, Robertico, and I will be leaving for training to disembark in Cuba and set her free. We believe that victory will come quickly. Juancito, once we're gone, you will be the man of the house. You will have to protect your mother and Lauri. Adela, I have no doubt that you will face this situation bravely. Lauri..."

I never knew what he was about to say, because I interrupted him: "Robertico can't go. Not now."

And then I revealed the secret I had not shared with anyone:

"I am...we are going to have a baby."

Robertico hugged me like crazy, and kept asking me over and over again if I was sure. Johnny wanted to know if he could be the godfather. Vidal started singing a lullaby at the top of his lungs as he pretended to rock a baby in his arms. Adela, in between nervous laughter, asked if she seemed old enough to be a grandmother. My father-in-law disappeared for a few minutes and then came back with a bottle of cider, a left-over from New Year's Eve.

"We have to toast this future member of the family," he said.

In just a brief moment, we had gone from solemnity and sadness to excitement and joy. It didn't last long. My father-in-law kissed me on the cheek and whispered in my ear, "Robertico has to leave anyway."

I looked at my husband and I saw him nod affirmatively. I didn't dare complain in front of everybody else, but that night in the privacy of our room, I begged him not to leave me alone. It was useless.

"I am doing this for our child. So that he can be born and grow up in a free Cuba," he argued.

Shortly afterwards, I found out that Vidal had been a pilot. He was the first to leave. They called him one evening and two days later the whole family took him to the place where he was supposed to present himself. He didn't want us to get out of the car. Instead, we saw him nonchalantly walk away from us and listened as he hummed a song from *Luisa Fernanda:*

"With fortune I go forth...a soldier's good companion..."

That night I had a dream about Johnny and my own brother Pedritín. In my dream both of them were grown-ups and dressed in military uniforms, but they were fighting for opposite sides. I could hear the crackling of gunfire. Then, a long silence. Someone was telling me that one of them was dead, and I didn't know which one. I woke up in a sweat and couldn't get over my anxiety, so Robertico tried to calm me down.

"Nothing like that is going to happen. You'll see. Everyone, including your family, is going to welcome us back as heroes. Remember those films they made when World War II ended? We'll be welcomed back like that, with hugs, and garlands, and cheering."

Days passed, rumors increased. Robertico couldn't stand selling burgers at Royal Castle, but no one had contacted them. Finally, my father-in-law dialed a number that a friend had given him. He was told there was a group leaving for a training camp the next morning, and if they wanted to join them that they should be there at 8:00 o'clock sharp. There was hardly any time for anything. The next morning we drove in silence to the same place where we had dropped off Vidal just a few weeks earlier. This time we did get out of the car. As we hugged goodbye, we squeezed each other tightly, even though it was just for a second.

"We'll be back together again before the baby comes," Robertico promised me as he said goodbye.

Adela got behind the wheel. She had gotten her driver's license, but my father-in-law hardly ever allowed her to drive. We were driving home in silence, each one lost in our own thoughts, when suddenly at the corner Adela put her hands on her head and exclaimed:

"Oh, I can't believe it! I forgot to ask Roberto how to put the car in reverse!"

We cracked up laughing.

Within a week Adela was a different person. I never saw her cry or complain about anything ever again. The first thing she decided was that the house was too big for the three of us. We moved to an apartment in an area that everybody called "Pastorita" after some woman in Cuba who was in charge of housing. All the neighbors were Cuban and we felt more at home. Johnny started to make new friends and seemed happier. My mother-in-law found a job sewing in a factory. I did my part keeping house, doing the grocery shopping, cooking, cleaning, doing the laundry, helping Johnny with his homework. I was making a few dollars teaching English at home to some of the neighbors. Obviously, no one made too much money, so I didn't charge that much. I would have preferred to work outside the home, but Adela insisted that in my condition it was best not to do too much. The days seemed so long and I missed Robertico terribly, especially at night. To make matters worse, I hardly ever got any mail from home. I began to feel a little better once I started to feel the baby move. It made me think that I wasn't totally alone.

On the 13th of April, 1961, I received a brief note from Robertico. He said the trip had been long, that they had begun to train, and that he had run into several old classmates. He told me to take good care of myself and to pray for them. At the end of the letter he added, "I don't have any fears whatsoever. I am fulfilling my duty to my country." For the very first time, it dawned on me that he was lying to me or, at least, to himself. My husband in fact was scared.

Two days later, on a sunny Saturday morning, we learned that American planes had bombed Cuban air bases. More than feeling like celebrating, I was surprised that the news made me feel confused and troubled. What if they killed one of my loved ones? I thought about my cousin Armando, who had fought in the Sierra Maestra and wore the olive green uniform of the Revolution. Where could Robertico possibly be? How could they be sent on an invasion with just a few weeks of training?

Pastorita looked like a garrison: short wave radios, news, rumors, people coming and going, lots of coffee, hopes, nervous laughter, and so much anxiety that you couldn't keep it inside. Three days and three nights of contradictory news when time seemed to stand still. Nothing mattered to us but the fate of our men and of Cuba.

∽

Cuba. Castro Hails Victory. *Premier Castro announced in a communique April 20 that government troops had captured "the last points held by the [anti-Castro] foreign mercenary invasion forces…"*

Castro's communique also said that the Cuban air force planes had bombed and sunk several ships in which invaders had tried to escape. It said that "a large quantity of arms manufactured in the U.S. were captured, including several Sherman heavy tanks."

(*Facts on File* 21.1069, 146)

∽

When I heard the news over at a neighbor's house, I immediately ran home to look for Adela. I found her in the bedroom, kneeling by the bed with a rosary in her hands. I realized that she already knew. She must have heard me come in because, without turning around, she called me to her side. We prayed together in silence. Then she hugged me and, without shedding a tear, she said to me:

"You are not alone, child. I'll always be by your side."

There were reports of many arrests and executions. Sorí Marín, who just a few days before had been the Minister of Agriculture and who was rumored to have signed many death sentences, was shot. Castro threatened to execute all the invaders. The leaders in exile appealed to the OAS, the UN, and the Pope, asking for their intervention. Fidel paraded the prisoners in front of the TV cameras. Some of them showed just how exceptionally brave they were. We caught a brief glimpse of Roberto and Robertico. We were so nervous we couldn't sleep.

A few evenings later Vidal knocked on the door. He explained that he had flown several missions, but had been able to return to base without incident, and from there he had returned to Miami. He knew nothing of Robertico or of his father. We told him they were in prison. Adela told him he could sleep on the couch.

One of the few joys during that time was the arrival in the United

States of my brother Ricardo. He surprised me one afternoon with a call from the airport. He was only going to be in Miami for a few hours. He was on his way to New York where he had some friends who had promised to help him get started. I was hysterical until I found someone to drive me to the airport. On the way I thought my heart was going to leap out of my chest. We hugged long and hard, and I couldn't stop crying. I don't think I realized until right at that moment just how very much I missed my family.

Seeing Ricardo was like recovering my past in one fell swoop. The *cafés con leche* Mamá would bring me in bed, the aroma of Papá's cigars, the voice of Mamá Luya telling me stories, the memory of Pedritín playing ball on the street, Menchu marking the steps of the "cha cha" in our first school dance. I could see everything in my head like a slow-motion movie. I had so many questions I wanted to ask, and yet I couldn't utter a word. Before I knew it, Ricardo was catching his flight to New York, but before he took off, he handed me an envelope:

"Papá sent you this."

I waited until I got home to open it. I found $500 and a short note in my father's wide handwriting that simply said, "Buy the baby a crib from his grandparents." I hadn't had any doubts that Robertico would be back before the baby came, but the negotiations to release the *Brigadistas* kept dragging on and my due date was getting closer all the time. Adela and I were getting along and I had grown close to Juancito; but still, I couldn't stand being apart from my family. So it dawned on me that Menchu could come up for the birth of her nephew. I called her, but after a long silence on the phone, without any explanation she just blurted out that it was absolutely impossible. I kept nagging her and insisting since she wouldn't explain why until finally she lost her patience:

"Lauri, don't you get it? For many people here, you're having a child with an enemy of the Revolution."

A slap in the face would have hurt less.

"Menchu! How can you say that? You've known Robertico for years. Besides, it's *my* child, *your* nephew, *our* parents' first grandchild."

"Then come back here to have the baby," replied my sister.

"That's impossible."

"It's not impossible. What's happened is that you chose the other side."

"I chose to follow the man I love. It has nothing to do with politics."

"Everything has to do with the Revolution."

"Oh, Menchu, don't say foolish things. This is costing money."

When we hung up I felt a knot in my throat but I couldn't cry. Something very unyielding had started to grow inside me. It was the wall that would separate me little by little from my twin sister and the rest of my family.

❧

How I long to see the patio of my home again,
for exile to end,
to hell with the millions,
but give me back what's mine,
overturn the Law of Urban Reform,
How I want to hang my old pictures,
to go back to my books, my spoons
to my Malecón, to my country.

(Pura del Prado 62)

❧

One afternoon Juancito and I were watching an episode from *The Millionaire,* a program about different people who were given a million dollars by a very rich man and how it changed their lives, sometimes for the better, sometimes for the worse. It was always one of my father-in-law's favorite programs, so as Juancito and I watched it, we thought of him, but we didn't talk about it. At the precise moment when the anonymous donor of such an astronomical sum was knocking on the door of the next happy winner, I felt something warm and humid in-between my legs. The first thing I thought of was that I had wet myself. It took me a few minutes to realize that I was in labor. But it couldn't be. I still had three weeks to go. Robertico wasn't home yet. He was in prison in Havana, in that city of light and sun, where we were born and raised, where we had fallen in love; and here I was in Miami, alone, with a ten year old child, on the verge of giving birth. Everything seemed like a dream. Finally, I managed to yell:

"Johnny, run next door and see if one of the neighbors can take me to the hospital."

They put me in a room in front of a window. It was raining. I was able to doze off in between contractions but otherwise I listened to the rhythmic, monotonous sound of the rain against the window panes. Could Robertico hear the rain from his prison cell? And what if he wasn't released soon and I had to raise the baby by myself? In the middle of all of these thoughts, Vidal poked his head in the door, blew me a kiss, and left as white as a sheet.

"Hospitals have always made him nervous," commented Adela disapprovingly. The neighbors had called her at the factory, and she had come directly to the hospital. I would have preferred to have my mother or my sister with me. More than anyone else, I missed my grandmother. I tried to remember the lullabies she used to sing me to sleep with as a child. I started to sing, very softly, as if the child inside me could hear:

> *Señora Santa Ana*
> *why weeps the baby boy?*
> *'Tis a tasty apple*
> *that gives him so much joy.*

Adela joined in:

> *I will give you one.*
> *I will give you two.*
> *One for the baby*
> *and another just for you.*

Not one do I want.
Not for two do I pine.
My lost one I want,
the one that is mine.

We were silent for a while until I said, "You know, Adela, rather than having a million dollars, I'd prefer to have our lives back."

"Oh, honey, don't talk that way. You have to think of the future, of your little boy." We always referred to the baby as a boy. I guess we were all sure that it was going to be a boy.

It was now after midnight, and I had barely dilated any more. The nurse told me to be prepared for a long night. Adela was exhausted and Johnny was with the neighbors. I asked her to go home, and she agreed as long as I promised to call her as soon as it seemed to be time, regardless of what hour it was.

At 5:30 in the morning the pain woke me up. I hadn't felt anything like it before. It was so intense I couldn't breathe. I was only able to call the nurse once it passed a bit. I don't know why she's taking so long. I try to focus on pleasant things: Menchu and me on the beach, with our red pails and shovels, building sand castles. I can feel the sand on my feet... the sun on my shoulders. Oh, oh, here comes the pain again! Oh, oh my God, oh...I don't like to complain, but...oh...oh fuck! My mother would kill me if she'd heard me.

"Nurse, please, nurse, come quickly."

I feel this enormous weight in-between my legs, as if the head were coming out. I want to push. The nurse examines me, but I don't understand what she's saying. I ask her to call my mother-in-law. The doctor arrives and they prep me to go to the operating room. I tell him they can't take me yet, that no one from my family is here yet, that I can't give birth by myself.

"Si no deja que el médico se la lleve, va a parir sola de verdad," the nurse explains in Spanish that I really am going to give birth by myself if they don't get me to the operating room.

I remember when my brother Pedritín was born. Menchu and I were nine. They took us out of school and we went to see him. I don't know if it was Menchu or I that said he had lion's hands. Everyone thought it was such a cute thing to say. Mamá looked beautiful, lying on the sheets with her initials that they had brought from home, wearing her sky blue night gown with a lace robe.

And look at me now, all sweaty, wearing this hospital gown I can hardly keep together so my behind doesn't show when I walk to the bathroom; alone, surrounded by strangers speaking a language which isn't mine, which I barely understand when I'm nervous. My poor child is coming into the world like this. They inject me in the vein. I drift off…

"We'll be together by the time the baby's here," I hear my husband's words. My God! Robertico, why have you abandoned me?"

My son was born at 6:07 a.m., September 8, 1961. I named him Pedro Pablo de la Caridad. Robertico and I had already decided to name him Pedro for my father and Pablo for his grandfather. I added the "Caridad" part on my own, in honor of the patron saint of Cuba since he was born on Her day. The minute they put him in my arms I was able to forget about the labor pains and I felt an unbelievable elation. I couldn't forget, however, how far away all my loved ones were.

They put me in a room with three other women. One of them was a tall and heavy black woman that had just delivered her sixth child. The other one was a blond, skinny American girl. Apparently, her baby girl had been born with some type of defect. The doctor closed the curtain when he came in to talk to her and her husband. Afterwards, they both cried a lot. The third one was Cuban like me, although a little older. We immediately hit it off.

Vidal and Juancito came every afternoon. They would bring me a candy bar or a bag of M&Ms, that is, until the nurse told them that chocolate wasn't good for me because it could constipate me. Adela would come around six o'clock after she got off from the factory. The day after the baby was born she said to me, "I called your brother and your family in Cuba to let them know. They were so happy and said to give you a kiss for them."

Something must have shown in my face because she added, "Oh yeah and Menchu asked if the baby had lion's hands."

Vidal became an excellent baby sitter. He would get home from work around 7:00 in the morning and would sleep until 1:00 or so. Later in the afternoon he would mind the baby so that I could rest for a while. He would sing to him *"Under the shade of the silk and lace parasol..."* and pieces from other operettas, and Pedro Pablo would fall fast asleep in his arms.

"He is going to think Vidal is his father," I would think, somewhat sadly.

Over the next year, I remember the bittersweet taste of watching my son grow up away from his father and my family. The first time he sat up, his first tooth, his first words, his first steps, all of them were cause for celebration and tears. Life became routine, interrupted only by news about the negotiations to free the *Brigadistas,* an occasional telephone call from Ricardo telling me about his life in New York, and letters from the Island, which were more infrequent now. As for the few letters that I did have from Robertico, I read them every night before going to sleep. From home, it was my mother who wrote the most. Those thin sheets of paper always left me with the feeling that they were keeping something from me, but no matter how much I tried to read between the lines, I still couldn't put my finger on what it was.

Pedro Pablo turned one without his father ever having seen him. He looked precious in his new outfit, a hand-me-down from the grandchild of one of my Spanish students. We bought him a cake from a neighbor who made them at home and invited three or four kids from the neighborhood. Adela, who had made great strides in the kitchen, insisted on making small tea sandwiches and chicken salad, and she stretched the food budget for the whole month just to make it all possible. Although we had been teaching him how to blow out candles for a month, when we sang "Happy Birthday" to him, he got upset and started to cry.

✧

Kennedy's Address. *The U.S.'s announcement that aggressive rocket bases were being built in Cuba was made by President Kennedy in a nationwide radio-TV address at 7 p.m. EDT October 22... He said he therefore had ordered the following "initial steps" be taken. "All ships of a kind bound for Cuba from whatever nation or port, will, if they are found to contain cargoes of offensive weapons, be turned back... I have reinforced our base at Guantanamo, evacuated today the dependents of our personnel there and ordered additional military units to be on a stand-by alert basis..." Mr. Kennedy concluded... "My fellow citizens, let no one doubt that this is a difficult and dangerous effort on which we have set out. No one can foresee precisely what course it will take or what costs or casualties will be incurred."*

(Facts on File 22.1147, 361–36)

∽

The exiles were sure there would be an invasion of Cuba. The Americans were afraid of a nuclear war. In Johnny's school they even gave them instructions on where to hide. I couldn't sleep. I was afraid that any action that the United States took might provoke retaliation against the *Brigadistas* in jail. I also worried about what could happen to my family if they bombed Havana. I had terrible nightmares where I dreamed the Island was entirely leveled and full of debris and ashes. But, in the end, nothing happened. The Russians returned the missiles on a ship and, for us Cubans, nothing really changed.

"Kennedy betrayed us again..." was all you heard from the exile community.

Finally, my father-in-law, my husband, and the other *Brigadistas* were exchanged for tractors and baby food. They all came back a lot thinner. Roberto looked twenty years older. All of Pastorita came out to welcome them, and I was so proud of them all. With the little we had, Johnny and I went out and bought a bottle to celebrate.

"To the heroes," we toasted with enthusiasm.

I could sense that my husband and father-in-law weren't really comfortable. They barely put the glass to their lips. Robertico couldn't wait to meet his son, who had fallen asleep. We tiptoed into the room so we wouldn't wake him up. His father looked at him for a long time, and with his index finger caressed his fine hair, his ears, his little nose, his lips still moist from his last bottle. He turned to me, and said in an astonished voice:

"This is a miracle. You're the real hero."

Christmas was here again, and we were together. Somehow Vidal was able to get hold of a pig and we roasted it in the backyard. The American across the street complained to the police about the noise and the smell of pork. Didn't he have anything better to do than to spoil our Christmas Eve?

The next day we found out that President Kennedy was coming to Miami to address the *Brigadistas* in the Orange Bowl. People couldn't talk about anything else. I will always remember that day: it was sunny but very windy. I really didn't believe that the President was going to make an appearance, but just in case we wore our Sunday best. The Orange Bowl was packed and crazy. Some were saying that Kennedy was a traitor. Others were sure that he had a secret plan to finish off Castro. The buzz continued until they played both national anthems. The crowd came to its feet. The *Brigadistas* wore their uniforms and so did the Americans. Everyone stood at attention. Finally I caught sight of Kennedy. His hair was reddish and windblown. I don't remember a single thing he said, but I do remember the crowd chanting, "war, war," and Jackie saying a few words in Spanish. The climax came when the *Brigadistas* presented Kennedy with the Cuban flag. You could hear his Bostonian accent echoing throughout the Orange Bowl:

"I can assure you that this flag will be returned to this brigade in a free Havana."

The translated words were repeated from one person to the next.

Two days later, we once again sat around the TV and watched the crowds in Times Square say goodbye to the old year and welcome in

1963. We ate our grapes and toasted with cider. And my father-in-law once again lifted his glass:

"Next year…"

But his voice cracked and he was unable to finish. Perhaps he had lost faith in our return.

My husband and his father started looking for a job at the beginning of the year. Or at least, so they said. One afternoon when Adela and I were on our way downtown with Pedro Pablo, we ran into them at Walgreens. There was a crowd around them, and they were describing how they had fought in the Bay of Pigs. I was able to observe Robertico without him seeing me. He was pretending he had a machine gun in his hands and was imitating its sound… "rrrrrr…" Suddenly, he felt like a stranger to me.

Robertico kept telling me that no one would hire them because everybody knew they were veterans of the Bay of Pigs, and they couldn't ask them to work at a burger joint or deliver newspapers. I just couldn't accept that the American who had been his boss at Royal Castle would think that way, but Robertico insisted that though he'd be willing to work anywhere or do anything, there was no way he was going back to flipping burgers. It was beneath him.

It was becoming more and more difficult every day to live with my in-laws, especially now that we had a child. I found out that churches were helping refugees relocate outside Miami. They would find them sponsors and work in other cities. Without Robertico knowing about it, I put our names on the list.

On January 6th, the Feast of the Epiphany, my father-in-law's mother arrived from Cuba. She was a tall woman and still attractive for her age. She immediately took charge of the household. Well actually, she took charge of everything. She was constantly saying that Johnny needed a haircut. (What's more, she insisted on calling him Juancito, even though he hated it.) She moved all the furniture around. And within a week, she started looking for a new place to live because, according to her, Pastorita was full of scum. Adela would look at my father-in-law with desperation, hoping he'd say something, but he wouldn't intervene. The situation grew more tense every day. Doña Asunción (that's what she insisted on being called) had also decided she would handle the money and wanted Adela and Vidal to turn their pay checks over to her. She even tried to take the little bit I earned selling magazines by phone while Pedro Pablo napped. One afternoon Doña Asunción stumbled over a small toy that Pedro Pablo had left on the living room floor. It was a brand new toy truck that I had just bought for him the day before at the supermarket. The old bat, who was agile for her age, reached down, picked the truck up off the floor, and looked me in the eye, saying:

"Laura, you are totally irresponsible. In this household there's not enough money to go around buying toys."

"No, you're the irresponsible one wanting my child to grow up without toys."

"That's all I need. Some brat disrespecting me!"

I took a bottle out of the refrigerator and shut myself in the bathroom with the baby. I don't know which of the two us cried more. The baby didn't want the cold milk, and I didn't want to come out and face the "witch," as Johnny and I had started to call her. I sat there and began to sing to Pedro Pablo in the hopes that he'd fall asleep and, also, to block out all the shouting that was going on:

> *Señora Santa Ana*
> *why weeps the baby boy?*
> *'Tis a tasty apple*
> *that gives him so much joy.*

Two days later they called from the Church. They wanted to know if Robertico, the baby and I would go to a place called Columbus, in Ohio. There was a possible lead on a job for Robertico, and even though it was cold in the winters, they'd give us some winter coats. They also told me that there was a family who could put us up for a while until we got on our feet. I told the nun we'd take it, although I really didn't like the idea of living with strangers.

"It's just that since the day we were married we've never been on our own…"

She promised me that she'd look into it and see if they could work something out, but I assured her that we would go no matter what.

That night Robertico told me that some of the *Brigadistas* were going to get together to start planning what to do next. That's when I told him about the possibility of us moving to Ohio. He looked at me in disbelief and insisted that his place was here in Miami. Never, not even when I asked him not to take part in the invasion, had we had a more heated discussion.

"So why did you ever insist on having a child? It's not like you ever think of him first or worry if there's enough money to buy him milk or even care if your grandmother won't let him play with his toys…" I said in a harsh tone.

"I want my son to have a country."

"He was born in this country."

"Yes, but he's Cuban!" he yelled as he slammed the door.

CHAPTER THREE
"...Fi-del! Fi-del! Fi-del!..."

IT IS THE AFTERNOON OF THE 26TH OF JULY. The Civic Square bustles and boils over with people. Five hundred thousand Cubans from the countryside and as many from Havana mingle in the enormous esplanade. The open space is a sea of hats and of machetes held high against the blue sky. The tropical sun lights up Martí's statue and obelisk. It generously bathes the human contingent and radiates off the buildings nearby.

On the terrace of the National Library stand the leaders of the Revolution and the foreign dignitaries. Two gargantuan hands, on which a dove perches momentarily, bear the symbolic "26." To the side, the National Flag furls in the wind.

Raúl Castro, always combative, speaks:

"Everyone here needs to come to order because the people are in the plaza... The best army the Republic can count on is the one in front of us right now."

There is great suspense in the air. From the stage, someone directly addresses the masses:

"I would like to take this uproar that is bursting forth from all parties and change it into a question, a question that I put directly before you the people. Do you, or do you not, want Fidel to continue heading the government?"

A million voices answer in unison: "¡Sí!"

Next comes the acclamation of el líder máximo, the Maximum Leader—Fi-del, Fi-del, Fi-del; and the hats thrown into the air—Fi-del, Fi-del, Fi-del; and the brandishing of the machetes—Fi-del, Fi-del, Fi-del; and the ovations—Fi-del, Fi-del, Fi-del; and the joy in every soul's eyes—Fi-del, Fi-del, Fi-del; and the impetuous movement of the sea of people—Fi-del, Fi-del, Fi-del; these acts and others confirm that it is the will of the Cuban people, and the people alone.

"The people have spoken and have ordered Fidel to fulfill his obligation."

(*Bohemia* 51:3, 85–86)

౸

I'm empty inside, as if all my organs had been taken out, as if this woman who gets up, showers, eats, drinks, talks, studies, walks, goes to bed and gets up again were a robot, stripped of her memories, her dreams, her aspirations. No. It's worse than that. If there were only emptiness inside me, I wouldn't feel anything. What's really happened is that I've been split in two. My other half left with Lauri. My life was truncated. My soul is like a stump, like a huge bloody stump with big chunks of unhealed pieces that they keep picking at.

Attending the university is an act of sheer will. Lauri and I had always dreamed about the day that we would climb the famous steps together. I feel like I'm stealing part of her life, that this doesn't belong to me alone. I can barely concentrate on my studies the way I should. At times it seems like the only thing we do is listen to Fidel's long speeches. They go on for hours and hours. I ride the bus and Fidel is speaking. I get home and Fidel is speaking. We have dinner and Fidel is speaking. I go out on the front porch and Fidel is speaking. I go to bed and Fidel is speaking. Papá turns off the TV and Fidel is still speaking. The next door neighbor turns off the radio and Fidel is still speaking... I go to sleep and Fidel is still speaking. Although I always hear it, I don't always listen. When I do, sometimes things become clear. Other times, however, he appears to go round and round the same issue and always says the same thing. And finally winds up saying nothing. Still, he must be saying something because the next morning everyone asks, "Did you hear Fidel?", as if it had been the most important thing in the world.

My friend Lázaro thinks that Fidel Castro is some kind of messiah. Once, Fidel showed up at the university. He wanted the students to vote for a guy named Cubelas for president of the Federation of University Students. He was there talking to the students all night long until the next morning. When Lázaro told me about it his eyes lit up and became very small. I don't know why, but it scared me.

Some of the old professors didn't come back this year because they didn't want to accept the new Council. The university president, however, did stay. I heard someone say he is a senile old man who wants to die being president, and that they'll keep him on as long as he does what he's told. My brother Ricardo just keeps shaking his head, saying, "What a disgrace!"

To me it looks like Ricardo has aged all of a sudden. He's only five years older than we are, but he looks like a grown-up now. Although the university refused to accept the credits he had earned at Villanova, he's just a few credits short for his law degree. Even so, he doesn't want to take the bar exam at the University of Havana.

"If all of this changes, the credits won't matter. And if it doesn't, I'll have to leave," he explains to Papá.

It wasn't until recently that I found out Ricardo had fought against Batista. All those times he mysteriously disappeared, which Lauri and I assumed were romantic interludes, it turns out he was really going out, selling bonds and handing out propaganda. He even planted bombs! Papá keeps reminding him, but he always responds, "This isn't what I fought for."

I wish Ricardo would explain things to me, but when I ask him, he just looks at me with what's clearly an expression of painful sadness in his eyes. Then he pats me on the head and says, "Go back to reading your poetry. This is men's business."

I hate it when he talks to me that way. Yesterday, I got so mad that I threw a book at him. I missed, so he just laughed as he sauntered away.

There are a lot of changes taking place around here and fast too. The year began with the Agrarian Reform Law. Lázaro is its most ardent defender. He strolls down Plaza Cadenas talking to anybody who will listen about how the peasants have been oppressed and how we need to give the land back to them. Sometimes he invites me to have a soda with him, and all he talks about is the Agrarian Reform.

"Man, you talk as much as Fidel," I tell him in jest.

He'll change the topic for a while and ask me about my classes and my family. He flirts with me a little. But then he charges again. There comes a time when I stop listening to his words, but I do like the sound of his voice. I watch his gestures, how he moves his hands, the enthusiasm in his expression. I nod my head as if I were agreeing, but then he realizes I'm not paying attention to him and he gripes at me:

"I don't like women who say 'yes' to everything."

"Me neither" is my response, but that's not actually true. My mother is like that and I adore her. Almost all the women I know are like that; or if not, they're the exact opposite, like Aunt Paquita who died arguing with Uncle Manuel. I wouldn't want to be like her for anything in the world.

"Women should know how to think for themselves," Lázaro tells me.

With that in mind I decide to ask him about some of the things that have been troubling me lately, like the revolutionary trials.

"And what if it turns outs that one of these men who have been condemned and shot is innocent? They're freezing bank accounts of honorable people, like the parents of my friend Eva. Do you know what they told her mother when she went to their safety deposit box and tried to get out a small crucifix that Eva and her sister had worn for their First Communion? That it belonged to the Revolution! How is it possible to sweep away people's rights overnight?"

"Revolutions are like that, Menchu. They can't be any other way. Besides, in Cuba people didn't have any rights…our guarantees under the Constitution had been abolished…many of our friends were tortured… others were found dead… Are you going to defend Batista now?"

"No, but at least back then there was still a sense of solidarity. You know very well that people stuck together, like that time when you got arrested and they let you go because Robertico's father made a call to a friend of his who was one of Batista's officials…"

Lázaro's eyes had become beady again, so small they seemed like two horizontal lines.

"Hah! You don't know the first thing about politics."

"Didn't you just say that you liked women who could think?"

Lázaro then walked up to me and kissed me. He thrust his tongue into my mouth, and he ran it over my gums, my teeth, my tongue. It was a kiss full of fury and saliva that took my breath away. I tried to move back. The weight of his body trapped me against the wall of the interior patio of the house. I could feel his erection pushing in between my legs.

I tried to get free, to scream. We struggled. Just then we heard Papá cough in the living room. He let go and then looked at me mockingly:

"I'm sorry, but tonight you're irresistible."

"If you disrespect me one more time, I swear…"

"It won't happen again." And while he was saying that, he moved closer to me and touched my breast, right at the nipple.

∽

They came from everywhere, in irrepressible waves. Under the ardent sun, led by their teachers, they got off the buses, got into single files, perspired, sang, and laughed. The bands deafened the air with their music. Flags waved in the breeze. The loudspeakers, broadcasting over the noise of the crowd, issued recommendations. The green lawns, stepped on by thirty thousand pairs of shoes, gave out a strong smell of the countryside, of life. They screamed and laughed. They were confident. They were the children of Cuba, the students rejoicing in a free motherland.

The Revolution had called them to the former military installation at Columbia. What was Columbia for them prior to January 1st? The same as it was for the adults, an evil place, a lair of hate and death. How could they have ever thought that they could get past the fortified posts and get to the walled enclosure? And now here they were, in Columbia. Here they were trampling the famous polygon, the cradle from where so many orders to imprison and to kill were given. Here they were, children, weak creatures, who, with no weapons other than their hands waving flags and no armor other than their blue uniforms, had won the battle against the tyrant. Where before there was death, now there was life. Where before there were threats, now there were hymns. Where before there were rifles, now there were books, pencils, and pens.

The Revolution had brought about a miracle.

(*Bohemia* 51:49, 66)

∽

Lázaro has become an agitator at the university. He's impatient. He says everything from the past has to be swept away, and it has to be done quickly. Yesterday he climbed onto a makeshift platform and started to harangue a group of fellow students:

"No sector of the country has enjoyed the trust and empathy of the Cuban people as much as this university. For its brilliant and continued service to the Motherland, for its radical way of facing the Cuban problem, not only in times of liberal corruption but in times of insolent oppression, for its actions in 1923, 1930, 1933, 1952, and 1956…each time a citizen walked up our front steps and looked at the statue of our Alma Mater, severe and ever vigilant over the old city abused by despots and denigrated by crooks, they would see in her a symbol and a promise of civic resurrection…"

As students began to applaud, his voice—firm and strong—seemed to come from deep inside him:

"Throughout the years, the University of Havana has prided itself on being the critic and censurer of our national life, an attitude that now imposes on it the highest responsibility: to live by the example we demand of others. Our task," he said with his index finger raised high in the air, "is not to affix blame; however, if the process of rectification drags on for too long, it will be a slow death indeed. Educational normality must return to this highest center of Cuban culture."

When he finished, all the students gathered around. They patted him on the back as they complimented him on his oratory skills.

"Hey, you've become a real Cortina…" joked one, referring to the famous orator.

"You sound more like a disciple of Fidel," stated another.

I saw his eyes skimming over the group. I knew he was looking for me. A part of me wanted to run up and hug him; at the same time, part of me was afraid. I left before he could spot me.

⁓

El Cobre is a small town laid out at the foot of a mountain. At the top of a hill, overlooking the edge of town, one finds the Sanctuary of Our Lady of Charity. It was here that the patroness of Cuba was first carried by the zealous hands of fishermen who had found her floating in the waters of the Caribbean. It is here where believers from every corner of the Island come to adore her. At the steps to the Sanctuary one finds the destitute who seek alms from the faithful who pass; the motley signs that along with their vendors interminably announce today's lottery numbers; the weathered display of religious wares—medallions, rosaries, souvenirs, prayer cards—that are marked "cheaper than inside."

A young lieutenant from Niquero, twenty years of age, clean shaven, climbs the steps on his knees, steps that will lead him to the dark-skinned virgin. His shirt wet with perspiration clings to his body, which has endured the trip on foot from Santiago. His knees, which never bent to the tyrant in the foothills of the Sierra Maestra, are now bent as he fulfills his promise.

He rests and moves his handkerchief back and forth as he pats his face.

"Some type of promise?" someone asks.

"Yes sir."

"For what?"

"I made a promise the day before I went up into the mountains... I vowed to the Virgin that I'd walk all the way from Santiago and climb Her steps on my knees."

"So She would protect you?"

"No, so that She would protect Fidel..."

(Bohemia 51:38, 62)

∽

Lázaro said that religion is the opiate of the masses.

Another student quipped back:

"Hey, man, that's a Marxist phrase."

Papá asked Ricardo if he is conspiring against the government. All color drained from my brother's face and the outside of his nostrils became snow white. They always get that way when he lies.

"Of course not, Papá. I am only working with the Catholic Congress."

"You better watch what you're doing, Ricardo. Things aren't like they used to be."

"Don't worry, viejo, I know what I'm doing."

"Ay, mijo" Mamá intervened. "Don't take any risks, son."

When I told Lázaro that I was going to go to the Catholic Congress with my brother, he was furious.

"Do whatever you want to... The Church has always allied itself with the powerful. It did so with the Spanish colonists..."

"You can't say it allied itself with Batista..."

"Some joined the Revolution at the last minute, just in case... But look, Menchu, that's not it. The Catholic Congress is a counterrevolutionary movement. Can't you see that? It's a group of privileged elitists that can't stand the idea of us all being equal."

"My brother isn't an elitist, and in my house you've always been treated as if you were our equal."

"You see? 'As if I were your equal'...because you don't really think that I am your equal, but all that is over and done with..."

"Lázaro, how can you talk about my family that way?"

"It's not just your family, Menchu, it's the entire middle class, the bourgeoisie. Can't you see how they've exploited the rest of us, how little they have cared about the country? When it comes to education, the Revolution and its plans are going to change a lot of things... A new generation is going to be born, a new man..."

I went with Ricardo to the assembly anyway. There was a huge crowd and the religious songs truly inspired me. One of the speakers said that, to combat materialism, we had to practice a militant spirituality, without fear, even if it cost us our lives. I was surprised how many people knew my brother.

It's been different this Christmas. Mamá keeps crying, waiting for news from Lauri. Ricardo comes and goes without saying much. And with Papá you never know. Sometimes I hear him talking with friends about the Revolution and he seems somewhat enthusiastic. Other times, when Ricardo's giving his point of view on things, he seems to agree with him. Since he's basically an optimist, he's sure things are going to get better. Pedritín brought a drawing home from school that has hats made of guano in the shape of a Christmas tree with a garland around it that reads "The Year of Liberation." Also, the weather has been awful. It's been so rainy and windy. We sat around the dinner table on Christmas Eve, as we always do, but no one was really in the mood to celebrate. We were getting ready for cider and dessert when Lázaro arrived. Papá lifted his glass:

"To Cuba," he said.

"To Laurita being back here with us next year," Ricardo answered him with a painful irony in his voice.

Mamá ran to the kitchen so we wouldn't see her cry.

At midnight, against a backdrop of horns and ringing bells, the austere melody of the National Anthem could be heard from one end of the Island to the other. The radio, bands, and loudspeakers sent the patriotic hymn through the airwaves, accompanied by thousands of voices from every corner of the country.

The celebration was as much a welcome as a goodbye. 1959 was now a memory, and it had gone down in history as a stellar year in the destiny of the Motherland.

(Bohemia 52:2, 63)

Last night Papá and Ricardo got into a big argument. At first I thought it was about politics since that was usually the theme of their conversations. But later I heard Ricardo saying,

"I can't believe you can do something like this to Mamá. There's no better woman in the world who's more willing to please others..."

"I know you're right...I adore her. This has nothing to do with that, Ricardo. It's just that all men need an escape...getting out every once in a while doesn't hurt anybody. And this woman, well, she's something else, she's so sensuous, you can't resist her. Look, what happened was..."

"I don't want to hear the details, all right?"

I ran away frightened and angry. Since then I haven't been able to look Papá in the eyes. Every time I think of him all I see is him in bed with a woman with big tits and an enormous ass, and I feel like vomiting. I wonder if Mamá knows. She seems so sad, but then she's been that way ever since my sister left.

Sometimes I feel like everything is caving in around me, that I'm walking in quicksand and that I could be swallowed up by it at any time. Lázaro comes over almost every night, and we sit on the front porch and talk. He's always so sure of himself, so enthusiastic, so optimistic about the future. He has an answer for every one of my doubts. Around 11:00 Mamá usually sticks her head out the door and says:

"Good night, Lázaro. Remember Menchu has classes in the morning."

Then I walk him to the sidewalk and we say good night with a kiss. Once in a while, just before leaving, he pushes me softly against the side of the house, where we can't be seen, and there he holds me tight and kisses me. I like his kisses. God, I like his kisses! I like them so much that sometimes I think I'm going to die. Then I break into a run and go inside the house. Am I falling in love with Lázaro? God, I wish I could to talk to Lauri!

Last week we went to the wake for María Aurora's father. A few months ago they took over his company when they nationalized all the businesses. As María Aurora herself told me, he tried to explain to the auditors that his match factory had been founded by his father, a Spanish immigrant, who had nothing to do with politics, and that he himself had sold bonds for the 26th of July movement.

"This has nothing to do with politics, old man. This is revolutionary justice. Don't be a dumbass."

He told them that they would have to remove him by force, and that's what they did. When he got home he was livid. María Aurora said that the veins in his neck were sticking out so much that she thought they were going to explode. They heard a noise around dawn, and María Aurora's mother got up and found him on the kitchen floor. It was a massive heart attack. His widow kept mumbling inconsolably:

"The Revolution killed him."

And then she would sigh:

"I don't know what we're going to do now…"

When I told Lázaro about it, he seemed to take it hard.

"It's a shame, Menchu… Please tell them that if they need anything, they can count on me." It almost seems as if he had read their mind because two days later María Aurora called me to see if he could help them obtain the necessary paperwork to leave the country.

Everything is happening so quickly that sometimes I feel as if I'm caught in the eye of a hurricane. The only constant is Mamá Luya, sitting in her armchair in the dining room, just up from her nap, with her powdery face and Coty pink lips. She smells of perfume and of my childhood. Suddenly, another year has gone by.

July 8, 1961
The Year of Education

Dear Dora,

I'm sending this letter to let you know that I'm teaching others to read and write, I am thirteen years old, and I'm in the first grade. I just began school this year. My name is Marina Díaz Barrio. I give classes by candlelight since I don't have a lantern.

I've read letters people send in to Bohemia, you know, like when they said you could write in for the Three Kings Day I wrote one but I didn't send in a photo since I wasn't able to get my picture taken. And today I'm writing to let you know that I'm ready and willing to take up arms to defend my beloved country. Also, I want you to know that I have four pupils and I think two are on the brink of being able to read.

Also, I wanted to say that the only hope of seeing Fidel was to go to Havana on the 26th of July but now they're telling us that none of us are going to be able to go to Havana, not the tutors and not those who can read. Well, I've seen pictures of Fidel because we have a lot of them at home.

I live in Las Villas. I wanted you to publish my letter in Bohemia so that Fidel would read it because I know he reads Bohemia. I just want to be able to say "thank you, Fidel." I have great admiration for you and all your comrades.

Right now I am learning about dressmaking. I also know how to knit and I'm going to learn how to embroider, I really want to know how to do all of this so I can teach others.

Fidel, I won't give up for all the tea in China. Always Forward! (And please excuse my handwriting.)

Fatherland or Death! We shall overcome!
Marina Díaz Barrio

(*Bohemia* 53:34, 21)

∽

There are many things that trouble me, but the issue of education isn't one of them. Marta Lola and I have registered to go to the countryside to participate in the literacy campaign. Nothing seems better than to aspire to be a country where everyone can read and write. Ricardo is opposed to me going. As he usually does, Papá just says, "We'll see," and Mamá doesn't say anything. But I've already made my decision: I'm going.

Lauri called to tell us that she's expecting a baby. I can't believe it! It seems like yesterday that we were just two teenagers dancing rock and roll and infatuated with boys... How did we grow up so fast? In such a short time we've had no choice but to become women.

There are all kinds of rumors going around, that the Revolution is going to take away parents' legal rights over their children, and that there's going to be an invasion by the *gusanos,* or "worms," as they're calling the people who've left the country these days.

There were three air raids on Saturday, one in Santiago, one in San Antonio de los Baños and one here in Havana. The country is geared for war. They say that an invasion by the Americans is imminent. Lázaro came to my house very early in the morning. It was the first time I had seen him wearing the militia uniform. Thank goodness Ricardo wasn't up yet!

"This is imperialist treachery, the cowards…" he said indignantly. And once more his eyes became so small that they again seemed like two horizontal lines.

"I came to say goodbye," he announced.

"But where are you going?" I asked alarmed.

"Where do you think? To defend the Revolution."

The rumors of an invasion turned out to be true. My heart was in my throat thinking something could happen to Lázaro. Up to now I really hadn't understood how much he means to me. The idea of losing him horrified me. When he finally came home from the front, I hugged him and burst into tears.

"There, there…there's no need to cry."

Now I feel that Lázaro has been right all along. The Revolution might not be perfect, but it isn't right for a country as big and powerful as the United States to attack us.

Ricardo hasn't come home for days. Mamá and Papá whisper to each other. I think he's in hiding but they don't want to tell me anything. Thousands of people have been arrested. They've rounded up all of the invaders. You can't imagine how absolutely shocked we were when we saw Robertico and his father among them! We couldn't believe it.

"They are nothing but 'worms,' counterrevolutionaries," said Lázaro with disgust.

Mamá, who rarely said anything that had to do with politics, let him know she was offended:

"That's enough, Lázaro. That's my daughter's husband you're talking about."

Mamá wanted to call Laurita but couldn't get through.

"What's going to become of my daughter? And expecting a child…" she said sadly.

Many of my classmates from the university have been arrested. All Catholic publications have been banned. They're also going to nationalize all the private schools. The rumor about parents losing legal rights over their children is spreading more and more.

Life has become a constant and continuous separation. I feel like I'm a gigantic hand waving goodbye to something or someone all the time. Most of my classmates are leaving the country. So are my old teachers. My uncles, aunts and cousins are also taking off. Many of them have left without even saying goodbye, as if they were running away. And afterwards, it's as if the sea has swallowed them up. Nobody even mentions their name. Ricardo doesn't live at home anymore, but every time he comes over he tells us that we should all leave too. Papá assures him that nothing is going to happen to us and that things are going to get better… Mamá doesn't contradict him—she always agrees with Papá—but I know that deep down she's dying to see Laurita. I couldn't stand being away from Lázaro. And also, the idea of going to the countryside to teach people to read and write, for the first time, makes me feel like I'm doing something worthwhile.

"Don't you realize that Pedritín is precisely at the age to be indoctrinated," Ricardo insists. "A lot of families are sending their young kids away, even if they have to send them out of the country alone."

"There's no way I could ever do anything like that," Mamá says emphatically.

"He would be with Lauri."

"Either we all leave, or we all will stay."

But that's not the way it turned out. Ricardo left, and without even saying goodbye. In a way, it was even more difficult than when Lauri left. I don't know why, but I don't think I'll ever see him again.

My only support has been Lázaro. The only time I get mad at him is when he talks bad about my brother-in-law.

"Robertico stooped as low as you can go, being a mercenary for the Yankees, joining up with the imperialists to invade your own country, using American weapons against his fellow Cubans, fighting against the Revolution, this Revolution which is as green as our palm trees and will make it possible for all children to have shoes and schoolbooks. But the Revolution is generous and has forgiven him. Let's see if the Yankees come rescue him."

Mamá insisted on visiting Robertico in jail and even took him some things to eat. She looked miserable when she returned. Her only comment was, "It's so sad to see any man in prison. Besides, he's my son-in-law."

I felt bad that I didn't go with her, but sometimes I think Lázaro is right, that I've been blind. We had a privileged lifestyle. Private schools. A tutor if we were not doing well in math or fell behind in English. Ballet lessons. French. Art. Going to the symphony on Sundays. Never thinking about how much illiteracy there was in the country. Fancy restaurants. Summers at the beach house. Eating mangoes on the seashore, their sticky, sweet juice sliding down our necks. With so many starving children! Running then to jump into the ocean. The waves breaking right at the level of our mouths. Without ever considering how many didn't have access to the beaches! Easter week at Uncle Maximo's ranch. His horse, Jardinera. I want to ride her. It's my turn! Without ever thinking how the landowners exploited the poor peasants! A shot of espresso in the middle of the afternoon. The men playing dominoes. The women relaxing in rocking chairs, and all the cousins running around. With our backs to the problems of the masses. As night fell, the glow of lightning bugs. If you put one on its back and it jumps three times before it flies, you'll have three children. Baseball games between La Habana and Almendares. Formental can really slug the ball! The ice cream from Tropicream and from Picolino. *A Prado y Neptuno iba una chiquita, cha-cha-cha…"* Mamá, why won't you let us shave our legs? *"El Silver tiene lo que más yo quiero…"* The clubs. The dances. My God, how could I have been so blind! The only poor person I knew was the old woman who begged for alms outside our church. Papá would give us a quarter to put in her hand, and in return, she'd give us a smile and a little prayer card. It's true that Mamá was never one of those society women who spent her days playing canasta and being photographed for the social pages in the paper, and Papá never exploited anybody. Everything we enjoyed was due to his hard work. But it's not fair for some to have so much and others to have so little! And the four kids that belonged to our black cook, Hilda, were more like folkloric characters than real people. Lázaro's right. There's been too much racial discrimination in this country. Finally, Blacks will now be able to swim at the beaches.

Yesterday my sister called. She asked me to go up and be with her when she has the baby. At first I didn't say much. Lázaro wouldn't take his eyes off me while I was talking to her. Finally I had to tell her straight out that I couldn't. Maybe I was too insensitive.

Lauri, I wish I could have told you how traveling to the United States would have put me in a bad situation and how it could have caused me all types of problems in the university, how it would have offended Lázaro who's so good to all of us. I don't know if you would have understood. Anyway, you hung up without giving me enough time to explain.

CHAPTER FOUR
"I Wanna Hold Your Hand!"

WE ARRIVED IN COLUMBUS IN THE MIDDLE OF FEBRUARY, 1963. It was twenty-eight degrees outside. When we got off the airplane steam came out of our mouths when we tried to speak. I was surprised to see the branches on the trees so bare. To me they looked like arms that were raised to God imploring him to send warmth. The Stones, who were our sponsors, lived in a red brick townhouse. It was surrounded by so many others that were just alike, I was always afraid that I'd confuse which one was theirs. The basement became our living quarters. From the small high windows you could see the ground and the dry brown grass in the yard. The house only had one bathroom, so if we really needed to go, we had to use a bucket. Robertico said it reminded him of prison.

It snowed just a few days after we arrived. It was the first time we had ever seen snow, and we went out and played in it like kids, throwing snowballs at each other, and even making a snowman. Things seemed softer with everything white. I was in awe of the landscape that seemed virginal to me. It was the same feeling I had when I had my First Communion. It was almost like a blinding flash, as if you had discovered the existence of a superior being, something beyond comprehension. Time stood still as I watched each flake fall from the sky. Every second was identical to the previous one, and to the next one, and I asked myself if eternity was going to be like this. Nonetheless, as the days went by, the snow became filthy and was piled up on the side of the streets. It turned into a gray heap of muck that became a nuisance to everybody.

They found a job for Robertico as a bill collector. He had to go door-to-door trying to collect payment for bills that were long overdue. A lot of times people would slam the door in his face. Roberto complained about the cold and his aching feet. Once, even a dog ran after him. He was always in a bad mood. Besides, they didn't pay him very much. I would spend almost every waking moment with Pedro Pablo locked in the basement, not daring to take him out except for in the morning when the sun was out, especially since he had a runny nose all winter long. Mrs. Stone loaned us a vaporizer that helped him breathe a little easier during the night.

On Sundays we would go to church with Peter and Kathy, our sponsors, and their nine-year old daughter, Elizabeth. What caught my eye was how well dressed the older women were, always wearing their hats and gloves without fail. Roberto always said they put on so much rouge that they looked like clowns.

I had dreamed about being alone with Roberto and the baby, but now it turned out that I not only missed my family, but I had started to miss Miami, Johnny, Vidal, and even my in-laws. Besides, Roberto had become a different person. So many times during his absence I had longed for him, I had remembered our nights of making love, I had wanted nothing more than to take refuge in his arms, but now he was right by my side and he seldom touched me. In bed, I'd hug him, rub his back, the back of his neck, or I'd reach over and try to touch him. But he'd usually mutter something under his breath about being tired and a minute later he'd begin to snore. So many times I fell asleep crying. There were times I even masturbated. I had done it often while he was gone, but now, with him sleeping right there next to me, it made me feel both hurt and angry. At least it helped me fall asleep.

Some weekends the Stones would take us downtown. I felt that compared to Havana, Columbus was dreadful but, of course, I didn't say so. What always made me shudder most was the penitentiary. It was built with bricks that were an indescribable dark color, with just a few small windows and surrounded by tall barbed wire. It was guarded by men with long rifles, and the whole place had a sinister aspect that terrified me. The prison made me think of Cuba. Sometimes I would dream that my mother was inside and I could hear her screaming and begging to be let out. I would've preferred never to have gone by it, but I didn't say anything. I tried not to hurt the Stone's feelings and, as for Roberto, I didn't want to add more fuel to the fire. He was angry enough on his own. He used to say he couldn't stand Americans and having to speak English all the time.

I wanted to work, but it was impossible with the baby. One day I mentioned it at church and I was shocked when they asked me if I wanted to help out in the nursery, a sort of a pre-kindergarten. I could take Pedro Pablo with me, and since the church was only three blocks from the house, we could walk there. I accepted the offer right away. At least, Pedro Pablo would have other children to play with, and we both would get out of the house some. My second surprise came a week later when they gave me a pay check. I couldn't believe it!

With what I saved from my very modest salary and with the little that I had left from the money my father had sent me with Ricardo, we bought our first car, a 1953 Ford that was falling apart. It was faded red, and we named it *El Mamey,* after the Cuban fruit we both loved.

I offered to help Roberto with his job. I could drive the car—Vidal had taught me how after the baby was born, and he'd sometimes lend me his car—and Roberto could get out and go make the collections. That way he could work faster. We'd go in the evenings and weekends, which is when you found people at home. Most of the time Pedro Pablo would fall asleep in the back seat. I also started doing the weekly report Roberto had to submit to his employer and I began keeping track of all the bills. I don't know if it was because of my help or just plain luck, but he started collecting more and, as a result, making a little more too. The summer had arrived, and the trees had turned green, and Pedro Pablo had begun to say a few words in English. With the money we were saving it looked like we were going to be able to move into our own apartment soon. There was nothing I wanted more. Even Roberto, every once in a while, was becoming the same Roberto he had been before. Plus, Mrs. Stone offered to babysit one evening so we could go out. We went to the movies and to have a soft drink afterwards. And later, we made love like we were newlyweds.

One day in late July, we got a call from Miami. Doña Asunción had died. Johnny had found her on the floor after school with her eyes wide open and the telephone in her hand. It was a massive heart attack. The first thing I thought of was how terrible it must have been for the child.

Roberto decided to go to his grandmother's funeral. I couldn't believe it. The woman was a witch, and she had made life so miserable for Pedro Pablo and me, and Roberto wasn't even that close to her. But by the time he told me, he had already purchased the ticket and was packing his bag. I asked him how much the ticket had cost. He had spent almost everything we had saved for the deposit on the apartment. I wanted to kill him, but I swallowed hard and kissed him goodbye.

I expected him to come back sooner, but two weeks went by. When he called from Miami he seemed distant, and I was even afraid he wasn't ever going to come back. What would I do if he abandoned us up here in this city so far away from everything? Finally, he called and told me that he was coming home the next day:

"I have a surprise for you. You are going to like it," he said.

Pedro Pablo and I went to pick him up at the airport. As soon as I saw him I felt at ease again inside. During the last few months I had started to resent him and even wondered if I loved him as much as I used to.

The minute we got in the car he said:

"Laurita, we're moving. We're getting out of Columbus."

A friend of his had helped him track down an old schoolmate, Pancho, who lived in the outskirts of Washington, DC. Pancho had told him that a lot of Cubans lived there, that it was a tight knit group, and that they always helped each another. He promised that he'd find him a job there.

I argued that it was crazy to leave Columbus without having a job lined up. At least here we had help from the Stones and from the church, and that we both had a job. But Roberto had already made up his mind. He had left the most convincing point for last:

"We'll finally have our own apartment."

"And how are we going to pay the rent? How are we going to come up with the money for the deposit?"

"Don't you worry. Everything's already taken care of. Don't you trust me anymore?"

Although we had lived in Columbus only a few months, and they had been difficult ones at that, I still cried when I said goodbye to my friends at church, to Peter, Kathy and Elizabeth, and even to Roberto's boss who demanded those dreadful weekly reports.

Roberto, on the other hand, was barely in the car heading for DC when he said:

"I'm never coming back to this boring town again!"

In my mind I was content as long as the three of us were together, but I guess he obviously didn't feel the same way. I felt that strange restlessness that sometimes overtook me. It was a peculiar type of pain, an ache that crept around in my chest without finding exactly where to settle.

More than 200,000 persons, mostly Negroes but including thousands of whites, held a massive peaceful demonstration in Washington August 28 to focus attention on Negro demands for immediate equality in jobs and civil rights.

The demonstrators gathered in the early morning at the Washington Monument, while 13 of their leaders called on Congressional leaders. Then, led by the organizers of the demonstration, the marchers moved in 2 paths, down Constitution Avenue and Independence Avenue, to the Lincoln Memorial. The demonstrators eventually filled almost the entire mall between the monument and the memorial. The leaders, after completing the march, went to the White House and conferred with Pres. Kennedy, and then returned to address the Lincoln Memorial gathering.

The Washington marchers came from throughout the nation; they included large delegations from churches and unions, but by and large the demonstrators were average Negro Americans from country areas… Thousands of placards demanded "And End to Bias," "Integrated Schools," "An End to Police Brutality"—all of these ending with the word, "Now!"…the crowd spontaneously broke into song… The marchers were also entertained by celebrities, among them Ossie Davis, Joan Baez, Bobby Darin, Odetta and

Jackie Robinson.

Law enforcement was handled by 5,000 police, National Guardsmen and Army reservists. No marchers were arrested. (…) Mr. Kennedy said that "the cause of 20 million Negroes had been advanced by the program conducted so appropriately."

(*Facts on File* 23.1191, 299)

∽

After driving for I don't know how many hours, we got to Maryland at night. Four couples with their children were waiting for us in the apartment complex. It was crazy. Pancho introduced us:

"This is Anabel, who's a hairdresser…this is her husband, José, who works in a department store…and this is Eddy, who works in a bank, and his wife Isabel, who's a secretary. They live in the same building where you're going to live…and these are Anabel and José's children, and this…"

I was exhausted and sure that I'd never be able to remember all the names. Besides, everyone was talking at the same time about a demonstration that had taken place that very day for the Blacks. Finally, they took us to our apartment, and it seemed so lovely and immense.

"I remember you told me that you didn't have any furniture so we were at least able to find you a mattress," Pancho said to Roberto as they took Pedro Pablo's crib down from the top of *El Mamey*. The crib, along with our clothes, was everything we owned in the world.

The three of us slept on the mattress that night.

Before falling asleep, I said to Roberto:

"You know, *mi amor*, I haven't been this happy in a long time."

He answered with a snore.

∽

Spokesman for a unity movement which aspires to act as liason between Cuban refugees and Washington said yesterday they have the financial backing of wealthy exiles.

The commission, formed May 20 of 150 exiles from politics, labor, and business, announced a three-point program for the elimination of Castro, eradication of communism and re-establishment of the 1940 Constitution.

The committee said it would choose seven committee men in between 10 or 12 days to act as representatives in dealing with the Unites States and other governments.

It also said no members of the movement would receive salaries.

(Wilkinson A1)

∽

"Juan Fernando... God damn it! I told you to come to breakfast... Juan Fernaaaaando..."

My neighbor's yelling woke me up, and it didn't make a very good impression on me either. I guess without knowing it I had become used to the monotonous silence of Columbus. Besides, I had never heard that type of language in Cuba and certainly hadn't heard anyone talk to their children that way.

Just as in Miami, the Cuban colony in Silver Spring—the suburb where we had come to live—was very mixed. Exile had brought together people from many diverse educational backgrounds. One thing was certain, however; we all helped one another. Anabel would give all the women and children haircuts. Pepe, who was a mechanic, would fix everyone's cars. Frank, who was trying to renew his dentistry certification, started to pull teeth even before he got his license. The children's clothes were handed down from one household to the next as soon as they were too small. Since my English was better than most, I was always translating documents or writing letters for the neighbors. And every time a new family arrived from Cuba, we all pitched in to help them.

Roberto found a job at a bank. It was downtown, a block away from Eddy's job, so they decided to car pool and alternate the driving. I thought it was a miracle that we could count on a fixed income and that Roberto could work in an office and not out on the street as a collector.

There was an older Cuban woman in the complex who was able to babysit Pedro Pablo, so I started looking for a job, but without much success. Finally, one day at the drugstore I ran into Marta Garay, an old friend of Mamá's. I was so ecstatic to see her that before I knew what I was doing I had told her all my problems.

"Don't worry, I'm going to help you," she said.

And that's what she did. She found me a job in a real estate office. The owner was a Jewish woman. When she interviewed me, she asked me if I could type and take dictation, if I knew how to use a mimeograph, an adding machine, and a million other things I didn't even understand. I said yes to everything, even though my knowledge was limited to a six-week course I had taken in Havana one summer. I had to take two buses to get to the office and at the beginning it wasn't easy, but I learned a lot and I was so happy that nothing else mattered. During the day the realtors had a lot of free time while they waited for the phone to ring, so they would chat about politics. I started to become interested in what was going on in the country.

The men of the neighborhood formed a baseball league and the Sunday games became our favorite entertainment during the spring and summer. After the games, we'd have a barbecue. We were so poor that each of us could only have just one hot dog each. One day, a young man who was not from the neighborhood stopped by, and Roberto asked him if he wanted something to eat. He devoured two hot dogs, and my friend Silvia and I didn't get a thing. We wanted to kill my husband.

The men used to get together on Friday nights to play dominoes. Sometimes they'd play until the early morning hours. The women would get mad and plan all kinds of ways to get back at them, like leaving them for hours with the kids, but in the end it was just talk.

My brother Ricardo came once in a while to spend the weekend with us.

We'd laugh at all the things that happened to him when he first got here, and we'd stay up late nostalgically remembering our lives back in Cuba. He invited us to go visit him in New York. I immediately fell in love with the city, but Roberto complained about the traffic and how dirty he thought the streets were.

Washington, in contrast, was a tranquil, majestic city with wide avenues and many trees. When people came to visit us, we'd always take them to see all the monuments. Once we climbed the eight hundred and ninety-eight steps of the obelisk built in George Washington's honor. The Lincoln Monument seemed like a Greek temple to us. It has a gigantic statue of the slain president whose eyes seemed to follow you everywhere. In the circular building built on the banks of the Potomac River dedicated to Thomas Jefferson, we'd read inscriptions of things the author of the Constitution had written. There's one inscription in particular that we Cubans like to read. In it, Jefferson swears his opposition to any kind of tyranny.

We also visited Mount Vernon, the home of the first American president. Washington's mansion is immense, with well-tended gardens and a spectacular view. What I liked best was the inside of the house. Everything was very plain, almost austere. The White House was also very plain until Jackie Kennedy started to restore it. I remember how impressed I was by the number of groups who were protesting in front of the presidential mansion for all types of reasons. In that respect, freedom of speech in this country is really admirable.

At the Capitol, we sat in the gallery, watched Congress in session, and we also saw how they printed money at the mint. I was really moved by the changing of the guard at the Tomb of the Unknown Soldier in Arlington Memorial Cemetery, as well as the many plain white crosses marking the remains of so many who had died defending freedom. On holidays, family members bring flowers and small flags, giving the hallowed ground the look and feel of home.

We explored Georgetown—one of the richest neighborhoods and where there's a famous Jesuit University—and strolled down its lovely little streets. There are so many wonderful boutiques and colorful cafes. All of them are expensive, of course, but Ricardo treated us to a light lunch a time or two. We even found a bookstore there that sold books in Spanish. We also enjoyed the *barrio latino* near Columbia Road, where we were always pleased to hear people speaking Spanish and to find Cuban spices or a bunch of luscious plantains in the markets.

Along 16th Street and Massachusetts Avenue is where you'll find all the embassies. Washington has always had a very active diplomatic life, one which we only caught a glimpse of through the media. Americans seemed very simple to me, almost provincial. At first, I couldn't stand how they were constantly talking about the weather, and how they made such a big deal if it was going to be sunny or not, but later I understood how much the weather affects our day-to-day life, even our disposition. Although they're courteous and well mannered, they always seemed distant to me and a little superficial…and sometimes even uninformed about things. They didn't know a single thing about Cuba. But if there's one thing about them, at least they're honest. I was always amazed back then how someone could leave a pile of newspapers with a box next to it, and people would take a copy and never fail to drop the correct change in the box to pay for it. That would never have happened in Cuba. Not only would people have taken the paper without paying, but sooner or later someone would have taken the whole bundle *and* the box.

Lovers of their traditions and of democracy, Americans celebrate Thanksgiving and Election Days with the same regularity as the turning of the leaves in the Fall. In comparison to passionate Latinos, the North Americans in fact seemed really boring to me. However I admired their work ethic—a Protestant influence—which you could even see in their children. At a very young age a lot of them start doing different types of work, like mowing the lawn, babysitting, or delivering newspapers to earn some money for their expenses.

Washington has so many great museums at a good price, and we became really familiar with them over the years since we were trying to do everything possible to get ahead. We bought furniture on an installment plan and traded the old Ford for a shiny Volkswagen. Most of us were terribly homesick and missed our country so much. I felt so bad because I wasn't getting much mail from home anymore. When tropical storm Flora hit Cuba, it took three days for my call to get through. Thank God everyone was all right. For Roberto, there was no other topic of conversation than Cuba, and his mood fluctuated according to the news. If the exiles were planning any type of commando attack, all he could think about was our return. If the newspapers expressed any opinion favorable to the Revolution, he would send a letter to the editor. He spent most of his time deriding the Revolution: the Committees for Defense, the rationing books, the "volunteer" work, the Pioneers, the political divisions in the Communist party or the so-called *microfacción* crisis, the Russians. He was obsessed with it. Once, when we had just finished making love, and he got out of bed and threw a fit:

"Damn it, Lauri, they shot Virgilio and he had never been with a woman," he said as he furiously punched the wall.

Our surroundings weren't too peaceful either. The Civil Rights movement in the United States was getting stronger every day. I couldn't understand how the greatest democracy in the world could treat Blacks the way it did, and how the previous year the president had had to send the National Guard to the University of Mississippi in order for a black student to be able to attend college there. We all talked about how we didn't have those types of prejudices in Cuba, but Anabel's father said we shouldn't be fooled by all of it because Martin Luther King was a communist.

Due to the increasing tensions of the Cold War, they've installed a "hotline" between Washington and Moscow to avoid starting a nuclear war by accident. It would be the end of the world!

∽

John Fitzgerald Kennedy, 46, the 35th President of the United States, was assassinated in Dallas, Texas November 22. He was struck in the head and neck by 2 rifle bullets at 12:30 p.m. CST, as he rode in a motorcade, and was pronounced dead at Parkland Hospital in Dallas at 1 p.m. He is the 4th American president killed while in office.

Traveling in the same car as the President, Governor John Connelly was also wounded and is in critical condition. Mrs. Kennedy and Mrs. Connelly, sitting next to their respective husbands, were unharmed.

Lee Harvey Oswald, 24, a pro-Communist ex-Marine who once tried to trade his American citizenship for Soviet citizenship, was arrested less than 2 hours after the assassination. Despite his denials, he was arraigned as the President's Murderer.

Vice President Lyndon B. Johnson, 55, who was riding only 2 cars behind President Kennedy's, was sworn in as President at 2:39 p.m. the same day aboard Air Force One while on the runway at Love Field airport in Dallas. Mrs. Kennedy, for whose arrival the ceremony was delayed for about 5 minutes, stood at Mr. Johnson's left, her clothes still spattered with her husband's blood.

Seven minutes after the ceremony the Presidential Plane left Love Field to fly Mr. Johnson, his wife, Mrs. Kennedy and the body of the late President Kennedy back to Washington. It arrived at Andrews Air Force Base at about 6 p.m. EST.

(Facts on File 23.1204, 409)

∽

I will never forget as long as I live the day Kennedy was killed. I had gone downtown that day to have lunch with Bobby—that's what everyone called him down at the bank. All of a sudden everything in the room changed. There was surprise and astonishment on everybody's face. We could hear voices, but they were all talking at the exact same time so we couldn't make out what they were saying. Some people ran from one place to another; others were frozen in place.

"Kennedy's been shot," someone said. Finally we learned that he was dead. A gray shadow fell over the capital on that winter day. We were all so overtaken by grief that we didn't know how to react. I saw people hugging each other who were crying uncontrollably. Others fell to their knees and began to pray.

A suspect was apprehended immediately. There were rumors going around that Cuba was somehow involved in the assassination. Some of our neighbors were glad because they said that the Americans would surely have to get rid of Fidel now; as for me, however, I was ashamed to think that any Cuban could be capable of something so terrible. We spent two days at home watching the funeral on television. John-John saluted his father's casket as if he were a tiny soldier. The alleged assassin, Lee Harvey Oswald, was killed, too, and right in front of the TV cameras! There were a lot of theories about what had happened, but the bottom line was that nobody knew for sure. Robertico's buddies from the Brigade kept calling all the time. Everybody wondered how all of this was going to affect Cuba. Some felt that there was no reason to be upset because they insisted that Kennedy had betrayed them. But I couldn't stop thinking about that day when we saw him at the Orange Bowl, how his red hair shone in the sun. I had to drag the rocking chair out of our bedroom in the middle of the night, because I kept imagining that I could see the President sitting there, rocking back and forth.

The news was always about the war in Vietnam and the fight for Civil Rights. The Chinese exploded an atomic bomb. Martin Luther King, Jr. won the Nobel Peace Prize. It seemed like we were the only ones who had Cuba on our minds.

Although most of us couldn't vote, the majority of Cubans liked Goldwater, the Republican candidate for President. But secretly I rooted for Johnson, an old politician from Texas who talked with a Southern accent. At least he seemed to care for the poor and promised that he would try to end the war.

Ricardo invited us to come to New York to welcome in the New Year. The city was bright with Christmas lights. It smelled of pine trees and roasted chestnuts. Pedro Pablo enjoyed looking at the windows at Macy's and at the people skating at Rockefeller Center. He was so cute and knew the lyrics of all of the Beatles' songs. He would sing all the time.

I wanna hold your hand!
I wanna hold your hand!
I wanna hold your hand!
And when I touch you.
I feel happy inside.
It's such a feeling that, my love,
I can't hide. I can't hide!
I wanna hold your hand!
I wanna hold your hand!
I wanna hold your hand!

We also visited St. Patrick's Cathedral. Every time I go into a church, I pray for the same thing: that we can return to our country soon. We also visited with my aunt and uncle. Tío Julio is already working in a hospital. It was hard to look at him; he looks so much like Papá! Tía Alicia is always so kind and affectionate. My cousins—Julio Eduardo and Carlitos—and I reminisced about the family get-togethers that we used to have every Sunday at my other grandmother's house, and how we and our cousins used to play games in the driveway of the house on C Street. Julio Eduardo confided in me that he had a girlfriend and that he wanted to study Medicine like his Dad. I hadn't seen them since I left Cuba. Bobby barely remembered them. I had forgotten how good it feels to be with family.

It was such a moving experience for us to be together in Times Square at midnight. I thought about my family in Havana. For a split second, Menchu, I thought I spotted you in the crowd. Although I knew it was impossible, I spent all evening looking for you, as if I were really going to find you there.

Contrary to Johnson's campaign promises, the war seemed to go on forever. As we watched the nightly news on TV, it seemed like the war was being fought in our own living room. No wonder the anti-war movement started becoming stronger and more popular. The racial problem also became more intense. Malcolm X was killed in New York.

In Alabama they ignored the new laws that allowed Blacks to vote, and the President had to send in the National Guard. But even that wasn't enough to stop the violence. The Ku Klux Klan shot a white female because she gave a black woman a ride in her car.

Pedro Pablo has already turned four, and I don't want him to grow up as an only child. We've been trying for some time, but I haven't gotten pregnant. I went to a gynecologist who assures me that there's nothing wrong. Bobby says that this whole thing about having another child has become an obsession for me.

This summer we went on vacation for the first time since we were married. I would have liked for just the three of us to have done something together, but a bunch of families from the apartment complex were going to Miami, so we all went together and travelled as a caravan. We stayed together in the same little hotel in Miami Beach so it wouldn't cost as much. I was so happy to see my in-laws again, and Vidal, and Johnny, who's gotten so tall. I couldn't believe how much the city has changed, too. There are signs in Spanish everywhere. The vacation didn't turn out the way I had hoped, and I fought a lot with Roberto. The men played dominoes all day long while the women watched the kids and talked about stupid stuff. After we finished supper, we'd go visit friends and family and, once again, it was always the same story: he'd be with the men talking about Cuba, and I'd be with the women and the kids.

The best part was seeing the ocean again, walking on the beach, feeling the waves swirl around my feet. The sea holds so many memories for me! It brings to mind the summers at Veneciana beach when we'd go to the pier and try to catch crabs...and Tía Flor swimming in the ocean with us, all holding hands to form a circle, jumping with each crashing wave... What was the name of that friend of ours that Tía Flor nicknamed "Little Fish"? I'm sure you must remember, Menchu. It reminds me how blue the water always was at Varadero. And how we used to like to collect seashells and make sand castles... I've never seen sand more fine...just like it was for Pilar in Martí's, "The Little Pink Shoes." Remember how that poem used to always make us cry?

Especially the part where the nanny takes off her glasses?

I became so sad that I got sick. I needed to call Cuba, but it was almost impossible from the hotel. I asked Bobby to make the call from his parents' house, but he came up with a million excuses. Finally, he told me:

"I can't do that to my dad. A call from his house to a bunch of communists could really cause him some problems."

"Bobby! A bunch of communists? We're talking about my parents, and my sister, and my little brother! You don't understand because you have your family here. I had never even been away from my parents before…" I broke into a fit of crying that was so agonizing, it frightened Pedro Pablo. I had to calm myself down because I don't like to fight in front of our son, but I'd never be able to forgive him for that.

During the trip several couples mentioned that they wished their sons were more informed about Cuban culture so when we got back we launched a center for Cuban culture, the *Casa Cuba*. We started out by putting on a small theatrical piece that I wrote about the Three Wise Men. The most difficult part was for the kids to learn the carols. Pedro Pablo looked so cute, and he did the best job. Everything turned out so well, but I was peeved that Bobby got there late.

∽

Vietnamese War. U.S. aircraft bombed a target 5 miles south of Hanoi in one of a series of air strikes that day. Eight U.S. planes were downed, a record number for a single day. Their loss brought to 435 the number of American aircraft lost over North Vietnam…

A North Vietnamese Foreign Ministry statement…charged that U.S. planes had "attacked densely populated areas in the southern suburb of Hanoi and other densely populated areas inside the city…

According to figures released by the U.S, military command in Saigon November 23, at least 48,000 Communist troops had infiltrated into South Vietnam from North Vietnam during January-September…

A total of 45,000 Viet Cong were said to have joined the Saigon government's side since South Vietnam instituted its "Open Arms" program for Communist defectors in 1963…

All 27 Americans aboard a U.S. Air Force C-47 transport were killed November 26 when the plane crashed shortly after takeoff from Tansonhut airbase near Saigon.

The Viet Cong proposal, announced November 26 by the National Liberation Front clandestine radio, said the guerrilla forces would suspend military operations for Christmas from 7 a.m. December 24 to 7 a.m. December 26 and for New Year's from 7 a.m. December 31 to 7 a.m. January 2, 1967.

(Facts on File 26.1362, 457)

On Monday, I registered for classes at Montgomery College. It's not that I've given up on ever studying at the University of Havana, but we don't how long all of this is going to go on, and I need to make good use of my time. Now that Pedro Pablo is in the first grade, he doesn't have to spend so many hours at the babysitter's. I've been lucky because his sitter is a Cuban woman and her entire family loves him. And besides, they all speak Spanish to him. It always hurts me so much when I take him to school and I see him pledging allegiance to the American flag. It's hard to talk to Bobby about it. Since he quit his job at the bank and started selling insurance on commission, he never knows when he's going to get home or even how much he's going to earn. But he says it's a place to start and that it's a field with a lot of room for opportunity. Besides, he couldn't stand his American boss any longer.

My cousins signed up for the draft because Tío Julio says that you have to follow the laws of the country. Julio Edward was drafted into the Marines, so we went to New York to see him off. Tía Alicia invited all of us to have lunch with them on Sunday. We spent the afternoon reminiscing about Cuba, my classes, our school when we were kids, and Carlitos' studies… It was all so natural and at the same time so contrived, as if the next day that young man, who just a few years ago ran around grandma's patio with me, weren't going to put on a military uniform and soon be under fire from Vietnamese bullets in a land so far away that we hadn't even studied it in geography class.

Before we left, in a very subtle way Julio Edward called Pedro Pablo and me back to his room so he could give him a couple of records. One of the 45s was Petula Clark's *Downtown* and the other was one of the Beatles.

"I wanted you to have this," he told Pedro Pablo, "because when you were real little you used to go around singing this, and every time I hear it I always think about you." And then he started singing along:

> *I wanna hold your hand!*
> *I wanna hold your hand!*

Pedro Pablo was so happy he ran off to show his father the records. As for me, he gave me one of his photos.

"So you can show off your cousin," he said jokingly, trying to keep the situation from becoming too serious.

"You bet, the most handsome cousin in the world…" I wanted to quip back with the same flippant tone but my voice cracked. All I could think about was the day I said goodbye to Bobby when he went off to the Bay of Pigs. I hugged him so he couldn't see my tears.

Back in the car, my husband tried to cheer me up:

"Don't worry; nothing's going to happen to him. Besides, he's fighting for our cause."

"What? How is it possible that going off and perhaps getting killed in Vietnam could in any way be a form of fighting for Cuba?"

"Because he'll be fighting against communism… You'll see. He'll be back before you know it."

But there was something about our goodbye that left me with a sense of dread. I worried that I would never see my cousin again, that young man with eyes as dark as a well, his broad forehead, his enigmatic smile. My fear stuck in the middle of my chest like the stinger of a wasp.

Ever since Julio Edward went off to war we've been on pins and needles. Every night at the end of the news they put up the names of those who were killed that day with this music in the background that I'll never forget as long as I live. If I don't get to watch the news that evening, I wake up in the middle of the night with the sick feeling that something has happened to my cousin. In my nightmares, the guerrillas and the militia blend together. Sometimes I see the faces of the people I went to school with when I was kid. I also see Johnny, and Bobby, and even Vidal and my father-in-law. They're always dressed in uniforms. And there are also pregnant women dressed in rags. And children, so many crying children. Some of them look like Pedro Pablo, others like Pedritín. There's always a lot of noise, and fire, and gunshots, and dust, and tanks, and rifles, and planes. Then I feel a loud explosion, and then there's nothing but silence, just silence, a deafening silence... And a white and blinding light, like the one that was burned on my retina the day I left Havana.

The gynecologist has prescribed some really expensive pills for me. He says that if I take them, and we have sex on the indicated days, that he believes that within three or four months I should get pregnant. I want to have another child so badly that I've even considered adopting one. Why not an orphan from Vietnam? Bobby says I'm crazier than hell, that we already have a son, and there's no way. I think I'm ovulating right now, and he didn't get home until 4:00 in the morning last night! I was so furious with him that I pretended to be asleep. This morning he told me that he was working on a plan to bring together all the different groups of exiles.

Finally this afternoon, when Pedro Pablo was over at the neighbors, we made love. At first it was difficult for me because I was still so furious with him, but as soon as he began touching me, it was like all my rage started to dissolve and slip from my body... He slowly fondles my nipples and I feel a tingle between my legs that keeps rising deep inside of me. He runs his tongue over them and sucks them, he lets his saliva run over them, and then he sucks on them even harder, like a hungry child. The pleasure makes me writhe and jerk, and I want to feel him on top of me, I want to feel him inside of me. But he keeps on with his caresses and goes further, he goes from one breast to the other, he takes each one in his hands, he softly bites my nipples, he kisses my lips, my eyes, my ears, my hair. He goes back to my nipples and he moistens them, he kisses them, he runs his tongue over them, he puts them in his mouth and he sucks them, first softly, and then with more pressure...then wildly.

I feel his naked body against mine. He rubs his erection against my clitoris...he moves it around the edges of my vagina...until finally he's inside of me. We move in unison. I feel the warm wetness between my legs.

He lifts himself and searches for my mouth. His lips slide down my neck until they once again find one of my nipples. He clenches it with his lips, and the pleasure swells.

"Come... Come on, my love," I plead.

Our fused bodies rise and fall on the bed. I feel the bed posts straining. I sink my nails into his back and scream. I scream because of the intense pleasure between my legs. I scream because I'm alive and I have a man who makes love to me...and a son and four walls. He thrusts himself with more force and moves his hips in a circle. I scream again. I shriek because of the intense pleasure between my legs. And because I always have to hold back these goddamn tears.

∽

U.S. and North Vietnamese troops suffered heavy causalities between July 2–7 near the U.S. Marine base at Conthien, just south of the western end of the demilitarized zone.

The first clash erupted July 2, about 1 ½ miles northeast of Conthien, when 500 troops of the 90th Regiment of North Vietnam's 324B Division ambushed the U.S. Marine 9th Regiment's 3rd Platoon. 35 Marines were killed in the surprise attack.

(*Facts on File* 27.1394, 271)

✑

I got a letter from Julio Edward, and he received the one I sent him with the picture of Pedro Pablo. He says that he and some Cuban buddies eat black beans and rice in camp. Tía Alicia even sends him *merenguitos,* those sweet meringue deserts that we used to always snack on. And Susana, his girlfriend, writes him every day. He's about to finish the thirteenth month of his tour. Hopefully he's going to be back sometime in early July. He says that he can't wait to see all of us again. With his typical sense of humor, he ends the letter with "Make way, watch out, here I come!" Carlitos says that they've already put a bottle of champagne in the refrigerator for his return. I can't wait to go see him.

It's the 4th of July and no one is working. The heat is unbearable. We've waited until it got dark to start grilling. The kids have spent the whole day playing together. They're all wound up because they can't wait to go see the fireworks. Bobby and the neighbors are talking about Che Guevara and arguing about if he's really dead. Yesterday I left a urine sample at the doctor's to see if I'm pregnant, but I don't even want to think about it. For days I've been feeling bad. It's hard to describe, but it feels like some type of strange uneasiness, as if I had a bunch of butterflies inside me right around the same place as my heart.

"That's how I felt every time I had an exam," one of my neighbors, Silvia, tells me.

I was standing in the doorway when the phone rang. It took me so long to overcome my dread that Bobby, who was seated, had already started to get up and answer it when I told him:

"Leave it, I'll get it. "

I'll never forget that there are eleven steps from the doorway to the phone.

"Lauri?"

As soon as I heard Ricardo's voice I feared the worst.

"Oh no, Ricardo, no. Julio Edward?"

They buried him with full military honors. The cousins are playing in the patio of grandma's house in Vedado. The coffin is covered with an American flag and a Cuban flag.

"Who wants to play red rover?

"No, how about statues instead?"

"No, let's play tag."

"I know, hide and seek."

Two soldiers with white gloves fold the two flags ceremoniously and present them to Tía Alicia.

"No, we've already played that one. How about cops and robbers?"

"I'm the policeman!"

It seems like my aunt and uncle have become old.

Julio Eduardo is singing:

> *I wanna hold your hand!*
> *I wanna hold your hand!*

"When you were real little you used to go around singing this, and every time I hear it I always think about you," he tells my son.

Carlitos has grown up all of a sudden.

And Susana, the girlfriend, so very young, all dressed in black with eyes red from crying, looks like a child-widow.

They said farewell to Julio Eduardo Soler Barraqué with a twenty-one gun salute and the melancholy tribute of a cornet. He was born in Havana on the 19th day of March, 1944, and he died in Vietnam on July 2nd, 1967 having served his country for twelve months and twenty-nine days. He had not yet turned twenty-four years of age.

In one blow I suddenly understand the verses by Martí:

"Why does the sun have light?"

When we returned home the first thing I did was call the gynecologist. He told me I'm pregnant. I hope that it's a girl.

CHAPTER FIVE

"…Within a Hundred Years There Will Be No Greater Honor…"

THE HIGHWAY THAT LEADS DOWN TO THE VALLEY SNAKES ITS WAY THROUGH THE STEEP MOUNTAINS. Far below the windy road, the rounded dome-like hills—the *mogotes*—look like herds of elephants. Some stand alone; others are linked together; all in never-ending rows making their way to the circus. From the scenic lookout, you can take in the entire valley as it spreads out and extends beyond the edge of the earth. What an unbelievable sight!

The sierra stretches out from one side of the horizon to the other while the Pizarras Mountains hide behind a covering of piney forest. Down below, the verdant crops blanket the valley in every possible shade of green, interrupted at times only by the yellowish gray of an occasional hut.

The sight of the massive *mogotes* stirs up a sense of uneasiness. Balanced in such a precarious way, you'd think you're about to witness a terrible catastrophe. In the highest parts, a dense veil hangs from the crevices of the exposed rocks, shrouding them in greenish-black, yellow, and grey hues. Thin creeping vines weave their designs among the treetops. A thick moss covers the edge of the boulders, from which defiant wild orchids—purple, white, and violet—sprout forth abundantly.

As the sun goes down a soft murmur begins to emanate from the very core of the mountain range. It starts out as a hum that grows louder as the night goes on. It's the mysterious and marvelous night that sings its song. You can almost feel the flutter of the insects, the croaking of the frogs, the chirping of the crickets, all of which echo incessantly in soft harmony. According to the peasants, or *guajiros* as we call them, the iguanas start singing their melody in the evenings.

For the past two months we've been working on the "literacy campaign." Despite the suffocating heat, the mosquito bites, and the sleeping and bathing conditions, we're thrilled to be a part of such an important project. Marta Lola and I are exhausted. Some of the other girls make fun of us.

"You two aren't used to this, are you?" Maruja asks us with a sarcastic disdain in her voice.

"Don't tell me. You two sleep on silk sheets embroidered with golden thread," adds Angelita with her mischievous eyes glaring at us.

"Get out of here! I've never even seen sheets like that…"

"Why do you assume that rich people…"

"Hey! We're not rich! Ok?"

"Enough already. Drop the crap and let's read a while."

Marta Lola says she doesn't understand how they can possibly think that we're different from them. We even dress identically. She's even started to talk dirty like they do so they won't accuse her any more of being bourgeois.

The conditions are difficult. For the most part the kids are shy and respectful, but they're not in the habit of studying much, and they get distracted easily. In every group, though, there's always one or two that make it worth the while. They always raise their hand to ask a question, and you can see in their little anxious faces that they're eager to learn. We also have some adult students: rough country folk with their leathery hands and dirty fingernails; young women who dream about going to the city; ageless mothers who have given birth to children one after another. Their faces light up when they learn how to write their names.

The beauty of the countryside overwhelms me and makes it easier to put up with the inconveniences. I've never seen more beautiful sunrises or sunsets. At night we sit around in a circle and sing songs. The *guajiros* make up poems on the spot. And the air you breathe is so pure.

Yesterday, Lázaro arrived. I hadn't seen him since I left Havana. He brought me one letter from Mamá and another from Pedritín. As we strolled around the camp he caught me up on the most recent events since we don't get much news here. His enthusiasm is contagious. He thinks Cuba is destined for wonderful things.

"Menchu, we're a part of history now, and not just Cuba's, but the world's. This Revolution is going to be the first of many and they're going to keep on happening across this entire continent... There won't be any more kids without a school, without shoes, without food... There won't be any more injustice, or rich people, or poor, or Blacks or Whites. We'll all just be equal."

He also told me that he had come to say goodbye. He had been selected among other journalists to accompany a delegation to Moscow as a journalist.

"But you haven't even finished your studies yet..."

"I know but they chose me based on the work I've done for the Revolution."

"Moscow's so far away... Aren't you going to freeze?"

"I don't think it's that cold in the summer, silly... Besides, it's only for a few days..."

After that he took me to a nearby spot in the woods. When he held me I felt a sense of relief, as if I had just gotten home after taking a long trip. Then he gently kissed my eyes, my hair.

"I know I probably don't smell that great," I told him with a smile.

"You smell like Cuba...and you smell amazing."

I gave in to his tender caresses. All at once his embrace became stronger. He gently laid me on the ground.

"Lázaro, they can see us..."

"Shh...don't say anything," and he pressed his mouth against mine.

He opened my blouse and slid his arms around me again. I felt his hands unclasping my bra. Then he leaned back and looked at my bare breasts.

"You're so beautiful." He ran his finger over my lips which I moistened so I could kiss him again. He slid one single finger down my chin, down my neck, to the top of my breast...

"Lázaro, no, please don't," I told him but I was incapable of resisting him.

A sensation that I had never felt before began to burn between my legs.

"Your breasts are like two gardenias," and he brought his lips closer to kiss them. I felt a startling shock of pleasure so intense that a squeal of ecstasy slipped out, which he squelched with his kisses.

"I love it that you want to scream...but they can hear us..."

I tried to push him away to get up, but he got on top of me so quickly that it took my breath away. I don't know how he got my pants down. I felt his hard penis between my legs. Then he took it in his hand, and he rubbed it hard against my vagina.

"Do you like that baby?"

I couldn't answer him. All of a sudden something broke inside of me and I could feel that piece of throbbing meat thrusting inside of me. He moved like a mad man. In that very moment I was overwhelmed with an indescribable fragrance—an aroma of man, of countryside, of sweat—that awakened desires in me that I never knew I had. I wrapped my arms around his back and began to move up and down until I found his rhythm. It was as if we rode together, and both of us had turned into horse and rider at the same time, a runaway minotaur in full gallop.

"You sway with the grace of the cane fields," he whispered in my ear. "You're as sweet as sugarcane, as juicy as our pineapples, as ripe as the *mamey* fruit..."

All at once his caresses, his kisses, every muscle in his body tensed up and took on a fierce, almost violent, passion. And with a serious and profound tone in his voice, as if it came from deep within him, he stated bluntly:

"I'm going to make love to you until your pussy hurts."

When we got back to camp, night had fallen, and he was right. I hurt.

In April of 1962, the Young Communist League (YCL) and the Pioneers Union of Cuba (PUC) were formed under the auspices of two corresponding and joint initiatives for the purpose of bringing future generations into the creative endeavors of the Revolution. Tomorrow's pillars of Cuba are taking shape in a healthy and sound environment, free from vices and self-centeredness, trained in the love of country, study, and work, and skilled in the noble practices of camaraderie and human solidarity. On this the first

anniversary of the Revolution, reflecting upon what the YCL and PUC have accomplished in such a short time, the future of socialist Cuba radiates with pride and hope in welcoming this multitude of young men, women, and children that constitute the greatest treasure of the Revolution.

(*Bohemia* 58:12, 3)

෨

Mamá's real nervous because Pedritín is eager to head off to the countryside with his comrades and do volunteer work. She's been asking Papá to get him a doctor's excuse so he can get out of it, but he says the same thing every day.

"Tomorrow, I promise, I'll get it. It's just that my friend, Dr. Ortega, was really busy today and he forgot to sign it."

As the day grows closer, Mamá gets more impatient.

"Pedro, please. I'm begging you. Get it done already!"

Even though Pedritín wanted to go so badly, I finally confronted Papá:

"You're not going to get him the doctor's excuse, are you?"

"Of course I am... You know it's just that..."

"Don't lie to me, Papá."

"Oh, Menchu, look, people just don't want to get mixed up in other people's business but, ok, I'll go and insist that..."

"I don't agree with what you're doing and you're going to hurt Mamá even more if you keep on deceiving her."

"What in the world are you talking about?"

"Nothing... Look, you didn't want to leave the country because you had your own personal reasons... As far as I'm concerned, fine, but as for Mamá she needs to hear the truth."

"Don't you dare tell your mother a word about this."

"Of course I'm going to tell her."

"Menchu...please."

Just at that moment Mamá came out of the kitchen.

"So what's all the fuss about *mija*?"

"Mamá, you better start getting used to the idea of Pedritín going to work in the coffee and sugar cane fields, and you'd be better off if you went ahead and smiled and helped him with his Pioneer scarf, and start accepting that later on he'll join the Young Communists and, finally, one day he'll be a member of the Party."

"But, Menchu, what are you talking about?"

"What I'm saying Mamá is that in this country there's been a Revolution, and that we're not leaving, and that I'm young and my little brother is nothing but a child, that we can't keep on living like this, and that if we want to wind up being somebody in life, if we want to study, have a good job, travel, have people respect us, and—above all—do something good for this country, we have to get in line with the Revolution, and do it with our eyes shut, with blind faith, because we just don't have any other choice."

"Menchu, I don't understand, Papá is going to get him a doctor's excuse…"

"Tell her, Papá, tell her the truth. You're not going to get him anything, are you? And if he were to get it for him, Mamá, what would you do next month, and the month after that, and after that? Are you going to keep him shut up in the house like an invalid?"

Two large tears welled up in her eyes. She lifted her head and, after a moment, she looked at us and said.

"You're right. It's the best thing for everybody."

Pedritín took off for the coffee harvest not long after that, and he came back as one of the top workers in his institute.

A sight that just a few years ago no one would have thought possible is taking place throughout the entire Island. Millions of Cubans have taken to the countryside to do their part in assisting with the nation's agricultural needs. In the past, all national events typically took place in the cities, and in particular

the capital. Daily life and the true backbone of the country were officially
ignored. Rural Cuba only existed for exploitation and when it was convenient
for elections. Today what was previously our great unknown is at the very
heart of our national attention. Brigades of workers, students, members of the
Ministry of the Revolutionary Armed Forces, all have joined forces to work
together methodically and diligently in order to bring about greater agricultural
production in general, to give rise to the greatest sugarcane harvest ever seen,
and to impart scientific knowledge to the rural community for the betterment
of their fellow compatriots. Signs that read "We're in the Fields" are frequently
posted on deserted office doors where workers have heeded the honorable call of
their native land. And the sum totals are mounting. The yield continues, and the
bell curve has yet to reach its peak. Ambitious plans are successfully being carried
out on farms throughout the state. The battle for sugar takes on larger proportion
each year. All of Cuba has enlisted to be on the frontlines. The coordinated efforts
of an entire people will guarantee victory in this our peaceful battle. And in this
matter, as in all things, we can once again say "We shall overcome!"

(*Bohemia* 59:39, 3)

∽

I switched rooms with Pedritín. Now I have the one in the back,
which is smaller, but that way Lázaro can come in through the patio
and spend the night with me without my folks seeing him.

He told me all about his childhood, a childhood filled with
uncertainty and adversity:

"My mother was a dressmaker. My father was an important politician,
and she was his mistress. He had his wife and other sons, but he always
provided for us. He would always bring cash for Mami along with gifts
for me, even though I always hated it when he would rub his hand
in a distracted way across my head, like he was petting an animal or
something. I remember spending time with him only twice. The first
time I was probably five or six years old and we went to the movies. We

sat in the last row, and he never took off his hat. When I told Mamá about it, my grandmother interjected that he was afraid people would probably see him with me.

I didn't think that could possibly be true because that very same day he told Mamá that she should send me off to study at a private school. I don't know if he paid for it or not, or if they just let me in based on his recommendation, but I never felt comfortable there. The kids always stared at me. I thought it was because of my raggedy clothes and my old beat up shoes, and so one night when he came to visit my mother I made sure I stayed awake and waited for them to come out of the bedroom, and when he did I pounced on him before he could get away. I let go with one single gulp of breath: 'The kids at school all make fun of me because my uniform is all old…and besides it's too small.' It must have struck him funny because he took out a few bills from his wallet and told my mother: 'Tomorrow go buy the kid what he needs.' And then he just smiled at me.

Despite my new clothes, only one kid would hang out with me. It didn't matter anyway since I left the school not long after that. One Sunday, which was sort of strange, my father showed up unexpectedly. He seemed really excited.

'You and Lazarito get dressed because I'm going to take you out,' he told my mother. We got ready in a heartbeat. We crawled into his big impressive car and the next thing you know, we get out at this theme park, the one they call Coney Island. He bought me a pineapple drink, which was really cold, and some cotton candy. They hung back a bit, and seemed to be excited about something while I went on ahead, jumping over puddles and savoring all my treats. Suddenly, Fonseca—we always referred to him by his last name—said that he didn't feel very well and that we should probably head back. We made the trip back in silence, as if a grey cloud had eclipsed the bright light of that particular Sunday.

When we got back, my mother insisted that he go in and lie down for a while. He didn't want to, but he finally gave in: 'That'll probably help a bit.'

My mother loosened up his clothes, and he stretched out on the bed, without even pulling back the covers. She went in to fix him some bicarbonate, and I heard him say, 'I'm sure it's just something I ate.'

I went up to him. He opened his eyes and he looked right into mine. I had never noticed just how big his eyes were. And then I noticed a small stream of blood that was coming from the corner of his mouth. It trickled all the way down to his starched white *guayabera*. When my mother came back from the kitchen, he was already dead.

Then the rough years came. I didn't mind switching schools so much, but it really hit my mother hard when we had to give up the house and move to a pretty rough *barrio*. She worked all day glued to a sewing machine with my grandmother always tormenting her: 'You should look for another Fonseca. If I were young...'

Years later a lawyer told me that I had the right to part of my father's inheritance. Finally, just to avoid the whole scandal, his family gave in and gave us a portion of the money. It wasn't much, but it was enough to buy the house that we live in now."

"Did you ever meet your brothers?" I asked him.

"No. Only once did I ever see them, and that was from a distance. And, as you can imagine, they've left the country."

It is the word that symbolizes the aspiration of a large part of humanity, and for which hundreds and hundreds of millions of human beings are concretely working today. And within a hundred years, there will be no greater honor nor will there by anything more natural and logical than to be called a "Communist."

We are headed toward a communist society. And if the imperialists do not want soup, well, we will give them three bowls of soup. From this day forward, let it be known, that when they call us Communists, they are addressing us in the most honorable way that one can be called.

(Fidel Castro 3 October 1965)

❧

Lázaro and my cousin Armandito have become good friends. I also get along real well with Magaly. The four of us go out together pretty often. These days there are always plays, art exhibits, and the ballet to attend. They're also publishing tons of books and a lot of foreign writers have come to visit. All over the Island there's a great cultural awakening. All of that despite having to be on alert for an invasion. Lázaro is right. We'd be better off if the Yankees would just leave us alone.

"Fidel is completely correct when he says 'Within the Revolution, Everything; Outside the Revolution, Nothing!' because everything that is truly good can take place within the Revolution, and what else is there outside of it but the lack of respect from our enemies? Do you think that the Americans have the right to violate our air space fifty-eight times in less than two months?" Lázaro's eyes become minuscule when he gets excited. Sometimes I make fun of him.

"You still think you're a student leader..."

"Menchu, you can't let your guard down for a moment."

Armandito and Magaly are happy because they're expecting a baby by the end of the year. I asked Lázaro if he'd like to have kids. He kept quiet for a long time, as if he had to think hard about it. Finally, he answered me in a serious tone:

"Yes, Menchu. I would like to have children, so that we really could create the New Man, a son of the Cuban Revolution."

"Me too, but I would like it to be *our* child too."

"Obviously, silly. But we have to get married first."

"So are you asking me to marry you?"

"Look, Menchu, Family is a bourgeois institution, but in this country, those values still exist and I don't want my son to suffer what I had to go through for being an illegitimate child."

We were able to get the papers in order in just a few days, and we got married without telling anyone, not even my parents. Lázaro kept living at his house and me in mine. He was sure that if I went to his house to live, his grandmother would make my life miserable, and if he came to mine, he would wind up fighting with my family. It would be better just to wait until we could have a place of our own. In East Havana they were building some new apartments, and we got on the waiting list to get one. In any case, we spent almost every night together.

Papá must have seen him leave one morning because he yanked me aside. He was furious:

"Menchu, as long as I'm alive, this will be a respectable house. I can't control what you do out there, but I don't want that man ever in my house again. Do you hear me? And it'd be better if your mother didn't find out that I saw him coming out of your bedroom."

"So, a respectable house, huh? And what you do out there doesn't matter?"

"Menchu..."

"Don't try to give me your moral lessons, Papá. And it'd be better if my mother didn't find out about the things I know about you."

"Don't you disrespect me!"

"I haven't had any respect for you in a long time."

"The things that Lázaro and the Revolution have put in your head!"

"This has nothing to do with Lázaro or the Revolution. It's about you and that I've known for a long time that you've been cheating on Mamá."

"That's enough! Or I'll..."

Suddenly we realized that Mamá was standing in the doorway. Neither one of us knew just how long she had been listening to us.

"Leave her alone, Pedro. Mind your own business."

That afternoon Mamá called me to her room. She opened her wardrobe and took out a small box hidden in her underwear drawer. They were pearl earrings.

"Look at these, *mija*. Mamá Luya gave me these earrings when I married your father. Now that you're a married woman, I want to have them."

"But Mamá, how did you know? We haven't told anyone."

"I know my daughters well. And look, it'd be better if Lázaro came in through the front door, and he should come eat with us whenever he wants. I'll talk to your father."

By the end of the year—on December, 28th, 1963—Magaly gave birth to a baby boy, and they called him Ernesto.

"So I guess you named him after your uncle," remarked Mamá.

"No, Mariana," Lázaro explained. "It's for Che."

A few days later the doctor told me I was expecting.

✺

Like a bugle call, the watchword has found its way to every corner of the Island. And heeding the call to patriotism and collective work, with its face to the countryside the entire nation is going forth into the cane fields. Factories, governmental offices, schools, encampments, military bases, organizations of the masses, all have joined together in the great collective effort so that the name "the People's Harvest"—as the Revolution refers to the daily tasks of its sugar industry—may become a viable reality. The term "the People's Harvest" suggests something much more than the collective possession of the nation's treasures. It also signifies the direct participation of its citizens. What gives even greater meaning to the Fortnight is that the efforts of all serve as a tribute to the heroes of the Bay of Pigs. In this way, each year the victory that was won on that glorious beach will be repeated and prolonged in her cane fields. The same Cuba that cast its invaders into the sea is the same one, with this unprecedented mobilization, that now will bring imperialism to its knees with blows from her machetes.

(*Bohemia* 59:13, 41)

✺

When I went into labor, Papá offered to take me to the hospital in his car, and I asked for Mamá to go with us. Later on others showed up a little bit at a time—Lázaro, Mamá Luya, Tía Flor, my friend Marta Lola. Even Maruja, who's now the president of the CDR, came by with Pedritín.

"He was dying to see his sister so I brought him," she told us.

As the labor dragged on, they began to leave one by one. Lázaro had guard duty and even he took off.

"I won't leave you," said Mamá, and she sat at my side. I fell asleep but, half awake, I could feel her pat the sweat from my forehead and moisten it with a wet cloth.

"You're so good to me, Mamá."

"Oh, *mija,* at least I can be with you. Your poor sister had to give birth all by herself."

"I know Mamá, but that's all in the past. Pedro Pablo must be two by now, right?"

"He'll turn two on the 8th of September. God knows when I'll get the chance to see him…"

"You miss them a lot, don't you?"

"So much, *mija.*"

"Me too."

The contractions get worse. I try to think about something pleasant. Lauri and I are at the beach with the buckets and shovels that we got for our birthday, making castles with towers and subterranean tunnels that the water passes through…I feel the sand under my feet…that fine sand of our beaches…the hot sun on my shoulders… Oh God, here comes the pain again…oh, oh God… We're swimming in the sea with Tía Flor. Doris is also there, that friend of ours who could swim so well that we nicknamed her "Little Fish…" Another contraction's coming, this time worse than ever… I try not to complain but…oh…oh fuck…!

"Menchu!" Mamá scolds me, but then she smiles.

I feel a tremendous pressure between my legs. I want to push. The nurse examines me and calls the Doctor. Lauri and I are jumping over the waves. The water soaks us.

"Her water has broken," I heard someone say.

When the contractions get unbearable, I squeeze Mamá's hand. The pain on her face is so bad I feel like I shouldn't complain. They finally take me into the delivery room. A little later I hear a cry and, instinctively, I know it's a girl. I look at the clock. It's 10:15 p.m., the 9th of June, 1964. My daughter has been born. We've named her Tania.

∾

There's love in those hands.

But when you don't wash them and keep them clean, they can spread germs that cause serious illnesses, including gastroenteritis. For the sake of your health…clean hands!

Gastroenteritis can and must be avoided.

                                                                          MISAP Health Education

Clean hands…clean clothes…clean food…clean house…clean hands… clean clothes…

                                                                          (*Bohemia* 56:50, 74)

∾

Lázaro is becoming more and more active professionally. His work as a journalist allows him to attend important events. He's travelled everywhere on the Island. He's also gone to Moscow three times, this last time he accompanied Che Guevara. I don't understand why, but they haven't published any of his work from this last trip. But last night, when the baby had finally fallen asleep and the house was quiet, he read his article to me:

"It was the night before we returned. The whole group had stayed up chatting, talking about a thousand things. Dawn was approaching. One by one each went to bed until finally Che and I were the only ones left. We smoked in silence, lost in our thoughts, because everything had already been said—our ideas, analyses, hypotheses, every theme had been exhausted. The only thing that remained was that rare emotion of a man when he confronts himself, his destiny, perhaps his life or perhaps his death. Then, in a soft voice, more for himself than for me,

Che began to talk about Fidel. Not about the politician, not about his exceptional gifts, not about his supreme intelligence with which he was overseeing the crucial situation of the country. He did not speak about any of those things because they have already been said. No, he spoke about his devotion, about the feeling that the extraordinary greatness of his friend produced in him. He confessed—I don't think he was confessing to me as much as he was just talking out loud—that he had not understood Fidel nor his greatness, that he had doubted him, that he had feared that Fidel would get off track.

There was a deep bitterness in his words, a reproach of himself, a pain that welled up from such a mistake. It dawned on me that that he couldn't pardon himself. That distant Fidel of the early years, that guerrilla leader, that confused agitator, had begun to grow little by little, he had begun to transform before his eyes into a great revolutionary leader, who symbolized for Che the capacity of Man, of every man, to fulfill his most stirring destiny. And he had doubted Fidel. He had doubted the man!

Then, surprisingly, Che turned to me and said:

"Do you know what the real challenge is for a leader? He must be able to see things with cold objectivity, to make painful decisions without blinking an eye. But he must also have a passionate spirit and, even though it might sound ridiculous, I'd say he has to be guided by great feelings of love. Our revolutionaries on the front lines must embody that type of love for the people, for the most sacred of all causes, and make it unique and indivisible. They can never descend upon the places where the ordinary man holds sway, armed merely with a small dose of affection.."

Che is that 'new man,' the leader that combines cold reason with a love that goes beyond our feelings for our family, companions, and children. A love that surpasses power, that goes further, that has a greater commitment. A love that is willing to surrender all, even one's life."

His voice cracked as he finished reading. Then, with an abrupt gesture, he neatly folded the paper and gave it to me:

"I'm not going to publish this. Keep it for Tania...for the future... so that she can see that her father was a witness to the one of the most beautiful moments in her country's history."

I placed the sheet of paper in the night stand. The next morning, I read it again. I asked myself what did Tania and I mean to Lázaro in comparison to Che, Fidel, the Revolution. Maybe I was jealous, but I felt that same uneasiness that sometimes crept up on me, that tickle behind my sternum, that threat of pain that would move around in my chest without settling down.

∽

In Guisa, Oriente, with its geographic and historic backdrop of epic proportions, the Federation of Cuban Women celebrated its fourth anniversary. More than six thousand women from the countryside, the majority from the Sierra Maestra, gathered with the leaders of the FCW, headed by Vilma Espín.

As the Cuban flag flew over the agrarian countryside, urban and rural members alike, followers and militants, all offered a dose of jovial responsibility. Far in the past are the civil distinctions between the sexes as well as the discriminative epithet of "weak" added to the noun "woman." Today, as social and political fighters, and workers in the forefront and militia, they serve as an example to their sisters throughout the Americas.

(Bohemia 56:35, 62)

∽

Finally, after so many complications with my college plans and Tania's birth and all, I finally graduated with my architecture degree. For my first job I was hired as an adviser to the sub-commission in Trinidad for the National Commission of Monuments. To commemorate its founding 450 years ago in 1514 by Diego Velázquez, they wanted to restore the city's colonial appearance. Our job is to make sure that the modern improvements are in keeping with the original architecture. A few days ago we had our first meeting in Trinidad. Set against the majestic backdrop of the green peaks of the Escambray Mountains, caressed by the breeze from the sea, the city has a lot to offer: its proximity to the mountains and the beach, the existence of deep caverns, and exquisite parks, even a small lake. But it's a diamond in the rough. Despite its historic town square, its Church of the Holy Trinity, the neoclassic structure that houses the library, its cobblestone streets, there's also an infinity of huts and shacks and even dwellings whose walls are put together with straw and mud. In La Barraca—a poor section of town made up of adobe houses—I could easily imagine gliding past me the dark and slippery shadow of Caniquí, Trinidad's legendary thief who allegedly had supernatural powers. In contrast, up above, across all the old rooftops television antennas weave together like a great spider web.

∽

Populations continue to grow and multiply, all the while the size of our lands remains the same. Mankind will have to do everything possible to increase its productivity, to maximize what the land yields, to take advantage of today's advances in technology, since only those who are not revolutionaries, those who do not have the slightest idea of the possibilities of Man's intelligence and willpower can conceive of a world in which their fellow humans die from hunger.

And of course, there are two things that are indispensable: Revolution and Technology. And that which we do here today will not only be useful for us, but someday it will be of value to others who must also resolve similar conflicts.

(Fidel Castro 12 August 1967)

∽

Things are so crazy these days that I feel dizzy at times. To cope with everything I take Tania over to Mamá Luya's house since nothing ever changes over there. She still takes her siesta after lunch. When she gets up, it's always the same ritual: she takes out her corded girdle from the wardrobe and laces it up, she puts on her printed dress, powders up her face, puts on her lipstick, and then she heads out to the patio. She always has an aroma about her of jasmine and my childhood. Sometimes I water the garden since it's hard for her to be on her feet too long these days. Tania always wants her to pick her up and carry her. She likes to run her hand over Mamá Luya's face, over that smooth skin that feels like a baby's, which somehow the years haven't managed to wrinkle. I don't know how she and Tía Flor manage to do it, but they always have some little snack to offer us when we come over. But what Tania likes the most are all the songs that her great-grandmother teaches her... *"There once was a little bitty boat, a little bitty boat there was..."* as Tania shows her with her little fingers pinched together the size of the imaginary boat. To fall asleep, however, there was no other song that would do other than 'the one about the apples' as she called it:

> *Señora Santa Ana*
> *why weeps the baby boy?*
> *'Tis a tasty apple*
> *that gives him so much joy.*

> *I will give you one.*
> *I will give you two.*
> *One for the baby*
> *and another for you.*

> *Not one do I want.*
> *Not for two do I pine.*
> *My lost one I want,*
> *the one that is mine.*

"It seems like it was just yesterday that I would sing lullabies to you and your sister," Mamá Luya always sighs and remarks. "Poor Lauri... so alone up there in the cold," she inevitably adds.

Maruja likes to teach songs to Tania too. Every time she's playing out on the patio, Maruja comes up to her and sings:

> *Listen to me, you who say that your country is not so beautiful,*
> *Listen, you who say that what is yours is not so good,*
> *I invite you to find anywhere in the world*
> *another sky so blue as the sky that is yours,*
> *a moon so bright as the one you see*
> *that shines upon the sweetness of the sugarcane,*
> *a Fidel that quakes in the mountains,*
> *a ruby field with a single star and its five stripes,*
> *Cuba, how beautiful is Cuba,*
> *for he who defends her loves her the most.*

—Eduardo Saborit, "Cuba, How Beautiful is Cuba"

Tania struts around with her hands on her hips, imitating her, repeating over and over:

"Cuba, how beautiful is Cuba…"

❧

There has been a lot of discussion recently about Viet Nam. On numerous occasions we have analyzed what their heroic struggle truly means, what Viet Nam itself means to the world, to other liberation movements, and to all nations who find themselves besieged by imperialists. We have affirmed how in Viet Nam a battle is being fought for all mankind, and by heroically and victoriously waging war against the most powerful, aggressive, and odious imperialists of the world, Viet Nam is also fighting on our behalf.

It is perhaps unnecessary to reiterate our zeal and solidarity with Viet Nam because it is only natural and logical that a country such as ours—one that is also threatened by similar dangers—should feel towards Viet Nam the most profound solidarity.

Viet Nam today is involved in a fight to the death, a crucial struggle that continues to take on greater significance and intensity.

And it is for that reason that we wish to offer a gesture that goes beyond mere words. And that is, that we will dedicate this year to Viet Nam and ask that it be recognized as the Year of Heroic Viet Nam.

And this gesture, which says it all, constitutes the proposal before you: may the year 1967 henceforth be known as the Year of Heroic Viet Nam. All those in favor raise your hand.

Fatherland or Death! We Shall Overcome!

(Fidel Castro 2 January 1967)

∽

Among the intellectuals there's been a lot of commotion lately about a book by somebody named Debray. Lázaro spends all his time trying to keep up with the occasional bits of news we get about Che, who has once again taken up the revolutionary cause in other parts.

We found out that my cousin Julio Edward is fighting in Vietnam— for the other side, obviously. His folks left for the U.S. in '61, and it looks like he was drafted into the army, or maybe he volunteered, I'm not sure. No one talks about it much, but every time there's news about the war, I think we all have him in our thoughts, even if we don't say it out loud. Lázaro, Maruja, and Marta are thrilled when the Yankees experience big setbacks, but I can only manage to fake a smile. It's not a matter of politics. What would happen if they killed my cousin? I remember when the family used to get together on Sundays and we would play games at our other grandmother's house on C Street there in Vedado. Maybe it's better that she died. She already lost one grandson in World War II. Why did I say that? It's not going to happen again.

I'm always asking Papá if he's heard anything from Tío Julio. He usually shrugs me off. My father is a Cantinflas type. One really never knows what he's up to. Lately he's become real friendly with Lázaro and he seems more revolutionary than Fidel himself. Other times I hear him and his friend Eneido whispering about stuff, and it sounds like they're being critical of the Revolution, but when I try to join in they immediately stop talking. He won't even be frank with his own daughter! It's not like I'm going to turn him in...

Finally, around the beginning of July, we got the news. Julio Edward was killed one day short of completing his tour of duty. When Armandito came to tell us, Maruja came in from the doorway and remarked:

"So what was a Cuban boy doing getting involved in a war run by the Yankees?"

My mother stared her down with that cold steel look of hers, just like her own mother's:

"Maruja! Show some respect for the dead. No matter what, he's still my husband's nephew."

Papá remained motionless. Later on, he got up and made coffee, as if nothing had happened. But later that night, he shut himself in the bathroom. And I think I could hear him crying.

CHAPTER SIX
"If You're Heading to El Cobre…"

MY SECOND CHILD WAS BORN ON FEBRUARY 8TH, 1968, on the same day that Governor George Wallace announced that he was running for president on the platform of opposing the Civil Rights movement. I wanted to name the baby Julio Eduardo, but Roberto insisted that he be named after him. The previous week my in-laws had come up to take care of Pedro Pablo while I was in the hospital and to give me a hand once I got back home. Adela insisted on tending to the baby all by herself. I know she means well, but I would have preferred to be alone with my husband and kids.

"My little flower child…" I whisper to the baby, and Bobby gets mad. To him, all hippies are communists.

The night before his parents were going to head back home, he asked them, "So, what do you think about coming up here and moving in with us? With a loan from the VA or the FHA we could buy a house, you could help take care of the kids and we could all live more comfortably…"

My mother-in-law answered without thinking twice:

"The truth is that since Johnny left for college in Gainesville, we're very lonely…"

I wanted to kill my husband. He should have asked me first. And on top of it all, I find out that he had already looked at a house and was working on making an offer.

"Of course, if you or Mamá don't really care for it…"

I had to like it. He had already put down a deposit, and we weren't in any position to lose the money. We argued all night long. I don't know how many times I've told him that we have to make these kinds of decisions together. I don't think he even understands what I mean. But later on, sure enough, he comes up to me, and with each of his caresses on the back of my neck, my anger dissolves a little at a time. We end up making love and, as usual, he gets his way.

We'll make the move in June, once Pedro Pablo has finished the school year. At least the house is really pretty.

ༀ

A 16-year-old Negro boy was slain in Memphis March 28 shortly after violence and looting broke up a protest march led by the Reverend Dr. Martin Luther Jr. in support of the city's predominantly Negro striking sanitation workers. Governor Buford Ellington (D., Tennessee) called up 4,000 National Guardsmen and ordered a curfew. The violence came in the 6th week of what had begun as a labor strike and had developed into a general civil rights protest by the city's Negro community.

(*Facts on File* 28.1431, 131)

ༀ

Recently, I've spent a lot of time in front of the TV while I nurse Bobby Jr., and I've come to realize what a great divide there is in this country. Are we headed for another Civil War? I think about Cuba, and especially about Hilda, our cook from Jacomino, and how she was always talking about her four little *negritos,* as she herself called her own children. Menchu and I tutored her oldest daughter to help her pass the entrance exam for high school. I can still see her, dressed in our hand-me-downs, with her hair in braids, sitting on our terrace out back, doubled over her books.

She wanted to learn so badly! And she passed the exam with flying colors, and Papá got her a scholarship. I wonder what life was like for them. We never saw where they lived. It never dawned on us. I also wonder how they're doing now. There are so many things I have questions about. Are Blacks really better off now because of the Revolution, as they say? Could King really be a communist like a lot of Cubans believe? I wish there were someone I could talk to about these types of things… I can't really talk to Bobby because the only thing that interests him is overthrowing Fidel. My boss is a real leftist, so I can't trust his opinion either.

~

The Reverend Dr. Martin Luther King Jr., 39, Nobel Prize winner and acknowledged leader of the nonviolent civil rights movements was shot to death by a sniper in Memphis, Tennessee, April 4.

The news of King's assassination evoked expressions of dismay and shock across the U.S. and throughout the world. The killing precipitated rioting and violence in Washington, Chicago and other U.S. cities. 34 persons were killed and thousands injured and arrested in the disorders by April 10. More than 20,000 regular federal troops and 34,000 National Guardsmen were sent to the troubled cities after King's death as local authorities called for help to end the disorders.

President Johnson, reflecting the nation's grief, delivered a nationwide TV address in which he lauded the slain Negro leader and appealed to "every citizen to reject the blind violence that has struck Dr. King, who lived by nonviolence."

The bullet that killed King hit him on the right side of the neck at 6:01 p.m. CST as he leaned over the 2nd floor railing outside his room at the Lorraine Motel in the predominantly Negro section of Memphis. He was pronounced dead at St. Joseph's Hospital at 7 p.m.

(Facts on File 28.1432, 139)

~

We were coming back from the doctor's office—Bobby Jr. was due for his two-month shots—when the riots began. I didn't get this secondhand; I saw it with my own eyes. I saw their wrath as the Blacks broke store windows, they threw stones at cars driven by Whites, they overturned police cars, they set fire to their own neighborhoods. I was terrified that something was going to happen to my sons. We went up 16th in order to avoid 13th which runs through a black neighborhood. In any event, Bobby made me get on the floor of the back seat with the kids until we got to Silver Spring. And we didn't even see the worst of it. My dear friend Luisa was coming home from the store in her carpool and they split her head open with a rock. What's going to happen to this country?

∽

Senator Robert Francis Kennedy (D., New York) was shot by a gunman in Los Angeles June 5. The suspected assassin…was immediately arrested at the scene of the crime.

Kennedy was shot shortly after leaving a rally celebration of his victory in the California presidential primary. The Senator was gunned down less than 5 years after the assassination of his older brother, President John F. Kennedy, and only 2 months after that of the Reverend Martin Luther King. As a shock wave of sorrow, shame and indignation engulfed the nation, President Johnson expressing the grief of his countrymen, announced he was creating a special commission of distinguished citizens to study violence in the U.S. with a view to finding out "how we can stop it."

Kennedy, who had arrived comatose at the hospital, underwent 4 hours of surgery to remove bullet fragments from his brain. His press secretary announced a minute before 2:00 a.m. June 6 that Kennedy died at 1:44 a.m.

(Facts on File 28.1441, 226–227)

∽

There is as much tension in our home as there is in the nation's capital. Moving day was one problem after the next. To begin with, Bobby offered the master bedroom to his parents, the only room with a bathroom in it. I understand that they're older, but it's my house…

What bothers me the most is that he doesn't consult me. Thankfully, my father-in-law wouldn't accept his offer, and Adela pointed out that Bobby Jr.'s crib wasn't going to fit in the other smaller bedroom with us.

Anyway, it irritates me that Bobby never sides with me. Yesterday Adela insisted on giving Pedro Pablo a cookie even though I had already told her that he shouldn't have any sweets right before dinner. She looked at Bobby for support so, of course, he chimed in:

"Well, let's give him half a cookie."

I didn't say anything until we were alone:

"I'm sure you thought you came up with a solution worthy of King Solomon, but I would appreciate it if you didn't diminish my authority in front of my son."

"I don't know what's the matter with you, Lauri. You used to get along fine with my mother in Miami."

"Things were different then. I was in her home, but now she's in mine. Besides, your mother has changed a lot. And so have I."

"All right, it won't happen again."

But it keeps on happening all the time, and Bobby never sides with me. It's all my fault, and yet as soon as he touches me I melt and put it out of my mind. But next time...

My father-in-law is dying to work at the Organization of American States. I don't know how many people he's contacted.

"I just want to get in, even as a doorman. I'll take care of the rest." I find that mixture of humility and arrogance very touching.

I was finally able to quit my job at the real estate office. The owner was a very difficult woman and really made my life miserable. I didn't have any other choice however but to put up with it since we needed the money. Now I'm working for a very rich contractor who has a lot of connections. I told Roberto:

"If you want me to, I'll talk to my boss to see if he knows someone who can help you at the OAS."

He came up and put his hand on my shoulder.

"That would mean so much to me Lauri."

I thought he was going to cry.

With my in-laws at home, I've decided to go back and take a few more classes. That way I'll be able to finish school faster. I love my classes, especially the ones in literature. I even find physics to be poetic. After I take classes at the local college, what I'd really like to do is to enroll in the university. In that sense, it's been a blessing having Bobby's folks live with us.

We're also able to go out more. Besides everything going on at the *Casa Cuba,* some evenings we go to the movies with some other couples. Other times we get together in the basement of someone's house. Occasionally we even have small parties. One evening while we were doing the *escoba* dance, the one where everyone keeps changing partners while dancing, I'm pretty sure that Eddy was flirting with me. I think he rigged it so that we would always wind up as partners, and I know that he was dancing closer than he should. Half-joking, half-serious, he'd say things like how I was a hippie in spirit. Maybe it was just my imagination; regardless, I had a very good time.

Bobby is doing well selling insurance, but sometimes I get so mad at him. He spends all of his time talking on the phone to his friends in Miami about Cuba. When the Russians occupied Czechoslovakia, he called his buddies every day and talked about how Castro had supported the invasion and how that wasn't going to sit well with either the Americans or the Cuban people and on and on… No wonder our telephone bill is so high. And yet I think twice before calling Cuba since I know how expensive it is!

The Holidays this year were so special. Johnny came up and spent his Christmas vacation with us. I can't believe just how much he has grown up. He has become an intelligent and studious young man, and I love talking to him. Pedro Pablo adores him. My boss got my father-in-law an interview with some OAS official and on the 23rd he got a call asking him to report to work in January.

"Lauri, I am forever in your debt. You're the daughter I never had," and he gave me a big hug. The truth is he always shows me a lot of affection.

Those were not the only pleasant surprises. Just as we were about to sit down for dinner on Christmas Eve, there was a knock at the door. It was Vidal carrying an armful of presents! He told Pedro Pablo how he used to rock him when he was a baby, and he sang Bobby Jr. to sleep with an aria from *Los Gavilanes:*

> *Recalling you night and day,*
> *beloved hamlet,*
> *my hope renewed*
> *and my sorrows lessened.*

> *Recalling you, calm sea,*
> *Recalling you, blue firmament,*
> *sweeter was my suffering*
> *and diminished my discontent.*

Everyone fell silent. The only thing you could hear was Vidal's deep baritone voice:

> *Recalling you night and day*
> *beloved hamlet*

"That's the way we Cubans live," said my father-in-law. And he was right.

Something very odd happened to me on New Year's Eve. It was like some type of vision or even a hallucination. I had this sensation that we were shipwrecked, the last Cubans to survive a terrible catastrophe. In Cuba they've tried to erase history, to pretend that nothing and no one existed prior to 1959, to steal a people's collective memory. How can a nation exist without a past? We are the last ones who can remember the country as it was before the Revolution. We are the ones who have been called upon to conserve and transmit a precious legacy. We are, for all intents and purposes, the last generation of Cubans. I felt like turning off the music, and interrupting all the couples that were dancing to the

Orquesta Aragón, and begging them to understand the seriousness of our historic responsibility. But suddenly everything started to spin and to become foggy. Something even more terrifying occurred to me—maybe we're merely shadows, maybe we don't really exist, no one sees us or hears us, maybe the Cuba we remember only exists in our dreams, that the corner store that sells Cuban products, that our little performances starring Martí as the main character, that the yellowed photographs that we never get tired of poring over, that the acts of patriotism, the clay pots, the flags, our furnishings, the newspapers in Spanish, this very music that we're listening to right now—*"And if you're heading to El Cobre, be sure and bring me..."*—that all of it has been a lie, maybe that Cuba, the real Cuba, is the other one, the one that consists of olive green uniforms and slogans, of ration books and Defense Committees, of political prisoners and the dead, the one in which some or many or—I don't know—maybe just a few are blind to the horrors because they sincerely believe that they are building a new and better Cuba—*Patria o Muerte, Venceremos!*

∽

Cuban welder Armando Socarrás Ramírez, 22, survived a nine-hour, 5,600-mile flight from Havana to Madrid on June 4 in the unpressurized, unheated wheel well of an Iberian Airline DC-8 jetliner. The stowaway survived a severe oxygen shortage and temperatures of 40 degrees below zero at the flight's 29,000 feet altitude. A fellow stowaway, Jorge Pérez Blanco, 16, fell as the jet took off.

Socarrás, who left Cuba for political reasons, was brought to the U.S. July 25 by the International Rescue Committee to join an uncle living in New Jersey.

(Facts on File 29.1502, 516)

∽

All of us went to New York for my cousin Carlitos's wedding. I like that city more all the time because you can see something different every day. I think I especially enjoy its pace of life. There is something vibrant in the air. As soon as we get close to the Lincoln Tunnel, my blood starts to stir in my veins.

Although it's been over three years since Julio Eduardo's death, the wedding reception was very simple, without music or dancing, as they tend to do here. In spite of the occasion, Aunt Alicia and Uncle Julio looked sad. She was still dressed in black, and he wore a black tie. Burying a child must be the most painful thing in the world. If something were to happen to mine, I think I'd go mad. I never know what to say to them. I don't know if I should tell them that Pedro Pablo still remembers Julio Eduardo, that I can't hear the Beatles without crying, that many times I dream of him, that I have his picture on my nightstand... I always end up hugging them tight because the right words just won't come out.

Every day, there are more and more protest demonstrations against the war. Young people are burning their draft cards. Many have moved to Canada to avoid going to Vietnam. They say it's an absurd war, that there's no way to win, that it should be left to the Vietnamese. Others, especially the Cubans, argue that someone has to protect the world from communism. I don't know what to think. Part of me wants the Americans to win because that way, I guess, my cousin's death wouldn't have been in vain. Besides, communism is terrible. At the same time though, I don't want there to be any more deaths.

I also feel confused at times about the whole business with Cuba. I see people who've been through so much... It's so sad to live apart from your country... I get so angry when I read all the propaganda—how before Castro came to power Cuba was an American brothel, how the Revolution has provided everybody with bread and education—but I also think about my family there. I can't help it. When people make generalizations about Cubans on the Island as if everyone were the same, as if everybody were Castro's accomplice, I jump all over them. I know my brothers collaborate with the Government. They don't have any other choice! People don't understand that in Cuba everybody works for the State. There's no alternative. That doesn't mean that everybody's a Communist or that they're bad people. The truth is they probably know less about the terrible things that the regime is doing than we do. Bobby doesn't see it that way and the other day we argued about it when we were over at some friends' house.

I don't like to bring it up to him, but I can't stand his little digs about my family, so I ended up reminding him that my mother was the only one who visited him in prison and brought him food. My friend Silvia is the only one who understands me because her parents are still in Cuba, too.

The Monday morning after we returned from New York, the telephone rang while I was helping Pedro Pablo get ready for school. When the operator informed me it was a call from Cuba, as always, I was excited to hear the voices of my loved ones and, at the same time, I was scared that something bad had happened. When I heard Menchu's voice, I knew something was wrong:

"Mamá Luya got sick last week. We took her to the clinic, but...she had a stroke."

"How is she, Menchu? How is she?"

"Tía Flor wanted to bring her home..."

"And?"

"She died on Friday. We were with her...she didn't suffer."

"But...how is that possible, Menchu? She's dead?"

"We tried to call you, and Ricardo too, but no one answered."

"We were at Carlitos's wedding in New York. How's Mamá? Can I talk to her?"

"She seemed all right at first. But after the funeral she fell apart. She's sleeping now."

"You've already had the funeral?"

"Yes, on Saturday."

"And Tía Flor?"

"You can imagine..."

I couldn't hold back the tears any longer.

"Oh, sis, what a tragedy, what a terrible tragedy…"

"Lauri, Mamá Luya wasn't the same person that she was when you left, she was almost eighty-five…"

"Sis, did you get my letter with the pictures? Did Mamá Luya get to see them?"

"Yes, yes, a few days ago. She really liked them. We put them on her night stand."

"And Papá? And Pedritín?"

"Fine…they're fine. They're not home right now. Sorry, we've been waiting for them to put the call through and it just came in."

I continued to cry. We were saying our goodbyes when Menchu said:

"Lauri, Mamá Luya said that Pedro Pablo looked like the two of us. The truth is that both boys are very handsome."

I had to hang up because I couldn't talk for my sobbing.

I cry because my grandmother has died and I hadn't seen her in ten years…because I didn't even find out until after they had buried her…because as she lay dying, I was at a wedding, not knowing she was exhaling her last breath…

I cry because she never met my kids, and she never got the chance to teach them the same lullabies she had taught my sister and me, songs like *"Había una vez un barquito chiquitico… There once was a little bitty boat, a little bitty boat there was…"*

I cry for her house in La Sierra, with its flowerbeds of impatiens and caladiums out front…because I will never again see Mamá Luya wake up from her nap and put on that absurd girdle with all those ties and ribbons that she would pull out of her armoire, and see her put on her print dress and sit there out back on the terrace, with her lips touched up with her light pink Coty lipstick…

I cry for the stories that she'll never get to tell me again…because never again will I hear her voice, nor will I smell her fragrance of jasmine, nor will I feel the softness of her skin, nor will she look at me with her steely blue eyes…

I cry because she is dead, under the ground, in the same grave where so often we put flowers for my grandfather and I can't even go there to be with her...

I cry for my parents, and for Menchu, and for Pedritín, and for Julio Eduardo who came from Cuba to die in Vietnam and is buried in New York, where snow covers his grave in winter and I don't even know if he's cold...

I cry because in Miami Johnny had to go to school wearing the shirts from his LaSalle uniform and they would laugh at him...and because Menchu didn't want to come for the birth of my first child... and because she just told me that Pedro Pablo looks like us and because my husband thinks that everyone there is a Communist...

I cry because Mamá Luya will no longer make me pudding and let me eat it warm right out of the pan, because she won't ever come take care of me again when I'm sick...because in school my own child pledges allegiance to another flag...and he sings *twinkle twinkle little star*... Why didn't you wait for me, Mamá Luya? Why won't you be waiting for me on the stairs when I get back, just like you were the day I last saw you when I left? Why? Why? Why am I here surrounded by English everywhere, while in Havana—that city of slogans and light— you and my innocence have died?

∽

Farewell to the land, goodbye to the fruit that nourishes,
So long dear grandfather who on the front porch slumbers.
Over the empty days wafts yesterday's wind.
Stoically I swallow, but I shall never fail to remember.

(Torres 22)

∽

The years go by quickly. These days they're measured more by the seasons than by the calendar. They seem to start with the beginning of the school year like a composition book with all its pages blank. I always remember how Mamá would take us to the *Moderna Poesía* to buy school supplies and how she would then sit at the dining room table to cover our books... Nowadays book covers come pre-cut... Then before long you need a sweater in the evenings and soon the leaves will turn red, golden, and brown only to then fall brittlely to the ground... on Sundays we all work together raking the leaves in the yard...even Bobby Jr. likes to help...the sky is bluer and there's a transparent quality to the air that makes everything look sharper... Halloween arrives and Adela makes costumes for the boys so they can go through the neighborhood and trick-or-treat for candy at the houses decorated with jack-o-lanterns, witches and ghosts... Soon it's Thanksgiving Day, dinner with turkey, sweet potatoes and a special prayer written by me to be read before we eat... Christmas...the season for office parties, exchanging gifts, get-togethers with friends, going with the kids to see the tree at the White House...and that unrelenting homesickness for the ones back there... Without a doubt someone will invariably say, "Christmas in Cuba was always better," just as sure as someone else will make our customary New Year's Eve toast, "Next year in Havana..." It's winter now and the days have become shorter, the branches on the trees grow bare...to me they still seem like arms raised in prayer...at the front of the house we planted two pine trees that stay green all year long, that is until one frigid January morning when we woke to find one of them lying on the ground...overcome by the weight of the snow it lay there stiff, reminiscent of a soldier slain in battle...in the spring, nature is reborn...the first thing to bloom is the forsythia and later on small patches of green slowly start covering the trees...then the azaleas bloom in all their splendor, followed by the cherry trees with their flowers as ephemeral and beautiful as the flight of a butterfly...our jackets come off next...baseball's here...the squirrels scurry through the trees...and on Easter the kids draw pictures of bunnies, we get dressed up in our new clothes and go to Mass, we prepare a huge meal, and my son asks me "what does resurrection mean?"...summer...long days, there's life after work, the inflatable pool in the back yard, hamburgers on the grill...the annual pilgrimage to Miami...we return with extra pounds, a box filled with books in Spanish, the smell of the sea, the taste of mangos, the heat from of the sun, and friends who warm our heart...

∞

Richard Milhous Nixon announced last night that he will resign as the 37th President of the United States at noon today.

Vice President Gerald R. Ford from Michigan will take the oath as the new President at noon to complete the remaining 2 ½ years of Nixon's term.

After two years of bitter public debate over the Watergate scandal, Nixon bowed to public pressure and the leaders of his party to become the first President in American history to resign.

"...as President, I must put the interest of America first," he said.

While the President acknowledged that some of his judgments "were wrong," he made no confessions of "high crimes and misdemeanors" with which the House Judiciary Committee charged him in the bill of impeachment.

The president-to-be praised Mr. Nixon's sacrifice for the country and called it "one of the saddest incidents I have ever witnessed."

(*Washington Post* 9 August 1974: A1)

∞

Although at times I still have my differences with Adela, I have grown fond of her. Some nights, while Bobby's out playing dominoes and the boys are already asleep, Roberto reads and she and I talk while we fold the laundry. Sometimes I tell her about my life in Cuba, and she tells me about her childhood growing up... I learned how when she was ten years old she went to Spain with her mother, who was returning to her hometown for the first time, and how on the return trip to Cuba her mother fell gravely ill. They put her in quarantine and Adela could only see her through a glass window. She died and they buried her at sea. Adela was physically incapable of crying or even uttering a word until the ship reached Havana and she spotted her father waiting for her on the dock.

I have come to admire my father-in-law too. He wakes up early, and before leaving for work, he sits down with a book and studies English. He has made great strides, all by himself. His way of thinking also surprises me at times. When Augusto Pinochet staged his *coup d'état* in Chile, a group of Cubans wanted to publish a letter of support, and they asked me to translate it. I did so, but when it came time to sign it like they wanted me to, I refused. I guess they thought that it was because of my family in Cuba, but then I explained why:

"It's just that I don't endorse *coup d'états*, and I'm not in favor of overthrowing any country or throwing out its constitution. Look what Batista's *coup* did to us in Cuba..."

A heated argument ensued, and much to my surprise, my father-in-law intervened on my behalf. He was the one who in the end came up with a solution:

"I think that the letter would be more effective, and perhaps even more acceptable to Lauri, if your support were not unconditional, but rather showed a strong desire for Pinochet to quickly restore rights, call for elections, and return the country to democracy."

Recently I started helping out an organization that publishes a bulletin on human rights in Cuba. What happened was that one of its leaders asked me out to lunch one day. I only knew that she was an older woman who had been a feminist in Cuba and part of Castro's first cabinet. At first I was hesitant, but I quickly found her charming, and I agreed to help out in any way I could. I started out by folding papers and stuffing envelopes with letters that described the political prisoners on the Island. Sometimes a group would come to our house and we'd all do the work together. My in-laws and even Pedro Pablo helped out at times. Later on they asked me to translate some of the reports. As I read the stories of the political prisoners, the repression that was taking place on the Island ceased to be an abstract concept. After that they started having names and faces that would jump out at me from the pictures. They are treated so brutally that it's terrifying. Hunger, forced labor, overcrowding, sharing their space with rats and their own feces, stuck in tiny cells they call "mousetraps," or *ratoneras,* abused by guards who strip search them, who rip off their clothes, who insult them, who beat them, who rob them of their meager possessions, who punish them if they complain, who stick them in dark solitary confinement, who deny them medical attention, who detain them beyond their sentence. But they don't give in; and they don't give up. There are also female political prisoners. They also mistreat them savagely, they push them, kick them, strip them, humiliate them, torture them with the noise coming from loudspeakers that doesn't stop for days, they knock them down with high-powered water hoses. One of the prisoners stated that the guards are so sadistic that they get erections from beating them. Sometimes they kick them in their private parts and bite their breasts. And in the middle of this horror a woman—whom they had jailed and abused even though she was pregnant—gave birth to a baby girl. They named her *Milagritos* since she was their "little miracle."

∽

According to some estimates, the highest number of political prisoners in Cuba was reached during the 1960s with 60,000 inmates. According to figures from Amnesty International, about 20,000 had been released by the mid-1970s. As a base of comparison, in a country the size of the United States those figures would be the equivalent of 1,410,000 and 466,000 political prisoners respectively. Such figures would place Cuba as the leading country in the world with the greatest number of political prisoners per capita, even greater than the Soviet Union itself.

(Greve and Pérez A1)

❧

There are times that I really worry about Bobby. You can tell that he's just not adapting, that he has become so bitter and nothing makes him happy. He's always complaining about having to live in exile. But at least he has all of his family here! Cuba is painful for me, too. It hurts to always feel like a foreigner, with your roots exposed, with this feeling that everything is temporary, that life is back there in a future that never seems to get here. What has happened to us is very hard, but there are so many who have it so much worse. Others have had family members killed or they're still in prison. It hasn't been bad for us in the United States, after all we have two sons…but you'd think that neither they nor I matter at all to Bobby. As much as I love Cuba, at times I'm jealous. He's obsessed with one thought. From the time he gets up until the time he goes to bed, all he does is talk about Cuba. When I try to bring it up to him, he gets mad and he sulks for days. I don't know what's worse. There are times when I ask myself if all couples go through hard times after they've been married a while, and if I'll ever feel like I did when we first arrived in Miami and we were so poor and so madly in love. After all is said and done, I was the one who left everything behind to follow him! But on the other hand, I couldn't have stayed in Cuba without him…and I certainly can't imagine my life without my children. I can't wait to graduate and become a teacher. That way I can get home earlier and spend more time with them. All my worries vanish when I'm with them, and my life takes on a renewed purpose. Sometimes, when I check in on them to make sure they're covered up, I see them sleeping and my eyes fill with tears. At that very moment life seems like a miracle.

❧

The American evacuation from Vietnam, which took place amidst scenes of chaos, panic, and suffering, is over.

It came only hours before the government in Saigon that it had long supported finally fell, surrendering unconditionally to North Vietnam, which had fought for this ultimate triumph for 30 years.

The final act of American involvement, that had lasted for a generation took the lives of 56,737 military personnel, cost more than $160 billion and affected virtually every aspect of national life, occurred in the early morning hours of Wednesday.

As the last helicopters were taking to the air with Ambassador Graham Martin and other survivors of the once overpowering American presence, President Ford issued a statement. He said the evacuation "closes a chapter in the American experience," and called upon the nation to close ranks, to avoid recrimination about the past.

(*Washington Post* 30 April 1975: A1)

༺༻

I was talking long distance with my cousin Carlitos about the situation with the Vietnamese refugees when my father-in-law came home so visibly upset I had to hang up:

"Roberto, what's wrong?"

"Adela has cancer, *mijita*," he said as he collapsed on the couch.

The biopsy from a lump she had found on one of her breasts had come back positive and they needed to operate right away.

"Why hadn't you said anything to us?"

"I didn't want any of you to worry…and with you being in the middle of exams and all…"

The hospital has a strange smell. I can't help but wonder if it's the smell of death. The doctor assures us that the operation has been successful but that she's going to need radiation. She has to go every day for six weeks. I go with her. I'm moved to see how quickly she has changed. This strong, domineering woman, who now sits beside me waiting for her turn, has become so vulnerable.

"Do you want me to go in with you?"

I'd really prefer to go in with her than stay in the waiting room staring at the faces of the other patients, pale with the threat of death detectable on their semi-closed eyelids.

It's the first time I see her naked chest and the long angry scar. I feel a wave of nausea welling up in my mouth, but I don't look away. The technicians draw an area on her skin with a purple marker where she will receive the radiation. When the treatment is about to begin, they ask me to leave.

"I'll be right outside the door," I say.

Adela is a very strong woman and she handles the radiation well. But near the end, it burns her skin and she loses her appetite.

"The worst part is that they get that machine so close to me that I'm afraid it's going to come down on top of me," has been her only complaint.

She very quickly put herself in charge again at home. The doctors asked to talk to us.

"The cancer was very advanced. We took out the glands, but most likely the cancer will metastasize."

"How much time does she have?" asked Roberto.

"Three, four years at most."

I keep on insisting on finding out if there isn't some other possible treatment. How can we just sit here and do nothing and wait for her to die?

But, in fact, there was nothing that we could do.

"She should live her life as normally as possible...of course, she shouldn't carry anything heavy with that arm."

Adela's illness changed all of us. She took charge of the kids and spoiled them way too much. I knew that she shouldn't, but how could I object? I also worried about how her passing would affect the boys. I tried to talk to Bobby about it but to no avail.

"Mamá is strong. Nothing is going to happen."

I don't know if he didn't want to face reality or what, but Bobby started spending more and more time away from home. He played tennis, dominoes, or attended meetings sponsored by who knows what

Cuban group. He was obsessed with the idea of returning to Cuba to fight. He even slept with a revolver under his pillow. Imagine, and with my fear of any kind of weapon…but begging him didn't do any good. Sometimes I wondered if he wasn't ill. Yet, at work, and with his friends, he was so charming. Now, I had become the one who didn't want to be alone with him. We seldom made love anymore.

I found refuge in my kids and my students. It was a big change for me being a teacher after having always worked in an office. Had it not been for them, I think I would have gone crazy.

I also felt so bad for my father-in-law. Adela would constantly belittle him, and he would never say anything back to her. Sometimes I was struck by the idea that she would live to be a hundred and would continue to blackmail us with the threat that she could die any second.

In the last few months her behavior became very erratic. She became irate with me at times and would insult me for no reason. And in front of the kids! She would accuse me of terrible things, even of having had an affair with my old boss!

"If you keep behaving this way, Adela, you're going to have to move out," I told her one day after I had had enough.

What a mistake! Adela became indignant and said she was leaving even if she had to sleep on a park bench. Bobby threw it in my face that this was the way I paid back his mother after all that she had done to help me go back to school. The kids were caught in the middle. I finally gave in after my father-in-law said, "Look, *mijita,* I know you're right, but forgive her. She's not herself. I don't know what's going on."

We found out soon enough. The cancer had gone to her brain and was eating away at her skull. The last few months were hell. Besides work, the children, and the house, I took care of Adela. I bathed her, shampooed her hair, clipped her nails, held her head when she vomited, cleaned up her urine and feces, talked to the doctors, I even learned to give her injections. She never thanked me and only smiled when Bobby or the kids stuck their heads in the door or when Johnny—whom she started to call Juancito again—called on the phone. Only once, when she was in terrible pain and I had just given her a shot of pain killer, did she say, "Don't leave me alone."

I walked toward the bed and gently took her hand. I desperately wanted her to say something, just one word that would heal my wounds and would let me look back fondly on everything we had gone through together. She squeezed my hand tightly but didn't say anything.

The cancer must have reached her lungs because it became hard for her to breathe. She started spending the night in a recliner in the living room. I was so afraid that we were going to get up one morning and find her dead in the living room.

"Bobby, we should see about putting her in a hospice...this is so hard on the kids..."

"Let's wait a bit... With the new medicine, you'll see, she'll get better..."

"I can't stand this anymore, Bobby."

One night I heard her talking and jumped out of bed. She was delirious! She was speaking to the captain of a ship and was asking him about her mother's health. She was talking like a little girl. After a few minutes she said, "Oh, Mommy, how good of you to come."

I didn't ask Bobby this time. I called an ambulance.

She died on a frigid January morning. When we got back home from the hospital, we noticed that the other pine tree had fallen due to the weight of the snow, and it lay there rigid and motionless on the white blanket just as Adela did between the sheets.

CHAPTER SEVEN
"The Ten Million Are On Their Way!"

A FEW DAYS AGO THE RUMOR STARTED GOING AROUND THAT THEY HAD KILLED CHE. At first we thought it was just a bunch of talk, lies made up by the counterrevolutionaries that wanted him dead. But when the foreign cables started coming in, hinting at the possibility that they had captured him, Lázaro began to get nervous. For three days, rather than coming home, he stayed up at *Bohemia,* glued to the teletype. At first we didn't hear anything from official sources. But finally we got the news. He was dead. We were stunned. After all, Che wasn't even a Cuban and he had risked his life fighting for our country. Some people wonder why they didn't give him more help, why he had to die so alone. Lázaro is completely beside himself. I had never seen him cry before.

"He was a great man, Menchu, the most virtuous man I've ever met."

There was a big gathering that night in the Plaza of the Revolution. Lázaro wanted to take Tania.

"It's a historic moment, a tragedy for all Mankind. Besides, Che died for her, so that she could live in a better world…"

"But the poor thing has a cold and it's getting chilly at night," objected Mamá, who wound up staying home with her.

All the rest of us went. I had never seen the Plaza so full nor heard a silence so profound while in the middle of such a huge crowd.

❧

History should not appeal only to those who by vocation or profession offer history classes or write textbooks. History should be of interest to one and all: everyone has to know what, how, and why things have happened. Only by knowing and understanding history well can we have the ability to understand why we are who we are and where we are. And equally so, we will comprehend better where we are headed and how far we can go. Revolutionary history is a continuous line. With the Revolution we have not severed the history of Cuba. We have simply pruned the rotten branches from the tree of Cuban history. The powerful trunk and its healthy branches have not been cut. The history of Cuba, from the roots of its tree to today's new pines, is a continuum that carries on. As we come to know it more deeply, we will be able to better understand why our Revolution is what it is and why it must be that way.

(*Bohemia* 60:38, 3)

∽

Mamá gets out the photo albums every afternoon and shows them to Tania, and sometimes to Ernestico too when Armandito and Magaly bring him by. They start out with the old yellow photos, the ones of Mamá's grandparents. She goes along telling the kids:

"This is my mother and this one here is my father..."

There are photos of Mamá Luya when she was a child with her brothers. Then come the ones of when my parents were dating, the ones from our childhood: Ricardo with his sailor suit, Lauri and me always dressed alike, Pedritín at the beach... There's a second album with photos of those who have left us. Mamá once again repeats the whole thing to my daughter:

"This is your Uncle Ricardo. This is your Aunt Lauri. Look at how she looks just like your Mamá... These are her sons, Pedro Pablo and Bobby, who are your cousins..."

Every photo is accompanied with some story or memory or hope.

"Someday you're going to meet your cousins...and we're all going to get together and have a big party, with lots of balloons, and snacks, and cookies, and chicken salad, and cake, and cold drinks... Just like the birthday parties we used to have for your Mamá and Laurita."

"This is your grandfather's brother, and these are also your cousins..." She keeps on going, pointing out Tío Julio and Tía Alicia, there with Carlitos and Julio Eduardo, standing in front of St. Patrick's. Tania pays close attention and protests if her grandmother forgets a small detail or changes one of her stories in the slightest.

"That's not the way it goes, *Abuela.*"

And Mamá starts all over again and explains how Tía Lauri took off in a big ol' plane and now she lives far, far away in a country where it snows and gets really cold.

Yesterday Lázaro arrived earlier than usual and saw them in the patio. They were so caught up in the ritual of looking at the photo albums that Tania didn't run to give him his customary hug.

"The child has to know her roots, Lázaro," Mamá told him with a certain tone of pride in her voice.

"You're right, Mariana, but keep in mind that, every tree has a few rotten branches as they say," Lázaro quipped back.

The old woman didn't back down.

"Rotten? You mean forgotten," she replied between her teeth. Fortunately Lázaro had already taken off and didn't hear her.

∽

When our country belonged only but to a few privileged individuals, the word homeland, patria, had no meaning. When the land belonged to the speculators and the estate magnates, the so-called latifundistas, *the soil on which we lived had no meaning. Even the air we breathed was scarcely ours, and that was only because they could not include it in a property registry or lock it up in a warehouse. But today the concept of homeland, of patria, is different. When the soil belongs to everyone, when the riches are possessed by all, when opportunity is shared equally, when the true homeland beckons to belong to all, then only those who have no sense of loyalty whatsoever to our homeland, only the privileged ones, or those who aspire to be so, only they are the ones who abandon their country to go elsewhere.*

For this reason we lose absolutely nothing when these people leave. For this reason we have done nothing to block them from leaving and going off to enjoy the alms of the imperialist master. We shall develop our own homeland. We—

all of us who today truly possess a homeland and all who truly understand the concept of homeland—we shall make it great with our own efforts.

(Fidel Castro 15 March 1968)

∽

"Eneido, come on in. Papá should be back in a bit. He went to stand in line at the butcher shop because Mamá's legs are hurting her, but he shouldn't be too much longer. Come on in and have a seat…"

"Thanks, Menchu, but I really shouldn't stay. You never know how long those lines are going to last."

"What's wrong Eneido?" Mamá asked as she came in from the patio.

I realized right at that moment that he was sweating profusely and that he looked all shook up.

Mamá got him to come in and sit down. Without asking him, I gave him a glass of water. He drank slowly, almost unaware of his own actions.

"Since I was a boy, Mariana, since I was a boy…" he murmured.

Then he suddenly put his head in his hands and began to cry.

"There, there, Eneido. Tell us what happened."

Right at that moment Papá came home and we found out.

"They're going to take over all the small businesses. It's part of the revolutionary offensive to build socialism and communism together at the same time," Papá said, and then added. "They've appropriated Eneido's store."

Eneido lifted his head. Now a bit calmer, he explained:

"Since I was a kid, I had always dreamed of having my own business… My store was tiny, and these days, it's been hard to keep it stocked…but it's my life…I've had it for more than thirty years… Everybody in the neighborhood knows me…I'm well respected… My brothers took off, but I stayed because that little store was all that I had. What am I going to do now?"

In the space of a few months Havana was like a completely different city. The *churro* vendor, the snow cone cart, the tamale man, all of them disappeared. The candy man no longer came by tempting us with his "coconut kisses." You didn't see the guy selling his assortment of cone-shaped lollipops in all sorts of colors, and you didn't hear the cheerful little bell of the ice cream man. The place down at the corner that sold all types of fried foods closed its doors. The *bodega*—the one where you could still get anything from a cold beer to a bar of *guayaba* candy—also shut down. No one came by offering to sharpen your scissors any more. The street vendors all died out.

> *"Wherever, However and For Whatever,*
> *Commander-in-Chief, At Your Service!"*

There was one man who refused to follow orders. The bulldozers were positioned right in front of the Tropicana ready to tear down that den of corruption and vice, that symbol of the exalted classes. He wasn't even the owner. He was only the manager, but still he stood there in the doorway and told them that they would have to kill him if they wanted to tear it down. The militia didn't know what to do until the order came down from above to hold off. Everybody is talking about the incident… but obviously, very quietly.

"Well, the bulldozers should have flattened that counterrevolutionary," commented Maruja.

The rest of us remained silent.

❧

The Year of the Ten Million, our decisive effort continues on. The commemoration made on May Day is being felt in the furrows and the fields. Rather than being in the plaza, all are in the countryside. Rather than waving a sign or flag, all are waving a machete. It is no longer just a matter of goals and quotas; rather it is a fervent commitment that goes beyond production figures and predictions. The Day of the Worker—a perennial date

of reckoning and struggle, as well as an occasion to take note of the strength
of the proletariat—today has come to acquire a vigorous affirmative meaning.
The country has given itself into developing its riches. Sweat, which is gold, no
longer flows for the benefit of a group of exploiters. The sense of ownership, free
from self-indulgence and selfishness, extends to all the possessions of the nation.
In recognition of the glorious anniversary of May, Cuban men and women
alike answer the call to engage in simultaneous battles on all fronts and in the
trenches. The symbolic red flags show where the million are treading.

(*Bohemia* 62:18, 3)

∽

We get up at 4:30 in the morning in order to be in the cane fields
by dawn. You have to put on pants, thick boots, long sleeve shirts, and
a hat. Even with all that, the cane leaves still somehow get inside your
clothing and scratch up your skin. The heat's unbearable. You never stop
sweating. We put a jug aside in the shade of the unending foliage and
the cool water quenches our thirst for a moment.

Before noon, when the sun is directly overhead and at its hottest,
they take us to a shelter. There they give us something to eat and then
we return to the cane fields two hours later.

The cane stalks grow tall, in an orderly and unswerving line. They
extend as far as you can see, slipping over the horizon without end. It's
like an infinite ocean. A sea of cane fields.

Sometimes, when we're really tired, we sit down and chew on a
piece of cane. They say that it's terrible for your teeth, but it's sweet and
delicious, and it gives us a shot of energy right away. As night falls, we
head back to camp completely exhausted.

Despite being dead tired, there are times I just can't fall asleep.
Lázaro is in Oriente, Pedritín in Camagüey. It's been months since
I've seen them. Papá just retired from his position at the Ministry
of Construction, and he and Mamá are in Havana, standing in line

and taking care of Tania and Ernestico. And meanwhile, I'm here, surrounded by these women who are my comrades, with whom I share a bond of daily living, and yet at the same time it sometimes seems that we have nothing in common at all. Still, when I see everyone else so excited and dedicated to the work, I can't help but feel the same. If this really were the turning point, and if only we were truly building a new and better Cuba for our kids…! I don't know why, when I'm far away from Lázaro, I start to have my doubts… I miss you so much, Lauri. We almost never write anymore. I can't imagine what your life must be like. Sometimes it seems like it was all just a dream, that our entire childhood of beaches and outings, that those Sunday afternoons when we would play red rover, and hide-and-seek, and freeze tag and all types of games, that those nights listening to baseball on the radio, that those classrooms where we learned French and we cried while reciting Martí's poetry – *…oh Pilar, with your pail and rolling hoop and little pink shoes…* — that those nights when your would dance out on the terrace to the rhythm of the Cha-cha-chá from the record player – '*…When Miñoso bats the ball…*' — that our entire world so full of illusions never really existed, and that the only true reality is this one, this interminable cane harvest that Cuba has become, which sometimes I love, and sometimes I hate, and which stings me in the very core of my soul, just like the sharp blades of the sugarcane that that cut into my skin.

∽

More production…by increasing productivity.

Production can be considerably improved without necessarily increasing the number of workers, without extending the workday, without increasing the worker's level of intensity (that is, the physical and emotional effort), and without the need to resort to investment. Production can be considerably improved by eliminating errors, as much as in the application of techniques as well as in the organization of the workforce, and thus eliminating for

the worker weaknesses and oversights in carrying out his task. This is the
formula that the research from MINTRAB shows us: More production...by
increasing productivity!
   The Year of the Ten Million!

ᴄᴘᴏ

Each day in the news you see the name of some cane cutter or combine operator who has broken the previous harvest record. What really stands out is how all of us, the farm workers and volunteers too, have heeded the call of the Revolution. Everywhere you go people are praising the quality of the sugar that's delivered to the mills and the intense revolutionary consciousness of the people.

In the evenings, you see the trucks that bring the workers back home, some of whom have been away for months. They come back with their clothes all dirty and torn, their hands a mess, and their bodies aching. They're anxious about seeing their loved ones, taking a bath, sleeping in their bed, catching up on the harvest results, about that one millionth share that each one of us has put forth, that effort it took when the heat overcame us, that superhuman resolve when the thirst became unbearable, that heart wrenching feeling leaving your family so you can put the homeland first.

The harvest is over. Even though we're almost sure that we didn't reach the ten million tons, we're waiting and hoping for the news...eager to find out the results of this effort that has paralyzed the rest of the country.

"My teacher says that we probably got all the way to eleven million," says Ernestico with conviction.

"Well, I bet we got to twelve million," Tania raises the stakes with infantile enthusiasm.

"You kids don't get your hopes up," advises Mamá.

Finally, in a ceremony in front of the U.S. Interests Section, where he spoke in protest over the kidnapping of some fishermen, Fidel made the announcement. We indeed had not reached the ten million tons of cane. The news was devastating. But on this 26th of July, in the plaza that brims with excitement, while explaining in great detail the reasons, he offers the next plan:

"We will transform this setback into victory…"

When I turned around to make a comment to Lázaro, I could see in his face how disappointed he was. We returned home in silence.

For twelve years
Grandfather would come into the house
and shower me with toys.
You could see him coming
under his white hat
like a Wise Man
who hopes to go by unnoticed
his guayabera made of beige
and shiny thread
smelling of honey-caramel
and of blessings.

At twelve o'clock on the dot
he would always say the family
looked more like the neighborhood block
and he laughed as he wanted to applaud
and say that it was a party
because my mother was conspiring with the stove.

Seated in front of the café
his beard, his imagination, grew
he was Olympic

determined
a good friend
discreet
virile.

For me
Grandfather invented life
pulling out of his white hat
oceans, moons, and countries.

Just yesterday he was invincible
seated on his stool
as if time were an unhurried dove
as if he could still yawn
as if they hadn't traded his hat
for the bit of dirt
that now covers his head.

(Rivero 12–13)

❧

Mamá Luya suffered a stroke, and the doctors don't think she'll make it. Tía Flor refused to leave her at the hospital so she took her home. When I went by to see her yesterday, they were bathing her. It frightened me to see how frail she had become. She looked like a little bird in that bed. How was it possible that I had gone to visit her each week but I hadn't noticed that she had lost so much weight?

"Let's see *vieja* if you're not more comfortable like this," said Tía Flor as she fluffed her pillow and smoothed down her gray hair.

Mamá Luya opened her eyes, and she smiled at her daughter. So often there had been defiance in those eyes, but now there was such gratitude that it made me tear up. Then she focused her gaze on the dresser.

"Hmm? What can I get for you, Mamá?"

Mamá Luya can no longer speak, but Tía Flor understood by her glance what she wanted.

"Menchu, open up the top drawer and bring her the letter that came from your sister. She wants you to see the photos."

"Look how cute those kids are."

"Pedro Pablo looks like the twins when they were young, doesn't he Mamá?"

My grandma had fallen asleep clutching the photo to her chest.

Tía Flor wouldn't leave her side. Mamá and I insisted on taking turns, but the most we could get her to do was to rest a bit in the bed in the adjoining room. By the third day, Mamá Luya could barely open her eyes. Her eyes had glazed over, and she barely recognized anyone, not even Tía Flor. The house began filling up with people. Everybody offered to pitch in…but then they would start chatting, insensitive to the fact that a few steps away my grandmother was agonizing. Finally, one afternoon, Tía Flor put her foot down and threw everybody out. Only the three of us—Mamá, my aunt, and I—remained.

"You have to let people die in peace," she told us.

Then she went to the dresser and took out a rosary. She placed it between her mother's hands.

"Let's pray," she said. And she began:

"Our Father, who art in Heaven…"

When we finished, she pulled the chair up closer to the bed and she began to speak to Mamá Luya. I heard her tell the same stories that I had heard my grandmother tell so many times before, stories about her childhood in Spain, about how she had gotten married without her parents' permission, about the trip to the Island in a big steamer, about the birth and infancy of her children… Little by little Mamá joined in. They didn't talk to each other. Instead, they talked directly to her, as if they were sure she could hear them. Then she asked me if I didn't want to talk to her too… At first I couldn't speak… Finally the words just came blurting out:

"Oh, *abuelita*, if you only knew that when we were kids what Lauri and

I enjoyed more than anything in the world was to come here... We were always so happy when Mami and Papi would take off on a trip and you would come take care of us... When Tania was a baby, I would always put her to sleep by singing her the same songs you taught us, and I'm sure that Lauri has done the same thing with her kids... Even now, even though she's gotten so big, when she gets sick she still asks me to sing her the song about the pilgrims, "...*In the bottom of the sea...*," and the one about the '*little bitty boat*'...and the one about *Señora Santa Ana*..."

"Let's sing to her," said Tía Flor.

> *Alfonso XII, where are you heading?*
> *So melancholy you seem.*
> *I seek my Mercedes,*
> *Whom since yesterday I have not seen.*

Night fell upon the house as the three of us huddled against her bed and continued our hushed lullaby:

> *But Mercedes is dead,*
> *Dead, for see her I did,*
> *As four dukes carried her*
> *Through the streets of Madrid.*

Suddenly, the rhythm of her breathing changed. Tía Flor began to whisper to her again.

"Mamá. Don't be afraid. I'm here for you. You know that there are so many people that you love who are waiting for you...your parents, your brothers and sisters, Papá. Finally, you're going to be with Papá. You've been so wonderful...don't be afraid. You believe in God. You know that there's another life. You're in your bed, surrounded by your daughters and your granddaughter, by people who love you. We're praying for you. We've got your flowers from your garden. Can you smell them? But it's time to go, Mamá. Give me your hand. Don't worry about me. You're always saying how much I have helped in life. Let me help you in death as well. I'm going to miss you so very much…but you'll be so better off… you'll keep watch over all of us, and from where you're going to be you'll be able to see Ricardo and Lauri too. Yes, I'm going to take very good care of myself…I promise you, Mamá. Everything's fine… Go peacefully…"

Right at that moment Mamá Luya opened her eyes and tears rolled down her cheeks. The cloudy look in her eyes disappeared and, for one brief instant, her normal expression returned to her face. She was back. It even looked like she smiled at Tía Flor. I saw a slight movement of her fingers, as if she were squeezing her hand. Then she let out a deep breath—that last sigh of death—and she closed her eyes forever.

We buried her the next day in the Colón Cemetery, next to my grandfather. The day was appropriately gray. It wasn't until we returned to the house at La Sierra that I saw Tía Flor cry.

∽

The pointe slippers spin. They set their first steps in motion—plié, attitude, passé. They rise midway where they linger for a brief instant.

"Next, we will dance on the tips of our toes."

When they are older, when they finish their seventh year, they will join the National Ballet. Some of them will become professors; others will perform on stages throughout the world. From these will come the prima ballerinas: the next Pávlova, another Ulánova, or the next Alicia Alonso.

Alicia. Alicia. Everybody wants to be like Alicia. Alicia is their idol. Alicia is the figure of their dreams. Alicia, the movements that they must mimic. Alicia, the poetry that they want to emulate, poetry composed of limbs, torso, and head. Alicia is the name that is repeated. Alicia is the ballet itself, the epitome of beauty, the incarnation of the homeland.

(*Bohemia* 50:35, 17–20)

∽

Two days ago I turned thirty. I look at myself in the mirror. I don't need to know if I look younger or older, if I'm pretty or ugly, if I'm starting to gray or not, if I still have a twinkle in my eye, as Papá used to say when I was a girl. I want to look beyond this body and see who I am, what I believe in, what I dream about.

One thing I know—I'm a mother. When I take Tania to the ballet and I see her little face so intense—she's such a perfectionist—or when I watch her play or sleep, or when she hugs and kisses me, life seems like it's offering me a miracle. As for my parents, they have their defects, but the truth is I adore them. I went through a stage when everything that Papá did drove me crazy. I resented him. I still get annoyed with the way he acts, like he's some Cantinflas or something, without saying things directly. But maybe that's how he's managed to keep them from kicking him out of the Ministry. And poor Mamá, she's such a saint. She probably lets Papá take advantage of her and manipulate her too easily. She stands in line day after day without complaining. I know I should help her out more often. And she's always coming up with something new so we don't get bored with eating the same old thing. I know just how much she has suffered from Mamá Luya's death. I wish I knew how to make her feel better, but I think Ricardo and Lauri not being here, and not knowing her grandchildren, may have actually hurt her even worse. I have to confess that, at times, I've felt a little jealous. Pedritín is never at home anymore…I'm the one who has to take care of them, but all Mamá does is sigh because of Lauri… Sometimes my sister seems like a ghost to me, my other half that died, or maybe that never existed; and then there are other times that it seems like she never left, and that I could just walk in and start chatting with her about any silly thing that popped into my head because there are things that only she would understand. I can't even remember what Ricardo looks like anymore. I have to look at their photos just to recall his face, and yet I can still feel his touch, how his hand felt when he would take mine in his as we crossed the street, how his hugs made him seem like such a grown-up when I was just a girl… I always felt like he was my real protector, more so than Papá. And now, he's so far away. He's just a voice at the other end of a telephone line that from time to time comes out with things that seem so out of place, like 'how you doin'?', 'you need anything?', 'it's really cold up here…' Pedritín is around, but I hardly ever see him. It used to be because he was preparing for his studies, and now it's because he spends his time at the university or with the Communist Party Youth Corp or doing volunteer work. Besides, I'm afraid I don't even know him anymore. I really don't know what he feels or what he thinks. I like my work, and I've been lucky because they put me with the team that designs schools. When I'm drawing, I can forget about the rest of the world. When I'm all alone, with my head full of images, with my pencil in my hand, when the ideas start taking shape on paper, I well up with enthusiasm, a burst of energy, a rush of adrenaline… The whole business of seeing a piece of paper evolve into a real building, one that you can actually see and touch… Even better, it's something I am contributing to the country, to the Revolution.

Lázaro…it's been more than ten years since that afternoon when we first made love on the green grass, and yet even now I still get goose bumps if I merely brush up against him. But these days he seems so far away at times and so immersed in his worries.

I wish I had more friends. Almost all the girls I went to school with have gone away. Marta Lola was about the only one who had stayed behind but then she went off to study microbiology in the Soviet Union. There are times when I can't even go down the street where the old school was because it seems like it's full of the ghosts of all of those who have taken off. I don't even feel like celebrating my birthday anymore.

And then, obviously, there's Cuba and the Revolution. I truly believe that it's a privilege to live during these times, that we're constructing the future, that my daughter will be the beneficiary of these sacrifices. But then at other times the Revolution turns into a chatty old witch that torments me. It's like we're not living our own lives. It's as if all the problems of the world—from Ho Chi Minh's death to who should be allowed to enroll in the university—had all invaded my personal space.

FIDEL, THIS IS YOUR HOUSE. As if the world could be reduced to a slogan. *THE TEN MILLION ARE ON THE WAY.* As if they were on the bus with me. *WE'RE SOCIALISTS THROUGH AND THROUGH.* As if they were ingredients in our casseroles. *IF YOU DON'T LIKE IT, LUMP IT.* Just like they were sitting at the family table. *THE PARTY IS INDUSTRIOUS.* As if they were rifling through my daughter's clothing. *FIDEL, FIDEL, GIVE THE YANKEES HELL!* As if they went to the bathroom with me. *WHEREVER, HOWEVER, AND FOR WHATEVER. COMMANDER-IN-CHIEF, AT YOUR SERVICE!* As if they had gotten under the sheets between my husband and me. *BE PATRIOTIC. CONSUME CUBAN PRODUCTS.* Sometimes I just want to shout "Enough!" *FATHERLAND OR DEATH!* Enough. *WE SHALL OVERCOME.* All I am asking for is silence.

Last night Lázaro insisted on taking me to the movies and out to eat for my birthday. When I suggested that we call Armandito and Magaly he told me that he'd prefer for just the two of us to go. On our way back he wanted to take a stroll down the *Malecón.* We walked along the seawall in silence, holding hands like two teenagers.

"You want to go to the *Gato Tuerto*? You always run into your writer friends there."

"No. Let's just go home."

"Lázaro. Something's up. What's wrong with you?"

"It's...nothing," he sighed deeply as if he were trying to gulp in the entire ocean breeze.

We were already in bed, with the lights out, when he finally spoke up.

"Menchu, I'm worried. I believe the Revolution has chosen the right path...and that Marxism truly is the solution... I understand that we have to defend ourselves from our enemies, and the Americans are looking for whatever possible opportunity to infiltrate us. I think it's good that we have made ties with the Soviet Union. But I don't know. I don't like this whole business about the Padilla affair. Some of the things that the intellectuals have said in their letter are actually true. Besides, Sartre, Vargas Llosa, they've always been friends of the Revolution...and they're thinkers. I also don't understand the need for repression if we believe in our truths. There's also a lot of discontent among the students. A few months ago there was a confrontation in Oriente between some students and Fidel himself, and they kicked them out of the university. Now we're hearing that that they're coming up with new regulations and that only revolutionaries will be allowed to enroll."

"Sometimes I have my doubts too, Lázaro."

"Look, maybe we're too close to it, and we can't see things clearly."

"Yeah, maybe. Sometimes you can't see the forest for the trees, as Mamá Luya used to always say."

"Menchu, there's the possibility that they're going to give me an assignment with the *Prensa Latina.*"

"Oh no, Lázaro, separated again? Where are they going to send you this time? And for how long?"

"A few months...a year...maybe more... There's a position in the Soviet Union."

"That far away!"

"But I have a surprise for you. I've already asked for permission. You and Tania can come with me. So, you'll learn Russian and..."

"But how could I possibly leave my folks?"

"It won't be for that long. They're in good health. And your brother's here."

"I don't know..."

"Besides, I've found out that there are really good ballet classes for Tania."

"You knew that you could get me with that, didn't you? You're so bad. Like you didn't already have all of this planned out..."

That night we made love with a renewed passion, as if the zeal for life had been reborn in us. For a long time we remained silent, holding each other, naked. Outside, Havana slept.

∽

From this point forward—without any doubt or hesitancy whatsoever, without tentativeness or ambiguity—there will be room only for Revolutionaries.

As you already know, my dear intellectual bourgeoisies and liberal bourgeoisies and CIA agents and other intelligence agencies—that is, those from the spy services of imperialism—we will not let you in Cuba, just like we denied access to the UPI and the AP. The doors have been firmly shut for an indefinite and infinite period of time!

(Fidel Castro 30 April 1971)

∽

I'll always remember our stay in the Soviet Union as one of the happiest times in my life. My first impression however wasn't so good. Moscow is surrounded by a circle of dark, gray, and blockish buildings, which are infinitely the same. It looks like a bigger version of the Alamar section of Havana, only worse, since it lacks the boisterous charm of its residents and those quaint clotheslines of ours where we hang our underwear out to dry in the sun. But after you spend some time there, you come to understand that the Soviet capital is really a vast and beautiful city, full of marvelous Byzantine churches, with their onion-shaped cupolas and bearded priests who sing mass before a wall full of icons. The Orthodox saints seem so spiritual...and in a sense even nationalistic since they take on unique characteristics that don't exist elsewhere.

We visited the monasteries and cemeteries; we went to vigils; we took part in the Easter and Christmas celebrations; we had tea with Russians who were proud of their culture and their past, but who weren't sure if things were going to get better or if they would ever be able to travel to foreign lands. The museums are amazing—the Tretyakov Gallery in Moscow, the Hermitage in Leningrad, the monuments to the victims of Fascism in Kiev and Stalingrad, the museums in the various painters' houses, especially the one in Stanislavski's where everything is so meticulously kept and arranged. Tania and I would go quite often to the Bolshoi to see lavish ballet performances. Every once in a while

I was able to convince Lázaro to join us, and we'd go to the opera. We had never seen anything like it.

Tania learned Russian right away, and she was happy with her ballet classes. I struggled with the language, although the little bit I had studied in Havana helped me get along, and I could defend myself. Lázaro quickly mastered it and took the opportunity to start his graduate work. Known as "the whims of Stalin," the University of Moscow was an imposing building, designed in the same style as the Leningrad Hotel, the Ukraine Hotel, the Department of Foreign Affairs and others. There were also a lot of luxuries—great restaurants, elegant halls, sports fields, a hospital, even a center for dentistry. The Russians on campus seemed very cultured and philosophical. Everybody was always reading Pushkin, Lermontov, and Tolstoy, and everyone knew passages from their works from memory, even the physicists and mathematicians, who were considered every bit as much or more of the *intelligentsia* than the doctors and lawyers. In contrast, the run of the mill people are very rustic. They dress in ordinary clothing as humble people from the countryside, but they're typically cordial and polite. In their lifestyles they're somewhat aloof, but if they offer you their friendship, they're very loyal. They drink a whole lot, perhaps more than they should.

It is a country of contrasts, of imposing architecture and millennial culture, which at the same time lags significantly in the common advances that have made daily life easier. They were able to send men into orbit but can't invent a fan that works well. They regret that they're not in contact with Western Europe and the rest of the world. There are long lines to get into the movies just to see an American film, or a European one from the 1950s or the beginning of the '60s that we saw in Cuba when it came out. Coming across a bottle of Hungarian perfume in the stores is a real find, and if it's French it's a treasure. And how is it feasible that in an enormous city that has a gigantic metro with its opulent subway stations full of remarkable statues, how is it that you can't find one sheet of toilet paper? Everywhere you turn you find the stamp of Marxist atheism, and yet at the same time you see the traces of its religious past. One thing's for sure, they eat well. Tania loves the carrots with this special sauce that's a type of bitter cream they put on everything and that the men gobble up since they say it's good for one's virility.

I hated the winter. Six months of eternal snow and a cold so cruel that it got to 45 degrees below zero. It doesn't start to get light until 9:00 in the morning, and afternoon is over by 2:00, and by 3:00 there's already a darkness that threatens to end the light of the day, which is snuffed out completely by 6:00. Everybody scurries through the streets, bundled up, searching for refuge at the nearest metro stop. The same thing for me: I was weighed down with my overcoat, boots, hat, gloves, wool socks, and all.

We made friends with an older couple. They lived in a tiny but charming apartment. Ivan was a historian and Olga, his wife, was a scientist and very refined in spirit. We would talk about poetry and go out and pick mushrooms and strawberries in the woods. He tried to explain the situation that the country was in:

"The showcase of Socialism is Berlin, the German Democratic Republic which always stands in opposition to the Federal Republic, and which is backed by Moscow. But," he added, shaking his head back and forth, "those people are destined for suffering."

One day, on the 9th of May, all of us went down and stood out in front of the Bolshoi to see a group of elderly veterans, both men and women, who had survived the war. Their chests covered with medals, they had come together to commemorate the war, to celebrate that they were still living, and also to pay their respects for the ones they had lost.

"There are several generations of Soviets among the group there, all of them traumatized by the war in some fashion, some are pro-Stalin and others, even if they don't admit it publicly, are anti-Stalin. And yet, at least up until now, they're still united as one people."

Sometimes we'd go skiing. Lázaro and Tania would always have a good time, but I couldn't do anything but fall down. It was like a form of torture, and it was so cold that my eyes would fill with tears and my hands would go numb. Finally there came a time when I had enough. I could no longer tolerate the winter. I got fed up with picking mushrooms and berries for marmalade. I missed my mother and the sea.

∽

Throughout the first half of 1974, inclusive of the dates January 3rd through June 30th, the nation will embark upon an enrollment campaign to register all citizens—those by birth as well those naturalized—who were born subsequent to January 1st, 1959 for the Identification Credential and Minor Identification Card.

In order to carry out a successful operation, the physical presence of each citizen will be required with the exception of minors and the physically and mentally disabled.

It should be recognized that throughout the campaign the efforts of the CDR and the ANAP have been exemplary, given that it was they who went door to door in order to distribute to the people the instructions that would enable them to comply with the Identification Card process.

(Bohemia 65:52, 56)

∽

In January of 1974 they asked Lázaro to return to Havana to work on some special reports. It was the fifteenth anniversary of the Revolution and they expected Leonid Breshnev to travel to Cuba on the 28th, José Martí's birthday.

In spite of how badly we wanted to go back, it was hard for us to say goodbye to Ivan and Olga, and as I gazed through the airplane window at the byzantine cupolas rising from the snow below I couldn't help but tear up.

Havana seemed more radiant, more sensual, and in more decay than ever. My parents too had grown so much older, especially Papá who couldn't help but shuffle his feet as he walked.

I have vague memories of those years: the enthusiastic reception of Breshnev, the Soviet presence in Havana (not those refined and profound Russians, but the other ones, the coarse ones that the Cubans nicknamed the "boozers.") What's more is that in the middle of so much greenery and sun, they seemed out of place. The Soviet films were unbearable. No one could stand them. Russian classes were always being offered on the TV and radio. Tania even tried to teach her grandparents. Papá managed to learn a few words, but Mamá refused:

"Honey, I'm just too old to learn another language..."

It was about that time that Pedritín and Camilo—Maruja's son—got sent to Angola. During the Batista coup, Maruja had been a nurse's aide in Morón, in the Province of Camagüey. She had started out by helping her brother who belonged to a revolutionary cell. She stole syringes, bandages, cotton, anything from the hospital to help out with the wounded. Later on she took to the streets, placed spikes in the road, threw Molotov cocktails, and ultimately even tossed grenades. She fell in love with a revolutionary and wound up pregnant. When she was about to give birth they were on the run, and they had to deliver the baby in a barn that the rebels had taken from the Army. Two days later she handed her baby over to her mother, and a comrade took her by Jeep to Sancti Spiritus where she managed to reach Escambray and later on join back up with the insurgents. There she took care of the wounded and joined in the fighting like any other soldier. When she finally saw her son again, after the beginning of January, he was already walking. After she learned that the boy's father had been killed in action, she moved to Havana where they gave her a house in our neighborhood that had belonged to a family who had left Cuba. She began working in a clinic as a nurse and only two things in the entire world interested her: the Revolution and her son Camilo, who had just turned seventeen.

Six months later the news arrived that Camilo had died in combat. They told her that it would be better if they buried him there in Angola. She didn't object nor did she cry. Instead, she doubled her revolutionary fervor, but in her eyes there was something odd, something that scared me.

Mamá stayed glued to the news. Sometimes I thought it was going to be too much for her, that her heart was going to split. But my brother came back from the war two years later, safe and sound. Papá bought some beer and a suckling pig on the black market, and we celebrated like we never had before.

CHAPTER EIGHT
"...What Sorrow! What Suffering...!"

WE'VE BEEN BACK IN MIAMI NOW FOR OVER TEN YEARS. Bobby had always wanted to come back, and when Adela passed away he kept on insisting so much that I finally just gave in. Pedro Pablo still needed another year to finish high school, but he didn't seem to mind it if we moved. He wanted to study in Gainesville anyway like his uncle had, and he was better off if he was a resident of Florida. Bobby Jr. seemed to be getting more defiant all the time, but I figured he'd grow out of it. As for my father-in-law I didn't think he would want to quit his job at the OAS, and I felt bad leaving him behind. One day he caught me completely off-guard:

"Lauri, I'm thinking about going to Miami with you. I want to be a lawyer again. Besides, *mijita,* maybe I can still be useful. I know the kids are already grown, and you two need to be alone, but..."

"Roberto, you know that you're not a bother, quite the opposite," and I insisted that he move in with us, at least for a while.

We bought a very comfortable house in Westchester, a middle class area of town where a lot of Cubans lived. We put the kids in private school. Bobby got his license to sell insurance, and I got a job with the school system.

My father-in-law was already close to retirement but he was bent on getting back into law, and he did just that. The day he passed the Bar Exam we had a few friends over to celebrate. Even Johnny, his wife Kathy, and their newborn came from Georgia. We were so happy because we hadn't seen them since they had gotten married two years ago, and we were dying to see the baby. When everybody finally left, Roberto came up to me and said:

"You know this diploma really belongs to you too."

"Oh Roberto, please."

"No really, *mijita,* you've always believed in me, you helped me learn English, and you've been my inspiration. You're like one of those little ants, always working, studying, making sure your kids got the education they needed. I love you, Lauri, and admire you very much."

And then he gave me one of his typical pats on the back.

A few months later he insisted on moving out and there weren't any arguments to the contrary.

"I'm just moving a few blocks away and besides, if you ever need me…"

And in fact, even then he still kept on being like a father to me and was always the best grandfather ever to my kids.

The first few years were great. Robertico—in Miami he didn't want anyone calling him Bobby—seemed to be back to his old self. He wasn't so bitter. We would go out with couples our own age. We went to Europe twice and once to Mexico. Our relationship got better. We only fought about Cuba. There was one instance in particular when I really lost my cool. One of their old friends went back to Cuba in '78 to participate in negotiations with Castro. And even though he ultimately left the negotiations early and came back and made some very dignified statements, they still kicked him out of the Brigade.

"But to get you guys out of Cuba they had to negotiate with the authorities, so why do you want to punish him for doing the same thing for other prisoners?"

Robertico got so mad at me that the vein in his neck looked like it was going to explode.

For me, going back to Miami was like a reunion with Cuba itself. The *flamboyán* trees, the coffee, the blazing sun, the *guayaba* pastries, the ocean, pineapple juice, the hibiscus, tamales, the red and white impatiens, green plantains, rocking chairs on the porch, *mamey* drinks, the caladiums, our tasty snacks of ham, cheese, pork and pickles on a cracker, the architecture, the sweet taste of *Materva,* the ocean—once again the ocean!—*medianoches* and other sandwiches, Spanish, avocados, the music, waitresses who ask you "*¿qué más quieres, mi amor?*"—"what else can I get you dear?"—sugar cane juice, the heat, yucca treats, palm trees, dishes like "fried brains," the ocean, mangos, always the ocean, and the Island—so close and yet at the same time always so far away.

And the exiles, those individuals who are so much a part of me and yet the very ones who also really rub me the wrong way…always fixated on just one theme, always talking, shouting, jumping up and down, always plotting to overthrow Castro day and night…the exiles who at midday relax at the cafés with their suitcases packed full of memories, packed and ready to return to paradise, even though they—or is it we?—aren't sure if that particular paradise is a memory or a dream.

Over the years, news from my family became more and more sporadic. Mostly I heard from Mamá whose letters talked a lot about what they were able to get with this month's rations, or if someone had died, or if some cousin of mine had gotten married or had a child… It was challenging to stay in touch since we couldn't go there, and they couldn't come here. Almost twenty years had slipped by. Some families were able to get around it all by meeting up in Canada or Mexico, but they were the exceptions. Most of us just suffered silently. It was such a hostile environment that people tended not to speak about their families back there.

Finally, by 1979 the Cuban government began to allow exiles to come back to visit. They began to offer trips to the Island for what they called the "community," a euphemism that the government used to identify us. Yesterday we had been thrown out as *gusanos,* or "worms," and yet today we were welcomed back as butterflies. Anyway, I didn't waste any time thinking about it.

"Robertico, I want to go see my family."

He flew into an outrage like I had never seen before.

"Listen to what I'm going to tell you…and listen up good…if you go back there…" and then he just lost it.

"Robertico, don't be like that. Look, a lot of people are going back, and my parents aren't getting any younger."

"If you go back there…if you go back to Cuba…I'll kill you!"

I tried bringing it up a few more times, but finally it got to where I couldn't even mention it.

One time I went with him to a ceremony that the *Brigadistas* have every year on April 17th across from a park in Little Havana where there's this monument and a torch that's always lit. I listened silently to all the grandiose speeches full of patriotic rhetoric. I observed each member of the Brigade—many of them now older men with their pudgy bellies—and listened as the roll was called for the fallen.

"Alberto González Recio".

"*¡Presente!*"

"Hernán Koch"

"*¡Presente!*"

"Vicente León"

"*¡Presente!*"

Some of the women were dressed in black. I thought about the mothers whose sons weren't coming back, about the girlfriends that had lost their first love, about the widows, about the children that barely knew their fathers or maybe had never met them at all. Later on we went by the headquarters of one of the patriotic organizations. On their walls they had hung all types of photos of the *Brigadistas*—some with their camouflaged uniforms on during their training sessions, others posing for the camera holding up the Cuban flag—and on each smiling face you could see the faith that they had in their victory and their mission.

For a brief second I think I understood Robertico, his frustrations, his bull-headedness.

"Just wait, you'll see. They're going to welcome us back as heroes just like they did in those films in World War II," he had once told me right before he left for the Bay of Pigs.

My husband had thought he was going to be the savior of his people. He had bet it all on the invasion, and he had lost. He was taken prisoner; no one gave him a medal when he got home; and then I had taken him off to snowy Columbus where he had to go from house to house as a bill collector. But he just couldn't stop thinking about his fellow companions who had either been taken prisoner or were dead. And even though we had barely begun to live, all of his dreams had already been toppled.

And what if he hadn't come back? I would be right here in this ceremony with Pedro Pablo, dressed in black, crying not for the "Bobby" that I've known for these past 18 years, but for the one back then, for that younger Robertico, the one that I loved unconditionally. And the ones who didn't come back, would they be the same today as the ones whom these women had spent their life idealizing?

I felt this terrible pain down deep inside for so many reasons, but more than anything I hurt for Cuba, and for all the broken lives, and for Robertico, and because the only thing in the world that could have possibly made him happy was Cuba, not my love, not the love of his children, not even the love from his parents. I hated that I hadn't understood him sooner. It hurt me to see the hero that he never became and the anti-hero that he refused to be. But above everything else it hurt so bad to feel how our love was dying, and it weighed me down. I suffered as if I were bearing the sorrow of an unborn child in my womb.

∽

With anti-Castro signs and Cuban flags in hand, hundreds of Cuban exiles at rallies throughout Miami this Friday voiced their opposition to the visit to the United Nations by the President of the Cuban Council of State, Fidel Castro.

The protest carried out last night in Bayfront Park was organized in response to an earlier one held in New York at the same exact hour that Castro delivered his speech before the General Assembly of the U.N.

Catholic priest and anti-Castro activist, Father O' Farill asserted that the true representatives of Cuba are its exiles since only they can proclaim the truth about Cuba.

(*El Miami Herald* 13 October 1979)

∽

After being in Miami for two or three years, they made me Assistant Principal in the school where I was teaching, and they gave me a raise.

I began working on my Master's at night. It was like a whole new world had opened up to me. I had always felt like some type of chessboard: some parts of me were bright and enlightened and others remained obscured in the shadows because there was so much I didn't know. Going back to school in Washington had helped me a lot but I still had big gaps in my education and I was anxious to fill them. I began to hang out with a great group of people, and although they were younger than me, I could really identify with them. I also started sending off an occasional article to newspapers and a few were actually published. I had always liked to write and it was thrilling to see my name in print.

My biggest concern in those days was Bobby Jr. From the very moment he started Junior High he began to change. He became aloof and even down-right rebellious. At first we chalked it up to his age, and we tried to be patient. But when he turned sixteen, things became more serious. He'd skip school occasionally, and we wouldn't know where he was. One time they called us from a store where he had been caught shoplifting a pair of tennis shoes. A young man who had always gotten good grades now all of a sudden was starting to fail classes. When he got his driver's license and Robertico refused to get him a car, things got even worse. The plan was that we would lend him mine every once in a while, and if he showed that he was responsible, we would buy him his own within a year. You can't imagine how many wrecks he had! I always told him that the important thing was that he wasn't hurt, but still that didn't diminish all the inconveniences and costs that came with each wreck. He totaled the Honda that I had bought used but in decent condition. The absolute worst part was all those late nights when it'd get to be 2:00, 3:00, or 4:00 in the morning and still no sign of him. I always imagined the worst. I conjured up images of him bleeding to death or already dead in some ditch, that he had been mugged or even murdered. I went back and forth between waking up Robertico, calling one of his friend's house, notifying the police, or just waiting for him to show up. As was always the case in anxious moments, I would pass the time praying. I would make up games with the clock. 'He better get here before 3:00, and by God when he does I'm not going to utter a word to him!' But 3:00 came and went and nothing. And that's how it went night after night. I tried everything. I tried talking to him, asking him to tell me what was wrong, assuring him that I had faith in him. I brought up everything I could think of that might make him open up, even his grandmother Adela who had loved him so much! Sometimes I would lose my patience, and I would let him have it and even punish him. For the most part, however, I appealed to his reason and to his heart. But he always just sat there and listened to me in an exasperating silence, and never changed his ways. I made his grandfather intervene. I met with his teachers and with his school counselors. I talked with his friends' parents. One time, I even got Pedro Pablo to come from Gainesville to talk him. But that didn't do any good either.

"He's just going through a stage…he'll get over it," Robertico would sometimes say, and he would look the other way. Other times they'd fight and yell.

The boy could never hold his tongue:

"So why all of a sudden all the questions about who I go out with, where I'm going, and who my friends are when you've never been interested in me before. You've never tried to get to know who I am or what I'm all about. The only thing you've ever cared about was bringing down Fidel, but you've even failed at that."

Robertico slapped him right across the face. The boy just stood there like he was paralyzed.

"Don't you dare hit him," I jumped in between the two of them.

In the confusion of it all, however, Robertico grazed my mouth with his ring and I began to bleed a little.

"Look at what you did. You hit Mami!"

"It was nothing…it was an accident…come on you two…stop fighting…"

I kept asking myself over and over where I had gone wrong. I felt guilty and at the same time betrayed by him. Sometimes I was afraid that he was on drugs, and I was tempted to go through his things in his room. But I had always respected both of my sons' space and I didn't give in to spying on him. I had never felt so confused. I didn't know what to do.

✀

In the early hours of Saturday morning a man entered a Fraternity party and opened fire with a pistol. Among the casualties, two students were killed and five injured.

19-year-old Mark Houston was taken into custody without resistance following the shooting. The two fatalities were students Terrell Johnson and Patrick McGindy. 20-year-old John Leroy Aiken remains in critical condition after undergoing surgery. Three other students remain in stable condition. The motive for the crime has yet to be determined.

(*El Nuevo Herald* 6 October 1979)

✀

By the beginning of 1980 I had given up on convincing Robertico to let me go to Cuba, so I began to make arrangements for my parents to come visit me instead. I wanted to see the two of them together, but it was difficult to get permission for both to come at the same time. I suggested that they decide who would come first.

"I don't want to die without seeing you again or without meeting my grandchildren," my father told me. I went right away and applied for his visa. It suddenly hit me that Papá had turned seventy-five. Even though the recent photos they had sent gave away his age, in my mind I always pictured him the way he looked twenty years ago. The paperwork took forever, and I couldn't think about anything else. I gradually started buying clothes for everybody, first for him, and then for Mamá, for Menchu and Pedritín, and for Tania. Maybe my family had given themselves over to the Revolution, but—good God!—they were my flesh and blood. Besides, what else could they have done? I started making plans where I wanted to take Papá. Obviously, he'd want to spend a few days in New York with Ricardo, especially if he came during baseball season. Imagine him at a Yankee's game! He was as big of a fan of that team as he was of La Habana. When I pictured all those things it took me back to El Cerro Stadium and I saw Formental batting, and Mike Anderson, and Miguel Ángel pacing back and forth nervously at third... I remembered my father teaching us how to ride a bike, taking us to Casa Suárez to buy candy, and bringing home that black and white RCA television, the first one we ever had.

This time I didn't have any premonition whatsoever. Not even when I heard Menchu's voice at 6:00 in the morning. I just thought it had something to do with the upcoming trip.

I didn't cry a single tear when I found out that my father had died from a heart attack. More than pain, I felt an immense rage against Fidel Castro, the Revolution, Che, the olive-green uniforms, the militia, the Defense Committees, the Pioneers, the 26th of July Movement, all of it, absolutely every single thing that had happened in Cuba since 1959. It was a deep feeling, but I felt it all over. I also felt another type of anger, one that was more sordid and poignant.

I didn't let Robertico touch me.

"It's your fault...it's your fault that I didn't get to see him before he died."

I stormed off to work before the knot in my chest could break apart into tears.

∽

Armando Ruiz was an actor in Cuba. He usually played roles in classical Spanish plays. But last year he played the role of a bus passenger while his father pretended to be a bus driver on the streets of Havana.

Their prop: a stolen municipal bus. The pair, along with 10 friends and relatives, used it to crash through the gates of the Venezuelan Embassy in Havana last May.

Their role as regular passengers was fake, but the escape was real—the first in a string of violent escapes that has culminated in the attempt of 10,000 Cubans to seek asylum in the Peruvian Embassy in the Cuban capital.

Ruíz spent more than 100 days in the Venezuelan Embassy waiting to leave Cuba. Now in Miami and unemployed, he is going on a hunger strike in support of the would-be refugees.

"We know how hard it was for a dozen to get the courage to flee," Ruiz said. "Imagine 10,000."

(*Miami Herald* 9 April 1980: 20A)

After I finished up at school each afternoon I volunteered to help out with the Mariel refugees. More than 100,000 had arrived in just a few weeks. It was true that Castro had opened up the prisons and insane asylums and had thrown out some of the true "dregs" of society, but for the most part they were hard-working people. I did see some pathetic cases, like the old man who had thrown together a make-shift house in the stairwell of the Orange Bowl and he couldn't understand why they wanted to take him to go live in a shelter. Some were covered in mosquito bites since they had to wait for hours outside in the open. Others showed me the scars from the dogs that had been let loose on them. There were terrible stories, like this woman whose baby was stolen from her while she was getting on the boat, and she became so distraught that she threw herself into the water and drowned. On television, you could see all types of despicable behavior. Cubans throwing rotten eggs at other Cubans and saying horrible things. With my own eyes, I saw a child who couldn't have been more than seven, and both of her arms had been broken. How is it possible that there are human beings who could bring harm to an innocent child? Have the Cuban people sunk so low?

I think back on the country I left, the Havana of my youth, the way

I saw it out of a school bus window. My Havana that consisted of school desks and parks, of beaches and children's games. The Havana of my first communion. *Hey-ho, Alánimo, hey-ho, Alánimo*...of bougainvilleas and hibiscus...*the queen is passing by*...the protective shadow of my grandmother... And now, this other Havana full of violence on every corner... *Marlborough went off to war*...a malignant Havana...*what sorrow! what suffering!*...with death always lurking and threatening... *and what news of his homecoming...?* My Havana and my farewell...*oh do-re-mi-do-re-fa and who knows of his homecoming...?*

∽

Give me your tired, your poor, Your huddled masses yearning to breathe free, The wretched refuse of your teeming shore. Send these, the homeless, tempest-tossed to me, I lift my lamp beside the golden door!

Emma Lazarus,
Inscription on the Statue of Liberty

∽

There were also some good times back in those years, like when they called us from Key West to tell us that Tía Flor had gotten out with the Mariel boatlift. That woman is incredible. We immediately took off to look for her and to bring her home. Seeing her, hugging her, hearing her speak, it was like recovering a tiny bit of my family. As soon as we were alone, I began to ask her about everybody back home.

"Your mother has really aged, Lauri. Your father's death did her in. She's dying to see you, but she wouldn't have been able to survive the crossing. And, also, she doesn't want to leave your brother and sister behind."

"But tell me something, are they really caught up in all of it, Tía?"

"Lauri, it's all very complicated. But, yes, they believe sincerely in what they're doing. Your brother hasn't known anything else. Menchu was also just a young lady…she stayed behind…fell in love with Lázaro… life is complicated…you have to understand that. Back in the beginning even I had my hopes, almost everybody in Cuba did, and don't even bring up your Tío Luis…he was that way until he died… But they're good people, your brother and sister. Trust me."

The time I spent with Tía Flor was marvelous. We spent hour after hour chatting. I wanted to know everything, what time they got up, what they ate, what shape the house was in. I also asked her about Papá's death. And then afterwards we talked a lot about the country and what might happen next. I remembered Tía Flor as a very happy and exuberant woman who wore those immense necklaces all the time, and who always smoked with one of those long cigarette holders. I also found out just how intelligent and sensible she was. For some time, I had secretly feared that I wouldn't be able to relate to my family once I was reunited with them. I had heard a lot about cases like that. But with Tía Flor, I was so relieved; it was like I had just seen her yesterday. I began making plans to close in the garage and build her a bedroom, but she refused.

"Lauri, I've always dreamed of living in New York."

"But it's really cold up there. And what are you going to do?"

"Live…work…"

"Tía…but at your age?"

"Hey, I'm a lot younger than your mother…"

And so she got on a bus without knowing a word of English and took off for the city of skyscrapers to start over at the age of sixty.

∽

I am just one of many who have taken advantage of this opportunity—or rather this disaster—in order to make it here, and in no way do I feel a sense of victory nor, shall we say, a great happiness. Instead, it's a feeling of relief to be alive and to have gotten out of there, but it's the same feeling a person gets when you're able to get out of a burning house. What I mean is, the house burned down, and I was able to save myself…but still, the house burned down.

—Reinaldo Arenas, shortly after arriving in the United States through the 1980 Mariel boatlift

(Ulla and Ott *"In Their Own Words"*)

&

Another one of the happy moments was Pedro Pablo's wedding. It seemed like a dream. I couldn't believe that he was a grown man now, especially since I could remember the day he was born as if it were just yesterday. He had always been a rather formal boy and never caused me any grief. He had finished his studies and had gotten a good job. I would have preferred it if he had married a Cuban girl, and if the wedding had been in Miami, but I understood that since she was from Jacksonville they needed to have it there. Susan is a great gal, but it's never the same… not just due to the language but because of one's entire way of being… even though according to Pedro Pablo she's a transplanted *gringa*…and you can tell that they're so much in love. The most wonderful part was that all of our family was able to attend the wedding. My father-in-law, Vidal, Johnny and his family, my cousin Carlitos, Ricardo and his wife and children, and Tía Flor. Even the Stones—those Americans from Columbus who had taken us in—sent a gift. My two sons looked so handsome dressed in their tuxes! I felt so proud when I danced with them. But as in all the important moments, it hurt me that my own family wasn't there. My own family? Maybe it's time to realize that this family, the one gathered here, on this side, is really my family now. And yet, I feel incomplete as if something were missing. We're always dreaming about going back to Cuba, and it turns out that our life is really this one. We're living it without realizing it, as if we were off somewhere else.

All during the ceremony I kept thinking about my own wedding. Oh, the dreams I had! Where does love go when it's over? Had things come to an end between Robertico and me?

Going back in my mind now and trying to remember, I think it was after Pedro Pablo's wedding that things really got worse. Robertico began to drink more than his fair share. He didn't really get wasted drunk, but I preferred to ignore him rather than confront him. He was also not doing so well in business, but since I had gotten some raises I was able to make ends meet. Everywhere you went people were talking about *perestroika, glasnost,* and the inevitable transformation of the Soviet Union and its satellites. Regardless, he kept on seeing communists everywhere he looked.

One day we really got into it:

"Don't tell me that all of you are going down to Flagler Street again..."

"Where do you get off telling me what to do?" He really got worked up. Actually, he was always in a bad mood. I told him he should go see a therapist and he took it as a personal attack.

At the beginning of the year my father-in-law announced that he was getting married again. I was so happy for him. Roberto is a wonderful man and deserves to be happy. Besides, Olga is such a lovely woman, and so modest. But the idea really infuriated Roberto. The same guy who never mentions Adela's name, the same one who didn't even order the tombstone for her grave—I had to do it—the same guy who hardly entered her room when she was dying of cancer, and then to come out with this bit that Roberto's marriage was a betrayal to the memory of his mother. Sometimes my husband is like a complete stranger, a person who's totally removed from my life.

Things got worse once I graduated and began to teach at the university. Robertico had never struck me as the envious type, and although he never helped out much around the house or with the kids, I just thought it was because that's the way Latin men are and not because he didn't love me. I didn't believe, I couldn't believe that it was my success that truly bothered him. But sometimes it seemed that every time something good came along, Robertico always tried to rain on my parade.

One of the touchy subjects back in those days was my insistence on going back to Cuba to see my family. Sometimes he would try to get me to see his side:

"Lauri, and what about the years when I was a prisoner? And the memory of the martyrs like Pedro Luís Boitel, and the ones they tortured, and the ones that have been in jail for years and years? You know the stories of the Valladares, about Martín Pérez, about Húber Matos and all the anonymous men and women...you yourself worked with Human Rights in Washington...and the years in exile, so many women working in sweatshops, everything that's happened? Are you going to betray all of that? And the dead, Lauri, the memory of the dead?"

"I don't think the dead are going to mind one bit if I go see my family."

"Don't disrespect the memory of the martyrs of the homeland..."

"Look, Robertico..." but he interrupted me.

"Maybe the dead don't matter to you, but they do to me. And they should matter to you too because otherwise what will they say about us?"

"It doesn't matter to me what anybody says. I have a clean conscience."

"How can you say that? How can you even think about going back there while the same tyranny exists, while those same people...?"

"Oh, Robertico, this conversation is absurd. Do you think that the regime is going to fall because I make the sacrifice of never seeing my mother again? If your family were there you would understand what I'm saying..."

When all else failed, he would try to seduce me. He would get all loveable and affectionate for a few days. He would come looking for me in bed and make passionate love to me, even tenderly. Sometimes I think Robertico was only able to express his love for me through sex, that he's a good man, and that he loves me even though he's never figured out how to make me happy. Other times I think maybe it's just me who's reading into his caresses something that really isn't there.

When he started up with the same old story the next day, and he saw that I hadn't changed my mind, he got in bad mood all over again.

"Look, Roberto, I haven't gone to Cuba yet because I didn't want to go against your wishes and because I thought that one day you would understand…besides, I had always had this dream that my mother could come here instead, but now that she's almost blind I know it's impossible, and that I'm the one who will have to go. I don't want the same thing to happen like it did with Papá. I don't want her to die without having seen her one more time. Look, your father was also at the Bay of Pigs and he understands why I want to go…"

"Don't talk to me about my father…"

"Why not? Your father's an amazing man who has worked hard and who has been successful…he's part of our historic exile community that has a lot to be proud of."

"Yeah, sure, he was a great success but as far as you're concerned I'm nothing but a failure, right?"

"I didn't say that."

"No but you thought it."

"No, Robertico. Besides that's not what we're talking about."

He just sat there for a long time and wouldn't say a word. The silence became thick. I got up to go to the kitchen. He put his hand on my shoulder and stopped me. I turned around, and he looked me square in the eyes. I don't know if what I saw in his gaze was pride or fear, humility or desire for control, love or hate. Maybe all of that and more.

"Promise me that you will not go back to Cuba until Castro's gone."

I tried to shake loose from his grip and avoid a response, but he insisted.

"Lauri, are you going to promise or not?"

"Roberto, don't ask me to do that. I can't…I can't promise you I won't."

I can still hear the sound of the front door slamming behind him.

It was the last time that I ever saw him.

Now he is lying here in a casket covered in a Cuban flag. Johnny comes up to me and asks if I want a coffee. There are so many people around me, everybody's talking at the same time, and I'm so alone, so absolutely alone. I'm here, but I'm really not.

✐

This past Friday borders guards of the German Democratic Republic (GDR) dismantled portions of the Berlin Wall, the supreme symbol of the Iron Curtain for the past twenty-eight years. The ruling Communist Party indicated that it would hold free elections and form a democratically elected, coalition-based government.

Thousands of elated Germans crossed from one side to the other, pushing baby carriages and hugging their neighbors from the other side. Some used pickaxes and hammers to chip away pieces of the despised wall in order to keep them as souvenirs.

Throughout the city one could hear the resounding music of tolling church bells, which the gathering masses regarded as 'liberty bells.'

(El Nuevo Herald 11 November 1989: A1)

CHAPTER NINE
"Out With the Scum!"

A FEW MONTHS AGO THEY STARTED ALLOWING THOSE WHO HAD FLED THE ISLAND TO COME BACK FOR A VISIT. The ones who took off—so often without even saying goodbye and who eventually fell into the black hole of oblivion—are now a part of what we call "the community abroad." The orders from above indicate that we're supposed to be nice to them.

It's been twenty years now since Lauri left and eighteen for Ricardo. I wonder if they'll come see us. Every time a family member returns from abroad the whole neighborhood gets in an uproar. They come back loaded down with gifts and stories of what they've accomplished up there. "But you wouldn't believe my house, all the color televisions, a new car each year, and what an event my daughter's fifteenth birthday was, and then there was this vacation we took on this wonderful cruise ship..." And they even bring out the photos to prove it. One guy who lost his bodega down on the corner, Benito, came back and has been telling people all about the four stores he now owns in Haileah. They all come across as happy and even a bit chubby, and their Spanish is jumbled up with English. All of them invariably say how much they miss Cuba and that there's no sky bluer than ours. But then they take off again.

Maruja came by one afternoon all flustered because one of them had showed up at her house:

"If you don't mind, I only want to take a peek around the house... I left when I was really young and I barely remember it." He was the son of the former owners.

She was so taken aback that she let him in. The young man began to reminisce:

"This was my room here...and that's where my parents slept... This," he pointed out as he broke into tears, "is the room that my grandfather died in..."

"I'm sorry *señora*. I didn't think it would get to me so much."

Maruja offered him a glass of water and even made him a cup of coffee.

Later that night she asked me out of the blue:

"Do you think if they come back they could take my house away from me?"

"No, Maruja, I don't think so, but keep in mind that those people lived here before you and I were even born. Mamá told me their story. It took them a lot of years of hard work to scrape together to build that house."

"I've worked for a long time too…"

"That's true…and don't worry. They're not coming back."

Many of them don't plan on coming back even for a brief visit. Even Ricardo told me on the phone not too long ago, "As long as things remain the same, we won't be coming back."

Lauri hasn't come back for a visit either, nor my classmates, my old professors, nor my uncles, my cousins.

"Those people won't dare come back as long as we sustain the Revolution," Lázaro predicted. "And the truth is that they will probably die without having returned to Cuba because the Revolution is irreversible."

"I can't bear to think that I may never see my brother and sister again."

"You have to be realistic."

It is also possible now for the elderly to make visits to the United States. Lauri is going to invite one of our parents as soon as she can, and then the other next year. She hinted that maybe I could come down the road. I'd do it if for nothing else than just to see her… But what am I talking about? Lázaro would never allow it. Regardless, I can't imagine they'd give me permission because of my age. My parents should go first and then we'll see. I immediately told Mamá that she should get her paperwork together and apply for permission, but somehow Papá convinced her that he should be the first to go.

"I'm not in good health and I don't want to die without seeing my kids again," he argued while putting his hand on his chest.

"I think you just might have a 'special friend' in Miami," I overheard Lázaro quietly teasing him.

But what if that were true? What if that woman that he had an affair with lived in Miami now, and he wanted to go see her? How despicable would it be if he kept Mamá from seeing her kids for something like that? The old man has already turned seventy-five, but he still looks in good shape, and he's always been a womanizer. Lázaro assures me that he was just kidding around. Who knows? Men always stick up for each other. I wish I could just come out and directly ask Papá about it, but I haven't found the right moment.

I'll never know the truth now.

Papá died one night in March in front of the television in the living room. Mamá knew immediately that something was wrong when she couldn't wake him to go to bed. Once again the funeral parlor. Once again a phone call to Lauri and Ricardo. Another burial in the Colón Cemetery. This time I couldn't manage to cry. Who was this man that had died? Who was my father? What did he believe in? Whom did he love? As I looked at him in the casket, he suddenly seemed like a stranger to me.

Mamá took it all in stride, like she does everything. It hit Pedritín hard however. After the burial he gave me a big hug. I had never seen him cry like that before.

∽

As was to be expected, hundreds of eccentrics—made up almost entirely of lumpen, dissenters, dead-beats, and parasites—presented themselves in the patio of the Peruvian Embassy within a few hours of the withdrawal of the Cuban sentry. Within 48 hours more than three thousand had gathered, the majority hailing from Havana and the nation's western provinces. Many unfortunately brought with them family members including children.

Judging by their clothes, mannerisms, and language seldom has there ever been such a "select" group gathered in a given place.

Not a single one had been persecuted politically or in need of the sacred right of asylum.

Nonetheless each one has the full confidence that the Revolutionary government has spoken in earnest when it signaled this as an opportune moment to emigrate to other more appropriate settings. As in the past, once again Cuba has gladly opened its doors to the vile rabble opposed to Socialism and the Revolution.

(*Bohemia* 72:15, 50)

൭

A few days after Papá's death rumors started going around about how they had removed the guard at the Peruvian embassy. In just a few hours Havana was in an uproar. Entire families, who had been out and about, rushed into the embassy to seek asylum without even going home to pack a toothbrush. Many of them ran off without even saying goodbye to their spouse or children. In three or four days, more than ten thousand men, women, and children had packed the embassy in Miramar.

"I bet you that a lot of those people were in the Plaza of the Revolution just a few days ago. I don't get why they're leaving. Just to eat better? To go around in fancy cars? To dress better only to find that you're still as unhappy as everybody who comes back to visit? Yeah, you go through some rough times here, but capitalism is much worse... Besides, this is their home. As they say, 'our wine is bitter...but at least it's our wine.'"

"Lázaro, to get by in Cuba you have to make a lot of sacrifices and not everybody is as dedicated as you are to the Revolution," Mamá tells him during one of those rare moments when she emerges from the silence that she has lived in since Papá died.

The situation is getting tense. Lázaro, who has access to the international press, told me that the whole business with the Embassy has had ramifications, that it's being seen as a rejection of the Revolution.

"So now it turns out that they're supposedly heroes who seek liberty when what they really want is to live in a society of consumerism and to get fat like those guys who come here from Miami. Heroes? What they really are is…"

The Cubans who leave are no longer referred to as "worms" as before. Instead, they're called *lumpen,* misfits, queers, whores, dykes, scum. Some left the Embassy and went back to their houses to wait for their papers of safe-conduct. People painted vulgar graffiti on the walls of their homes and threw eggs at them.

Yesterday afternoon Ernestico came home outraged:

"Aunt Menchu, you know that there are people like Tania and me in the Lenin School who are there because of our grades, but the majority of them are sons and daughters of Ministers, Deputies, Directors, and other big shots… You should see how they dress, the watches they wear… Their parents travel abroad. And now they're all supposedly infuriated and are badmouthing the ones who are trying to leave. If they can have it all, why does it bother them if other people want a better life?"

He didn't stop rambling as he paced back and forth in the living room:

"Do you remember my friend Guillermo who graduated two years ago? They kicked him out of the university. A few days ago they called the students into the Assembly for a Deeper Revolutionary Awareness and they accused him of severe ideological and political deviation. You know what his big crime was? Go ahead. Guess. You'll never guess."

"I don't have any idea, Ernesto, but calm down."

"Get this. They kicked him out for wearing a pair of jeans that had an American flag on them that his godparents had sent him. And just for that the State Security Agency has deemed him to be a threat to society and indictable under the new 'Propensity for Dangerous Crime' law. And Aunt Menchu, Guillermo was just the first case in the college…"

"Well, maybe…"

"Maybe nothing! Do you know what the other case was about? Go ahead, guess, go ahead… No, forget it, you wouldn't guess in a million years. How could it possibly occur to anyone in their right mind to expel someone from the university because they were seen putting toy sailboats in the fountain? A toy sailboat! Get this. They were informed that it was an 'irresponsible act of ideological escapism.'"

"Calm down Ernesto, there's got to be a reasonable explanation…"

"Explanation? Aunt Menchu, Guillermo is the son of a farmer and a maid from Santa Clara who back in the days of capitalism earned fifteen pesos a month. He was born in '59. Guillermo's a son of the Revolution, and look at him, look at what's happening to him… I just don't understand. I don't understand what this country's coming to."

And he slammed the door and ran out of the house.

⁓

Despite that in our country homosexuals are neither persecuted nor harassed, there was no small number of them among those who took shelter in the Peruvian Embassy, along with others given to gambling and drugs who have also been unable to find an accepted outlet for their vices.

Demand, discipline, and rigor stand in opposition to weakness, delinquency, idleness, and parasitism. In this our working citizens think as one.

Let the deadbeats leave! Out with the deviants! Out with the dregs! Out with the delinquents! Out with the scum!

A man does not rise before dawn and work tirelessly for hours in the furrow, in the workshops, and in the factories only to serve and feed parasites. This is not the way we choose to carry out our worthy and heroic mission among nations. We did not spill our blood in Cuba and other corners of the world so that we might defend, honor, and extol with our flag those types of "Cubans."

(*Granma* in *Bohemia* 72:15, 50)

⁓

They've said that anybody who wants to leave can. Well, sort of. First they have to give you a discharge paper from your job and then some other document. I've heard that to get permission to leave, you first have to declare that you're a delinquent or a homosexual or a prostitute, but

I can't believe that's true. Everybody's gone nuts, especially the single men. They run home, grab a few things, kiss their mom goodbye, and then find a way to get to Mariel. Entire families have gone as well. They lug their children, their old folks, even their dogs. I'm afraid that Ernestico is going to do something stupid. After the business with Tía Flor nothing would surprise me. She came over one morning, and you could tell she was anxious and in a hurry.

"Mariana...Mariana...Menchu...I've got news. There's something I have to tell you. I'm leaving Cuba. I've already got everything arranged. I'm leaving for Mosquito tonight."

"Flor! Are you crazy?"

"No, I've thought about it a lot. I spent so many years taking care of Mamá, and I'm ready to live. I'm fifty-seven and..."

"Sixty, Flor," interrupted Mamá.

"Fine. Sixty. It doesn't matter, I feel young, and I want to see the world, not stand in line. I want to be able to savor a fine whisky, smoke with a cigarette holder without them calling me bourgeois...read novels by Vargas Llosa or Cabrera Infante or whomever I feel like...go by bus or take a taxi...walk around the city with people who are well dressed... to speak out loud...to go to a museum...to wear a brand new dress right off the rack...to meet interesting people...you know, live."

"And the house, and Mamá's things?"

"Lázaro and Menchu can move in. They've never really had a place of their own."

"I can't leave Mamá alone."

"Well then let Tania move in with her...and Pedritín too...and you two take the house, but I'm not staying in that hell hole that's made up of four walls, a set of dishes, and some old photo albums. Life is something else...and in this country there isn't any life."

She gave us a big hug and before we knew it she was already heading out the door.

"What are you going to do when you get there?"

"I'll call Laurita...and later on...live, sis, just live."

✑

On Monday morning two ships, originating from Florida, left Mariel for the United States with forty-eight social misfits. According to sources, on Tuesday eleven more ships, originating from the same source, will depart for that country this time with the intent to transfer more than three hundred individuals. A nice pace!

These ships have come on their own accord and were received with the utmost courtesy. Their crew members requested that they be allowed to transport a number of those who were guests in the Peruvian Embassy and others who have relatives in the United States. Their request was fully obliged.

Meanwhile, the Yankee State Department has been frantically issuing statements against such trips to Cuba, threatening participants with penalty of arrest, confiscation, and similar measures. Thus it seems they have begun to reap the fruits of their politics of aiding and abetting illegal departures from Cuba, including hijacking ships with their crews as hostages. And now it seems they have become our border patrol. In short, we have extended ourselves to the Floridian peninsula.

(Bohemia 72:17, 45)

✑

We're surrounded by violence. A few days ago there was a really ugly scene. Apparently a bunch of people who wanted to leave the country had gathered in front of the U.S. Interests Section. I don't know how it began but things got heated and a brawl broke out. Even the women got into it and started hitting each other with their handbags. Lázaro told me all about it. He had been walking by, just by chance, and with his journalistic curiosity and all, he got right in the middle of the whole thing.

"Menchu, I don't like what I'm seeing... Things are getting out of hand... You know how much it disgusts me to see people leaving like this, *en masse*...people who owe everything to the Revolution and who aren't willing to make a sacrifice for the future of their country...but still I don't think all this violence is going to get us anywhere either."

They say that President Carter has issued a statement saying that they'll accept any Cuban who wants to go and, naturally, that's stirred things up even more. So many of the people I love have gone away. It's like things were twenty years ago when people would disappear without even saying goodbye, and then later on you'd find out that they had taken off. Each disappearance left a hole in me emotionally. I thought I'd never have any more friends ever again, but I did. I found new friends to care for only now to have my heart torn out once more. Amelita, my friend from work, left. So did Ivan, the artist who was so clever... he learned everything so quickly and with so much enthusiasm. There have also been stories in the news that some of them have capsized and drowned. I'm just glad that Tía Flor called us from Lauri's house as soon as she got there to let us know she was all right. I miss all of them so much. Every day we feel a little bit more alone.

At least we have Havana. When I miss my friends too much, I head out into the streets and I take long walks. Behind those faded façades of the houses in Vedado, I can still glimpse the architectural beauty of the stained glass semi-circles and the lattices. On other days I head to the cemetery. I stroll amid the crypts and read the inscriptions on the tombs until I arrive at the pantheon where Papá and so many other relatives are buried. That's when I start to reminisce and remember those Sundays when the whole family would get together at grandmother's house and all the cousins would play hide-and-seek and freeze-tag...and then all of my memories become motionless, frozen in time, just like when we pretended to be statues. I can see Julio Eduardo's face so clearly... I stand in front of Mamá Luya's tomb and my grandfather's. I find a bench and sit there for a long time and just think about so many things...even though what I really want is to clear my head and remember nothing. The park is another of my sanctuaries. I contemplate the trees with their century-old trunks...and inevitably I wind up at the sea. I look across the horizon and it seems like there's some type of barricade that divides in two the things I love the most. Over there, my brother and sister, my uncles and aunts, my cousins that I don't even know, and so many friends… Back here, my mother, Lázaro, my daughter, Pedritín, the dead I've buried, the countryside, my city, my country… And that line in the sea that separates us hurts so much.

∞

Due to inclement weather yesterday, no vessels departed on Sunday from Mariel to the United States. In an effort to take greater measures for increased safety, all vessels will now depart in convoys so that they may offer mutual assistance and support. Additionally, a Cuban military ship will escort the flotilla up to a given distance from Florida. There will not be any safer means of transportation in the world than that of the Mariel-Floridian route.

(*Bohemia* 72:18, 68)

∞

Ernesto came bursting in more upset than ever.

"Where's Uncle Lázaro?"

"I don't know. He should be here any time now."

"I need to see him. He has to help me. They're doing something terrible to Guillermo and his family. He says it doesn't matter what they do to him and the rest of them, but he wants to get his little sister out of the house. Oh, Tía Menchu, it's horrible. They brought in all the kids from school to yell insults at them…even Tania's there."

I took off for Guillermo's with Ernestico. We almost ran the two blocks between our house and his friend's. Sure enough. A mob had gathered in front of their house. Many of them were just kids dressed in their school uniform.

"Lumpen!"

"Scum!"

"Traitors!"

"Deviants!"

"Counter-revolutionaries!"

"Cowards!"

"Leeches!"

We finally caught sight of Tania. She was chanting insults from the back of the crowd. She seemed more scared than agitated. I had been in such a hurry to get there, but now I didn't know what to do. Just at that moment, my daughter saw me, and ran up to me.

"Your grandmother's sick," I lied opening my eyes real wide in hopes that she'd realize that it was an excuse to get her out of there.

She followed me without asking any questions and without looking at me as if she were a pet that had done something wrong.

"Mamá's ill," I explained to Maruja as we passed in front of her even though I'm sure she knew it wasn't true.

We started heading for home, but Ernesto wanted to stay so he could try to calm down the raucous crowd that had begun to throw eggs along with insults at his friend's house.

"These people are good people," he kept on saying over and over without anyone paying attention to him. Finally I was able to pry him away and convince him to come back home with us. None of us spoke on the way back. When Lázaro got home we ate in absolute silence and hardly lifted our eyes from our plates. You could feel a shameful complicity in our silence. When we finished eating, Ernesto and Lázaro went off into the back room. Much later, they came out and left the house and didn't return until dawn. I didn't ask any questions, but the next morning, when we had a second alone just the two of us, Ernesto told me that Guillermo and his family had gone out the back, that he and Lázaro had waited for them in the alley, and that they took them to some relatives' house in Bauta from where they'll leave for Mariel.

"If it weren't for uncle Lázaro, they would have killed them today... I'll never forget what it was like when they handed over the little girl through the fence... It was like a movie, Aunt Menchu, like a nightmare..."

Lázaro didn't say anything about it until that night when we went to bed:

"I told Ernesto that he'd be better off if he went to study in the Soviet Union. I'm going to try to arrange a scholarship for him."

A few months later we said our goodbyes at the dock. I don't know who was more sad, if it was Mamá or Tania.

"It'll do him good," said Armandito, who held a high position in the Revolutionary Armed Forces, and who still doesn't understand the apprehensions of his son.

"Don't forget to bundle up," Magaly reminded him.

'And another one leaves...' I thought to myself. But I didn't say anything.

∽

I would say that what we see before us today is a battle, a battle that we wage in defense of the integrity of our country. The mere presence of you here today, your mere presence in this Plaza is a battle, and an important battle in defending the integrity and the security of Cuba, for if the enemy should confuse us that would be dangerous; and if the enemy should deceive us that would be dangerous.

Thus, work has already begun on drafting a strategic plan to instruct the nation on how to survive and withstand a total blockade, and what each of us as citizens must do should there be a complete blockade. Suppose that they prevent food from entering, that fuel is kept out, what must each of us do to survive?

There's been talk of a blockade, knowing how difficult it would be for a country without petroleum to survive a naval siege. And we must continue to develop our plans lest such a situation arise. Indeed Regan, or Reagan, or Rigan—I don't know how you pronounce it—who's undoubtedly going to be the Republican candidate, has declared that he supports the plan for a naval blockade against Cuba. Clearly none of this will be easy, we must warn them. But we have the obligation as revolutionaries and as pragmatists to have a response ready for each of these scenarios. But the one thing they will never be able to imagine is a day when Cuba surrenders, because we will never surrender. We shall never surrender!

(Fidel Castro 1 May 1980)

∽

Given the impending U.S. invasion, paramilitary groups—known as the Territorial Regional Militia—have been formed. Maruja is on call at all hours. The country is on the brink of war. We're all standing guard continuously, and when we're not on guard, we're in line. We shall never surrender! We just got through celebrating the twentieth anniversary of the Bay of Pigs. The police are apprehending anybody who wears jeans with U.S. symbols and proceeding to cut them off. *We shall never surrender!* You have to get in line because the eggs have arrived. You stand in line to get a sesame ice cream in Coppelia. You run and get your spot in this line or that line because they're going to have cooking oil. You get in another line because the meat has come in. And you stand, and you stand, and you always have your tote bag ready just in case, hanging off your shoulder as if it were just another body part. *We shall never surrender!*

Mamá became ill. She had a high fever and a rash practically all over her body. Her head and legs ached, she was vomiting, and it even affected her eyes. I thought she was going to die. She was so weak. It's all because of the standing water, which has become a breeding ground for mosquitoes. We haven't been able to fix the drainage in the patio, and she's out there every day hanging up clothes on the line. I hated to leave her alone, but since I'm in the Combatant Mothers for Education movement, I had promised to go around and give talks on hygiene. At least they've started to fumigate now. There's been a dengue fever outbreak all over the Island.

I finally took Mamá to the clinic and the doctor told me that she needed to be admitted right away. She seemed to be getting along okay but the red rash was getting worse. They put her in the hospital for four or five days and took blood samples every day. I had to get up early every morning and get my place in the hot water line. When we finally got our turn at the hot water tap, we'd fill up an old oil can that had a handle improvised from a clothes hanger, and then everybody would go back to the ward and use that for the bath water for the patients. Like everybody else, Mamá, was in one of the two wards. One was full of beds and the other full of cribs and mothers since mostly that's all there was—babies and old folks. I was so exhausted that every once in a while I'd fall asleep in one of the chairs.

I was able to buy a chicken on the black market to make some soup. It's the only thing that sounds good to her. *But we shall never surrender!*

∽

We share the conviction of the Cuban people and put forth the most profound suspicion that the plagues that have befallen our country, and especially the most recent outbreak of dengue hemorrhagic fever, have been introduced into our country by the CIA. We challenge the government of the United States to address its stance in this area, to say whether or not the CIA has once again been authorized or not to organize attempts against the participants of our Revolution and to afflict plagues against our plants, our animals, and our citizens.

(Fidel Castro 26 July 1981)

∽

After Tía Flor left for the United States, Lázaro and I moved into her house in La Sierra. Mamá stayed with Pedritín in Vedado until my brother's girlfriend moved in… She's not a bad girl, it's just that Mamá felt uncomfortable. Anyway, when she got sick I brought her here to care for her and now we've decided it'd be best if she moved in with us. Tania stayed back in Vedado so she could be closer to the university. Who could have guessed that she was going to major in the sciences? She studies bio-chemistry and spends her whole life behind a microscope. I worry sometimes because she seems so lost in her thoughts. She almost never goes out. Her only other passion is the ballet. She hardly has any friends except for her cousin Ernesto, who comes back from Russia every summer. When he's here they go out a lot, and they spend hours just chatting. Even though she was just a little girl, Tania is nostalgic about the time we spent in the Soviet Union. She has been awarded a grant to do her graduate work there. I agonize at the thought of being separated from her...but at least it makes me feel better knowing that Ernestico would be there with her.

Pedritín spends all his time going back and forth to Nicaragua. Lázaro travels sometimes too. For a while the economy had gotten a little bit better and they could buy a lot of things through the free market. Everybody has gotten in the habit of listening to Radio Martí. Mamá for example has become a big fan of the radio soap operas. As for me I used to like listening to the music specials, or just keeping up with what was going on in the world.

But things have gotten bad again and they have launched a campaign to rectify errors and negative tendencies, as they say. Raúl himself has announced that this time we are truly going to lay the foundation for the new socialistic and communistic society to which Mamá immediately responded:

"So if I may ask, what have we been doing up until now?"

Lázaro, however, answered very seriously:

"Mariana, the problem is that Cuba has failed to apply Marxist principles the way they were intended... But I don't have much faith that they're not going to do the same thing again."

"Look, Lázaro, with or without Marxist principles, we've been at this for almost thirty years...and now they're talking about even more sacrifices and that we should be ready to get by on just herbs."

Sure enough, they don't provide the typical afternoon snack at the office anymore; they've canceled the free meals for workers; they've gone back to rationing milk and rice again; and they're going to raise bus fare.

∽

As we assess our situation during these times, we cannot lose sight of the strict obligations that correspond to each revolutionary. The price of public transport in our cities has increased by ten cents per fare. Will this small increase suffice? No, reality says it will not. Nonetheless there are still citizens who ridicule the law by not paying their fare. Over and above the measure of increasing prices, we must all make this decision our own by impeding dishonest offenders because they harm the national economy and because they create an unacceptable image of lawlessness.

(*Bohemia* 79:2, 20)

∽

So many things are happening! They've started to bring the remaining soldiers home from Angola. And in the Soviet Union there are a lot of changes taking place.

With a sadness so deep that it seeps through his voice, Lázaro keeps on saying, "Everything is collapsing around us."

They have arrested General Arnaldo Ochoa, both of the de la Guardia twins from the Ministry of the Interior, and a whole bunch of people. Lázaro couldn't believe it.

"But Ochoa is a hero! I don't get it. It seems like it was just yesterday that they were decorating him with medals. He's a courageous man… not like Tortoló who made us look so bad with that mess in Grenada."

They have accused him of corruption and misuse of economic funds. They say that drugs were also somehow involved. Lázaro says that's impossible because Ochoa would have never been involved in something like that.

"Where there's smoke…" Mamá left her implication hanging.

We lived each minute of the trial. The prosecutor asked for the death penalty for Ochoa and the other defendants. Within a week, they came back with the verdict. Ochoa, de la Guardia, and two others would be executed. The others were sentenced to fifteen to thirty years in prison.

Lázaro was outraged.

"I know Ochoa, Menchu. I interviewed him several times. He's a loyal person…a fighter… This just can't be. How is it possible that they're going to put him in front of a firing squad?"

But the majority supported the decision.

"It's the only way to teach them a lesson. So they'll learn…"

When I read in *Granma* that they had shot them I felt a chill run down my spine. It seemed like all of a sudden the entire house became dim as if a giant black bird had just flown over us.

Mamá asked me what day it was.

"July 13th."

"It was thirty years ago today that Lauri left us."

"I know Mamá. I remembered what day it was too."

That night Lázaro came home with a bottle of rum and he went outside and sat in a chair on the patio. And he began to drink. I went outside to be with him, but he asked me to leave him alone. When he came to bed it was already dawn, and he had drunk the whole bottle. I had never seen my husband like that.

Three days later the poet Nicolás Guillén died.

"It just goes to show you," my mother observed. "Don't you remember the same thing happened during the whole Mariel business when Haydée Santamaría committed suicide?"

"What in the world are you talking about, woman!" Pedritín grumbled. "Guillén was always a communist… He was dedicated to the Revolution like nobody else."

"Well, you just never know when a person's going to start to feel ashamed."

⁓

They're going to execute a man
whose hands are tied.
There are four soldiers
who are poised to shoot.
Four soldiers
who are hushed,
who are bound,
as bound as the one
who they are going to shoot.

"Can you escape?"
"I can't run!"
"Quick! They're going to fire!
"What can we do?"
"Maybe the rifles aren't loaded…"
"They've got six shots of burning lead!"
"Maybe the soldiers won't shoot."
"God, you're such an idiot!"

They fired.
(But how could they do that?)
They killed.
(But how could they do that?)
There were four soldiers
who were hushed
by the lowering of his officer's sword;
there were four soldiers
who were bound,
as bound as the man
that the four were bound to kill.

(Guillén 13–14)

❦

They have required all ten thousand students studying abroad in socialist countries to pay their tuition in dollars. Ernesto had already graduated but was still taking courses. Tania still needed a few more courses but they let her take her exams early so she could finish. She was by herself when we picked her up.

"Ernesto's not coming back," she announced.

I imagine that his parents had already guessed as much because they didn't even bother to go to the airport. It didn't seem like it surprised Lázaro either:

"He's better off."

We got a call from Miami. Robertico had an accident and died. My poor sister. A widow, and so young! She couldn't even bring herself to come to the phone. We spoke with her son Pedro Pablo. God, how I wish I could just hug her! These are the moments when being separated hurts the worst.

On *Radio Rebelde* they read a cable in a mournful and alarming tone that said that the Berlin wall has come down, but a lot of people are saying that the whole thing has been blown out of proportion by the Western press and that this is just Socialism's way of rectifying errors and strengthening itself. Maybe Lázaro will have more information, but I don't like to ask him too much and get him all riled up. He still hasn't gotten over the whole business about Ochoa.

Today is the 7th of December, the anniversary of Maceo's death, a date set aside to remember all the nation's fallen heroes. They've used today's occasion to honor those who died in the Angolan war. Fidel spent more time in his speech criticizing the new path taken by the Socialist bloc—especially the Soviet Union—than he did commemorating the heroes of Angola.

I saw Maruja bite her lip.

"I've been waiting all these years for them to bring my son's body home, a humble *mulatto* boy who went off to Angola and died defending the Revolution. My only son, Menchu. And in the end, for what? Sometimes I think no one cares."

I didn't know what to tell her.

CHAPTER TEN
"With a Sad and Heavy Heart"

IT'S DEEP INSIDE OF ME. IT THUNDERS IN MY EARS, IN MY HEAD. It wakes me up at night. It attacks me in the middle of the street. The gunshot. That sound, my God, how can I describe that sound? A crack, so startling, so sudden, so final. There's no way to forget his face as I watched him for the last time through the window of the door, as I watched him at the very instant when he raised the gun to his temple and pulled the trigger. His face contorted and...I just can't. I keep having to go to the bathroom to throw up. I just want to be able to close my eyes and not see him. It's as if the inside of my eyelids were tinted red. Everything I see is red, the same shade of red as the blood stain that I still haven't been able to get rid of entirely. To have the gall to come to my house, to my driveway, seems like the greatest act of self-centeredness I can imagine, his last chance to ridicule me. I keep going to the bookshelves and pulling down the photo albums...our wedding, when the kids were young, our vacations. I try to remember us making love. I try to picture him at his happiest moments because I know that he had them. He must have, right? And as much as I try, the smiling face I see in the photos and in my mind inevitably turns into a grimace, that contorted face he made just before he blew his brains out. It's such a trite phrase. I had never really thought about it before, but that's exactly what happened. I think I'm going to throw up again... I wish I could just cry instead. It's so strange. I haven't shed a single tear. Sometimes I feel like I've been drugged. And then all of a sudden I hear the gunshot again. I feel like I'm going crazy. Everything I see is red, whether I have my eyes wide open or closed shut. Red. A red that dissolves into a blinding light through which I imagine the tiles of the rooftops of Havana. But I just can't see them. I hear the gunshot again. It thunders in my head, in my ears. A dry, hollow sound. It's deep inside of me. Inescapably like death itself.

I keep waking up sweating and out of breath. It takes me a few minutes to realize that I'm in my own bed, in Miami. Yes. The other side of the bed is empty. Yes. My husband is dead. No. He died from a massive coronary when he was 52 and not from blowing his brains out. They found his car wrapped around a tree like an accordion and Robertico drooped over the steering wheel. Why can't I get out of this nightmare? He didn't commit suicide. He didn't commit suicide, I keep telling myself. Or did he? Why do I have this guilt complex, then, as if I had killed him? I try to make sense of it all. I had fallen out of love with him a long time ago. There were times when I had even thought about getting a divorce. And then…there were others…go ahead Laura, tell the truth… there were moments when I saw him sleeping next to me, and I wished he were dead. But no one dies just because you want them to. If that were the case Fidel Castro would have been buried in the ground a long time ago! But on the other hand, I loved my husband. I must have loved him. If not, why else would I have stayed with him for all these years and allowed him to keep me from my visiting my family in Cuba?

For months after Robertico's death I had that same recurring nightmare. Although I couldn't have received more support from my family and friends, I felt tormented. Both of my sons instantly became grown men. They were the ones who took care of all the details. And Bobby Jr. turned into a different person overnight. He even enrolled in some courses at the university. He started talking about going off to study like his brother and uncle had done.

"If Mami is doing okay and I can leave her by herself…" he would say as if suddenly our roles had been reversed, and he was the one who had to take care of me. About a year later I almost had to kick him out of the house so he would go to Gainesville.

"You go ahead, honey. I'll be just fine," I lied.

It wasn't true that I'd be fine. The visits to the psychiatrist didn't help my depression and the pills didn't do anything either. Everybody attributed the pain to losing Robertico; but it wasn't his absence that made me feel so glum, it was the guilt. And, on top of it all, I had been harsh with him the last time I saw him. He had taken off without us really dealing with the problem that had been at the root of everything all these years. With his very last words in life he asked me not to go back to Cuba. And although I hadn't promised him anything, that conversation stuck in my mind. It was like he was still controlling me even after his death. Maybe the worst thing that I did was not to tell anybody about it. I don't think I was truly honest even with the psychiatrist. I guess deceiving myself was a way of coping.

It was my father-in-law who helped me the most. He and Olga would frequently invite me out to eat or to go to the movies.

"You need to get out more," they insisted. Roberto would call me every day. And he often took me out for lunch or he'd stop by. We would share a coffee or a Scotch depending on the hour. We tended to talk about the boys, about Johnny, about Cuba of course. But when he tried to talk about Robertico's death or my state of mind, I put up my defenses.

"There can't be any pain that's worse than losing a son, Roberto. I know that you're suffering too... Don't worry about me."

Finally one day, after drinking down his Scotch in one gulp, my father-in-law told me point blank:

"Lauri, we need to talk. I've known you since you were a teenager. You've been like a daughter to me...a good daughter. The tragedy in Cuba has affected all of us. If someone had told us that we were going to go through some of the crazy things that we've lived through, we wouldn't have believed them. Some have suffered more than we have. Their family members have been executed or been put in prison for years. Or they've drowned trying to cross the Straits. But each Cuban has his quota of pain, his own intimate problem. The worst part has been that families have been separated. I left my two sisters in Cuba, and I know that I'll never see them again. But we were all grown up when I left. You were just a child, you were barely an adult when you married my son and wound up facing a life that hasn't been easy. I've seen how determined you can be, how you fought to get ahead at work, to study, to be a good parent, how you've put your own touches on your home, whether you were decorating the Christmas tree or how you would seat us around the table in a certain way, the way you celebrate birthdays and the pictures you take, how you took care of Adela until the day she died. And through all of it, you were heartbroken because your parents and family, and especially your twin sister, were back there. Robertico loved you, and he was a good man. But he didn't know how to express it. And, after it was all said and done, he could never accept it here. He just couldn't allow himself to give up on Cuba. Being separated from your family has caused you so much suffering, but somehow you managed to create a new life here for yourself and your sons. He didn't. Maybe you'd have been better off if he had just left you years ago and then he would've put all his energy into fighting for Cuba, but he didn't. He also never learned how to let go of fighting for Cuba so he could give you and your boys what you needed. Since his death I've struggled a lot because I feel guilty that I never sat down with him and talked to him about all of this, but maybe back then I didn't see things so clearly. And who knows, maybe he wouldn't have listened to me anyway. Yeah, you're right. I've suffered too. It's been so hard for me to deal with his death, and I don't know why…" and then his voice began to quiver, "…I don't know why I can't get his face out of my mind when he was a little seven year-old boy, all snaggletooth, and so proud of himself for having learned how to ride his bike without training wheels. Lauri, *mijita*, Robertico was a tormented man, just one of so many of the anonymous victims of this whole ordeal, but you're a heroine, you have to keep going forward… Or you're really going to let me down. Robertico has now finally found peace in death that he never found in life. I only wish I could live long enough to take his body back to Cuba one day so he could be buried there. But you have to get out of this rut. You can't go on like this."

"Oh, Roberto, don't say that…"

"I have to say it. I'm speaking to you as a father would to his daughter. You've always lived your life for others. It's time to love yourself, Lauri. Travel. Make a new home for yourself. Do something you've always wanted to do. Write. Plant a garden. Live, Lauri, live it up. You're still young, and very attractive, and such a nice person, and you deserve it.

You deserve to be happy because you've never had the chance, right?"

For the first time since the accident, I cried. I wept while Roberto hugged me and stroked my back with the same tenderness of a father and a mother at the same time.

"Go ahead, *mija,* cry. What you need to do is have a good cry. But then you have to promise me that later on you're going to do what I say."

∾

Dear Lauri,

It was so great to see you again. I hope the trip was enjoyable for you as well. Looking back on our days in school, that young girl that I remember so well has grown into such a complete woman: beautiful, intelligent, kind. I've thought about you so often since our recent lunch date. I'd love to see you again. I occasionally travel to Latin America and I could arrange a layover in Miami, if you would like me to. Let me know what you think. Meanwhile, if you come to New York, don't forget to let me know.

A big hug and a kiss,
Gastón

∾

After I received his letter, I read it just once and then placed it in the back of a desk drawer.

Gastón and I had been schoolmates when we were kids. We both liked to write, and in high school we had worked together on the school paper. We had stayed in touch while in exile, but we hadn't seen each other for years. Barely a few weeks after Robertico's death, I had to travel to New York—where he was living now—for a conference on Spanish in the United States. We caught up with each other, and he asked me out for lunch. I don't know how it happened, but we wound up in bed. He was very caring and affectionate, and when it was time to say goodbye he told me:

"When we are faced with our own mortality, we have to celebrate that we're alive and embrace life. It's a natural instinct. You shouldn't feel guilty. After all, I was the one who took advantage of the situation because I think that I've been in love with you since we were kids..."

I avoided reliving that afternoon in my mind for some time but, now that I've broken down the very walls that I myself had constructed, I went back and re-read Gastón's letter and decided to give him a call.

"It turns out that I'm heading to Buenos Aires in two weeks and I have a layover in Miami. I'll work it where I can spend the night, and that way we can go out to eat... I'll give you a call as soon as I know the exact date," he told me.

Over the next twelve months Gastón managed to come through Miami a dozen times. We would always go out to eat at the same French restaurant in Coral Gables, and then we would head to his hotel. I think during those few nights with him I became more aware of my own sexuality than I had during the entire time I was married. I felt like I didn't have any inhibitions. I could reveal my fantasies to him...and even make them come true, like when we bathed ourselves in champagne. I would have never dreamed of doing anything like that with Robertico. Gastón was a man of the world who had travelled everywhere. He had been married three times and hadn't been faithful to any of his wives.

"You know I've been looking for you for a long time," he told me.

The last thing I needed was to get involved with a womanizer. I also understood that sometimes things happen without you realizing what's going on. I knew, however, that I wasn't in love with Gastón. I didn't feel jealous when I thought about what he might be doing when we weren't together, and when he told me every once in a while about some sexual escapade that he had recently had, far from hurting me, it actually aroused me. I looked forward to each one of our encounters, his elegance, the sex, all of it. It was good for me. I knew he was incapable of hurting me. The fact that he didn't live in the same city was also an advantage. I just didn't want things to get too complicated. So, the day he spoke to me about how we should get married, I decided I should be frank with him:

"Gastón, you're so good to me…but I don't want to get married…at least, not right now, not with you, not with anybody…"

"I don't think you love me, Lauri."

"Don't say that."

"You don't love me the same way I love you."

"Maybe…"

After that he began to visit less frequently until finally he stopped arranging stopovers in Miami altogether.

An invitation to convene a reunion of "all sectors that constitute the Cuban people" was issued this past Thursday in Havana by Gustavo Arcos Bergnes—Secretary General of the Cuban Committee for Human Rights.

"Our hope is to bring about in a civilized, honest, and respectful manner a gathering of Cubans in which all distinct schools of thought, both within and outside of Cuba, are invited," urged Arcos in a document delivered by telephone and recorded in Miami by pro-human rights activists.

After debating Gustavo Arcos Bergnes' proposal to convene with the Cuban government, the fifty-three organizations—all of which are comprised of exiles—agreed to respect the position of the "Cuban Freedom Fighters" but not to include them in the discussion.

Speaking on behalf of all of the exile organizations, the document issued by the Cuban Patriotic Summit added "A monologue with the dictator is impossible."

Previously, in December, 1989, a similar document had been sent to the National Assembly for the People's Power in which the leaders of the Cuban Committee for Human Rights called for a national dialogue. With the same purpose in mind, Arcos sent a personal letter directly to Castro. There was no response in either case.

(El Nuevo Herald 8–15 June 1990)

∽

The whole business of waiting for months, all the illusions and apprehensions, wondering constantly whether it's a boy or a girl—because the parents, despite the advantages of modern science, decided to wait and not find out the sex beforehand—the question of picking out strollers and diapers, trying to guess on what day he or she will be born, who the baby is going to look like…and then, so suddenly, that little bundle that the nurses bring in, with his round little head barely visible, and my heart skips a beat, and a wave of love overcomes me and floods my heart and warmly reaches all the way to my eyes which well up with tears—pleasant tears of gratitude, of love, and of astonishment before the miracle of life.

Tyler was born on December 31st, 1992. It doesn't seem strange to me to be a grandmother, but I can't believe that Pedro Pablo is a father! It seems like it was just yesterday that Johnny and I were watching *The Millionaire* in that tiny apartment when I went into labor.

As with everything in exile, even the sweetest moments can leave a sour taste. For those Cubans who die outside of Cuba, it hurts; but the same is true for the ones who are not born there. How can you nurture a love for Cuba in an infant? How am I going to make sure he learns Spanish when he has an American mother and is going to be surrounded by English? If it was so difficult with my own kids, what in the world is it going to be like with my grandkids? I understand that this is a great country and, of course, I'm appreciative…but it hurts me to see that my kids and grandchildren have not grown up as Cubans. But, then, what are they? It's clear to me that Pedro Pablo and Bobby Jr. aren't really Americans…even though they've pledged allegiance to a different flag in school, although they speak English without an accent, even if for them Cuba only exists in their imagination.

Susan puts Tyler in my arms, my first grandchild. I think back and reminisce about my mother, about Mamá Luya, about Adela, and I begin to sing softly,

Señora Santa Ana
why weeps the baby boy?
'Tis a tasty apple
that gives him so much joy.

I will give you one.
I will give you two.
One for the baby
and another just for you.

Not one do I want.
Not for two do I pine.
My lost one I want,
the one that is mine.

❧

According to dissident and diplomatic sources, thousands of Cubans shouting anti-government slogans fought police with sticks and stones all along the Havana Malecón on Friday, August 5th. According to estimates by correspondents, twenty to thirty thousand Cubans gathered along the four-kilometer-long Malecón before the incident erupted. They were apparently drawn there by rumors that a fleet had left the United States and was coming to pick up anyone who wanted to leave Cuba.

Some hours after the riots, Fidel Castro indicated that he would allow another Mariel if the United States did not punish those who fled the Island by sea.

During what has constituted one of the gravest moments for the Castro government, thousands of demonstrators attacked and threw stones at the windows of several stores that catered to foreign tourists and a hotel near the Bay of Havana. The police opened fire, leaving several people seriously wounded.

Hundreds of people came down Galiano and Neptuno Streets breaking store windows and shouting "Freedom! Freedom!"

Rafael Dausá, spokesman for the Cuban Interests Section in Washington,

D.C. roundly denied that such an incident had occurred. "Havana is completely calm," he insisted. "These allegations are entirely false."

(*El Nuevo Herald* 6 August 1994: A1)

∽

No matter how much I try not to, I've become obsessed with the whole issue. I believe that people have a tendency to flee because of something much deeper than fear of political repression. Cubans are merely trying to save themselves and their family members because the concept of "nationhood" has disappeared. The Revolution has always tried to be synonymous with Cuba, while Castro himself has been viewed as the homeland. But *that* Revolution failed. The future they promised never arrived and it's been a complete failure. Things never got better and, in fact, they've only gotten worse. Communism has been toppled. There's no longer any ideological justification for it. The only thing they can offer is "Socialism or Death." And it's a thousand times better to run the risk of death searching for the "American dream" than it is fighting for a nation where you can't even find a bicycle, a plate of hot food, and certainly not hope.

The ones that are fleeing from Cuba these days on make-shift rafts, or the *balseros* as they're called, don't have any intention of ever going back. They don't dream of bringing about democracy, or liberty, nor a free-market economy. They can't understand what it means to dream about a better future for the nation because for them Cuba began when Castro headed up into the Sierra Maestra Mountains and not like it did for us when Father Varela taught us how to think. There's neither a plan for continuity nor a concept of a statehood that goes beyond the Revolution in time and space. The only way out is on a raft. You have to do whatever you can to escape from a country whose head honcho has threatened to sink it into the sea.

And exile? Has nostalgia and distance managed to distort our recollection of Cuba? Has perhaps geography clouded our vision? We're missing our roots, our land, our countryside. We've idealized the past, and we're not exactly certain about the present. How can we construct the future then? Even the ones to come in this latest wave of events have lost contact with the country's reality.

No one knows how this current crisis of the *balseros* will end. It seems like all avenues are closed, and any potential solution is complicated. Cuba, like the rafters themselves, is adrift and ultimately may drown or be eaten by the sharks.

There are times I stay up all night long thinking about such things.

∽

At the 17th hole of the golf course at what was the most tranquil military base of the United States, a group of shirtless rafters play baseball to pass the time while they await the news that will determine their fate.

The individuals present are not limited to one sector or color of society nor solely one socio-political ideology. Instead, one finds a microcosm of Cubans made up of all social and ideological stances, men and women, transients and laborers, and—above all—young people who protest and throw up their hands whenever it is suggested that they are economic refugees.

"We wouldn't go back even if they promised us ham, which we haven't seen in thirty years."

The majority share the same tent and two enemies: an old one, Fidel Castro, and of course a new one, President Bill Clinton, whom they blame for their precarious situation.

(*El Nuevo Herald* 12 September 1994: A1)

∽

I listen everyday to the list of names on the radio of the *balseros* that they've picked up out in the ocean. It's bizarre to think that any of my family would come over that way, but still I welcome every one of them who makes it.

The other day I received a surprising call from the newspaper where I've published some articles over the past few years. They're sending an investigative team down to Guantánamo to do a story on the refugees and at the last minute one of the reporters got sick. So, they offered me the job and, needless to say, I jumped at it and immediately went out and bought rolls of film for my camera.

Thursday, October 20th, 4:45 a.m. My colleagues arrive at the house. I make everyone a Cuban coffee. We take off for the Ft. Lauderdale airport.

The Fandango airlines plane is a twin engine twelve-seater. They serve coffee and doughnuts before we take off. During the flight, it's unbearably cold. Very cloudy. Looks like snow. Below, all you can see is the ocean. I think about the *balseros* on their rafts. We make a stop at Exuma to get some gas. We're still an hour and a half away. I go over my list in my head to make sure I brought everything I need: tape recorder, camera, notebook, pen. I go over my notes, the places I'd like to see, the questions I intend to ask. It doesn't really seem like I'm heading to Cuba. I'm just going to an American military base. Still, it makes me think back on what it was like leaving thirty-five years ago and it makes me shudder. As I've done so many times over the years I picture in my mind what my room looked like when I was a little girl and the exact image of the way it was the day I left it. There on the bed I can see my prized Cuban geography book and my cute straw sunhat with its pink bow, both of them symbols of the country and the genteel life style I left behind.

All of a sudden, there's a lot of fuss:

"Look, on the right, you can see it, there it is, over there..."

At first, I don't see anything, and then a few seconds later you can clearly see the outline through the clouds. The eastern most point of Cuba, Maisí. A rush of emotions overtakes me. I've dreamed about this country for over three decades. Its constant presence has been at the center of my sleepless hours, my rage, my most intimate conflicts, my entire life. Over the years I've wondered if Cuba really existed or if it was just a figment of my imagination, an idea, a myth. And, now, here it is, right in front of my eyes. The Island. I reminisce about all the loved ones I would have liked to have shared this moment with. And more than anything, it hits me at that moment that Mamá Luya and my father are buried down below. It dawns on me that my mother, and all my family, breathe the air below this sky. But there's no way for them to know that I'm here, that I'm so close and yet so far. Is there any way they could feel my presence? Is it possible that the wind might carry my thoughts?

As the plane gets closer, the silhouette of the mountains and the long coastline of the eastern province become better defined. The image makes it seem like Cuba is opening up her arms to me. I take photo after photo. I try to contain myself, but tears stream down my cheeks. I can't explain what I'm feeling. The bay clearly comes into sight. Just like other times when I've felt happiest, I feel like I could die.

The plane touches down on Cuban soil, and they take us over to the ferry. I can't describe the shade of blue that you see in the water and the sky. If only I were a painter... How is it possible that everyone around me right now is oblivious to this miracle I'm living? I'm back in Cuba!

As we come closer to the base, I can make out the American flag. Now I understand better than ever the pain of that Cuban poet who a century ago said that he returned "from that distant shore with a sad and heavy heart" when he found another country's flag flying that wasn't his.

The first thing we see is about five hundred or so Haitians that they're sending back. Before they get them on board, they take off their black bracelet that marks them as refugees. Almost barefoot and in tattered rags, they stagger along with their belongings, with their kids, and with an uncertain look about the future on their face. The Captain told us that they pray and sing a lot. It's not a joyous return but a return nonetheless. When will it be our turn to go back?

We finally arrive at the encampments. We see the small school, the clinic, even an improvised art gallery. They tell me that they have a mayor and an interpreter. Some of them get together to study English; others, to study the Bible. Every one of them has something to add. They want the world to know that they're a respectable wave of immigrants, that there are a lot of professionals, that they're *political* and not economic refugees. They're well kept, articulate, and respectful. All of them want to send messages to their relatives. And they want us to tell their stories of frustration and courage. They also ask us what we think is going to happen to them, if they will ever make it into the U.S.

In an improvised wooden crib, a small baby is crying, and I ask her mother what her name is:

"She doesn't have one."

I'm shocked.

"My husband says that we're not going to name her until the very last Cuban gets out of here," explains the mother.

The woman picks up her baby daughter and cradles her. Her milk has stained her blouse around the nipples. She confides to me in a whisper:

"I call her Consuelito because that's what she is, "my little comfort." If it weren't for her…"

It brings to mind my own grandson. He has so much! I try to encourage her:

"You'll see. You'll be out of here in no time."

And I hide my face behind my camera so she won't see me crying.

Later in the night, after the balseros have set sail, the world that flickers behind them in the distance changes forever.

As soon as they cast off, their neighbors go to their homes and steal whatever they can: televisions, beds, sofas, refrigerators.

The government gets involved only later, informed by the neighbors who keep a watchful eye out and who consider it their obligation to report them missing. The authorities place a paper seal over the door which declares that the house is now property of the state.

And the families who remain behind find themselves in a nightmarish labyrinth: innumerable nights of lying awake wondering if their sons and husbands have survived, and innumerable days of trying to combat the reality of having lost their loved ones, with less money each day to buy the essentials, with less food in the governmental stores, and with less hope to help them survive.

"Who knows how many marriages have been destroyed?" remarks Mayda whose husband, Miguel, took off this past Wednesday in a make-shift raft. "And how many more wives will have to be left behind before this is all over?"

(*El Nuevo Herald* 13 September 1994: A1 and A6)

Not long after Robertico's death the political organizations that he belonged to began inviting me to their gatherings. They wanted to be kind and honor his memory and for me to represent him as his widow. But before long I realized that it was just a token gesture and that they weren't interested in the least in anything that I had to say. The mere suggestion, for example, that maybe it would be a good strategy to lift the embargo provoked a violent reaction by some of the leaders. It was like waving a red flag in front of a bull.

Little by little I began distancing myself from them. Other groups popped up however who said they were interested in establishing a dialogue, national reconciliation, a referendum, and negotiations and the like. They started gaining a lot of support and everybody began talking about "a post-Castro Cuba." Leaders from all over the world have made visits to Cuba to talk with Castro about theories for a transition, but nothing has come of it. On the contrary, he keeps on responding with the same old thing, "the Special Period." Every day there are more blackouts, less gasoline, and less food. People are literally dying on their bicycles. They're wasting away more and more all the time. An epidemic of neuropathy has hit the Island. Mamá has almost gone blind. I send her everything I can. My arms hurt just from wanting to hug her so much. But then I hear Robertico's voice in my head:

"Lauri, promise me that you'll never go back to Cuba as long as Castro's in power."

I can't explain these things to my sister over the telephone. How could she understand?

The regime goes on. Tourists, dissidents, Fidel, the Church, Robaina, prostitution, Raúl Castro, the American dollar, Alarcón, experimental capitalism, the Pope, baseball, Brothers to the Rescue, Cuban music, Madeleine Albright, academics, the European Union: the headlines are full of news from and about Cuba, but the years go by and nothing happens.

Menchu has finally decided to come. And here I am at the airport, standing in front of the gate, with my heart about to leap out every time I get a glimpse of one of the passengers coming through the doors, searching for her anxiously among the crowd, waiting to finally embrace my sister, my twin sister whose life is a mystery to me, my sister that I haven't seen since that July afternoon when I left my country.

CHAPTER ELEVEN
Then…Give Me Death!

LÁZARO COULDN'T BELIEVE IT. We piled in the old broken down Lada and went down 42nd Street to 5th Avenue until we could see the huge eye-sore of the Soviet Embassy. It was true. There it was, waving in the breeze, silhouetted by our blue Caribbean sky—the Czarist flag. The red flag with the familiar hammer and sickle had been taken down.

It was December 26th, 1991.

When I look back and try to remember, I can see now that things had been in motion for a long time. I can't pinpoint the date exactly. Maybe it was the fallout from the Mariel boatlift, or maybe that night when he got so drunk after they shot Ochoa. I think the letter that Tania brought back from Ernesto saying that he was not coming back to Cuba really hurt him. Even though I wound up tearing it into pieces, I read it so many times that I remember it almost word for word.

Dear Aunt Menchu and Uncle Lázaro,

I am writing to you two because I know you'll understand. I think I speak for a lot of us in my generation, those of us who were born with the Revolution, with the Bay of Pigs, Hurricane Flora, Socialism and the rallying cry of "Homeland or Death" on our tongues. Our parents didn't baptize us. We were raised atheists. It was only our grandmothers who in secret would whisper a prayer for us and show us some engraving or illustration of the Virgin. (Did you know that Tania can say the "Our Father" in Latin?) We were the results of a lack of contraception, the outcome of a zealous desire to bring new beings into the world for the Fatherland and, in some cases, the products of love. We grew up with the first phase of the embargo. We were kids when the singers and ballerinas were first sent to the fields, when the homosexuals along with all the Protestant and Catholic seminarians were catalogued as social deviants and sent off without exception to the UMAP labor camps where they tried to make them into "useful men for the Fatherland." We were fed peas and croquettes. The shouts of "We shall overcome" hung in the air. Our fathers—and sometimes our mothers too—would get dressed in their olive green uniforms, and they would leave us to fend for ourselves while they went off for guard duty. So often our meals were cold because we couldn't heat them since we were always either missing parents or lacking electricity. We were Pioneers. We repeated "Let's be like Che..." over and over. We listened to long and tedious speeches by the Commander-in-Chief in which he told us how fortunate we were to live in "the very best country in the world" and "the most democratic" one, where human rights were thoroughly respected, where we had "the resplendent future of Communism" ahead of us. When we were little we didn't have chocolates or candy. Instead our only taste of sweetness came from the sugar cane our parents gave us when we went along with them on that famous "ten million ton" harvest, which as we know didn't amount to much. We didn't know what ham was unless it was the artificial kind, the one that showed up when we were teenagers along with the Soviet jellies and Bulgarian juices. We often travelled in the back of pickups with our parents to go do our volunteer work. We attended their so-called "country schools." They gave us scholarships. We came to know the spoiled little "daddy's boys" with their fancy clothes and tape players that they used to listen to the Beatles. They made us cut our hair and wear baggy khakis and work clothes. They drafted the guys into the military and made the girls work in the FCW. All of us had to join the CDR, and the most promising ones signed up for the Young Communist League. We often had to bathe and shampoo our hair with detergent and rain water. We didn't get more than three toys a year, and even then we only got what was left over when it came our turn. We didn't know what Christmas was, or what a real vacation felt like. We only had the Malecón, our famous esplanade where we could catch some sun, kiss a girl, pick at a guitar and play some songs by Silvio or Pablito, and where we could chat about what might be out there beyond Cuba and our ration books. Our classes would always start and end in the same way, and they constantly followed the same "Marxist-Leninist" methodology. There wasn't room for impertinent questions, which could come at a high price. One day, after various classmates disappeared, we learned that they had gone off to the North, and we never heard anything else about them again. They told us that all of us were equal, and yet they made us throw eggs and insults at anybody who didn't think like we did. We went from middle school to high school, and although we made it to college we didn't get to study what we wanted, rather "we chose the field they assigned us." The others—the "internationalists"—went off on missions to Africa or Nicaragua. Many have gone to war. Sometimes they didn't come back. All of the spoiled "daddy's boys" usually settle down in Mexico or Canada or Spain where they spend their exile in luxury, but when they feel the slightest bit nostalgic they come back to the Island for a quick fix but they still live the good life. Others of us studied abroad in the Soviet Union or Eastern Europe. We got a taste of different worlds and, after that, Cuba seemed so small, like a prison. We read Orwell, and the Island reminded us of an 'animal farm.' We understood Marx from a different angle, and to us it seemed that the way he was adapted in the New World distorted what he was really saying. Moreover, after we found out about the crimes that Stalin had committed it gave us chills. In the end we wound up repeating that same prayer that grandmother had taught us.

Well, guys, I better go. I don't know what path my life will take, or if we'll ever get to see each other again. I know that some door will open for me. I can't thank you enough for everything you've taught me. I always think of you fondly. I know that you two are good and idealistic people. I just don't know how they could have robbed you of the Revolution.

A big hug,
Ernesto

When we finished reading the letter, Lázaro looked at me and asked: "Do you think they stole the Revolution from us, Menchu?"

I didn't know what to tell him.

✎

I know deep down that all of you understand very well the moment we are living in, the dangers that confront us, the threats that surround us. I can see that you have understood very well the unwholesome happiness of those who think that the hour is at hand to take revenge against the work of the Revolution, against the Revolution itself and its Revolutionaries. You recognize the insalubrious hope of those who believe that they will be able to subdue us and bring our nation to its knees, those who imagine that it could be possible to oblige us to live once again within a repugnant capitalistic society.

I ask those countries, those others who present different societal and democratic models, models that they wish to impose on us: what type of participation and democracy do they offer? In our case, the young Pioneers have gathered here at this conference to discuss a variety of problems with the Party and with the government. Workers too have the opportunity to meet and confer with the Party and the government, as do farmers, women, or neighborhood organizations. So I ask you, in those countries do students get the opportunity to meet periodically to discuss a wide range of problems with members of its government, its administration, with members of the State? And not only are you here to discuss the specific problems that interest students, but those that concern the entire country and the whole nation.

(Fidel Castro 6 December 1991)

∞

Another turning point for Lázaro was when they made all of those changes in the media. *Granma* became the only daily newspaper. The rest started out coming out weekly, and *Bohemia* was cut down to a format of just sixty-four pages. Some of the cultural sections that Lázaro had contributed to recently were completely eliminated. He must have gotten home early that day because when I came home from work he was already sitting there in his chair, out back on the patio, with his bottle of rum. I figured he wanted to be alone so I barely said hello to him, but quite the opposite, he wouldn't stop talking.

"Can you imagine, Menchu, that *Workers* is actually defending the idea that we should establish some type of joint corporations with foreign capitalists? I'm sure they don't really think that, that is if they're still allowed to think. That must be the word that has come down from the top. On the one hand, we say that we'll go down with the Island before we ever give in, even if we're the last bastion of Socialism now that Poland and Czechoslovakia are selling out. And in the spirit of our independence we always say 'our country will always be an eternal Baraguá.' But then at the same time—and I have it from a reliable source—an official high up in the party is going to get with Salinas who's going to ask the Americans to lighten up. And don't forget, the Spaniards have already started building up hotels in Varadero. Why did we fight a Revolution, Menchu? Just so we could go back to capitalism? You'll see…in a few years this is all going to be worse than in '58…you'll see."

"Lázaro, the world has changed…there's a new generation…full of young people who…"

"Yeah, young people who shit on us, just like in that art exhibit—if you can call it art—the one where this supposed 'artist' dropped his drawers, took out a copy of *Granma,* and literally shit on it."

"But there are others who…"

"Yeah, like the guy who's going around saying that the Party didn't bring about the Revolution rather it was the other way around…as if the Party didn't have a universal dimension that existed well before all this…"

"Lázaro, maybe Marxism's fine in theory, but maybe it doesn't work in everyday life."

"Don't say that. What's happened is that they don't know how to apply its principles correctly, and we've had so many foreign enemies."

"But it hasn't worked in the Soviet Union or…really anywhere… I think it's just the opposite, that what's happening is probably good for the Revolution, the Cuban Revolution, as green as our palm trees, like Fidel used to say."

"Those were different times, Menchu."

"Yeah, now that we're in the 'Special Period' we're in peace time, or is it that we're at war…who knows, or maybe we've come all the way to the evacuation plan they're talking about, 'Option Zero' as they say…

yeah, the zero of everything…everyday there are more blackouts and less to eat… Mamá is so skinny… At least Lauri sends her vitamins."

"Ochoa's dead and Juan Escalona, of all people, President of the Popular Assembly?" he exclaimed, completely oblivious to what I had just said as if I were thinking to myself.

"Don't talk so loud, Lázaro…"

"The Nobel Peace Prize to Gorbachev? At what price? A few weeks ago the Soviets and the Americans made a joint declaration saying that Iraq should withdraw its troops from Kuwait…"

"I don't know what we're going to find to eat today…"

"And then there are the priests who, little by little, are sneaking around, leaving their cards and handing out their propaganda…"

"Lázaro, you shouldn't drink so much…"

But he kept on drinking, not only that night, but every night. Sometimes he would sit there for hours in silence, with a lost look, drinking one shot after another until he'd finally fall asleep. Other times, he felt like talking…and he'd ramble about the debate between *Granma* and the UNEAC or whether or not certain firms had been financed entirely with foreign capital, about how *Granma* had said that we're an underdeveloped agrarian society and it was true, about how the "Ready Response Brigades" were like Machado's secret police, how if they wanted to remove the Soviet troops they should go ahead and do it since what good did they do anyway, about how they hadn't discussed the things they really should have discussed in the IVth Congress …

At first I tried to reason with him, but it was useless. He was obsessed. It became impossible to hide things from the neighbors. He wasn't careful about what he said, not even with Maruja. He's lucky that she's such a softy and didn't turn him in. Even she tried to talk some sense into him:

"Lázaro, these are difficult times, but the Revolution has brought about a lot of good. Look at me, just a country girl from Morón who has become a Head Nurse… I even gave a son to the Revolution, and I'm not complaining. Better times are coming. You have to think about Tania and the grandkids you're going to have one day. That's who we're working for, for the future."

"Maruja, you don't get it. The future is already here."

We started growing apart. I became more resentful of having to take care of all the daily struggles out and about, while he sat at home on the patio, drinking rum and feeling sorry for himself. I couldn't stand the smell of his rum-drenched breath, his sweaty clothes, his raspy voice, the way he shuffled his feet. The few times he came looking for me to make love, I turned him away. I was lucky that he would usually just fall asleep right away. It was the worst time of my life.

∽

If we are willing to do all this, we do it all as free men and free women, masters of our country and not as slaves. If we are willing to put up with sacrifices, it is for a greater good and not to live life humiliated and exploited. If we are willing to make sacrifices for one, two, three, five years, we do it because we know that we stand for the Revolution, Socialism, Justice, and the Future, and what we strive for is to preserve the right to that future.

And to those weaklings, cowards, and those sellouts who never felt the kiss of our country in their soul or the idea of justice in their mind or in their heart, to those who say that the struggle is a lost cause, to those we must once again say, the only lost cause, the only thing that destroys all causes, is not to have a country, not to have the Revolution, and not to have Socialism.

There remains no hope for the one who would give up on his country, the Revolution, and Socialism. Whereas we will defend that very hope, the one bestowed upon us by the Nation, by the Revolution, and by Socialism, with our last drop of blood. We prefer death over giving up on the Revolution and Socialism because the alternative is moral death, the most horrid of all deaths.

(Fidel Castro 6 December 1991)

∽

One morning Lázaro got up, shaved, took a bath, put on some clean clothes, and said rather bluntly:

"I've been a coward. I'm not going to drink anymore. I'm going to take a different path."

At first I didn't believe him, but as time went by I saw that the man that I had fallen in love with was coming back to me. He was once again considerate and tender with me. He was balanced and realistic with what he said. He was courteous and well-mannered towards Mamá. I even noticed that he was making a conscious effort to get closer to his daughter. But I wasn't convinced. I knew him too well, and it seemed like he was hiding something. It even dawned on me that maybe he was getting ready to take off on a raft like so many others. He had that look on his face, that look of veiled enthusiasm that he always had when he had his hands on some project that inspired him.

But I never could have imagined what was about to happen.

My brother Pedro called me real early one morning. Lázaro had been to see him, and he seemed to be acting strangely. He was talking as if he were trying to say goodbye. He had asked if he could stop by and leave some papers that he wanted him to have. God, why didn't I go with him too?

When I got to the house in El Vedado, by brother told me that Lázaro had just left that very second.

"He gave me this envelope and he told me not to open it unless something happened to him. He wouldn't stop for me, but maybe we can still catch him."

Just at that moment we heard a noise and turned around. Through the window that looks out onto the back patio we saw Lázaro at that very instant that he pulled the trigger of the gun that he was holding to his temple. He fell dead a few feet from that passageway where we used to hide and kiss when we were young. His suicide note was short:

Forgive me Menchu. I've tried as hard as I could these past months not to leave you with bad memories. I just can't do it anymore. We are not and never will be like Che. We'll never be able to build the Cuba we had dreamed of for our daughter. I don't know if the Revolution betrayed us or if we betrayed it. But, there's one thing I'm sure of, I was always loyal to you.

Lázaro
January 1, 1992, "The Year of Fire"

∽

According to the Annual Bureau of Statistics, the number of suicides in Cuba has risen from 1,011 in 1970 to 2,220 in 1989. Without significant fluctuations, the latter statistic points to a rate of 21.1 suicides for every 100,000 inhabitants. According to the Director of the National Program for the Prevention of Suicide, for every action realized there are ten to fifteen failed attempts to take one's life. Suicide now constitutes one of the top ten causes of death in Cuba.

(Bohemia 83:5, 29)

∽

I go to the *bodega*—or what's left of what used to be a *bodega*—or an old supermarket, and all I see are empty, dirty shelves, long faces, and hundreds of people poorly dressed—old folks with their hair undone, young people on bicycles, tired workers, even children with empty bags—all of them waiting for the arrival of "something," anything, but it never arrives… The famous "Special Nutritional Plan" is like God: everyone speaks about it, but no one's ever seen it. The average Cuban has lost everything except his sense of humor. As for our great plantain products brought about by a new, intensive irrigation system "Micro Yet," we only see them on the cover of *Bohemia*—which is becoming more and more scarce due to the lack of paper—or on TV when there isn't a power outage.

Last week the last burner on our electric stove went out. Everybody in the neighborhood is cooking with wood, that is, if you can find it. Some are burning their furniture, the window frames. There's an eighty-nine day backlog for delivering gas canisters. And it's almost impossible to find gas for sale out on the street and when you do it's usually gone before sunup. To get hot water, I have to rely on a neighbor to heat some for me. At least that way, Mamá can have some hot soup or rice, even if it's just once a day. I worry about her more than anything else. I've lost sixty pounds, and as for Mamá, she refuses to tell me how much she weighs now. I look at myself in the mirror and I only see some foreboding bags under my eyes and yellow skin. The doctors say that an "8" for your hemoglobin count is high, given the circumstances...

"Try not to lose any more weight," they advise, but they don't prescribe a special diet.

On the street corners, small aimless groups come together. Each day there are more people without a job—many of the factories have closed down due to the lack of raw materials and other resources. Public transportation is disappearing given the lack of gasoline, parts, and tires. I bought a bicycle but, like a lot of others, I gave it up. The effort it took to go long distances drained my last bit of energy. Besides, it's dangerous. The other day the son of a friend of mine from work was killed. He was nineteen. He was going along hanging on to the back of the bus when he smashed his head against an electric pole on 23rd Street.

The buildings are in the same condition as the people. Houses go unpainted. Many have been shored up for years. Just walking down the sidewalks in Old Havana means risking your life. Every so often a balcony tumbles to the sidewalk. Then you have the mudslides during the rainy season. They don't even make it into the papers anymore. They're so common they're not newsworthy.

When our neighbor across the street, Gregorio, started losing weight, he went to see the doctor at the clinic. He explained to him that his feet were swollen and that he felt like a ball was swelling up on the left side of his stomach.

"It's nothing. Drink some water with sugar and get some rest."

Gregorio asked them to take some x-rays.

"There's no reason to do so. I'm sorry," they answered.

He insisted so much that they finally gave in and wrote an order for x-rays, but he would have to find a place that could take them. After two months they diagnosed him with cancer. Six weeks later, at only forty-five years old, he passed away. He left behind a small apartment that he hadn't finished paying for—he only needed 150 pesos more—and a small tape-recorder with a cassette that his mother couldn't bring herself to listen to.

The whole neighborhood turned out for the funeral. Many of us saw ourselves reflected in the face of our neighbor, laid out before us in a gray 'one size fits all' casket. We couldn't even bring him an arrangement. There weren't any flowers that day.

"He was so young to come down with cancer," everyone lamented.

"That young man starved to death," Mamá declared. No one argued with her.

∽

Currently in Cuba the average life expectancy from birth is estimated at 75 years.

(*Bohemia* 83:7, 18)

∽

I walk for blocks under the unforgiving sun in search of something to eat. Even the famous so-called "Taíno" soup—that soup that's made up of food that's been thrown away—has become a scarce commodity. Eggs are in short supply. Pizzas—when you can find them—don't come with cheese. Hamburgers—called these days "McCastros"—are getting thinner and greasier and yet the lines to buy them are getting longer. About the only thing you can find are popsicles made from lemon, grapefruit, or orange syrup. That's not to say you can choose which flavor. There's only one available at a time.

If it weren't for what we can get every once in a while on the black market with the money that Ricardo and Lauri send us, we wouldn't be alive. And even then you have to be careful. The other day they were selling breaded steaks that turned out to be mop cloths that had been convincingly wrapped in grounded crackers. I'm lucky I didn't buy any. Pedritín has good connections and gets along better. He always shares with Tania. In that sense, he's a really good kid. He even brings us something occasionally. Even then, there are times I think I'm going to faint or maybe even die. Maybe that would be better. At times the smallest thing, a smell, a phrase, an image reminds me of Lázaro, and it hits me right in the heart like a dagger. But I don't want to remember him, I can't. It hurts too much. And I have to keep on going. I have to survive. Getting up each morning is an act of faith, although I don't know what I have faith in anymore. Maybe in life, life itself.

Cuba was dying…the majority of those born on the Island lived in a state of poverty given that 950,467 found themselves without a profitable occupation.

The tobacco and sugar industries were perishing. The large plantation owners were coming to an end; the lands were passing into the hands of foreigners or were being consolidated into the hands of the few. The tobacco magnates left the country, either in economic or political exile, in search of solutions for the societal issues. The nineteenth century was coming to a close and Cuba was dying…

(*Bohemia* 83:7, 18)

∽

I just passed by a dead dog. It was dirty and gaunt. There are thousands of stray dogs running aimlessly through the streets of Havana. Sometimes they run in packs to protect themselves; others go alone desperately looking for a few scraps. When the Soviets returned home after the collapse of the "real" Socialism, they simply abandoned their cats and dogs. Up until then their pets had lived better than most Cubans, pampered with special food bought at the exclusive diplomatic stores. Since the "Special Period" began, the Cubans too have had to let their own pets loose on the street simply because they didn't have anything to feed them. Others prefer just to put them down. I know a retired professional woman who had five beautiful cats. When she could no longer find any fish, not even on the black market, she asked a veterinarian friend to euthanize them. She buried them right there in her patio and put a rose bush over them. Maybe that's the way to do it. The strays are so hungry and filthy and they have that glassy look in their eyes. Dazed, they meander among the few remaining cars on the street. Every once in a while you hear a squeal, and one of them falls beneath the wheels of a truck or bus crammed with passengers. Someone usually takes pity on it and drags it by the paws or tail, and they throw it into a corner of the sidewalk or in a dumpster where little by little the carcass starts to decompose—they no longer come by for the trash that often. It's such a pathetic end for man's best friend.

The rosebush that the woman planted over the cat's grave also died. There was no way to water it.

∽

Gray, black, chestnut, and roan mares with regal glossy withers and sparkling eyes roam freely. Nature was bountiful to this creature immortalized by poets: its sinewy head, extended neck, high haunches, the slender front legs, and a height between 1.52 and 1.65 meters. They come from pure-blooded

British stock. Their breed began in Cuba in 1918 and by 1943 at least 271 had been born, but beginning with the Revolution their existence took on new meaning.

(*Bohemia,* 84:31, 22–24)

∽

Ever since she came down with dengue fever, Mamá has had problems with her vision. Recently she's been complaining again about not being able to see. She hasn't been able to see well enough to sew, or knit, or even read for some time. She certainly can't write to Lauri and Ricardo so she dictates the letters to me. Even the images on the TV have become blurry for her. What keeps her entertained the most is listening to radio programs or visiting with anyone who drops by, especially relatives. Without a doubt, her favorite is Tania. That girl puzzles me. I can never figure out for certain what she's thinking. She barely shed a tear at her father's funeral. But Mamá is so loving with her, and anyway, it makes me happy to see them together. Those are the two things I love the most in the world.

I thought Mamá needed some new glasses and that maybe my brother or sister could bring some new ones, but they've diagnosed her with neuropathy. It's a vitamin deficiency that attacks the eyes, and since hers were already bad… And with her being so undernourished… I've learned that a lot of people here have it. The doctor at the clinic told me it's almost an epidemic.

At least it's easier these days to call. I immediately got in touch with Lauri and asked her to send the vitamins. She always replies more quickly than Ricardo when we need something. I don't like to have to ask, but when it's for Mamá, I don't hesitate. I can't believe that she might go blind.

∽

(Havana) – Cuba is the leading manufacturer of generic pharmaceuticals in Latin America and plans to increase its technological capacities, according to the Director of the Center for Medicinal Research and Development.

Currently there are close to nine hundred pharmaceutical products that have been developed in local laboratories, and new plans are underway for the production of insulin and chemical reactors, contraceptive pills, and a production unit for hemo-derivatives.

Among the most singular contributions are the hemo-derivatives, given the nation's capacity for a strong infrastructure that relies on voluntary donations and a network of blood banks capable of processing normal and hyper immune plasma.

(Bohemia 85:23, 25)

The lights go out so frequently that everyone says that rather than blackouts we have illuminations. The heat is unbearable. People sleep on the balconies. I sometimes have to put a mattress out on the patio. And the food and transportation situation aren't getting any better. What the people want is to leave. They've started building rafts right there in the very patios of their houses, in plain sight for everyone to see. They've even said good riddance to anybody who wants to go. They're no longer called worms, or scum, or lumpen like they were back in 1960 and 1980. Now they just want them to leave.

Entire families are taking off, everybody from the old folks to the babies in their arms. Some of them even take their pets. Other times four or five kids from the neighborhood will decide to join together. There are other cases where people beg strangers to take them along. In the same small raft you get people who until that very moment had never seen each other. Some study the tides and the right hour to depart, but others take off as soon as they get things together. Many times you'll see people saying goodbye, especially the women and kids waving from the beach until the makeshift boat disappears over the horizon.

I look out over the water, and I wonder if they're scared or not. I wonder what it's like to spend the night at sea, listening to the only sound you can hear, the ocean's heavy breath, without another horizon other than the darkness. How can you make sense of the heartbreaking irony of dying of thirst when you're surrounded by water? And the torment of seeing the raft surrounded by sharks, sensing their razor-sharp teeth tearing into your skin! I can't imagine how frightening it must be for your loved ones! How many of them will never make it? It seems like you'd have to be crazy to launch out into the sea…especially in an inner-tube… crazy, absolutely crazy… Or maybe you're crazy to stay in Cuba during this long, interminable, scorching, and exhausting summer of 1994.

If we did not belong to a nation of giants, if we did not have young people like you, the fate that would await us would be to become another Puerto Rico, or another Miami, which they say is one of the worst centers of crime, prostitution, and drugs in the world. If we did not have a people such as ours, we would lose the Revolution, we would lose Socialism.

(Fidel Castro 6 December 1991)

Five years have gone by, and we survived, but at what price? Just to give the nod to the tourists? Just so we can open up our beaches to them while we close them off from Cubans? Houses are falling apart but there are plenty of resort hotels for the Canadians, Italians, and Spaniards. They come so they can take in the sun and the *mulattas,* to get drunk on our rum and palm trees, to sway their hips to the music or in bed. The prostitutes are everywhere, decent girls who probably go to bed for a pair of jeans or slacks, for a tasty meal, or to go someplace pretty, like one of those locales reserved for the tourists where they can't go with their Cuban boyfriends. There are also men who prostitute themselves. Some young men sell their own bodies, even though they're not really homosexuals. Others sell off their daughters or sisters or even their mother.

But, as is always the case, it's a different story when you're talking about the "daddy's boys." Just like many of the former officials of the military or Ministry of the Interior, they're preparing for a possible return to capitalism. They've already got positions in the new "mixed firms" that are incorporating some basic capitalistic principles. In fact, they're the new capitalists of Socialism. They study English, information technology, principles of marketing; they even travel to Spain, Mexico, or Canada to enroll in special training courses.

Others earn an honorable living. There are many professionals who work as taxi drivers. Everyone wants a job that is somehow related to tourism. It's the only way to obtain dollars. The dollar rules in Cuba. Lázaro was right. If he could only see what Cuba's like today...! You even see people begging on the streets.

Not everybody is begging. Others are fighting with both fists. If they have the room for a small mom-and-pop restaurant, some families have opened *paladares* in their homes. Or if not they make artisan crafts. Still others rent out rooms in their homes to tourists. Some occupy themselves with finding antiques, while others are in charge of selling them, obviously, to the foreigners.

"Those antiques probably belong to people who left," Mamá says reproachingly.

"Oh, woman, that was a long time ago..."

The ones who have it the best are the ones who receive dollars from relatives elsewhere. Or as they say, those who have faith are those who have *F.E.*, or family in the exterior. I can't complain about my brother and sister. There was a time we had grown apart, but now they call often enough, and they send money every two or three months. If it weren't for them, Mamá and I would be bad off since I'm retired now and the two pensions don't amount to anything.

It was right after I retired that Mamá told me:

"You need to go back to Church, Menchu."

"Would you go back with me?"

"I never left."

"What do you mean?"

"I mean that I never stopped believing in God, that I've always prayed, that I rely on my Saints every single minute. I said *novenas* when Lauri and you were pregnant, whenever any of the grandchildren were sick, when Pedritín was in Angola. I pray every night for the ones I love...for those who have passed on...even Lázaro, for Robertico and for Maruja's boy, the poor thing. I mean, after all, we saw him grow up."

I began to attend San Agustín. Seeing those images again from my childhood brought about some type of mysterious reaction even though I didn't know exactly what it was...I felt at home. Maybe I hadn't left God entirely behind me either. Later on I began to work with volunteers who take care of more than four hundred elderly people "adopted" by the Church. They're entirely alone and there's no way they can get by on their ration book. So we usually cook what we can and take food by for them, help them with the washing, or even help them bathe themselves.

"Menchu, as for old folks you already have enough on your plate just dealing with me," Mamá would say from her armchair next to the dining room window where Mamá Luya used to sit.

The priest was an intelligent, cultured old man. He began to lend me books that we would discuss afterwards. Then came the long year of 1998 when we had to get everything ready for the Pope's visit. Those were some good times. We had a purpose, and we had hope. And John Paul II finally arrived. What a glorious day! I can't think of anything that had been that moving for years. I was even able to take Mamá in a wheel chair, and we received communion from the Pope.

But it's been a little over a year now since the Pope came and went, and everything's the same as before. Sometimes a little better, other times worse, but always the same. In Cuba everything changes, and everything remains the same. Always the same.

One morning I was surprised when Tania showed up.

"And what are you doing here instead of being at work?"

"I need to talk to you and *abuela*."

"It's must be because you're either getting married, or pregnant, or you're leaving," Mamá uttered.

"Oh, Mamá, for goodness' sake!"

"Well, it's almost like that."

"*Mija,* for the love of it, just tell us already."

"I've been awarded a scholarship to study for a year in Barcelona…"

Being separated from Tania broke my heart, but in the end I was happy to see her get out of this place. Now, when she writes us, you can tell she's happy. What a girl! She loves the cold… She says that the city is beautiful. And she wants me to come visit her, but how could I afford it?

For years Lauri's been insisting that I apply for my papers so that I could go visit her in Miami. She was going to come down for the Pope's visit but in the end things didn't work out. We knew a lot of people back then who were making the trip. I always told Lauri, however, that I couldn't leave Mamá by herself. Maybe down deep I was afraid of what it would be like to see her again. I know that's irrational, but it frightened me to think that we might not be able to connect anymore they way we used to.

When my cousins Lucrecia and Anita came back for a visit, all we could do was just cry, and hug, and remember everything about the past when we were kids, as if no time had ever passed and we had never been separated. So, I finally decided that I would make the trip and go see Lauri. It was Maruja that gave me the final push. She promised me that she would take care of Mamá. And now, here I am in an airplane, with the lights of Miami below me, on the verge of embracing my sister, that other half of me who I haven't seen in nearly forty years, since her husband took her away on another plane on a sunny day in July.

CHAPTER TWELVE
No More Farewells

I COULDN'T STOP CRYING AS I EMBRACED MY SISTER IN THE MIAMI AIRPORT. I cried for so many reasons. I ached for never having gone to the Tropicana, for the blueness of Varadero, for the death of my father who I said goodbye to forever when I was eighteen, for my aging mother who maybe I'd never get to see again, for my kid brother who had turned communist, because I even missed the clerk at Casa Suárez with his balding head and splotchy hands, all the way down to the neon billboard of the woman in her Jantzen bathing suit diving into the sea. Finally I stepped back so I could see her better. It caught me by surprise how skinny, gray, and old she looked. It was as if someone had magically fast-forwarded the calendar, and I was seeing myself ten years down the road. I immediately started looking for her luggage so she wouldn't see my reaction.

Over the next few days I took her around to show her the different parts of Miami, like South Beach, Key Biscayne and Coconut Grove. With a certain amount of pride I showed her Little Havana, with its signs in Spanish and its smells of tobacco and coffee, so she could see how we as Cubans mull over our expatriated nostalgia in an effort to duplicate the country we left behind. I even took her by our first house and the apartment where we had lived with my in-laws right after we got here from Cuba.

"Hey do you think we could stop for a coffee?" she asked me during one of our trips out.

"Sure…but you know they say that drinking too much coffee isn't good for your health…"

"It seems like everyone here is obsessed with their health and yet that they're all clearly obese and are always going around talking about their operations and illnesses. In Cuba we eat whatever we can get our hands on, but we walk a ton, ride our bikes, and are so afraid of ending up in a hospital that we're actually in good health."

I had to control myself to keep from snapping back with a response. I was delighted that we were together again, but even though she tried, there were just things she didn't get. She didn't seem too excited about anything. She wasn't really complimentary or even grateful for things. To think that I was making so many sacrifices so she'd feel at home and so she could have the best of everything. And then to come out with these absurd comparisons as if anything in Cuba could possibly be better than things here in the U.S. It also annoyed me that she didn't know to pick up the second call if one came in on the call waiting… And she didn't seem to have any sense of time…and if I dared to throw out the scraps from dinner it clearly irritated her. I had to do it when she wasn't looking.

But at the same time, it's also true that I was just as unaware that sometimes I did or said things that made her feel equally bad. Every week I insisted that she run errands with me and go shopping at Publix, and when we did we'd always have the same conversation:

"Menchú, what flavor yogurt do you like?"

"It doesn't matter to me, Lauri."

"Menchú, which ice cream?"

"You go ahead and pick, Lauri."

"Menchú, should we get Coke, Diet-Coke, Coke-Free, or…"

"Lauri! It really doesn't matter to me…"

I couldn't understand how she could be so indifferent about everything until one day she got really upset and almost screamed at me:

"You could feed almost all of Havana with this! I can't even bear to look at it when I think of everybody back there… And besides, don't you get it? I don't know what to choose!" And she ran out of the store crying.

In general, however, we got along so well, as if we had never been separated. We had some good times with the kids and with Tyler, who became good friends with his great aunt. We spent an unforgettable afternoon with some childhood friends reminiscing about the good old days.

The best moments were at night when we could spend time together alone. After eating and watching a bit of television, we'd get in our pajamas and spend our time reading each other's diaries. Every once in a while one of us would read a passage that would move us so much that we'd start to cry and have to console each other.

"Oh stop it, silly. That was such a long time ago."

At other times we'd stop long enough to ask each other a question or make a comment:

"You know," I told her one day, "one of the things that hurts me the most is how little I really know mom and dad, and of course, how little they know me. All these years I've had somewhat of an idealized memory of them. I've always imagined them in the same way a little girl or teenager would… The things you've written about Papá are really shocking."

"Lauri, you need to understand. Papá wasn't necessarily a bad person…"

"I know he wasn't bad, but he hurt Mamá and it was his fault that they never left Cuba."

"Maybe it was never meant to be. Maybe it was our destiny."

"Destiny! That's one of those things that Cubans believe in that drives me nuts… You make your own destiny. It's always *'We'll see…'* or *'If we're lucky…'* It's like everyone wants to leave things to chance."

"So, do you think picking up and leaving was the answer?"

"No, not at all. Just the opposite, I think if every single one of us had stayed in Cuba things would have been different."

"But then why be mad at Papá for keeping us there?"

"I don't know, Menchu, because the worst part of all has been that families were separated… Well, maybe we should talk about something else. By the way, another thing I wanted to ask you about, that part about Julio Eduardo not having any business being in a war for Americans, was it really Maruja who said that?"

"Lauri, it's like I told you before, it was a time of revolutionary fervor, and Maruja, well, she's a good person but you've got to understand her circumstances…"

"No, no, I get that. What I'm talking about is that we had always heard that it was Papá who had made that comment and even said even worse things…"

"¡*Por Dios,* Lauri! He had his shortcomings but he would have never been capable of doing that."

"Do you realize that Uncle Julio and Papá have been at odds all these years over that?"

"That's why?"

"Well, that and because Papá never bothered to get in touch with him when Julio Eduardo was killed."

"Well, I don't know about that…maybe he wrote a letter and it was lost…but I promise you that Papá never said anything remotely similar to that. In fact, he was so upset that he carried a photo of Julio Eduardo in his wallet until the day he died. I know because they gave it to me at his funeral. And every year, near the anniversary of his death, he never failed to go to the pantheon at El Cacahual."

"El Cacahual? Isn't that where Maceo is buried?"

"Yes, it is."

"But what does Maceo have to do with Julio Eduardo?"

"Papá believed that Julio Eduardo had died as a hero…and that we should pay tribute to his memory."

"My God, Menchu, two brothers who didn't write or speak to each other for so many years over a simple misunderstanding…and now Papá's gone…but when you head up to New York to visit Ricardo you've got to tell Tío Julio all of this. Oh, the twists and turns of life! When I think back on when we were kids and we'd get together every Sunday at grandmother's. Remember?"

"Of course."

"Who could have imagined back then what life was going to hold for us? It's so absurd to think that Julio Eduardo was going to die in a war in Vietnam."

"Yeah, just as absurd as Pedritín who was in a war in Angola for two years. In his case we were lucky, but a lot of his friends were killed. The whole ordeal with Camilito was devastating. Imagine, we had watched him grow up since he was two."

Sometimes we'd go for a drive and things would come back to me that I had forgotten a long time ago.

"Menchu, how did that song go that we used to sing on the bus? You know, the one that Señora Nina taught us."

"Oh Lauri, I can't remember those things…"

"Yes you do, I know you must…it was something about elephants…"

"Wait a minute. I think I've got it."

> *An elephant swung on the web of a spider,*
> *A friend she did call to swing there beside her.*

> *Two elephants swung on the web of a spider,*
> *Another she called to swing there beside her.*

> *Three elephants…*

One memory led us to another and soon we were singing along, recalling old melodies from our childhood.

I also had a thousand questions about different family members that Menchu patiently answered:

"And what about Gilda? She was too young to die. What happened?"

"Well, you know how domineering her mother was. She finally married Rubén but they actually kept living apart with their own parents."

"She was still living in Old Havana?"

"How can you remember all these things? But you're right. Yeah, and he kept on living in Lawton. Can you imagine? Anyway, the thing was he told her he wanted to leave Cuba and asked her to get her papers ready, but she told him that she couldn't go because of her mother. Well, they never talked about it again, but a year later he just took off without a word. She suffered so much that the only way to get her mind off it was to take care of the animals. You remember how she loved dogs. They had several of them over at Rubén's house, and after he took off she had to find a home for them. One day she was over at the house of the people who had agreed to take them in, and she decided to fix up the patio where they were going to keep the dogs. It was right after lunch, and the sun was brutal. Everybody told her to wait until later that evening when it would be cooler and they'd help, but you know how stubborn she was. Anyway, sure enough, she had a stroke! I took care of her in the hospital…Magaly and I took turns… She only lasted a week."

"And her mother?"

"Her mother lived for five more years and all she ever did was complain about what Gilda had done to her…"

"But what did Gilda do?"

"She up and died."

"That woman was crazy…"

"And the strangest thing was that right in the middle of the funeral one of those Chinese dogs came in…"

"A Chinese dog?"

"Yeah, one of those ugly ones that have a mustache…"

"But what did it do?"

"Well, nothing really, it just sat there all night long next to the coffin. Armandito said it had come to pay his respects on behalf of all dogs."

"That poor girl… She had it so bad…I really loved her. Remember how she used to tell us stories?"

"Yeah, but she wasn't always so nice, but I guess it's understandable. She had a rough life…"

"What's so funny?"

"I'm just thinking about that Chinese dog…"

"You know, Cuba really is a surreal country."

There were times when we laughed so much, but at the same time the heartaches that had built up over the years also made me feel the need just to hold my sister tight and tell her how much I had missed her all these years.

"I know, I know. I've missed you too…"

Then we would sit there on the bed for hours, just hugging each other and crying, rocking back and forth and randomly conjuring up so many memories, like the way our mother and grandmother would rock us in those chairs so typically Cuban.

I needed my sister to understand what it meant to live outside of one's country:

"You don't know what it's like to live in exile, what it's like to travel somewhere and when they ask you where you're from you have to explain that you're from Cuba but that you don't reside there... It's like being an orphan. Worse. It's like your parents have abandoned you, that you never had parents, that you don't have a name..."

"But at least you've gotten to travel... Sometimes the Island itself is like a big prison..."

I told her how one of the things that bothered me the most when I first got here was how I would go places, to the movies, shopping, and I wouldn't know anyone. In Columbus we never even saw a single Cuban.

"The thing is that here you can work and you know if you work hard you can have almost anything you want, well, except to live in your own country."

"You know, Lauri, it just dawned on me that it's the exact opposite in Cuba. There you have the consolation of getting to live in your own country but you work and you work, and you just don't get anywhere..."

"That's true, but at least your daughter was born and raised in her own country. She got to meet Mamá Luya and Papá... Here you try to explain it all to your kids so they'll know their roots and where they come from, but you're never really sure if it sinks in... You can never really share with them the things that have been important to you... They have a different flag, a different anthem, and another language even if they do speak Spanish... Don't get me wrong. I'm really grateful to this country and I admire it, but it will never be *mine*."

My sister also helped me understand what it meant to all of those who stayed behind to have to say so many farewells, something I had never thought about.

"Lauri, those of you who left aren't the only ones who long for the old days. Look at all of our old schoolmates that you have here. Marta, Eloísa, and I are the only ones of us left, and out of the cousins only Armandito…and Gilda who died so suddenly… It's true that all of you here nostalgically reminisce about us, but it's different for us. In our mind you are constantly present. For example, I'm sure you've forgotten about that wall in the patio at Mamá Luya's house where you scribbled our names. Well, it's there just like you left it, and I see it every day. And Mamá…Mamá doesn't stop talking about you and Ricardo, and more than anything else really about you."

"Sometimes I feel so guilty…"

"After you told me all about Robertico I understand why you never came back, but a lot of time has passed and you shouldn't let him control you any longer from the grave."

"You know, Menchu, over the last few years, I've realized that I spent the first part of my exile in a state of shock, like I'd been drugged or something, almost like a robot… I think I, and maybe others too, felt that way because it was how we coped with the fact that our lives had been turned upside down. But you're right. I've made up my mind. I'm going to go see Mamá…I'm going to Cuba."

"Really? Are you sure? Think about it because I don't want you later on to feel…"

"No, I swear I'm going, even though just thinking about it makes my legs weak…"

"I know what you mean. I was scared to come too."

"What? Were you afraid of me?"

"Well, you know…"

"Hey!" And I began to tickle her like I did when we were kids.

"Lauri, please!" She begged me to stop. "Please!"

We knew we had to laugh to ease the tension. Both of us had sensed that no matter how bad it might hurt, there were things we had to get off our chests and tell each other.

"Oh Menchu…what happened? How is it possible that we've been separated for so long?"

"Life, Lauri, I guess just life…"

"It wasn't life, Menchu. It was Fidel Castro. It's all his fault."

"Oh let's just drop it…"

"I just don't get it, Menchu. How is it possible at this stage of the game that Cubans can't see that they were wrong?"

"Lauri, we're not got going to get anywhere arguing about it."

"But we're not arguing…"

"So, what do you want me to say? That I shouldn't have fallen in love with Lázaro because he was a Marxist? That all the hours I spent teaching others to read, that all the cane I cut, that all the schools I designed, that the only place I've ever visited, the Soviet Union, that all the hardships I've endured, that all the sacrifices we've made don't amount to anything? That my life hasn't amounted to anything? That the lives of the twelve million Cubans still back there don't amount to anything? That we should tuck our tail, be humble, and tell all the exiles 'we were wrong, dear brothers, you have all the answers, please come back and save us, come back with your markets overrun with food, come on back and teach us all about patriotism with your outdated speeches?'"

At first I was outraged, but later on I tried to put myself in her shoes, and I wound up asking her to forgive me.

"It's not a question of forgiveness, Lauri. It's about understanding each other. You haven't done anything to make me mad, but some of the things that I've heard since I've been here… Don't all of you realize that for better or worse that's my life, that's the real Cuba, not the one that all of you have invented?"

"But…but that's exactly the worst part. We've spent the last forty years sighing for Cuba, filling our homes with photos from Cuba, with pictures of *flamboyán* trees in Cuba, writing poems about Cuba, composing hymns praising Cuba, telling our kids stories dealing with Cuba, fooling ourselves that that country isn't devouring us, thinking about Cuba day and night, always listening for news from Cuba, creating a *Casa Cuba* wherever there's a Cuban community, feeling like we're strangers in a foreign land everywhere we go. And now you come out and tell me that we don't even have the right to have an opinion about it! We don't belong in either place, and we're not going to, not here, not there. We're...we're...scum!"

"Now you're the one exaggerating... In fact, you're the ones that have it all. Just look at this beautiful house you have."

"Menchu, be serious. This house is a pile of crap. What the hell does it matter if you have a house but you don't have a homeland? I don't have a country. Don't you get it? I love Cuba, but it doesn't love me... Oh, just so you know, as far as the rest of the world is concerned, you know which wave of exiles they've welcomed with open arms? The most recent ones, the ones who have already made a name for themselves in Cuba, the ones who until yesterday were a part of the Cuban government, the ones who get their kicks writing about the conditions there, because, hey, poverty sells, sex sells, wagging your tail on stage sells, beating drums sells...but what about all the dead, and the prisoners, and the ones that have drowned, and the ones like Robertico who never made it, and all the anonymous exiles, and my sons who are Americans but not really...the ones who have names like Fernández and have dark hair... what about them? No one wants to think about them. They don't matter."

"Listen to you. You would have thrown those ideas right back in Robertico's face if he had said all that."

"Yeah, but in some ways he was right."

"We're all right in some ways, but no one has all the answers."

"If I had just one wish for Cuba, you know what it would be? That no Cuban would ever have to live in exile. Never, Menchu, never again."

"You know what I would do? I would make all goodbyes illegal. There'd be no more farewells... Hey, stop that. Don't you start crying, sis, for the sake's of Papá's memory, please don't. Look at us, silly, this is all like a dream, here we are, together again, remembering so many things."

"A dream? Our life has been like a nightmare! It was hard to see when we were right in the middle of it, but the rhetoric during the Cold War was so cruel. That's when I was in Washington..."

"Yeah, that was during my Moscow days...but don't think about those things now. What's important is that now we know there are more things that unite us than separate us."

"Yeah, as far as you and I are concerned, but I wonder if Robertico and Lázaro would have ever understood each other."

"I don't know. I don't even know if you and I would understand each other if both of them were still alive."

"But women are different... And Pedritín, I wonder if we'll be able to get along."

"I'm sure you will if you just try..."

"And if he tries too, right?"

"The fact that he sent you a necklace is a good sign. You know I have my own doubts about how I'm going to get along with Ricardo."

"You'll do fine, you'll see... In fact, Ricardo's just a big softy."

"Pedritín's the same. That's why it's like a drama. There are so many good people who've been assigned some role like they were the bad guys in the movies."

"That makes me think about all the Westerns we used to watch..."

"Remember how we adored Roy Rogers?"

"It was the same here too. My father-in-law, and even Pedro Pablo, used to love to watch that show about Wyatt Earp."

"You haven't told me what he's up to."

"He died not long ago..."

"Your father-in-law?"

"No, Roy Rogers. Roberto's still hanging in there with his eighty plus years. He's doing fine... Well, somewhat...Olga takes good care of him. The whole question here about the elderly is a serious problem."

"It couldn't be worse than back there. Get this. One of my friends from work just had a hernia operation because every time his grandmother needed to go to the doctor he had to carry her up and down the stairs. Needless to say she was pretty tall and more than a little overweight... Can you imagine? He's probably better off that she passed away. The old folks have been through so much."

"Remember how we'd call you *'Mechita'* because you were always blowing a *'fuse'* over the slightest little thing?"

"I guess that's one advantage of getting old. I've learned how to be patient."

"For me I've learned to have confidence in myself. If you only knew when you were young what you know now."

"I've also learned how to be alone."

"The whole ordeal with Lázaro really hurt you deeply, didn't it?"

"Yes. I still miss him. And my daughter too. Now I just have Mamá, but it's like our roles have been reversed, like she's my daughter and I'm the mother. When I'm with her I complain at times, more than anything because she needs constant attention, but now that I've been here for a while I miss her so badly."

"First thing tomorrow we're going to go down to the agency and get the papers in order for my trip...and...then I'm going to take you out to eat at Versailles. I can't believe that you've already been here for two weeks and we haven't gone there yet..."

"Fine, and when you come to Havana I'm taking you out to Palenque... It's like a huge hut. You go down 5th Avenue, past the Yacht Club and..."

"Just thinking about it gives me goose bumps and knots in my stomach."

"We shouldn't say anything to Mamá until the very last minute or there'll be no living with her."

"All this business of making plans has made me hungry. Do you think it's time to make a trip to the kitchen?"

We both loved chocolate and every night we'd serve ourselves tremendous helpings of ice cream. Sometimes Menchu would say with a nostalgic tone:

"The ice cream in Cuba is so good..."

"Oh yeah, and you have as many flavors as Baskin Robbins," I added playfully.

"No, we don't have as many flavors, but the ones we have are delicious."

Every conversation opened the door to another memory:

"Hey, remember Tropicream that was down on 12th Street?"

"Of course…"

"We used to go when we were kids."

"And the matinees at the Miramar Cinema…"

"Obviously, that's where I met Robertico… You didn't go that day… Have you ever wondered what would have happened if Robertico had fallen in love with you rather than me?"

"No, I've never really thought about it, but I imagine that I would have had your life and you mine."

"Yeah, our lives are interchangeable…and just because of an accident of fate, like you not going to the movies one afternoon…"

And then at other times, we'd go from superficial matters to questions that we might not have even dared to ask ourselves before her visit.

"Lauri, you haven't truly been happy, have you?"

"No, and it's not just because of Robertico. I've always had this sense that all of this is just a passing phase, that my real life is back in Cuba. And now look. My life has passed me by… But on the other hand, I wouldn't trade it for yours either. I wouldn't have my boys…and you… you haven't been happy either, have you?"

"Maybe happiness doesn't really exist."

"Perhaps there are only happy moments. Now those we've had."

"Like right now. This is one of those moments."

"Yeah. Another thing that I've learned with my years is that no one makes someone else happy. You make your own happiness, and it comes from a lot of different parts. Does that make sense? When I got married I was so in love with Robertico. I thought he was responsible for my happiness, that the things that we did separately didn't really count for anything…and as time has gone by I've realized that it just doesn't work that way."

"I had a friend who used to always say that you have to learn to love life unconditionally, on its own terms, for itself."

"That's so true."

"You know what the worst part of getting old is?"

"That your tits start to sag."

"No, Lauri, seriously…the worst thing for me is all the people who have died. I remember when we were kids and they would always take us to church for All Souls' Day, I used to always pray for Uncle Nel, and for that girl who died in the fifth grade from leukemia, and for our grandfather that we never got to meet… When we were kids that's who we thought of when we went to pay our respects to those who had passed away, but these days…"

"Oh I know…Mamá Luya…Robertico…Lázaro…Julio Eduardo…Adela…"

"Gilda…Camilito…"

"Vidal…"

"Robertico's uncle died?"

"Yes, and he was so young."

"Did he die of cancer?"

"I'm not sure, but I think it was AIDS. It didn't occur to me until much later, but he was a homosexual and he died suddenly around the beginning of the epidemic."

"The poor guy. And even people our own age have started to die."

"Just last year three of my friends…"

"I can't imagine the day we lose Mamá."

"And Tía Flor too…"

"But you know what? There are always others being born. I can't believe that you're already a grandmother… That's how life is… But let's talk about something else."

After a while we started sharing secrets about our lives that were so intimate that we hadn't even dared to write them down in our diaries.

"So, tell me, besides Gastón, have you ever had any other lovers?"

"Well…nothing serious. How about you?"

"Nothing serious either, but…yes…"

"Wow, you've really kept that quiet. Do tell!"

"Well, he's from Spain and he travels to Cuba on business every once in a while."

"Oh sis, maybe you'll get married and later on live in Spain since Tania is already there."

"And even Ernestico's in Madrid now too, but…that's not going to happen, Lauri."

"Why not?"

"Well, he's charming, good-looking, sophisticated, and he has travelled, he's wealthy…"

"But he's married."

"No…although I'm sure he must have something going on somewhere."

"Then what?"

"What I'm sure he finds attractive about me is the world I live in. That man is in love with Cuba, not with me. In his culture, I'd be out of place. We'd lose the magic that we have now, and neither one of us would be happy."

"It's true that we get more mature with age."

"Okay, so now, your turn."

"All right, but promise me you're not going to be shocked."

"Shocked? Me? With the things I've seen in my life!"

"It's embarrassing …"

"Don't be silly."

"Well, I'm seeing a young man, a man much younger than me…"

"Sounds good to me."

"He's barely older than Pedro Pablo…but he's very mature."

"And?"

"And he's a wonderful lover. I'm telling you, when it comes to the bedroom, a fifty-year old man is definitely not the same as a thirty-year old. I had forgotten."

"And are you in love with him?"

"No, and neither is he, but we enjoy spending time together and we really care for each other. I can't explain it. I guess it's a part of growing older, or realizing that some things in life just don't fit neatly into the script they give you. Does that make sense?"

"Sure it does. And I think it's great. Do your sons know?"

"Heavens no! The good thing is that neither one of us want to complicate things. Besides, I'd feel awkward going out in public with him. They'd think he was my son!"

Every day that went by I came to appreciate more and more how well we understood each other. We had been separated when we were teenagers and reunited as adult women, but it was like no time had ever passed.

"Oh Menchu, I haven't talked like this to anyone since I left Cuba."

"Me neither, Lauri."

"Promise me that we'll never again be separated like that."

"Things are going to be different from now on."

"If there were only changes in Cuba."

"There will be some day...I only hope that they don't destroy Cuba and that they don't humiliate people in the process."

"Me too, but it's going to take such a long time. What are we going to do in the meantime?"

"If I only knew..."

"We've got to get to bed soon. It must be around 3:00 in the morning."

"*¡Por Dios!*...time really flies. It's almost dawn."

We had already turned out the lights when I heard her ask me:

"Hey Lauri, do you remember when Mamá used to dress us alike?" And I went to sleep with the image in my mind of two little girls dressed in identical organza dresses, scampering happily in a garden in Havana under the plentiful shade of an almond tree.

The next morning while we were eating breakfast, I looked long and hard at my sister. In just a few weeks she had changed. All of a sudden it seemed like I was looking into my own face.

"Look at you, you're not skin and bones like you were when you got here, or as Mamá would say, you've gotten plump... But that hair! We're both going to get our hair done," and I immediately called to set up an appointment.

After the hair salon we hit the stores.

"Choose whatever you want, Menchu…and quit looking at the price tags."

We went into the fitting room with identical pairs of white pants and a black and white checkered blouse.

"It reminded me of an outfit we had when we were kids."

"Me too."

Finally, with the same hairdo and dressed alike, we looked into the mirror and were dumbfounded. It's like we were seeing double. After all these years, we were finally identical again.

"Do you think Mamá will be able to tell us apart?" I asked her.

"We'll find out soon enough, won't we?"

CHAPTER THIRTEEN
Together Again

WHEN MENCHU RETURNED TO CUBA, I felt so empty inside that I was afraid I was going to fall into a state of depression. I missed her so badly. At first I found it difficult to explain to everyone what it had meant to be together again with my sister. I was afraid no one would understand. But once I finally decided to talk about my feelings, I found out that a lot of people had gone through a similar experience. After all is said and done, family is the one thing that has outlasted the ideological differences. I was moved by my sons' enthusiasm when I told them I had decided to go back to Cuba for a visit. My father-in-law also supported my decision:

"You're doing the right thing, *mijita*. A lot of time has passed and you should go back home and see your mother. Besides, it's time for all of us to start going back to Cuba…"

Before she left, Menchu and I had gone to the travel agency to fill out the paperwork. Now I had to wait anxiously for maybe four weeks, which is how long it took sometimes before you could get a visa. It infuriated me to have to ask for a visa to enter my own country, but at least I would be traveling with an American passport, I told myself.

I was so nervous. It felt like I had a flock of birds inside of me, from my throat to my stomach. I tried to keep my mind on other things. I took refuge in pondering the moments I had shared with Menchu, the wonderful trip we had taken to New York to visit Ricardo and Tía Flor, and so many delightful moments we had shared in Miami.

Finally, the agency called, but I couldn't believe what they told me. My visa had been denied. I had spent the last forty years not wanting to go back to Cuba, but it had never dawned on me that they wouldn't let me in my own country. I felt so angry, so hurt, and so helpless…I didn't know what to do. I finally called Menchu:

"Calm down… These things happen. Let me see what I can find out…"

I waited for what seemed to be an interminable month until one day

I finally heard her voice again:

"Lauri, I've got news, they're going to issue you a visa!"

The truth is I didn't know travelling to Cuba could be so complicated. They finally issued me a ticket for Friday, the 2nd, just a mere few days before the fortieth anniversary of that July 13th so long ago when I had left my home behind. For the first time in so many years Menchu and I were going to celebrate our birthday together.

As soon as I announced that I was going to Cuba, I found out just how many people had already gone back. People that I would have never imagined…and all of them kept giving me advice:

"Make sure and get a canvas suitcase because they don't weigh as much…"

"For gifts, take some coffee, seasonings, soap, and stuff like that, but not shampoo. It weighs too much…"

"It's better to buy things for them there than to spend two dollars a pound for excess luggage."

"Don't forget to go to Publix and weigh your suitcase so you don't go over the 44-pound limit…"

"Put some Kleenex in your purse because you're not going to find toilet paper anywhere…and also some wipes in case the water goes out…"

"Don't forget to take plenty of aspirin and antacids, antihistamines, band-aids…anything you think you might need…you're not going to find anything there…and if you don't need it, just leave it with your relatives."

Then the favors started rolling in:

"Can you take this letter and this bottle of vitamins to my sister, please?"

"Hey, this is for my godmother… It's just a few water filters…"

"And these reading glasses are for my uncle, if you don't mind."

During the day I'd keep myself busy, carefully picking out the right clothes I was going to take so I wouldn't call too much attention to myself, and also doing the typical things you always have to do before any trip—canceling the newspaper, asking the neighbor to pick up the mail and water the plants—but at night I couldn't sleep. I'd close my eyes and all I could see were glimpses of Havana…a street…a roof…a window…a face…the sea…always the sea, and so much light, a light so bright it would wake me up. Images that I thought that I had forgotten kept parading through my mind. The city of my childhood, which had fallen asleep in my subconscious, came back to life once again. Those sites, however, were washed out by images of another Havana, the one in ruins that I had seen so many times in documentaries. Occasionally, when I could finally fall asleep, sometimes I'd feel like I was falling into an abyss and it would jolt me awake. Then there were the nights when I'd see the faces of my brothers, and sister, and cousins… They looked just like they did when they were kids, like they did when I left home, but then their faces slowly changed and took on the look of a teenager, and then an adult… In my dreams, however, I couldn't make out my mother, even though I could feel her presence and smell her particular aroma. After hours of trying to get to sleep without any luck, I'd get up and study a map of Havana that I had bought. With the map in hand I'd retrace with my finger the route from my house to school, to the music conservatory, to the beach, to my grandparent's house, over all the streets that I had spent so much time on… Other times I'd search the Internet for information. I couldn't get over the number of travel ads I saw for tourism to Cuba.

When I got back from Miami, I couldn't do anything except think about my sister. I was so anxious to see her again, but I had so many questions now after our visit. She had such an idealized view of Cuba, would she be disillusioned with the way it really was here? With so much poverty, would she be able to see the true character of this Island and its people? She was so used to being well off, how could she possibly adapt to such difficult conditions that had become commonplace for us, even if it were for just a few days? What would it be like when she finally got to see Mamá again? Sometimes it reminded me of the story of the prodigal son. Would I be jealous of my sister? And how would her visit affect Mamá? Would her heart be able to handle it? How would Lauri get along with Pedritín? And what about Maruja? I was afraid that my sister would say something that would rile up my best friend, or vice versa.

When Lauri called and said that they had denied her visa, I immediately went to see a friend of Lázaro's who had connections in high places in the government. That's when I found out that my sister had been on the "Deny Entry" list for years.

"You know that Laura is not a terrorist and that's she not going to come here and hurt anybody."

"Maybe not now, but back then...who knows?"

"But she's incapable of hurting a flea."

"But what about her husband?"

"Her husband's dead and buried!"

"Okay, but then there's her father-in-law..."

"He's an old man who's over eighty now!"

"Well, all right honey, let me see what I can do..."

Fortunately, everything got worked out, and I managed to start getting things ready for Lauri's visit. I would have liked to have been able to fix the house up a bit more, but it was impossible to find any paint. At least I was able to find someone to help me, and we gave the house a good cleaning. In one of the closets where Mamá and I still had things stored from the house in Vedado, I found the bedspread that Lauri had gotten for her wedding but had never had the chance to use. I also got out the photos of our fifteenth birthday party and an old doll that we had named Leonor in honor of Martí's story. And of course, both pictures of Rafael's *Madonna* that had adorned the walls above our beds when we were girls. I tried to prepare Tía Flor's old room as best as possible so it would look just like old times.

I keep wondering if Mamá suspects something. Sometimes I worry that the shock may be too much for her heart and that I should

Uva de Aragón 269

somehow prepare her for the surprise. But then if something went wrong and Lauri couldn't come, the disappointment would be even worse.

I know what a good time we had, and that we enjoyed that special connection again, but it's one thing to do it there and quite another thing here... As the day approaches, I can't help but feel more and more nervous.

∽

I didn't want to bother anybody so I took a taxi to the airport. I had to be there at 7:00 in the morning, even though it was such a short flight and it left at 1:00 in the afternoon! I had mixed feelings of sadness and anger when I saw so many Cubans lined up with their canvas suitcases. A couple of them were carrying bicycle tires. A few others, plastic flowers for the gravesites of their loved ones. It was obvious that some of them had made the trip before. A few, like me, were going back for the first time in years.

By 10:00 everything had been taken care of. I ate breakfast, bought a newspaper, and called my kids.

"Mamá, everything's going to be just fine. Give Aunt Menchu a kiss for me," Pedro Pablo said in a supportive voice.

"Don't forget to bring me some sand from a beach," Bobby Jr. reminded me.

I also called my father-in-law.

"*Mija,* you're not going to have any problems, you'll see..."

He must have read my mind because the truth is that I was really nervous. I hadn't admitted it to anyone, of course, but when I thought about Bobby having fought in the Bay of Pigs, when I recalled my years in Washington as a Human Rights activist, and that I had occasionally worked with Radio Martí, all of it made me nervous. I even imagined myself locked up in a cell, surrounded by men in militia uniforms who were confronting me with recordings of my own voice criticizing their government. They exhibited photos and newspaper clippings and hounded me with questions. I told myself that it wasn't going to be like that, that others a lot more radical than I had gone back and nothing had happened to them, and that I personally wasn't anyone special. But, just on the off chance, I had left a copy of my will and a letter for the boys on top of the dresser. When I get back I'll laugh about all this…I think.

Thank goodness Menchu was able to come here to Miami first. Without me having set foot in Cuba, she's been my bridge to the Island. I've learned so much from her about life there and, more importantly, I've come to realize that the two of us are identical. And not just because of our physical appearance. Menchu is the reflection of what I never was as well as what I might have been.

Actually, my biggest fear isn't that something bad is going to happen to me. It's just that I've spent so many years searching for things that could connect me to life in Cuba, struggling so I wouldn't become a distorted figure, like in an old yellowed photo, so I wouldn't come off as having distanced myself from those on the Island. I've spent so much time gazing into the eyes of those who have recently arrived just so I could catch a glimpse of my homeland, stretching out my hand despite so many and such drastic differences. Did I pull it off, I wonder? Maybe after all, regardless of the precautions, perhaps I really am carrying some excess baggage with me. But what suitcase could possibly hold all the pain I've endured for having lived in exile? In what suitcase could I possibly put all of my accumulated nostalgia and suffering from having been uprooted? No, without a doubt what I fear the most is that I'm going to feel like a foreigner in my own country. If that's the case, then I won't truly belong anywhere. Here, in the United States, I'll never really feel at home. So…is it in fact true, then? Am I finally going home?

∽

Pedritín offered to take me to the airport to pick up Lauri. I would have preferred to have gone alone, but I don't have a car, and I didn't think it was right to go in a taxi. Besides, even though he made it sound like he was doing me a favor, I think down deep he really wanted to go to pick up her up too. Mamá seems to be as calm as ever, but I can't believe she doesn't suspect anything. She's always able to pick up on things.

∽

The plane finally takes off. Miami gets smaller in the distance. I feel my heart pounding in my chest. They serve us a small snack, but I can't eat a bite. Hardly a few minutes have gone by when I hear someone say:

"There it is!"

I press my face against the glass of the window. This time it wasn't like the long trip to Guantánamo when we had to take a round-about route since we weren't allowed to fly over Cuban air space. This time we had barely lost sight of the Everglades when among the clouds you could start to make out the northern coast of Cuba. My God, it was like a time machine. Forty years recovered in forty minutes. For four decades my home has been so far away when in reality it's been so close. The plane banked and, suddenly, I caught a glimpse of Havana, the unmistakable shape of its bay, the dome of the Capitol that shone in the brilliant sun and, like a sentry that protects the castle in a fairy tale, *El Morro* fortress—the faithful guardian of the city and of my memories as a young girl.

All the passengers began to sing the National Anthem. I couldn't join in however because I wasn't able to utter a sound. Deep down inside me, I gave thanks to the Virgin because Cuba and my mother had waited for me for so many years.

I immediately recognized the old airport, but the plane kept on taxiing until we reached the new, smaller terminal. The sign read *Aeropuerto José Martí* in huge blue letters. My legs trembled as I stepped for the first time on my native soil. I felt like the palm trees were bidding me welcome—Martí's palm trees who "wait as lovers do," Heredia's palm trees that keep his melancholy eyes from conceding "Niagara's majesty." I felt a strange desire to kneel down and kiss the ground. But forget it, as little as I exercise these days, I'd do it and I wouldn't be able to get back up. How in the world can the Pope do it, especially at his age? It's weird how the strangest things pop into your head at the most serious times. I was already standing in front of the Immigration window when I started to have second thoughts again. What if they didn't let me in? The Immigration officer seemed so young...

"Be sure not to lose this piece of paper. You'll have to hand it in when you leave," he told me in a kind and even affectionate tone.

"You can come on through... And...welcome back to your country..." I heard him say as a buzzer sounded and I pushed open the door leading to Customs.

The first one I saw was Pedritín. Unlike the photos they had sent me, he looked just like I had pictured him in my dreams. He still had the same boyish face he had when he was younger. We gave each other a huge hug, and I felt all the built-up hard feelings dissolve into tears. In one fell swoop I had recovered my baby brother and I was overcome with the same limitless euphoria that I had experienced the day he was born.

"Hey! So what about me? Don't I get a hug?!" exclaimed Menchu. And I gave her a big hug too.

"Wow, we couldn't have planned it better, huh?" she added.

That's when I realized that we were dressed identically. We had both picked out the pants and blouse we had bought together in Miami.

We climbed in Pedritín's Lada. My first impression wasn't a good one. Cuba seemed like an underdeveloped country, so different than the way I had remembered it. To keep up my spirits I reminded myself that when you first arrive in a city you seldom think it's pretty. I also had a hard time recognizing a lot of my previous landmarks until Menchu blurted out:

"Look Lauri..." she said, pointing to a building on the right.

"Oh my, it's the *Río Cristal!* Remember when we used to go on Sundays with Tía Flor and all her writer friends?"

"How could I forget. Rómulo Gallegos was always there."

"And Andrés Eloy Blanco too…"

Passing the Sports Complex brought other memories to mind.

"Papá used to always take us here every year to see the circus."

"Yeah, and then Mamá of course would always disinfect us with alcohol!"

"How is Mamá, Menchu?"

"Well, she's okay. She's getting to be more and more like Mamá Luya every day. She sleeps in her room and even takes a siesta these days. I swear sometimes I think she *is* Mamá Luya. Her sight has improved a bit thanks to the vitamins you've been sending, but not completely. One thing for sure, her mind is really sharp."

"I need to make a stop and run some papers by the post office. We'll take a drive so Lauri can see some of the sites before we head home," Pedritín said.

"That's probably a good idea since that'll give Mamá a chance to get up from her nap before we get there," added Menchu.

We went past the Plaza of the Revolution with its imposing monument of Martí and mural of Che Guevara. We went down G Street or rather Avenue of the Presidents.

"Isn't that where our doctor's office was?" I asked. With every little bit more and more landmarks were coming back to me.

When we came to the esplanade at the end of the street and I spotted the *Malecón*, I had to take out a Kleenex.

"Pace yourself, sis, you still have a lot of emotions to go through."

Pedritín headed into the tunnel and came out the other side at the fountain where Fifth Avenue begins.

"Isn't this where Kasalta used to be? They would always bring us here for our birthdays and we loved to eat veal parmesan and spaghetti."

"No, this isn't where it *used to be*. It's still here. It's just that they're remodeling it."

"I can't believe it."

"But, wasn't there a clock around here somewhere?" Menchu added.

"Sure, it's right over there."

"I can't get over what a memory my little sister has."

"Pedritín, I…I've never forgotten any of this…and not the Church of Santa Rita… Oh, Menchu, why this is where Gracielita lived and we used to ride bikes in that park…"

"Now it's called Emiliano Zapata."

"Look! Look, it's the Grau's house… And they still have those huge clay pots out front."

Pedritín took a right on La Copa.

"We're going this way because they put in a new post office over here," Menchu explained.

"But isn't that Lucrecia's and Anita's house?"

"Well, yeah, but now it's the Serbian Embassy."

Pedritín parked and I climbed out of the Lada.

"Menchu, oh the times we used to come here to play with them. How I remember Uncle Ernesto… He died right here in this house… And over there was the shopping center and the Lisboa Restaurant, right?"

"It's still there."

"It's like time stood still." I had gone from crying to laughing to astonishment.

While Pedritín mailed the letters, Menchu and I strolled around the block reminiscing about our cousins' old neighborhood.

"That's where the Morenos lived. Remember?"

"And this is where Luis' bodega was…"

"And over there was the Fuentes' hardware store…"

"These apartment buildings really are in bad shape…"

Pedritín had caught up to us by now and when he honked the horn I jumped in quickly.

"Menchu! Hurry up. Let's go. I can't wait any longer to go see Mamá."

At times it seemed like I was a young girl again and that we were merely heading to my grandmother's house. Everything seemed so familiar that it was like I had never left. We finally got there and I saw the house, in need of a coat of paint, I couldn't help but feel a twinge in my heart from pain and shame.

The grates surrounding the garden out front, the greenish-black paving stones that led up to the entry way, the little lamp post, everything was exactly like I had left it. Never in my life had I felt a stronger emotion but, at the same time, I had never been more at peace.

"Let me go in first by myself. Since we're dressed alike, and she won't be able to see me that well, and also since she's not expecting me, she'll think I'm you."

"As you're walking in, start out by saying, 'What's up, old woman? Did ya have a good nap?' And then give her a kiss."

I followed my sister's instructions.

"Fine, dear, I slept just fine, but I had the strangest dream. I'll tell you about it in just a minute, but first be a doll and go get me a glass of water."

I went right to the kitchen. My eyes welled up with tears when I saw the same aluminum glasses we had used when I was a kid, the kind where each one's a different color. I had never given them a second thought, but now I remembered them perfectly and that Mamá's was the green one. But it wasn't there. Then it dawned on me to open the refrigerator, and I found it right where it was supposed to be.

"Here you go, Mamá."

"Thanks *mija*."

I sat in the chair next to my mother. I was dying to hug her, to throw myself in her lap and just sob, but I controlled myself.

"So, aren't you going to tell me about your dream?"

"I don't remember it exactly…you know how dreams are…but it had something to do with a man who had two sons, and one of them goes away for many years, and the other one stays behind…"

I held my breath. Had she possibly recognized me?

"And what else?"

"Oh, I don't know…I guess it's just more of my typical ramblings… but come a bit closer…you've got the light behind you and I can barely see you…"

I sat there at her feet on the floor, just as I had done when I was a girl with my grandmother. She stroked my hair and said:

"You know with this eyesight of mine I can't focus well…"

"Is that so?"

"You know, it's strange, you're right here at my side, but I could swear that I just saw you in the hallway. It must be your sister, don't you think."

✦

When Mamá recognized her, Lauri began to cry so hard that Pedritín had to bring her a glass of water.

I immediately jumped out of my hiding place and tried to tone things down a bit out of fear of what might happen to Mamá if she got too emotional.

"I knew we couldn't trick you, you old woman, even with you not seeing so well."

"It's tough to fool the heart of a mother... Besides, they've gone to so much trouble with all these preparations, who else would they have done that for if not for you? Don't think that just because I hadn't asked them that I hadn't realized what was going on."

We spent the whole afternoon laughing, crying, reminiscing, and making plans for the coming days.

Lauri couldn't drag herself away from Mamá. She kept going up to her and hugging her constantly.

"I just can't believe it. It seems like I'm dreaming."

"I know *mija*. Me too."

Far from being jealous like I thought I was going to be, I was so happy and deeply relieved. It was as if this strange void, this sort of internal chill that had hurt me down deep for all these years, had started to evolve into a warm flame, a comforting salve.

✦

The first thing we did the next morning was to go to the cemetery. While we were waiting for them to prepare a couple of vases of flowers there at the corner of 12th and Zapata, I had the strange sensation that things were running together, that the past was being superimposed onto the present. I could see my mother the way she looked when she was younger. Ricardo was once again a young man. Papá was leading Menchu and me along by the hand to go put flowers on Uncle Nel's grave.

When we got to the gravesite, it surprised me how much time had robbed the black marble of all of its shine and color. I once again felt that sharp pain and void that my father's passing had left in my soul forever, and the wound opened once more. And I cried, I cried the very tears that I had not been able to let loose the day I received word of his death. Being able to put flowers on his grave and praying there with my sister under the warm native sun at last eased my pain a bit.

Next we visited our grandparents' grave. I could envision Mamá Luya with such absolute clarity there on the landing of the stairs, her steel gray look staring right through me, just the way I had last seen her forty years ago when I left Cuba that 13th of July. And I began to bawl again.

"There, there, Lauri, don't beat yourself up…"

Over the next few days we went everywhere—our old school, the church where we had our first communion, the beach where we learned to swim. It was like our old house in Vedado where we had spent our childhood had been suspended in time. The same planters out front, the same bluish stained-glass window in the middle of the door, the same black and green tiles… I don't know why the floors made such an impression on me… Maybe the universe of a child is much closer to the ground. That's where we would sit and play jacks, do our homework, and paint. And that's where we would make bets to see who could walk the farthest without stepping on one of the cracks.

∽

It's amazing how Lauri can remember everything. When we passed by the Center for Culture, she immediately said:

"That's where the old High School used to be…"

When she saw monuments like the Giraldilla, the one dedicated to the students, and El Templete, she got so excited, you would have thought she'd come across an old friend. Pedritín was shocked to learn that she knew more about Havana's history than he himself did.

"This is where the Spaniards celebrated the first Mass..."

"Hemingway used to come to this hotel often..."

She took picture after picture, and kept on repeating, just as we do: "It's not easy; it's just not easy..."

Standing in front of the Cathedral, the Palace of the Governors, the Church of San Francisco, she was like a pilgrim entering the Holy Land.

"Menchu, Old Havana is gorgeous..."

"Yeah, they're doing a good job restoring it. Before I retired I helped out with some of the plans for the renovation..."

Lauri gloated over everything. One afternoon while we were having some ice cream and lemonade at a cafe in the Plaza de Armas she moaned happily:

"Wow, Menchu, you were right. The ice cream here really is delicious."

"It's probably because of the sugar..."

Something amazing happened in the Bodeguita del Medio. Lauri insisted on treating us to a *mojito.* All of a sudden she got up from the bar as if there were a spring in her seat and she went right over to the photos that are behind the glass.

"Look! Look, Tía Flor's in this photo!"

And sure enough, there she was, right in the middle of a bunch of people, including the poet Guillén.

"All these years and we had never even noticed that picture. Then Lauri gets here and in no time flat she immediately recognizes it," said Pedritín astonished once again.

"Oh, kiddo, the truth is I never really left."

⧸⧹

My homeland welcomed me back; its branches embraced me; its breeze caressed me; its streets flirted with me; the hibiscus winked at me; the coleus danced for me. The waves crashed against the *Malecón* bathing my skin, while the salty mist ran down my face and blended with my tears. On each street a memory appeared: the house of a particular friend, a Doctor's office, the cinema we'd always go to. It even seemed like the deer at the entrance gates at the zoo were going to jump up and welcome me back.

There's no doubt about it, Havana is deteriorating. It reminds me of one of those great dames from long ago who now, past her prime, shows her age with caked-on makeup, the kind who's poorly dressed, with her scars and wrinkles all showing, and yet the kind that has still kept her elegance and dignity intact. Perhaps I found my greatest comfort in gazing at the trees: at those almond trees in front of my house whose shadows sheltered my childhood dreams, at the tall pines at Veneciana beach, the Seagrape trees, the slender palms, the thick trunks of the *jaguey* trees in the Park of the Hanged where we played so many afternoons during our youth.

Every so often Lauri would say the same thing over and over to us:
"You know, it's not just some made-up nostalgia that a bunch of exiles cling to. It's really true. Our skies in fact are bluer, our beaches are truly more beautiful, and our air is actually cleaner."

With so many flattering remarks, she immediately won over Pedritín, who without giving it a second thought forgot about all the trash-talk he had been throwing around, and instead he gushed all over her.

It made me happy too. All my worries had been for nothing. Lauri acted differently in Havana than she had in Miami. It really did seem like she had never left. She was always generous with everybody, but in a tactful way so she wouldn't offend them.

"Menchu, do you think that Maruja would be offended if I left her a little 'thank you,' you know besides the small soaps I brought for her? Maybe even a little bit of money? It was so nice of her to take care of

Mamá when you came to visit me..."

The reunion with the cousins was also wonderful. We were all able to get together at the house in Vedado on our birthday. Lauri got along really well with Magaly. And as for Armandito, forget it, it was like the two of them had just seen each other yesterday. All they did was talk baseball all night long. She even hit it off with Pedritín's wife.

I was so sorry that Tania couldn't have been there with us.

"And Ernestico too," added Mamá.

∞

During the twenty-one days I spent in Cuba I lived life to the fullest, as if I were trying to make up for lost time. I would fall into bed exhausted, and I'd sleep like a baby. Nothing had ever happened to me like this. I didn't miss Miami. I didn't even miss my kids, although I thought a lot about how great it would be to come back with them.

I don't know what I enjoyed more, the strolls with my brother and sister, or the moments I would spend chatting with Mamá. I told her everything that had happened in my life, but not in the same way I had told Menchu. When I could, I would soften the tough times and emphasize the positive ones. More than anything else, I told her all about my sons and about Tyler. I did everything I could to wait on her and relieve my sister a bit. After a few days, she even began to get us mixed up:

"Menchu...I mean, Lauri..."

"Look at that, I thought you were the only one who could tell us apart," we would kid her.

"I get you mixed up in my heart because I love you both exactly the same."

It surprised me just how generous Cubans are in spite of their poverty. At every house we visited, they would offer us coffee or juice or even some flan. Imagine doing that under their circumstances. That's what breaks my heart the most. I wish I could help all of them. I was able to give out a few little gifts, but of course it was Mamá and Menchu that I worried about the most. At least I was able to buy them a fan, and they ate better while I was there. I also left the pantry stocked so they could get by until I could send them some money again. However it seemed that everything I did for them really didn't amount to much.

Everybody complained about the regime constantly. Only once did I dare say something to Menchu.

"I don't understand something. If everybody's tired of the way things are, why don't they do something?"

"Lauri, it's not that easy. Besides, haven't you noticed that there are still a lot of people who are in favor of all this?"

"Yeah, it's probably the ones who have something to gain…"

"Well, yeah, but maybe it's also the ones who fear change…"

A week before Lauri was scheduled to go back, she told me she wanted us to spend a few days at the beach in Varadero. I tried to change the subject, but she insisted.

"You think Mamá would want to come with us? Or maybe Maruja wouldn't mind watching her for a bit? It would only be for two days…"

"It's not that Lauri…"

"Then what's the matter?"

"You want to spend the night there, right?"

"Yeah, because it's too far to go and come back in just one day, don't you think? We could just get a hotel…"

I didn't have any other choice but to tell her the truth.

"Look, the thing is, I can't stay at the same hotels you go to."

"Menchu…I can't believe it!"

"Yeah, it's true, when Alfredo my friend from Spain visited we had some problems…and that's why now we always rent a house…it's better than causing problems…"

"Don't worry about it all. We're not going."

"No, if you want to go by yourself, I understand..."

"Absolutely not, sis. We'll go some other time."

⚮

More than not going to Varadero, it aggravated me that it didn't seem to bother anybody that they weren't allowed to go places that were reserved for foreigners only. But I didn't say anything.

That wasn't the only thing that made me angry. One night, Armandito and Magaly invited us to a performance of the National Ballet at the Grand Theater of Havana, formerly the National Theater.

"Oh, Menchu, remember how we used to come here all the time when we were kids...?"

I immediately noticed, however, that everyone was dressed so elegantly, like I hadn't seen anyone else in Havana until then. When we went into the theater, I also noticed that Armandito had tossed a few coins to some kids hanging around the car, telling them:

"Keep an eye on it for me, comrades."

Magaly must have noticed that it didn't sit well with me.

"What's the matter, Lauri? You're so quiet. Don't you like the ballet?"

"No, it's not that. Quite the contrary. I really appreciate you bringing me."

When they dropped us off, and we were alone, I couldn't hold it in any longer:

"Sis, I don't understand it at all... Forty years of Revolution and so many sacrifices made by so many people, and for what?! Today, there's a new upper class... Those people we saw, all dressed up, with their fancy shoes and perfume... They're not the same as Maruja and all the other friends you've introduced me to... You and I looked like we were Magaly's poor relatives."

"Well, since Armandito is in the military, and now that he's gotten into one of those new 'for-profit' enterprises..."

"Look, I'm happy that they're doing well, but if that's what it's all about, it must be easy to be a revolutionary. Do you know who I've thought about a lot lately?"

"I don't know."

"My in-laws…and what they took from them, and I'm not talking about their money Menchu, I'm talking about their life, the life they led, their careers, their house, their neighborhood… If it had all happened to make Cuba a better place, maybe it would've been worth it, but look, look around you, it's been a disaster! Damn it to hell, you don't know how much all of this hurts me!"

"Lauri, what you have to keep in mind is that a lot of the social differences you see are symptoms of the current crisis, but even at that the ones who can't afford decent clothing and shoes still have received a great education, healthcare, welfare, and social and cultural opportunities that weren't accessible to them fifty years ago. I could list for you the names of the sons and daughters of maids who have gone on to get their doctorate…or the children of illiterate famers who have risen to the ranks of overseeing research centers."

"Menchu, don't give me that… Yes, okay, I'm not denying anything you say, but at what price? In the United States, the same is true, even the lowliest can become president, but not at the price of repression and not by taking away from some just to give to others nor by taking away all civil liberties."

"Sis, please! Let's not fight…"

"Well, the truth is I really don't want to fight either…after all, this trip has taught me a lot…like why you were so bewildered at the supermarket…sometimes you seemed…I don't know…almost ungrateful. It's just that I went to so much trouble so you could have a good time and so that nothing was missing and, I'm not bringing it up just so I can throw in your face, but everything there is expensive, and money comes from working hard, it doesn't grow on trees, but now I guess I realize…it's just that Cubans are very…well I don't know if it's that they're stubborn…maybe they're just a little bit too proud."

"Maybe…but we can't lose our dignity… Or else…"

"Another thing I've learned is that the cliché I hear so often, that

Cubans have torn down the past, just isn't true… Quite the opposite, what you do find is that there isn't anything that's new."

"Maybe you're right. The most uncertain thing around here is the future."

"Oh, Menchu, what a cross we Cubans have had to bear."

And as I watched the dawn appear over Havana from the little room at Mamá Luya's house, where we had so often scampered about as children, I felt an agonizing pain in my chest. It was the pain of my heart breaking for Cuba.

The date for her departure grew nearer. We were probably fortunate that there was a stream of people who kept coming to the house to tell Lauri goodbye and to ask her to take letters and all types of things back to Miami. With so many people around we didn't have the chance to become sad.

"I'll come back as soon as I can," Lauri kept promising Mamá, "and I'll bring your grandchildren."

"Now I can die in peace."

"Don't you dare say that! For goodness sake, I need you now more than ever. Besides, I'm going to convince Ricardo to come too."

The afternoon before I left, Menchu wanted to take me over to Casablanca. We took a ferry across the harbor to the *parador*. The view of Havana from the other side of the bay was spectacular.

"Come on, let me treat you to an ice cream…my last ice cream in Cuba."

"Well, your last one on *this* trip."

I felt like I needed to tell my sister something:

"Menchu, I understand that you don't want to leave. Before I didn't get it, but now I do… And even though it breaks my heart to see what you have to endure—and I'll help however I can—down deep I'm happy that you're here."

"And I understand too why you can't stay…"

"At least, not at the moment, you understand, don't you?"

"Of course. It's one thing to come for a few days, but it's difficult…"

"It's not because of the food situation or shortage of water…"

"I know. I also learned a lot about things when I went to Miami."

"Really?"

"I've come to the conclusion that all the talk around here about the first wave of exiles just isn't fair at all… All you ever hear is that they were traitors who sold out to the Americans and things like that. It's touching to see how all of them have fought to keep the memory of Cuba alive and to pass it down to their kids. I know that you love Cuba."

"That's why I always say being Cuban is an incurable disease that you get in your blood, and sometimes it's even contagious."

"You're right, there's something magical about Cuba…that's why all the foreigners fall in love with it."

"You don't know what this trip has meant to me…"

"And to us too…"

"No, Menchu, you can't understand. Obviously, the most important thing has been to see all of you. But it's more than that. Coming back to my country has allowed me to put my whole life into perspective. You won't believe it, but it's even helped me understand and forgive Robertico, something that I hadn't been able to do up until now."

"I'm so happy for you, sis…"

"Even more so, I no longer have doubts about who I am, and I don't feel any more like my country has rejected me. Even if I were to die tomorrow, even if I could never come back again…"

"Hey! Don't say stuff like that."

"Menchu, listen to me, what I'm trying to say is that this huge wound that I've been carrying around inside of me all these years is finally starting to heal. So many times I had thought that the Revolution had taken everything from us, but it didn't. No one realized that we had paradise right here, inside of us, all along. All my fears were pointless. I truly feel like I've been at home, regardless of all the other stuff. It's a victory, a small one, and a private one, but for me it's enough."

"I'm so glad, Lauri...there just shouldn't be any ill feelings among Cubans."

After we finished our ice cream, we sat a bit longer and admired the silhouette of the city and the ever-changing colors of the sunset and its reflection across the bay. Before we left, we made our way up the hill to the statue of Christ.

I lifted my eyes and gazed up at the white, colossal figure.

"Come on, let's say an 'Our Father.'"

After that we stayed there a long time, hand in hand, in silence.

~

The night before Lauri left, we got to bed early. We didn't say too much. We were tired and perhaps felt like we didn't need words any longer to express ourselves.

I could tell that Lauri was trying to downplay the goodbyes in order to make it easier on Mamá. Maybe she could tell that I was having a hard time too.

~

Even though my plan was to come back as soon as I could, when I went to hug Mamá I shuddered in fear that it was going to be the last time. Now that she was once again in my life, I didn't want to lose her once more. As if she could read my mind, she told me very calmly:

"Lauri, don't be upset, *mijita*. Come back when you can... I'll always be here waiting for you."

~

Pedritín had told us that he was going to send a friend by to take us to the airport because it was going to be impossible for him to get away at that hour. But he showed up right on time.

"How could I let you head back without me saying goodbye? Come on, I'll drive you out to Rancho Boyeros."

It seemed like that the clock was running too fast to all of us. We didn't want to leave each other again. We all felt the same pain in the middle of our chests, as if our hearts were being torn in two.

∞

When the plane took off, I kept watching out the window until the distance and my tears kept me from seeing the outline of the Island, and then everything turned into blue, the blue of the sky and of the sea.

∞

I saw the plane take off. I followed it with my gaze as it climbed. When it disappeared into the clouds, I was still waving goodbye to my sister.

Back at home, Mamá was waiting for me to eat.

"Come on, you old woman, you have to eat so you can keep up your strength for Lauri's return."

"That's right, Lauri and her kids, and Ricardo and his, and Tania and Ernestico...we'll finally all be together again."

"Maybe next Christmas..."

"Maybe so..."

We ate in silence while on the news they talked about the preparations for the upcoming Summit of the Ibero-American Presidents that was going to be held in Havana at the end of the year. Out of the blue, Mamá told me:

"Uff, *mija*, turn that nonsense off. It's always the same song and dance."

∞

I cried until fatigue overcame me. I closed my eyes, but I couldn't sleep. All I can see is the blinding light of Havana. It's burned onto my retina. It still hurts my eyes.

Memoria del silencio

UVA DE ARAGÓN

A Fernando, porque me instó a escribir una novela.
A mi hermana Lucía, sin quien no la hubiera podido escribir.
A mi madre, que sólo alcanzó a leer los primeros capítulos,
y a mis hijas, que espero lean los últimos.

AGRADECIMIENTOS

A Gloria, Lisandro, Nara, Toni,
Armando, Patricia, Eloísa, Gemma,
Marta, Margarita, Álvaro,
"el gordo", Antonia, Mercy y Pepe,
por sus valiosos consejos.
A Isabel, por tantas copias que hizo.
A aquellos a quienes les robé jirones
de sus vidas para contarlos aquí.
Y a mis padres y abuelos
porque me transmitieron
el amor a Cuba y a la literatura.

Gracias a Sara E. Cooper & Cubanabooks,
y en especial gracias a Jeffrey C. Barnett,
traductor, amigo y cómplice,
sin cuya comprensión y dedicación
a esta novela, esta nueva edición bilingüe
no sería hoy realidad.

Al pintor Humberto Calzada
por su generosidad
al permitirme utilizar su obra

*"A Painted Memory II, Acrílico sobre fotografía por
Victoria Montoro Zamorano" para la cubiera*

UNA NOTA DE LA AUTORA

Todas las palabras parecen insuficientes para expresar mi gratitud a Jeffrey C. Barnett por su interés en mi obra y especialmente por el tiempo, esfuerzo, dedicación y amor que ha puesto en la traducción de mi novela *Memoria del silencio*. Ha logrado una obra maestra. También deseo agradecer a Sara Cooper y a Cubanabooks el entusiasmo con que aceptaron la publicación de este libro.

Recientemente, una adaptación de la novela al teatro se estrenó, bajo la dirección de Virginia Aponte, en la Universidad Católica Andrés Bello en Caracas, Venezuela, con una asombrosa acogida de la prensa, los estudiantes y el público en general. Esta experiencia me llevó a comprender que esta historia cubana transciende las fronteras nacionales. Es una gran recompensa para un autor comprobar el valor universal de su obra.

Mi esperanza es que esta edición bilingüe logre que la novela tenga un mayor alcance, y que puedan leerla muchos estudiantes y profesores en el mundo académico, al igual que otros lectores. Si contribuye a una mejor comprensión de la historia contemporánea de Cuba y su diáspora, así como del sufrimiento de todos los pueblos divididos por ideologías o desplazados por guerras u otros conflictos, todos mis esfuerzos al escribirla serían más que justificados

Además de la dedicatoria original, deseo ofrecer esta nueva edición a los cubanoamericanos nacidos en Estados Unidos o que vinieron a este país muy pequeños, y que prefieren leer en inglés, su primer idioma. Esta es la historia de sus padres y abuelos, y, en gran medida, también la de ellos. En especial, quiero dedicar este libro a mis nietos Zachary, Cristian, Brandon y Nikulas.

Uva de Aragón
Miami, 10 de abril de 2014

CAPÍTULO UNO
Reencuentro en Miami

—YO TÚ EN VEZ DE PONERME ESE PITUSA, que estuviste medio año para conseguirlo, me pondría la ropa peor, la más ripiada.

—¿Estás loca?

—Claro que no, Menchu, pero si total, seguro que tu hermana te va a comprar mil cosas. Es más, yo tú llevaba la maleta vacía.

—Chica, mira que tú estás mal. Yo no voy a Miami para que mi hermana me compre nada.

—Y entonces, ¿a qué vas? No te me irás a quedar por allá...

—Por Dios, Maruja, ¿tú crees que yo voy a abandonar a Mamá?

—Entonces, si no fuera por la vieja, ¿te quedarías?

—No, tampoco. Hace mucho que decidí que no me iría de Cuba jamás.

—Así me gusta, compañera. No puede uno venderse a los dólares de la Yuma. Aquí, socialismo o muerte.

—Oye, es muy temprano para esa cantaleta. Mira que ni un buchito de café tengo en el estómago.

—No te pongas brava, tú sabes que es jugando. La verdad es que me da miedo que te vayas a ir tú también. Eres la única amiga que me queda...

—Y tú no te me pongas sentimental que se me aflojan las piernas. Si supieras, estoy loca por ir, y al mismo tiempo tengo miedo. Quizás Laurita y yo no nos entendamos... Hemos tenido unas vidas tan distintas. ¡Si alguien nos hubiera dicho cuando éramos niñas que nos íbamos a separar a los 18 años y a no vernos más por casi cuarenta...! ¡Tan unidas que estábamos! Imagínate, siendo *jimaguas*... Mamá nos vestía iguales. Nadie nos podía distinguir. Sólo la vieja.

—Para que tú veas, y ahora Mariana a veces te confunde con tu hermana. Es que ya ella no está tan clara...

—Yo quisiera convencer a Laurita de que la viniera a ver.

—A eso vas entonces, ¿a pedirle a tu hermana que venga a ver a la vieja? Si no lo hace por su propia voluntad y se lo tienes que pedir, bastante mala hija es.

—No, si se ocupa de mandarnos todo lo que puede.

—Sí, mi amiga, mandar sí, pero no sólo de pan vive el hombre. ¿Y el cariño?

—Cada cual tiene sus ideas... Por eso voy... Ya es hora de que podamos abrazarnos y respetar cada una nuestra manera de pensar.

—Es que tú eres muy buena, Menchu.

—No, Maruja, yo no soy mejor que los demás. Cuando Robertico se llevó a mi hermana fue como si se llevara a la mitad de mi vida. Ahora lo único que tenemos en común son los recuerdos de la infancia, y al menos eso quisiera hacer, pasarnos una noche como cuando éramos pepillas, hablando sin parar, recordando aquel primer guateque al que fuimos y como nadie nos sacaba a bailar, y cuando nos escapábamos a la bodega del chino después de la escuela a comprar africanas, a dos quilos cada una, y hacíamos pajaritas con los papeles de distintos colores y aquellos lazos gigantescos que nos ponía Mamá en la cabeza. Creo que con esa tela hoy se hace uno un vestido...

—No tienes por qué tener miedo. Se van a llevar de lo mejor.

—Es que he oído tantos cuentos de gente que son un estorbo allá para la familia. A veces regresan antes de que se les termine el tiempo del permiso y están felices de volver a su casa.

—Oye, ahí está Pedritín con el carro para llevarte al aeropuerto.

No quise demorar mucho la despedida porque me costó tanto decidirme a dejar a Mamá que si lo pensaba mucho no me iba. El camino lo hicimos en silencio. Pedritín no estaba de acuerdo con que yo fuera a ver a Laurita a Miami. No comprendía que los vínculos familiares fueran más importantes que todo lo demás. Para él todo el que se había ido para el Norte era un traidor, un pro-yanqui, y los yanquis eran los peores enemigos, los que amenazaban al país y ponían en peligro la soberanía nacional. Mucha soberanía y muy poco en los fogones, dicen algunos. No sólo de soberanía vive el hombre. Pero era inútil hablar esas cosas con mi hermano menor. Él era tan chiquito cuando vino la

Revolución… Bueno, yo tampoco admito las críticas sino en lo más recóndito de mí misma. Porque las dudas duelen, pecho dentro, como si uno llevara un niño muerto en las entrañas… Hieren los ojos esas casas despintadas y apuntaladas de Centro Habana. Las vidrieras vacías. Los carros antiguos. Hasta los afiches amarillentos del Che Guevara. Y eso que últimamente las cosas han mejorado bastante, sobre todo para los que tienen dólares. Por lo menos hay más movimiento en la calle, la gente anda siempre en algo… ya sea legalmente o en la bolsa negra… En fin, tras los bolsillos de los turistas, jineteando o bisneando… Y a la Habana Vieja la están poniendo preciosa… ¡Qué trabajo me costó decidirme a vender los libros de Tía Flor! Iván me los llevó a la Plaza de Armas y le dieron 200 dólares por ellos. Bueno, a lo mejor se quedó con una buena tajada. Ya ni en los amigos se puede confiar. De todas formas, con eso comimos mejor los últimos meses y hasta pude dejar algo para la vieja mientras yo estuviera fuera. La verdad es que no quería que Lauri me viera tan desmejorada… Una también tiene su orgullo. Lo malo ha sido lo bravo que se puso Pedritín. Ni que él leyera tanto para que le importaran así unos libros que lo único que hacían era coger polvo…

Me puse a mirar las calles… las casas… los árboles… la gente. ¿Cómo se sentirán los que hacen este recorrido pensando que a lo mejor nunca volverán? ¿Habría presentido mi hermana el día que se fue que sería por tanto tiempo, quizás para siempre…? Yo no podría vivir fuera de mi país. Es un consuelo saber que en un mes regresaré.

Pedritín me acompañó a despachar la maleta y a pagar los impuestos de aeropuerto. Nos despedimos frente a las casetas de Inmigración. De pronto me entregó un pequeño paquete y me dijo:

—Dale esto a Lauri de mi parte. Para que vea que en Cuba todavía hay cosas buenas.

Luego me abrazó fuerte, como recuerdo lo había hecho solamente en otra ocasión, en el cementerio, después de que enterramos al viejo. Y se marchó sin virar ni una vez la cabeza, pese a que yo le gritaba:

—Pedritín, cuídame mucho a la vieja…

Estuvimos más de cuatro horas esperando. Resulta que le dicen a uno una cosa, y luego es otra. Es decir, se suponía que los pasajeros llegaran a las 10 a.m. y el avión saliera a la 1 p.m. Pero no era cierto. El vuelo estaba para las 2 de la tarde. Además, salió con retraso. Y yo con el estómago tan vacío... Por fin me decidí a subir a la cafetería a tomar un café. Noté a algunos pasajeros que se apretujaban en el balcón interior desde donde alcanzaban a ver a los familiares que habían quedado atrás. Agitaban las manos en señal de despedida, muchas veces con los ojos llenos de lágrimas. Comprendí que eran los que se iban con salida definitiva, y me recordó a cuando Laurita se fue. Y luego Ricardo, aunque a él no pudimos ni venir a despedirlo. Por más que me quise controlar, se me puso un nudo en la garganta. Traté de mirar al resto de los viajeros para distraerme. Había muchas mujeres cincuentonas como yo, o incluso más viejas, emperifolladas con su mejor vestidito, intentando inútilmente disimular su pobreza. Los que habían venido a Cuba de visita y ahora regresaban a sus casas en Miami se distinguían enseguida. Y no tanto por la ropa sino porque estaban más gordos, tenían mejor color, y protestaban más. Yo sí que no decía ni jota. Total, para qué ponerme el hígado a la vinagreta si íbamos a despegar cuando al piloto, o al controlador aéreo, o al tipo de Seguridad o al que fuera, le saliera de los mismísimos cojones.

Si me oyera Mamá. Nunca nos dejó decir malas palabras. Ni a los varones. Aunque Ricardo y Pedritín las decían de todos modos. A Laurita y a mí nos las enseñó Tía Flor. ¡Con qué gusto le dije por primera vez a mi primo Luisito "comemierda"! No me importó que me oyera la vieja y me amenazara con lavarme la boca con jabón. ¿Qué edad tendríamos entonces? Como nueve años por lo menos... Seguro que Lauri se acuerda.

Ya estamos a punto de despegar. ¡Qué calor, Dios mío! Mira que hace años que no me monto en un avión. Bueno, sólo he volado dos veces, aquella vez de niña que Papá nos llevó a todos a Nueva York, y cuando fui a Moscú con Lázaro. ¡Cómo hacíamos planes de jovencitas Lauri y yo sobre los lugares a los que queríamos ir! A Roma, a Venecia, a St. Michael, por la novela aquella que habíamos leído que nos impresionó tanto, a Grecia, y a París. Siempre soñábamos con ir a París, y con unos trajes muy elegantes y unos perfumes muy exóticos…. y unos hombres maravillosos a nuestros pies.

La vida de Laurita tampoco habrá sido un paraíso. ¿Habrá sido feliz con Robertico? ¿Se habrá acostumbrado a la viudez? Todo fue tan rápido… Tantas cosas que no sabemos la una de la otra. Antes nos escribíamos mucho. Yo creo que a diario. Después, ¿qué pasó? Es cierto que las comunicaciones se hicieron muy difíciles, pero de todos modos…

De nuevo se me humedecieron los ojos cuando observé las costas de Cuba que iban quedando atrás. "La tierra más fermosa," dijo Colón al ver por primera vez nuestro suelo. ¿Tendremos alguna maldición los cubanos por ser nuestra Isla tan bella? No creo que sea falso nacionalismo. Cuba tiene una magia especial que seduce a la gente. ¿Qué pensará Lauri de nuestro país? Algunas cartas, algunas llamadas telefónicas, casi siempre en momentos de crisis, no bastan para conocerse dos personas. Somos en verdad dos extrañas.

Tantos años separadas, como si estuviéramos muy lejos la una de la otra, y de pronto, en apenas unos minutos, se divisa Miami. Tiene más edificios de lo que pensaba. Siento que el corazón se me quiere salir por la boca. Me tiemblan las piernas cuando bajo del avión. ¿Y si no la reconozco entre tanta gente? Hace mucho tiempo que no nos vemos. ¡Qué bobería! ¿Cómo no voy a conocer a mi hermana gemela?

Fue ella quien me gritó primero:

—¡Menchu…! ¡Menchu…!

—¡Laurita!

Mi miedo era infundado. Casi antes de vernos, nos reconocimos. El abrazo fue largo y apretado. Todo lo que nos rodeaba —gentes, barullo, luces, voces— se me borró. Por un instante, la vida se detuvo. Sólo existíamos nosotras dos llorando sin parar. Habíamos compartido íntimamente nuestra infancia y adolescencia, y ahora nos reencontrábamos para develar el misterio de lo que había del otro lado de ese muro de agua y de incomprensiones que había separado a los cubanos. Y yo, qué cosa más absurda, no dejaba de pensar en aquella fiestecita en que nadie nos sacaba a bailar.

Laura fue la primera que reaccionó.

—¿Dónde está tu maleta?

El aeropuerto era un hervidero de cubanos. Por fin salimos de allí. Me preguntó si quería esperarla mientras ella iba a buscar el carro, pero no sé por qué me dio miedo quedarme sola y preferí acompañarla. El parqueo era inmenso, de no sé cuántos pisos. En el camino me sentí un poco aturdida. Tanto tráfico, el radio encendido, y, aunque ya debería estar acostumbrada, el estómago tan vacío, me producían una sensación de desmayo. Estuve a punto de preguntarle si faltaba mucho, si podíamos parar a tomar café. Pero no veía ningún establecimiento comercial cerca y no me decidí a pedírselo.

Cuando por fin salimos de la autopista, Lauri me dijo:

—Ya estamos llegando. Esta zona se llama Westchester. Es casi toda de cubanos, y me queda muy cerca de la universidad donde enseño.

Dobló varias veces hasta que nos detuvimos frente a una casa pintada de color crema con las ventanas marrón oscuro. En el jardín del frente crecían crotos, marpacíficos, arecas.

—Las sembré —me dijo Laura mostrándome un cantero de vicarias— porque me recuerdan a Cuba… la casa de Mama Luya en el reparto La Sierra…

Ese sencillo comentario me confirmó que mi hermana había seguido emocionalmente unida a nosotros, a pesar de los años transcurridos y de tantas trabas de los gobiernos de ambos lados para separar a las familias.

En cuanto abrió la puerta y entramos a la sala, me volvió a abrazar:

—Me parece mentira que estés aquí… Ya te enseñaré todo lo demás —continuó— pero primero voy a llevarte a tu cuarto. Era el de los muchachos que lo tengo ahora para los huéspedes, o para cuando me dejan a mi nieto. En honor a ti, compré cortinas y sobrecamas nuevas… A ver, Menchu, ¿a qué te recuerda?

—Ay, mi hermana, a nuestro cuarto de niñas… Las sobrecamas son de los mismos colores… ¡Y hasta las *madonnas* de Rafael que teníamos en las cabeceras! ¿Cómo las has podido encontrar?

—No tienen valor, son unas reproducciones de la Galería de Arte de Washington... pero cuando las vi, no pude resistir comprarlas. Las tuve muchos años guardadas, y ahora las enmarqué para ti. Cuando regreses, si quieres te regalo la tuya...

—No, por Dios, si quedan tan bien aquí... Además, yo todavía tengo aquellas, las originales.

—No lo puedo creer... ay, Menchu, estoy loca por preguntarte mil cosas, y recordar juntas otras mil. Hoy mismo estaba pensando en Alicia, la conserje del colegio, cuando le cantábamos los pasodobles que nos enseñó Tía Flor y nos daba más merienda...

—Y yo me acordé esta mañana de esas noches cuando éramos pepillas, que las pasábamos sin dormir habla que te habla...

—Par de cotorras, nos decía Mamá. Y no hay Navidad que yo no recuerde cuando acompañábamos a Papá a la casa Suárez a comprar dulces... Jamás he comido un turrón de yema más rico.

—¡Y aquellas yemitas cubiertas de chocolate!

—El dependiente era calvo y tenía las manos manchadas. Cogía el papel de envolver de un rollo grande. ¡Si me parece que lo estoy viendo!

—¡De lo que te has venido a acordar!

—Ha sido muy duro para mí no tener con quién compartir estos recuerdos. Pero ya habrá tiempo. Mira, aquí tienes dos gavetas de esta cómoda para guardar tus cosas, y estos percheros en el clóset... No sé qué quieres hacer, si bañarte, desempacar, descansar... dime lo que quieres hacer...

Laurita se empeñaba en complacerme, pero no sé por qué me sentía incómoda. No pude evitar una risa nerviosa. Por fin le dije:

—... lo que me apetece es un poquito de café...

—En seguida te lo cuelo, y con espumita y todo. ¿Te dieron de comer en el avión? ¿No tienes hambre?

—La verdad es que tengo un poco de debilidad.

—Pobrecita. Te he preparado uno de tus platos favoritos para la comida... pero ahora ¿quieres un yogurt, una fruta? Mira, tengo plátanos, manzanas, mandarinas, uvas. ¿O prefieres una coca cola y galleticas con queso? Bueno... ¿un juguito?

—Cualquier cosa, Laurita... de verdad que me da lo mismo. Y tranquilízate ya, que te pareces a Cachucha.

—¡El tiempo que hacía que no me acordaba de ese personaje!

En la cocina Laura sirvió un vaso de jugo de tomate para cada una y hasta cortó unas rodajitas de limón. Luego puso queso holandés y galleticas en una tabla. Yo observaba cada uno de sus gestos... y me sentía por momentos como si estuviera frente a un espejo.

—¡Cuánta finura...!

—Por Dios... esto es hoy porque es el primer día, ya después...

—¿Te acuerdas como le gustaba a Papá el jugo de tomate?

—Sí, siempre lo ponían los domingos para empezar el almuerzo...

—Después de que veníamos de misa y escuchábamos los discos de los Panchos...

—Eran aquellos discos de 78 que se ponían uno arriba del otro e iban cayendo...

—Ahora hasta los *cassettes* están pasados de moda... todo viene en CD. Mira, si yo tengo aquí uno de los Panchos... Te lo voy a poner...

—No, Laurita, ahora no, que empezamos a llorar otra vez. Ven, siéntate conmigo. ¡Qué rico está este queso!

—Trata de imitar al de Cuba, se llamaba Gallo Azul... ¿no? Pero cuéntame, ¿cómo dejaste a Mamá?

—Bastante bien... A ella no le gusta nada separarse de mí, pero estaba tan contenta de que nos reuniéramos que ni protestó.

—¿Y Pedritín?

—Bien... me llevó al aeropuerto.

Lauri iba de un lado para otro hablando sin parar, con un nerviosismo que no recordaba en ella.

—Lauri, no des tantas vueltas y siéntate ya.

Ay, Menchu, te he extrañado tanto todos estos años... Hay tantas cosas que quiero preguntarte... que me cuentes día a día tu vida... aunque nos quedemos en vela como cuando éramos muchachitas...
—me dijo con la voz temblorosa.

—Vamos, mi hermanita, no te pongas así... Si parece un milagro que estemos juntas. En ocasiones hasta tenía miedo de que nunca más nos volviéramos a ver.

—¡Yo también!

No tuve ya dudas de nuestra conexión.

—¿Dónde pusiste mi maleta?

Busqué entre la ropa lo único que había podido traerle, y le expliqué:

—Tantas veces que hubiera querido pedirte consejos, compartir contigo... Cuando se hizo tan difícil enviar y recibir cartas empecé a llevar un diario... también recortaba cosas de la prensa y las pegaba en estas libretas, o copiaba algún poema que me gustaba... no escribía todo los días... a veces hasta pasaron años en que no lo tocaba... pero todas las cosas importantes de mi vida están aquí, Lauri. Y las he escrito para ti.

—¡Si tienes la misma caligrafía Palmer tan bonita que nos enseñaron en el colegio...! Gracias, mi hermanita... Éste es el mejor regalo, saber qué te acordabas de mí —me dijo conteniendo la emoción y luego añadió, en un tono entre confidencial y solemne:

—No me vas a creer lo que te voy a decir. Yo también he llevado un diario de mi vida. Y también lo escribía para ti. Igualito que el tuyo, incluye pasajes de la prensa y poemas que he copiado para ti... ¡Es increíble! Lo único que el mío está mecanografiado... y ya en los últimos años lo hacía en la computadora. Precisamente en estos días lo he releído y lo he ordenado para ti. Pero te juro que no he cambiado ni un punto ni una coma.

Salió del cuarto y regresó al instante con una carpeta que puso en mis manos.

—¿Puedo leerlo?

—Todavía no... te lo voy a poner en la mesa de noche para cuando estés sola, antes de dormir... yo haré lo mismo con el tuyo... Y espero que algún día escribas el capítulo sobre este reencuentro en Miami...

—Claro... y tú tendrás que añadir el de tu regreso a Cuba...

—Ya hablaremos de eso... ahora ven... déjame enseñarte el resto de la casa.

—Espera. Se me olvidaba que tengo algo más para ti.— Y saqué del bolso el paquete que me había dado para ella mi hermano.

—Te lo manda Pedritín.

—¿Para mí? ¿Qué es?

—No tengo idea…

Lauri acarició suavemente el papel cebolla. Por fin se atrevió a abrirlo. Era un collar hecho de conchas de mar. Se quedó mirándolo largamente. Luego, se lo llevó a la nariz y aspiró.

—Tú sabes, creo que aún huele a las playas de Cuba… Coño, Menchu, ¡qué desgracia la de los cubanos!

Y comenzó a sollozar incontrolablemente, como si quisiera liberarse de una pena muy honda. La abracé y lloramos juntas, hasta que ella se separó y corrió para la cocina.

—¡Por Dios, por un poco se me quema la comida!

CAPÍTULO DOS
Cubans, Go Home!

LO QUE SIEMPRE RECUERDO DE LA HABANA ES LA LUZ. Cuando trato de reconstruir aquel 13 de julio de 1959, cierro los ojos y veo una luz cegadora que me hiere los ojos. Vamos en el *pisicorre*. Robertico y yo nos sentamos en el último asiento. Como está colocado al revés y el cristal de atrás es amplio, así contemplamos mejor la ciudad que dentro de pocas horas vamos a dejar. Papá va al timón con Mamá a su lado. En el asiento del centro, con nuestras maletas, Menchu y Pedritín. Hay un sol vertical que hace que todos los colores se tornen más brillantes, como si una especie de fuego animara por dentro edificios y calles, y hasta el mismo aire, un vapor denso que emana del asfalto y parece contener punticos amarillos, azules y rojos.

Ayer nos casamos. La ceremonia fue en la Parroquia del Vedado. Yo sé que Robertico estaba triste por la ausencia de sus padres. El brindis lo hicimos en casa. Todo muy sencillo. No era lo que Mami y Papi hubieran querido para la boda de una de sus hijas. Ni lo que yo había soñado. Pero era mejor no llamar la atención. Papá hasta sugirió que en las invitaciones Robertico no usara su apellido compuesto, Fernández-Luaces, sino Fernández, a secas. ¡Con qué vehemencia se negó! ¡Cómo me gusta cuando se enoja…! Disfruto oyendo su voz hasta tal punto que me pierdo en ella y a veces no distingo las palabras. Amo cada uno de sus gestos, el movimiento de sus manos, la forma en que frunce el ceño. Vinieron casi todas mis compañeras a la boda. Lo difícil fue no poder decirles que al día siguiente Robertico y yo no nos íbamos de luna de miel a Varadero, como habíamos dicho, sino a Estados Unidos, y que el viaje podría ser mucho más largo que las dos semanas previstas. Yo pienso que para septiembre volveremos y podré matricularme en la universidad. Es más, le he pedido a Menchu que cuando ella haga su solicitud de ingreso, haga la mía también. Mi hermana sabe imitar mi firma perfectamente… Y yo la de ella, claro.

La noche de bodas fue… no sé… distinta a lo que me imaginaba. Me sentí feliz cuando Roberto me tomó en sus brazos y me besó... luego, como no tengo punto de comparación... no sé... sin duda no fue como en las películas... claro, quizás él estaba nervioso, y yo, ¡ni se diga! No se me ocurrió que me iba a quitar el *déshabillé* tan pronto. ¡Con lo que tardamos Mamá, Menchu y yo para escogerlo! Y en unos segundos estaba en el suelo como un trapo sucio. Claro, yo no estaba allí para modelar ropa interior... Pero hubiera preferido que no hubiera tenido tanta prisa.

¡Todo pasó tan rápido! Luego no pegué los ojos en toda la noche. Yo no estoy acostumbrada a dormir con nadie en la misma cama. Incluso cuando de niña me enfermaba y Mamá prefería que durmiera en su cuarto, me costaba mucho trabajo conciliar el sueño. Lo más lindo fue por la mañana, cuando, después de tomar el desayuno y de mirar las olas romper contra el Malecón, regresamos a la cama e hicimos otra vez el amor. Esa segunda vez me gustó más.

Íbamos a ir directamente al aeropuerto, pero Roberto me adivinó el pensamiento.

—Si nos apuramos, podemos coger un taxi a tu casa para que veas a tu familia y tu padre nos lleve al aeropuerto. Seguro que acaban de regresar de misa. ¿Por qué no los llamas y les dices que vamos para allá?

Cuando llegamos, subí al piso alto y recorrí cada habitación. No sé qué extraño presentimiento me hizo pensar que nunca más volvería a aquella casa donde había nacido y vivido los 18 años de mi existencia. Al mismo tiempo me reproché ser muy dramática, una chiquilla tonta con influencia de Hollywood.

Por fin voy a mi cuarto. Contemplo las dos camas, con sus sobrecamas de flores rosas y azules. Echadas sobre estos lechos, Menchu y yo hemos compartido sueños y preocupaciones, nos hemos quedado hasta las tantas leyendo novelas de Louise M. Alcott y de Alejandro Dumas, las rimas de Bécquer, las leyendas de Ricardo Palma, *Los zapaticos de rosa de Martí*... Aquí hemos estudiado durante horas y horas y hemos escuchado escondidas los juegos de pelota de La Habana y el Almendares cuando Mamá nos creía ya durmiendo...

Veo sobre la mesita de noche mis cuadernos escolares y el libro que usé para mi último examen de bachillerato, apenas hace unos días. Es la *Geografía de Cuba* de Leví Marrero. Lo tomo entre las manos. Lo hojeo. Miro las páginas subrayadas, los mapas de Cuba coloreados, y la letra de las canciones de Lucho Gatica escritas por Menchu en las páginas interiores de la contraportada. Ya Robertico me grita que es hora de irnos. Dejo el libro sobre la cama y voy en busca de la pamela que compré para el viaje y que ayer, con la prisa, se me olvidó llevarme. ¡Se ven tan bonitas las mujeres con sombrero! Pero es inútil. O no me la sé poner o no me queda bien. Oigo las voces familiares que me apuran. Tiro el sombrero sobre la cama. Antes de irme, una última mirada a mi alcoba de niña y adolescente. El juego de cuarto estilo provenzal francés que nos regalaron al cumplir los 15. Las *madonnas* de Rafael sobre las cabeceras. Y, sobre el lecho de sobrecama floreada que acunó mis sueños de juventud, el libro de *Geografía de Cuba* y la pamela blanca, con su gran lazo rosado.

Mamá Luya no quiere venir al aeropuerto. Papá dice que es mejor así, porque no vamos a caber todos en la máquina. Me despido de ella en los altos de la escalera. Aspiro su fragancia a jazmín y siento la suavidad de su cutis contra el mío. En el rellano, alzo la vista y la contemplo. Su cabeza cana y sus ojos gris acero. Sé que en cuanto me vaya se echará a llorar, pero ahora me sostiene la mirada y me sonríe. Le tiro un beso y corro escaleras abajo, temerosa de que si la vuelvo a ver la abrazaré llorando y no habrá quien me separe de ella.

Por el camino me concentro en mirarlo todo —calles, árboles, casas, gente— como queriendo grabarlo para siempre en mi memoria. Me entran las dudas. Pasamos el Palacio de los Deportes. Sé que Robertico y yo nos queremos, pero la idea de separarme de mi familia y de irme de mi país me llena de angustia. Ya estamos llegando. Es mi luna de miel… debo estar feliz… pronto regresaremos… me digo a mí misma.

En Rancho Boyeros me sorprende encontrarme a mi hermano Ricardo. Me abraza muy fuerte y se va enseguida, no sé si porque está apurado o por ocultar su emoción. De la despedida final apenas recuerdo nada más. Sólo las lágrimas calladas, los abrazos, las advertencias discretas, y un dolor en el medio del pecho como si se me hubiera partido en dos.

Cuando por fin el avión despega, me quedo mirando por la ventanilla hasta que las lágrimas y la distancia no me dejan ver más el contorno de la Isla y todo se convierte en azul de cielo y mar. Adiós, Cuba.

Lloro hasta que me vence el cansancio. Apoyo la cabeza en el hombro de mi marido y cierro los ojos. Pero no puedo dormir. Sólo veo la luz cegadora de La Habana. La llevo prendida a la retina. Todavía me hiere los ojos.

Cuba. Fidel Castro anunció su renuncia como Primer Ministro de Cuba el 17 de julio durante una comparecencia por televisión. Declaró que las "diferencias morales" entre él y el Presidente Manuel Urrutia Lleó no le dejaban "otra alternativa… sino renunciar." Acusó a Urrutia de "una actitud rayana en la traición" al demorar las acciones de la Revolución, la distribución de las tierras (…) y de no firmar las regulaciones que sentencian a la pena de muerte a los contrarrevolucionarios. Urrutia presentó su renuncia más tarde ese 17 de Julio y buscó refugio con su familia en Bauta, un pueblo cercano a La Habana. (…)Oswaldo Dorticós Torrado, Ministro de las Leyes de la Revolución, de 40 años, fue nombrado por el gabinete como Presidente. (…) El Capitán Antonio Núñez Jiménez, de 36 años, director ejecutivo del Instituto de Reforma Agraria de Cuba, declaró en una conferencia de prensa en Nueva York el 19 de julio que Urrutia había tratado de chantajear al gobierno cubano con acusaciones falsas de que estaba dominado por comunistas. Núñez negó haber sido jamás comunista. Castro, que había estado bajo constante presión por todo su gabinete para que retirara su renuncia, informó a 500,000 de sus partidarios en un acto para conmemorar el 6to aniversario del Movimiento 26 de Julio, que asumiría de nuevo el cargo de Primer Ministro para cumplir "la voluntad del pueblo."

(*Facts on File* 19.978, 243)

Cuando llegamos a Miami fuimos a vivir con mis suegros a una casa bastante grande en la zona del Soutwest. Además de Adela y Roberto, que ocupaban la habitación principal, vivían con nosotros Juancito, mi cuñado, que tendría entonces unos 9 años, y Vidal, el hermano de Adela, un poco menor que ella. Juancito compartía una habitación con su tío, y Robertico y yo ocupábamos la otra. Los cuatro utilizábamos el mismo baño.

A los pocos días, parada frente al clóset que nos habían asignado, comprendí que aquellos lindos vestidos de mi ajuar de boda no me iban a servir para nada. Mi padre me había dado algunos dólares, y aunque no tenía experiencia alguna en administrar el dinero, el instinto me decía que debía gastar lo menos posible. Con todo, un mediodía que mi suegra anunció que iba al *downtown,* me brindé a acompañarla y aproveché para comprarme algunas cosas de andar, más frescas y más modestas. Era la primera vez que escogía mi ropa sin consejos de Mamá. Adela estuvo muy prudente, haciendo comentarios como "eso te queda bien" o "tiene buen precio," pero sin apurarme ni forzarme. Cuando terminamos, antes de tomar la *guagua* de regreso, me invitó a una Coca Cola en Walgreens. Había muchos cubanos reunidos allí. Se intercambiaban noticias de Cuba y de dónde podía buscarse trabajo. Me encontré con el papá de mi amiga María Cristina y me saludó muy cariñoso. Siempre he recordado aquella tarde. Fue una de las más bonitas de aquellos primeros meses.

Mi suegro había sido un hombre poderoso en La Habana, un abogado importante que les llevaba los asuntos legales a diversos empresarios, especialmente de la industria fosforera. Cuando vio entrar a Castro en la ciudad se viró para su mujer y le dijo:

—Vámonos de este país. Este hombre va acabar con todo.

La mayoría de las personas que se fueron tan al principio estaban vinculadas al régimen anterior. Él aseguraba con vehemencia que nunca había sido batistiano ni había sido favorecido en nada. Yo pienso que era verdad, porque en el exilio vivían bastante mal. Aunque algún dinero debieron sacar, porque hasta el momento nadie trabajaba en la casa. Lo único que se hacía era hablar de Cuba, de la Revolución, de Castro, de los americanos. Y del regreso.

Todos vivían pegados al radio. Y brincaban cada vez que sonaba el teléfono. Adela, una mujer bonita, de unos cuarenta y pico años, hacía torpemente de ama de casa. Trataba de limpiar, hacer los mandados, lavar, cocinar, pero era un verdadero desastre. Cuando no se le quemaba el arroz, le quedaba duro. Tampoco sabía freír huevos. Una vez lavó los calzoncillos del marido con una camiseta roja de Juancito y se tiñeron de rosado. Mi suegro dijo que eso era para maricones y que mejor volviera a ponerlos blancos porque él no los usaba así, y no había dinero para comprar otros. Adela lloraba con tanta angustia como si se le hubiera muerto un pariente. Yo me acordé de cuando se perdió nuestra perrita, y Menchu y yo no hallábamos consuelo, y Papá nos regañó porque nos decía que los perros eran perros y las personas eran personas. Me acerqué a mi suegra y le pasé la mano tímidamente por el pelo desteñido y le dije:

—No se apure, Adela, que los calzoncillos son calzoncillos.

Pero ella seguía llorando a moco tendido y me reprochaba:

—Sí, pero Roberto es Roberto.

El de mejor humor siempre era Vidal. En realidad se llamaba Alberto Castaño, pero de jovencito le gustaba mucho cantar y lo apodaron así por el personaje de *Luisa Fernanda*. En Miami el barítono frustrado tomó un curso por correspondencia y aprendió a arreglar televisores. Ponía anuncios en las tablillas de los supermercados: "Vidal fix television for little money." Cuando lo llamaban por teléfono se acicalaba como si fuera a un baile. Esperaba a que nadie lo viera y le robaba un poco de colonia a mi suegro y se la ponía con los dedos en las sienes y en los bigotes finos y negros. Regresaba a veces sudado y con tres dólares en el bolsillo, que era lo que cobraba. Algunas veces traía también tubos. Cuando Juancito le preguntaba si eran los que estaban descompuestos, aseguraba que no, que al armar de nuevo el televisor le sobraban y que no sabía qué hacer con ellos. Todos nos reíamos, creyendo que exageraba. Hasta que un viejo americano, bajito y regordete, vino a reclamarle que había robado los *bombillos* de su aparato, y Vidal se los devolvió, explicándole en su inglés de fuerte acento:

—*Sorry. I cannot put back, I cannot put back.*

Juancito era un niño triste, muy distinto a su hermano —siempre optimista—, que sufría porque no entendía lo que decían en la escuela y porque él, con sus pantalones anchos, sus camisitas azules (Adela le hacía usar las de su antiguo uniforme de La Salle) y su bella melena oscura, se veía fuera de lugar entre aquellos americanos pecosos, de camisas a cuadros remangadas y cabellos rubios, cortos y tiesos. Yo lo ayudaba con la tarea por las noches. Cuando sacaba buenas notas, me premiaba con un beso en la mejilla y me decía:

—Eres muy buena, Lauri. No sé que haría sin ti.

Entonces me acordaba de Pedritín, que era casi de su misma edad, y de mi padre, que había hecho tanto para que aprendiéramos inglés, y de toda la familia. Se me llenaban de lágrimas los ojos sin poderlo evitar. Los abría mucho para que Juancito no me viera llorar. Me consolaba pensando que todo lo podía aguantar porque llegaría la noche y me perdería en los brazos de Robertico. Era el único puerto seguro.

Sólo recuerdo contento a Juancito por aquella época la tarde en que Vidal regresó feliz porque había arreglado dos televisores en una casa y además le habían dado una generosa propina. Exhibía el billete de diez dólares como un trofeo y nos miraba a todos, como quien está a punto de escoger a un jugador para tirarle la pelota. Por fin dijo:

—Vamos, Juancito, que te voy a llevar a pelar y a comprar una camisa de cuadros como las de tus compañeros de escuela.

Adela protestó que ella necesitaba tinte pero Vidal no le hizo ningún caso y Juancito volvió con el pelo corto y tieso, y estrenó a la mañana siguiente su camisa flamante. Cuando regresó de la escuela me confió en voz baja:

—He hecho un amigo en la clase. Me ha dicho que de ahora en adelante me va a llamar Johnny.

Mi suegra cada vez estaba más rara. Pasaba de los gritos al silencio más absoluto. De mandarnos a todos como si fuera un general, a llorar como el ser más indefenso del mundo. Yo me apegué mucho a mi suegro.

Era feo, gordo y sentimental. A veces se llevaba las manos a la cabeza y decía:

—¡Qué será de Cuba y de Adela!

Robertico se pasaba el día en la calle buscando trabajo. Hasta que lo encontró. Despachaba *fritas* en un lugar llamado Royal Castle. Por la noche las que ya estaban preparadas y no se habían vendido, se las repartían entre los empleados. Las *fritas* no eran muy grandes y no tenían *papitas a la juliana* adentro, como en Cuba, pero al menos mataban el hambre. No sé cómo se las arreglaba mi esposo para que siempre alcanzara por lo menos a una por cabeza, y a veces hasta sobraban para que repitieran Vidal y Juancito, siempre los más hambrientos.

Todos vivíamos pendientes del cartero. Nuestra mayor ilusión era recibir cartas de La Habana. Cualquier comentario sobre la situación del país, lo leíamos en voz alta. Si alguna de mis amigas hablaba con entusiasmo de los *guajiros* que habían ido a celebrar el 26 de julio a La Habana y que habían sido hospedados en casas particulares, mi suegro se indignaba y arremetía contra la ingenuidad de la clase media del país. Si un amigo de Robertico le contaba sobre la manifestación de Acción Católica, mi esposo se quejaba indignado:

—¡Yo debía estar allá!

Pero si alguna amiga de Adela comunicaba los rumores que circulaban sobre el cierre de las escuelas privadas y hasta sobre que los padres perderían la Patria Potestad de sus hijos, agradecíamos nuestra suerte:

—¡Menos mal que salimos a tiempo!

Invariablemente, las cartas nos dejaban peor (yo prefería las de Menchu, y, claro, las de Mamá), pero, a pesar de todo, nos alegraba recibir aquellos sobres cuya caligrafía amiga equivalía a la sonrisa de un ser querido.

Uno de nuestros pasatiempos favoritos era ir al aeropuerto a ver llegar a otros cubanos. Especialmente a partir del verano de 1960 el número fue aumentando vertiginosamente. Siempre recordaré a aquellas niñas con sus cintillos en la cabeza, sus *sayitas* anchas sobre *sayuelas* almidonadas, sus zapaticos de charol con *escarpines* blancos, eternamente abrazadas a una muñeca, la incertidumbre reflejada en sus rostros infantiles. Las madres a menudo llevaban collares de perla y un bolso tipo sobre debajo del brazo. Los padres, de traje y espejuelos de pasta oscura. Los varones todos me recordaban a Pedritín. Parecían familias endomingadas que regresaban de misa. Eran refugiados que no tenían la menor idea del cambio de 360 grados que darían sus vidas. Después empezaron a llegar muchos niños solos. Algunos tenían un letrero alrededor del cuello con sus señas. Creo que por eso, sin ponernos de acuerdo, nunca nadie volvió a sugerir ir al aeropuerto. Dolía demasiado.

∞

El Presidente Eisenhower (...) autorizó el 2 de diciembre el gasto de hasta $1 millón para ayuda y relocalización de 30,000-40,000 refugiados anti-castristas en Nueva Orleans y en Miami y otras áreas de la Florida. (...) El Representante Francis E. Walter (D., Pa.) informó al Consejo del Comité Intergubernamental de Migraciones Europeas en Ginebra que unos 36,000 cubanos han recibido asilo en Estados Unidos y que en el presente están llegando al país un promedio de 1,000 refugiados por semana.

(*Facts on File* 20.1049, 443)

∞

En aquella etapa todo el mundo se ayudaba. Las puertas de las casas estaban a menudo abiertas. No es una metáfora. No había entonces miedo a ladrones ni a violadores. Y se compartía lo que cada cual tuviera, ya fuera un pomo de mantequilla de maní, cortesía del Refugio, o una caja de galleticas dulces, inesperado regalo de alguna norteamericana caritativa.

A pesar de lo feliz que me sentía al lado de Robertico, de lo hermosas que eran nuestras noches de amor, extrañaba mucho a mi familia, a mis amigos, todo lo que había dejado atrás. Las primeras Navidades no habían sido tan malas, pues estábamos convencidos de que muy pronto regresaríamos a Cuba. Ahora se acercaban las segundas y yo sentía una gran tristeza que trataba inútilmente de disimular. Una tarde encontré en un clóset de la casa una vieja edición de *Little Women*, uno de las primeras novelas que Menchu y yo habíamos leído. Comencé a releerla, y me invadió tal congoja, que salí de la casa casi corriendo. Quería evitar que me vieran así. En mi confusión, cometí la imprudencia de cruzar por el medio de la calle sin mirar si venía alguien. Un pequeño camión dio un frenazo. El chofer sacó medio cuerpo por la ventanilla, y me gritó furioso:

—*Cuban, go home!*

Hubiera querido decirle que no había nada que deseara más en el mundo, pero ya él se alejaba a toda prisa mientras yo, sentada en el *contén,* lloraba sin consuelo. Creo que en ese momento preciso cobré conciencia de que sin quererlo me había convertido en una refugiada, una exiliada. Me fui de Cuba recién casada con la idea de que regresaría pronto y que podría empezar a estudiar en la Universidad, como siempre había soñado. Pero mi suegro tiene razón. Castro está acabando con el país. Los arrestos y fusilamientos horrorizan. Y tienen el respaldo de los cubanos, que gritan pidiendo paredón. Y del mundo entero que los aplaude. Ya han nacionalizado varias industrias. El padre de María Aurora, que era cliente de mi suegro, se ha muerto de un infarto cuando defendía su fábrica de fósforos.

∽

Cuba. Sindicalistas reciben asilo. *Por lo menos 12 líderes del Sindicato de Trabajadores Eléctricos pidieron asilo en la Habana en las embajadas de Argentina, Perú, Ecuador y Brasil el 14 de diciembre. Los líderes obreros buscaron refugio en las sedes diplomáticas pocas horas antes de que se llevara a cabo una demostración pública para aprobar la "purificación" de los sindicatos.*

El Presidente del Banco Nacional Cubano, Ernesto Guevara y el Vice Presidente del Consejo de Ministros Soviético Anastas I. Mikoyán firmaron en Moscú el pasado 19 de diciembre un acuerdo para expandir el comercio *entre Cuba y la Unión Soviética a $168 millones en 1961.*

Ese mismo día en La Habana, el Primer Ministro Fidel Castro anunció que la Unión Soviética había prometido comprar a Cuba 2,700,000 toneladas de azúcar a 4 centavos en 1961 y que China y otros países del bloque comunista se habían comprometido a comprar 1,000,000 y 300,000 toneladas respectivamente, al mismo precio.

Guevara firmó una declaración en Moscú apoyando la política exterior del Primer Ministro Soviético Kruschev, incluyendo el respaldo a movimientos de liberación nacional en la América Latina.

(*Facts on File*, 20.1051, 462)

◦∞

En el verano de 1960 había empezado a comentarse que los americanos preparaban una invasión a Cuba. Alrededor de las Navidades se intensificaron los rumores. Los exiliados no hablaban de otra cosa. Muchos visitaban a mi suegro. Todos opinaban a la vez y en voz muy alta. En fin de año, frente al televisor que mostraba las multitudes alegres en Times Square, alzamos nuestras copas de sidra. Mi suegro brindó al compás de las doce campanadas:

—¡Este año en La Habana!

Nos abrazamos esperanzados.

En enero vino un frente frío. La casa no tenía calefacción. Nos dijeron que en una iglesia estaban regalando ropa de invierno. Roberto le peleaba a Adela:

—El frío apenas durará y no es necesario gastar en colchas. Te prohíbo aceptar nada de caridad. Nosotros no somos unos muertos de hambre.

Adela y yo cruzamos una mirada cómplice. Me fui a la iglesia con Johnny (todos habíamos comenzado a llamarle así) y regresamos con cuatro mantas y dos *sweaters,* uno para el niño y otro para Robertico. Eran los dos que estaban más en la calle y pasaban más frío.

Esa noche, bajo el calor de la manta que guardaba un ligero olor a naftalina, Robertico me hizo el amor de una forma distinta. Muy lentamente, como si quisiera eternizar cada segundo, y con una intensidad cargada de fiera tristeza. Noté que no se ponía el preservativo que era lo que usábamos para que yo no cayera en estado. Pero no dije nada. Cuando terminamos, ya no teníamos frío y nos quedamos abrazados desnudos durante un largo tiempo. Empezaba a dormirme, cuando me dijo:

—Si hay una invasión a Cuba, mi padre y yo vamos a ir. Tendrás que ser muy fuerte.

Yo asentí con la cabeza.

—Sé que no es el momento, pero, por si me muero, me gustaría dejarte un hijo.

Nunca antes se me había ocurrido que Roberto me faltara. Sentí un escalofrío. Me puse el *ropón* y regresé a sus brazos.

—No seas tonto. Tú nunca te vas a morir.

Ya nunca más usamos condones. De todas formas, Robertico los detestaba.

No sé cuándo ni cómo se inscribieron, pero una noche mi suegro apagó el televisor, se aseguró de que estábamos todos presentes y nos habló muy serio.

—Los hombres de esta familia van a cumplir su sagrado deber con Cuba. Muy pronto Vidal, Robertico y yo nos iremos a entrenar para desembarcar en Cuba y liberarla. Creemos que la victoria será rápida. Juancito, cuando nos vayamos, tú serás el hombre de la casa. Tendrás que proteger a tu madre y a Lauri. Adela, no me cabe la menor duda de que tú sabrás afrentar estos momentos con valentía. Lauri...

Nunca supe lo que me hubiera dicho, porque lo interrumpí.

—Robertico no puede irse. Ahora no.

Y entonces revelé el secreto que aún no había compartido con nadie.

—Voy... vamos a tener un hijo.

Robertico me abrazó emocionado preguntando incesantemente si estaba segura. Johnny quería saber si podía ser el padrino. Vidal cantaba a toda voz una canción de cuna mientras simulaba mecer a un bebé.

Adela, entre risas nerviosas, preguntaba si ella parecía tener edad para ser abuela. Mi suegro desapareció unos minutos y regresó con una botella de sidra que había quedado de fin de año.

—Hay que brindar por ese nuevo miembro de la familia —dijo.

En unos breves instantes habíamos pasado de la solemnidad y la tristeza al alboroto y la alegría. No duró mucho. Mi suegro me dio un beso en la mejilla y me dijo al oído:

—Robertico tiene que irse de todas maneras.

Miré a mi esposo y vi que asentía con la cabeza. No me atreví a protestar delante de los demás pero esa noche, en la intimidad de la habitación, le rogué que no me dejara sola. Fue inútil.

—Lo hago por nuestro hijo, para que pueda nacer y crecer en una Cuba libre —me argumentó.

Descubrí en esos días que Vidal había sido piloto. Fue el primero en marcharse. Lo llamaron una noche y dos días después toda la familia lo llevamos al lugar donde debía presentarse. No quiso que nos bajáramos del carro. Lo vimos alejarse, ligero el paso, tarareando:

—Con la fortuna… me he desposado… buena compañía para ser soldado…

Esa madrugada soñé con Pedritín y Johnny. Los dos eran ya hombres, vestían uniformes militares y se encontraban en trincheras opuestas. Se oía el estallido de las balas. Luego, un largo silencio. Alguien decía que había un muerto. Yo no sabía cuál de los dos era. Me desperté sudada y presa de una gran angustia. Robertico trataba de consolarme:

—Nada de eso va a suceder. Verás como todos, incluyendo a tu familia, nos reciben como a héroes. ¿Recuerdas las películas del fin de la segunda guerra mundial? Así nos darán la bienvenida, con abrazos, guirnaldas, aplausos.

Pasaban los días, aumentaban los rumores, Robertico ya no soportaba vender fritas en el Royal Castle, y nadie los llamaba. Por fin, mi suegro marcó un teléfono que le dieron unos amigos. Les dijeron que había un grupo que salía al día siguiente, que si querían irse con ellos, se presentaran a las ocho de la mañana. Apenas hubo tiempo para nada.

Muy temprano manejamos en silencio al mismo lugar donde pocas semanas atrás habíamos despedido a Vidal. Esta vez nos bajamos del carro. Los abrazos fueron breves pero apretados.

—Estaremos juntos antes de que nazca el niño —me prometió Robertico al despedirse.

Adela cogió el *timón* para regresar. Había sacado la *cartera* pero mi suegro apenas la dejaba manejar. Íbamos en silencio, cada uno sumido en sus pensamientos. Al llegar a la esquina, Adela se llevó las manos a la cabeza y exclamó:

—¡Tan presente que lo tenía y se me olvidó preguntarle a Roberto cómo se pone la marcha atrás!

Nos echamos a reír.

A la semana, Adela era otra persona. Nunca más la vi llorar ni quejarse por nada. Lo primero que decidió fue que esa casa era muy grande para los tres. Nos mudamos a unos apartamentos que llamaban Pastorita, por no sé qué mujer en Cuba a cargo del asunto de viviendas. Todos los vecinos eran cubanos y uno se sentía más acompañado. Johnny empezó a hacer amigos y se le veía contento. Mi suegra encontró un trabajo cosiendo en una factoría. Yo me ocupaba de hacer los mandados, cocinar, lavar la ropa, y de ayudar a Johnny con las tareas. Ganaba mi dinerito enseñando inglés. Claro, nadie estaba bien económicamente así que cobraba muy poco. Hubiera preferido trabajar, pero Adela me decía que en mi estado era mejor cuidarse. Los días se me hacían infinitamente largos y extrañaba mucho a Robertico, sobre todo por las noches. Además, apenas recibía cartas de mi casa. Hallé algún consuelo cuando empecé a sentir al niño moverse en el vientre. Me parecía de alguna forma que estaba menos sola.

El 13 de abril de 1961 recibí una breve nota de Robertico. Me decía que el viaje había sido largo, que habían comenzado a entrenarse, que se había encontrado con viejos compañeros de estudio. Me pedía que me cuidara y que rezara por ellos. Al final añadía: "No siento ningún temor, estoy cumpliendo el deber con la Patria". Se me ocurrió por primera vez que me mentía, o se mentía a sí mismo. Mi esposo tenía miedo.

Dos días después, una soleada mañana de sábado, supimos que aviones norteamericanos habían bombardeado bases aéreas cubanas. Me extrañó no sentir alegría sino una gran confusión. ¿Y si mataban a alguno de mis seres queridos? Me acordé de mi primo Armando, que había peleado en La Sierra Maestra, y vestía uniforme verde olivo. ¿Dónde estaría Robertico? ¿Cómo podían mandarlo a una invasión con apenas unas semanas de entrenamiento?

Pastorita parecía un cuartel. Todo era radios de onda corta, noticias, rumores, ir y venir de apartamento en apartamento, buchitos de café, ilusiones, risas nerviosas, y una inmensa ansiedad que no cabía en el pecho. Fueron tres días y tres noches de noticias contradictorias, en los que el tiempo pareció detenerse. No existía para nosotros más que la angustia por saber el destino de nuestros hombres, y de Cuba.

∽

Cuba. Castro anuncia victoria. El Primer Ministro Castro anunció en un comunicado el 20 de abril que las tropas revolucionarias habían capturado los últimos puntos en poder "de las fuerzas invasoras de mercenarios extranjeros."

El comunicado informó que las fuerzas aéreas cubanas habían bombardeado y hundido varias embarcaciones en las cuales los invasores habían tratado de escapar. Decía que "se había confiscado un gran número de armas hechas en Estados Unidos, incluyendo varios tanques Sherman."

(Facts on File 21.1069, 146)

∽

Cuando escuché la noticia en casa de los vecinos, me fui de inmediato a la nuestra a buscar a Adela. La encontré en su habitación, de rodillas junto a la cama, con un rosario en las manos. Comprendí que ya lo sabía. Al parecer me había sentido entrar porque sin virarse me llamó a su lado con la mano. Rezamos juntas en silencio. Luego me abrazó, y sin derramar una lágrima me dijo:

—No estás sola, criatura. Yo estaré siempre a tu lado.

Había noticias de muchos arrestos y ejecuciones. Fusilaron a Sorí Marín, hasta unos días antes Ministro de Agricultura y que decían había firmado no sé cuántas sentencias de muerte. Castro amenazó con fusilar a los invasores. Los líderes del exilio se dirigieron a la OEA, a la ONU, al Papa, pidiéndoles que intervinieran. Fidel también hizo desfilar a los prisioneros ante las cámaras de televisión. Algunos se portaron muy valientemente. Vimos a Roberto y a Robertico, pero sólo de refilón. Estábamos tan nerviosas que no podíamos dormir.

Pocas noches después tocó a la puerta Vidal. Explicó que había volado en varias misiones pero que había regresado sin percance a la base y lo habían devuelto a Miami. Nada sabía de Robertico ni de su padre. Le explicamos que estaban presos. Adela le dijo que podía dormir en el sofá.

Una de las pocas alegrías de aquellos meses fue la llegada de mi hermano Ricardo. Me llamó sorpresivamente desde el aeropuerto. Nada más se quedaría unas horas. Iba rumbo a Nueva York, donde lo esperaban algunos amigos que habían prometido ayudarlo a encaminarse. Me volví loca hasta que encontré quien me llevara a verlo. En el camino creía que el corazón se me iba a salir. El abrazo fue largo y apretado. Yo no paraba de llorar. Creo que hasta ese momento no me había percatado de cuán dolorosamente extrañaba a mi familia. Ver a Ricardo fue recuperar de golpe mi vida pasada. Los cafés con leche que me traía Mamá a la cama, el aroma del tabaco de Papá, la voz de Mamá Luya haciéndome cuentos, la imagen de Pedritín jugando pelota en la calle, Menchu marcando los pasos del cha cha chá en nuestros primeros bailecitos. Todo se me mezclaba en la cabeza como una película en cámara lenta. Tantas preguntas que le quería hacer y no atinaba a articular palabra. Cuando me vine a dar cuenta, ya Ricardo estaba tomando otro avión. Antes de marcharse me entregó un sobre:

—Papá te manda esto.

Esperé a estar en casa para abrirlo. Encontré 500 dólares y una breve nota en la ancha caligrafía de mi padre que decía simplemente: "Cómprale la cuna al niño en nombre de sus abuelos."

Nunca había tenido dudas de que Robertico regresaría antes de que yo diera a luz. Pero las negociaciones para la liberación de los brigadistas se prolongaban y la fecha del parto se acercaba. Aunque no tenía queja alguna de Adela, y me había apegado mucho a Juancito, desde que no tenía a mi esposo, extrañaba más a mi familia. Se me ocurrió que quizás Menchu podría venir para el parto. Se lo dije por teléfono. Después de un largo silencio me contestó que era imposible. Yo insistía. Ella no me daba una respuesta directa. Ante mi persistencia, perdió la paciencia:

—Lauri, ¿pero tú no entiendes? Para muchos aquí vas a tener un hijo de un enemigo de la Revolución.

Una bofetada no me hubiera hecho mayor efecto.

—¿Cómo puedes decir eso, Menchu? Tú conoces a Robertico hace años. Además, es mi hijo, tu sobrino, el primer nieto de nuestros padres.

—Entonces ven a dar a luz aquí —me dijo mi hermana.

—Eso es imposible.

—No es imposible. Lo que pasa es que tú escogiste el otro bando.

—Yo sólo escogí seguir al hombre que amo. Eso no tiene que ver con la política.

—Todo tiene que ver con la Revolución.

—Ay, Menchu, no digas boberías que la llamada cuesta dinero.

Cuando colgamos sentía un nudo en la garganta pero no pude llorar. Algo muy duro empezó a crecerme dentro. Era el muro que me iría separando poco a poco de mi hermana gemela y de toda mi familia.

Pero qué ganas tengo de volver al patio de mi casa,
que se acabe el exilio,
al diablo los millones,
que me devuelvan mi inventario,

que me des-selle la Reforma Urbana
colgar mis viejos cuadros,
volver a ver mis libros, mis cucharas,
mi Malecón, mi Patria.

(Pura del Prado 62)

∽

Era temprano en la tarde y yo estaba viendo con Juancito un episodio de *The Millionaire*, un programa sobre personas a quienes un hombre muy rico les regalaba un millón de dólares y cómo les cambiaba la vida. A veces para bien, a veces para mal. A mi suegro le gustaba mucho y ahora el niño y yo, cuando lo veíamos, pensábamos en él, pero no nos lo decíamos. Justo en el momento en que el donante anónimo de tan astronómica suma tocaba a la puerta del afortunado ganador, sentí algo húmedo y baboso entre las piernas. Lo primero que pensé fue que me había orinado. Demoré unos minutos en darme cuenta que estaba de parto. No podía ser. Faltaban tres semanas para la fecha prevista. Robertico no había regresado. Estaba preso en La Habana, en esa ciudad de luz y sol donde habíamos nacido y donde nos habíamos enamorado; y yo estaba en Miami, sola con un niño de diez años, a punto de tener un hijo. Todo me parecía irreal. Por fin atiné a gritar:

—Johnny, corre, mira a ver si uno de los vecinos me puede llevar al hospital.

Me pusieron en una habitación frente a una ventana. Llovía. Entre contracción y contracción, me dormía un poco. Escuchaba, sin embargo, el sonido rítmico, incesante, monótono, de la lluvia contra los cristales. ¿Se sentiría la lluvia en la prisión donde estaba Robertico? ¿Y si no lo soltaban hasta que el niño fuera grande y yo tenía que criarlo sola? En medio de mis angustias, Vidal asomó la cabeza, me tiró un beso y se fue más blanco que una sábana.

—Los hospitales siempre lo han puesto muy nervioso —comentó

Adela con sorna. Los vecinos la habían avisado en la factoría y había venido directamente para el hospital. Yo hubiera preferido tener a mi madre o a mi hermana a mi lado. Sobre todo, extrañaba a mi abuela. Trataba de recordar los canciones con que arrulló mi infancia. Me puse a cantar en voz muy baja, como si el niño en mi vientre ya pudiera oírme:

> *Señora Santa Ana,*
> *¿por qué llora el niño?*
> *Por una manzana*
> *que se le ha perdido.*

Entonces Adela se me acercó y cantó conmigo:

> *Yo te daré una*
> *Yo te daré dos*
> *Una para el niño*
> *Y otra para vos*
> *Yo no quiero una*
> *Yo no quiero dos*
> *Yo quiero la mía*
> *que se me perdió.*

Nos quedamos un momento en silencio hasta que yo le dije:

—Si usted supiera Adela, que antes de ganarme un millón de dólares preferiría que nos devolvieran nuestra vida.

—Ay, mijita, qué boberías dices… Tú tienes que pensar en el futuro, en tu niño —siempre hablábamos del niño. Estábamos todos seguros de que sería varón.

Eran más de las doce de la noche y yo apenas había dilatado. La enfermera nos dijo que lo mío iba para largo. Adela se veía extenuada y Johnny estaba con unos vecinos. Le pedí a Adela que se marchara, y lo hizo con la promesa de que la llamaríamos en cuanto se acercara el parto, a la hora que fuese.

A las cinco y media de la madrugada me despertó el dolor. Nunca había sentido nada así. Era tan fuerte que no podía respirar. Sólo cuando pasó pude llamar a la enfermera…

No sé por qué se demora tanto. Trato de pensar en cosas agradables. Menchu y yo estamos en la playa, con unos cubos y unas palas, haciendo castillos con torres y puentes. Siento la arena entre los pies… el sol cálido sobre los hombros… Ahí viene de nuevo el dolor… ay, ay, aaayyy… no me gusta quejarme… ¡coño! Si me oye mi madre diciendo esas palabras… *Nurse, please, nurse, come quickly.* Siento un peso entre las piernas como si se me fuera a salir la cabeza. Quiero pujar. La enfermera me examina y me dice algo que no entiendo. Yo le pido que le avise a mi suegra. Llega el médico y me preparan para ir al salón. Le digo que no, que no hay nadie de mi familia, que no puedo parir sola.

—Si no deja que el médico se la lleve, va a parir sola de verdad —me dice una enfermera en español.

Recuerdo cuando mi hermano Pedritín nació. Menchu y yo teníamos nueve años. Nos sacaron de la escuela y lo fuimos a ver. No sé si fue Menchu o yo la que dijo que tenía manitas de león. A todo el mundo le hizo mucha gracia. Mamá se veía linda, con sábanas con sus iniciales que había traído de la casa, su ropón azul cielo y su *mañanita* de encaje.

Mírame a mí ahora, toda sudada, con este trapo de ropón que me han dado que no me lo puedo cerrar y se me ve el *fondillo* cuando voy al baño, sola, rodeada de gente extraña que habla un idioma que no es el mío y que cuando me pongo nerviosa no entiendo. Mi pobre hijo, venir a nacer así. Me inyectan en la vena. Siento que me adormezco.

—Estaremos juntos antes de que nazca el niño —oigo las palabras de mi marido. Dios mío, Robertico, ¿por qué me has abandonado?

Mi hijo nació a las 6:07 de la mañana del 8 de septiembre de 1961. Lo inscribí como Pedro Pablo de la Caridad. Ya Robertico y yo habíamos decidido ponerle el nombre de mi padre y el de su abuelo. Yo añadí el de la patrona de Cuba sin consultarle, puesto que había nacido en su día. En cuanto lo cargué no me acordé más de los dolores del parto y sentí una emoción muy grande. No olvidaba, sin embargo, lo lejos que estaban todos los seres que más quería.

Me pusieron en una habitación con tres mujeres más. Una de ellas era una negra alta y gruesa que había venido a parir su sexto hijo. La otra era una americanita rubia y muy delgadita. Al parecer su niña había nacido con algún problema. El médico cerró la cortina cuando vino a hablarle a ella y al esposo. Luego los dos lloraban mucho. Enseguida se la llevaron para otro cuarto. La tercera era cubana como yo, aunque un poco mayor. Enseguida nos hicimos amigas.

Todas las tardes venía Vidal con Juancito. Me traían una barrita de chocolate o un paquete de M&M, hasta que la enfermera dijo que el chocolate no era bueno porque me podía estreñir. Adela venía como a las seis, cuando salía de la factoría. Al segundo día me dijo:

—Llamé a tu hermano y también a tu casa para avisarles. Se pusieron muy contentos y te mandan muchos besos.

Alguna sombra debió cruzar mi frente. Entonces añadió:

—Menchu preguntó si el bebito tenía manos de león.

Vidal resultó un excelente niñero. Llegaba de su trabajo como a las siete de la mañana, dormía como hasta la una y por las tardes me cuidaba al niño para que yo descansara. Le cantaba "A la sombra de una sombrilla de encaje y seda…" y no sé cuántas cosas más, y Pedro Pablo se dormía feliz en sus brazos.

—Se va a creer que es su padre —pensaba yo, algo triste.

Del próximo año recuerdo el agridulce sabor de ver a mi hijo crecer lejos de su padre y de mi familia. La primera vez que se sentó, el primer diente, sus primeros balbuceos, los primeros pasos fueron todas ocasiones de celebración y lágrimas. La vida se fue haciendo rutina, sólo interrumpida por las noticias de las negociaciones para liberar a los brigadistas, alguna llamada de Ricardo contándome de su vida en Nueva York, y la correspondencia, ya menos frecuente, que nos llegaba de la Isla. Las pocas cartas que recibí de Robertico las leía todas las noches antes de dormirme. De casa, era mi madre la que más escribía. Aquellos pliegos de papel aéreo siempre me dejaban la inquietud de que ocultaban algo, pero por más que intentaba leer entre líneas no alcanzaba a precisarlo.

Pedro Pablo cumplió su primer año sin que su padre lo hubiera podido conocer. Estaba precioso con un trajecito nuevo que había heredado del nieto de una americana a quien yo le daba clases de español. Le compramos un *cake* a una vecina que los hacía en su casa e invitamos a tres o cuatro niños del barrio. Adela —que había adelantado mucho en la cocina— insistió en que había que hacer bocaditos y ensalada de pollo y estiró el presupuesto del mes para la celebración. Aunque llevábamos un mes enseñándole a apagar la velita, cuando le cantamos *Happy Birthday* el niño se asustó, empezó a hacer pucheros y rompió a llorar.

∞

Discurso de Kennedy. *El anuncio de parte de Estados Unidos que bases de misiles estaban siendo construidas en Cuba fue hecho por el Presidente Kennedy en un discurso transmitido a todo el país por radio y televisión a las 7 p.m el 22 de octubre…. Dijo que por tanto había ordenado que los siguientes "pasos iniciales" se tomaran. "Todos los barcos con camino a Cuba desde cualquier nación o puerto, si contienen una carga de armas ofensivas, serán obligados a regresar… He ordenado el fortalecimiento de nuestra base en Guantánamo, evacuado hoy todas las familias se nuestro personal allí y ordenado que unidades militares adicionales se mantengan en estado de alerta…" El Presidente Kennedy concluyó… "Mis conciudadanos, que no haya dudas que este es un esfuerzo difícil y peligroso el que hemos asumido. Nadie puede prever precisamente qué camino tomará o el costo o las bajas en que habrá."*

(Facts on File 22.1147, 361–36)

∞

Los exiliados aseguraban que habría una invasión a Cuba. Los norteamericanos temían el comienzo de una guerra nuclear. En la escuela de Johnny hasta dieron instrucciones de dónde esconderse. Yo no podía dormir. Temía que cualquier acción de Estados Unidos provocara una represalia contra los presos. También pensaba que si bombardeaban La Habana algo le podría pasar a mi familia. Tenía unas pesadillas terribles en las que veía la Isla arrasada, llena de escombros y cenizas. Pero no pasó nada. Los rusos sacaron los misiles en un barco y los cubanos nos quedamos en las mismas.

—Kennedy nos vendió otra vez... —se lamentaban los exiliados.

Por fin a mi suegro, a mi marido y a sus compañeros los cambiaron por tractores y compotas para niños. Regresaron más delgados. Roberto parecía veinte años más viejo. Todo Pastorita salió a recibirlos. Yo me sentía muy orgullosa de que volvían de la guerra. Del poco dinerito que teníamos, Johnny y yo habíamos comprado una botella.

—Por los héroes —brindé con entusiasmo.

Me pareció que mi esposo y su padre se sentían incómodos. Apenas se llevaron la copa a los labios. Robertico tenía prisa por conocer a su hijo, que se había quedado dormido. Entramos despacio al cuarto para no despertarlo. Su padre lo miró largamente, le pasó el índice por el pelo fino y oscuro, las orejitas, la nariz de porroncito, los labios aún húmedos de leche. Se viró a mí asombrado.

—Esto es un milagro. La verdadera heroína aquí eres tú.

De nuevo era Navidad y estábamos juntos. No sé cómo Vidal consiguió un lechoncito y lo asamos en el patio. El americano de la acera de enfrente se quejó a la policía de la bulla y el olor a puerco. ¡Mira que aguarle a uno la Nochebuena!

Al día siguiente supimos que el Presidente Kennedy venía a reunirse con los brigadistas en el Orange Bowl. En todas partes se hablaba de lo mismo. Siempre recordaré que había sol y mucho viento. Yo no creía que el Presidente fuera a ir pero por si acaso nos pusimos nuestra mejor ropa. El estadio estaba lleno. Todo el mundo hablaba. Algunos decían que Kennedy era un traidor. Otros aseguraban que tenía un plan secreto y estaba decidido a terminar con Castro. Hasta que empezaron a tocar los himnos. La multitud se puso de pie. Los brigadistas vestían de uniforme. Y los americanos también. Todos estaban en atención. Por fin vi a Kennedy. Tenía el pelo muy rojo y el aire se lo despeinaba. No recuerdo nada del discurso. Pero si sé que se oían gritos de "¡Guerra! ¡Guerra!" y que Jackie dijo unas palabritas en español. El momento culminante fue cuando los brigadistas le entregaron al Presidente la bandera cubana. Se oyó su acento bostoniano entre las multitudes:

—*I can assure you that this flag will be returned to this brigade in a free Havana.*

La traducción corría de voz en voz...

—Ha prometido devolverles la bandera en una Habana libre.

Dos días después contemplamos de nuevo en el televisor a las multitudes de *Times Square,* comimos las uvas y brindamos con sidra. Mi suegro repitió:

—El próximo año...

Pero se le quebró la voz y no pudo terminar. Quizás había perdido la fe en el regreso.

Mi esposo y su padre comenzaron a buscar trabajo a principios de año. O al menos, eso decían. Una tarde que Adela y yo nos fuimos con Pedro Pablo al *downtown* nos los encontramos en el Walgreens. Estaban rodeados de gente y les contaban cómo habían peleado en Bahía de Cochinos. Me quedé observando a Robertico sin que me viera. Actuaba como si tuviera en las manos una ametralladora e imitaba su sonido..."rrrrrrr...". De pronto, me pareció un extraño.

Robertico me decía que nadie les daba trabajo porque todo el mundo sabía que eran veteranos de Bahía de Cochinos y no podían pedirles que vendieran fritas o repartieran periódicos. A mí no me cabía en la cabeza que el americano que era su jefe en el Royal Castle se fuera a poner con esas cosas, pero él me decía que trabajaría en lo que fuera, menos volver a ese lugar. Era como mentarle la madre.

Cada vez se hacía más difícil, ahora que teníamos al niño, seguir viviendo con mis suegros. Me enteré de que las iglesias estaban ayudando a relocalizar a las familias. Les buscaban patrocinadores y trabajo en otras ciudades. Sin Robertico saberlo, puse nuestro nombre en la lista.

El Día de Reyes llegó la madre de mi suegro de Cuba. Era una mujer alta y aún bonita, aunque ya estaba mayor. En el acto se hizo cargo de la casa. En realidad, se hizo cargo de todo. Opinaba que Johnny estaba muy mal pelado. Además, se empeñaba en decirle Juancito, aunque a él no le gustara. Cambió todos los muebles de lugar. Y a la semana se puso a buscar una casa adonde mudarnos porque según ella en Pastorita los vecinos eran unos chusmas. Adela miraba a mi suegro con desesperación, para que hiciera algo. Pero él no intervenía en nada. Cada día la situación era más tensa. Doña Asunción (así había que decirle) también había decidido que ella administraría el dinero, y pretendía que Adela y Vidal le dieran sus cheques. Hasta me fiscalizaba unos pesitos que yo ganaba vendiendo por teléfono subscripciones a revistas mientras el niño dormía. Una tarde Doña Asunción tropezó con un camión rojo que Pedro Pablo había dejado regado en la sala. Estaba nuevecito, puesto que yo se lo había comprado el día anterior en el supermercado. La vieja, que tenía una agilidad increíble para sus años, recogió el juguete del suelo y me buscó con la mirada.

—Laura, eres una irresponsable. En esta casa no hay dinero para gastarlo en estas cosas.

—Irresponsable es usted que quiere que mi hijo crezca sin juguetes.

—¡Es lo único que me faltaba! ¡Qué venga esta mocosa a faltarme el respeto!

Tomé un biberón del refrigerador y me encerré en el baño con el niño. No sé cuál de los dos lloraba más. El niño no quería la leche fría y yo no quería salir y encontrarme con la bruja, como Johnny y yo habíamos apodado a su abuela. Entonces me puse a cantar a ver si Pedro Pablo se dormía y para no oír los gritos que continuaban afuera:

Señora Santa Ana
¿Por qué llora el niño?
Por una manzana
que se le ha perdido...

Dos días después me llamaron de la iglesia. Querían saber si Robertico, el niño y yo nos iríamos a Columbus en Ohio. Había la posibilidad de un trabajo para él. Y aunque el invierno era frío, nos darían abrigos. También me informaron de una familia que podía hospedarnos hasta que pudiéramos independizarnos. Le dije a la monjita que sí, aunque le confesé que no me gustaba mucho la idea de vivir con gente desconocida.

—Es que desde que nos casamos nunca hemos podido estar solos...

Me prometió que vería qué se podía hacer. Le aseguré que de todas maneras nos iríamos.

Esa noche Robertico me dijo que algunos brigadistas se iban a reunir para planear los próximos pasos. Yo le conté lo de la iglesia y la posibilidad de irnos a Ohio. Me miró extrañado y me aseguró que su lugar estaba en Miami. Nunca, ni cuando le pedí que no fuera a la invasión, habíamos tenido una discusión tan fuerte.

—¿Para qué quisiste tener un hijo, si apenas lo miras ni te preocupas si hay dinero para comprarle leche o si tu abuela lo deja jugar en paz? —le reproché.

—No quiero que mi hijo tenga una patria esclava.

—Él nació en este país.

—Pero es cubano.

Y se fue dando un portazo.

CAPÍTULO TRES
"¡Fí-del, Fí-del, Fí-del!"

ES LA TARDE DEL 26 DE JULIO. La Plaza Cívica bulle y se hincha de pueblo. Medio millón de campesinos y otro tanto de habaneros se confunden en la explanada enorme. Un mar de sombreros de yarey, cruzado de machetes de un extremo a otro, cubre la extensión. El sol patrio ilumina la estatua y el obelisco del Apóstol, baña generoso el contingente humano, fulge en los edificios próximos.

En la terraza de la Biblioteca Nacional están los líderes de la Revolución y los invitados extranjeros. Dos manos gigantescas, en las que se posa una paloma, llevan la cifra simbólica 26. En el borde, la Bandera Nacional abre sus alas al viento.

Raúl Castro, siempre combativo, pronuncia:

—Todos tienen aquí que andar muy derechos, porque Liborio está en la plaza... El mejor ejército con que cuenta la República es el que tenemos delante.

Hay un grave suspense en el ambiente... Desde la tribuna, alguien interroga al pueblo:

—Hay un clamor que brota de todos, y yo quiero convertirlo en consulta directa. ¿Quieren ustedes o no que Fidel siga al frente del gobierno?

Un millón de voces a una sola vez gritan ¡Sí!

Lo que viene después: la aclamación del líder máximo —Fí-del, Fí-del, Fí-del; los sombreros lanzados al aire —Fí-del, Fí-del, Fí-del; los machetes entrechocándose —Fí-del, Fí-del, Fí-del; las ovaciones —Fí-del, Fí-del Fí-del; el regocijo en todas las pupilas —Fí-del, Fí-del, Fí-del; el movimiento impetuoso del océano popular —Fí-del, Fí-del, Fí-del, sólo es confirmación del acto de voluntad de los cubanos.

—Esta vez manda el pueblo y le ordena a Fidel cumplir con su deber.

(*Bohemia* 51:3, 85–86)

∽

Por dentro estoy hueca. Como si me hubieran vaciado todos los órganos, como si esta mujer que se levanta, se baña, come, bebe, habla, estudia, camina, se acuesta y se vuelve a levantar, fuera un ser autómata a quien han despojado de su vida interior, sus recuerdos, sus sueños. No. Es peor que eso. Si no hubiera más que una gran oquedad en mi interior, no sentiría. Lo que han hecho es partirme en dos. La mitad de mí se fue con Lauri. Todo quedó trunco. Mi alma es como un muñón. Un inmenso muñón sangriento al que van arrebatando más y más trozos de carne viva.

Voy a la universidad a fuerza de voluntad. Lauri y yo habíamos soñado mil veces con el día en que subiéramos juntas la famosa escalinata. Siento que le estoy robando parte de su vida. Que esto no me pertenece a mí sola. De todas formas, apenas logro concentrarme en los estudios. A veces me parece que todo lo que hacemos es escuchar los largos discursos de Fidel. Duran horas y horas. Voy en la guagua y Fidel está hablando. Llego a casa y Fidel está hablando. Comemos y Fidel está hablando. Salgo al portal y Fidel está hablando. Me acuesto y Fidel está hablando. Papá apaga el televisor y Fidel sigue hablando. El vecino de al lado apaga el radio y Fidel sigue hablando. Me duermo y Fidel sigue hablando. Aunque lo oiga siempre, no siempre lo escucho. Cuando lo hago, a veces todo se me hace claro, y otras, por el contrario, me parece que le da vueltas y vueltas a las cosas y dice siempre lo mismo. Y en definitiva, no dice nada. Aunque algo debe decir, porque a la mañana siguiente todo el mundo pregunta, ¿oíste lo que dijo Fidel? como si fuera lo más importante del mundo.

Mi amigo Lázaro piensa que Fidel Castro es una especie de Mesías. Una vez se apareció en la Colina de la Universidad. Quería que votaran por un tal Cubelas para Presidente de la FEU. Estuvo hasta la madrugada hablando con los estudiantes. Cuando Lázaro me lo contó los ojos le brillaban y se le ponían pequeñitos. No sé por qué me dio miedo.

Algunos de los viejos profesores no regresaron este año porque no quisieron aceptar el nuevo Consejo Universitario. Pero el Rector se quedó. Oí decir que es un viejo senil que quiere morirse siendo Rector, y que lo dejarán mientras no estorbe. Mi hermano Ricardo se pone las manos en la cabeza y dice:

—¡Qué vergüenza! ¡Qué vergüenza!

A mí me parece que Ricardo ha envejecido de pronto. Es sólo cinco años mayor que nosotras, pero ya no parece un muchacho. Aunque no le aceptaron las asignaturas que estudió en Villanueva, sólo le quedan tres más para ser abogado y no quiere presentarse a exámenes en la Universidad de La Habana.

—Si esto cambia, estas notas no valdrán. Y si no cambia, yo tendré que irme —le dice a Papá.

Ahora es que vine a enterarme de todo lo que luchó Ricardo contra Batista. Esas salidas misteriosas que Laurita y yo atribuíamos a citas amorosas eran para vender bonos, distribuir propaganda. ¡Hasta puso bombas! Papá se lo recuerda de continuo. Y él le responde:

—No fue para esto para lo que luché.

Yo quisiera que me explicara las cosas, pero cuando le pregunto, me mira con una gran tristeza en los ojos, me pasa la mano por el pelo y me dice:

—Tú a tus lecturas de poesía que esto es cosa de hombres.

Me da tanta rabia cuando me contesta así que ayer le tiré un libro a la cabeza. Fallé y se fue riéndose de mí.

Los acontecimientos se suceden con rapidez. El año comenzó con la Reforma Agraria. Lázaro es su defensor más entusiasta. Se pasea por la Plaza Cadenas hablando a cuantos quieran escucharle de lo oprimido que han estado los *guajiros* y de la necesidad de que la tierra les pertenezca. A veces me invita a tomar un refresco y no hace más que hablar de la Reforma Agraria.

—Chico, tú hablas tanto como Fidel —le digo en broma.

Por un rato cambia el tema. Se interesa por mis estudios, por mi familia. Me dice algún piropo. Al poco tiempo vuelve a la carga. Hay un momento en que dejo de oír sus palabras. Me gusta sentir el sonido de su voz, observar sus gestos, el modo que mueve las manos, el entusiasmo de su expresión. Muevo la cabeza asintiendo, pero él se da cuenta de que no lo atiendo, y me lo reprocha:

—No me gustan las mujeres que dicen que sí a todo.

—A mí tampoco —le contesto. No es del todo cierto. Mi madre es así y yo la adoro. Casi todas las mujeres que conozco son así; o son lo contrario, como Tía Paquita, que se murió peleando con Tío Manuel. A ella no quiero parecerme por nada del mundo.

—Las mujeres deben saber pensar —me dice Lázaro.

Entonces le pregunto las cosas que me inquietan. Como lo de los juicios revolucionarios.

—¿Y si uno de estos hombres a los que han condenado y fusilado fuera inocente? Están congelando cuentas de gente decente, como los padres de mi amiga Eva. ¿Sabes lo que le dijeron a su mamá cuando quiso coger de la caja bancaria una medallita con la que Eva y su hermana hicieron la Primera Comunión? ¡Qué eso pertenecía a la Revolución! ¿Cómo es posible barrer de la noche a la mañana con un estado de derecho?

—Las revoluciones son así, Menchu. No pueden ser de otro modo. Además, en Cuba no había un estado de derecho… las garantías estaban suspendidas… muchos amigos nuestros fueron torturados… otros aparecieron muertos… ¿Es que vas a defender a Batista?

—No, pero al menos entonces quedaba algo de solidaridad humana. Tú bien sabes que cuando a ti te detuvieron, te soltaron porque el padre de Robertico llamó a un amigo suyo Ministro de Batista…

A Lázaro se le han puesto otra vez los ojos tan pequeños que parecen dos rayas.

—Bah, ¡tú no sabes nada de política!

—¿No dices que te gustan las mujeres que piensan?

Lázaro se me acercó entonces y me besó. Me metió la lengua en la boca y me acarició con ella las encías, los dientes, la lengua. Fue un beso lleno de furia y de saliva que me cortó el aire. Quise desprenderme de él. El peso de su cuerpo me atrapó contra el muro del patio interior de casa. Sentí su sexo bajo el pantalón que arremetía entre mis piernas. Traté de zafarme, de gritar. Forcejeamos. En eso sentimos a Papá tosiendo en la sala. Me soltó. Me miró socarrón.

—Perdóname. Es que esta noche estás irresistible.

—Como me vuelvas a faltar el respeto, te juro…

—No sucederá de nuevo —y mientras me decía esto, se me acercó despacito y me tocó un pecho, justo al nivel del pezón.

∽

Venían de todas partes, en oleadas incontenibles. Bajo el ardiente sol, guiados por sus maestros, se apeaban de las guaguas, formaban filas, sudaban, cantaban y reían. Las bandas atronaban el aire con su música. Ondeaban las banderas. Los magnavoces, sobreponiéndose al vocerío, emitían recomendaciones. El césped verde, pisoteado por treinta mil pares de zapatos, emitía un fuerte olor a campo, a vida. Ellos gritaban y reían. Tenían confianza. Eran los niños de Cuba, los escolares jubilosos de una Patria Libre.

La Revolución los había convocado para Columbia. ¿Qué era Columbia para ellos, antes del primero de enero? Lo mismo que para los adultos, un sitio siniestro, una madriguera de odio y muerte. ¿Cómo podían haber pensado jamás en trasponer aquellas fortificadas postas y llegar hasta el recinto amurallado? Y he aquí que estaban en Columbia. He aquí que pisoteaban el famoso polígono, de donde tantas veces surgieron, como aves de maldad, las órdenes de encarcelar y de matar. He aquí que ellos, niños, ellos, criaturas débiles, sin más armas que sus débiles manos que agitaban banderas ni más coraza que la coraza azul de sus uniformes, le habían ganado la batalla al monstruo. Donde había antes muerte, ahora palpitaba la vida. Donde antes sonaban las amenazas, oíanse ahora himnos. Donde antes había rifles, balas y cañones, había ahora lápices, libros y libretas.

La Revolución había realizado el milagro.

(*Bohemia* 51:49, 66)

∽

Lázaro se ha convertido en un agitador en la Universidad. Está impaciente. Dice que hay que barrer con todo lo anterior y hay que hacerlo enseguida. Ayer se encaramó en una tribuna improvisada y comenzó a arengar a un grupo de compañeros:

—Ningún sector de la vida nacional ha disfrutado tanto como esta Universidad de la confianza y la simpatía popular. Por su brillante hoja de servicio a la Patria en todo momento, por su modo vertical y radical de plantear el problema cubano, tanto en épocas de corrupción liberal como en las de la opresión insolente, por sus gestas de 1923, 1930, 1933, 1952 y 1956... cada vez que un ciudadano pasaba frente a la colina y miraba la estatua del Alma Mater, severa y vigilante sobre la ciudad vejada por los déspotas y mancillada por los viles, veía en ella un símbolo y una promesa de resurrección cívica...

De pronto los muchachos empezaron a aplaudirlo. La voz, fuerte y profunda, parece salirle de muy dentro:

—A través de los años la Universidad de La Habana se ha erigido siempre en crítica y censura de la vida nacional, actitud que ahora le impone una altísima responsabilidad: la de dar ejemplo de lo que exige a otros. Fijar culpas —y su índice se alzaba en el aire— no es nuestro cometido, pero la depuración, si es lenta, será un suicidio a plazos. La normalidad docente debe regresar al más importante taller de cultura de Cuba.

Cuando terminó todos lo rodeaban. Le palmoteaban la espalda, celebraban su oratoria:

—Oye, estás hecho un Cortina... —le bromeó uno.

—Más bien pareces un discípulo de Fidel... —le comentó otro.

Vi que su mirada se alzaba sobre el grupo. Sabía que me buscaba. Tenía ganas de correr a él y abrazarlo; al mismo tiempo, sentía miedo. Me alejé sin que me viera.

✺

El Cobre es un mínimo pueblo que se ha armado con un pedazo de tierra al pie de una montaña. Al fondo, sobre una pequeña loma, sobrio, armónico, el santuario de la Virgen de la Caridad. Hasta allí fue llevada la Patrona de Cuba que manos fervorosas de pescadores encontraron un día sobre las aguas del Caribe. Hasta allí van a adorarla los creyentes de todas las esquinas del país. Escalinata del Santuario. Un ramillete de mendigos tendiendo la mano al paso generoso de los creyentes. Abigarrados cartelones con los números de los bonos que no cesan de pregonar los vendedores. Sobre callosas manos, el tablero de mística mercancía que exhibe medallitas, rosarios, medidas de la patrona de Cuba, estampas "más baratas que allá dentro."

Un joven rebelde, afeitado, veintidós años, teniente "de en vuelta de Niquero", asciende de rodillas los escalones que lo conducirán hasta las plantas de la virgen morena. La sudada camisa pegada al cuerpo que resistió, a pie, la trayectoria desde Santiago. Las rodillas, que subieron las estribaciones de La Sierra Maestra para no doblarse ante el Tirano, se doblan ahora en fervoroso cumplimiento de una promesa.

Descanso. El pañuelo se mueve incesantemente por el rebelde rostro.

—¿Una promesa? —alguien le pregunta.

—Sí, señor.

—¿Con qué motivo…?

—La hice un día antes de subir a la montaña… Le prometí a la virgencita venir a pie desde Santiago y subir de rodillas sus escaleras.

—¿Para que te protegiera?

—No… Para que protegiera a Fidel…

(Bohemia 51:38, 62)

Lázaro ha comentado que la religión es el opio de los pueblos. Un compañero le contestó:

—Oye, chico, eso es una frase marxista.

Papá le preguntó a Ricardo si está conspirando contra el gobierno. Vi a mi hermano palidecer y las aletas de la nariz se le pusieron muy blancas. Siempre le pasa cuando dice una mentira.

—Claro que no, Papá. Yo sólo estoy trabajando en el Congreso Católico.

—No te metas en líos, Ricardo, que ahora no es como antes.

—No te preocupes, viejo, que yo sé lo que hago.

—Ay, mijo —intervino Mamá— no te expongas.

Cuando le conté a Lázaro que iba a ir al Congreso Católico con mi hermano se puso furioso.

—Haz lo que quieras... La Iglesia siempre ha estado con los poderosos. Estuvo con la colonia española...

—No podrás decir que estuvo con Batista...

—Algunos se sumaron a la Revolución a última hora, por si acaso...

—Pero mira, Menchu, no es eso; es que ese movimiento es contrarrevolucionario. ¿No te das cuenta? Son unos niños *bitongos* que no pueden soportar que ahora todos seamos iguales.

—Mi hermano no es un niño bitongo y en mi casa siempre se te ha tratado como si fueras igual que nosotros.

—¿Tú ves...? "Como si fuera igual que ustedes... ", porque no piensan que soy igual, pero ya todo eso se acabó.

—Lázaro, ¿cómo puedes hablar así de mi familia?

—No es tu familia, Menchu, es toda la clase burguesa. ¿No te das cuenta de cómo han explotado a los demás, de lo poco que se han preocupado por el país? Los planes de la Revolución con respecto a la educación van a cambiar muchas cosas... Va a crecer otra generación, un hombre nuevo...

De todas maneras, fui con Ricardo a la procesión. Había mucha gente y los cánticos religiosos me emocionaron. Uno de los oradores dijo que frente al materialismo había que ejercer la espiritualidad militante, sin temores, y aún a riesgo de ofrendar la vida. Me sorprendió la cantidad de personas que saludaban a mi hermano.

Estas Navidades han sido distintas. Mamá anda siempre lloriqueando, pendiente de las noticias de Lauri. Ricardo entra y sale sin dar muchas explicaciones. Con Papá nunca se sabe. A veces lo oigo hablar con amigos y parece entusiasmado con la Revolución. Otras, cuando Ricardo le argumenta, parece coincidir con él. Como es tan optimista siempre asegura que las cosas mejorarán. Pedritín trajo de la escuela un dibujo de un árbol de Navidad hecho con sombreros de guano y una gran guirnalda que decía "Año de la Liberación". Además, el tiempo ha estado espantoso, con lluvias y viento. Nos sentamos a la mesa en Nochebuena, como siempre, pero ninguno tenía ánimo de celebración. A la hora de los turrones y la sidra, llegó Lázaro. Papá quiso brindar:

—Por Cuba —dijo.

—Porque el año próximo Laurita esté con nosotros —le contestó Ricardo, con un punto de dolorosa ironía en la voz.

Mamá se escondió en la cocina para que no la viéramos llorar.

A las doce de la noche, sobre un fondo alegre de claxons y campanas, las notas marciales del Himno Nacional envolvieron la Isla de extremo a extremo. La radio, las orquestas, los altoparlantes, dieron al aire la música gloriosa de Perucho, rodeada por cientos de miles de voces en todos los rincones del país.

La celebración tenía tanto de saludo como de despedida. 1959 quedaba en el recuerdo y en la historia como un año estelar en el destino de la patria.

(*Bohemia* 52:2, 63)

Anoche Ricardo y Papá discutieron muy exaltados. Al principio pensé que era de política, pues es de lo que más hablan. Pero luego escuché que Ricardo le decía:

—No puedo creer que tú le hagas algo así a Mamá. No hay mujer más abnegada, más complaciente.

—Tienes razón. Si yo la adoro… Esto es otra cosa, Ricardo. Todos los hombres necesitamos nuestro desahogo… una canita al aire de vez en cuando no le hace daño a nadie… Y es que la muchachona es un pollazo, un verdadero bombón… difícil de resistir. Mira, lo que pasó…

—¿No me irás a contar los detalles ahora?

Me alejé espantada. Desde entonces no he podido mirarle a los ojos a Papá. Cada vez que pienso en él me lo imagino en la cama con una mujer con unas tetas y unas nalgas enormes y me dan ganas de vomitar. Me pregunto si Mamá lo sabrá. Se le ve triste, pero siempre está así desde que se fue mi hermana.

A veces siento que todo a mi alrededor se está derrumbando, que camino por una tierra movediza que en cualquier momento podrá tragarme. Casi todas las noches Lázaro viene y nos sentamos en el portal a hablar. Está siempre tan seguro de sí mismo, tan entusiasta, tan confiado en el futuro. A cada una de mis dudas parece tener una respuesta. Como a las once, Mamá se asoma al portal y nos dice:

—Buenas noches, Lázaro. No te demores mucho que Menchu tiene clases por la mañana.

Entonces lo acompaño hasta la acera y nos despedimos con un breve beso. Algunas veces, antes de irse, me empuja suavemente hasta el costado de la casa, donde no pueden vernos, y me abraza y me besa. Me gusta, me gusta que me bese, me gusta tanto que a veces me parece que me voy a morir. Entonces salgo corriendo y me meto en la casa. ¿Me estaré enamorando de Lázaro? ¡Cuánto quisiera poder conversar con Lauri!

La semana pasada fuimos al velorio del padre de María Aurora. Hace pocos meses nacionalizaron las empresas y por fin ocuparon la suya. Según me contó la propia María Aurora, él trató de explicarles a los interventores que su fábrica de fósforos la había fundado su padre, un inmigrante español, que no tenía nada que ver con política, que él había vendido bonos del 26.

—Esto tampoco tiene que ver con política, viejo. Es la justicia revolucionaria. No se ponga majadero.

Él contestó que tendrían que sacarlo a la fuerza. Y a la fuerza lo sacaron. Llegó a su casa hecho una furia. María Aurora decía que la vena del cuello se le salía tanto que parecía que le iba a explotar. Por la madrugada sintieron un ruido. La mamá de María Aurora lo encontró en el suelo de la cocina. Dicen que fue un infarto masivo. La viuda no se consuela y comenta bajito:

—Lo mató la Revolución.

Después, añade, entre suspiros…

—Yo no sé lo que vamos a hacer ahora…

Cuando se lo conté a Lázaro, pareció impresionado.

—Es una pena, Menchu… Diles que si necesitan algo, que cuenten conmigo.

Tal parece que fuera adivino porque dos días después María Aurora me llamó a ver si Lázaro podía ayudarlos a tramitar los papeles para salir del país.

Los hechos se suceden con tanta rapidez que a veces me da la sensación de estar parada en el vórtice de un huracán. Lo único que parece permanecer intacto es Mama Luya sentada en el butacón del comedor de su casa, recién levantada de la siesta, con la cara empolvada y los labios pintados muy claros con su creyón de Coty. Huele a colonia y a mi infancia. De pronto, se ha ido otro año.

Julio 8 de 1961
Año de la Educación

Señora Dora,

Le hago esta carta para decirle que estoy alfabetizando, tengo trece años y estoy en primer grado. Empecé este año en la Escuela. Y me llamo Marina Díaz Barrio. Estoy dando clases con mechón porque no tengo farol.

He leído cartas que mandan a BOHEMIA, mire, cuando dijeron que podían escribir para los Reyes yo escribí y no mandé la fotografía porque no pude retratarme. Y hoy le escribo para decirle que estoy dispuesta a coger las armas para defender a mi Patria querida. También le diré que tengo cuatro alumnos y ya pronto pienso dar a dos por alfabetizados.

También le diré que la única esperanza de ver a Fidel era ir a La Habana el día 26 de Julio y ahora dicen que no podremos ir a La Habana ni los alfabetizadores ni los analfabetos. Así que he visto a Fidel en retrato porque tengo muchos en mi casa.

Yo vivo en Las Villas. Yo quisiera que publicara mi carta en BOHEMIA para que Fidel la lea porque sé que lee BOHEMIA. Yo quisiera poderte dar las gracias, Fidel. Siento un gran afecto por ti y tus compañeros.

Estoy en el corte y la costura. También sé tejer y voy a aprender a bordar, tengo un gran empeño de aprender para enseñar luego.

Fidel, yo no me rindo por la manteca. P'alante y p'alante y perdóname la letra.

¡Patria o muerte! ¡Venceremos!
Marina Díaz Barrio

(*Bohemia* 53:34, 21)

༄

Hay muchas cosas que me inquietan, pero lo de la educación es distinto. Marta Lola y yo nos hemos apuntado para ir al campo a la campaña de alfabetización. Nada me parece mejor que aspirar a un país donde todos sepan leer y escribir, y sean cultos. Ricardo está opuesto a que vaya. Papá, como siempre, dice, "vamos a ver…" y Mamá se queda callada. Pero yo estoy decidida a ir.

Lauri llamó para decirnos que espera un niño. ¡Me parece mentira! Hace un par de años éramos unas pepillas bailando "rock and roll" y danzones, y suspirando por los muchachitos. Y ahora… De un día para otro nos hemos tenido que hacer mujeres.

Hay rumores de todo tipo, que si la Revolución les va a quitar a los padres la patria potestad de los hijos, que si viene una invasión de gusanos (así les dicen a los que se han ido).

El sábado hubo tres ataques aéreos, en Santiago, en San Antonio de los Baños y aquí en La Habana. El país está en pie de guerra. Dicen que vendrá una invasión americana. Lázaro llegó a casa muy temprano. Era la primera vez que lo veía con el uniforme de miliciano. ¡Menos mal que Ricardo no estaba aún levantado!

—Esto es una traición imperialista, cobarde… —decía indignado. Y los ojos se le ponían pequeñitos, como dos rayitas.

—Vine a despedirme —me anunció.

—¿Pero adónde vas? —le pregunté alarmada.

—¿A dónde va ser? A defender la Revolución.

Los rumores de invasión no eran falsos. Yo estaba con el corazón en vilo pensando que algo le podía pasar a Lázaro. Hasta ahora no había comprendido cuánto significaba para mí. La idea de perderlo me horrorizó. Cuando por fin regresó del frente de batalla y lo abracé, me eché a llorar.

—Vamos, vamos… que no es para tanto…

Ahora pienso que tiene razón. Aunque no todo sea perfecto en la Revolución, no es justo que un país tan grande como Estados Unidos nos ataque.

Hace días que Ricardo falta de la casa. Mamá y Papá cuchichean. Yo creo que está escondido y no me lo quieren decir. Han arrestado a muchas personas. Ya han cogido a todos los invasores. ¡Cuánta fue nuestra sorpresa cuando vimos entre ellos a Robertico y a su padre! No lo podíamos creer.

—Son unos gusanos… unos contrarrevolucionarios —comentó Lázaro con un gesto de repugnancia.

Mamá, que apenas habla de estas cosas, le respondió en voz firme:

—No ofenda, Lázaro, que es el esposo de mi hija.

Mamá quiso llamar a Laurita pero no pudimos comunicar.

—¿Qué será de mi hija, ahora? ¡Y esperando un niño…! —se lamenta.

Muchos compañeros de la universidad están detenidos. Clausuraron las publicaciones católicas. También van a nacionalizar todas las escuelas. Los rumores sobre lo de la patria potestad aumentan.

La vida se ha convertido en un continuo desgarramiento. Me siento como una gigantesca mano de despedida. Casi todos los compañeros de clase se están yendo. También los antiguos maestros. Se van los tíos, los primos. Muchos, sin decir adiós, como si huyeran. Después, es como si se los hubiera tragado el mar. ¡Nadie los menciona! Ricardo ya ni vive en casa, pero cada vez que viene nos dice que nos debemos ir todos. Papá le asegura que no nos pasará nada, que las cosas van a mejorar... Mamá no discute, siempre está de acuerdo con él, aunque en el fondo esté loca por ver a Laurita. A mí la idea de separarme de Lázaro me angustia. Y no sé, con esto de ayudar a alfabetizar, me parece por primera vez que hago algo útil, importante.

—No te das cuenta de la edad de Pedritín. Lo van a adoctrinar —insiste Ricardo.

Muchas familias están mandando a los hijos solos fuera del país.

—Eso sí que yo no lo hago por nada del mundo —opina Mamá.

—Estará con Laurita...

—O nos vamos todos o nos quedamos todos.

Pero no ha sido así. Ricardo se fue. Y sin apenas despedirse. En cierta forma, fue peor que cuando Laurita. No sé por qué pienso que nunca más lo volveré a ver.

Mi único sostén es Lázaro. Sólo me pongo brava con él cuando me habla mal de mi cuñado.

—Roberto se prestó a lo más bajo, a ser un mercenario de los yanquis, a venir con los imperialistas a invadir el país, a disparar con armas americanas contra sus propios compatriotas, a atentar contra esta Revolución más verde que las palmas que hará que todos los niños tengan zapatos y cuadernos. Pero la Revolución es generosa y lo perdonó... A ver si los yanquis lo vienen a rescatar...

Mamá insistió en ir a ver a Robertico al Príncipe y hasta le llevó algunas cosas de comer. Se le veía acongojada al regresar. Sólo comentó:

—Es muy triste ver a hombres presos. Además, es mi yerno.

Me dio pena no haberla acompañado. Pero a veces creo que Lázaro tiene razón, que he estado ciega. Nosotros teníamos una vida privilegiada. Escuela privada. Una maestra especial si no entendíamos las matemáticas o nos atrasábamos en el inglés. Clases de ballet. Francés. Dibujo. Los conciertos los domingos. Sin pensar por un momento en la cantidad de analfabetos en el país. El Carmelo. La Casa Potín. Los veranos en la playa. Comer mangos sentados sobre la arena, el jugo dulce y pegajoso deslizándose por el cuello. ¡Con tantos niños pasando hambre! Correr entonces a meterse en el mar. El susto de las olas al nivel de la boca. Sin jamás percatarnos de que los pobres no tenían acceso a las playas. La Semana Santa en la finca de Tío Máximo. La yegua Jardinera. Yo quiero montarla. ¡Es mi turno! Sin pensar por un momento en los *guajiros* explotados por los latifundistas. El cafecito de mediodía. Los hombres jugando dominó. Las mujeres dándose sillón y todos los primos correteando. ¡De espaldas a los sinsabores del pueblo! Por las noches, la luz de los cocuyos. Si lo pones bocabajo y da tres brincos antes de volar, tendrás tres hijos. Los juegos de La Habana y el Almendares. ¡Cómo batea el negro Formental! Los helados de Tropicream y los del Picolino. A Prado y Neptuno... tarán tarán... iba una chiquita... Mami, ¿por qué no nos dejas afeitarnos las piernas? El Silver tiene lo que más yo quiero... El club. Los bailecitos. ¡Qué ciega estaba, Dios mío! Los únicos pobres que conocía eran el Caballero de París y la viejita que pedía limosna a la salida de la iglesia. Le regalábamos una peseta que nos daba Papá, nos recompensaba con una sonrisa y una estampita, y nos sentíamos felices... Es verdad que Mamá nunca fue una de esas burguesas de canasta y crónica social, ni Papá jamás explotó a nadie. Todo lo que disfrutamos era fruto de su trabajo. ¡Pero no es justo que algunos tengan tanto y otros tan poco! Los cuatro negritos de Jacomino, hijos de Hilda la cocinera, no eran para mí seres reales, sino una especie de referencia folclórica. Lázaro tiene razón. En este país ha habido mucha discriminación racial. Ahora al fin los negros pueden bañarse en las playas.

Anoche llamó mi hermana. Me pidió que fuera a acompañarla para cuando dé a luz. Primero le di evasivas. Lázaro no me quitaba los ojos de encima. Por fin tuve que decirle que no rotundamente. Quizás haya sido muy dura.

Lauri, hubiera querido explicarte cómo eso me comprometería, los problemas que me traería en la universidad, cómo señalaría a toda la familia, cómo ofendería a Lázaro que es tan bueno con nosotros. No sé si me hubieras entendido. De todas formas, colgaste sin darme tiempo a nada.

CAPÍTULO CUATRO
"I Wanna Hold Your Hand!"

LLEGAMOS A COLUMBUS A MEDIADOS DE FEBRERO
DE 1963. Había 28 grados. Al bajarnos del avión echábamos humo por
la boca al hablar. Me sorprendió que las ramas de los árboles estuvieran
tan desnudas. Se me antojaron brazos alzados que imploraban a Dios.
Nuestros patrocinadores, el matrimonio Stone, vivían en un *townhouse*
de ladrillos rojos, rodeado de tantos otros iguales que yo siempre temía
confundirme de casa. Nos instalaron en el sótano. Por las pequeñas
ventanas se veía la tierra y la hierba seca del jardín. Había un solo
baño y como ellos lo usaban primero, si teníamos alguna emergencia
hacíamos nuestras necesidades en un cubo. Robertico decía que le
recordaba la prisión.

A los pocos días de llegar, nevó. Nunca habíamos visto nieve y
jugamos como niños tirándonos pelotas y construyendo un muñeco.
Cuando nevaba se suavizaba el contorno de las cosas. Había una especie
de virginal pureza en todo el paisaje que me sobrecogía. Sentía algo similar
a cuando hice la Primera Comunión, una especie de flechazo luminoso,
de adivinación de una inteligencia suprema más allá de mi comprensión.
Viendo caer aquellos copos blancos me parecía que el tiempo se detenía.
Que cada segundo era idéntico al anterior y al próximo al mismo tiempo,
y me preguntaba si así sería la eternidad. Pero cuando pasaban los días, la
nieve se ensuciaba y se acumulaba a los lados de las calles. Se formaba un
fango gris que era un estorbo para todo.

A mi esposo le consiguieron trabajo de cobrador. Tenía que ir de casa
en casa tratando de que le pagaran cuentas atrasadas. Con frecuencia le
tiraban la puerta en la cara. Roberto se quejaba del frío y de que le
dolían los pies. Una vez hasta le cayó atrás un perro. Siempre estaba de
mal humor. Además, le pagaban muy poco. Yo me pasaba muchas horas
encerrada con Pedro Pablo en el sótano. Apenas me atrevía a sacarlo
un rato por la mañana cuando había sol, pues durante todo el invierno
siempre tenía agüita por la nariz. Mrs. Stone —Kathy— nos prestó un

vaporizador y con eso respiraba mejor por las noches.

Los domingos íbamos a misa con Peter y Kathy, la pareja que nos hospedó, y su hija Elizabeth, de 9 años. Lo que más me llamaba la atención era lo arregladitas que estaban las viejitas, siempre con guantes y sombrero. Roberto decía que se ponían tanto colorete que parecían unos payasos.

Había soñado estar a solas con Roberto y el niño pero comencé a extrañar no sólo a mi familia sino también Miami, a Johnny, a Vidal, e incluso a mis suegros. Además, Roberto parecía otra persona. Tantas veces durante su ausencia que lo había deseado, que había recordado nuestras noches de amor, que había querido refugiarme en sus brazos, y ahora lo tenía a mi lado, y apenas me tocaba. A veces, en la cama, lo abrazaba, le pasaba la mano por la espalda, por la nuca, trataba de buscarlo, pero él, por lo general, murmuraba algo sobre lo cansado que estaba y al minuto comenzaba a roncar. En muchas ocasiones, me dormí llorando. Y en otras, hasta llegué a masturbarme. Lo había hecho ya muchas veces durante su ausencia, pero ahora, con él durmiendo a mi lado, me daba una mezcla de dolor y rabia muy grandes. Al menos, me ayudaba a conciliar el sueño.

Algunos fines de semana los Stone nos llevaban al centro de la ciudad. A mí me parecía que en comparación con La Habana, aquello era una basura, pero no lo decía. Lo que más me impresionaba era la prisión. Estaba construida con unos ladrillos de un color oscuro indescriptible, con apenas unas pocas ventanitas pequeñas, y rodeada de una cerca de alambres de púa. Siempre estaba custodiada por hombres uniformados con armas largas. Todo el lugar tenía un aspecto siniestro que me aterraba. Aquella prisión me hacía pensar en Cuba. A veces soñaba que mi madre estaba dentro y gritaba para que la dejaran salir. Hubiera preferido no pasar por allí, pero no hacía ningún comentario. Trataba de no herir a los Stone y con Roberto no quería echarle más leña al fuego. Bastante huraño estaba siempre. Decía que no resistía estar rodeado de tantos americanos y tener que hablar todo el tiempo en inglés.

Deseaba trabajar, pero con el niño me era imposible. Un día lo comenté en la iglesia y para mi sorpresa me preguntaron si quería ayudar en el *nursery,* una especie de escuelita que tenían para niños de *pre-kinder.* Podría llevar a Pedro Pablo. Y como la iglesia estaba a tres cuadras, iríamos caminando. Acepté entusiasmada. Por lo menos, el niño tendría con quién jugar y saldríamos un poco de la casa. La segunda sorpresa fue cuando, a la semana, me entregaron un cheque. ¡No lo podía creer!

Con lo que ahorré de mi modesto sueldo y con algo que aún me quedaba del dinero que mi padre me había mandado con Ricardo, compramos nuestro primer carro, un destartalado Ford del 53. Era de un color rojo desteñido y le pusimos El Mamey.

Le propuse a Roberto ayudarlo con su trabajo. Yo podía manejar el carro —Vidal me había enseñado después de que nació el niño y a veces me prestaba su *transportation*— mientras él se bajaba a cobrar. Así perdería menos tiempo. Íbamos por las noches y los fines de semana, que era cuando la gente estaba en la casa. Pedro Pablo casi siempre dormía en el asiento de atrás. También comencé a llenarle el informe semanal que tenía que entregar a la compañía y a llevarle todas las cuentas. No sé si fue por eso o por pura suerte, pero empezó a cobrar y a ganar más. Ya era verano, los árboles desnudos se habían llenado de verde y el niño comenzaba a decir palabritas en inglés. Con el dinero que estábamos ahorrando pronto podríamos mudarnos a nuestro propio apartamento. Nada me hacía más ilusión. Hasta Roberto, a veces, parecía el de antes. Incluso una noche Mrs. Stone se ofreció a quedarse con el niño para que saliéramos. Fuimos al cine y a tomar un refresco. Y luego hicimos el amor como cuando recién casados.

Un día de julio nos llamaron de Miami. Doña Asunción había muerto. Johnny la había encontrado al regreso de la escuela tirada en el suelo de la sala con los ojos muy abiertos y el teléfono entre las manos engarrotadas. Había sido un infarto. Lo primero que pensé fue en la impresión que habría sido para el niño.

Roberto decidió ir al entierro de su abuela. Yo no podía entenderlo. La mujer era una bruja, nos había hecho sufrir mucho al niño y a mí, y él nunca había mostrado ningún especial cariño por ella. Pero cuando me lo dijo ya tenía el pasaje en la mano y hacía la maleta. Le pregunté lo que había costado el boleto. Era casi todo el dinero que teníamos para el depósito del apartamento. Lo hubiera querido matar, pero me callé y lo despedí con un beso.

No volvió enseguida como yo había pensado. Pasaron dos semanas. Cuando llamaba desde Miami sonaba distante y hasta temí que nunca regresaría. ¿Qué haría si nos abandonaba en aquella remota ciudad? Por fin anunció que llegaría al día siguiente.

—Te tengo una sorpresa. Te va a gustar —me dijo.

Fui a buscarlo al aeropuerto con Pedro Pablo. La alegría que me dio verlo me devolvió la paz interior. En los últimos meses sentía un cierto resentimiento contra él y me había llegado a preguntar si ya no lo quería como antes.

En cuanto nos montamos en el carro me dijo:

—Laurita, nos vamos de Columbus.

Por mediación de un amigo mutuo, había localizado a Pancho, un antiguo compañero de estudios, que vivía en las afueras de Washington. Pancho le había contado que allá había muchos cubanos y que se ayudaban unos a otros. Le había prometido encontrarle empleo en esa ciudad.

Yo le argumentaba que era una locura irnos sin algo seguro, que en Columbus teníamos el apoyo de los Stone, de la iglesia, que ambos teníamos trabajo. Pero Roberto estaba decidido. Había guardado para el final el argumento más convincente:

—Tendremos nuestro propio apartamento.

—Pero, ¿cómo lo vamos a pagar? ¿Cómo vamos a dar el depósito?

—No te preocupes. Ya eso está resuelto. ¿Es que no confías en mí?

Aunque habíamos vivido en Columbus apenas unos meses y habíamos pasado tantos apuros, lloré al despedirme de mis amigos de la iglesia, de Peter, Kathy y Elizabeth, y hasta del americano gruñón a quien había que entregarle todas las semanas el informe de los cobros.

Roberto, por el contrario, cuando nos montamos en el carro lo primero que dijo fue:

—Aquí no vuelvo más nunca. ¡Qué pueblo más aburrido!

Pensé que a mí me bastaba con estar los tres juntos para ser feliz, pero obviamente a él no, y sentí de nuevo ese desasosiego que a veces me invadía. Era una especie de cosquilleo detrás del esternón, una amenaza de dolor que se me movía dentro del pecho sin acabar de asentarse.

∽

Más de 200,000 personas, principalmente Negros pero incluyendo miles de blancos, llevaron a cabo una manifestación pacífica en Washington el 28 de agosto con el objetivo de reclamar la atención pública sobre las demandas de igualdad en los trabajos y en los derechos civiles que los Negros han planteado.

Los manifestantes se reunieron temprano por la mañana en el monumento a Washington mientras 13 de sus líderes se entrevistaban con miembros del Congreso. Seguidamente, con los organizadores de la marcha a la cabeza, tomaron dos caminos, uno por Constitution Avenue y el otro por Independence Avenue hasta el Lincoln Memorial. Los manifestantes llenaban prácticamente todo el espacio entre los monumentos a Washington y a Lincoln. Al terminar la marcha, los líderes fueron a la Casa Blanca donde se entrevistaron con el Presidente Kennedy. Regresaron para dirigirse a la multitud allí congregada.

Los manifestantes venían de todas partes del país, incluyendo numerosas delegaciones de iglesias y sindicatos, pero la mayoría eran afroamericanos de zonas rurales. Muchos llevaban pancartas que decían "Abajo la discriminación," "Integración en las escuelas," "Abajo con la brutalidad policíaca" —todas terminando con la palabra "¡Ahora!" ...la muchedumbre comenzó espontáneamente a entonar canciones... También entretuvieron a los manifestantes personalidades como Ossie Davis, Joan Baez, Bobby Darin, Odetta y Jackie Robinson.

El orden fue mantenido por 5,000 policías, miembros de la Guardia Nacional y reservistas del ejército. No hubo ningún arresto. El Presidente Kennedy declaró que se había reforzado la causa de 20 millones de Negros por la forma ordenada en que se había llevado a cabo la marcha.

(Facts on File 23.1191, 299)

⨎

Llegamos a Maryland de noche, después de manejar no sé cuantas horas. Nos estaban esperando cuatro matrimonios con sus hijos en uno de los apartamentos. Se formó tremendo alboroto. Pancho nos presentaba.

—Ésta es Anabel, que es peluquera, éste es su esposo José, que trabaja en una tienda y éste es Eddy, que trabaja en un banco, y su esposa Isabel, que es secretaria. Viven en el mismo edificio donde van a vivir ustedes, y éstos son los hijos de Anabel y José, y éste…

Yo estaba rendida y segura de que jamás me acordaría de tantos nombres. Además, todo el mundo hablaba con mucha excitación sobre una marcha que los negros habían tenido ese día. Por fin nos llevaron a nuestro apartamento, que a mí me pareció precioso y grandísimo.

—Como me dijiste que no tenían muebles les conseguimos al menos un colchón… —le dijo Pancho a Roberto mientras bajaban del techo del Mamey la cuna de Pedro Pablo, que era, con nuestra ropa, lo único que poseíamos en el mundo.

Esa noche dormimos los tres en el colchón.

Antes de conciliar el sueño le dije a Roberto:

—Sabes, mi amor, hacía tiempo que no me sentía tan contenta…

Me contestó con un ronquido.

⨎

Un vocero de un movimiento de unidad que aspira a actuar como liason entre los refugiados cubanos y Washington, declaró ayer que contaban con el apoyo de exilados ricos.

La comisión, constituida el 20 de mayo por 150 exiliados del sector político, laboral y empresarial, anunció un programa de tres puntos para la eliminación del régimen de Castro, la erradicación del comunismo y el restablecimiento de la Constitución de 1940.

El comité dijo que escogería a siete miembros del comité dentro de 10 ó 12 días para que actuaran como representantes del grupo al tratar con los Estados

Unidos y otros gobiernos.
   También dijo que ningún miembro del movimiento recibiría salario alguno.

(Wilkinson A1)

∾

—Juan Fernando... ¡Coño!... te he dicho que vengas a desayunar... Juan Fernaaando...

Me despertaron los gritos de mi vecina. Acostumbrada ya, sin saberlo, al silencio sepulcral de Columbus, aquello me causó una tremenda mala impresión. Además, yo nunca en Cuba había oído decir malas palabras ni llamar a los niños de esa manera.

Al igual que en Miami, la colonia cubana en Silver Spring, el barrio adonde fuimos a vivir, era muy variopinta. El exilio había reunido a personas de distintos niveles de educación. Eso sí, todos nos ayudábamos. Anabel les cortaba el pelo a las mujeres y a los niños. Pepe el mecánico arreglaba los carros viejos de todos. Frank, que revalidaba su carrera de dentista, comenzó a sacarnos muelas antes de que le llegara la licencia. La ropa de los niños iba de casa en casa según le iba quedando chiquita a unos y sirviéndoles a otros. Como yo era de las que mejor sabía el inglés, siempre estaba traduciendo documentos o escribiendo cartas que me pedían los vecinos. Y cuando llegaba alguna familia de Cuba, todos cooperábamos para encaminarlos.

Roberto encontró trabajo en un banco. Era en el centro de la ciudad, a una cuadra de donde trabajaba Eddy, así que decidieron ir juntos y turnarse manejando. A mí me parecía una maravilla contar con un sueldo fijo y que Roberto estuviera en una oficina y no en la calle de cobrador.

En los apartamentos vivía una señora cubana que podía cuidarme a Pedro Pablo y comencé a buscar trabajo, sin éxito. Por fin un día me encontré en una farmacia a Marta Garay, una vieja amiga de mi madre. Me dio tanta alegría que en un instante le conté todos mis problemas.

—No te preocupes, yo te voy a ayudar —me dijo.

Y así fue. Por mediación suya me coloqué en una oficina de bienes raíces. La dueña era una señora judía. Cuando me entrevistó me preguntó si sabía mecanografía y taquigrafía, usar mimeógrafo, máquina de sumar y un montón de otras cosas que no entendí. A todo le dije que sí aunque mis conocimientos de oficina se limitaban a un curso que había hecho un verano en La Habana. Tenía que coger dos guaguas para llegar y al principio pasé mil apuros, pero aprendí mucho y me sentía tan contenta que no me importaba. Los vendedores tenían tiempo libre esperando que sonara el teléfono y conversaban mucho de política. Empecé a interesarme por las cosas del país.

En el barrio los hombres formaron una liga de pelota, y en la primavera y el verano nuestro mayor entretenimiento eran los juegos de los domingos. Después hacíamos un *barbecue*. Éramos todos tan pobres que los *hotdogs* estaban contados a uno por cabeza. Un día se acercó inesperadamente un muchacho que no era del grupo. Roberto le ofreció si quería algo. Se devoró dos *hotdogs* y mi vecina Silvia y yo nos quedamos sin comer. Por poco matamos a mi marido.

Los hombres también se reunían los viernes a jugar dominó. A veces les sesiones se prolongaban hasta bien entrada la madrugada. Las mujeres nos quejábamos y planeábamos todo tipo de venganzas, como irnos de paseo y dejarlos durante horas con los niños. Pero en definitiva no hacíamos nada.

Mi hermano Ricardo venía de vez en cuando a pasarse un fin de semana con nosotros. Nos reíamos muchísimo con sus cuentos de los apuros que había pasado recién llegado. Nos quedábamos levantados hasta tardísimo, recordando con nostalgia nuestra vida en Cuba. Nos invitó a que fuéramos a verlo a Nueva York. Yo en seguida me enamoré de la ciudad, pero Roberto se quejaba del tráfico y decía que todo estaba muy sucio.

Washington, por el contrario, era tranquila, majestuosa, señorial, con anchas avenidas y muchos árboles. Cuando venía gente de fuera, siempre los llevábamos a ver los monumentos. Una vez subimos los 898 escalones del alto obelisco construido en honor de George Washington.

El monumento a Lincoln es una especie de templo griego con una gigantesca estatua del presidente asesinado, cuyos ojos parecen seguir al visitante a todas partes. En el edificio circular construido a las orillas del Potomac en memoria de Thomas Jefferson pueden leerse citas del autor de la Constitución, entre ellas una en que jura su hostilidad contra todas las formas de tiranía. A los cubanos nos gustaba leerla.

También en esos tiempos visitamos Mount Vernon, donde vivió George Washington, el primer presidente norteamericano. Es una mansión grande, con unos jardines inmensos y bien cuidados, desde donde se divisa una hermosa vista. Lo que más me impresionó fue el interior de la casa, todo muy sencillo, casi austero. La Casa Blanca era igualmente simple hasta que Jackie Kennedy se dio a la tarea de restaurarla. Recuerdo cuánto me impresionó observar a diversos grupos de personas con pancartas protestando frente a la mansión presidencial por las razones más disímiles. En ese sentido, la libertad de expresión es admirable en este país.

Observamos sesiones del Congreso en el Capitolio así como la impresión de billetes y monedas. Siempre me conmovía el cambio de guardia ante la tumba del soldado desconocido en el Cementerio de Arlington, y la infinidad de sencillas lápidas blancas donde yacen los restos de tantos que han muerto defendiendo la libertad. Los días de fiestas patrióticas los familiares les traían flores y banderas, y el camposanto cobraba calor de hogar.

En Georgetown, uno de los barrios más ricos, donde también había una famosa universidad jesuita, descubrimos unas calles muy agradables para caminar, con tiendecitas y restaurantes, todo muy caro, aunque en alguna ocasión Ricardo nos invitó a merendar en uno de los cafés. Encontramos hasta una librería en la que vendían libros en español. También nos gustaba ir al barrio latino, cerca de Columbia Road, donde nos sorprendía gratamente escuchar hablar español y poder comprar en la bodega una latica de *bijol* o un hermoso racimo de plátanos verdes.

A lo largo de la Calle 16 y de la Avenida Massachusetts están las embajadas. Washington ha tenido siempre una vida diplomática muy activa a la que sólo nos asomábamos a través de los discretos comentarios de la prensa. Los americanos me daban la impresión de ser gente muy simple, casi provinciana. Al principio me chocaba que siempre estuvieran hablando del *weather* y que hicieran tantos aspavientos cuando había un día soleado, pero después comprendí cómo el clima afecta la vida diaria y hasta nuestro estado de ánimo. Aunque corteses y educados, siempre me parecían distantes y un poco superficiales. A veces hasta incultos. De Cuba no sabían nada. Eso sí, son muy cívicos. En esos años me llamó la atención cómo un vendedor podía dejar en una esquina un montón de periódicos y una caja de cartón, y los ciudadanos pasaban, tomaban un ejemplar y dejaban sus monedas para pagarlo. Eso no hubiera podido pasar en Cuba, donde no sólo la mayoría de la gente se hubiera llevado los periódicos sin pagar, sino que algún pillo hubiera acabado robándoselo todo.

Amantes de las tradiciones y de la democracia, los norteamericanos celebran el Día de Acción de Gracias y las elecciones con la misma inexorable regularidad que la caída de las hojas cada otoño. Comparados con los latinos, tan exuberantes, los sajones se me hacían inmensamente aburridos. Admiré, sin embargo, una ética del trabajo —influencia del protestantismo— que se observaba hasta en los niños. Desde muy jóvenes desempeñaban labores diversas —como cortar el cesped, repartir periódicos, cuidar a niños más pequeños— para ganar algún dinerito para sus gastos.

Washington ofrece estupendos museos que fuimos conociendo a través de los años, porque entonces nuestros mayores esfuerzos estaban dedicados a salir adelante. Compramos muebles a plazos y cambiamos el viejo Ford por un flamante VW. La mayoría sentíamos una gran añoranza por nuestro país. Yo sufría porque recibía pocas cartas de casa. Cuando el ciclón Flora, demoró tres días que me dieran la llamada. Menos mal que todos estaban bien. Para Roberto no había otro tema de conversación que Cuba, y sus estados de ánimo fluctuaban de acuerdo a las noticias. Si los exiliados preparaban algún ataque comando, se ilusionaba pensando en el regreso. Si en los periódicos aparecía algo favorable a la Revolución, él mandaba una carta al editor. La mayoría de las veces se la pasaba hablando mal de la Revolución: que si los Comités de Defensa, que si el racionamiento, que si el trabajo voluntario, que si los pioneros, que si la *microfracción,* que si los rusos. Era como una obsesión. Una vez, acabábamos de hacer el amor, y se levantó de la cama hecho una furia:

—Coño, Lauri, a Virgilio lo fusilaron sin que se hubiera templado a una mujer —y dio un puñetazo sobre la cómoda.

Tampoco nuestro entorno era sosegado. El movimiento de los derechos civiles cobraba cada día más fuerza en Estados Unidos. Yo no entendía cómo en la gran democracia del mundo se trataba así a los negros, como el año anterior el Presidente había tenido que mandar a la Guardia Nacional para que un negro pudiera estudiar en la Universidad de Mississippi. Todos comentábamos que en Cuba no había esos prejuicios. Pero el padre de Anabel decía que no nos fiáramos, que Martin Luther King era comunista.

Las tensiones de la guerra fría hicieron que se instalara una "línea caliente" entre Moscú y Washington para evitar que, por accidente, fuera a comenzar una guerra nuclear. ¡Sería el fin del mundo!

✎

John Fitzgerald Kennedy, de 46 años, el trigésimo quinto presidente de los Estados Unidos, fue asesinado en Dallas, Texas, el 22 de noviembre. Dos balas de rifle lo hirieron, una en la cabeza y otra en el cuello, a las 12:30 p.m. (Central Standard Time) mientras desfilaba en un auto descapotable y fue declarado muerto en el Parkland Hospital a la 1 p.m. Es el cuarto presidente americano asesinado durante su mandato.

El Gobernador John Connally, que viajaba en el mismo auto que el Presidente, fue alcanzado por otra bala y se encuentra en estado grave. La Sra. Kennedy y la Sra. Connally, sentadas al lado de sus respectivos esposos, no resultaron heridas.

Lee Harvey Oswald, de 24 años, un ex-Marine pro comunista que en una ocasión intentó cambiar su ciudadanía norteamericana por la soviética, fue arrestado menos de dos horas después, y fue acusado del asesinato del Presidente, pese a negar su culpabilidad.

El vicepresidente Lyndon B. Johnson, de 55 años, quien iba sólo dos automóviles detrás del que llevaba al Presidente Kennedy, juró como Presidente a las 2:39 p.m. del mismo día, a bordo del avión presidencial en la pista del aeropuerto Love Field en Dallas. La ceremonia se demoró unos 5 minutos para esperar la llegada de la Sra. Kennedy, quien se situó parada a la izquierda del Sr. Johnson. Su vestido aún se veía salpicado con la sangre de su esposo.

Siete minutos después de la ceremonia, el avión presidencial partió de Love Feld para llevar a Mr. Johnson, a su esposa, a Mrs. Kennedy y el cadáver del Presidente Kennedy de regreso a Washington. Llegaron a la Base Aérea Andrews como a las 6 p.m. (Eastern Standard Time.)

(Facts on File 23.1204, 409)

∾

Nunca olvidaré el día que mataron a Kennedy. De casualidad yo había ido al centro a almorzar con Bobby (en el banco todos llamaban a Robertico así). De pronto el ambiente se enrareció. Había asombro y estupor en todos los rostros. Se oían voces que hablaban al unísono pero no podíamos distinguir lo que decían. La gente se movía de un lado a otro; al mismo tiempo todos estaban como paralizados.

—Han disparado a Kennedy —alguien dijo. Por fin supimos que estaba muerto. Una sombra gris se posó sobre la capital norteamericana aquel día de invierno. Todos estábamos tan sobrecogidos que no atinábamos a reaccionar. Vi a personas abrazarse llorando. Otras cayeron de rodillas y comenzaron a rezar.

En seguida apresaron a un sospechoso. Circulaban rumores de que Cuba estaba involucrada en el magnicidio. Algunos de nuestros vecinos se alegraban, porque decían que entonces seguro que acabarían con

Fidel, pero a mí me daba mucha vergüenza que fuera a ser un cubano el responsable de algo tan espantoso. Nos pasamos dos días en la casa viendo los funerales por televisión. JohnJohn saludó el féretro de su padre como un soldadito. Mataron a Lee Oswald, el presunto asesino. ¡Delante de las cámaras de televisión! Había muchas teorías sobre lo que había pasado, pero en definitiva nadie sabía nada. Los compañeros de Robertico de la Brigada llamaban continuamente. Todos se preguntaban cómo esto afectaría lo de Cuba. Algunos insistían en que Kennedy nos había traicionado, que no había por qué llorarlo. Pero yo no podía quitarme de la cabeza su imagen cuando lo vi en el Orange Bowl, el pelo rojizo brillando bajo el sol. Por la madrugada tuve que sacar el sillón del cuarto porque me parecía que veía a Kennedy meciéndose en él.

Sólo se oían noticias de la guerra de Vietnam y de la lucha por los derechos civiles. Los chinos explotaron una bomba nuclear. A Martin Luther King le concedieron el premio Nóbel de la Paz. Parecía que sólo a nosotros nos importaba Cuba.

Aunque casi ninguno tenía voto, los cubanos simpatizaban con Goldwater, el candidato republicano a la presidencia, pero yo me alegré cuando ganó Johnson, un viejo político tejano que hablaba con acento sureño. Al menos parecía preocuparse por los desamparados y prometía que trataría de terminar la guerra.

Ricardo nos invitó a esperar el año en Nueva York. La ciudad estaba toda iluminada. Olía a pinos y a castañas asadas. Pedro Pablo disfrutó mucho viendo las vidrieras de Macy's y a la gente patinando en Rockefeller Center. Estaba graciosísimo y se sabía todas las canciones de los Beatles. Se pasaba el tiempo cantando:

> *I wanna hold your hand!*
> *I wanna hold your hand!*
> *I wanna hold your hand!*
> *And when I touch you,*
> *I feel happy inside.*
> *It's such a feeling that, my love,*

I can't hide, I can't hide!
I wanna hold your hand!
I wanna hold your hand!
I wanna hold your hand!

También fuimos a San Patricio. Siempre que entro a una iglesia pido lo mismo: que pronto podamos regresar a nuestro país. Visitamos a mis tíos. Tío Julio ya está trabajando en un hospital. Me impresionó verlo, porque se parece tanto a Papi. Tía Alicia siempre tan cariñosa. Julio Eduardo, Carlitos y yo recordamos los domingos en casa de Otra Mamá, cuando todos los primos jugábamos a los Pasos Americanos en el zaguán de la casa de la calle C. Julio Eduardo me confío que tenía una noviecita, y que quería estudiar medicina, como su padre. Yo no los veía desde que me fui de Cuba. Y Bobby apenas se acordaba de ellos. Se me había olvidado lo bien que uno se siente con la familia.

Fue emocionante estar todos juntos en *Times Square* a las doce de la noche. Pensé mucho en mi gente en La Habana. Hubo un momento, Menchu, que me pareció verte claramente en medio de la multitud. Aunque sabía que era imposible, me pasé toda la noche buscándote, como si de veras te fuera a encontrar allí.

Contrariamente a lo que auguró en su campaña Johnson, la guerra en Vietnam parecía no tener fin. Todas las noches, en la televisión, cuando daban las noticias, era como si los tiros resonaran en la sala de la casa. No en balde cobró fuerza el movimiento estudiantil en contra de la guerra. El problema racial también se agudizó. Mataron a Malcolm X en Nueva York. En Alabama no lograron que se respetaran las nuevas leyes que permitían a los negros votar. El Presidente tuvo que mandar a la Guardia Nacional. Pero ni con eso pudo evitar la violencia. El Ku Klux Klan mató a una mujer blanca que llevaba en su carro a una mujer negra.

Ya Pedro Pablo cumplió cuatro años y no quisiera que se quedara solo. Hacía tiempo que no nos estábamos cuidando, pero no salía en estado. Fui a un ginecólogo que me aseguró que estaba bien. Bobby decía que eso de tener otro hijo se ha convertido en una obsesión para mí.

Este verano fuimos de vacaciones por primera vez desde que nos casamos. Yo hubiera preferido estar los tres solos, pero un grupo grande de familias de los apartamentos iba a Miami y fuimos juntos en caravana. Nos hospedamos todos en el mismo hotelito en Miami Beach, y así nos salió más barato. Me dio mucha alegría ver a mis suegros, a Vidal y a Johnny que está altísimo. También la ciudad está muy cambiada, llena de letreros en español por todas partes. Las vacaciones no fueron lo que yo esperaba y hasta me peleé con Roberto. Por el día los hombres se pasaban el tiempo jugando dominó y las mujeres cuidando a los niños y hablando boberías. Después de comer, íbamos a visitar amigos y familiares, y era la misma cosa, él hablando de Cuba con los hombres, y yo con las mujeres y los niños.

Lo mejor fue ver el mar, caminar por la playa, sentir las olas batirse contra mis pies. ¡Cuántos recuerdos me trae el mar! Pienso en los veranos en la Playa Veneciana… cuando íbamos a pescar jaibas al muelle… y Tía Flor bañándose en el mar con nosotros, todos cogidos de las manos formando un círculo, saltando con cada gran ola… ¿Cómo se llamaba aquella amiguita nuestra a la que Tía Flor le puso de apodo "el Pececito"? Seguro que tú te acuerdas, Menchu… ¡Y qué azules las aguas de Varadero! Cómo nos gustaba recoger caracoles y hacer castillos en la arena… Nunca he visto una arena tan fina. Como la de Pilar… ¡Cómo llorábamos con ese poema de Martí! Sobre todo la parte en que el aya de la francesa se quitaba los espejuelos.

De pronto sentí una tristeza tan grande que el dolor se hizo físico. Quise llamar a Cuba, pero desde el hotel era muy difícil. Le sugerí a Bobby hacerlo desde casa de sus padres y me dio mil excusas. Finalmente me dijo:

—A mi padre puede perjudicarle una llamada desde su casa a unos comunistas.

—¿Qué comunistas, Bobby? Son mis padres, mi hermana, mi hermanito menor. Tú no entiendes porque tienes aquí a tu familia. Yo nunca antes me había separado de ellos… —Rompí a llorar con tal desconsuelo que Pedro Pablo se asustó. Me tuve que controlar porque no me gusta pelear delante del niño, pero esto no se lo voy a perdonar.

En el viaje varias parejas comentamos lo alejados que estaban nuestros hijos de la cultura cubana y al regresar fundamos una Casa Cuba. Comenzamos montando una obrita de teatro, que yo misma escribí, sobre los Reyes Magos. Lo más difícil fue que los niños se aprendieran los villancicos. Pedro Pablo se veía de lo más gracioso y lo hizo de lo mejor. Todo quedó de lo más bien, aunque yo estaba molesta porque Bobby llegó tarde.

∽

Aviones norteamericanos bombardearon una zona de 5 millas al sur de Hanoi en una serie de ataques aéreos. Ocho aviones americanos fueron derribados en combate, el número mayor en un solo día, lo cual eleva la cifra a 435 aviones que los americanos han perdido sobre Vietnam del Norte....

Un Ministro de Política Exterior de Vietnam del Norte dijo que los aviones estadounidenses "han atacado zonas densamente pobladas en los suburbios al sur de Hanoi y en otras zonas de la ciudad...."

De acuerdo con cifras reveladas por los mandos militares en Saigón el 23 de noviembre, al menos 48,000 tropas comunistas se han infiltrado en Vietnam del Sur de enero a septiembre....

Desde que Vietnam del Sur instituyó la política de "brazos abiertos" para los desertores en 1963, unos 45,000 Viet Congs se han cambiado de bando y se han unido al gobierno de Saigón....

Los 27 americanos a bordo del U.S. Air Force C-47 murieron el 26 de noviembre cuando el avión se estrelló poco después de despegar de la base de Tansonhut cerca de Saigón....

La propuesta de Viet Cong, anunciada por la radio clandestina del Frente Nacional de Liberación, dijo que las fuerzas guerrilleras suspenderán las operaciones militares por la Navidad desde las 7 a.m del 24 de diciembre hasta las 7 a.m. del 26 de diciembre y por Año Nuevo desde las 7 a.m del 31 de diciembre hasta las 7 a.m del 2 de enero de 1967.

(Facts on File 26.1362, 457)

❧

El lunes me matriculé en Montgomery College. No es que haya desistido de estudiar algún día en la Universidad de La Habana, pero no sabemos cuánto va a durar esto y hay que aprovechar el tiempo. Como ya Pedro Pablo está en primer grado, no tiene que quedarse tantas horas en casa de la *babysitter*. He tenido suerte porque es una señora cubana y toda la familia quiere muchísimo al niño. Además, le hablan en español. A mí me da un dolor inmenso cuando voy a la escuela y lo veo jurando la bandera americana. Con Bobby no puedo contar, porque desde que dejó el banco y trabaja a comisión vendiendo seguros, nunca se sabe a qué hora va a llega ni cuánto va a ganar. Pero él dice que es sólo al principio, que es un campo en el que hay mucha oportunidad, y que ya no resistía más al jefe americano que tenía.

Mis primos se presentaron para el *draft*, porque Tío Julio dice que hay que acatar las leyes del país. A Julio Eduardo lo reclutaron los marines, así que fuimos a Nueva York a despedirnos de él. Tía Alicia nos invitó a almorzar el domingo. Nos pasamos la tarde hablando de Cuba, de mis clases, del colegio del niño, de los estudios de Carlitos, todo tan natural y tan falso, como si al día siguiente aquel muchacho que hace pocos años corría conmigo por el zaguán de la casa de abuela no fuera a vestir un uniforme militar y a estar pronto bajo las balas de los vietnamitas, en unas tierras tan ajenas a nosotros que ni siquiera las estudiábamos en la clase de geografía.

Antes de marcharnos, Julio Eduardo nos llamó discretamente a su cuarto a Pedro Pablo y a mí. Al niño le regaló su disco de 45 revoluciones de Petula Clark con la canción Downtown y otro de los Beatles.

—Es que tú cantabas esto cuando eras muy chiquito y siempre me hace pensar en ti —le dijo a Pedro Pablo. Y se puso a tararear:

I wanna hold your hand!
I wanna hold your hand!

El niño se fue feliz a enseñarle los discos a su padre. A mí Julio Eduardo me dio una foto suya.

—Para que presumas de tu primo —me dijo con humor, como queriendo quitarle solemnidad a la ocasión.

—Sí, el primo más lindo del mundo... —quise contestarle con el mismo tono ligero, pero la voz se me quebró. Pensaba en el día en que despedí a Bobby cuando se fue a la invasión. Lo abracé para que no me viera las lágrimas.

Al regreso, en el carro, mi marido trató de animarme:

—No le va a pasar nada. Además, estará luchando por la causa.

—Yo no entiendo como ir a que te maten en Vietnam sea una forma de servir a Cuba.

—Estará combatiendo contra el comunismo... Ya verás que está de regreso en lo que canta un gallo.

Pero aquella despedida me dejó el temor de que no vería más a aquel primo de ojos oscuros como un pozo, frente amplia y enigmática sonrisa. Y aquel miedo se me clavó en medio del pecho como el aguijón de una avispa.

Desde que Julio Eduardo se fue al frente vivimos en vilo. Todas las noches, después del noticiero, ponen por televisión la lista de las bajas con una música de fondo que se me quedará grabada para siempre en el alma. Si alguna noche me duermo sin ver las noticias, me despierto de madrugada con la inquietud de que le ha pasado algo a mi primo. En mis pesadillas, los guerrilleros y los milicianos se confunden. A veces tienen las caras de mis compañeros de aula. Veo a Johnny, a Bobby, y hasta a Vidal y a mi suegro. Siempre van de uniforme. También hay a mujeres embarazadas, vestidas con harapos. Y niños, niños que lloran y lloran. Algunos se parecen a Pedro Pablo, otros a Pedritín. Siempre hay mucho ruido y fuego y disparos y polvo y tanques y rifles y aviones. Hasta que siento una explosión muy grande y entonces no hay nada más que silencio, un silencio muy, muy hondo... Y una luz blanca y cegadora, como la que llevo prendida a la retina desde el día en que dejé La Habana.

El ginecólogo me ha mandado unas pastillas carísimas. Dice que si las tomo y tenemos relaciones sexuales en los días indicados, él cree que en tres o cuatro meses saldré en estado. Yo deseo tanto tener otro hijo que hasta he pensado en adoptar uno. ¿Por qué no un huérfano de la guerra de Vietnam? Bobby dice que estoy más loca que una chiva, que ya tenemos un hijo, que de ninguna manera. Se supone que en estos días esté ovulando, ¡y anoche llegó a las cuatro de la mañana! Yo estaba tan furiosa que me hice la dormida. Hoy me dijo que estaban haciendo un plan para la unidad de todos los grupos exiliados.

Por fin esta tarde, cuando Pedro Pablo estaba en casa de los vecinos, hicimos el amor. Al principio me costó trabajo porque estaba muy brava con él, pero en cuanto me toca es como si toda la ira se me deslizara fuera del cuerpo. Bobby se pasa rato acariciándome los pezones y yo siento un cosquilleo entre las piernas que me va subiendo por el vientre... Luego me los chupa mucho tiempo, les pasa la lengua, los llena de saliva, los chupa de nuevo como una criatura hambrienta. Yo me retuerzo de placer y quiero sentirlo arriba de mí, que me penetre. Pero él dilata las caricias, va de un pecho al otro, los toma entre sus manos, me muerde suavemente los pezones, me besa los labios, los ojos, las orejas, el pelo. Regresa a los pezones y los moja, los besa, les pasa la lengua, se los mete en la boca y me los mama, con suavidad primero, con mayor presión... con locura.

—Ven, mi amor —le ruego.

Siento su cuerpo desnudo sobre el mío. Me frota el miembro erecto contra el clítoris... va tanteando los bordes de la vagina... hasta que está dentro de mí. Nos movemos al unísono. Siento la humedad entre las piernas.

Se separa y me busca la boca. Sus labios van besándome el cuello hasta llegar de nuevo a uno de mis pezones y prenderse a él. El placer se multiplica.

—Ven, mi amor, ven ya —le pido.

Los cuerpos, muy unidos, cabalgan sobre el lecho. Siento crujir los muelles de la cama. Me prendo a su espalda y grito. Grito por un placer intenso que siento entre las piernas. Grito porque estoy viva y tengo un hombre que me hace el amor y un hijo y cuatro paredes. Él aumenta la presión de su cuerpo sobre el mío, el movimiento circular de las caderas. Grito de nuevo. Por un placer intenso que siento entre las piernas. Y por estas malditas ganas de llorar que siempre estoy aguantando.

∽

Las tropas norteamericanas y de Vietnam del Norte sufrieron numerosas bajas entre el 2 y el 7 de julio cerca de la base de los U.S. Marines en Conthien, justo al sur del extremo oeste de la zona desmilitarizada.

El primer combate tuvo lugar el 2 de julio a una milla y media de Conthien, cuando 500 tropas de la división 324B del regimiento 90 de Vietnam del Norte tendieron una emboscada al tercer pelotón del regimiento noveno de los marinos norteamericanos. Treinta y cinco americanos murieron en el sorpresivo ataque.

(*Facts on File* 27.1394, 271)

∽

Recibí una carta de Julio Eduardo. Le había llegado la mía con la foto de Pedro Pablo. Me cuenta que varios compañeros cubanos y él comen arroz y frijoles negros en los campamentos. ¡Tía Alicia les manda hasta merenguitos! También Susana, su novia, le escribe a diario. Ya está terminando los 13 meses en el frente. Debe estar de regreso para los primeros días de julio. Dice que no puede esperar de ganas que tiene de vernos a todos. Con su humor criollo, termina la carta diciendo "¡Abre, que voy, cuidado con los callos!". Carlitos dice que han puesto una botella de champán en el refrigerador para cuando vuelva su hermano. Yo quiero ir enseguida a verlo.

Es el Día de la Independencia. Nadie trabaja hoy. Hay un calor intenso. Hemos esperado a que caiga la tarde para encender el *barbecue*.

Los niños se han pasado el día jugando. Están embulladísimos para ir a ver los fuegos artificiales. Bobby y los vecinos especulan sobre si el Che Guevara está vivo o muerto. Ayer dejé en el laboratorio una muestra de orina a ver si he salido en estado. Pero no quiero ni pensar en eso. Aunque hace días que no me siento muy bien. Es un malestar impreciso, una especie de nerviosismo raro, como si me revolotearan mariposas dentro, justo al nivel del corazón.

—Así yo me sentía cada vez que tenía exámenes —me dijo mi vecina Silvia cuando se lo conté.

Estaba parada en el portal cuando sonó el teléfono. Me demoré en reaccionar, hasta el punto de que Bobby, que estaba sentado, se levantó para contestar. Por fin le dije:

—Deja, yo voy.

Nunca olvidaré que del portal al teléfono hay once pasos.

—¿Lauri?

En cuanto oí la voz de Ricardo temí lo peor.

—Ay, Ricardo, no. ¿Julio Eduardo?

El entierro fue con honores militares. Los primos estábamos jugando en el zaguán de la casa de la abuela en el Vedado. El féretro estaba cubierto con una bandera norteamericana y otra cubana.

—¿Quién quiere jugar al tieso-tieso?

—No, mejor a las estatuas.

—No, a los agarrados.

—Yo prefiero a los escondidos.

Dos soldados con guantes blancos doblan las banderas y se la entregan a Tía Alicia.

—No, que ya jugamos a eso. Mejor a los policías y los ladrones.

—¡Yo soy policía!

Mis tíos me han parecido más viejos.

Julio Eduardo está cantando:

I wanna hold your hand!
I wanna hold your hand!

—Es que tú cantabas esa canción cuando eras muy chiquito y siempre me hace pensar en ti —le dice a mi hijo.

Carlitos se ha hecho hombre de pronto.

Y Susana, la noviecita, toda vestida de negro y con los ojos rojos de llanto, parece una niña viuda.

Han despedido a Julio Eduardo Soler Barraqué con veintiún cañonazos y la música melancólica de un cornetín. Nació en La Habana el 19 de marzo de 1944 y murió en Vietnam el 2 de julio de 1967 después de servir en el frente 12 meses y 29 días. No había cumplido los 24 años.

Comprendo de golpe los versos de Martí.

¿Por qué tiene luz el sol?

Cuando regresamos a casa lo primero que hice fue llamar al ginecólogo. Me dijo que estoy en estado. Ojalá sea hembra.

CAPÍTULO CINCO
"Dentro de cien años no habrá honra mayor"

LA CARRETERA QUE LLEVA HACIA EL VALLE SERPENTEA POR LAS EMPINADAS CUESTAS. En el largo recorrido en curva, los *mogotes,* unos aislados y otros en cadenas, parecen manadas de elefantes, en interminables hileras circenses. Desde el mirador se divisa el valle, que se abre al borde del abismo. ¡Qué grandiosidad de paisaje!

Las sierras quiebran el horizonte de un lado y otro, mientras las Pizarras se pierden cubiertas de pinares. Abajo se ven las zonas cultivadas, el verde en toda su gama, sólo interrumpido a largos trechos por el gris amarillento de un bohío.

La presencia gigantesca de los mogotes es amenazadora. La maravilla de equilibrio es tal que se cree presentir una próxima y temible catástrofe. En lo alto, un velo tupido verdinegro, amarillo y gris, cuelga de las hendiduras de las rocas desnudas. Enredaderas finas tejen sus encajes entre las copas de los árboles. Una vegetación boscosa cubre la periferia de las rocas, entre las que abundan, desafiantes, la orquídeas silvestres— moradas, blancas y violetas.

Al atardecer se escucha un murmullo suave que sale de la misma entraña de La Sierra y va creciendo según avanzan las horas. Es la noche misteriosa y bella que entona un son. Casi pueden percibirse el aletear de los insectos, el croar de las ranas, el silbido de los grillos que se repite de eco en eco con suave tintineo. Los *guajiros* de la región aseguran que el llamado lagarto de La Sierra comienza con la tarde su melodía.

Llevamos dos meses en la campaña de alfabetización. Nos ilusiona ser parte de este proyecto, a pesar del calor sofocante, las picaduras de los mosquitos y las incomodidades para dormir y para asearnos. Marta Lola y yo estamos exhaustas. Algunas compañeras se ríen de nosotras.

—Es que ustedes no están acostumbradas… —nos dice Maruja, con un punto de desprecio en el tono burlón.

—¿Ustedes duermen en sábanas de seda bordadas con hilo de oro?

—pregunta Angelita, los ojitos pícaros llenos de brillo.

—¡Qué imaginación! Claro que no. Nunca ni he visto sábanas así...

—Como dicen que la gente rica...

—Nosotras no somos ricas.

—Basta ya de hablar boberías. Vamos a leer.

Marta Lola dice que no entiende cómo, si todas vestimos iguales, pueden decirnos que somos distintas, y hasta ha empezado a hablar de forma vulgar para que no la acusen más de ser burguesa.

Las condiciones son difíciles. Los niños por lo general son tímidos y respetuosos pero no tienen hábito de estudiar y se distraen fácilmente. En cada grupo, sin embargo, hay uno o dos que recompensan el esfuerzo. Siempre levantan la mano para hacer preguntas y se les ve en las caritas ansiosas la avidez de aprender. También tenemos alumnos adultos: *guajiros* recios, con las manos curtidas y las uñas sucias; mujeres jóvenes que sueñan con irse a la ciudad; madres sin edad que han parido hijo tras hijo. Se les ilumina el rostro cuando aprenden a escribir sus nombres.

La belleza de la campiña invade mis sentidos y alivia todas las incomodidades. Nunca he visto amaneceres y atardeceres más bellos. Por las noches nos sentamos en un círculo y nos ponemos a cantar. Los *guajiros* improvisan décimas. Se respira un aire muy puro en las montañas.

Ayer vino Lázaro. No lo veía desde que me fui de La Habana. Me trajo una carta de Mamá y otra de Pedritín. Mientras paseábamos por los alrededores del campamento, me fue poniendo al día de los últimos acontecimientos pues aquí no nos llegan todas las noticias. El entusiasmo de Lázaro es contagioso. Piensa que Cuba está destinada a grandes cosas.

—Menchu, somos parte de la historia, no sólo de Cuba, sino del mundo. Esta Revolución será el principio de otras que se expandirán por todo el continente... No habrá más niños sin escuela, sin zapatos, sin comida... No habrá injusticias, ni ricos, ni pobres, ni negros, ni blancos. Todos seremos iguales.

También me dijo que venía a despedirse. Lo han escogido para ir como periodista acompañando a una delegación a Moscú. —Pero si tú ni has acabado la carrera...

—Me han seleccionado por mis méritos revolucionarios.

—Moscú está tan lejos... ¿Habrá frío?

—No creo que haya mucho frío en verano, boba... Y serán sólo unos días...

Después me llevó hasta un monte cercano. Cuando me abrazó, sentí una sensación de alivio, como si hubiera llegado a casa después de un largo viaje. Luego me besó muy suavemente los ojos, los cabellos.

—No debo oler muy bien... —le dije entre risas.

—Hueles a los campos de Cuba... y me gustas mucho...

Me abandoné a sus caricias, llenas de ternura. De pronto el abrazo se hizo más apretado. Me empujó suavemente sobre la hierba.

—Lázaro, pueden vernos...

—Shh... no hables... —y apretó su boca contra la mía.

Me abrió la blusa. Me rodeó de nuevo con sus brazos. Sentí sus manos desabrochándome el ajustador. Se echó entonces para atrás y contempló mi pecho desnudo.

—Eres tan bella. —Me pasó el índice por los labios que se humedecieron para besarlo. Deslizó un solo dedo por la barbilla, el cuello, el comienzo del seno...

—Lázaro, no, por favor... —le decía, pero era incapaz de moverme.

Una sensación antes desconocida me ardía entre las piernas.

—Tus pechos son como dos gardenias... —y acercó sus labios para besarlos. Sentí un latigazo de placer tan intenso que se me escapó un grito, que él acalló con sus besos.

—Me gusta que grites... pero nos pueden oír...

Traté de apartarlo, de levantarme. Colocó su cuerpo sobre el mío con tal brusquedad que me cortó la respiración. No sé cómo me bajó los pantalones. Sentí su sexo erguido entre mis piernas. Entonces se agarró el pene con las manos y me lo frotaba con fuerza por la vagina.

—¿Te gusta, chinita?

No pude contestarle. De pronto algo se rompió en mí y aquel pedazo de carne palpitante me penetraba. Lázaro se movía con furia. En ese momento me llegó un olor indescriptible, a hombre, a campo, a sudor que despertó en mí deseos insospechados. o lo abracé por la espalda y comencé a moverme hasta igualar su ritmo. Era como si cabalgáramos juntos y ambos nos hubiéramos convertido en caballo y jinete a un mismo tiempo, en un galopante minotauro desbocado.

—Te mueves con la gracia de un cañaveral... —me murmuraba al oído—. Eres tan dulce como la caña, tan jugosa como nuestras piñas, tan suave como la pulpa de un mamey...

De pronto sus caricias, sus besos, cada músculo tensado de su cuerpo, cobraron una fiera pasión, casi violenta. Y la voz, ahora grave y profunda, como si le brotara de las entrañas, me anunció:

—Te voy a templar hasta que te duela el bollo.

Cuando regresamos al campamento, se había hecho de noche y era cierto que me dolía.

∽

En abril de 1962, en dos operaciones afines y paralelas se crearon la Unión de Jóvenes Comunistas y la Unión de Pioneros de Cuba, como vehículos para la incorporación de las nuevas generaciones a las tareas creadoras de la Revolución. Pilares de la Cuba del mañana se están formando en un medio sano y limpio, liberado de vicios y egoísmos, educados en el amor a la patria, el estudio y el trabajo, en el aprendizaje de las nobles prácticas del compañerismo y la solidaridad humana. En este primer aniversario, mirando lo que se ha hecho en tan poco tiempo, en el recuento de la obra de la UJC y la UPC, el porvenir de Cuba socialista se ilumina de orgullo y esperanza, para saludar a esa masa de jóvenes y niños que constituyen el mejor tesoro de la Revolución.

(*Bohemia* 58:12, 3)

∽

Mamá está muy nerviosa porque Pedritín quiere ir al campo a hacer trabajo voluntario con sus compañeros. Ella le ha pedido a Papá que le consiga un certificado médico para que lo excusen. Él le hace todos los días el mismo cuento.

—Mañana sin falta te lo traigo, Mariana. Es que hoy mi amigo el Dr. Ortega estaba muy ocupado y se le olvidó firmarlo.

A medida que se acerca la fecha, Mamá se impacienta.

—Pedro, por favor, acaba de resolver ese asunto.

De todas formas, el muchacho está loco por ir… Por fin yo hablo con Papá:

—Tú no le vas a conseguir el certificado, ¿verdad?

—Sí… tú verás… es que…

—No me digas mentiras, Papá.

—Ay, Menchu, es que la gente no quiere meterse en problemas, pero yo voy a insistir…

—Harás muy mal. Y haces muy mal en engañar a Mamá.

—¿Qué quieres decir?

—Nada, que tú no has querido irte del país por tus razones muy personales… Está bien. Pero entonces hay que hablarle claro a Mamá…

—No le digas a tu madre nada de esto.

—Claro que hay que decirle la verdad…

—Menchu… por favor.

Mamá salió de la cocina.

—¿Qué pasa, mija?

—Mamá, más vale que te hagas a la idea de que Pedritín va a ir a recoger café y a tumbar caña, y más vale que le pongas con gusto la pañoleta de pionero, y que te acostumbres a la idea de que después será de la Juventud Comunista y algún día del Partido.

—¿Qué dices, Menchu?

—Digo que en este país ha habido una Revolución, que nosotros no nos vamos a ir, que yo soy joven y mi hermano es un niño, que no podemos vivir contra la corriente, y que si queremos llegar a ser alguien en la vida, a estudiar, a tener buenos trabajos, a viajar, a que nos respeten, y sobre todo, a hacer algo por nuestro país, la única forma es sumarnos a la Revolución, y hacerlo con los ojos cerrados, con una fe ciega, porque no tenemos otro camino.

—Menchu, pero tu Papá le va a conseguir un certificado... —Díselo, Papá, díselo. No le va a conseguir nada. Y si se lo consigue, ¿qué vas a hacer el mes que viene, y el otro, y el otro? ¿Lo vas a tener en la casa la vida entera como si de verdad fuera un enfermo?

Dos grandes lágrimas asomaron a los ojos de mi madre. Irguió la cabeza y después de una breve pausa, nos habló:

—Tienes razón. Es lo mejor para ustedes.

Pedritín se fue por fin a la recogida de café y volvió trabajador vanguardia de su instituto.

Un espectáculo que nadie pudo anticipar hace pocos años tiene lugar en la Isla: el vuelco de millones de cubanos sobre el campo en función de faenas agrícolas. En el pasado, todo acontecimiento nacional debía cumplirse en las ciudades, particularmente en la capital. La realidad y la sustancia del país eran ignoradas oficialmente. El campo servía sólo en el momento de la explotación y en el del voto. Hoy se sitúa en primer plano lo que entonces se desconoció. Brigadas obreras, estudiantiles, del MINFAR, cooperan metódica y ardorosamente al auge de la producción agrícola, dan impulso impar a las zafras del pueblo y se adentran científicamente en el conocimiento vivo de la economía rural, en la aplicación del saber a la creación de la riqueza para su pueblo. "Estamos en el verde," se lee con simpatía en carteles situados a la puerta de oficinas desiertas, cuyo personal acudió a la cita de honor en la tierra natal. Y las cifras productivas crecen. El rendimiento se desarrolla, la curva ascensional agrícola no se detiene. Prosperan planes ambiciosos en enormes fincas del estado. La batalla del azúcar prosigue en mayor escala cada año. Es Cuba entera la que está de cara al campo. La acción integral de todo un pueblo garantiza la victoria en esta contienda de la paz. En ella también puede decirse: VENCEREMOS.

(*Bohemia* 59:39, 3)

∽

He cambiado de habitación con Pedritín. Ahora tengo la del fondo, que es más pequeña, pero así Lázaro entra por el patio y se pasa la noche conmigo sin que lo vean los viejos.

Me ha contado su infancia marcada por la carencia y la incertidumbre:

—Mi madre era modista. Era la querida de mi padre, un político importante. El tenía esposa, otros hijos. Pero se ocupaba de nosotros. Le daba dinero a Mami y me traía regalos, aunque no me gustaba cuando me pasaba la mano por la cabeza distraídamente, como si acariciara a un animalito. Recuerdo haber salido con él sólo dos veces. La primera tendría yo unos 5 ó 6 años y fuimos a un cine. Nos sentamos en la última fila y nunca se quitó el sombrero. Cuando se lo conté a Mamá, mi abuela, que no lo podía ver, comentó: "Tendría miedo de que lo vieran contigo."

Yo pensaba que no era verdad, porque ese mismo día le había dicho a mi madre que me mandara a estudiar en una escuela privada. No sé si mi padre la pagaba o si me habían admitido por recomendación suya, pero nunca me sentí a gusto allí. Los niños me miraban mal. Pensé que era por mis ropas raídas y mis zapatos viejos, y una noche que él fue a ver a mi madre, esperé sin dormirme a que salieran de la habitación, y lo abordé antes de que se marchara. Le solté de sopetón: "Los niños en la escuela se ríen de mí porque mi uniforme está muy viejo… y además me queda chiquito." Debió hacerle gracia, porque se sacó un billete del bolsillo y le dijo a mi madre: "Mañana le compras lo que necesite a este *fiñe.*" Y me sonrió.

A pesar del traje nuevo, sólo uno de los compañeritos compartía conmigo. De todas formas, pronto tuve que cambiar de escuela. Un domingo, cosa rara, mi padre llegó sorpresivamente. Parecía alegre.

"Vístanse tú y Lazarito que los voy a llevar a pasear", le dijo a mi madre. Estuvimos listos en lo que canta un gallo. Nos montamos en su máquina grande y oscura. Por fin nos bajamos en Coney Island. Me compró un jugo de piña, muy frío, y un algodón de azúcar. Ellos caminaban atrás, conversando animadamente, y yo iba delante, sorteando los charcos y saboreando la merienda. De pronto Fonseca (siempre nos referíamos a él por su apellido) dijo que no se sentía bien y mejor volvíamos. Regresamos en silencio, como si una sombra gris se hubiera posado sobre la luz de aquel domingo.

Cuando llegamos mi madre le insistió que entrara y descansara un rato. Dudó, pero por fin aceptó: "A lo mejor así se me pasa."

Mi madre le aflojó la ropa y él se tendió en el lecho, sin quitar la sobrecama. Ella fue a prepararle una sal de frutas. "Seguro que es una mala digestión." le oí decir.

Me acerqué. Abrió los ojos y los fijó en mí. Nunca había notado que tuviera unos ojos tan grandes. Vi entonces que un hilo de sangre le corría por la comisura de los labios. Llegó a alcanzarle la guayabera blanca. Cuando mi madre regresó estaba muerto.

Entonces vinieron los años malos. No me importó cambiar de escuela, pero mi madre sufrió mucho cuando nos tuvimos que mudar a una casa y a un barrio peor. Trabajaba todo el día pegada a la máquina de coser, con mi abuela siempre atormentándola: "Te debías buscar otro Fonseca. Si yo fuera joven…"

Años después un abogado me dijo que tenía derecho a parte de la herencia de mi padre. Por fin, para evitar el escándalo, la familia nos dio una cantidad de dinero. No era mucho, pero pudimos comprar la casa donde ahora vivimos.

—¿Conociste alguna vez a tus hermanos? —le pregunté.

—No, sólo en una ocasión los vi de lejos. Y claro, ya se han ido del país.

∽

Y es la palabra que simboliza la aspiración de una gran parte de la humanidad, y por ella hoy trabajan concretamente cientos y cientos de millones de seres humanos. Y dentro de cien años no habrá honra mayor, ni habrá nada más natural y lógico que llamarse comunista.

Hacia una sociedad comunista nos encaminamos. Si no quieren los imperialistas caldo, pues les daremos tres tazas de caldo.

De ahora en adelante cuando nos llamen comunistas, sepan que nos llaman de la manera más honrosa que pueden llamarnos.

(Fidel Castro 3 de octubre 1965)

∽

Lázaro y mi primo Armandito han hecho muy buenas migas. Yo también me llevo bien con Magaly. A menudo salimos los cuatro. Siempre hay obras de teatro, exhibiciones de pintura, ballet. Se están publicando muchos libros y un gran número de escritores extranjeros vienen de visita. En toda la Isla hay un gran auge cultural. Y eso que estamos siempre en pie de guerra. Lázaro está en lo cierto. Estaríamos mucho mejor si los yanquis nos dejaran tranquilos.

—Fidel tiene razón cuando dice que dentro de la Revolución todo y fuera de la Revolución, nada. Porque en la Revolución cabe todo lo bueno, y ¿qué hay fuera de ella sino la ignominia de los enemigos? ¿Tú crees que hay derecho a que los americanos violen nuestro espacio aéreo 58 veces en menos de dos meses? —A Lázaro se le ponen los ojos chiquiticos cuando se apasiona. A veces me burlo de él.

—Tú te crees que todavía eres líder estudiantil...

—Menchu, no se puede bajar la guardia en ningún momento.

Armandito y Magaly están felices porque esperan un niño para fin de año. Le pregunté a Lázaro si le gustaría tener hijos. Estuvo un largo rato en silencio, como si lo tuviera que pensar mucho. Por fin me contestó, en tono grave:

—Sí, Menchu. Me gustaría tener un hijo, para crear de verdad al hombre nuevo, a un hijo de la Revolución cubana.

—Yo quisiera también que fuera hijo mío...

—Claro, boba. Pero tenemos que casarnos.

—¿Me estás proponiendo matrimonio?

—Mira, Menchu, la familia es una institución burguesa, pero todavía en este país existen esos valores y no quiero que mi hijo sufra lo que yo sufrí por ser hijo natural.

En pocos días arreglamos los papeles y nos casamos sin decírselo a nadie, ni siquiera a mis padres. Lázaro siguió viviendo en su casa y yo en la mía. Él estaba seguro de que si me iba a la suya, su abuela me haría la vida imposible, y que en casa, acabaría peleando con mi familia. Mejor era esperar a poder vivir solos. En la Habana del Este estaban construyendo unos apartamentos nuevos y nos apuntamos para conseguir uno. De todas formas, casi todas las noches las pasábamos juntos.

Papá debió verlo salir una mañana porque me atajó. Estaba descompuesto:

—Menchu, mientras yo viva, éste será un hogar decente. No puedo controlar lo que hagas fuera de aquí, pero no quiero que ese hombre vuelva a entrar a mi casa. ¿Me oyes? Y mejor que no se entere tu madre de que lo he visto salir de tu habitación.

—¿Con qué un hogar decente...? ¿Es qué lo que tú haces fuera de la casa no cuenta?

—Menchu...

—No vengas a darme lecciones de moral, Papá. Y mejor que mi madre no se entere de las cosas que yo te sé.

—No me faltes el respeto.

—Hace mucho tiempo que te perdí el respeto.

—¡Las cosas que te han metido en la cabeza ese Lázaro y la Revolución!

—Esto no tiene nada que ver ni con Lázaro ni con la Revolución. Tiene que ver contigo, y con que hace mucho tiempo que sé que engañas a Mamá.

—¡Cállate! O te voy a...

De pronto nos percatamos de que Mamá estaba en el umbral de la puerta. Ninguno de los dos sabíamos qué tiempo hacía que nos oía.

—No le pelees a Menchu, Pedro. Ella sabe sus cosas.

Esa tarde Mamá me llamó a su cuarto. Abrió su escaparate y extrajo de entre su ropa interior una pequeña caja. Eran unas dormilonas de perla.

—Mira, mija. Estos aretes me los regaló Mamá Luya cuando me casé con tu padre. Ahora que eres una mujer casada me gustaría que los tuvieras tú.

—¿Cómo lo supiste, Mamá? No se lo hemos dicho a nadie.

—Conozco bien a mis hijas. Y mira, mejor que Lázaro entre por la puerta principal y que venga a comer con nosotros cuando quiera. Yo hablaré con tu padre.

A finales de año, el 28 de diciembre de 1963, Magaly dio a luz a un niño. Le pusieron Ernesto.

—Será por la memoria de tu tío... —comentó Mamá.

—No, Mariana —le aclaró Lázaro—. Es por el Che.

Pocos días después el médico me dijo que estaba en estado.

La consigna, como un toque de clarín, se extiende a todos los rincones de la Isla. Durante la Quincena de Girón, la nación entera, de cara al campo, se volcará en los cañaverales respondiendo a la cita del patriotismo y el trabajo. Fábricas, ministerios, escuelas, campamentos, militares, organizaciones de masas se aprestan al magno esfuerzo colectivo para convertir en realidad viva el nombre de Zafra del Pueblo, con el que la Revolución distingue la jornada azucarera. Cuando se dice Zafra del Pueblo no se expresa únicamente un sentido posesivo de las riquezas nacionales. Se está señalando también la participación directa del pueblo. Acrece la significación de esta quincena el hecho de que se ofrezca como un homenaje a los héroes de Girón. De este modo, cada año, la victoria ganada en la playa gloriosa se repetirá y prologará en los cañaverales. La Cuba que arrojó al mar a los invasores es la misma que ahora, en una movilización sin precedentes, habrá de abatir el imperialismo a golpe de mocha.

(*Bohemia* 59:13, 41)

Cuando me puse de parto, Papá se ofreció a llevarme en su carro a Maternidad. Yo quise que Mamá me acompañara. Luego fueron llegando Lázaro, Mama Luya, Tía Flor, mi amiga Marta Lola. Hasta Maruja, la presidenta del CDR, vino con Pedritín.

—Estaba loco por ver a su hermana y lo traje —nos dijo.

Pero el parto se demoraba y se fueron yendo. Lázaro tenía guardia y se marchó también.

—Yo no me voy —dijo Mamá, y se sentó a mi lado. Me quedé dormida. Sentía, entre sueños, cómo me secaba el sudor de la frente y me la humedecía con colonia.

—Eres muy buena, Mamá.

—Ay, mija, menos mal que puedo estar contigo. Tu pobre hermana tuvo que dar a luz sola.

—Bueno, vieja, ya eso pasó. Pedro Pablo tiene casi dos años, ¿no?

—Los cumple el 8 de septiembre. Sabe Dios cuándo lo conoceré...

—¿Los extrañas mucho?

—Mucho, mija.

—Yo también.

Las contracciones arrecian. Trato de pensar en cosas agradables. Lauri y yo estamos en la playa, con unos cubos y unas palas que nos han regalado por el cumpleaños, haciendo castillos con torres y túneles subterráneos por los que pasa el agua... Siento la arena entre los pies... esa arena fina de nuestras playas... el sol caliente sobre los hombros... Ahí viene de nuevo el dolor... ay, ay, ayyy... Estamos bañándonos en el mar con Tía Flor. También está Doris, aquella amiguita que nadaba tan bien que le pusimos de apodo "el pececito"... Viene otra contracción, esta vez más dolorosa aún... no me gusta quejarme... pero ¡coño!

—Menchu... —Mamá me regaña, pero sonríe.

Siento un peso entre las piernas. Quiero pujar. La enfermera me examina y llama al médico. Lauri y yo brincamos sobre las olas. El agua nos empapa.

—Se le ha roto la fuente —oigo que alguien dice.

Cuando vienen las contracciones fuertes, le aprieto la mano a Mamá. Pone tal cara de sufrimiento que prefiero no quejarme. Por fin me llevan al salón. Poco después oigo un llanto. Instintivamente, sé que es una niña. Miro el reloj. Son las 10:15 p.m. del 9 de junio de 1964. Ha nacido mi hija. Le hemos puesto Tania.

∽

En esas manos hay amor
Pero cuando no se mantienen limpias, cuando no se lavan a menudo,
pueden transmitir gérmenes de graves enfermedades ¡la gastroenteritis entre
ellas! Por su salud… manos limpias!
La gastroenteritis Puede y Debe Evitarse
MINSAP Educación para la salud
Manos limpias… ropa limpia… alimentos limpios… casa limpia…
manos limpias… ropa limpia…

(*Bohemia* 56:50, 74)

∽

Lázaro cada día está más activo. En su labor de periodista tiene oportunidad de asistir a importantes eventos. Viaja por la Isla. También ha ido tres veces a Moscú, la última vez acompañando al Che Guevara. De esta visita, no entiendo por qué, no ha publicado nada. Pero anoche, cuando la niña ya se había dormido y la casa estaba tranquila, me leyó su testimonio:

"Era la víspera del regreso. Habíamos estado todo el grupo conversando, comentando mil cosas. Se acercaba el alba. Los compañeros se fueron retirando. Quedamos solos el Che y yo. Fumábamos en silencio, ensimismados ambos porque todo estaba hablado, se habían agotado las ideas, los análisis, las hipótesis. Quedaba sólo esa rara emoción del hombre ante sí mismo, ante su destino, quién sabe si ante su vida o ante su muerte. Entonces, con voz contenida, más para sí mismo que para mí, el Che empezó a hablar de Fidel. No del estadista, no de sus dotes excepcionales, no de la inteligencia suprema con que estaba manejando la crucial situación del país; no se habló de nada de eso porque ya todo eso estaba hablado. Habló de su devoción, del sentimiento que le producía la grandeza extraordinaria de su amigo. Confesó —no creo que me lo confesó a mí, lo dijo simplemente— que él no había comprendido a Fidel ni su grandeza, que había dudado de él, que había temido que Fidel se quebrara en el camino.

Había una amargura profunda en sus palabras, un reproche a sí mismo, un dolor que nacía de este error. Comprendí que no se podía perdonar a sí mismo. Ese Fidel Castro de los primeros tiempos, ese líder guerrillero, ese agitador confuso, se fue creciendo, se fue convirtiendo paso a paso ante sus ojos en el gran revolucionario, y simbolizaba para el Che la capacidad del hombre, de cada hombre, para cumplir su más bello destino. ¡Y él había dudado de Fidel, él había dudado del hombre!

Entonces, sorpresivamente, el Che se viró hacia mí y me dijo:

—¿Sabes cuál es el verdadero drama de un dirigente? Debe tener una mente fría, tomar decisiones dolorosas sin contraer un músculo. Pero también debe tener un espíritu apasionado, y, a riesgo de parecer ridículo, diré que tiene que estar guiado por grandes sentimientos de amor. Nuestros revolucionarios de vanguardia deben idealizar ese amor a los pueblos, a la causa más sagrada, y hacerlo único, indivisible. No pueden descender con su pequeña dosis de cariño cotidiano hacia los lugares donde el hombre común los ejercita.

El Che es ese hombre nuevo, ese dirigente que combina la fría razón con un amor que no puede ejercitarse en la familia, en la compañera, en los hijos. Un amor que tampoco puede satisfacer el poder, que está más allá, que tiene mayor compromiso. Un amor que está dispuesto a darlo todo, incluso la vida".

Terminó de leer con la voz quebrada. Luego, con gesto brusco, dobló el papel en cuatro y me lo entregó.

—Esto no lo voy a publicar. Guárdalo para Tania… para el futuro… para que sepa que su padre es testigo de uno los momentos más hermosos de la historia de su país.

Coloqué la hoja en la mesa de noche. A la mañana siguiente, la leí de nuevo. Me pregunté qué significábamos Tania y yo para Lázaro en comparación con el Che, Fidel, la Revolución. Quizás estaba celosa, pero sentí de nuevo ese desasosiego que a veces me invadía. Era una especie de cosquilleo detrás del esternón, una amenaza de dolor que se movía dentro de mi pecho sin acabar de asentarse.

∽

En Guisa, Oriente, sobre un fondo geográfico e histórico que tiene contornos de epopeya, celebró su cuarto aniversario la Federación de Mujeres Cubanas. Seis mil y más campesinas, la mayoría procedentes de La Sierra Maestra, se apretaban en torno a las dirigentes de la FMC, encabezadas por Vilma Espín.

La Bandera Nacional flotaba sobre el paisaje agreste. Federadas del campo y la ciudad, entusiastas y combativas, ofrecían una tónica de jovial responsabilidad. Muy atrás quedaba ya la diferencia a nivel cívico entre ambos sexos y el epíteto discriminativo de "débil" agregado al sustantivo "mujer". Hoy día, luchadora social y política, trabajadora de vanguardia y miliciana, daba ejemplo a sus hermanas de América.

(Bohemia 56:35, 62)

∽

Por fin, después de tantas complicaciones con el cambio de planes de estudio y con el embarazo de Tania, me gradué de arquitecta. Mi primer trabajo es como asesora de la subcomisión de Trinidad de la Comisión Nacional de Monumentos. Con motivo de haberse cumplido 450 años que Diego Velázquez la fundó en 1514, se quiere restaurar la fisonomía colonial de la ciudad. A nosotros nos corresponde vigilar que las mejoras modernas no dañen la arquitectura original. Hace pocos días tuvimos la primera reunión en Trinidad. Enmarcada en el majestuoso escenario de las verdes cumbres del Escambray, acariciada por las brisas marinas, la ciudad tiene mucho a su favor: la proximidad de la montaña y el mar, la existencia de cuevas profundas, y de parajes bellísimos, incluso una laguna. Pero es un diamante en bruto. Porque además de la vetusta Plaza de Armas, de la iglesia de la Santísima Trinidad, del edificio neoclásico que acoge la Biblioteca, de las calles empedradas, hay un sin fin de bohíos y chozas, de viviendas construidas incluso con paredes rudimentarias de hierbas y tierra fangosa. En La Barraca, barrio pobre de casas de adobe, me ha parecido que se deslizaba la sombra oscura, fugitiva, del legendario Caniquí. En contraste, sobre los tejados viejísimos se levantan las antenas de televisión, como una gran telaraña.

La humanidad crece, la humanidad se multiplica; y no crece, sin embargo, la superficie. El hombre tendrá que hacer todo lo necesario por incrementar la productividad por superficie, poner el máximo de las tierras o de la superficie en productos, aprovechar todos los recursos de la ciencia; puesto que sólo quienes no sean revolucionarios, quienes no tengan la menor idea de las posibilidades de la inteligencia y de la voluntad del hombre podrán concebir un mundo en que la humanidad se muera de hambre.

Y desde luego, dos cosas son imprescindibles: revolución y técnica. Y lo que nosotros hagamos aquí no sólo será útil para nosotros sino serán experiencias que algún día podrán ser útiles también a otros pueblos que tengan que resolver problemas similares.

(Fidel Castro 12 de agosto 1967)

Vivimos en un torbellino tal, que a veces me siento mareada. Entonces me voy con Tania para casa de Mama Luya. Allí todo está igual. Ella sigue durmiendo la siesta después del almuerzo. Cuando se levanta, es el mismo ritual. Saca del escaparate la faja de cordones, se la amarra, se pone su vestido estampado, se empolva la cara y se pinta los labios muy claritos, se arregla la redecilla y se sienta en la terraza. Siempre huele a jazmines y a mi infancia. A veces le riego el jardín, porque ya le cansa estar mucho rato de pie. A Tania le gusta que la cargue, y le pasa la mano por la cara, por esa piel suave, de bebé, que los años no han logrado arrugar. No sé cómo se las arreglan Tía Flor y ella que siempre tienen alguna golosina que ofrecernos. Pero lo que más disfruta Tania son los cantos que su bisabuela le enseña. "Había una vez un barquito chiquitico, había una vez un barquito chiquitico…" y la niña muestra con los deditos el tamaño de la imaginaria embarcación. Para dormirse no quiere otra canción que la de las manzanas, como dice ella:

> *Señora Santa Ana*
> *por qué llora el niño*
> *por una manzana*
> *que se le ha perdido*
> *Yo te daré una*
> *yo te daré dos*
> *una para el niño*
> *y otra para vos.*
> *Yo no quiero una*
> *yo no quiero dos*
> *yo quiero la mía*
> *que se me perdió.*

—Parece que era ayer que les cantaba a tu hermana y a ti —siempre suspira Mama Luya.

—Pobre Laurita… tan sola por esos fríos —añade invariablemente.

También a Maruja le gusta enseñarle canciones a Tania. Cada vez que la niña está jugando en el portal y pasa por casa, se le acerca cantando:

> *Oye, tú que dices que tu patria no es tan linda,*
> *Oye, tú que dices que lo tuyo no es tan bueno,*
> *yo te invito a que busques por el mundo*
> *otro cielo tan azul como tu cielo,*
> *una luna tan brillante como aquella,*
> *que se filtra en la dulzura de la caña, un Fidel que vibra en las montañas,*

un rubí, cinco franjas y una estrella...
Cuba, qué linda es Cuba
quien la defiende la quiere más.

"Cuba, qué linda es Cuba", canción de Eduardo Saborit

Tania la imita y poniéndose las manos en las caderas, repite:
—Cuba, qué linda es Cuba...

∽

Hemos hablado mucho de Vietnam, hemos analizado en numerosas ocasiones todo lo que significa la heroica lucha de Vietnam, lo que significa para el mundo Vietnam y para los movimientos de liberación y para todos los pueblos hostigados por el imperialismo; cómo en Vietnam se libra una batalla por toda la humanidad; cómo Vietnam, al enfrentarse heroica y victoriosamente con los más poderosos, agresivos y odiados imperialistas del mundo, libra también una batalla por nosotros.

Nuestro fervor y nuestra solidaridad con Vietnam no hay que reiterarlos, porque es tan natural y tan lógico por sí mismo que un país como el nuestro también amenazado de similares peligros, sienta hacia Vietnam la más profunda solidaridad...

Y Vietnam está frente a una lucha a muerte, a una lucha decisiva, lucha que crece en profundidad y en intensidad.

Y por eso, más que palabras, queremos hacia Vietnam un gesto que lo diga todo, y es que este año, este año nosotros lo dedicaremos a Vietnam y que este año sea el Año del Vietnam Heroico.

Y eso, eso que lo dice todo, esa es la proposición que hacemos a ustedes: que el año 1967 sea el Año del Vietnam Heroico, y los que estén de acuerdo que levanten la mano.

¡Patria o muerte! ¡Venceremos!

(Fidel Castro 2 de enero 1967)

∞

En los círculos intelectuales hay mucho revuelo con el libro de un tal Debray. Lázaro sólo hace seguir las pocas noticias que nos llegan sobre el Che, que anda de nuevo por el mundo de guerrillero.

Hemos sabido que mi primo Julio Eduardo está peleando en Vietnam. Claro, del otro lado. Ellos se fueron en el 61, y al parecer lo reclutaron para el ejército americano. O fue de voluntario, no sé. Nadie habla mucho de eso, pero creo que cada vez que hay noticias de la guerra todos pensamos en él, aunque no lo digamos. Lázaro, Maruja y Marta Lola se alegran cuando los yanquis tienen muchas bajas, pero yo sólo logro fingir una sonrisa. No es por cuestión política. ¿Pero, y si hubieran matado a mi primo? Lo recuerdo cuando nos reuníamos la familia todos los domingos y jugábamos a los pasos americanos en la casa de Otra Mamá en la calle C en el Vedado. Quizás sea bueno que la pobre abuela se haya muerto. Ya perdió a un nieto en la Segunda Guerra Mundial… ¿Por qué he dicho eso? No va a pasar lo mismo.

Siempre le pregunto a Papá si ha tenido noticias de Tío Julio. Por lo general me contesta muy raro. Es una especie de Cantinflas mi padre. Uno nunca sabe qué quiere decir. Ahora es muy amable con Lázaro y a veces hasta parece más revolucionario que el propio Fidel. Otras veces lo oigo hablando bajito con su amigo Eneido y me parece que están criticando la Revolución, pero cuando me acerco se callan. ¡Ni conmigo es sincero! Ni que yo lo fuera a denunciar…

Por fin, a principios de julio, nos ha llegado la noticia. A Julio Eduardo lo mataron un día antes de que se le cumpliera el plazo para regresar a su casa. Cuando Armandito vino a decírnoslo, Maruja, que estaba en el portal, entró y comentó:

—¿Y qué tenía que ir a buscar un muchacho cubano a esa guerra de los yanquis?

Mi madre le clavó esa mirada suya gris acero, como la de su madre, y le dijo:

—Maruja, respete a los muertos. Como quiera que sea, es el sobrino de mi esposo.

Papá se quedó impávido. Después se levantó como si nada e hizo café. Pero por la noche se encerró en el baño. Me pareció oírlo llorar.

CAPÍTULO SEIS
"Y si vas al cobre quiero que me traigas…"

MI SEGUNDO HIJO NACIÓ EL 8 DE FEBRERO DE 1968, el mismo día que el Gobernador George Wallace anunció su candidatura presidencial y sus intenciones de barrer con el movimiento de los derechos civiles. Yo le quería poner Julio Eduardo, pero Roberto insistió en que se llamara como él. Mis suegros vinieron una semana antes para quedarse con Pedro Pablo mientras yo estaba en el hospital y para ayudarme cuando llegara a la casa. Adela se empeñaba en hacérselo todo al bebé. Sé que no lo hace por mal, pero yo hubiera preferido estar sola con mi esposo y con mis hijos.

—*My flower child…* —le digo al niño, y Bobby me pone mala cara. Para él todos los hippies son comunistas.

La noche antes de que se fueran sus padres, les preguntó:

—¿Qué les parece si ustedes vienen a vivir con nosotros? Con un préstamo de VA o de FHA podemos comprar una casa, y así nos ayudan a cuidar a los niños y vivimos todos más amplios…

Mi suegra en el acto contestó:

—La verdad es que desde que Johnny está estudiando en Gainesville nos sentimos muy solos…

Yo quería matar a mi marido. Debió haberme consultado primero. Para colmo, me entero de que ya había visto una casa y estaba en trámites de hacer una oferta.

—Claro, si a ti y a Mamá no les gusta…

Nos tuvo que gustar, porque hasta había dado un depósito y no estamos como para botar el dinero. Estuvimos peleando toda la noche. No sé cuántas veces le he dicho que estas decisiones las tenemos que tomar juntos. Creo que ni siquiera entiende lo que quiero decir. Pero luego se me acerca… Cuando empieza a acariciarme la nuca se me va disolviendo el enojo. Acabamos haciendo el amor, y siempre se sale con la suya.

Nos mudaremos en junio, cuando Pedro Pablo haya terminado el curso. Menos mal que la casa está bonita.

❧

Un muchacho negro de 16 años resultó muerto en Memphis el 28 de marzo cuando una manifestación de protesta presidida por el Reverendo Dr. Martin Luther King, Jr. terminó en violentos disturbios y asaltos. La manifestación era en apoyo a los trabajadores de sanidad, en su mayoría negros. El Gobernador Buford Ellington (Demócrata de Tennessee) pidió la ayuda de 4,000 miembros de la Guardia Nacional y declaró un toque de queda. La violencia estalló en la sexta semana de lo que comenzó como una huelga laboral, y se había convertido en una protesta en pro de los derechos civiles de la comunidad negra de la ciudad.

(*Facts on File* 28.1431, 131)

❧

En estos días en que me paso tantas horas frente al televisor mientras le doy el pecho a Bobby Junior, me he dado cuenta de la gran división que hay en el país. ¿Irá a haber otra guerra civil? Pienso en Cuba, en Hilda la cocinera y cómo siempre invocaba a sus cuatro negritos de Jacomino. Menchu y yo preparamos a la niña mayor para que hiciera el examen de Ingreso a Bachillerato. Todavía me parece que veo a Josefina con la ropa que nos había quedado chiquita a nosotras, con sus dos trencitas, sentada en la terraza de casa, doblada sobre los cuadernos. ¡Qué empeño tenía en aprender! Pasó el examen de lo más bien y Papá le consiguió una beca para estudiar. ¿Cómo vivirían? Nunca fuimos a Jacomino. Ni se nos ocurría. ¿Qué habrá sido de ellos? ¿Se habrán favorecido con la Revolución los negros como dicen? ¿Será comunista King como aseguran algunos cubanos? Quisiera tanto tener a alguien con quien discutir estas cosas… A Bobby ni le puedo hablar porque a él sólo le interesa tumbar a Fidel. Mi jefe es muy izquierdista, y tampoco me fío.

❧

El Dr. Martin Luther King, Jr., de 39 años, ganador del Premio Nóbel de la Paz y reconocido líder del movimiento a favor de los derechos civiles, fue asesinado por un francotirador en Memphis, Tennessee, el 4 de abril.

Se han recibido expresiones de asombro y pésame de distintas partes del país y del mundo. La noticia del asesinato de King precipitó disturbios en Washington, Chicago y en otras ciudades americanas. Treinta y cuatro personas resultaron muertas y miles heridas. Más de 20,000 tropas regulares y 34,000 de la Guardias Nacional fueron enviadas a las ciudades afectadas por los disturbios en respuesta a la petición de ayuda de las autoridades locales.

El Presidente Johnson se dirigió a la nación en un discurso televisado en el cual elogió al líder negro y pidió que "todo ciudadano debe rechazar la violencia sin sentido que mató al Dr. King, quien vivió a favor de la no violencia".

La bala mortal hirió a King en el lado derecho del cuello a las 6:01 p.m. mientras se encontraba en el balcón del segundo piso frente a la habitación donde se hospedaba en Hotel Lorraine en el área principalmente de personas de la raza negra en Memphis. Fue declarado muerto a su llegada al St. Joseph's Hospital a las 7:05 p.m.

(*Facts on File* 28.1432, 139)

∽

Regresábamos del médico con los niños —a Bobby Junior le tocaban las vacunas de los dos meses— cuando comenzaron los disturbios. Nadie me lo contó. Con mis propios ojos vi la furia de los negros rompiendo las vidrieras, tirándole piedras a los autos de los blancos, volcando perseguidoras, prendiéndole fuego a sus propios barrios. Sentí pánico de que algo le pasara a mis hijos. Subimos por la calle 16, para evitar la 13, que cruza por el mismo barrio de los negros. Con todo, Bobby me hizo ir con los niños agachada en el suelo del asiento de atrás hasta que llegamos a Silver Spring. Y eso que nosotros no vimos lo peor. Las imágenes que salieron por televisión son pavorosas. A la pobre

Luisa, que venía con su *carpool* de la tienda, le abrieron la cabeza de una pedrada. ¿Qué va a pasar en este país?

✌

El Senador Robert Francis Kennedy (D., N.Y.) fue baleado en Los Angeles el 5 de junio, minutos después de que había pronunciado un discurso en una fiesta en celebración por su victoria en las primarias presidenciales de California. El presunto asesino… fue apresado inmediatamente en la misma escena del crimen.

Este atentado al senador ha tenido lugar menos de 5 años después del asesinato de su hermano mayor, el Presidente John F. Kennedy y sólo 2 meses después del asesinato del Reverendo Martin Luther King. Mientras que una ola de dolor, vergüenza e indignación abate al país, El Presidente Johnson expresó el sentimiento de sus compatriotas al anunciar que creará una comisión especial formada por distinguidos ciudadanos para estudiar la violencia en los Estados Unidos en vistas a encontrar "cómo vamos a ponerle fin."

El Senador Kennedy, que llegó en estado de coma al hospital, fue sometido a una operación de 4 horas para extraerle del cerebro los fragmentos de las balas. Su secretario de prensa anunció un minuto antes de las 2:00 a.m. el 6 de junio que Kennedy murió a las 1:44 a.m.

(*Facts on File* 28.1441, 226–227)

✌

En la casa hay tanta tensión como en el resto de la capital norteamericana. La mudada fue un problema tras otro. Para empezar, Bobby les ofreció a sus padres el cuarto principal, el que tiene el baño dentro. Yo comprendo que ellos son mayores, pero es mi casa… Lo que más me molesta es que no me consulte. Menos mal que mi suegro se negó y que Adela dijo que la cuna de Bobby Junior —que todavía duerme con nosotros— no nos iba caber en el otro cuarto más chiquito.

De todas formas, me irrita que Bobby nunca me apoye. Ayer Adela insistía en darle una galletica a Pedro Pablo aunque yo le había explicado que no puede comer dulces antes de la comida. Ella buscó a Bobby con la mirada y él, por supuesto, intervino:

—Bueno, vamos a darle media galletica.

No dije nada hasta que estuvimos solos.

—Tú seguro que te crees que fue una solución salomónica, pero te agradecería que no me quitaras la autoridad con mi hijo.

—No sé qué te pasa, Lauri. En Miami te llevabas muy bien con mi madre.

—Era distinto. Yo estaba en su casa, pero ahora ella está en la mía. Además, tu madre ha cambiado mucho. Y yo también.

—Bueno, no sucederá más.

Pero vuelve a suceder de continuo. Bobby nunca me da la razón. Es culpa mía, porque en cuanto me toca me derrito y se lo dejo pasar todo. Aunque la próxima vez…

Mi suegro está empeñado en trabajar en la OEA. Ha llamado a no sé cuántas puertas.

—Que me dejen entrar aunque sea de portero, que ya yo me ocuparé de lo demás. —A mí me conmueve esa mezcla de humildad y prepotencia.

Por fin pude irme de la oficina de bienes raíces. La dueña era muy difícil y me hizo pasar muchas humillaciones. No tuve más remedio que aguantar, porque nos hacía falta el dinero. Ahora trabajo en la oficina de un constructor muy rico, que tiene muchos contactos. Le dije a Roberto:

—Si usted quiere, le hablo a mi jefe a ver si conoce a alguien que pueda ayudarlo.

Se me acercó y me dio unas palmaditas en el hombro.

—Te lo voy agradecer mucho, Lauri.

Me pareció que estaba emocionado.

Este semestre, como están mis suegros en la casa, he matriculado más asignaturas. Así podré terminar los estudios más pronto. Me gustan mucho las clases, especialmente las de literatura. También la física me ha parecido muy poética. Cuando termine en el *college,* quisiera ir a la universidad. En ese sentido es una gran ayuda vivir con los viejos.

También podemos salir más. Además de las actividades de la Casa

Cuba, algunas noches vamos al cine con otros matrimonios amigos. Otras veces nos reunimos en el sótano de alguna casa. Hasta hacemos algunas fiestas. Una noche que jugábamos al baile de la escoba, me pareció que Eddy flirteaba conmigo, que siempre se las arreglaba para que bailáramos juntos y que me apretaba un poco más de lo corriente. Me decía en tono de broma que yo era una hippie mental. No sé si eran ideas mías. De todas maneras, lo pasé muy bien.

A Bobby no le va mal con las ventas de seguros, pero a veces me pongo brava con él. Se pasa llamando a sus amigos en Miami para hablar de Cuba. Cuando la invasión de Checoslovaquia hablaban a diario. Que si Castro la había apoyado y eso le iba a costar con los americanos y con el pueblo… No en balde las cuentas son siempre altísimas. ¡Con lo que yo me aguanto en llamar a Cuba para no gastar!

Han sido unas Navidades muy especiales. Johnny las vino a pasar con nosotros. ¡Está hecho un hombre! Es muy inteligente y estudioso, y me encanta conversar con él. Pedro Pablo lo adora. Mi jefe le consiguió una entrevista a mi suegro con un funcionario importante de la OEA, y justo el día 23 lo llamaron para que empezara a trabajar en enero.

—Lauri, no sabes cómo te lo agradezco. Tú eres para mí la hija que nunca tuve —y me dio un abrazo muy fuerte. La verdad es que él es muy cariñoso conmigo.

No fue la única sorpresa agradable. Justo cuando nos íbamos a sentar a la mesa en Nochebuena, tocaron a la puerta. ¡Era Vidal cargado de regalos! Le hizo cuentos a Pedro Pablo de cómo él lo mecía cuando recién nacido. Y a Bobby Junior lo durmió cantándole un aria de *Los gavilanes:*

> *Pensando en ti noche y día*
> *aldea de mis amores*
> *mi esperanza renacía*
> *se aliviaban mis dolores.*
> *Pensando en ti, mar serena*
> *pensando en ti, bello cielo*

era más dulce mi pena
y menor mi desconsuelo.

Se hizo silencio en la casa. Sólo se oía aquella voz de barítono:

Pensando en ti noche y día
aldea de mis amores.

—Así vivimos los cubanos —comentó mi suegro. Y tiene razón.

La noche del 31 me pasó algo muy raro. Fue una especie de alucinación, de visión, en la que me invadió el temor de que nosotros éramos una especie de náufragos, los últimos cubanos sobrevivientes de una catástrofe. En Cuba han querido borrar la historia, aniquilar todo lo anterior a 1959, robarle al pueblo su memoria colectiva. ¿Cómo puede existir una nación sin pasado? Nosotros somos los últimos que podemos recordar al país antes de la Revolución, los llamados a conservar y trasmitir un preciado legado. Somos en verdad la última generación de cubanos. Sentí ganas de apagar la música, de hablarles a aquellas parejas que bailaban al ritmo de un disco de la Orquesta Aragón, de hacerles ver cuán grande es nuestra responsabilidad histórica. Pero de pronto todo comenzó a girar, a nublarse, y se me ocurrió otra idea más aterradora: que somos sombras irreales, personas inexistentes, que nadie nos oye ni nos ve, que la Cuba que nosotros recordamos no existe más que en nuestros sueños, que la bodeguita con productos cubanos, que las obritas de teatro con Martí como personaje, que las amarillentas fotografías que no nos cansamos de mirar, que los actos patrióticos, que los tinajones, las banderas, los taburetes en nuestros hogares, que los periodiquitos en español, que esta misma música que ahora escuchamos —Y si vas al Cobre, quiero que me traigas… —es todo mentira, y que Cuba, la Cuba real, es la otra, la de verde olivo y consignas, la de libreta de racionamiento y comité de defensa, la de fusilados y presos, en la que algunos, o muchos, o una sola persona, no sé, viven ciegos al horror porque creen firmemente —¡Patria o muerte! ¡Venceremos!— que están construyendo una Cuba mejor.

❧

El soldador cubano Armando Socarrás Ramírez, de 22 años de edad, sobrevivió un vuelo de nueve horas y 5,600 millas de La Habana a Madrid el 4 de junio en el hueco, sin presión ni calefacción, de una rueda de un jet DC-8 de la Aerolínea Iberia. El polizón sobrevivió a pesar de sufrir severa falta de oxígeno y temperaturas de 40 grados bajo cero a una altitud de 29,000 pies. Jorge Pérez Blanco, de 16 años, que intentó escaparse con él, cayó al vacío poco después de despegar el avión.

Socarrás, que se fue de Cuba por razones políticas, fue trasladad a Estados Unidos por el Comité de Rescate Internacional para reunirse con un tío que vive en New Jersey.

(*Facts on File* 29.1502, 516)

❧

Fuimos todos a Nueva York a la boda de mi primo Carlitos. Cada día me gusta más esa ciudad, donde se ven tantas cosas distintas. Creo que me agrada especialmente su ritmo. Hay algo que vibra en el ambiente. A mí, nada más acercarme al Lincoln Tunnel la sangre empieza a bullirme en las venas.

Aunque ya hace más de tres años de la muerte de Julio Eduardo, la recepción fue muy sencilla, sin música ni baile, como se estila aquí. A pesar de la ocasión, Tía Alicia y Tío Julio se veían tristes, todavía de medio luto ella y de corbata negra él. Perder a un hijo debe ser el dolor mayor del mundo. Si algo le pasara a los míos, creo que me volvería loca. Yo nunca sé qué decirles a mis tíos. No sé si contarles que Pedro Pablo aún recuerda a Julio Eduardo, que no puedo oír el disco de los Beatles sin llorar, que muchas veces sueño con él, que tengo su fotografía en mi mesa de noche… Siempre acabo abrazándolos muy fuerte, porque nunca me salen las palabras.

Cada día hay más protestas contra la guerra. Los jóvenes queman sus tarjetas del *draft* en las manifestaciones. Muchos se van al Canadá para evitar ir a Vietnam. Dicen que es una guerra absurda, que no se puede ganar, que allá los vietnamitas. Otros, entre ellos muchos cubanos, argumentan que hay que defender al mundo del comunismo. Yo no sé qué pensar. En parte deseo que los Estados Unidos ganen. Es, no sé, como si de esa forma la muerte de mi primo no fuera en vano. Además, el comunismo es horrible. Por otra parte, no quisiera que hubiera más muertos.

Con lo de Cuba también a veces me siento confundida. Veo personas que han pasado tanto, es tan triste vivir fuera del país de uno, me enojo de tal forma cuando leo tanta propaganda —que si Cuba antes era el burdel de los americanos, que si la Revolución ha dado pan y educación a todos...— pero también pienso en mi familia allá. No lo puedo remediar. Cuando hablan mal de la gente en la Isla, como si todos fueran iguales, como si todos fueran cómplices de lo que está sucediendo, en seguida salto. Yo sé que mis hermanos colaboran con el gobierno. ¡No les queda más remedio! La gente no entiende que todo el mundo trabaja para el estado. No hay otra alternativa. Eso no quiere decir que sean comunistas ni malas personas. Lo más probable es que sepan menos que nosotros sobre muchas de las cosas que hace el régimen. Bobby no lo ve así y el otro día hasta discutimos en casa de unos amigos.

No me gusta sacárselo en cara, pero no soporto sus pullitas sobre mi familia y acabé recordándole que mi madre era la única que lo iba a visitar y a llevarle comida cuando estuvo preso. Sólo Silvia me comprende porque ella también tiene a sus padres allá.

El lunes después de llegar de Nueva York, tempranito por la mañana, mientras estaba ayudando a Pedro Pablo a vestirse para el colegio, sonó el teléfono. Cuando la operadora me anunció una llamada de Cuba, como siempre, me asaltó la ansiedad de escuchar las voces queridas y el miedo de que fuera alguna mala noticia. Al oír a Menchu supe que había pasado algo:

—Mama Luya se enfermó la semana pasada, la llevamos a la clínica, le diagnosticaron una embolia.

—¿Cómo está, Menchu, como está?

—Tía Flor la quiso traer para la casa...

—¿Y?

—El viernes se nos murió. Estábamos con ella... no sufrió...

—Pero cómo, Menchu, ¿se murió?

—Tratamos de llamarte, y a Ricardo también, pero no contestaba nadie.

—Estábamos en la boda de Carlitos en Nueva York. ¿Cómo está Mami? ¿Puedo hablar con ella?

—Parecía bien, pero después del entierro se ha derrumbado. Ahora está dormida.

—¿Pero ya la enterraron?

—Sí, el sábado.

—¿Y Tía Flor?

—Te imaginarás...

Ya no pude contener el llanto.

—Ay, mi hermana, qué desgracia tan grande, qué desgracia tan grande...

—Lauri, ya Mama Luya no era la misma, tenía casi 85 años...

—Mi hermana, ¿y recibieron mi carta y las fotos? ¿Las vio Mama Luya?

—Sí, sí, hace unos días. Le gustaron mucho. Se las pusimos en la mesa de noche.

—¿Y Papá? ¿Y Pedritín?

—Bien... bien. No están ahora en casa, pero fue cuando dieron la llamada.

Yo seguía llorando. Ya nos despedíamos, cuando Menchu me dijo:

—Lauri, Mama Luya decía que Pedro Pablo se parece a nosotras. La verdad es que están muy lindos los dos.

Tuve que colgar, porque el llanto no me dejaba hablar.

Lloro porque mi abuela se ha muerto y hacía diez años que no la veía... porque lo supe cuando ya la habían enterrado... porque mientras agonizaba yo estaba en una boda, ajena a que ella exhalaba su último suspiro... Lloro porque nunca conoció a mis hijos ni les pudo enseñar las mismas canciones que a mis hermanos y a mí... Había una vez un barquito chiquitico... había una vez un barquito chiquitico... Lloro por la casa de La Sierra, con sus canteros de vicarias y crotos... porque ya no veré a Mama Luya despertarse de la siesta, ponerse aquella absurda faja de cordones que sacaba del armario oscuro y su vestido estampado, y sentarse en la terraza, los labios recién pintados con aquel color clarito de Coty… Lloro por los cuentos que ya no me hará… porque nunca más oiré su voz, ni oleré su fragancia a jazmines, ni sentiré la suavidad de su cutis, ni fijará en mí su mirada azul acero. Lloro porque está muerta, sin moverse, bajo la tierra, en esa tumba que tantas veces visitamos juntas para ponerle flores a mi abuelo, y ni siquiera allí puedo ir a acompañarla… lloro por mis padres, y por Menchu, y por Pedritín y por Julio Eduardo que vino de Cuba a morir en Vietnam y está enterrado en Nueva York, donde en el invierno la tierra se cubre de nieve y no sé si tendrá frío… lloro porque Johnny tenía que ir al colegio en Miami con la camisa de La Salle y se reían de él… y porque Menchu no quiso venir para mi primer parto… y porque acaba de decirme que Pedro Pablo se parece a nosotras y porque mi esposo cree que los de allá son todos comunistas… Lloro porque Mama Luya ya no me hará natilla ni me dejará comerla calientica de la cazuela ni vendrá a cuidarme cuando me enferme… y porque mi hijo saluda en la escuela otra bandera… y canta twinkle twinkle little star… ¿Por qué no me esperaste, Mama Luya? ¿Por qué cuando regrese no estarás ya en el descanso de la escalera como cuando te vi la última vez? ¿Por qué? ¿Por qué? ¿Por qué estoy aquí, rodeada de inglés por todas partes, cuando en La Habana —esa Habana de luz y consignas— han muerto Mama Luya y mi infancia?

Adiós a la tierra, al fruto que alimenta,
al abuelo cabizbajo en el portal.
Tose el viento de ayer sobre los huecos días.
Se traga en seco, pero no se olvida.

(Torres 22)

Los años se suceden con rapidez. Más que el calendario, lo miden las estaciones. Parece comenzar en septiembre con el curso escolar, como un cuaderno con las páginas en blanco. Yo siempre recuerdo cuando Mamá nos llevaba a la Moderna Poesía a comprar los materiales para el colegio y como se sentaba en la mesa del comedor a forrarnos los libros... Hoy en día los forros vienen cortados... Por las noches ya hay que usar un suéter y pronto las hojas de los árboles se irán tiñendo de rojos, carmelitas y dorados hasta caer secas a la tierra... los domingos todos trabajamos recogiendo las hojas del jardín... hasta a Bobby Junior le gusta ayudar... el cielo es muy azul y hay una transparencia en el aire que hace que todo se me antoje más nítido... llega Halloween y Adela les hace los disfraces a los niños y vamos por el barrio y cómo disfrutan con los caramelos y las casas adornadas de fantasmas y brujas... ya enseguida es el Día de Thanksgiving, cena de pavo, boniatos y una oración que siempre escribo para leerla antes de sentarnos a la mesa... las Navidades... época de fiestas de oficina, intercambio de regalos, compra de juguetes, reuniones con amigos, ir con los niños a ver el árbol de la Casa Blanca... y esa persistente nostalgia por los de allá... qué va, las Navidades en Cuba eran mejores, alguien dice siempre, como alguien repite inevitablemente el mismo brindis de la noche del 31... el próximo año en La Habana... es invierno y los días son cortos, y las ramas de los árboles se desnudan... todavía siempre me parecen brazos alzados rezándole a Dios... a la entrada de la casa sembramos dos pinos que se mantienen verdes todo el año... hasta una helada mañana de enero en que uno de ellos, vencido por el peso de la nieve, amaneció muy tieso sobre la tierra, como un soldado muerto en batalla... en la primavera renace la naturaleza... los narcisos trompones son los primeros en florecer y unos diminutos brotes verdes van cubriendo los árboles... después retoñan las azaleas y los cerezos, con sus flores tan efímeras y bellas como el vuelo de una mariposa... Ya podemos soltar los abrigos... comienza la liga de pelota... las ardillas trepan por los árboles... y el día de Easter los niños pintan conejos en la escuela y estrenamos ropa nueva y vamos a misa, y preparamos un gran almuerzo, y mi hijo me pregunta qué quiere decir resurrección… verano… días largos, hay otra vida después del trabajo, la piscinita en el patio para los niños, el *barbecue*… el peregrinaje anual a Miami… y volvemos siempre con libras de más, un cajón de libros en español, y el olor del mar, el sabor de los mangos y el calor del sol y los amigos entibiándonos el corazón…

❦

Richard Milhous Nixon anunció anoche su renuncia como trigésimo séptimo presidente de los Estados Unidos.

El Vice Presidente Gerald R. Ford de Michigan jurará como el nuevo presidente a las doce del día para completar los 2 años y medio del término de Nixon.

Después de dos años de amargo debate público sobre el escándalo de Watergate, Nixon cedió a las presiones de la opinión pública y de los líderes de su partido para convertirse en el primer presidente americano en la historia que ha renunciado a su cargo.

"…como Presidente, debo poner los intereses de los Estados Unidos en primer lugar", dijo.

Mientras que el Presidente reconoció que algunos de sus juicios "estuvieron equivocados", no confesó ninguno de los delitos y faltas graves citadas por el Comité Judicial de la Cámara en el acta de acusaciones contra él.

El futuro presidente elogió el sacrificio que Nixon hacía por el país y calificó el momento como "uno de los incidentes más tristes de que he sido testigo".

(*Washington Post* 9 de agosto 1974: A1)

❦

Aunque todavía a veces tengo problemas con Adela, le he ido tomando cariño. Algunas noches, cuando Bobby va a jugar dominó, los niños duermen, Roberto está leyendo, y ella y yo estamos doblando la ropa, nos ponemos a conversar. A veces le cuento de mi vida en Cuba. Ella me habla de su infancia y juventud... me ha impresionado saber que cuando tenía como 10 años acompañó a España a su madre, que volvía por primera vez a su aldea, y al regreso, en el barco, la madre se puso muy grave. La tenían en cuarentena y ella sólo podía verla por unos cristales. Murió y la echaron al mar. Ella no pudo llorar, ni hablar siquiera hasta que llegó a La Habana y vio a su padre esperándola en el puerto.

A mi suegro he llegado a admirarlo. Se despierta temprano y antes de irse al trabajo, se pone a estudiar inglés. Ha adelantado mucho, él solo. A veces me sorprende también su manera de pensar. Cuando Augusto Pinochet dio el golpe de estado en Chile un grupo de cubanos querían publicar una carta de apoyo y me pidieron que se la tradujera. Deseaban que la firmara con ellos. Me negué. Creo que pensaron que era por mi familia en Cuba, pero les aclaré:

—Es que no estoy de acuerdo con los golpes de estado, ni con el militarismo, ni con romper el ritmo constitucional de los países. Miren lo que el golpe de Batista nos trajo en Cuba...

Discutimos acaloradamente y para mi sorpresa, mi suegro intervino a mi favor. Fue él quien dio la solución:

—Yo creo que la carta sería más eficaz y quizás Lauri la firmaría si el apoyo no fuera incondicional, sino que mostrara un deseo ferviente de que Pinochet restaurara pronto las garantías, convocara a elecciones, y reintegrara el país a la democracia.

Hace poco comencé a colaborar con una organización que publica un boletín sobre los derechos humanos en la Isla. Una de las dirigentes me invitó un día a almorzar. Sabía que era una mujer mayor, que había sido feminista en Cuba y del primer gabinete de Fidel. Fui con un poco de reserva pero la señora me cautivó y acepté ayudar en lo que pudiera. Empecé doblando papeles y poniéndolos en sobres. Son cartas que se mandan a distintas personalidades hablándoles de la situación de los presos políticos. A veces viene un grupo a casa y hacemos el trabajo juntos. Mis suegros y hasta Pedro Pablo también ayudan. Luego me pidieron que tradujera algunas de las denuncias. Al enfrentarme con estos relatos de los prisioneros cubanos, de pronto la represión en la

Isla dejó de ser un concepto abstracto. Desde entonces tiene nombres, apellidos, rostros que me saltan de fotos. La crueldad contra ellos es espantosa. El hambre, el trabajo forzado, el hacinamiento, conviviendo con ratas y con sus propias heces, metidos en celdas mínimas, ratoneras le dicen, expuestos a requisas, los desnudan, los insultan, los golpean, los despojan de sus más mínimas pertenencias, los castigan si protestan, van a las celdas tapiadas, sin ver la luz del sol por días y días, ni a otro ser humano, les niegan atención médica, los mantienen presos después de cumplidas sus sentencias. Pero no los doblegan. Muchos se plantan. Es decir, no ceden. También hay mujeres presas. También a ellas las maltratan salvajemente, las empujan y patean, las desnudan, las humillan, las torturan con altoparlantes cuyos sonidos no cesan en días y días, las tumban al suelo a manguerazos, por la fuerza del agua. Una ex-prisionera declaró que los carceleros son tan sádicos que tienen erecciones mientras las golpean. A veces las han pateado en sus partes y les han mordido los senos. Y en medio del horror, una mujer, a quien prendieron y maltrataron a pesar de estar en estado, parió una niña. Le pusieron Milagritos.

Según algunos estimados, la cifra más alta en el número de prisioneros políticos en Cuba se alcanzó en los años 60 con 60,000 reclusos. Según cifras de Amnistía Internacional, a mediados de la década de los 70 el total de los liberados hasta esa fecha alcanzaba alrededor de 20,000. En una base comparativa, esas dos cifras serían el equivalente, en un país del tamaño de Estados Unidos, de entre 1,410,000 y 466,000 prisioneros políticos para esa época. Eso convertiría a Cuba en uno de los países con mayor número de prisioneros políticos per cápita, incluso mayor que el de la propia Unión Soviética.

(Greve and Pérez A1)

A veces me preocupa Bobby. Noto que no se adapta, que se ha amargado, que nada le hace ilusión. Siempre se está quejando del exilio. ¡Y él tiene aquí a toda su familia! A mí también me duele Cuba. Y duele sentirse extranjera, con las raíces al aire, con esta sensación de que todo es temporal, que nuestra vida está allá, en un futuro que nunca llega. Lo que nos ha pasado es muy duro, pero hay tanta gente que ha sufrido más, que ha tenido familiares fusilados o que aún están presos. En Estados Unidos no nos ha ido mal y tenemos dos hijos... Parecería como si para Bobby ni ellos ni yo contáramos. Con lo que amo a Cuba, y a veces siento celos. Mi marido es un loco de un solo tema. Se levanta y se acuesta hablando de Cuba. Cuando le digo estas cosas, se pasa entonces días sin hablar, sumido en el silencio, y con un humor de perros. No sé qué es peor. Hay momentos en que me pregunto si todas las parejas después de unos años tienen etapas así, si volveré jamás a sentir la emoción de aquellas primeras noches en Miami, que éramos tan pobres y nos amábamos con tanta furia. ¡Yo que dejé todo para seguirlo! Pero no, no hubiera querido vivir en Cuba... y no puedo pensar en la vida sin mis dos hijos. Estoy loca por graduarme y poder trabajar de maestra para llegar más temprano y dedicarles más tiempo. Cuando estoy con ellos, se disipan mis inquietudes y todo tiene de nuevo un propósito. A veces, cuando entro al cuarto a ver si están tapados, y los contemplo dormidos, se me llenan de lágrimas los ojos. La vida entonces me parece un milagro.

∽

La evacuación norteamericana de Vietnam, que se llevó a cabo en medio de escenas de caos, pánico y sufrimiento, ha terminado.

Sucedió sólo horas antes de que el gobierno de Saigón, al que los Estados Unidos había apoyado largamente, se rindiera incondicionalmente a Vietnam del Norte, que había peleado por este triunfo durante 30 años.

En las primeras horas de la mañana del miércoles terminó la participación norteamericana en un conflicto que duró una generación, costó la vida de

56,737 miembros de las fuerzas armadas, y más de $160 mil millones y afectó virtualmente todos los aspectos de la vida nacional.

Mientras que el último de los helicópteros llevaba a bordo al embajador americano Graham Martin y a otros sobrevivientes de la poderosa presencia americana en la zona, el Presidente Ford declaró que "se cerraba un capítulo de la historia americana" e hizo un llamado a la nación para que cerraran filas y evitaran recriminaciones sobre el pasado.

(*Washington Post* 30 de abril 1975: A1)

∽

Estaba hablando por larga distancia con mi primo Carlitos, comentando sobre los refugiados vietnamitas, cuando mi suegro entró de la calle tan descompuesto que tuve que colgar.

—¿Qué le pasa, Roberto?

—Adela tiene cáncer, mijita —me dijo, desplomándose sobre un butacón.

La biopsia de un bultico que se había encontrado en un seno resultó positiva y van a operarla enseguida.

—¿Cómo no nos habían dicho nada?

—Para no preocuparlos… como tenías exámenes en estos días…

El hospital huele muy raro. ¿Será el olor de la muerte? El doctor asegura que la intervención quirúrgica ha sido un éxito. Pero Adela necesita tratamiento de radioterapia. Tiene que ir todos los días durante seis semanas. La acompaño. De pronto, me conmueve ver a esta mujer tan dominante y tan mandona, sentada aquí a mi lado, aguardando su turno, tan vulnerable…

—¿Quiere que entre con usted?

En realidad, lo prefiero a tener que quedarme en el salón de espera, viendo los rostros de los otros pacientes, demacrados, pálidos, con la amenaza de la muerte temblándoles en los párpados semicerrados.

Es la primera vez que le veo el pecho plano surcado por una gran cicatriz. Siento un amago de náuseas que me sube hasta la boca, pero no retiro la mirada. Los técnicos dibujan sobre su piel con un creyón morado la zona en que recibirá las radiaciones. Cuando va a empezar el tratamiento, me piden que salga.

—Yo estoy aquí cerquita —le digo para animarla.

Adela es una mujer fuerte y resiste las radiaciones bien. Pero al final se le había quemado la piel y no tenía ningún apetito.

—Si tú supieras que lo peor es cuando me acercan tanto esa máquina que me parece que me va a caer arriba —ha sido su única queja.

En seguida retomó el mando de la casa. Los médicos pidieron hablar con nosotros.

—Estaba muy avanzado. Le extirpamos los ganglios, pero lo más probable es que el cáncer haga metástasis.

—¿Cuánto tiempo? —preguntó Roberto.

—Tres, cuatro años lo más.

Insisto en saber si no hay ningún otro tratamiento posible. ¿Cómo vamos a cruzarnos de brazos a esperar que le llegue la muerte?

Pero no había nada que se pudiera hacer.

—Que viva su vida normal... claro, sin hacer peso con ese brazo...

La enfermedad de Adela nos cambió a todos. Ella se volcó en los niños y los consentía demasiado. Sabía que les hacía daño, ¿pero cómo pelear con una mujer condenada a muerte? Me angustiaba cómo les afectaría a mis hijos el desenlace. Trataba de hablar con Bobby, pero era inútil.

—Mamá es muy fuerte. No le va a pasar más nada.

No sé si fue por no enfrentarse a la verdad, pero Bobby estaba cada vez más tiempo fuera de casa. Se iba a jugar al tenis, al dominó, o a reuniones sobre Cuba de no sé qué nuevo grupo. Estaba obsesionado con la idea de regresar a Cuba a pelear. Hasta llegó a dormir con una pistola debajo de la almohada. Yo que siempre le he tenido pánico a las armas de fuego... pero mis súplicas eran inútiles. A veces pensaba que estaba enfermo. Sin embargo, en su trabajo, con los amigos, podía ser encantador. Ahora era yo la que prefería no estar a solas con él. Ya casi nunca hacíamos el amor.

Mi refugio eran mis hijos y mis alumnos. Fue un gran cambio trabajar de maestra en vez de en una oficina. Si no hubiera sido por ellos, me hubiera vuelto loca.

También me daba pena mi suegro. Adela siempre le estaba peleando y él ni le contestaba. A veces me sorprendía pensado que esa mujer iba a vivir cien años y nos iba a tener a todos chantajeados con la idea de que se moría en cualquier momento.

En los últimos meses su comportamiento fue muy errático. Conmigo se puso violenta varias veces. Me insultaba. ¡Y delante de los niños! Me acusaba de cosas horribles. ¡Hasta de haber tenido un *affair* con mi antiguo jefe!

—Si usted sigue comportándose así, Adela, va a tener que mudarse de mi casa. —le dije un día que ya no aguantaba más.

¡Para qué fue aquello! Ella, ofendida, que se iba aunque durmiera en un parque; Bobby, que si había puesto en la calle a su madre enferma con lo que ella me había ayudado para que yo pudiera estudiar; los muchachos en el medio, con caras de azoro. Cedí por la intervención de mi suegro:

—Mijita, yo sé que tienes razón. Perdónala. Ella no es así. No sé lo que le pasa.

Pronto lo supimos. El cáncer le carcomía los huesos de la cabeza. Los últimos meses fueron un infierno. Además de mi trabajo, los muchachos y la casa, atendía a Adela. La bañaba, le lavaba la cabeza, le cortaba las uñas, le aguantaba la frente cuando vomitaba, le limpiaba la mierda y los orines, hablaba con los médicos, hasta aprendí a inyectarla. No solía ni darme las gracias y sólo se alegraba cuando Bobby o los niños asomaban la cabeza a su habitación o cuando la llamaba Johnny, a quien ella empezó a llamar Juancito otra vez, como en Cuba. Sólo en una ocasión, cuando sufría muchos dolores y yo acababa de inyectarle el calmante, me suplicó:

—No me dejes sola.

Me acerqué a su cama y le tomé tímidamente una mano. Yo quería desesperadamente que me dijera algo, una palabra siquiera que aliviara mis heridas y me permitiera recordar con cariño tantas cosas que habíamos vivido juntas. Me apretó la mano fuertemente. Pero no habló.

El cáncer debió haberle atacado el pulmón porque le costaba respirar. Entonces le dio por dormir en un butacón de la sala. Yo tenía pavor de que una mañana nos la encontráramos muerta.

—Bobby, tenemos que internarla... los niños no pueden seguir viendo esto...

—Vamos a esperar un poco... Con la nueva medicina tú verás que va a mejorar...

—Yo no puedo más, Bobby.

Una noche la oí hablando y me tiré de la cama. Deliraba. Hablaba con el capitán de un barco. Preguntaba por el estado de salud de su madre. Tenía voz de niña. Después dijo:

—Ay, Mami, qué bueno que has venido.

No le consulté a Bobby. Llamé una ambulancia.

Murió una helada mañana de enero. Al regresar a casa del hospital, vimos que el otro pino se había quebrado bajo el peso de la nieve y yacía tieso e inmóvil sobre el blanco manto, como Adela entre las sábanas.

CAPÍTULO SIETE
"Los diez millones van"

Desde hacía días se rumoraba que habían matado al Che. Al principio pensamos que eran comentarios infundados, *bolas* de contrarrevolucionarios que lo quisieran ver muerto. Cuando empezaron a llegar cables del extranjero insinuando la posibilidad de que lo hubieran cogido preso, Lázaro se inquietó. Estuvo tres días sin venir a casa, en la redacción de *Bohemia,* al tanto del teletipo. De parte de las autoridades, un silencio total. Por fin confirmaron la noticia. Lo habían matado. Ha causado una gran impresión. Después de todo, el Che no era cubano y arriesgó su vida luchando por nuestro país. Algunos no entienden que no lo ayudaran más, que muriera tan solo. Lázaro está deshecho. Nunca antes lo había visto llorar.

—Era un hombre puro, Menchu, el hombre más puro que he conocido.

Convocaron a un acto en la Plaza de la Revolución para esa noche. Lázaro quería llevar a Tania.

—Es un momento histórico, una tragedia de la humanidad. Además, el Che ha muerto por ella, para que viva en un mundo mejor.

—Pero la niña tiene catarro y por las noches refresca... —argumentó Mamá, quien por fin se quedó en la casa con ella.

Los demás fuimos todos. Nunca había visto la Plaza tan llena ni un silencio tan hondo en medio de una multitud tan grande.

∽

La historia no debe interesar solamente a los que por afición, o por profesión, dan clases de historia o escriben libros de historia. La historia debe interesar a todos: todos tenemos que saber qué fue, cómo y por qué fue la historia. Porque en la medida que lo sepamos y lo comprendamos bien, estaremos en posibilidad de comprender por qué somos lo que somos y por qué estamos donde estamos; y también comprenderemos de mejor manera hacia dónde vamos y hasta dónde llegamos. La historia revolucionaria es una línea continua. Con la Revolución no hemos cortado la historia de Cuba. Lo que hemos cortado son las ramas podridas del árbol de la historia de Cuba. El poderoso tronco y las ramas sanas, ésos no han sido cortados. La historia de Cuba, desde la raíz del árbol hasta los "pinos nuevos" de hoy, es una línea en ascenso, en progreso. A medida que la conozcamos más profundamente, podremos comprender mejor por qué nuestra Revolución es como es y por qué nuestra Revolución debe ser como es.

(*Bohemia* 60:38, 3)

⁓

Todas las tardes Mamá saca el álbum de fotografías y se lo enseña a Tania. A veces también a Ernestico, cuando Armandito y Magaly lo traen por acá. Comienzan por las fotos antiguas, amarillentas, de los abuelos de Mamá. Ella les va diciendo a los niños:

—Ésta es mi madre y éste mi padre...

Hay fotos de Mama Luya de niña con sus hermanos, de su boda con mi abuelo, de Mamá y Tía Flor recién nacidas. Luego vienen las del noviazgo de mis padres, las de nuestra infancia: Ricardo con su trajecito de marinero, Lauri y yo siempre vestidas iguales, Pedritín en la playa... Hay un segundo álbum con las fotos de los que se han ido. Mamá le repite a mi hija:

—Éste es tu Tío Ricardo. Ésta es tu Tía Lauri, mira como se parece a tu Mamá... éstos son sus hijos, Pedro Pablo y Bobby, que son tus primos...

Acompaña cada imagen con algún cuento, algún recuerdo, alguna ilusión.

—Algún día vas a conocer a tus primos... vamos a reunirnos todos y hacer una gran fiesta, con muchos globos, y, bocaditos, pastelitos, croquetas, ensalada de pollo, cake, refrescos... como cuando les celebrábamos el cumpleaños a tu Mamá y a Laurita.

—Éste es el hermano de tu abuelo, y éstos también son tus primos —continúa, y señala a Tío Julio y a Tía Alicia, con Carlitos y Julio Eduardo, parados frente a San Patricio. Tania la escucha con atención y si Mamá olvida algún detalle, o varía en lo más mínimo alguna de las historias, protesta:

—Así no es el cuento, Abuela.

Y Mamá empieza de nuevo y le explica como Tía Lauri se fue en un avión muy grande, y ahora vive muy lejos en un país donde nieva y hace mucho frío.

Ayer Lázaro llegó más temprano de lo que solía y las vio en el portal, tan enfrascadas en el ritual de mirar las fotos, que Tania no corrió a abrazarlo como de costumbre.

—La niña tiene que conocer sus raíces… —le dijo mi madre, con un tono de orgullo en la explicación.

—Sí, Mariana, pero acuérdese que hay ramas podridas… —le contestó Lázaro en tono burlón.

La vieja no se quedó callada.

—Querrá decir prohibidas… —replicó entre dientes. Afortunadamente, ya Lázaro había entrado a la casa y no la oyó.

Cuando la patria era de unos cuantos privilegiados, la palabra Patria no tenía ningún sentido; cuando la tierra era de los especuladores o de los latifundistas, el suelo en que vivíamos no tenía ningún sentido; si acaso, era nuestro el aire que podíamos respirar, y eso porque no lo podían inscribir en un registro de propiedad ni lo podían encerrar en un almacén. Pero desde luego, hoy el concepto de la patria es diferente. Cuando el suelo es de todos, cuando la riqueza es de todos, cuando la oportunidad es de todos, cuando la patria de verdad está llamada a ser de todos, sólo los que no tienen la más elemental noción de la patria, sólo los privilegiados o aspirantes a privilegiados hacen eso: abandonar su patria para marcharse.

Por eso nosotros no perdemos nada cuando esos señores se van, por eso no hemos hecho nada para impedir que se vayan allá a disfrutar de las limosnas del amo imperialista; que esta patria la desarrollaremos, la haremos grande con el esfuerzo de los que en verdad tienen hoy una patria. Y de verdad tienen hoy un sentido de patria.

(Fidel Castro 15 de marzo 1968)

∽

—Pase, Eneido. Papá está al llegar. Fue a hacer la cola en la carnicería, porque a Mamá le dolían las piernas, pero ya no puede demorar mucho. Pase… siéntese…

—Gracias, Menchu, pero mejor me voy… esas colas nunca se sabe lo que duran.

—¿Qué te pasa, Eneido? —le preguntó Mamá que había salido al portal.

Me di cuenta entonces de que estaba sudando copiosamente y de que se veía muy descompuesto.

Mamá logró que entrara y se sentara. Sin preguntarle, le dio un vaso de agua. El hombre la tomó despacio, ajeno casi a sus propias acciones.

—Desde que era un niño, Mariana, desde que era un niño… —balbuceaba.

De pronto escondió la cabeza entre las manos y se echó a llorar.

—Vamos, Eneido, ¿qué pasó?

En eso llegó Papá de la calle y nos enteramos.

—Van a intervenir todos los negocios pequeños. Es parte de la ofensiva revolucionaria, para construir el socialismo y el comunismo a la vez.

—Le quitaron la quincalla a Eneido —añadió.

Eneido levantó la cabeza. Más sereno, nos explicó:

—Desde pequeño soñaba con tener mi propio negocio… La quincalla es chiquita, y en estos tiempos me ha costado mucho tenerla surtida… pero es mi vida… Más de treinta años hace que la tengo… Todos me conocen en el barrio… soy una persona decente… mis hermanos se fueron y yo me quedé porque esa tiendecita era todo para mí. ¿Qué voy a hacer ahora?

En pocos meses La Habana era otra. Desaparecieron los churreros, los granizaderos, el tamalero. Ya no pasaba el dulcero ofreciendo besitos de coco. No vi más el tablero con pirulíes de todos los colores. Ni el heladero dejó oír su alegre campanilleo. Cerró el fritero de la esquina. Desapareció también la bodega del barrio, donde todavía se podía ir a comprar una cerveza fría, o una barra de dulce de guayaba. Nadie volvió a ofrecerse para afilar las tijeras. Murieron los pregones.

DONDE SEA, COMO SEA Y PARA LO QUE SEA, ¡COMANDANTE EN JEFE, ORDENE!

Hubo un hombre que no quiso acatar órdenes. Los *bulldozers* estaban parados frente a Tropicana para arrasar con ese centro de corrupción y juego, símbolo de las clases dominantes. No era siquiera el dueño, sino el administrador. Pero se paró frente al establecimiento y dijo que había que matarlo para que derrumbaran aquello. Los milicianos dudaron, hasta que vino la orden de que se detuvieran. Todo el mundo hablaba del incidente. Claro, en voz baja.

—Pues debieron haberle pasado los *bulldozers* por encima a ese contrarrevolucionario —comentó Maruja.

Los demás nos quedamos callados.

∞

Año de los Diez Millones, prolongación del esfuerzo decisivo, la conmemoración del primero de mayo se sienta en los surcos y cañaverales, al viento el penacho de humo de los centrales azucareros. Al campo en lugar de la Plaza. Las mochas ocupan el sitio de las pancartas y banderas. Ya no se trata de metas o consignas sino de un compromiso vivo que desborda cifras y almanaques. El Día de los Trabajadores, antaño fecha de recuento y lucha, ocasión para medir las fuerzas del proletariado, gana hoy un vigoroso sentido afirmativo. El pueblo se entrega al desarrollo de sus riquezas. El sudor, que es oro, no se vierte para beneficio de grupos explotadores. El sentido de lo propio, liberado de ambiciones y egoísmos, se extiende a todos los bienes de la nación. Saludo a las gloriosas efemérides de mayo, los hombres y mujeres de Cuba responden 'presente' a la cita múltiple de las batallas simultáneas en todos los frentes y trincheras. Las simbólicas banderas rojas señalan los pasos del millón.

(*Bohemia* 62:18, 3)

∽

Nos levantamos a las 4:30 de la madrugada para estar en los cañaverales al amanecer. Hay que ponerse pantalones, botas gruesas, camisas de manga larga, sombrero. Con todo, la paja de la caña se cuela entre la ropa y hiere la piel. El calor se hace insoportable. No se para de sudar. Escondemos el porrón a la sombra de las matas sin mochar y el agua fresca nos alivia por un momento la sed.

Antes de las doce, cuando el sol ya cae vertical y fuerte, nos llevan al albergue. Allí nos dan algo de comer y regresamos a los cañaverales dos horas después.

Las cañas crecen altas, en línea recta. Si miras hacia el horizonte, se te pierde la vista sin ver el final. Es como un mar infinito. Un mar de cañas.

A veces, cuando estamos muy fatigadas, nos sentamos a chupar un trozo de caña. Dicen que acaba con la dentadura, pero es fresca y dulce, y enseguida nos da energía. Al anochecer, regresamos agotadas al campamento.

A pesar del cansancio, hay ocasiones en que no me puedo dormir. Lázaro está en Oriente, Pedritín en Camagüey. Hace meses que no los veo. Mamá y Papá —el viejo se acaba de retirar de su puesto en el Ministerio de la Construcción— en La Habana, haciendo cola y cuidando a Tania y a Ernestico. Y yo aquí, rodeada de estas mujeres que son mis compañeras, a quienes me une una convivencia diaria, y que sin embargo a veces me parece que no tienen nada que ver conmigo. Sin embargo, la incorporación a la zafra de todo un pueblo es tan entusiasta que no puedo dejar de contagiarme. ¡Si de verdad éste fuera el esfuerzo decisivo, si de verdad estuviéramos construyendo una Cuba mejor para los hijos...! No sé por qué, cuando estoy lejos de Lázaro me entran las dudas... Pienso en ti, Lauri. Ya casi nunca nos escribimos. ¿Cómo será tu vida? A veces me parece que todo fue un sueño, que nuestra infancia de playas y excursiones, que aquellas tardes de domingo jugando al tieso-tieso, a los escondidos y a las estatuas, que aquellas noches escuchado los juegos de pelota en la radio, que aquellas aulas donde nos enseñaban francés y llorábamos recitando los poemas de Martí —ay, Pilar, con su balde y su aro y sus zapatos color de rosa— que aquellas noches de bailecitos en la terraza al ritmo de un cha cha chá que emanaba del tocadiscos —cuando Miñoso batea de verdad...— que aquel mundo nuestro, tan lleno de ilusiones, no existió nunca, y que la única realidad es este interminable cañaveral que ahora es Cuba, que a veces amo y a veces detesto, y que me pica cada pulgada del alma, como las briznas filosas que se me clavan en la piel.

MÁS PRODUCCIÓN... AUMENTANDO LA PRODUCTIVIDAD

La producción puede elevarse considerablemente... sin aumentar el número de trabajadores, sin aumentar la jornada diaria de trabajo, sin aumentar la intensidad media (es decir, el esfuerzo físico y nervioso) del trabajador, sin necesidad de recurrir a inversiones. La producción puede elevarse considerablemente eliminando errores, tanto en la aplicación de la técnica como en la organización del trabajo, así como suprimiendo el trabajador debilidades y negligencias en el desempeño de su tarea. Ésta es la fórmula que nos revelan las investigaciones de MINTRAB: ¡Más producción... aumentando la productividad!

¡Año de los Diez Millones Van!

(*Bohemia* 62:18, 32)

Cada día asoma a la actualidad el nombre de algún machetero u operador de combinada que supera las metas precedentes de corte y alza. Se destaca cómo los trabajadores agrícolas y los voluntarios hemos respondido al llamado de la Revolución. En todas partes se habla encomiásticamente de la calidad con que llega la caña a los ingenios, y de la alta conciencia revolucionaria del pueblo.

Por las tardes se ven los camiones que devuelven a los trabajadores a sus hogares, algunos después de muchos meses de ausencia. Regresan con la ropa sucia y raída, las manos deshechas, el cuerpo adolorido. Están ansiosos de ver a sus seres queridos, de darse un buen baño, de dormir en su cama y de saber el resultado de la zafra, de esa millonésima que cada uno hemos puesto, de ese esfuerzo decisivo cuando el calor nos vencía, de ese impulso sobrehumano cuando la sed se hacía insoportable, de ese arrancarse del corazón a la familia para pensar primero en la patria.

Ha terminado la zafra. Aunque estamos casi seguros de que no se han alcanzado los 10 millones, estamos a la expectativa… deseosos de saber el resultado de este esfuerzo que ha paralizado al resto del país

—Mi maestra dice que a lo mejor se ha llegado a 11 millones —asegura Ernestico con convicción.

—Pues yo creo que son 12 millones —le sube la parada Tania, con entusiasmo infantil.

—No se hagan ilusiones —les aconseja Mamá.

Por fin, en un acto frente a la Sección de Intereses de Estados Unidos, en protesta por el secuestro de unos pescadores, Fidel dio la noticia. No hemos alcanzado los 10 millones de arrobas de caña. El impacto ha sido devastador. Pero el 26 de julio, en una plaza que bulle de expectativa, cuando explica largamente las causas, ofrece la próxima orientación:

—Hay que convertir el revés en victoria…

Cuando me viré a hacerle un comentario a Lázaro, vi que tenía el rostro descompuesto. Regresamos a la casa en silencio.

∽

Durante doce años
abuelo entró en la casa
llenándome de espadas y pelotas.
Se le veía venir
bajo el sombrero blanco
como un rey mago
que quiere pasar inadvertido
su guayabera de hilo
beige
brillosa
oliendo a caramelo de miel
y a bendiciones.

A mediodía en punto
comparaba la familia
con una gran manzana
y reía que daban ganas de aplaudir
de decir que era fiesta
porque mi madre conspiraba con el fuego.

Frente al café
le crecía la barba
la imaginación
era olímpico
resuelto
buen amigo
político
sexual.

Para mí
el abuelo inventaba la vida
sacando mares, lunas y países
de su sombrero blanco.

Aún ayer era invencible
en su taburete
como si el tiempo fuera una paloma lenta
como si todavía pudiera bostezar
como si no le hubieran cambiado su sombrero
por el poco de tierra
que ahora le cubre la cabeza.

(Rivero 12–13)

✍

A Mama Luya le dio una embolia. Los médicos tienen pocas esperanzas. Tía Flor se negó a dejarla internada y se la llevó para la casa. Cuando llegué a verla ayer, la estaba bañando. Me asusté de lo delgada que estaba. Parecía un pajarito en aquella cama. ¿Cómo es posible, si la visito todas las semanas, que no me diera cuenta de lo que ha bajado de peso?

—A ver, viejita, así estás más cómoda, ¿no? —y Tía Flor le arregló la almohada y le alisó el pelo blanco.

Mama Luya abrió los ojos y le sonrió a su hija. Había en su mirada, otras veces desafiante, tal gratitud, que se me humedecieron los ojos. Luego fijó la vista en el aparador.

—A ver, Mamá, ¿qué quieres ahora?

Mama Luya ya no puede hablar pero Tía Flor entendió en el acto lo que pedía.

—Menchu, abre la primera gaveta y tráele la carta que llegó de tu hermana. Quiere que veas las fotos.

—¡Qué graciosos están los niños!

—Pedro Pablo se parece a las jimaguas cuando chiquitas, ¿verdad, Mamá?

Mi abuela se había dormido apretando la foto contra su pecho.

Tía Flor no se separaba de su lado. Mamá y yo insistíamos en turnarnos, pero lo más que lográbamos era que se tirara un rato en la cama de la habitación contigua. Al tercer día, Mama Luya ya apenas abría los ojos, tenía la mirada nublada y parecía no conocer a nadie, ni siquiera a Tía Flor. La casa se fue llenando de gente. Todos se brindaban para ayudar… pero luego se ponían a conversar, insensibles al hecho de que a unos pasos agonizaba mi abuela. Hasta una tarde que Tía Flor se levantó con paso decidido y botó a todo el mundo. Sólo nos quedamos Mamá, ella y yo.

—Hay que dejar que la gente se muera en paz —nos dijo.

Entonces fue al aparador y sacó un rosario. Se lo puso entre las manos a su madre.

—Vamos a rezar —nos dijo. Y comenzó:

—Padre nuestro, que estás en los cielos…

Cuando terminamos, acercó la silla a la cama y comenzó a hablarle a Mama Luya. Le oí los cuentos que tantas veces le había escuchado a mi abuela, sobre su infancia en España, sobre cómo conoció a mi abuelo que acababa de llegar de Cuba, sobre cómo se casaron sin permiso de sus padres y el viaje a la Isla en un gran vapor, sobre el nacimiento y la infancia de sus hijos… Poco a poco Mamá fue entrando en la conversación. No hablaban entre ellas dos, sino que se dirigían a Mama Luya, como si estuvieran seguras de que pudiera oírlas. Luego me invitó a que le hablara yo. Al principio no me salía la voz… Por fin brotaron las palabras:

—Ay, Mamá, si supieras que cuando niñas lo que más nos gustaba a Lauri y a mí en el mundo era venir aquí… Qué felices éramos cuando Mami y Papi se iban de viaje y tú venías a casa a cuidarnos… Yo dormía a Tania de chiquita con los mismos cantos que tú nos enseñaste y estoy segura de que Lauri ha hecho lo mismo con sus hijos… Todavía, con lo grande que es, cuando Tania se enferma me pide la canción de los peregrinos, y "En el fondo del mar… ", y la del barquito chiquitico… y la de la Señora Santa Ana…

—Vamos a cantarle —dijo Tía Flor.

¿Dónde vas, Alfonso XII,
dónde vas, triste de ti?

Voy en busca de Mercedes
que ayer tarde no la vi.

Cayó la noche sobre la casa mientras las tres rodeábamos la cama de mi abuela.

Si Mercedes ya está muerta
muerta está que yo la vi
Cuatro duques la llevaban
por las calles de Madrid...

De pronto el ritmo de su respiración cambió. Tía Flor comenzó de nuevo a hablarle.

—Mamá, no tengas miedo. Déjame ayudarte. Tú sabes que te espera tanta gente que tú quieres, tus padres, tus hermanos, Papá. Por fin te vas a reunir con Papá... Tú has sido muy buena... no tengas miedo. Tú crees en Dios. Sabes que hay otra vida. Estás en tu cama, rodeada de tus hijas y tu nieta, de gente que te quiere. Estamos rezando por ti. Aquí tienes unas rosas de tu jardín. ¿Puedes olerlas? Pero ya es hora de irte, vieja. Dame la mano. No te preocupes por mí. Tú siempre dices que te he ayudado mucho en la vida. Déjame ayudarte a morir también. Te extrañaré mucho, mucho, pero... estarás mejor, Mamá... y velarás por todos, y desde donde vas a estar podrás ver también a Ricardo y a Lauri. Sí, yo me voy a cuidar mucho... Te lo prometo, Mamá. Vete tranquila...

Entonces Mama Luya abrió los ojos y le vimos las lágrimas rodar por las mejillas. La mirada vidriosa se aclaró y por un brevísimo instante le regresó la expresión al rostro. Era ella de nuevo. Incluso me pareció que le sonreía a Tía Flor. Le vi un leve movimiento de los dedos, como si le apretara la mano. Luego exhaló profundamente —ese último suspiro de la muerte... —, y cerró los ojos para siempre.

La enterramos a la mañana siguiente en el Cementerio de Colón, junto a mi abuelo. El día estaba apropiadamente gris. No fue hasta que regresamos a la casa de La Sierra que vi llorar a Tía Flor.

✍

Las pequeñas zapatillas giran, marcan los primeros pasos, plié, gran plié, attitude, passé. Se elevan, en medias puntas, así permanecen breves momentos.

—Después bailaremos en la punta de los pies.

Cuando sean grandes, cuando terminen el séptimo año, se incorporarán al Ballet Nacional. Algunas serán profesoras, otras se subirán a los escenarios de distintos países. De ellas saldrán las primeras bailarinas: Una Pávlova, una Ulánova, una Alicia Alonso.

Alicia. Alicia. Todas quieren parecerse a Alicia. Alicia es el ídolo. Alicia es la figura de los sueños. Alicia, los movimientos que deben repetir. Alicia, la poesía que quieren copiar, hecha extremidades, tórax, cabeza. Alicia es un nombre que se repite. Alicia es todo el ballet, toda la belleza, toda la Patria.

(*Bohemia* 50:35, 17–20)

✍

Hace dos días cumplí 30 años. Me miro al espejo. No me interesa saber si me veo joven o mayor, si soy bonita o fea, si tengo brillo en el pelo o no, si los ojos me siguen echando chispas, como me decía Papá cuando era niña. Quisiera mirar más allá de este cuerpo y saber quién soy, en qué creo, con qué sueño.

Sé que soy madre. Cuando llevo a Tania al ballet y veo su carita concentrada —siempre lo quiere hacer todo tan bien… —, cuando la observo jugar o dormir, cuando me abraza y me besa, la vida se me antoja un milagro. Los viejos tienen sus defectos, pero la verdad es que los adoro. Tuve una etapa en que todo lo que hacía Papá me sacaba de quicio. Estaba resentida con él. Todavía a veces me molesta esa forma de ser suya, como si fuera Cantinflas, sin decir las cosas de frente. Pero quizás por eso logró que no lo botaran del Ministerio… La pobre Mamá es una santa. Quizás demasiado sacrificada, demasiado manipulada por el viejo. Aunque cuando se para bonito… Se mete las colas día tras días sin protestar. Debería de ayudarla de vez en cuando. Y siempre inventando para que no nos aburramos de comer tantos chícharos. Sé que ha sufrido mucho la muerte de Mama Luya. Quisiera saber cómo consolarla. Pero creo que sufre más por la ausencia de Ricardo y de Lauri, y por no conocer a esos nietos. Confieso que a veces me da un poco de celos. Pedritín ya nunca está en casa… la que se ocupa de ellos soy yo, pero Mamá sólo suspira por Lauri… Mi hermana a veces me parece un fantasma, la otra mitad de mí que murió, o que nunca existió, y otras veces me parece que nunca se ha ido y que voy a poder comentar con ella cualquier bobería. Porque hay cosas que sólo ella entendería… Ricardo se me borra de la memoria. Tengo que mirar las fotos porque se me olvida su rostro, y sin embargo, recuerdo el tacto de su piel, de su mano tomando la mía para cruzar una calle, de su abrazo ya de hombre cuando yo era todavía una chiquilla. Siempre sentía que él, más que Papá, era mi protector… Y ahora está tan distante. Es sólo una voz en el hilo del teléfono, de cuando en cuando, unas palabras absurdas, de cómo estás, les hace falta algo, aquí hay mucho frío… Pedritín está aquí pero casi nunca lo veo. Antes porque estaba becado, ahora porque está en la universidad, o en una reunión de la Juventud, o haciendo trabajo voluntario. Además, me temo que no lo conozco, que de veras no sé lo que siente y piensa. Mi trabajo me gusta, y he tenido suerte de que me hayan puesto en el equipo que diseña las escuelas. Cuando estoy dibujando, el resto del mundo se me borra. A solas con las imágenes en la cabeza, y el lápiz entre los dedos… Cuando las ideas van tomando forma en el papel, siento un entusiasmo interno, un brote de energía, un impulso de adrenalina… Después ver ese dibujo transformado en un edificio concreto, que uno ve, toca… Además, es algo con lo que contribuyo al país, a la Revolución.

Lázaro… hace ya más de diez años desde aquella tarde que hicimos el amor por primera vez sobre la hierba, y todavía el mero roce de su piel me estremece. Pero a veces lo noto tan ausente, tan absorto en sus preocupaciones.

Me gustaría tener más amigas. Prácticamente todas mis compañeras de estudios se han ido. Me quedaba Marta Lola y ahora se fue para la Unión Soviética a estudiar microbiología. Hay veces que no puedo pasar por la calle donde estaba el colegio porque me parece que está lleno de los fantasmas de los que se fueron. Ya ni me interesa celebrar los cumpleañoss.

Y está, claro, Cuba, la Revolución. De verdad pienso que es un privilegio vivir estos momentos, que estamos construyendo el futuro, que mi hija será la beneficiara de estos sacrificios. Pero a veces la Revolución se me vuelve una bruja parlanchina que me atormenta. Es como si no tuviéramos vida privada, como si todo los problemas del mundo, desde la muerte de Ho Chi Minh hasta quién debe estudiar en la universidad, invadieran mi intimidad. FIDEL ÉSTA ES TU CASA. Es como si las consignas flotaran por todas partes. LOS 10 MILLONES VAN. Fueran conmigo en la guagua. SOMOS SOCIALISTAS PA'LANTE Y PA'LANTE. Hirvieran en las cazuelas. Y AL QUE NO LE GUSTE QUE AGUANTE, QUE AGUANTE Se sentaran a la mesa con la familia. LA ORI, LA ORI, LA ORI ES LA CANDELA. Se pasearan por las ropas de mi hija. FIDEL, SEGURO, A LOS YANQUIS DALES DURO. Me acompañaran en el baño. DONDE SEA, COMO SEA Y PARA LO QUE SEA ¡COMANDANTE EN JEFE, ORDENE! Se acostaran en la cama entre mi marido y yo. CONSUMA PRODUCTOS CUBANOS, QUE ASÍ TAMBIÉN SE HACE PATRIA. A veces quiero gritar, basta ya. PATRIA O MUERTE. Basta ya. VENCEREMOS. Lo único que pido es silencio.

Anoche Lázaro insistió en llevarme al cine y a comer como regalo de cumpleañoss. Cuando le sugerí que llamáramos a Armandito y a Magaly prefirió que fuéramos solos. Al regreso quiso que camináramos un rato por el Malecón. Paseamos en silencio, cogidos de la mano, como dos adolescentes.

—¿Quieres ir al Gato Tuerto? Ahí siempre te encuentras a tus amigos escritores.

—No, mejor vamos a casa.

—Lázaro, a ti te pasa algo, ¿verdad?

—No, nada —y respiró profundo, como si hubiera querido tragarse de una bocanada toda la brisa del mar.

Ya estábamos en la cama, con las luces apagadas, cuando al fin habló.

—Menchu, estoy preocupado. Creo que la Revolución va por buen rumbo... que el marxismo es la solución... Comprendo que hay que defenderse de los enemigos, y que los americanos sólo buscan la ocasión para penetrarnos. Me parece bueno que estrechemos lazos con la Unión Soviética. Pero no sé. Lo del Caso Padilla no me acaba de gustar. Algunas cosas que han dicho los intelectuales en su carta son ciertas. Además, Sartre, Vargas Llosa, han sido amigos de la Revolución... y son gente que sabe pensar. Yo tampoco entiendo la represión si creemos en nuestras verdades. También hay mucho descontento entre los estudiantes. Hace unos meses hubo un careo en Oriente entre unos muchachos y el propio Fidel, y los expulsaron de la universidad. Ahora hay rumores de que se preparan nuevas normas y de que sólo podrán estudiar los revolucionarios.

—Yo también a veces dudo, Lázaro.

—Mira, quizás estamos muy cerca y no podemos ver con claridad.

—Sí, a veces los árboles no te dejan ver el bosque, como decía Mama Luya.

—Menchu, hay una posibilidad de que me den un puesto en Prensa Latina.

—Ay, Lázaro, separarnos de nuevo... ¿A dónde te van a mandar ahora? ¿Por cuánto tiempo?

—Unos meses... un año... tal vez más... Hay una plaza en la Unión Soviética.

—¡Tan lejos!

—Pero te tengo una sorpresa. Ya pedí permiso. Tania y tú pueden venir conmigo. Así aprenderán ruso...

—Pero ¿cómo voy a dejar a los viejos?

—No será por mucho tiempo. Y ellos están bien de salud. Tienen a tu hermano.

—No sé...

—Además, he averiguado que hay clases de ballet muy buenas para Tania.

—Tú sabías que con eso me ibas a convencer... ¡Qué malo eres! Si ya lo tenías todo arreglado...

Esa noche hicimos el amor con renovada pasión, como si renaciera entre nosotros el gusto por la vida. Nos quedamos después mucho rato en silencio, abrazados desnudos. Afuera, La Habana dormía.

⁂

Tendrán cabida ahora aquí y sin contemplación de ninguna clase ni vacilaciones, ni medias tintas, ni paños calientes, tendrán cabida únicamente los revolucionarios.

Ya saben, señores intelectuales burgueses y liberalistas burgueses y agentes de la CIA y de la inteligencia del imperialismo, es decir, de los servicios de Inteligencia, de espionaje del imperialismo: en Cuba no tendrán entrada, como no se la damos a UPI y AP. ¡Cerrada la entrada indefinidamente por tiempo indefinido y por tiempo infinito!

(Fidel Castro 30 de abril 1971)

⁂

Siempre recordaré nuestra época en la Unión Soviética como una de las más felices de nuestra vida. La primera impresión no fue buena. Moscú está rodeada por un anillo de edificios cuadrados, grises, oscuros, infinitamente iguales. Una especie de Alamar, pero peor, sin la ruidosa sandunga de los criollos ni esas pintorescas tendederas nuestras con la ropa interior secándose al sol. A medida que uno se adentra en ella, sin embargo, comprende que la capital soviética es una ciudad hermosa, enorme, llena de maravillosas iglesias bizantinas, con sus cúpulas como cebollas, y adentro, los popes barbudos que cantan la misa delante del iconostasio. Los santos ortodoxos me parecen muy espirituales... Y hasta diría que nacionalistas, pues adquieren características no conocidas en otras latitudes.

Visitamos los monasterios, los cementerios; fuimos a velorios, a cenas pascuales y navideñas, tomamos el té con rusos que vivían con ansias de mejorar, de poder viajar al extranjero, pero muy orgullosos de su cultura y de su pasado. Los museos son riquísimos, la Galería Tretiakov en Moscú, el Ermitage en Leningrado, los monumentos a las víctimas del nazismo en Kiev y en Stalingrado, los museos en las casas de los pintores, de Stanislavski, todo muy bien cuidado y guardado. Tania y yo íbamos a menudo al Gran Teatro Bolshoi a ver fastuosas producciones de ballet. Algunas veces convencí a Lázaro y fuimos a la ópera. Nunca habíamos visto nada así.

Tania enseguida aprendió ruso, y estaba feliz con sus clases de ballet. Yo sufría con el idioma, aunque lo poco que había estudiado en La Habana me ayudó, y podía defenderme. Lázaro ya lo dominaba y aprovechó para tomar cursos de posgrado. La Universidad de Moscú era un edificio imponente, conocido como uno de "los caprichos de Stalin", de igual que el hotel Leningrado, el hotel Ucrania, el Ministerio de Asuntos Exteriores y otros. Ofrecía muchas comodidades, grandes restaurantes, pasillos lujosos, campos deportivos, hospital, hasta un centro odontológico. Los rusos en esa esfera me parecieron cultos y espirituales. Todo el mundo leía a Pushkin, a Lermontov, a Tolstoi, se sabían pasajes de memoria, incluso los físicos y los matemáticos, entre los cuales se encontraba un importante sector de la *intelligentsia,* quizás más que entre los abogados y los médicos. Por otra parte, la gente común y corriente era muy tosca. Se vestían como campesinos, usaban unos zapatos muy ordinarios, pero eran cordiales y hospitalarios. Vivían como reconcentrados en sí mismos, aunque si te ofrecían su amistad, eran muy leales. Tomaban muchísimo, más de la cuenta.

Es un país de contrastes. De imponente arquitectura y milenaria cultura, a la vez que con atrasos significativos en adelantos que alivian la vida cotidiana. Envían hombres al cosmos, pero no pueden hacer un ventilador que funcione bien. Se siente la falta de comunicación con

Europa Occidental, con el resto del mundo. Hay largas colas en los cines para ver una película norteamericana o europea de los 50 o principios de los 60, que los cubanos vimos cuando se estrenó. Un perfume húngaro constituye un acontecimiento en las tiendas y si es francés aquello es la locura. ¿Cómo es posible que en una urbe con metros gigantescos, con paradas majestuosas, llenas de estatuas imponentes, no haya papel de inodoro? El paradigma del ateísmo marxista, y sin embargo, las huellas de la religión están en todas partes. Eso sí, se come bien, sin dificultades. Tania se ha aficionado a las zanahorias con *esmetana,* una especie de crema agria que le ponen a todo, y que los hombres devoran gustosos puesto que aseguran que fortalece la virilidad.

Odié el invierno. Seis meses de nieves eternas y de un frío cruel, de hasta 45 grados bajo cero. No es hasta las 9 de la mañana que comienza a aclarar, las tardes concluyen a las 2 p.m. y ya a las tres una oscuridad amenazadora le roba luz al día, que se apaga totalmente antes de las seis. Todos andan de prisa por las calles, encorvados, buscando el refugio de la entrada del metro. También a mí me pesaban los abrigos, las botas, el gorro, los guantes, las medias de lana.

Hicimos amistad con un matrimonio mayor. Algunos fines de semana nos invitaban a su casa. Vivían en un apartamentico estrecho pero muy gracioso. Iván era historiador; su esposa Olga, científica, y muy refinada de espíritu. Hablábamos de poesía y recogíamos setas y fresas en el bosque. Él trataba de explicarnos la situación del país:

—La vitrina del socialismo es Berlín, la República Democrática Alemana, siempre en oposición a la Federal, y quien la sostiene es Moscú.

Y añadía moviendo la cabeza de un lado a otro:

—Pero éste es un pueblo hecho al sufrimiento.

Un 9 de mayo nos llevó frente al Bolshoi, donde se reunían los sobrevivientes de la guerra, hombres y mujeres, viejitos y viejitas, con los pechos cubiertos de medallas, que se congregaban para rememorar, alegrarse de estar vivos y entristecerse por sus muertos.

—Aquí hay varias generaciones de soviéticos conviviendo, con traumas de la guerra, pro Stalin unos, contra Stalin otros, aunque no declarados. Y aún así, en esta fecha al menos, unidos…

Algunas veces íbamos a esquiar. Lázaro y Tania lo pasaban bien, pero yo no hacía más que caerme. Me pareció casi una tortura, con tanto frío me lloraban los ojos y ni sentía las manos. Hubo un momento en que ya no soportaba el invierno y estaba harta de recoger las famosas setas y las frutillas para hacer mermelada. Extrañaba a mi madre y al mar.

En el transcurso del primer semestre del año 1974, en las fechas comprendidas entre el 3 de enero y el 30 de junio se desarrollará la etapa de solicitud del Carné de Identidad y la Tarjeta de Menor en todo el país para todos los ciudadanos cubanos por nacimiento o naturalización nacidos antes del 1 de enero de 1959.

Para realizar este trámite será necesaria la presencia física de cada ciudadano, excepción de menores e impedidos físicos o mentales.

En esta actividad es de destacar la labor de los CDR y la ANAP en la base, ya que ellos son los encargados de entregar a la población el modelo de citación en sus domicilios para que concurran a hacer la solicitud del Carné de Identidad.

(Bohemia 65:52, 56)

En enero del 1974 le pidieron a Lázaro que volviera a La Habana. Era el decimoquinto aniversario del triunfo de la Revolución y se esperaba que Leonid Brezhnev fuera a Cuba para el día 28, natalicio de José Martí. Querían que hiciera unos reportajes especiales.

A pesar de las ganas que teníamos de regresar, nos despedimos de Iván y de Olga con tristeza, y cuando desde el avión vi las cúpulas bizantinas de las iglesias erguidas sobre el manto de la nieve, se me humedecieron los ojos.

La Habana me pareció más luminosa, más sensual, y más ruinosa que nunca. A mis padres también los vi más envejecidos, en especial a Papá, que caminaba arrastrando los pies.

De esos años tengo vagos recuerdos: la recepción delirante a Brezhnev, la presencia rusa en la Habana, no de los rusos refinados y espirituales, sino de los otros, reconcentrados y toscos, al punto de que los cubanos, que a todo el mundo le ponen un mote, les apodaron los bolos. Además, aquí, en medio de tanto verde y tanto sol, se veían fuera de lugar. Las películas soviéticas eran de una densidad insoportable. Nadie las aguantaba. Las clases de ruso las daban por radio y por televisión. Tania trataba de enseñarles a los abuelos. El viejo llegó a aprender sus palabritas, pero Mamá se negaba:

—Mijita, ya yo estoy muy vieja para aprender otro idioma...

Fue por esos tiempos que a Pedritín y Camilo, el hijo de Maruja, los mandaron para Angola. Maruja trabajaba como auxiliar de enfermera en Morón, en la provincia de Camagüey, cuando el golpe de Estado de Batista. Comenzó ayudando a su hermano, que pertenecía a una célula revolucionaria. Se robaba inyecciones, vendajes y algodones del hospital para curar a los enfermos. Luego pasó a tirar puntillas a la calle, lanzar cocteles Molotov y hasta a poner bombas. Tuvo amores con un combatiente y salió en estado. Cuando iba a dar a luz estaban tan perseguidos, que tuvo que parir en una rastra que los rebeldes le habían ocupado al ejército. A los dos días le entregó la criatura a su madre y un compañero la llevó en un jeep hasta Sancti Spíritus, desde donde logró llegar al Escambray para unirse a los alzados. Allí cuidó a los enfermos y combatió como un soldado más. Cuando volvió a ver a su hijo, después del primero de enero, ya caminaba. Supo que al padre de la criatura lo habían matado. Se mudó entonces para La Habana, donde le dieron una casa en la misma cuadra nuestra, de una familia que se había ido para el norte. Trabajaba de enfermera en un policlínico y sólo dos cosas le interesaban en la vida: la Revolución y su hijo Camilo, que acababa de cumplir 17 años.

A los seis meses llegó la noticia de que Camilo había muerto en combate. A Maruja le dijeron que era mejor enterrarlo en Angola. No protestó. Tampoco lloró. Redobló su fervor revolucionario. Pero en sus ojos había algo raro, que me asustaba.

Mamá vivía pendiente de las noticias. A veces pensaba que iba a ser mucho para ella, que se le iba a partir el corazón. Pero mi hermano regresó de la guerra dos años después, sano y salvo. Papá consiguió cerveza y un lechón en la bolsa negra, y celebramos con un fiestón.

CAPÍTULO OCHO
"Qué dolor, qué dolor, qué pena"

HACE MÁS DE DIEZ AÑOS QUE REGRESAMOS A MIAMI. Bobby siempre había querido volver, y cuando murió Adela insistió con tal obsesión que acabé por ceder. A Pedro Pablo le faltaba un año para graduarse de *high school* pero no le importó el cambio. Quería ir a estudiar a Gainesville, como su tío, y le convenía ser residente de la Florida. Bobby Junior se mostró más rebelde, pero supuse que se le pasaría. Pensé que mi suegro no iba a querer renunciar a su trabajo, y me daba pena dejarlo solo. Me sorprendió un día:

—Lauri, me voy para Miami con ustedes. Quiero hacerme abogado de nuevo. Además, mijita, a lo mejor todavía les puedo ser útil. Eso sí, ya los muchachos están grandes y ustedes necesitan vivir solos.

—Usted no nos molesta, Roberto, al contrario —e insistí en que se mudara con nosotros, al menos al principio.

Compramos una casa muy cómoda en Weschester, un barrio de gente de clase media, donde vivían muchos cubanos. Matriculamos a los muchachos en el colegio. Bobby sacó su licencia para vender seguros. Y yo encontré trabajo en el sistema escolar.

Mi suegro estaba cerca de la edad del retiro pero se empeñó en revalidar su carrera y lo logró. El día que le entregaron el título reunimos a algunos amigos en casa para celebrarlo. Hasta Johnny vino de Georgia con su esposa Kathy y su hijita recién nacida. Nos alegró mucho, porque no los veíamos desde que se habían casado hacía dos años y estábamos locos por conocer a la niña. Cuando todos se fueron, Roberto se me acercó.

—Este título es tuyo también.

—¡Por Dios, Roberto!

—Sí, mijita, tú siempre has creído en mí, me has ayudado con el inglés… y además eres un buen ejemplo, porque eres como una hormiguita, siempre trabajando, estudiando, ocupándote de educar bien a tus hijos. Yo te quiero y te admiro mucho, Lauri.

Y me dio una de esas palmaditas suyas en el hombro.

Pocos meses después insistió en mudarse solo y no hubo argumentos para retenerlo.

—Pero si me voy a sólo unas cuadras y además, siempre que me necesiten...

Y en efecto, siguió siendo como un padre para mí y un abuelo ejemplar para mis hijos.

Los primeros años fueron buenos. Robertico —en Miami no quería que le dijeran Bobby— parecía recobrar su antigua personalidad. Ya no estaba tan amargado. Salíamos con otros matrimonios de nuestra edad. Viajamos dos veces a Europa y una a México. Nuestra relación mejoró. Sólo peleábamos sobre Cuba. Cuando a uno de sus compañeros lo expulsaron de la Brigada por ir a Cuba al diálogo con Castro en 1978, a pesar de que volvió antes que los demás y publicó unas declaraciones muy dignas, no me cohibí de expresar mis opiniones:

—Pero si para sacarlos a ustedes de Cuba se dialogó con el régimen, ¿cómo lo van a castigar porque quiera hacer lo mismo para liberar a otros presos?

Robertico se puso tan bravo conmigo que la vena del cuello parecía que le iba a explotar.

Regresar a Miami fue para mí un reencuentro con Cuba. Los flamboyanes, el cafecito, el sol fuerte, los pasteles de guayaba, el mar, el jugo de piña, los marpacíficos, los tamales, las vicarias, los plátanos verdes, los sillones, los batidos de mamey, los crotos, las galleticas preparadas, la arquitectura, la materva, el mar, otra vez el mar, las medianoches, el español, los aguacates, la música, las camareras, ¿qué más quieres, mi amor?, el guarapo, el calor, las yuquitas, las palmas, las frituritas de seso, el mar, los mangos, siempre el mar, y la Isla tan cerca y tan lejos a la vez. Y el exilio, esta gente tan mía y que tanto me choca, locos de un solo tema, hablando, gritando, gesticulando, tumbando a Fidel de la noche a la mañana, recostados a un café de mediodía, con las maletas llenas de recuerdos, siempre preparadas para el regreso a un paraíso que ya no saben —¿sabemos?— si es memoria o sueño.

En los últimos años sólo había recibido noticias esporádicas de mi familia a través de las cartas de mi madre, que solían incluir lo que habían dado por la libreta ese mes, si alguien se había muerto, si algún primo se había casado o había tenido un hijo... La comunicación era muy difícil, pues ni los cubanos podían viajar a Estados Unidos, ni los exiliados a Cuba. Así llevábamos casi 20 años. Algunas familias lograban reunirse en Canadá o México, pero eran las excepciones. La mayoría sufría las separaciones en silencio. El clima era tan hostil que apenas uno se atrevía a hablar de la familia allá.

Por fin, en 1979, el gobierno de Cuba autorizó a los exiliados a regresar de visita al país. Comenzaron los viajes a la Isla de "la comunidad," eufemismo que utilizaba el gobierno de La Habana para identificarnos. A los que ayer habían botado como a "gusanos," ahora los recibían como a mariposas. De todas maneras, no lo pensé dos veces.

—Robertico, yo quiero ir a Cuba a ver a mi familia.

Se volvió hacia mí con una furia que nunca antes le había visto.

—Óyeme lo que te voy a decir... óyeme bien... si vas a Cuba... —estaba totalmente descompuesto.

—Robertico, no te pongas así. Mira, mucha gente va, y mis padres ya están mayores...

—Si vas a Cuba... Si vas a Cuba... ¡te mato!

Insistí un par de veces, pero no podía ni mencionarle el tema.

En una ocasión lo acompañé al acto que el 17 de abril celebran todos los años los brigadistas frente a un parque en La Pequeña Habana con un monumento y una antorcha siempre encendida. Oí en silencio los discursos henchidos de retórica patriótica; observé uno por uno a los miembros de la Brigada, muchos ya hombres maduros, con los vientres abultados y las cabezas canas; escuché pasar lista con los nombres de los muertos:

—Alberto González Recio

—¡Presente!

—Hernán Koch

—¡Presente!

—Vicente León

—¡Presente!

Algunas mujeres vestían de negro. Pensé en las madres cuyos hijos no regresaron, en las novias que perdieron al primer amor, en las viudas, en los niños que apenas recordaban a sus padres o ni siquiera lo habían conocido. Luego visitamos el local de una organización patriótica. De las paredes colgaban las fotos de los brigadistas, algunos entrenándose, con su uniforme de camuflaje; otros posando para la cámara, sosteniendo la bandera cubana, la fe en el triunfo y en el ideal que perseguían reflejado en los rostros sonrientes.

Por un momento me pareció comprender a Robertico, sus frustraciones, su inconformidad.

—Verás que nos reciben como a héroes, igual que a los americanos en esas películas de la Segunda Guerra Mundial —me había dicho antes de partir a Bahía de Cochinos.

Mi marido se había soñado salvador de la patria, lo había apostado todo en la invasión y había perdido. Había estado preso, nadie le había dado una medalla al regresar, y luego yo me lo había llevado a las nieves de Columbus a ir casa por casa de cobrador. Pero él no podía quitarse de la cabeza a los compañeros muertos o presos, ni todos los sueños que nos habían arrebatado cuando apenas empezábamos a vivir.

¿Y si no hubiera vuelto? Yo estaría en este acto con Pedro Pablo, vestida de negro, llorando no al Bobby de estos 18 años, sino al de entonces, al Robertico joven, al que yo amaba sin reserva alguna. Y los que no volvieron, ¿serían hoy los hombres que estas mujeres se habían pasado su vida venerando?

Sentí un dolor muy hondo, por tantas cosas, pero sobre todo, por Cuba, y por tantas vidas rotas, y por Robertico y porque no le hubiera bastado mi amor ni el de sus hijos ni el de sus padres, ni nada en el mundo que no fuera Cuba para ser feliz. Me dolía no haber comprendido a mi marido antes, me dolía el héroe que no había sido y el antihéroe que no se resignaba a ser, pero sobre todo, me dolía ese amor nuestro que se me iba muriendo dentro, y me pesaba, me pesaba mucho, como si llevara en las entrañas a un hijo muerto.

✌

Con letreros anticastristas y banderas cubanas, centenares de exiliados cubanos expresaron el viernes su oposición a la visita del presidente del Consejo de Estado de Cuba, Fidel Castro, a las Naciones Unidas (O.N.U.), durante un acto de masas celebrado en Miami.

La manifestación, que se llevó a cabo al anochecer en el Bayfront Park, se organizó en respaldo a otra que tuvo lugar más temprano en Nueva York, mientras Castro pronunciaba un discurso ante la Asamblea General de la O.N.U.

El padre O'Farrill, sacerdote católico y activista anticastrista, expresó que los verdaderos representantes de Cuba eran los exiliados porque ellos podían decir la verdad sobre Cuba.

(*El Miami Herald* 13 de octubre 1979)

✌

Como a los dos o tres años de estar en Miami, me nombraron *Assistant Principal* de la escuela donde enseñaba y me aumentaron el sueldo. Comencé a tomar cursos por las noches en la universidad para sacar la maestría. Fue como si se me abriera un mundo nuevo. Siempre me había sentido como una especie de tablero de ajedrez —con zonas de luz y otras oscuras—, de tantas cosas que ignoraba. Los estudios en Washington me habían ayudado mucho, pero aún tenía grandes lagunas en mi educación que estaba ansiosa por llenar. Además, me uní a un grupo de compañeros muy bueno y aunque todos eran menores que yo, me fui compenetrando con ellos. También había comenzado a enviar algunos artículos al periódico y me los publicaban. Siempre me había gustado escribir y ver mi nombre en letras de imprenta me daba una gran satisfacción.

Mi mayor preocupación en esos años era Bobby Junior. En cuanto entró en *junior high* comenzó a cambiar. Se puso esquivo, y hasta francamente rebelde. Al principio se lo achacábamos a la edad y tratábamos de ser pacientes. Ya cuando cumplió 16, los problemas fueron más serios. A veces no iba a la escuela y no sabíamos dónde estaba. En una ocasión nos llamaron de una tienda donde lo habían detenido robándose un par de tenis. Un muchacho que siempre había obtenido buenas notas comenzó a suspender asignaturas. Cuando sacó la licencia de manejar y Robertico se negó a que le compráramos un carro, las cosas se pusieron peor. El plan era que le prestaríamos el mío de vez en cuando, y si demostraba ser responsable, le compraríamos el suyo dentro de un año. ¡Ni sé cuántas veces chocó! Yo siempre decía que lo importante era que no le hubiera pasado nada a él, pero no me hacían ninguna gracia los inconvenientes y los gastos que me traía cada accidente. Acabó con el Honda que me había comprado de uso, pero en muy buenas condiciones. Lo peor de todo eran esas madrugadas cuando daban las dos, las tres, y las cuatro de la mañana y no había llegado… Me imaginaba siempre lo peor. Que había chocado y estaba desangrándose o muerto en una cuneta. Que lo habían asaltado, que lo habían matado. Me debatía entre despertar a Robertico, llamar a casa de alguno de sus amigos, avisar a la policía o esperar a que apareciera. Como siempre en los momentos de apuros, me ponía a rezar. Me inventaba juegos con el reloj. ¡Que venga antes de las tres, Dios mío, y no le digo nada cuando llegue! Pero pasaban las tres, y nada. Así, noche tras noche. Lo intenté todo. Hablar con él, pedirle que me contara sus problemas, asegurarle que tenía confianza en él, rogarle por todo lo que pensé que podía conmoverlo. ¡Hasta por su abuela Adela que lo había querido tanto! Algunas veces perdí la paciencia y lo regañé, y hasta lo castigué, pero, principalmente, apelaba a su razón, y a su corazón. Me escuchaba en un silencio exasperante. Pero no cambiaba. Hice que su abuelo interviniera. Consulté con sus maestros y con los consejeros de la escuela. Conversé con los padres de sus amigos. Una vez, hasta Pedro Pablo vino de Gainesville a petición mía. Tampoco dio resultado.

—Son cosas de la edad… ya se le pasará… —decía Robertico y se hacía la vista gorda. Otras veces le peleaba, le gritaba.

El muchacho nunca se quedaba callado:

—¿Y a qué vienen tantas preguntas sobre con quién salgo, a dónde voy, y quiénes son mis amigos si tú nunca te has interesado por mí, ni por saber quién soy, ni por conocerme? A ti sólo te ha importado tumbar a Fidel, pero ni eso has podido hacer en la vida.

Robertico le dio un bofetón. El muchacho se quedó paralizado.

—No le pegues… —y me metí en el medio.

En la confusión, Robertico me hirió en la boca con su sortija y empecé a sangrar.

—Mira lo que hiciste, ¡le diste a Mami…!

—No fue nada… fue sin querer… vamos… no peleen…

Me preguntaba una y otra vez en qué le había fallado a mi hijo. Me sentía culpable y al mismo tiempo traicionada por él. A veces temía que estuviera en drogas y me tentaba la idea de registrar su cuarto. Pero siempre había respetado la privacidad de mis hijos y me resistía a espiarlo. Nunca me había sentido más confundida. Ya no sabía qué hacer.

∽

Un hombre entró a una fiesta que celebraba una fraternidad estudiantil en la madrugada del sábado y abrió fuego con una pistola. Dos estudiantes resultaron muertos y cinco heridos.

Mark Houston, de 19 años, fue arrestado tras el tiroteo, sin ofrecer resistencia. En el incidente murieron los estudiantes Terrell Johnson y Patrick McGindy. John Leroy Aiken, de 20 años, se encuentra en estado crítico después de ser sometido a una operación. Otros tres estudiantes heridos están en condición estable. Se desconoce el móvil del crimen.

(*El Nuevo Herald* 6 de octubre de 1979)

∽

A principios de 1980, cuando me convencí de que Robertico nunca aceptaría que yo fuera a Cuba, comencé a tramitar la visita de mis padres Tenía muchas ganas de verlos a los dos, pero era difícil que los dejaran venir juntos. Sugerí que fueran ellos quienes decidieran cuál vendría primero.

—No quiero morirme sin volverte a ver y sin conocer a mis nietos— me dijo mi padre. Le solicité enseguida la visa. De pronto me di cuenta de que ya Papi tenía 75 años. A pesar de que las fotos que me habían mandado recientemente delataban su edad, siempre lo recordaba como hacía más de 20 años. Los trámites se demoraban, y yo no podía pensar en otra cosa. Poco a poco fui comprando ropa para cuando llegara. Primero para él, luego para Mamá, para Menchu y Pedritín, y para Tania. Mis hermanos se habían integrado a la Revolución, pero, qué caray, eran mi sangre. Además, no les habría quedado más remedio. Planeaba adónde llevaría a Papi. Claro que querría pasarse unos días en Nueva York con Ricardo… si coincidiera con la temporada de pelota… ¡¿Quién lo pudiera ver en un juego de los yanquis?! ¡Con lo fanático que era mi padre de ese equipo! Tanto como de La Habana… Cuando pensaba en estas cosas me remontaba al estadio de El Cerro, y veía a Formental bateando, y a Mike Anderson, y a Miguel Ángel pasearse nervioso junto a la tercera base… Recordaba a mi padre enseñándonos a montar en bicicleta, llevándonos con él a la Casa Suárez a comprar dulces, y trayendo a la casa aquel televisor blanco y negro de RCA que fue el primero que tuvimos…

Esta vez no tuve ninguna premonición. Ni siquiera cuando oí la voz de Menchu a las 6 de la mañana. Pensé que sería para alguno de los trámites del viaje.

No lloré cuando supe que mi padre había muerto de un infarto. Más que dolor, sentí una rabia inmensa contra Fidel Castro, la Revolución, el Che, los uniformes verde-olivo, los milicianos, los Comités de Defensa, los pioneros, el 26 de julio, todo, absolutamente todo cuanto había acontecido en Cuba a partir de 1959. Era un sentimiento profundo, pero difuso. Sentía otra ira más sórdida y concreta.

No dejé que Robertico me abrazara.

—Por tu culpa… por tu culpa se me murió mi padre sin que yo lo volviera a ver.

Y me fui a trabajar sin que el nudo que me apretaba el pecho se hubiera disuelto en lágrimas.

∽

Armando Ruiz era actor en Cuba. Usualmente actuaba en obras españolas clásicas. Pero el año pasado hizo el papel de pasajero de autobús, mientras que su padre hacía el papel de chofer en las calles de La Habana.

El apoyo en escena: un ómnibus municipal robado. La pareja, junto con otros 10 amigos y familiares, utilizaron el pasado mes de mayo un autobús municipal robado para penetrar los portones de la Embajada de Venezuela en La Habana.

Aunque desempeñaban papeles ficticios, era real su fuga, la primera en una serie de escapadas violentas que han culminado en el intento de 10,000 cubanos de obtener asilo en la Embajada de Perú en la capital cubana.

Ruiz pasó más de 100 días en la Embajada de Venezuela esperando salir de Cuba. Ahora en Miami, y desempleado, se ha declarado en huelga de hambre en respaldo de los nuevos refugiados.

—Sabemos lo difícil que es para que 12 personas reúnan el coraje para huir- dijo Ruiz. Imagínese 10,000.

(Miami Herald 9 de abril 1980: 20A)

∽

Cuando terminaba en la escuela, me iba todas las tardes a trabajar de voluntaria con los refugiados del Mariel. Más de 100,000 habían llegado en pocas semanas. Cierto que Castro había abierto las cárceles y los manicomios, y descargado en los botes "escorias" de verdad, pero la mayoría era gente decente. Vi algunos casos patéticos, como el de un viejecito que improvisó su vivienda debajo de una escalera en el *Orange Bowl* y no entendía que lo quisieran sacar del estadio para llevarlo a un albergue. Algunos venían llenos de picadas de mosquitos, pues habían tenido que esperar por horas y horas a la intemperie. Otros me mostraron las huellas de las mordidas de los perros que les habían echado encima. Había historias horribles, como la de la mujer a quien, ya en el barco, le habían arrebatado a su hijito de brazos y en su desesperación se había tirado al mar y ahogado. En la televisión se han visto los actos de repudio. Cubanos tirándoles huevos podridos a otros cubanos y gritándoles insultos. Y con mis propios ojos vi a un niño, de no más de siete años, que llegó con los bracitos fracturados. ¿Cómo es posible que haya seres humanos capaces de hacerle daño a una criatura? ¿Se ha envilecido tanto el pueblo cubano?

Pienso en la Patria que dejé, en La Habana de mi infancia, vista por el marco de un ómnibus escolar. Mi Habana de pupitres y parques, de playas y juegos inocentes. Mi Habana de primera comunión. Alánimo... Alánimo... de buganvilias y marpacíficos... la reina va a pasar... la sombra protectora de mi abuela... Y ahora, esta otra Habana de violencia acechando en cada esquina... Mambrú se fue a la guerra... una Habana del dolor de ir creciendo... qué dolor qué dolor qué pena... con la muerta agazapada, amenazante... y no sé cuando vendrá... Mi Habana en el adiós... ay, ay que do re mi... que do re fa... y no sé cuando vendrá...

∽

Dadme vuestras cansadas y pobres masas humanas amontonadas que anhelan respirar en libertad; a los infelices desechos de vuestras playas atestadas; mandadme a estos, los azotados por las tempestades. Yo alzo mi luz junto a la puerta dorada.

Emma Lazarus
Inscripción en la Estatua de la Libertad

∽

También hubo algunas alegrías en esos años, como cuando nos avisaron de Cayo Hueso que Tía Flor había llegado por el Mariel. Esa mujer es increíble. Enseguida la fuimos a buscar y la trajimos para casa. Verla, abrazarla, oírla hablar, fue como recuperar un poco a mi familia. En cuanto estuvimos a solas, comencé a preguntarle por todos en casa.

—Tu madre está muy avejentada, Lauri. Lo de tu padre acabó con ella. Está loca por verte, pero no hubiera resistido esta travesía. Ni tampoco quiere dejar a tus hermanos.

—¿Y de verdad ellos están con eso, Tía?

—Lauri, todo es muy complicado. Pero sí, creen en eso con sinceridad. Tu hermano no ha conocido otra cosa. Menchu también era jovencita... se quedó allá... se enamoró de Lázaro... la vida es muy compleja... tienes que entenderlo. Si también yo al principio me hice mis ilusiones, bueno, casi todo el pueblo de Cuba, y tu Tío Luis ni se diga... hasta que murió... Pero son gente muy buena tus hermanos. Créeme.

Los días con Tía Flor fueron maravillosos. Nos pasamos horas y horas hablando. Yo quería saberlo todo, a qué hora se levantaban, qué comían, en qué condiciones estaba la casa. También le pregunté sobre la muerte de Papá. Y después hablamos mucho sobre el país y lo que podría pasar. Recordaba a Tía Flor como a una mujer alegre y exuberante que se adornaba con unos collares inmensos y fumaba con una larga boquilla. Comprendí que era también inteligente y sensata. Hacía tiempo que temía secretamente que al reencontrarme con mi familia no pudiéramos entendernos. Sabía de muchos casos así. Me dio tranquilidad que con Tía Flor me parecía que había dejado de verla el día anterior. Empecé a hacer planes para cerrar el garaje y construirle una habitación, pero se negó.

—Lauri, yo siempre he soñado con vivir en Nueva York.

—Pero hace mucho frío... ¿Y qué vas a hacer allá?

—Vivir... trabajar...

—Tía... pero a tus años...

—Oye, yo soy mucho más joven que tu madre...

Y se fue en un ómnibus a la ciudad de los rascacielos a comenzar de nuevo a los sesenta años, sin apenas saber inglés.

∽

Soy uno de los tantos que ha aprovechado más o menos esta oportunidad o este desastre para llegar aquí, y en realidad la sensación que yo siento en ningún momento es de triunfo ni, digamos, de una gran alegría, sino es una sensación hasta cierto punto de paz por estar vivo y por haber salido de allí, pero es la misma sensación que puede sentir una persona que sale de la casa cuando se está quemando, o sea, la casa se quemó de todos modos y yo me salvé la vida... pero la casa se quemó.

Reinaldo Arenas, poco después llegar a Estados Unidos por el Mariel.

(Ulla y Ott *En sus propias palabras*)

∽

Otro momento feliz fue la boda de Pedro Pablo. A mí me parecía mentira. Me costaba trabajo darme cuenta de que ya era un hombre, si me acordaba como si hubiera sido ayer del día en que nació. Siempre fue un muchacho muy formal, nunca me dio trabajo. Ya había terminado los estudios, tenía un buen trabajo. Yo hubiera preferido que se casara con una cubana, que la boda fuera en Miami, pero comprendí que si ella era de Jacksonville tuviera que ser allá. Susan es una muchacha muy buena, pero nunca es lo mismo... no por el idioma... sino por la forma de ser... aunque Pedro Pablo siempre dice que es una gringa aplatanada... se veían tan enamorados... Lo más lindo fue que toda la familia pudo asistir. Mi suegro, Vidal, Johnny y su familia, mi primo Carlitos, Ricardo con su esposa y sus hijos, Tía Flor. Hasta los Stone, aquellos americanos que nos acogieron en Columbus, le enviaron un regalo. ¡Mis dos hijos se veían preciosos vestidos de etiqueta! Me sentía tan orgullosa cuando bailaba con ellos. Como en todos los momentos importantes, me dolía la ausencia de los míos. ¿Los míos? Quizás ya sea hora de que comprenda que esta familia reunida acá, de este lado, son los míos. Y sin embargo, me siento incompleta, como si algo me faltara. Siempre soñando con regresar a Cuba, y nuestra vida es ésta. La estamos viviendo sin darnos cuenta, como si estuviera en otra parte.

Durante toda la ceremonia no pude dejar de pensar en mi boda. ¡Tantas ilusiones como yo tenía…! ¿Adónde va el amor cuando se acaba? ¿Se había terminado ya entre Robertico y yo?

Trato de precisar los recuerdos y pienso que fue después de la boda de Pedro Pablo que las cosas empeoraron otra vez. Robertico comenzó a beber más de la cuenta. En realidad, no se llegaba a emborrachar y yo prefería disimular que enfrentarme a él. También vendía mucho menos pero como mi sueldo iba mejorando, yo iba tapando los huecos. En todas partes se hablaba de la *perestroika* y el *glassnot* y la inminente transformación de la Unión Soviética y sus satélites, pero él seguía viendo comunistas hasta en la sopa. Un día me puse a chotearlo:

—Si van a entrar por la calle Flagler…

¡Para qué fue aquello! Se alteró mucho. En realidad, siempre estaba de mal humor. Le sugerí que fuera a un psiquiatra y fue como mentarle la madre.

A principios de año mi suegro nos anunció su casamiento. Yo me alegré muchísimo. Roberto es un hombre muy bueno y merece ser feliz. Además, Olga es una mujer encantadora, y muy discreta. Pero Robertico lo tomó muy mal. Él que nunca habla de Adela, que fui yo la que tuve que ocuparme de mandarle a hacer la lápida para la tumba, que casi ni entraba en su habitación cuando se estaba muriendo de cáncer, y venir a salir con que el matrimonio de Roberto era una traición a la memoria de su madre. A veces mi marido me parece un desconocido, una persona totalmente ajena a mi vida.

La situación entre nosotros se puso peor después de que me gradué y comencé a enseñar en la universidad. Nunca se me había ocurrido que Robertico fuera envidioso, y aunque no me hubiera ayudado mucho con la casa y con los muchachos, siempre pensaba que era porque los latinos eran así, y no porque no me quisiera. No creía, no podía creer que le molestaran mis éxitos. Pero a veces me parecía que cada vez que me pasaba algo bueno, Robertico se las arreglaba para amargármelo.

Uno de los temas más sensibles en todos estos años había sido mi insistencia en ir a Cuba a ver a mi familia. A veces trataba de convencerme:

—Lauri, ¿y los años que yo estuve preso, y la memoria de los mártires como Pedro Luis Boitel, y los torturados, y los que han estado en presidio por años y años? Ahí tienes las historias de Valladares, de Martín Pérez, de Húber Matos y de tantos hombres y mujeres anónimos... tú misma trabajaste en Washington por los derechos humanos... ¿y los años de exilio, tantas mujeres trabajando en factorías, tanto que hemos pasado? ¿Tú vas a traicionar todo eso? ¿Y los muertos, Lauri, y la memoria de los muertos?

—Yo creo que a los muertos no les va a importar mucho que yo vaya a ver a mi familia.

—No les faltes el respeto a los mártires de la patria...

—Mira, Robertico... —pero me interrumpía.

—Pues si a los muertos no les importa, a mí sí. Y a ti te debería importar por el qué dirán de nosotros...

—A mí qué me importa lo que diga nadie. Yo estoy tranquila con mi conciencia.

—¿Cómo puedes decir eso, cómo puedes ni pensar en regresar a Cuba mientras exista allí la misma tiranía, mientras esa gente...?

—Ay, Robertico, esta conversación es absurda... ¿Tú crees que el régimen se va a caer porque yo haga el sacrificio de no ver más nunca a mi madre? Si tu familia estuviera allá tú me entenderías...

Cuando le fallaban todos los argumentos, trataba de seducirme. Por unos días se volvía amable y cariñoso. Me buscaba en la cama y me hacía el amor apasionadamente y hasta con cierta ternura. A veces creo que sólo en el sexo Robertico ha podido expresarme su amor, que es un hombre bueno y que me quiere, aunque no haya sabido hacerme feliz. Otras veces pienso que soy yo la que quiero leer en sus caricias un significado que no tienen.

Cuando al día siguiente él sacaba el tema de nuevo y veía que yo no había cambiado de idea, volvía a su mal humor.

—Mira, Roberto, no he ido a Cuba hasta ahora porque no he

querido hacerlo contra tu voluntad, porque creía que algún día ibas a comprenderme... además, siempre tuve la ilusión de que mi madre pudiera venir, pero ahora que está casi ciega sé que es imposible, que tengo que ir yo. No quiero que pase como con Papi y que se me muera también sin haberla visto. Mira, tu padre también fue a Bahía de Cochinos y él entiende que yo quiera ir...

—No me hables de mi padre...

—¿Por qué no? Tu padre es un hombre muy digno, que se ha esforzado, que ha triunfado... es parte de ese exilio histórico que tiene mucho de que sentirse orgulloso...

—Claro, mi padre es un triunfador, y yo... yo para ti soy un fracasado, ¿no?

—No he dicho eso.

—Pero lo has pensado.

—No, Robertico. Además, eso no es lo que estamos discutiendo.

De pronto se quedó callado mucho rato. Ya el silencio se hacía denso. Me levanté con intención de ir para la cocina. Me detuvo su mano en el hombro. Me viré. Me miró muy fijo a los ojos. No sé si en los suyos había orgullo o miedo, humildad o afán de control, amor u odio. Quizás todo eso y más.

—Prométeme que no vas a regresar a Cuba hasta que Fidel se caiga.

Intenté zafarme y evadir una respuesta, pero insistió:

—Lauri, ¿me lo vas a prometer o no?

—Roberto, no me pidas eso. No puedo... no puedo prometértelo.

Todavía oigo retumbar en la casa el portazo.

Fue la última vez que lo vi.

Ahora yace en un féretro cubierto por una bandera cubana. Johnny se me acerca a preguntarme si quiero un cortadito. Tanta gente a mi alrededor, todos hablando al mismo tiempo, y yo tan sola, tan absolutamente sola. Estoy aquí y no estoy.

Guardias fronterizos de la República Democrática Alemana (RDA) demolieron el viernes partes del muro de Berlín, símbolo desde hace 28 años de la Cortina de Hierro. El Partido Comunista, en el gobierno, dijo que aceptaría la celebración de elecciones libres y la formación de un gobierno democrático de coalición.

Millares de felices alemanes cruzaron a un lado y al otro de la frontera, empujando coches de bebés y abrazando a vecinos del otro lado. Algunos usaron picos y martillos para hacer añicos los pedazos del odiado muro y guardarlos de recuerdo.

El tañido de las campanas se escuchaba como música de fondo, y el pueblo las llamó las campanas de la libertad.

(*El Nuevo Herald* 11 de noviembre 1989: A1)

CAPÍTULO NUEVE
"¡Que se vaya la escoria!"

DESDE HACE UNOS MESES HAN PERMITIDO A LOS QUE SE FUERON DEL PAÍS REGRESAR DE VISITA. Los que huyeron, muchas veces sin atreverse a decir adiós, y cayeron después en el hueco negro del olvido, son ahora parte de "la comunidad en el exterior." La orientación que ha bajado es de ser amables con ellos.

Han pasado veinte años desde que Lauri se fue, y dieciocho desde que partió Ricardo. ¿Vendrán? Cada vez que llega un familiar del exterior, se alborota el barrio entero. Vienen cargados de regalos y de cuentos de todo lo que han alcanzado en el norte. Que si una casa, que si tantos televisores en colores, que si un carro del año, que si la fiesta de quince para la hija, que si vacaciones en tal crucero… Y hasta enseñan las fotos para probarlo. Benito, al que le quitaron la bodega de la esquina, ha contado que tiene cuatro mercados en Hialeah. Se les ve gordos y contentos, y hablan mezclando palabras del inglés con el español. Todos, invariablemente, dicen que extrañan Cuba y que no hay cielo tan azul como el nuestro. Pero se marchan de nuevo…

Maruja vino una tarde muy agitada a contarme que le habían tocado a la puerta.

—Sólo quisiera ver la casa… yo me fui muy pequeño y apenas me acuerdo… —Era el hijo de los antiguos dueños.

Ella se quedó tan sorprendida que lo dejó pasar. El muchacho comenzó a recordar.

—Éste era mi cuarto… Aquí dormían mis padres… En esta habitación murió mi abuelo. —De pronto, se echó a llorar.

—Perdóneme, señora, no pensé que me afectara tanto.

Maruja le ofreció un vaso de agua y hasta le hizo café.

Luego, esa noche, me preguntó súbitamente:

—¿Tú crees que puedan regresar y quitarme la casa?

—No creo, Maruja, pero piensa que esa gente vivía ahí antes de nosotras nacer… Mamá me lo ha contado. Construyeron esa casa con el fruto del trabajo de muchos años.

—Yo también he trabajado muchos años...

—Es cierto... Pero no te preocupes, no van a regresar.

Muchos no tienen intenciones ni de venir de visita.

—Mientras las cosas no cambien, nosotros no podemos ir... —me dijo Ricardo por teléfono hace poco.

Tampoco ha venido Lauri, ni mis compañeros de aula, ni mis antiguos profesores, ni mis tíos, ni mis primos.

—Esa gente no vendrá mientras exista la Revolución —pronosticó Lázaro—. Lo más probable es que se mueran todos sin volver a Cuba... porque la Revolución es irreversible.

—No puedo pensar que nunca más vaya a ver a mis hermanos.

—Tienes que ser realista.

También existe ahora la posibilidad de las visitas a Estados Unidos de personas mayores. Lauri va a invitar a uno de los viejos ahora y el año que viene, al otro. Me insinuó que quizás más adelante yo pudiera ir. Lo haría sólo por verla... Aunque qué va, Lázaro no estaría de acuerdo. Bueno, de todas formas, no creo que me dieran el permiso, por la edad... primero que vayan mis padres, y ya después veremos. Enseguida le dije a Mamá que presentara sus papeles, pero no sé cómo ni por qué, Papá la convenció de que él debe ir primero.

—No estoy bien de salud y no quiero morirme sin volver a ver a mis hijos —argumenta, y se lleva la mano al pecho.

—Yo creo que tú tienes alguna amiguita en Miami... —oí a Lázaro jaraneando en voz baja con él.

¿Y si fuera cierto? ¿Y si aquella mujer con quién engañó a Mamá viviera ahora en Miami y él quisiera ir a verla? Me parecería tan monstruoso que privara a mi madre de ver a sus hijos por una cosa así. Ya el viejo cumplió 75 años... pero se ve bien, y siempre ha sido mujeriego. Lázaro me asegura que fue una broma inocente. Quién sabe... Los hombres siempre se tapan unos a otros. Quisiera preguntarle directamente a Papá, pero no encuentro el momento propicio.

Ya nunca sabré la verdad. Mi padre murió una noche de marzo

frente al televisor de la sala. Mamá se dio cuenta cuando no pudo despertarlo para que se fuera a la cama. Otra vez la funeraria. Otra vez avisar a Ricardo y a Lauri. Otro entierro en el Cementerio de Colón. En esta ocasión no pude llorar. ¿Quién era este hombre que había muerto? ¿Quién era mi padre? ¿En qué creía? ¿A quién amaba? De pronto, cuando lo vi en el ataúd, me pareció un extraño.

Mamá lo aceptó con la misma resignación que tiene para todo. Pedritín, sin embargo, estaba muy afectado. Después del entierro me dio un abrazo muy fuerte. Nunca antes lo había visto llorar así.

∽

Tal como se esperaba, a las pocas horas del retiro de las postas cubanas cientos de elementos constituidos por delincuentes, lumpens, antisociales, vagos y parásitos en su inmensa mayoría se dieron cita en el patio de la Embajada de Perú. Al cabo de 48 horas eran más de tres mil, procedentes fundamentalmente de la Ciudad de La Habana y las provincias occidentales del país. Algunos de estos elementos desafortunadamente llevaron también a familiares e incluso niños.

A juzgar por las vestimentas, los modales y el lenguaje, pocas veces se había reunido tan "selecto" grupo en algún lugar.

Ninguno de ellos era perseguido político ni estaba necesitado del sacrosanto derecho de asilo.

Ellos sin embargo tuvieron como siempre la confianza de que el gobierno Revolucionario hablaba en serio y que ésta era tal vez la oportunidad de emigrar hacia otros sitios más propicios. Como lo ha hecho siempre, Cuba le abría gustosa las puertas a toda la canalla que se ha opuesto al socialismo y a la Revolución.

(*Bohemia* 72:15, 50)

∽

Pocos días después de la muerte del viejo, comenzaron los rumores de que habían quitado la guardia en la Embajada de Perú. En apenas unas horas se formó un gran revuelo en La Habana. Familias enteras que estaban en la calle, sin regresar a su casa a llevarse siquiera un cepillo de dientes, se metieron en la sede diplomática a pedir asilo. Muchos se fueron sin despedirse de su esposa e hijos. En tres o cuatro días, más de 10,000 hombres, mujeres y niños abarrotaban la embajada en Miramar.

—Te apuesto a que mucha de esa gente estaba hace pocos días en la Plaza de la Revolución. No entiendo por qué se van. ¿Para comer mejor, rodar mejores carros, vestirse mejor pero seguir siendo unos infelices como todos esos que han vuelto? Aquí se pasarán dificultades, pero el capitalismo es mucho peor... Además, éste es el país de uno. Nuestro vino es agrio...

—Lázaro, para vivir en Cuba hay que sacrificarse mucho, y no todo el mundo tiene el mismo fervor que usted por la Revolución —le dice Mamá, en uno de los raros momentos en que sale del silencio en que vive sumida desde la muerte de Papá.

La situación está muy tensa. Lázaro, que puede leer la prensa internacional, me comentó que lo de la Embajada ha causado mucho impacto, que se ve como un rechazo a la Revolución.

—Ahora resulta que son héroes, que buscan la libertad, cuando lo que quieren es vivir en la sociedad de consumo, ponerse barrigones como todos esos tipos que han venido de Miami... ¡Héroes! Lo que son es...

Ya no se les dice gusanos a los que se van. Ahora son lumpens, antisociales, maricones, putas, tortilleras, escoria. Algunos regresaron a sus casas de la Embajada a esperar los salvoconductos. Y les pintorretearon las fachadas con malas palabras y les tiraron huevos.

Ayer por la tarde Ernestico llegó a casa indignado:

—Tía Menchu, tú sabes bien que en la Lenin hay gente como Tania y como yo que estamos ahí por nuestras buenas notas, pero la mayoría son hijos de ministros, de viceministros, de los dirigentes, en fin, los hijos de Papá... Hay que ver cómo se visten, los relojes que tienen... Sus padres viajan al exterior. Y ahora son unas fieras hablando en contra de los que se van. Si ellos pueden tener de todo, ¿qué más les da que otros aspiren a una vida mejor?

Hablaba sin parar, caminando de un lado a otro de la saleta.

—¿Te acuerdas de mi amigo Guillermo, que se graduó hace dos años? Lo expulsaron de la universidad. Hace unos días reunieron a los estudiantes en una Asamblea de Profundización de la Conciencia Revolucionaria y lo acusaron de desviaciones ideológicas y políticas de carácter grave. ¿Y tú sabes lo que eran esas desviaciones? Adivina, Tía, a que no adivinas…

—No sé, Ernesto, pero cálmate…

—Pues… ponerse una pitusa con una banderita americana que le mandó su padrino. Y por eso, Tía, los órganos de la Seguridad del Estado lo han señalado como un elemento peligroso para la sociedad y encausable bajo la Ley de Peligrosidad Predelictiva. Tía, y Guillermo era el primer expediente de la Facultad de Letras…

—Bueno, a lo mejor…

—A lo mejor, nada. ¿Y tú sabes cuál fue la otra acusación que le hicieron? A ver, adivina, adivina… No, olvídate, que ni en cien años lo adivinas… ¿Cómo a nadie en su sano juicio se le puede ocurrir que te expulsen de la universidad porque te vieron echando barquitos de papel en una fuente? ¡Barquitos de papel, Tía! Pues le dijeron que era un acto de irresponsabilidad y diversionismo ideológico.

—Cálmate, Ernesto, debe haber una explicación…

—¿Explicación? Tía, Guillermo es hijo de un *guajiro* y de una criada de Santa Clara que en la época del capitalismo ganaba 15 pesos mensuales. Nació en 1959. Guillermo es hijo de la Revolución, y mira, mira lo que le está pasando… No entiendo. No entiendo hasta dónde ha llegado este país.

Y salió de la casa a grandes zancadas.

∽

Aunque en nuestro país no se persigue ni hostiga a los homosexuales, entre los que se alojaron en el patio de la embajada peruana había no pocos de ellos, amén de aficionados al juego y a las drogas que no encuentran aquí fácil oportunidad para sus vicios. La exigencia, la disciplina y el rigor están reñidos con la blanduguería, la delincuencia, la vagancia y el parasitismo. Nuestro pueblo trabajador piensa unánimemente.

¡Que se vayan los vagos! ¡Que se vayan los antisociales! ¡Que se vayan los lumpens! ¡Que se vayan los delincuentes! ¡Que se vaya la escoria!

No se levanta un hombre de madrugada ni se trabaja intensamente durante muchas horas en el surco, en el taller, en los centros de producción y servicios para servir y alimentar parásitos. No se cumple una digna y heroica misión internacionalista, no se derramó nuestra sangre en Cuba y otros rincones del mundo para defender, honrar y prestigiar con nuestra bandera a ese tipo de "cubanos."

(Granma en Bohemia 72:15, 50)

∽

Han dicho que se vaya todo el que quiera. Bueno, te tienen que dar un documento de baja en el trabajo y no sé que otro papel. He oído que para que te permitan emigrar, tienes que declarar que has sido un delincuente, o que eres homosexual o puta, pero yo no puedo creer que sea así. La gente está como loca. Sobre todo los hombres solos. Vienen corriendo a su casa, recogen cuatro cosas, le dan un beso a la madre y se las agencian para llegar hasta el Mariel. También se han ido familias enteras. Se llevan a los niños, hasta de brazos, a los viejos, incluso los perros. Temo que Ernestico haga algún disparate. ¡Después de lo de Tía Flor ya nada me sorprende! Se nos presentó una mañana en casa, muy apurada y nerviosa.

—Mariana… Mariana… Menchu… Tengo que hablar con ustedes. Me voy de Cuba. Ya lo tengo todo arreglado. Esta noche salgo para El Mosquito.

—¡Flor, tú estás loca!

—No, lo he pensando muy bien. Dediqué muchos años a cuidar a

Mamá. Y ahora quiero vivir. Tengo 57 años y…

—Sesenta, Flor —la interrumpió Mamá.

—Bueno, sesenta, da lo mismo… pero me siento joven, y quiero ver mundo, no hacer más colas… tomarme un buen whisky, fumar con boquilla sin que me digan burguesa… leer los libros de Vargas Llosa… o de Cabrera Infante o de quien me dé la gana… coger una guagua o un taxi… caminar por una ciudad con gente bien vestida y bien calzada… hablar en voz alta… ir a un museo… estrenarme un vestido… conocer gente interesante… en fin, vivir…

—¿Y la casa, y las cosas de Mamá?

—Lázaro y Menchu se pueden mudar para allá. Nunca han podido vivir solos…

—Yo no puedo dejar a Mamá sola.

—Pues que se quede Tania con ella… y Pedritín… allá ustedes, pero yo no me voy a quedar en este infierno por cuatro paredes, una vajilla y unos álbumes de fotos viejas. La vida es otra cosa… y en este país no hay vida.

Nos dio un abrazo muy fuerte y sin que pudiéramos reaccionar ya estaba en la puerta de la calle.

—¿Qué vas a hacer cuando llegues?

—Llamaré a Laurita… y después… vivir, mi hermana, vivir.

En la mañana del lunes salieron de Mariel hacia Estados Unidos dos embarcaciones que, procedentes de la Florida, recogieron a 48 elementos antisociales. Se anunciaba que el martes saldrían 11 embarcaciones de la misma procedencia para trasladar a ese país a más de trescientos. ¡Buen ritmo!

Estas embarcaciones vinieron por su propia cuenta y fueron recibidas con toda cortesía. Sus tripulantes solicitaron llevar un grupo de los que fueron huéspedes de la embajada de Perú y a algunos familiares de residentes en Estados Unidos. Fueron plenamente complacidos.

Mientras tanto, el Departamento de Estado yanqui hace frenéticas declaraciones contra estos viajes a Cuba, amenazando con arrestar, confiscar, etc. Ahora empiezan a cosechar los frutos de su política de alentar las salidas ilegales de Cuba, incluido el secuestro de embarcaciones con sus tripulantes como rehenes. Ahora también se han convertido en nuestros guardafronteras. En dos palabras, le hemos retirado la custodia a la península de la Florida.

(*Bohemia* 72:17, 45)

∾

Estamos rodeados de violencia. Hace pocos días hubo un incidente bastante feo. Al parecer se congregó frente a la Sección de Intereses de Estados Unidos un grupo de personas que querían salir del país. No sé cómo empezó pero se caldearon los ánimos y se formó la piñacera. Hasta las mujeres se entraron a carterazos. Me lo contó Lázaro que de casualidad pasaba por allí y con esa curiosidad periodística que tiene para todo, en seguida se acercó.

—Menchu, no me gusta esto… las cosas se están yendo de la mano… Tú sabes que a mí me molesta que la gente se vaya así, en masa… personas que les deben sus carreras a la Revolución, que no son capaces de sacrificarse por el futuro del país… pero yo no creo que esta violencia conduzca a nada.

Dicen que el Presidente Carter ha declarado que aceptará a todos los cubanos que quieran ir para allá. Y, naturalmente, eso ha alborotado más a la gente. Tantos seres queridos que se van… Estamos como hace veinte años que las personas desaparecían sin decir adiós y de pronto te enterabas de que se habían ido. Aquellas ausencias me dejaron tullida emocionalmente. Pensé que nunca más tendría amigos. Pero he hecho nuevos afectos, y ahora, otra vez, el desgarrón. Se ha ido Amelita, mi compañera de trabajo… También el dibujante Iván… un muchacho tan dispuesto… que aprendía todo tan rápido y con tanto entusiasmo. Además, hay noticias de que algunos naufragaron y se ahogaron. Menos mal que Tía Flor ya llamó desde casa de Lauri a decirnos que había llegado bien. Los extraño mucho a todos. Cada día nos quedamos más solos.

Tenemos La Habana. Cuando me duelen demasiado las ausencias, me echo a la calle y camino. Detrás de estas fachadas despintadas de El Vedado, encuentro siempre la belleza arquitectónica de los medios puntos, los enrejados. Otras veces me voy al cementerio, camino entre las tumbas, leo las lápidas... hasta que llego al panteón donde están enterrados Papá y tantos de su familia. Me pongo entonces a recordar aquellos domingos cuando nos reuníamos toda la familia en casa de Otra Mamá y los primos jugábamos a los escondidas, y a tieso tieso... y de pronto las imágenes se quedan sin movimiento, congeladas, como cuando imitábamos a las estatuas. Veo tan claramente la cara de Julio Eduardo... Me acerco después a la tumba de Mama Luya y de mi abuelo. Me quedo sentada largo rato en un banco y pienso tantas cosas... aunque lo que quisiera es, precisamente, no pensar. El parque es otro de mis refugios. Contemplo los árboles con sus centenarios troncos... Inevitablemente, acabo siempre en el mar. Miro al horizonte y me parece una especie de reja que divide en dos las cosas que más amo. Allá, mis hermanos, mis tíos, los sobrinos que no conozco, tantos amigos... Acá, mi madre, Lázaro, mi hija, Pedritín, mis muertos, mi paisaje, mi ciudad, mi país... Y me duele esa línea en el mar que nos separa...

Ayer domingo, por condiciones del tiempo, no salió ninguna embarcación de Mariel hacia Estados Unidos. Para aumentar las condiciones de seguridad, las embarcaciones partirán en flotillas con el fin de auxiliarse y apoyarse mutuamente y, además, con una embarcación militar auxiliar cubana detrás hasta las aproximaciones de la Florida. No habrá transporte más seguro en el mundo que el de la ruta Mariel-Florida.

(*Bohemia* 72:18, 68)

Ernesto entró más descompuesto que nunca. Me preguntó sin preámbulos:

—¿Dónde está Tío Lázaro?

—No sé... Debe estar al llegar.

—Lo necesito urgentemente. Tiene que ayudarme... Le están haciendo un acto de repudio a Guillermo y a su familia. Él dice que no le importa lo que les pase a ellos pero que saque de la casa a su hermanita... Ay, Tía... es horrible... trajeron a los muchachos de las escuelas para que les griten... hasta Tania está allí.

Salí mandada para allá con Ernestico. Casi corrimos las dos cuadras que nos separaban de la casa de su amigo. En efecto, una turba se amontonaba en el portal, en la acera. Muchos eran muchachitos con uniforme escolar.

—¡Lumpen!

—¡Escoria!

—¡Traidores!

—¡Antisociales!

—¡Contrarrevolucionarios!

—¡Cobardes!

—¡Parásitos!

Por fin vi a Tania. Estaba en la parte exterior de la muchedumbre, coreando los insultos. Parecía más asustada que entusiasmada. Me había apresurado en llegar, pero ahora no sabía qué hacer. En eso mi hija me vio y corrió hacia mí.

—Tu abuela está enferma —le mentí, abriéndole mucho los ojos con la esperanza de que se diera cuenta de que era una excusa para sacarla de allí.

Me siguió sin hacer preguntas, la mirada huidiza como la de un animalito acorralado.

—Mamá se siente mal... —le expliqué a Maruja al pasar delante de ella, aunque convencida de que sabría que no era cierto.

Nos fuimos alejando. Ernesto se quedó atrás, intentando desanimar al coro vociferante que lanzaba huevos e insultos contra la casa de su compañero de estudios.

—Ésta es una familia decente… —repetía, sin que nadie le prestara atención. Por fin logré asirlo por un brazo y que regresara con nosotros a la casa. Nadie habló. Cuando llegó Lázaro comimos en absoluto silencio, sin levantar apenas los ojos del plato. Se palpaba entre nosotros una presencia extraña, una complicidad vergonzosa. Cuando terminamos, Ernesto y Lázaro se encerraron en la habitación del fondo. Muy tarde ya, salieron a la calle y no volvieron hasta el amanecer. No pregunté nada, pero por la mañana, en un momento que tuvimos a solas, Ernesto me ha contado que Guillermo y su familia salieron por el traspatio, que él y Lázaro los esperaron en la calle del fondo, y que los llevaron a casa de unos parientes en Bauta, desde donde se irán para el Mariel.

—Si no es por Tío Lázaro, hoy los hubieran matado… Nunca se me olvidará cuando nos dieron a la niña por la cerca… parecía una película, Tía, una pesadilla…

Lázaro no me comentó nada hasta por la noche, antes de dormirnos:

—Le aconsejé a Ernesto que se fuera a estudiar a la Unión Soviética. Voy a tratar de conseguirle una beca.

Pocos meses después lo despedimos en el muelle. No sé quién estaba más afectado, si Mamá o Tania.

—Le hará bien —dijo Armandito, que tiene un alto cargo en la FAR, y no entiende las inquietudes de su hijo.

—No andes desabrigado —le aconsejaba Magaly.

—Otro que se va… —pensaba yo. Pero no dije nada.

∽

Yo diría que ésta es una batalla que se ha librado hoy en defensa de la integridad de nuestra Patria. La sola presencia de ustedes, la sola presencia de ustedes, en esta Plaza es una batalla, y una importante batalla en defensa de la integridad y la seguridad de Cuba; porque lo peligroso es que el enemigo se confunda, lo peligroso es que el enemigo se engañe.

Ya se empieza a trabajar en la elaboración de planes de qué debe hacer el país para sobrevivir y resistir en caso de un bloqueo total, en caso de un bloqueo total, qué tiene que hacer cada uno de nosotros. Y suponiendo que no entren alimentos, que no entre combustible, qué tenemos que hacer para sobrevivir y resistir.

Hablan de bloqueos navales, calculando lo difícil que sería para un país sin petróleo sobrevivir a un bloqueo naval. Y nosotros tenemos que elaborar los planes de qué hacer en esa situación. Por cierto que Regan o Reagan o Rigan, no sé cómo se pronuncia, que es el candidato seguro del Partido Republicano, se ha declarado partidario de hacer bloqueo naval a Cuba. Claro que nada de eso es fácil, debemos advertírselo. Pero nosotros tenemos el deber como revolucionarios, como pueblo realista, de tener una respuesta para cada uno de estos problemas. Pero lo que sí no podrán imaginarse ellos es que Cuba alguna vez se rendirá, porque jamás nos rendiremos. ¡Jamás nos rendiremos!

(Fidel Castro 1 de mayo 1980)

∽

Se han organizado las Milicias de Tropas Territoriales ante el inminente ataque de Estados Unidos. Maruja hace guardia a todas horas. El país está en pie de guerra. Todos hacemos guardia a todas horas. Cuando no hacemos guardia, hacemos cola. ¡Jamás nos rendiremos! Hemos celebrado el XX Aniversario de la Victoria de Girón. La policía detiene a los jóvenes que llevan pitusas con símbolos norteamericanos y proceden a cortárselas. ¡Jamás nos rendiremos! Hay que hacer cola porque llegaron los huevos. Cola para tomar un helado de ajonjolí en Coppelia. Corre a marcar en tal cola porque van a dar aceite. Corre a marcar en la otra porque llegaron los productos cárnicos. Y siempre con la jaba a cuestas, como si fuera una extremidad más. ¡Jamás nos rendiremos!

Mamá se me enfermó. Tenía fiebre alta, una erupción por casi todo el cuerpo, dolor de cabeza y en las piernas, vómitos, y hasta le afectó los ojos. Creía que se me iba a morir. Estaba tan débil. Todo por el agua esa encharcada en el traspatio porque no hemos podido arreglar el desagüe. Es un criadero de mosquitos y ella que sale a tender todos los días… No me gustaba dejarla sola, pero soy del Movimiento de Madres Combatientes por la Educación y debía cumplir con mis deberes de ir a hablar en los círculos sobre higiene. Al menos ya empezaron a fumigar. Una epidemia de dengue se extiende por toda la Isla.

Por fin llevé a Mamá al Policlínico y la doctora me dijo que tenía que ingresarla de inmediato. Ella estaba tranquila pero cada vez se llenaba más de ronchas rosáceas. Estuvimos cuatro o cinco días en el hospital. Le hacían análisis de sangre a diario. Tenía que despertarme muy temprano para coger un turno en la cola del agua caliente. Nos daban unas latas de aceite, con un asa improvisada con percheros, y las llenábamos de agua de una llavecita y luego bañábamos a los pacientes con un jarrito. Estábamos en salas comunes, una llena de camas, y la otra de cunas y mamás, pues lo que más había eran ancianos y niños. A veces me dormía en un sillón porque me rendía el agotamiento.

Compré en la bolsa negra tres gallinas para hacer un buen caldo. Es lo único que la vieja toma con gusto. ¡Pero jamás nos rendiremos!

∽

Compartimos las convicciones del pueblo y albergamos la profunda sospecha que las plagas que han azotado nuestro país y especialmente el dengue hemorrágico pueden haber sido introducidas en nuestro país por la CIA. Emplazamos al gobierno de Estados Unidos a que defina su política en este terreno, a que diga si la CIA está autorizada de nuevo o no a organizar atentados a los dirigentes de la Revolución y a utilizar plagas contra nuestras plantas, nuestros animales y nuestra población.

(Fidel Castro 26 de julio 1981)

∽

Después de que Tía Flor se fue, Lázaro y yo nos mudamos para su casa en La Sierra. Mamá se quedó con Pedritín en El Vedado hasta que mi hermano le metió en la casa a una "novia"... No es mala muchacha, pero la vieja se sentía muy incómoda. De todos modos, cuando se enfermó la traje para acá para poder cuidarla y ya hemos decidido que se quede con nosotros. Tania siguió allá porque le queda más cerca de la universidad. Quién iba a decir que le iba a dar por la ciencia. Estudia bioquímica y se pasa la vida detrás de un microscopio. A veces me preocupo porque es tan callada... Casi no sale. Su única otra pasión es el ballet. Apenas tiene amigos, con excepción de su primo Ernesto que viene todos los veranos. Entonces salen mucho y se pasan las horas conversando. Aunque era una niña, Tania recuerda con nostalgia el tiempo que pasamos en la Unión Soviética. Se ha conseguido una beca para hacer allá estudios de posgrado. La idea de separarme de ella me angustia... pero al menos tengo la tranquilidad de que Ernestico está allá.

Pedritín se pasaba la vida viajando a Nicaragua. Lázaro también viajaba de vez en cuando. Por un tiempo la situación económica mejoró un poco y se podían comprar bastantes cosas en los mercados paralelos. La gente se entretenía oyendo Radio Martí. Mamá se aficionó a las novelas. Yo a veces oía los programas de música. También me gustaba enterarme de lo que pasa en el mundo.

Pero las cosas se pusieron malas otra vez y han lanzado una campaña de rectificación de errores y tendencias negativas. Raúl ha dicho que ahora es que vamos de verdad a empezar a construir el socialismo y el comunismo. Mamá enseguida comentó:

—¿Y se puede saber qué es lo que han estado haciendo hasta ahora?

Lázaro, sin embargo, le contestó muy serio:

—Mariana, el problema de Cuba es que no han aplicado de veras los principios marxistas... pero me temo que ahora tampoco lo van a hacer.

—Mire, Lázaro, con marxismo o sin marxismo, pero ya han pasado casi treinta años... y ahora hablan de más austeridad y de que nos preparemos para alimentarnos con hierbas...

En efecto, han suspendido las meriendas en las oficinas, los comedores gratuitos para los obreros, han racionado otra vez la leche y el arroz, y van a aumentar la tarifa de la guagua.

∽

A la hora de medir las medidas, no podemos perder de vista el papel que corresponde a cada revolucionario en su estricto cumplimiento. El precio del pasaje del transporte urbano ha aumentado a diez centavos. ¿Basta con esa disposición estatal? No, la vida dice que no. Todavía hay ciudadanos que burlan la ley y no pagan su pasaje en el ómnibus. Junto a la medida de aumentar el precio, tiene que existir la decisión de todos de impedir la deshonesta actuación de los infractores, porque dañan la economía nacional, porque crean una inadmisible imagen de desorden.

(*Bohemia* 79:2, 20)

∽

¡Están pasando tantas cosas! Comenzaron a regresar los soldados que quedaban en Angola. En la Unión Soviética hay muchos cambios.

—Eso se viene abajo — repite Lázaro, con una tristeza tan honda que se le filtra en la voz.

Detuvieron al General Arnaldo Ochoa, a los gemelos de la Guardia del Ministerio del Interior y a una pila de gente más. Lázaro no lo podía creer.

—¡Si Ochoa es un héroe, si parece que fue ayer que lo estaban condecorando! Un hombre valiente… no como Tortoló que nos hizo quedar tan mal cuando lo de Granada.

Los acusaron de corrupción y mal uso de recursos económicos. Parece que había algo de drogas por el medio. Lázaro insiste en que Ochoa no se involucraría en algo así.

—Cuando el río suena… —comenta mi madre.

Vivimos el juicio como en vilo. El fiscal pedía la pena de muerte para Ochoa y otros acusados. En una semana dictaron la sentencia. Ochoa, de la Guardia y dos más serían fusilados. A los otros los condenaron a 15 y 30 años de prisión.

Lázaro estaba indignado.

—Yo conozco a Ochoa, Menchu. Lo entrevisté varias veces. Es una persona fiel… un luchador… Esto no puede ser. ¿Cómo es posible que lo vayan a fusilar?

Pero la mayoría apoyaba la medida.

—Es la única forma de dar un escarmiento. Para que aprendan…

Cuando leí en Granma que ya los habían matado sentí un escalofrío. Me pareció que la casa se oscurecía de pronto, como si una gigantesca ave negra se hubiera posado sobre nosotros.

Mamá me preguntó qué día era.

—13 de julio.

—Hoy hace 30 años que se fue Lauri.

—Yo también me acordé, vieja.

En la noche Lázaro llegó con una botella de ron y se sentó en el sillón del patio de atrás. Se puso a tomar. Me le acerqué pero me rogó que lo dejara solo. Cuando vino a acostarse era ya de madrugada y había vaciado la botella. Nunca había visto así a mi marido.

Tres días después murió el poeta Nicolás Guillén.

—Siempre pasa —observó mi madre—. ¿No se acuerdan cuando en medio de lo del Mariel se suicidó Haydée Santamaría? Hay momentos en que es mejor morirse…

—¡Qué cosas dices, vieja! —le contestó Pedritín—. Si Guillén siempre fue comunista… comprometido con la Revolución como pocos…

—Uno nunca sabe cuando un hombre empieza a sentir vergüenza.

༄

Van a fusilar
a un hombre que tiene los brazos atados.
Hay cuatro soldados
para disparar.
Son cuatro soldados
callados,

que están amarrados,
lo mismo que el hombre amarrado que van
a matar.
—¿Puedes escapar?
—¡No puedo correr!
—¡Ya van a tirar!
—¿Qué vamos a hacer?
—Quizás los rifles no estén cargados...
—¡Seis balas tienen de fiero plomo!
—¡Quizás no tiren esos soldados!
—¡Eres un tonto de tomo y lomo!
Tiraron.
(¿Cómo fue que pudieron tirar?)
Mataron.
(¿Cómo fue que pudieron matar?)
Eran cuatro soldados
callados,
y les hizo una seña, bajando su sable,
un señor oficial;
eran cuatro soldados
atados,
lo mismo que el hombre que fueron
los cuatro a matar.

(Guillén 13–14)

∽

Les han exigido a los diez mil estudiantes que estaban en los países socialistas que paguen sus matrículas en dólares. Ya Ernesto se había graduado y seguía tomando cursos. A Tania le faltaban sólo unas asignaturas pero le adelantaron los exámenes para que pudiera terminar. Llegó sola.

—Ernesto no va volver —nos anunció cuando fuimos a buscarla.

Me imagino que sus padres lo sabían, porque no fueron al aeropuerto. A Lázaro tampoco le sorprendió.

—Es mejor para él.

Llamaron de Miami. Robertico tuvo un accidente y se mató. Mi pobre hermana. Viuda, ¡tan joven! Ni siquiera se pudo poner al teléfono. Hablamos con su hijo Pedro Pablo. ¡Cómo quisiera poder abrazarla...! Estos son los momentos en que la separación se hace más dolorosa.

Por Radio Rebelde leyeron un cable sobre la caída del muro de Berlín en tono luctuoso y alarmante, pero otros comentaron que la noticia había sido distorsionada por la prensa occidental y que lo que sucedía es que el socialismo estaba rectificando errores y fortaleciéndose. Quizás Lázaro tenga más información, pero no me gusta preguntarle mucho y echarle más leña al fuego. Bastante huraño está desde lo de Ochoa.

Hoy es 7 de diciembre, aniversario de la caída de Maceo, fecha señalada para recordar a todos los mártires de la patria. Han dedicado la ocasión para honrar a los muertos de la guerra de Angola. Fidel utilizó más tiempo de su discurso a criticar el camino emprendido por el bloque socialista, especialmente la Unión Soviética, que a hablar de los héroes de Angola.

Vi a Maruja morderse los labios.

—He estado esperando todos estos años para que me devuelvan el cadáver de mi hijo, un mulatico de Morón que se fue a morir a Angola pare defender la revolución. Mi único hijo, Menchu. Y en definitiva, ¿qué? A veces creo que a nadie le importa.

No supe qué contestarle.

CAPÍTULO DÍEZ
"Con el alma enlutada y sombría"

LO LLEVO DENTRO DE MÍ. Me retumba en los oídos, en la cabeza. Me despierta por las noches. Me asalta en medio de la calle. El disparo. Ese sonido —¿cómo se describe, Dios mío, un sonido?— sorpresivo, tan breve, tan de golpe, y tan definitivo. Ni puedo olvidar su rostro, como lo vi por última vez a través de la puerta de cristal, como lo vi en el instante preciso en que se llevó la pistola a la sien y disparó, y el rostro se contrajo y... No puedo más. Tengo que ir al baño y vomitar. Quiero cerrar los ojos para no ver, y es como si el interior de mis párpados estuviera teñido de rojo. Todo lo veo rojo, como el rojo de aquella mancha de sangre que nunca se ha borrado del todo. Venir a suicidarse al patio de mi casa me parece el mayor de los egoísmos, la burla final. Voy hasta el escaparate y saco los álbumes de la boda, de cuando los niños eran chiquitos, de los viajes... intento recordar cuando hacíamos el amor, trato de verlo en los momentos felices, porque los hubo, tuvo que haberlos, ¿verdad? y por más que quiera, siempre, inevitablemente, el rostro que me sonríe desde la foto y el recuerdo, se torna en la mueca última, en la faz contraída de ese último instante antes de que se volara la tapa de los sesos. Es una frase tan manida... volarse la tapa de los sesos. Nunca antes la entendí. Pero eso fue, en efecto, lo que sucedió... Creo que voy a vomitar de nuevo... En vez, quisiera poder llorar. Qué raro, no he derramado una lágrima. A veces, es como si estuviera anestesiada. Hasta que siento de nuevo el disparo. Creo que voy a enloquecer. Todo lo veo rojo, con los ojos abiertos, con los ojos cerrados. Rojo. Un rojo que se disuelve en una luz cegadora tras la cual adivino los tejados de La Habana. Pero no los alcanzo a ver. Oigo el disparo otra vez. Me retumba en los oídos, en la cabeza. Un sonido seco. Lo llevo dentro de mí. Definitivo, como la muerte.

Me despierto siempre sudando y sin respiración. Tardo varios minutos en darme cuenta de que estoy en mi cama, en Miami. Sí, el otro lado del lecho está vacío. Sí, mi marido está muerto. No, no se voló la tapa de los sesos. Murió de un infarto masivo a los 52 años. Encontraron su automóvil hecho un acordeón contra un árbol y a Robertico desplomado sobre el timón. ¿Por qué me asedia esta pesadilla? No se suicidó, no se suicidó, me repito a mí misma. ¿O sí? ¿Por qué este sentimiento de culpa, como si yo lo hubiera matado? Trato de entender. Ya yo no estaba enamorada de él. Es más, a veces hasta había pensado en algún momento en divorciarme. Y otras… confiésalo, Laura, otras, cuando lo veía durmiendo a mi lado, deseaba que se muriera. Pero nadie se muere porque otro lo desee. ¡Hace rato que Fidel Castro estuviera bajo tierra! Y, sin embargo, yo quería a mi marido, tenía que quererlo. ¿Por qué, si no, me había quedado con él y había renunciado por tantos años a visitar a mi familia en Cuba?

Durante meses después de la muerte de Robertico, tenía esa horrible pesadilla recurrentemente. Aunque no pude haber recibido más apoyo de mi familia y de mis amigos, me sentía atormentada. Mis hijos se portaron como dos hombres. Fueron ellos los que resolvieron todos los trámites. Y Bobby Junior se convirtió de golpe en otro muchacho. Hasta se matriculó en algunos cursos en la universidad. Hablaba de irse fuera a estudiar como habían hecho su tío y su hermano.

—Si Mami está bien y la puedo dejar sola… —comentaba, como si de pronto se hubieran invertido los papeles y fuera él quien debiera cuidarme a mí. Casi un año después, por poco lo tengo que empujar por la puerta para que se fuera a Gainesville.

—Vete tranquilo, hijo, que yo estoy bien…

Le mentía. No era cierto que estuviera bien. Ni las visitas al psiquiatra ni las pastillas que tomaba me habían aliviado la depresión. Todos se lo achacaban al dolor de perder a Robertico, pero más que sufrir por su ausencia, me sentía culpable. Y, sobre todo, estaba brava con él. Se había ido sin que hubiéramos resuelto el problema que nos había ido separando todos estos años. Lo último que me había pedido era que no fuera a Cuba. Y aunque nada le había prometido, me sentía profundamente afectada por esa discusión. Era como si aún después de muerto Robertico me dominara, me manipulara. Quizás lo peor que hice fue no contárselo a nadie. Creo que ni con el psiquiatra fui del todo sincera. Era una forma de engañarme a mí misma.

Fue mi suegro quien más me ayudó. Olga y él me invitaban a menudo a comer, al cine.

—Tienes que salir más —insistían. Roberto me llamaba todos los días. Y con frecuencia me llevaba a almorzar o pasaba por casa. Compartíamos un café o un scotch, según la hora. Hablábamos de los muchachos, de Johnny, de Cuba. Pero cuando intentaba hablar de la muerte de Robertico o de mi estado de ánimo, yo levantaba la barrera.

—No debe haber dolor peor que perder un hijo, Roberto. Yo sé que usted también sufre… No se preocupe por mí.

Hasta un día que mi suegro, después de apurar de un solo trago el scotch que le había servido, me dijo a quemarropa:

—Lauri, tenemos que hablar. Te conozco desde que eras una adolescente. Has sido más que una hija para mí… has sido una hija buena. La tragedia de Cuba nos ha afectado a todos. Si alguien alguna vez nos hubiera dicho que íbamos a pasar las cosas tan absurdas que hemos vivido, no lo hubiéramos creído. Otros han sufrido más que nosotros. Han tenido familiares fusilados o presos por largos años. O han muerto en el mar. Pero cada cubano tiene su cuota de dolor, su dilema íntimo. Lo peor ha sido la separación de la familia. Yo dejé en Cuba a mis dos hermanas que sé que nunca más veré. Pero ellas y yo éramos adultos. Tú eras una niña cuando te casaste con mi hijo y te enfrentaste a una vida que no fue nada fácil. Yo te he visto luchar por salir adelante en los trabajos, por estudiar, por aconsejar a tus hijos, por forjar un hogar, adornando el árbol de Navidad, sentándonos todos a la mesa, celebrándonos los cumpleaños, sacando fotos, cuidando a Adela hasta que murió. Y eso que tenías el corazón partido en dos, que tenías a tus padres, a dos de tus hermanos, incluso a tu hermana gemela, del lado de allá. Robertico te quería y era un buen hombre. Pero no lo sabía expresar. Además, nunca se adaptó. Nunca se resignó a perder a Cuba. Tú has sufrido por la ausencia de tu familia, pero supiste construir tu vida y la de tus hijos aquí. Él no. Quizás debió dejarte hace muchos años y dedicarse sólo a luchar por Cuba, pero no lo hizo. Tampoco supo dejar la lucha por Cuba para darte a ti y a sus hijos lo que necesitaban de él. Desde que murió muchas veces me he sentido culpable de no haber hablado con él estas cosas, pero quizás antes no las veía tan claramente. Y posiblemente tampoco me hubiera hecho caso. Sí, yo he sufrido su muerte y, no sé por qué… —y aquí la voz se le quebró— no se me aparta de la mente su carita a los siete años, sin dientes, y lo orgulloso que estaba cuando aprendió a montar en bicicleta sin rueditas… Lauri, mijita, Robertico fue un hombre atormentado, una de las tantas víctimas anónimas de este drama, pero tú eres una de las heroínas y tienes que seguir adelante… O me decepcionarías mucho. Ya mi hijo está en paz. Nunca tuvo paz Robertico… Yo quisiera vivir para trasladar algún día sus restos a Cuba… Pero tú tienes que salir de ese estado de ánimo… no puedes seguir así…

—Ay, Roberto, no me diga eso…

—Tengo que decírtelo. Te hablo como un padre a una hija. Tú siempre has vivido para los demás. Quiérete a ti misma ahora, Lauri. Viaja. Múdate de casa. O decórala. Haz alguna cosa que siempre hayas querido hacer. Escribe. Siembra el jardín. Vive, Lauri, vive. Que eres todavía joven… y muy bonita y muy buena, y te lo mereces. Mereces ser feliz. Porque tú nunca has sido feliz, ¿verdad?

Por primera vez desde el accidente lloré. Lloré largamente mientras Roberto me abrazaba, y con ternura de padre y de madre a la vez, me pasaba la mano por la espalda.

—Vamos, mijita, llora, que te hace falta llorar… pero después tienes que prometerme que me vas a hacer caso.

Querida Lauri,

¡Qué gran placer fue verte! Espero que para ti el viaje haya sido también una experiencia grata. Aquella muchachita que recordaba de nuestros años de estudiantes se ha convertido en toda una mujer: bonita, inteligente, simpática.

He pensado mucho en ti desde la tarde de nuestro almuerzo. Me encantaría verte de nuevo. A veces viajo a América Latina y podría hacer escala en Miami. Déjame saber si te agrada la idea. Y, naturalmente, si vienes a Nueva York, no dejes de avisarme.

Te mando un fuerte abrazo y un gran beso.

Siempre,
Gastón

∽

Al recibirla, había leído esta nota una sola vez y la había guardado en el fondo de una gaveta.

Gastón y yo habíamos sido compañeros en la escuela desde niños. A los dos nos gustaba escribir, y en el Bachillerato habíamos trabajado juntos en el periódico del colegio. En el exilio seguimos en contacto, pero hacía varios años que no nos veíamos. Apenas unas semanas después de la muerte de Robertico, tuve que viajar a Nueva York, donde él vivía, a una conferencia sobre el español en Estados Unidos, donde nos reencontramos. Me invitó a almorzar. No sé cómo sucedió pero acabamos en la cama. Fue muy tierno conmigo y al despedirnos me dijo:

—Cuando la muerte se nos acerca demasiado tenemos que celebrar que estamos vivos. Es un instinto natural. No te sientas culpable. En todo caso, he sido yo quien me he aprovechado de la situación, porque creo que desde niños he estado enamorado de ti…

Había evadido desde entonces el recuerdo de aquella tarde pero ahora, rotos esos muros que yo misma había construido, releí la nota que me había escrito Gastón y lo llamé.

—Precisamente dentro de dos semanas tengo que hacer escala en Miami de paso a Buenos Aires. Lo arreglaré para quedarme una noche, así podemos comer juntos… Te llamo en cuanto sepa la fecha exacta —me dijo.

Durante el próximo año Gastón se las arregló para pasar por Miami una docena de veces. Comíamos siempre en el mismo restaurante francés en Coral Gables y luego íbamos para su hotel. Creo que aprendí a conocer mi propia sexualidad mejor en esas noches con él que en todos los años de matrimonio... Me sentía sin barreras... Podía confesarle mis fantasías... y hasta convertirlas en realidad, como cuando nos bañamos en champán... Nunca me hubiera atrevido con Robertico. Gastón era un hombre de mundo, que había viajado mucho. Se había casado tres veces. No le había sido fiel a ninguna de sus esposas.

—Es que te buscaba a ti —me decía.

Lo menos que yo hubiera querido era enredarme con un hombre mujeriego. Entendí entonces eso de que las cosas a veces pasan sin uno darse cuenta. Sabía, sin embargo, que yo no estaba enamorada de Gastón. No sentía celos de lo que pudiera estar haciendo cuando no estábamos juntos y si me contaba de algunas de las experiencias sexuales que había tenido, lejos de sufrir, me excitaba. Pero la ilusión de verlo, sus galanterías y nuestra relación sexual me hacían bien. Lo sabía incapaz de hacerme daño. El que no viviera en la misma ciudad era también una ventaja. No quería que la cosa se complicara demasiado. El día que me habló de que nos casáramos, opté de inmediato por ser sincera.

—Gastón... me haces mucho bien... pero yo no quiero casarme... al menos, no por ahora, ni contigo, ni con nadie...

—Yo creo que tú no me quieres, Lauri.

—No digas eso.

—No me quieres de la misma forma que yo a ti.

—Quizás...

Y comenzó a venir con menos frecuencia, hasta que dejó de hacer escala en Miami.

Un llamado para efectuar en La Habana un encuentro con representantes de "todos los segmentos que componen el pueblo cubano" fue hecho desde esa capital el pasado jueves por Gustavo Arcos Bergnes, Secretario General del

Comité Cubano Pro Derechos Humanos.

"Efectuemos de manera civilizada, honesta y respetuosa, la próxima conferencia de cubanos en Cuba, invitándose a todas las representaciones de las distintas corrientes de opinión que están dentro y fuera de Cuba" exhortó Arcos en un documento leído por teléfono y que fue grabado en Miami por activistas a favor de los derechos humanos.

Rechazo al diálogo pero respeto a la postura de los "luchadores por la libertad de Cuba" fue el acuerdo de 53 organizaciones de exiliados después de discutir sobre la controversia suscitada por la convocatoria de Gustavo Arcos Bergnes a un encuentro con el gobierno cubano.

"El monólogo con el dictador es imposible" agrega el documento emitido por la Gran Cumbre Patriótica, que agrupa a las organizaciones.

Ya con anterioridad, en diciembre de 1989, dirigentes del Comité Cubano Pro Derechos Humanos en la Isla dirigieron un documento similar a la Asamblea Nacional del Poder Popular para solicitar un diálogo nacional. Con igual propósito Arcos escribió una carta a Castro. No hubo respuesta en ninguno de los dos casos.

(*El Nuevo Herald* 8–15 de junio 1990)

❧

Esa espera de tantos meses, llena de ilusión y temores, ese preguntarse de continuo si sería niña o niño —los padres, pese a los adelantos modernos, optaron por no saber de antemano—, ese escoger coches y pañales, ese anticipar en qué fecha nacería, a quién se parecería... y de pronto, este bultico que traen las enfermeras, de donde asoma una carita redonda, y el corazón me da un vuelco y es como una oleada de amor que derriba todas las paredes e inunda el corazón y llega cálida hasta los ojos que se desbordan de lágrimas —lágrimas buenas, de gratitud, amor y de asombro ante el milagro de la vida.

Tyler nació el 31 de diciembre de 1992. No se me hace raro ser abuela; pero no puedo creer que Pedro Pablo sea padre... ¡Si me parece que fue ayer que estaba viendo *The Millionaire* con Johnny en aquel apartamentico de Pastorita cuando me puse de parto!

Como todo en el exilio, hasta los momentos más felices tienen un sabor amargo. Porque nos duelen los cubanos que mueren fuera de la Patria, pero también los que nacen ¿Cómo sembrar en esta criatura el amor a Cuba? ¿Cómo asegurarme de que aprenda español cuando tiene madre americana y vivirá rodeado de inglés? Si me costó tanto trabajo con mis hijos, ¿cómo será con los nietos? Comprendo que éste es un gran país y le estoy agradecida… pero me duele que mis hijos y nietos no sean cubanos… ¿Qué son? Porque tampoco Pedro Pablo y Bobby Jr. son americanos… aunque hayan jurado en la escuela otra bandera, aunque hablen el inglés sin acento, aunque Cuba para ellos exista sólo en la imaginación.

Susan me pone en los brazos a su hijo Tyler, mi primer nieto. Pienso en mi madre, en Mama Luya, y también en Adela. Y le canto muy bajito:

Señora Santa Ana,
¿por qué llora el niño?
por una manzana
que se le ha perdido
Yo te daré una,
yo te daré dos,
una para el niño,
y otra para vos.
Yo no quiero una,
yo no quiero dos,
yo quiero la mía,
que se me perdió.

෨෨

Miles de cubanos que gritaban consignas antigubernamentales se enfrentaron el viernes con piedras y palos a la policía a lo largo del Malecón habanero, informaron desde la Isla agencias de prensa, disidentes y fuentes diplomáticas.

Según las fuentes, de 20,000 a 30,000 cubanos se habían congregado a lo largo de cuatro kilómetros del Malecón antes de que estallaran los incidentes, aparentemente atraídos por rumores de que una flotilla había partido de Estados Unidos para recoger a quien quisiera irse de Cuba.

Horas después de los disturbios, el gobernante cubano Fidel Castro dijo que podría permitir otro Mariel si Estados Unidos prometía no castigar a quienes huían en embarcaciones de la Isla.

Durante lo que constituye uno de los incidentes más graves ocurridos durante el gobierno de Fidel Castro, miles de manifestantes atacaron varias tiendas especiales para turistas extranjeros y un hotel situado cerca de la entrada de la bahía de La Habana. La policía abrió fuego y dejó varios heridos.

Centenares de personas descendieron por las calles Galiano y Neptuno, rompiendo los cristales de las tiendas y coreando: "¡Libertad! ¡Libertad!"

Rafael Dausá, vocero de la sección de Intereses de Cuba en Washington, D.C. negó rotundamente que hubiera ocurrido ningún incidente.

"La Habana está en completa calma" subrayó. "Eso es totalmente falso."

(*El Nuevo Herald* 6 de agosto 1994: A1)

∽

Por mucho que trato de desentenderme, el problema me obsesiona. Pienso que el síndrome de la huida tiene un móvil mucho más profundo que el miedo a la represión. Los cubanos no tienen otro interés que su salvación personal y la de sus familiares porque el concepto de nación ha desaparecido. La Revolución siempre ha querido ser sinónimo de Cuba. Castro es la Patria. Pero esa Revolución ha fracasado. El futuro que prometía ha llegado y es un desastre espantoso. Las cosas nunca mejoran sino que empeoran. El comunismo se derrumbó. Ya no hay coartada ideológica. La única oferta es "socialismo o muerte." Y es mil veces preferible arriesgarse a morir en busca del "sueño americano" que en la lucha por una nación que no da a veces ni siquiera una bicicleta, ni un plato de comida caliente, ni una esperanza.

Los cubanos que huyen de Cuba no quieren volver jamás. No sueñan con llevar al país la democracia, la libertad, una economía de libre mercado. No pueden identificarse con un proyecto nacional porque para ellos Cuba no empezó cuando el Padre Varela nos enseñó a pensar, sino cuando Castro se alzó en la Sierra Maestra. No hay una visión de continuidad, un concepto de nación que vaya más allá, en tiempo y en espacio, de la Revolución. El único camino es la balsa. Hay que escapar a toda costa de un país cuyo primer mandatario ha amenazado con hundirlo en el mar.

¿Y el exilio? ¿Ha logrado la nostalgia y la distancia distorsionar nuestra visión de Cuba? Quizás la geografía también nos llena de brumas la historia. Nos falta la raíz, la tierra, el paisaje. Hemos idealizado el pasado, y no conocemos a ciencia cierta el presente. ¿Cómo, entonces, construir el futuro? Aún los que han venido en los últimos años, ante la aceleración de los acontecimientos, pierden el contacto con la realidad del país.

Nadie sabe cómo terminará la crisis actual. Todos los caminos parecen cerrados. Todas las soluciones se hacen difíciles. Cuba, como nación, anda a la deriva. Y como los desesperados balseros, puede perecer ahogada o ser carnada para los tiburones.

Hay noches que me las paso en vela pensando en estas cosas.

Sobre el hoyo número 17 del terreno de golf de la que era la base militar más tranquila de Estados Unidos en el mundo, un grupo de balseros descamisados jugaban béisbol a mano limpia para matar el tiempo que pasa sin noticias sobre lo que va a ocurrir con su destino.

Aquí no hay gente de un solo sector o color o de una sola posición social o política; esto es más bien un microcosmos con cubanos de todos los rincones sociales y militancias, hombres y mujeres, vagos y trabajadores, y, sobre todo, jóvenes que protestan en coro y manotean cuando alguien se atreve a preguntar si son refugiados económicos.

"Ni aunque nos dieran jamón, que hace 30 años que el pueblo no lo ve, volveríamos."

La mayoría de ellos comparten la misma carpa y dos enemigos. Uno viejo, que es Fidel Castro, por supuesto, y el nuevo, que es el presidente Bill Clinton, a quien culpan de su precaria situación.

(*El Nuevo Herald* 12 de septiembre 1994: A1)

∽

Todos los días escucho por radio la lista de los balseros recogidos en alta mar. Es absurdo pensar que mi familia vaya a venir así, y, sin embargo, en cada cubano que llega los abrazo a ellos.

El periódico donde en los últimos años he publicado algunos artículos me llama sorpresivamente. Mandan un equipo a la base de Guantánamo para hacer un reportaje sobre los refugiados, y a última hora una de las reporteras se enfermó. Me ofrecen su puesto. Enseguida digo que sí y corro a comprar rollos para la cámara.

Jueves, 20 de octubre, 4:45 a.m. Los colegas llegan a mi casa. Hago café cubano. Partimos para el aeropuerto de Ft. Lauderdale.

El avión, de doce pasajeros, de la aerolínea Fandango, es de dos motores. Antes de irnos nos dan *coffee* y *doughnuts.* Hace un frío atroz durante el vuelo. Muchas nubes. Parece nieve. Abajo, la inmensidad del mar. Pienso en los balseros. Paramos en Exuma a echar gasolina. Queda hora y media de viaje. Confirmo mentalmente que he traído todo lo necesario para trabajar. Grabadora, cámara, libreta, pluma. Repaso mis notas, los lugares que deseo ver, las preguntas que quiero hacer. No pienso en que regreso a Cuba. Voy a una base norteamericana. Y, sin embargo, el recuerdo de mi salida de la Isla hace más de 35 años me punza. Como tantas veces a través de estos años, veo mi cuarto de niña, tal como lo dejé por última vez, con el libro de geografía de Cuba y la pamela de lazos rosados sobre la cama, símbolos de la patria y de un estilo de vida gentil que dejaba atrás.

De pronto, me avisan. "Mira, a la derecha, ya se ve... ya se ve...". Al principio, no distingo nada. Pocos segundos después, entre nubes, se perfila claramente Maisí. Una multitud de emociones me invade. Por más de tres décadas he soñado con este país. Su presencia ha presidido mi vida, mis desvelos, mis rabias, mis conflictos más íntimos. A veces, me he preguntado si Cuba existía realmente o si era sólo una idea, un mito. Y aquí está ahora, frente a mis ojos. La Isla. Pienso en tantos seres queridos con los que hubiera querido compartir este momento. Sobre todo, pienso que Mama Luya y mi padre reposan bajo esta tierra, pienso que mi madre y mis hermanos respiran bajo este cielo. No saben que estoy aquí, tan cerca de ellos, y tan lejos. ¿Sentirán de algún modo mi presencia? ¿Les llevará la brisa las ondas de mi pensamiento?

A medida que el avión se acerca, se hace más claro el contorno de las montañas, el litoral de la provincia oriental. Me parece que Cuba me abraza. Saco foto tras foto. Fluyen al fin las lágrimas que trato inútilmente de contener. No puedo explicar lo que siento. Ya se ve nítidamente la bahía. Como en los momentos de dicha más extrema, pienso que desearía morirme.

El avión toca tierra cubana. Nos llevan al *ferry*. No puedo describir el azul de esta agua, de este cielo. Si fuera pintora... ¿Cómo es posible que a mi alrededor todos permanezcan ajenos a este milagro que vivo? Estoy en Cuba.

Nos vamos acercando a la base. Diviso la bandera norteamericana. Comprendo mejor que nunca el dolor del poeta cubano que regresó hace un siglo de distante ribera con el alma enlutada y sombría, para encontrar una bandera que no era la suya.

Lo primero que vemos es la salida de medio millar de haitianos que regresan a su país. Antes de embarcarlos, les quitan el negro brazalete de refugiados. Con chancletas y mal vestidos, van con sus bultos a cuesta, sus niños, y una gran incertidumbre reflejada en los rostros. El Capitán nos contó que rezan y cantan mucho. No es un regreso jubiloso pero es un regreso. ¿Cuándo nos tocará a los cubanos?

Por fin, llegamos a los campamentos. Vemos la escuela, la clínica, hasta una improvisada galería de arte. Me cuentan que tienen un alcalde, un intérprete. Algunos se reúnen para estudiar inglés; otros, para leer la biblia. Todos tienen algo que decir. Quieren que el mundo sepa que es una emigración buena, que hay muchos profesionales, que son refugiados políticos, no económicos. Se ven limpios. Se expresan bien. Son respetuosos. Quieren mandar recados a sus parientes. Quieren que transmitamos al resto del mundo sus historias de valor y frustración. También no preguntan qué creemos que va a pasar con ellos, si los dejarán por fin entrar a los Estados Unidos.

En una improvisada cuna de madera, llora una criatura. Pregunto su nombre.

—No tiene.

Me sorprendo.

—Mi esposo —nos informa la madre— dice que no le va a poner nombre hasta que salga de aquí el último cubano.

La mujer carga a su hijita y la mece. La leche le ha manchado la blusa alrededor de los pezones. Me confía en voz baja:

—Yo le digo Consuelito, porque si no fuera por ella...

Pienso en mi nieto. ¡Tiene tanto! Trato de animarla:

—Usted verá como salen de aquí pronto...

Y escondo el rostro tras la cámara para que no me vea llorar.

Tarde en la noche, después de que los balseros se han lanzado al mar, el mundo que ven parpadear detrás de ellos en la distancia cambia para siempre.

Los vecinos que los han visto zarpar entran a las casas de los que se van, robando todo lo que pueden: televisores, camas, sofás, refrigeradores.

El gobierno entra en acción sólo después, informado por vecinos vigilantes que consideran un deber reportar la ausencia de los balseros. Las autoridades ponen un sello de papel en la puerta, reclamando la casa como propiedad del estado.

Y las familias que quedan detrás caen en un nuevo laberinto de pesadillas: innumerables noches de insomnio, preguntándose si sus hijos o esposos han sobrevivido, días enteros tratando de lidiar con la realidad de haber perdido a sus familiares, con menos dinero para comprar las cosas necesarias, menos comida en las tiendas del gobierno, menos esperanzas para ayudarlos a sobrevivir.

"¿Cuántos matrimonios habrán quedado destruidos?" se pregunta Mayda, cuyo esposo Miguel se fue en un bote improvisado el miércoles. "¿Y cuántas esposas más se tendrán que quedar solas antes de que esto cambie?"

(*El Nuevo Herald* 13 de septiembre 1994: A1 y A6)

∽

Después de la muerte de Robertico las organizaciones políticas a las que él pertenecía comenzaron a invitarme a sus actos. Querían ser amables, honrar su memoria, y que yo lo representara como su viuda. Pronto me di cuenta de que querían una figura decorativa, que no tenían la menor intención de escuchar nada de lo que yo dijera. Y la sugerencia siquiera de que a lo mejor sería una buena estrategia aliviar el embargo provocaba en algunos líderes una reacción violenta. Era como enseñarle una capa roja a un toro de lidia.

Me fui alejando. Surgían otros grupos que abogaban por el diálogo, la reconciliación nacional, un plebiscito, las negociaciones. Cobraron cierta fuerza. Todo el mundo hablaba del poscastrismo. Muchos líderes mundiales visitaron Cuba para ofrecerle a Castro fórmulas de transición. Pero nada. Él responde con el período especial. Cada día hay más apagones, menos gasolina, menos comida. La gente, literalmente, se muere en bicicleta. Cada vez están más flacos. Una epidemia de neuropatía recorre la Isla. Ya mi madre casi no ve. Mando todo lo que puedo. Me duelen los brazos de querer abrazarla. Me retiene la voz de Robertico:

—Lauri, prométeme que no irás a Cuba mientras Fidel no se caiga.

No le puedo explicar estas cosas a mi hermana por teléfono. ¿Cómo las va a entender?

El régimen subsiste. Turistas, disidentes, Fidel Castro, la iglesia, Robaina, las jineteras, Raúl Castro, los dólares, Alarcón, las empresas mixtas, el Papa, los peloteros, los Hermanos al Rescate, los músicos, Madeline Allbright, los académicos, la Unión Europea: todos aparecen en la noticia en relación con Cuba. Pasan los años y nada pasa.

Menchu por fin se decidió a venir. Y aquí estoy en el aeropuerto, parada frente a una puerta, con el corazón que se me quiere salir cada vez que se abre y veo salir a los pasajeros, buscándola ansiosa entre la multitud, esperando para abrazar por fin a mi hermana, a mi hermana gemela cuya vida es un misterio para mí, a mi hermana que no he visto desde aquel mediodía de julio en que dejé mi Patria.

CAPÍTULO ONCE
Preferimos la muerte

LÁZARO NO LO QUERÍA CREER. Por fin nos montamos en el desatartalado Lada, bajamos por la Calle 42 hasta la Quinta Avenida y llegamos a esa gran mole que es la Embajada Soviética. Y allí estaba, ondeando en la brisa, con nuestro cielo azul de fondo, la bandera zarista. El emblema rojo de la hoz y el martillo había sido retirado.

Era el 26 de diciembre de 1991.

Cuando trato de recordar, comprendo que todo comenzó mucho antes. No puedo precisar la fecha, si fue cuando los actos de repudio del Mariel, o acaso aquella noche que se emborrachó porque fusilaron a Ochoa. Creo que la carta de Ernestico que nos trajo Tania, en la que él explicaba que había decidido no regresar a Cuba, también le causó un profundo impacto. Aunque acabé rompiéndola, la leí tantas veces que la recuerdo casi palabra por palabra:

Queridos tíos:

Les escribo porque confío en que sabrán entenderme. Creo hablar por muchos de mi generación, los que nacimos con la Revolución, con Girón y el ciclón Flora, el socialismo y el grito de "Patria o muerte" en la garganta. Nuestros padres no nos bautizaron. Nacimos ateos. Sólo nuestras abuelas, a escondidas, nos enseñaban alguna estampita de la Virgen y nos rezaban en voz baja alguna oración. (¿Saben ustedes que Tania recita el Padre Nuestro en latín?) Fuimos producto de la falta de anticonceptivos, del entusiasmo por darle hombres nuevos a la Patria y, en algunos casos, del amor. Coincidimos con la primera etapa del bloqueo yanqui. Éramos niños cuando las coristas y los bailarines fueron enviados a la agricultura, cuando los homosexuales y los seminaristas, católicos y protestantes, catalogados de antisociales, compartían ecuménicamente en los campamentos de la UMAP, donde intentaban convertirlos en "hombres útiles a la Patria." Nos alimentaron con chícharos y croquetas, las llamadas "Venceremos" que se pegaban al cielo de la boca.

Nuestros padres —y nuestras madres a veces también— vestían uniforme verde olivo y nos dejaban solos para ir a hacer guardia. Comimos muchas veces los alimentos fríos, porque las ausencias (de padres o de electricidad) no nos permitían calentarlos. Fuimos pioneros. Repetimos sin cesar "Seremos como el Che…" Escuchamos largos y tediosos discursos del Comandante en Jefe en que nos anunciaba que éramos afortunados por vivir en "el mejor de los países," el "más democrático," donde se respetaban a cabalidad los derechos humanos, y que teníamos por delante "el futuro esplendoroso del comunismo…" No tuvimos caramelos, ni bombones, aunque probamos la dulzura de la caña cuando muy pequeños acompañamos a nuestros padres en aquella famosa zafra de los 10 millones van, que no fue a ninguna parte. No conocimos el jamón, a no ser el sintético, que llegó en nuestra adolescencia, con las compotas soviéticas y los jugos búlgaros. Viajamos muchas veces en camiones descubiertos con nuestros padres rumbo al trabajo voluntario, fuimos a la escuela en el campo, estuvimos becados, conocimos a los "hijos de papá", con su ropa bonita y su grabadora para escuchar a los Beatles. Nos obligaron a tener el pelo corto, a usar pantalones anchos, a vestir ropa de trabajo, a ir al Servicio Militar (los varones) e ingresar en la FMC (las hembras), ambos en los CDR, los más vivos en la UJC. Muchas veces nos bañamos con jabón de lavar, nos lavamos la cabeza con agua de lluvia y detergente. No tuvimos más que tres juguetes al año, y para eso los que quedaran cuando nos tocaba el turno. No conocimos las Navidades. Ni verdaderas vacaciones. Sólo teníamos el malecón para tomar el sol, para besar a una novia, para rasgar en alguna guitarra una canción de Silvio o de Pablito, para preguntarnos qué había más allá de Cuba y la libreta de racionamiento. Las clases comenzaban y terminaban todas iguales y seguían la misma metodología "marxista-leninista." No había espacio para preguntas impertinentes que podían tener un alto precio. Muchos compañeritos un día desaparecieron y luego nos enteramos de que se habían ido para el Norte y nunca supimos más de ellos. Nos dijeron que todos éramos iguales, pero nos hicieron tirar huevos e insultar a los que no pensaban como nosotros. Pasamos por la secundaria, el Pre, algunos lograron ingresar a la Universidad, casi ninguno para estudiar la carrera que quería sino "la que le dieron." Otros, los internacionalistas, fueron en misiones a África o a Nicaragua. Muchos han ido a la guerra. A veces no regresan. Los "hijos de papá" se acomodaron en México, en Canadá en España, donde viven su dulce exilio de terciopelo, pero cuando les aprieta la nostalgia visitan la Isla y disfrutan de los mismos privilegios que han tenido siempre. Otros también estudiamos fuera, en la Unión Soviética o la Europa del Este. Vimos otros mundos y Cuba se nos quedó estrecha, como una prisión. Leímos a Orwell y la Isla nos pareció la granja de los animales. Entendimos a Marx de otra forma y nos pareció que su adaptación criolla lo falsificaba. También supimos de los crímenes de Stalin y sentimos un escalofrío. De pronto, nos encontramos repitiendo aquella oración que nos enseñó la abuela.

Tíos, debo terminar. No sé qué rumbo tome mi vida, ni si alguna vez nos volveremos a ver. Confío en que me abriré paso. Les agradezco todo lo que me han enseñado. Pienso en ustedes con mucho cariño. Sé que son personas buenas e idealistas. No entiendo cómo es posible que les hayan robado la Revolución.

Un abrazo muy fuerte.
Ernesto

Cuando terminamos de leer la carta, Lázaro me miró y me preguntó:
—¿Tú crees que nos robaron la Revolución, Menchu?
No supe qué contestarle.

∞

Veo y comprendo que ustedes han captado muy bien el momento que estamos viviendo, los peligros que estamos viviendo, las amenazas que estamos viviendo. Veo que ustedes han captado muy bien la malsana alegría de aquellos que creen que se aproxima la hora de tomar revancha contra la obra de la Revolución, contra la Revolución y contra los revolucionarios; la malsana esperanza de aquellos que creen que podrán doblegar y poner de rodilla a nuestro pueblo, de aquellos que se imaginan posible obligarnos a vivir otra vez en la repugnante sociedad capitalista.

Yo les pregunto a esos países, a los que presentan como modelos de sociedad y democracia, modelos que quieren imponernos a nosotros, ¿qué clase de participación y democracia representan? Aquí los pioneros se reúnen a discutir con el Partido y con el gobierno todos sus problemas, los trabajadores se reúnen a discutir con el Partido y con el gobierno todos sus problemas, o los campesinos, o las mujeres, o los vecinos, y me pregunto si en alguno de esos países alguna vez los estudiantes se reúnen a discutir con el gobierno, con la administración, con el Estado, todos sus problemas; y no sólo aquellos problemas que les interesan a los estudiantes, sino los problemas que le interesan a todo el país, a toda la nación.

(Fidel Castro 6 de diciembre 1991)

∽

Quizás otro momento decisivo fue cuando hicieron todos esos cambios en los medios de difusión social. *Granma* quedó como el único periódico, los demás pasaron a ser semanarios, y *Bohemia* tuvo que reducirse a un formato de 64 páginas. Algunas secciones culturales con las que Lázaro había colaborado en los últimos tiempos quedaron eliminadas. Debió llegar temprano aquel día, pues cuando yo regresé del trabajo ya estaba sentado en el sillón, en el patio del fondo, con la botella de ron. Pensé que querría estar solo y apenas lo saludé, pero, por el contrario, le dio por hablar.

—¿Tú te imaginas, Menchu, que *Trabajadores* defienda que se establezcan empresas mixtas con capitalistas extranjeros? Estoy seguro de que no piensan así, si es que todavía piensan, sino que ésa es la orientación que ha bajado… Por una parte, que se hunda la Isla antes de ceder, aunque seamos el último reducto del socialismo, que si Polonia y Checoslovaquia se están vendiendo, que si nuestra Patria será un eterno Baraguá, y por otra —yo lo sé de buena tinta…— un alto dirigente del partido se entrevista con Salinas para pedirle a los americanos que aflojen… Y mira, ya en Varadero los españoles han inaugurado un hotel. ¿Para qué hicimos una Revolución, Menchu, para que regrese el capitalismo? Tú verás… en unos años esto va a estar peor que en 1958…

lleno de turistas... lo verás...

—Lázaro, el mundo ha cambiado... hay otra generación... una gente joven que...

—Sí, que se cagan en nosotros, como en esa exhibición de arte, si a eso se le puede llamar arte, en que un "artista" se quitó los pantalones y se cagó en el Granma.

—Pero hay otra gente...

—Sí, como ése que ahora dice que el partido no hizo la Revolución en Cuba sino al revés... como si el partido no tuviera una dimensión universal muy anterior a todo esto...

—Lázaro, a lo mejor el marxismo está muy bien en teoría, pero en la realidad no funciona.

—No digas eso. Lo que pasa es que no lo aplican bien y que hemos tenido muchos enemigos externos.

—Pero tampoco ha funcionado en la Unión Soviética ni en ninguna parte... yo creo que al contrario, que quizás lo que está sucediendo sea bueno para rescatar la verdadera Revolución, la cubana, tan verde como las palmas, como dijo una vez Fidel...

—Esos eran otros tiempos, Menchu.

—Sí, ahora estamos en el período especial en tiempo de paz... o en tiempo de guerra, quién sabe, o en la Opción Cero... sí... cero de todo... cada día más apagones y menos qué comer... Mamá está tan flaquita... Menos mal que Lauri le manda vitaminas.

—Ochoa muerto y ¡Juan Escalona Presidente de la Asamblea Popular! —exclama, ajeno a lo que acabo de decirle, como si concluyera alguna reflexión interior.

—No hables tan alto, Lázaro...

—El Nobel de la Paz a Gorbachev... ¿a qué precio? Hace unas semanas la URSS haciendo declaraciones conjuntas con los americanos para que Iraq retire las tropas de Kuwait...

—No sé que vamos a resolver para la comida hoy...

—También los curas están, poco a poco, como son ellos, solapados, colocando sus fichas... repartiendo su propaganda...

—No tomes tanto, Lázaro…

Siguió bebiendo, no sólo esa noche, sino todas. A veces se pasaba horas en silencio, con la mirada perdida, apurando un trago tras otro, hasta que se quedaba dormido. Otras veces le daba por hablar… que si la polémica entre Granma y la UNEAC, que si habían autorizado empresas con 100% de capital extranjero, que si Granma había dicho que somos un país agrícola subdesarrollado y era verdad… que si las Brigadas de Respuesta Rápida eran como la porra de Machado… que si querían retirar las tropas soviéticas que las retiraran, que total, para lo que servían… que si en el IV Congreso no se habían discutido las cosas que había que discutir…

Al principio trataba de razonar con él. Pero era inútil. Estaba como obsesionado. Ya era imposible ocultar la situación en el barrio. Él no se cuidaba, ni con Maruja. Menos mal que ella es un pedazo de pan con ojos y no lo denunció. Incluso a veces trataba de hablarle:

—Lázaro, son tiempos difíciles, pero la Revolución ha hecho mucho bien. Mírame a mí, una guajirita de Morón, que he llegado a ser jefa de enfermeras… Hasta un hijo le di a la Revolución y no me quejo. Van a venir tiempos mejores. Tienes que pensar en Tania y en los nietos que tendrás algún día. Para ellos trabajamos, para el futuro.

—Maruja, tú no te das cuenta. El futuro ya llegó.

Nos fuimos distanciando. Yo estaba resentida por todas las dificultades que pasaba a diario en la calle para resolver, y él pasaba el tiempo meciéndose en el traspatio y bebiendo ron. Me molestaba su aliento cargado de alcohol, el sudor de su ropa, la voz pastosa, el caminar lento. Las pocas veces que me buscaba para hacer el amor, lo rechazaba. Menos mal que enseguida se quedaba dormido. Fue la época peor de mi vida.

❧

Si estamos dispuestos a hacer todo eso, lo hacemos con hombres y mujeres libres, dueños de nuestro país y no como esclavos. Si estamos dispuestos a pasar sacrificios, es por algo muy superior, y no por vivir toda la vida humillados y explotados. Si estamos dispuestos a sacrificarnos uno, dos, tres y cinco años, lo hacemos porque sabemos que detrás de nosotros está la Revolución, está el socialismo, está la justicia, está el porvenir y lo que queremos es preservar el derecho a ese porvenir.

A aquellos blandengues, o cobardes, o de espíritu mercenario, a quienes jamás sintieron en su alma el beso de la patria o la idea de la justicia en sus mentes, en sus corazones, a esos que dicen que la lucha sería una lucha sin perspectiva, tenemos que decirles como ya expresé una vez, que lo único que no tiene perspectiva, lo único que destruye toda perspectiva es no tener patria, no tener Revolución y no tener socialismo.

A quien rinda la patria, la Revolución y el socialismo no le quedarán jamás la esperanza, y esa esperanza, la que nos dan la patria, la Revolución y el socialismo, la defenderemos hasta la última gota de sangre. Preferimos la muerte antes de quedarnos sin Revolución y socialismo, porque lo otro es la muerte moral, la más terrible de las muertes.

(Fidel Castro 6 de diciembre 1991)

✍

Una mañana Lázaro se afeitó, se bañó, se puso ropa limpia y me anunció:

—He sido un cobarde. No voy a beber más. Voy a buscar otro camino.

Al principio no lo creí, pero a medida que pasaron los días vi que resurgía el hombre que yo había amado. De nuevo era considerado y tierno conmigo; equilibrado y realista en sus comentarios; cortés y educado con Mamá. Incluso le noté un esfuerzo consciente por acercarse a su hija. Yo no las tenía todas conmigo. Lo conocía bien, y me parecía que me ocultaba algo. Hasta se me ocurrió pensar si estaría preparándose para irse en balsa. Tenía en el rostro esa expresión de velado entusiasmo que solía acompañarlo cuando tenía entre manos algún proyecto que lo ilusionaba.

Nunca sospeché lo que iba a suceder.

Mi hermano Pedro me llamó muy temprano una mañana. Lázaro

había estado a verlo. Lo había notado raro. Le hablaba como si se despidiera. Había quedado en regresar para traerle unos papeles que quería darle. ¿Por qué no iba yo para allá?

Cuando llegué a la casa de El Vedado, mi hermano me informó de que Lázaro acababa de irse.

—Me dio este sobre y me dijo que no lo abriera, a no ser que le pasara algo. No pude detenerlo.

Oímos un ruido y nos viramos. Por la ventana abierta vimos a Lázaro en el patio en el mismo instante en que se llevaba la pistola a la sien y se volaba la tapa de los sesos. Cayó muerto a unos cuantos metros de aquel pasillo donde cuando jóvenes nos escondíamos para besarnos. La nota de despedida era escueta:

Perdóname, Menchu. Hice un esfuerzo estos meses para no dejarte un mal recuerdo. No puedo más. No somos y ya nunca seremos como el Che. Ya nunca construiremos la Cuba que soñamos para nuestra hija. No sé si la Revolución nos traicionó o nosotros la traicionamos a ella. A ti, sin embargo, siempre te he sido fiel.

Lázaro
1 de enero de 1992, "Año del fuego"

❧

Según el Anuario Estadístico de Cuba, los suicidas en el país aumentaron de 1011 en 1970 a 2220 en 1989. Esta última cifra tiende a estabilizarse sin aumentos ni reducciones significativas, para una tasa de 21.1 suicidas por cada 100,000 personas. Según el director del Programa Nacional de Prevención del Suicidio, por cada hecho consumado hay de 10 a 15 intentos fallidos de quitarse la vida. El suicidio está entre las 10 primeras causas de muerte en Cuba.

(*Bohemia* 83:5, 29)

∽

Voy a la bodega, o a lo que queda de lo que fuera una bodega, o a un antiguo "supermercado" y veo sólo estantes vacíos y sucios, y caras largas y cetrinas de personas mal vestidas (ancianos despeinados, jóvenes en bicicletas, trabajadores cansados e incluso niños, con jabas vacías) todos a la espera de la llegada de "algo" que no llega... El Famoso "Plan Especial Alimentario" es como Dios: todo el mundo habla de él, pero nadie lo ve. El cubano lo ha perdido todo menos el sentido del humor. Los grandes plátanos productos del "micro-yet" —un sistema de riego intensivo— sólo los vemos en la portada de la revista *Bohemia,* que cada vez circula menos por falta de papel, y en la televisión, si no hay apagón.

Se nos rompió la semana pasada la cocina eléctrica, la última hornilla que funcionaba. Ya en el barrio están cocinando con leña... pero ¿dónde la consigues? Alguna gente quema los muebles, los marcos de las ventanas. Los balones de gas están a 89 días de entrega y el gas de la calle, en los barrios que hay, apenas se mantiene unas horas, casi siempre de madrugada. Cada día tengo que pedirle a un vecino que me haga el favor de colocar una olla de presión con un intento de caldo o arroz para poder comer algo caliente, aunque sea una vez al día. Lo hago por Mamá, sobre todo. Yo he bajado sesenta libras, y ella no quiere ni decirme lo que pesa. Me miro al espejo y veo sólo unas ojeras imponentes y la piel amarilla. Los médicos consideran que ocho de hemoglobina es alto, dada la situación...

—Evite bajar más de peso —aconsejan, pero no pueden recetar dieta especial.

En las esquinas, pequeñas concentraciones esperan, resignadas. Cada día hay más gente sin puesto fijo (muchos centros de trabajo han cerrado, por falta de materia prima y otros recursos) y el transporte (por falta de combustible, piezas de repuesto, gomas, etc.) sigue disminuyendo. Compré una bicicleta pero, como muchos, la he abandonado. El esfuerzo de utilizarla para grandes distancias agota las pocas energías. Además, es un peligro. El otro día se mató el hijo de un compañero de trabajo, de 19 años. Iba colgado de la guagua y le aplastaron la cabeza contra un poste del tendido eléctrico en la Calle 23.

El deterioro arquitectónico refleja el humano. Las casas sin pintar, muchas apuntaladas, algunas desde hace años. Caminar por las aceras de La Habana Vieja es arriesgar la vida. A cada rato se desploma un balcón. En la temporada de lluvia se suceden los derrumbes. Ya ni aparece en la prensa. Es tan común que no es noticia.

Gregorio, el vecino de enfrente, cuando comenzó a adelgazar fue a consultar al médico del policlínico. Le explicó que se le inflamaban los pies, que se sentía como si se le estuviera haciendo una pelota en el lado izquierdo del vientre.

—Eso no es nada. Tome agua con azúcar y cójase un descanso.

Gregorio pidió que le hicieran una placa.

—No hay condiciones para ello. Lo siento —le contestaron.

Tanto insistió que le dieron la receta pero tenía que resolver donde se la hicieran. Después de dos meses le diagnosticaron cáncer. Seis semanas más tarde, con sólo cuarenta y cinco años de edad, falleció. Dejó un apartamentico, sin poder terminar de pagarlo (le faltaban solamente 150 pesos), y una grabadora con un casete que su madre no se atreve a escuchar.

Todo el barrio fue al velorio. Muchos nos vimos reflejados en aquel vecino, acostado en una caja gris "igual para todos." No se le pudo poner ni una corona de flores. Ese día no había flores.

—Tan joven, que le diera un cáncer... —comentaban.

—Ese hombre se murió de hambre —sentenció Mamá. Nadie le contestó.

∾

Hoy la esperanza de vida al nacer en Cuba es de 75 años.

(*Bohemia* 83:7, 18)

∾

Camino varias cuadras bajo el sol implacable en busca de "algo" que comer. Incluso la famosa sopa *Taíno,* hecha con viandas de desperdicio, se ha vuelto un plato difícil. Hasta escasean los huevos. Las pizzas, cuando las hay, no tienen queso. Los hamburgers —bautizados McCastro— son cada vez más finos y babosos, y las colas para comprarlos, larguísimas. Sólo queda "helado de agua" con sabor de sirope (limón, toronja, naranja, no para escoger, sino como oferta única).

Si no fuera por lo que de vez en cuando conseguimos en la bolsa negra con lo que mandan Ricardo y Lauri, ya no existiríamos. Y hasta en eso hay que tener cuidado. El otro día vendieron por el barrio unos bistés empanizados que resultaron ser frazadas de trapear envueltas en galleta molida. Menos mal que yo no compré… Pedritín tiene buenas relaciones y resuelve mejor. Comparte siempre con Tania. En eso es muy bueno. Incluso nos trae algo de vez en cuando. Aún así hay momentos en que pienso que me voy a desmayar, que me voy a morir. Quizás sería lo mejor. A veces algo, un aroma, una frase, una imagen me trae el recuerdo de Lázaro y se me clava en el medio del pecho como un puñal. Pero no quiero recordarlo, no puedo. Duele demasiado. Y debo seguir adelante, sobrevivir. Levantarme cada mañana es un acto de fe, aunque no sé muy bien en qué creo. Quizás en la vida, en la vida misma.

∽

Cuba se moría… los nacidos en la Isla agonizaban en la pobreza mayoritariamente, porque 950,467 vivían sin ocupación lucrativa.

Las industrias tabacalera y azucarera fenecían. Se arruinaban hacendados; las tierras pasaban a extranjeros o se concentraban en pocos nombres. Los tabaqueros emigraban buscando, en un exilio económico y político, los modos de resolver de forma individual el problema social. Terminaba el siglo XIX y Cuba se moría…

(*Bohemia* 83:7, 18)

✧

Acabo de pasar junto a un perro muerto. Estaba sucio, muy delgado. Hay miles y miles de perros abandonados que recorren las calles de La Habana, desorientados. A veces andan en jaurías, protegiéndose unos a otros; algunos van solos, buscando desesperadamente por todos los rincones algo que comer. Al comenzar la repatriación, luego de la caída del "socialismo real," los soviéticos abandonaron a sus perros y gatos. Hasta entonces estos animales habían vivido mejor que muchos cubanos, alimentados con carne especial comprada en las diplotiendas. También, desde que empezó el Período Especial muchos cubanos han botado de las casas a sus animalitos porque no tienen qué darles de comer. Otros prefieren sacrificarlos. Conozco a una señora, ya jubilada, esposa de un profesional, que tenía cinco gatos bellísimos. Cuando no pudo conseguir más pescado, ni en la bolsa negra, pidió a un veterinario amigo que los inyectara, los enterró en su patio y sembró un rosal sobre ellos. Quizás hizo lo correcto. Los animales abandonados se ven hambrientos, escuálidos y sucios, con la mirada vidriosa. Caminan atontados entre los pocos vehículos que circulan. A cada rato se escucha un chillido, y alguno cae bajo las gomas de un camión o de una guagua atestada de pasajeros. Alguien se compadece y lo toma por las patas o el rabo, y lo tira en un rincón de la acera o en un latón de basura donde poco a poco se descompone el cadáver (ya la basura no se recoge todos los días). Triste destino del mejor amigo del hombre.

El rosal que la mujer plantó sobre la tumba de sus gatos murió también. No hay agua para regarlo.

✧

Yeguas moras, negras, castañas, alazanas, con lomos relucientes y brillantes ojos, corren en completa libertad.(…) La naturaleza fue pródiga con esta bestia a quien tanto han cantado los poetas: cabeza descarnada, cuello largo, grupa alta, extremidades anteriores delgadas y una alzada entre 1.52 y

1.65 metros. Son los caballos de pura sangre ingleses.(…) Su cría comenzó en Cuba en 1918 y hasta el año 1943 nacieron 271 ejemplares, pero fue a partir de la Revolución que esta actividad tuvo nuevas perspectivas.

(*Bohemia,* 84:31, 22–24)

∽

Desde que tuvo el dengue, Mamá quedó mal de la vista. Ahora otra vez empezó a quejarse de lo mal que ve. Ya hace tiempo que no puede ni coser, ni tejer, ni leer. Ni escribirle a Lauri y a Ricardo. Me dicta a mí las cartas. Hasta las imágenes del televisor las ve borrosas. En lo que más se entretiene es en oír el radio y cuando viene alguien de visita, especialmente la familia. Su preferida, sin duda, es Tania, y esa niña tan rara que nunca puedo saber a ciencia cierta lo que siente, que apenas derramó una lágrima cuando la muerte de su padre, es muy tierna con ella. De todas formas, me alegra verlas juntas. Son lo que más quiero en el mundo.

Creía que Mamá necesitaba espejuelos nuevos y quizás mis hermanos los podrían mandar. Pero le han diagnosticado neuropatía. Es una deficiencia de ciertas vitaminas que ataca a los ojos, y como ya ella los tenía mal… Y con lo mal alimentada que está… Me he enterado de mucha gente que lo tiene. El médico en el policlínico nos ha dicho que es casi una epidemia.

Menos mal que ahora las comunicaciones son más fáciles. Enseguida le pedí las vitaminas a Lauri. Ella responde siempre más rápido que Ricardo cuando necesitamos algo. No me gusta tener que pedir, pero cuando es para Mamá, no lo dudo ni un momento. No puedo pensar que se vaya a quedar ciega.

∽

La Habana. Cuba es el mayor productor de fármacos genéricos en América Latina y se ampliarán las capacidades tecnológicas, según informó la directora del Centro de Investigación y Desarrollo de Medicamentos.

Actualmente ascienden a 900 las formulaciones farmacéuticas que se obtienen en laboratorios y están en construcción nuevas instalaciones para la producción de insulina y reactivos clínicos, de tabletas anticonceptivas y una planta productora de hemoderivados.

Entre las líneas más novedosas están los hemoderivados, dada una fuerte infraestructura que se apoya en las donaciones voluntarias y una red de bancos de sangre para procesar plasma normal e hiperinmune.

(*Bohemia* 85:23, 25)

⁓

La luz se va por tantas horas que decimos que en vez de apagones hay alumbrones. El calor es desesperante. La gente duerme en los balcones. Yo a veces he tenido que poner una colchoneta en la terraza del frente de la casa. Y la situación de la comida y el transporte no mejora. La gente lo que quiere es irse. Han comenzado a fabricar las balsas en los patios de las casas, a la vista de todo el mundo. Hasta dijeron que el que quiera, que se vaya. Ahora no los llaman gusanos, ni escoria, ni lumpens como en el 60 y el 80. Sólo quieren que se vayan.

Se van familias enteras, con sus viejitos y sus criaturas de brazo. Algunos se llevan hasta los perros. Otras veces se reúnen cuatro o cinco muchachos jóvenes de un barrio para irse juntos. También hay personas que les suplican a otras que se los lleven y se montan en una misma balsa gente que, hasta ese momento, nunca se había visto. Algunos estudian las mareas, la mejor hora para zarpar, pero otros parten de cualquier costa y a cualquier hora. Muchas veces los van a despedir, se quedan las mujeres y los niños diciendo adiós en la playa hasta que la improvisada embarcación se pierde en el horizonte.

Miro el mar y me pregunto si no tendrán miedo. ¿Cómo será pasar la noche en el mar, escuchando su respiración solemne, sin otro horizonte que la oscuridad? ¿Cómo entender la desgarradora ironía de morirse de sed rodeado de agua por todas partes? ¡Qué angustia ver la balsa asediada por tiburones, presentir el desgarrón de esos dientes afilados sobre la piel! ¡Qué temor por los seres queridos que van con uno! ¿Cuántos no llegarán jamás? Parecería que hay que estar loco para echarse a la mar... hasta en una llanta... loco, sí, loco... o vivir en Cuba en este largo, interminable, caluroso y agotador verano de 1994.

∽

Si no tuviéramos un pueblo de gigantes, si no tuviéramos una juventud como ustedes, lo que nos esperaba era convertirnos en un Puerto Rico, convertirnos en un Miami, que dicen que es uno de los mayores centros de crimen, de prostitución y de drogas en el mundo. Si no tuviéramos un pueblo como el nuestro, perderíamos la Revolución, perderíamos el socialismo. (APLAUSOS).

(Fidel Castro 6 de diciembre 1991)

∽

Han pasado cinco años y hemos sobrevivido. ¿A qué precio? El de invitar a los turistas. El de abrirles nuestras playas y cerrárselas a los cubanos. Las casas se caen a pedazos pero los hoteles de lujo alojan a los canadienses, a los italianos, a los españoles. Vienen a beberse el sol y a las mulatas, a emborracharse de ron y palmeras, a menear las caderas en el baile o en la cama. Las jineteras están por todas partes. Muchachas decentes algunas que se acuestan por un par de pitusas o un blúmer, o por una comida sabrosa, o por ir a un lugar bonito, de esos reservados para los turistas adonde no pueden ir con sus novios cubanos. También los hombres se prostituyen. Algunos jóvenes, aunque no son homosexuales, venden su cuerpo. Otros venden los de sus hijas o sus hermanas, o hasta los de sus madres.

Pero, como siempre, otra es la historia de "los hijos de papá". Al igual que muchos antiguos oficiales de la FAR y del MINIT, se preparan para un posible retorno del capitalismo. Están ubicados en las empresas mixtas. Son los nuevos capitalistas del socialismo. Estudian inglés, computación, aprenden técnicas de márquetin, incluso viajan a España, México o Canadá, a pasar cursos especiales de entrenamiento.

Otra gente se gana la vida honradamente. Hay muchos profesionales que trabajan de taxistas. Todo el mundo quiere una plaza relacionada con el turismo. Es la forma de tener dólares. El dólar manda en Cuba. Lázaro tenía razón. ¡Si viera lo que es Cuba hoy…! Hasta hay gente pidiendo limosna…

Otros no. Otros luchan a brazo partido. Algunas familias han abierto paladares. O confeccionan artesanías. Hay quienes alquilan habitaciones a los turistas. Sé de quién se dedica a conseguirles antigüedades. Otros las venden. A los extranjeros, claro.

—Serán de la gente que se fue —dice Mamá de forma tajante.

—Ay, vieja, de eso hace tantos años…

Los que están mejor son los que reciben dólares de la familia. O como dicen, los que tienen fe, familiares en el extranjero. No me puedo quejar de mis hermanos. Hubo unos años en que estuvimos muy alejados, pero ahora llaman a menudo y mandan dinero cada dos o tres meses. Si no fuera por ellos, Mamá y yo la pasaríamos muy mal, pues ya yo me jubilé y con las dos pensiones solamente no nos alcanzaría para nada.

Fue precisamente poco después de dejar el trabajo que Mamá me dijo:

—Debes volver a la iglesia, Menchu.

—¿Volverías conmigo?

—Yo nunca me he ido.

—¿Qué quieres decir?

—Que siempre he creído en Dios, que siempre he rezado, que he invocado a mis santos a cada momento. Hice novenas cuando Lauri y tú estaban embarazadas, cuando alguno de los nietos se enfermaba, cuando Pedritín estuvo en Angola. Rezo todas las noches por los que quiero… y por mis muertos… incluyendo a Lázaro, a Robertico y al hijo de Maruja, pobre muchacho, si lo vimos crecer…

Empecé a ir a San Agustín. El reencuentro con aquellas imágenes religiosas de mi infancia fue ejerciendo algún misterioso efecto en mí, aunque no podía precisar cuál... Me sentí a gusto. Quizás yo tampoco me había alejado del todo de Dios. Después empecé a trabajar con otros voluntarios que atendían a más de 400 viejitos "adoptados" por la parroquia. Estaban absolutamente solos y con unas entradas que no les alcanzaban para comer. Así que cocinábamos para ellos y les llevábamos la comida. Y los ayudábamos a lavar la ropa, a veces a bañarse.

—Menchu, si para viejos ya tú tienes bastante conmigo —me decía Mamá, desde el butacón, al lado de la ventana del comedor, donde antes se sentaba Mama Luya.

El párroco era un hombre inteligente y culto. Comenzó a prestarme libros que después discutíamos. Vino entonces el largo año de preparativos para la visita del Papa. Fue una etapa buena. Teníamos una meta, una esperanza. Y llegó Juan Pablo II. ¡Qué jornada gloriosa! No recuerdo nada que nos conmoviera así desde hacía muchos años. Hasta logré llevar a Mamá en una silla de ruedas. El Papa nos dio la comunión.

Pero el Papa se fue, ha pasado más de un año y todo sigue igual. A veces un poco peor, un poco mejor. Pero igual. En Cuba todo cambia y todo se queda igual. Siempre igual.

Me sorprendió la visita de Tania una mañana.

—¿Y tú que haces que no estás en el trabajo?

—Tenía que hablar contigo y con mi abuela.

—Será porque te casas, estás en estado o te vas del país —fue el comentario de mi madre.

—¡Ay, Mamá, por Dios!

—Bueno, casi casi...

—Mija, por lo que más quieras, acaba de decirnos...

—He conseguido una beca por un año para hacer unos estudios especializados en Barcelona...

Separarme de Tania fue otro desgarrón, pero en el fondo me alegré de que saliera de este ambiente. Ahora nos escribe feliz. ¡Qué niña...! Le encanta el frío... Dice que la ciudad es preciosa. Quiere que yo vaya, pero, ¿con qué dinero?

Lauri llevaba años insistiéndome para que pidiera los permisos y fuera a Miami a verla. Ella iba a venir con lo del Papa y al final no pudo ser. Mucha gente conocida regresó entonces. Siempre le había contestado a Lauri que no podía dejar a Mamá sola. Quizás en el fondo le tema al encuentro. Sé que es irracional, pero me da miedo que no nos podamos entender.

Después de que regresaron mis primas Lucrecia y Anita, y verlas fue todo llanto, abrazos, recuerdos de infancia y un sentir que no había pasado el tiempo desde que nos separamos, me decidí por fin a ir a ver a Lauri. Maruja me dio el empujón final, me prometió ella misma cuidar a la vieja. Y aquí estoy, con las luces de Miami a mis pies, en el avión, a punto de abrazar a mi hermana, a esa otra mitad mía que no veo hace casi cuarenta años, cuando su marido se la llevó en otro avión como éste, un soleado mediodía de julio.

CAPÍTULO DOCE
Prohibidos los adioses

CUANDO ABRACÉ A MI HERMANA EN EL AEROPUERTO DE MIAMI, no podía dejar de llorar. Lloraba porque nunca había ido a Tropicana, por el azul de Varadero, por la muerte de mi padre de quien me despedí para siempre a los 18 años, por mi madre anciana a quien quizás no volvería a ver, por mi hermano menor que se había metido a comunista, por el dependiente de la Casa Suárez con su calva y sus manos manchadas, hasta por la mujer con la trusa Jantzen que desde el anuncio lumínico del Malecón se lanzaba al mar. Por fin me separé de Menchu para poder verla mejor. La encontré flaca, canosa, avejentada. Me pareció como si el calendario hubiera avanzado con prisa y me viera a mí misma diez años más tarde. En seguida me puse a buscar su equipaje para tratar de disimular la impresión que me había causado.

En los próximos días la llevé a conocer las distintas zonas de Miami, como South Beach, Key Biscayne y Cococonut Grove. Le mostré con cierto orgullo la Pequeña Habana, con sus letreros en español y su aroma a tabaco y a café, para que viera cómo los cubanos rumiamos nuestra nostalgia de exiliados intentando reproducir el país que dejamos atrás. Hasta la llevé a ver la primera casa y los apartamentos donde viví con mis suegros acabadita de llegar de Cuba.

—¿Podemos bajarnos a tomar un café? —me preguntó durante uno de esos paseos.

—Claro… Pero te lo digo por tu bien, tanto café no es bueno para la salud…

—Aquí todos viven obsesionados con la salud pero andan gordísimos y hablando siempre de operaciones y enfermedades. Allá comemos lo que se pueda, pero caminamos tanto, montamos tanta bicicleta, y tenemos tanto miedo a caer en un hospital, que estamos más saludables.

Tuve que contenerme para no contestarle. Me sentía feliz de que estuviéramos juntas pero por más que trataba había algunas cosas que no entendía. Nada parecía asombrar a mi hermana. Nunca elogiaba ni agradecía las cosas. Con lo que me estaba desviviendo por ofrecerle lo mejor de todo. Y entonces se apeaba con esas comparaciones absurdas, como si fuera posible que hubiera aspecto alguno de la vida en Cuba que pudiera ser mejor que en los Estados Unidos. También me irritaba que no supiera contestar la otra línea cuando estaba hablando por teléfono... Ni parecía tener sentido del tiempo... y si se me ocurría botar las sobras de la comida se disgustaba muchísimo. Tenía que hacerlo a escondidas...

La verdad es que a veces tampoco yo me daba cuenta de las cosas que podían herirla. Todas las semanas le insistía para que me acompañara al Publix a hacer los mandados y el diálogo era casi siempre el mismo.

—Menchu, ¿qué sabor de yogurt quieres?

—Me da lo mismo, Lauri.

—Menchu, ¿qué helado?

—Escoge tú, Lauri.

—Menchu, ¿Coca Cola de dieta o regular, con cafeína o sin cafeína?

—Lauri, de verdad que me da lo mismo...

Yo no comprendía cómo podía mostrarse tan indiferente a todo, hasta un día que me dijo muy descompuesta, casi gritando:

—¡Con esta comida se podría alimentar a toda La Habana! No puedo ni verla pensando en la gente allá... y además, ¿no te das cuentas de que no sé escoger? —y salió del mercado llorando.

Por lo general, sin embargo, nos llevábamos muy bien, como si nunca nos hubiéramos separado. Compartimos ratos muy agradables con los muchachos y con Tyler, quien hizo muy buenas migas con su tía abuela. Con las antiguas compañeras del colegio disfrutamos de una tarde inolvidable rememorando viejos tiempos.

Las mejores horas eran cuando estábamos solas por las noches. Después de comer y de ver un poco la televisión, ya en ropa de dormir, nos poníamos a leer los diarios que nos habíamos intercambiado. A veces alguna de las dos se sentía tan impresionada por algún pasaje, que empezaba a llorar, y la otra tenía que consolarla:

—Vamos, bobita, si eso fue ya hace mucho tiempo...

Otras veces interrumpíamos la lectura con alguna pregunta o comentario:

—Tú sabes —le dije en una ocasión a mi hermana— una de las cosas que más me duele es pensar lo poco que he conocido a mis padres y, claro, ellos a mí. He guardado todos estos años un recuerdo idealizado, los he visto siempre desde la perspectiva de una niña o de una adolescente... Las cosas de que me he enterado sobre Papá han sido un verdadero shock...

—Lauri, entiéndeme, Papá no era malo...

—No sería malo, pero hizo sufrir a Mamá y por su indecisión no se fueron de Cuba.

—Quizás fue nuestro destino.

—¡El destino! Ésa es una de las cosas qué más rabia me da de algunos cubanos... Uno se hace su propio destino, chica. Siempre con ese vamos a ver... con ese ojalá que... Mira que somos ojalateros...

—¿Y tú crees que irte fue la solución?

—No... al contrario, a veces pienso que si todos nos hubiéramos quedado las cosas hubieran sido distintas.

—Entonces, ¿por qué le reprochas a Papá que nos hayamos quedado?

—No sé, Menchu, porque lo peor ha sido la separación de la familia... Bueno, mejor lo dejamos ahí. Mira, otra cosita que te quiero preguntar... Eso de que Julio Eduardo no tenía nada que buscar en una guerra de los americanos, ¿lo dijo Maruja, como tú dices...?

—Lauri, ya te he explicado que era un momento de mucho fervor revolucionario, que Maruja es una mujer buena pero que sus circunstancias...

—No... si eso lo entiendo... Te pregunto porque aquí nos llegó la noticia de que había sido Papá quien había dicho eso y algo peor...

—¡Por Dios! Él tenía sus cosas pero hubiera sido incapaz...

—Te darás cuenta de que Tío Julio y Papá han estado todos estos años peleados por eso...

—¿Por eso?

—Y porque Papá no les escribió ni una miserable línea cuando mataron a Julio Eduardo.

—Eso no sé… quizás se perdiera la carta… pero te aseguro que Papá nunca dijo nada semejante… Y, es más, él que no era muy sentimental llevó una foto de Julio Eduardo en su cartera hasta el día que murió… lo sé, porque me la dieron a mí en la funeraria… Y cuando se acercaba el aniversario de su muerte se las arreglaba para llegar hasta El Cacahual…

—¿El Cacahual…? Ahí es donde está enterrado Maceo, ¿no?

—Sí…

—¿Y qué tiene que ver Maceo con Julio Eduardo?

—Papá decía que Julio Eduardo también había sido un héroe… y que iba allí a rendirle tributo. Cada cual…

—¡Dios mío! Dos hermanos tantos años sin escribirse ni hablarse por un mal entendido… ya Papá murió… pero cuando vayas a Nueva York a casa de Ricardo le tienes que contar esto a Tío Julio… ¡Qué cosas tiene la vida! Me pongo a pensar cuando éramos niños y nos reuníamos todos los domingos en casa de Otra Mamá… ¿te acuerdas, Menchu?

—Claro…

—¿Quién nos hubiera dicho entonces todas las cosas que nos iban a pasar? Es tan absurdo que Julio Eduardo se haya ido a morir a una guerra en Vietnam.

—Tan absurdo como que Pedritín haya estado dos años en una guerra en Angola. Tuvimos suerte con él, pero murieron muchos de sus compañeros. Lo de Camilito fue un golpetazo. Imagínate, lo vimos crecer desde que tenía dos años.

Algunas veces, cuando íbamos en el carro, me venían recuerdos que creía ya olvidados.

—Menchu, ¿y aquella canción que cantábamos en la guagua…? Sí… la que nos enseñó la señora Nina.

—Ay, Lauri… no me acuerdo…

—Sí, chica, te tienes que acordar… algo de unos elefantes…

—Ah, ya sé.

Un elefante se balanceaba sobre la tela de una araña

Cuando veía que resistía fue a buscar a un camarada
Dos elefantes se balanceaban sobre la tela de una araña
Cuando veían que resistía fueron a buscar a un camarada...
Tres elefantes...

Un recuerdo nos llevaba a otro y entonábamos juntas viejas melodías de la infancia.

También tenía mil preguntas sobre la familia, que Menchu contestaba con paciencia:

—¿Cómo fue la muerte de Gilda...? No era muy mayor...

—Bueno, tú sabes que su madre era muy dominante. Ella se casó por fin con Rubén pero hasta vivían en casas distintas...

—¿Ella seguía viviendo en La Habana Vieja?

—Cómo te acuerdas... Sí, y él en Lawton, te imaginas... Bueno, el asunto es que Rubén le dijo que se quería ir y le pidió que arreglaran los papeles. Ella le dijo que no podía por la madre. Más nunca hablaron de eso, y como un año después él se fue, así, de un día para otro. Ella sufrió mucho y se volcó en los animales. Tú sabes que le encantaban los perros. En casa de Rubén tenía varios y cuando él se fue, tuvo que buscar para dónde llevarlos. Un día estaba en casa de los amigos que se habían quedado con los perros, y se puso a arreglarles el patio, acabada de almorzar, bajo un sol terrible. Todo el mundo le decía que lo dejara, que cuando bajara el sol la ayudarían. Pero ya sabes lo cabezona que era. Nada, le dio una embolia. Yo estuve cuidándola en el hospital... Nos turnábamos Magaly y yo... Duró una semana.

—¿Y la madre?

—La madre vivió como cinco años más y lo único que hacía era quejarse de que Gilda le hubiera hecho eso a ella...

—¿Le hubiera hecho qué...?

—Morirse.

—Qué mujer...

—No, y lo más raro fue que de pronto en la funeraria entró un perro chino...

—¿Un perro chino?

—Sí, chica, de esos muy feos… como con bigotes…

—Bueno… ¿Y?

—Nada, que se pasó allí, junto a la caja, toda la noche. Armandito decía que era el delegado de los perros que había venido a rendirle tributo.

—La pobre… Mira que ha habido desgracias… yo la quería mucho. ¿Te acuerdas cómo nos hacía cuentos?

—Sí… pero era un poco amargada. No es para menos. Tuvo una vida difícil. ¿De qué te ríes…?

—De lo del perro chino…

—Es que Cuba es un país surrealista.

Había momentos, sí, en que reíamos, pero en otros la angustia acumulada por tantos años, resurgía con fuerza, y de pronto sentía necesidad de abrazar a mi hermana y de decirle cuánto la había extrañado en todos estos años.

—Yo sé, mi hermana, yo sé. Yo también te he extrañado mucho…

Entonces, sentadas sobre la cama, llorábamos abrazadas, balanceándonos y recordando, acaso inconscientemente, cuando nuestra madre y nuestra abuela nos mecían en aquellos sillones tan cubanos…

Para mí era importante que mi hermana entendiera lo que significaba vivir fuera del país de uno:

—Tú no sabes lo que es un exilio, lo que es viajar y cuando a uno le preguntan de dónde es, siempre tener que explicar, soy de Cuba, pero vivo en tal lado… Es como ser huérfana… peor… es como si te hubieran dejado en un torno de la beneficencia… como no tener padres, no tener apellido…

—Pero al menos has viajado… la Isla a veces es como una gran prisión…

Le conté cómo al principio una de las cosas que más me angustiaba era ir a los lugares, a los cines, o a las tiendas, y no encontrarme nunca a nadie conocido… En Columbus nunca habíamos visto ni a un cubano.

—Y trabajas, Menchu, y sabes que si trabajas puedes alcanzarlo todo, o casi todo, menos lo que más quieres, que es vivir en tu país.

—Te das cuenta, Lauri, es todo lo opuesto de Cuba… Allá uno tiene el consuelo de vivir en su país pero trabajas y trabajas y no alcanzas nada…

—Es cierto, pero al menos tu hija nació y se crió en su tierra. Conoció a Mama Luya… A Papá… Aquí uno trata de explicarles a los hijos, para que sepan cuáles son sus raíces, pero nunca sabes si te entienden… nunca puedes compartir con ellos las cosas que han sido tan importantes para ti… tienen otra bandera, otro himno, otro idioma… aunque hablen español… Y no me malinterpretes, le estoy muy agradecida a este país, lo admiro, pero nunca jamás será el mío…

Mi hermana a su vez me hizo comprender lo que significaron los adioses para los que se quedaron, algo en lo que yo nunca había pensado.

—Lauri, ustedes no cuentan con el monopolio de la nostalgia. Mira como tienes compañeras de la escuela aquí… Marta Lola, Eloísa y yo fuimos las únicas que nos quedamos, y de los primos sólo Armandito… ¡ah! y Gilda, que murió en seguida… Ustedes se acuerdan de nosotros, pero entre nosotros ustedes son una presencia constante. Seguro que te has olvidado cuando pintaste la pared del patio en casa de Mama Luya… Bueno, ahí está todavía lo que escribiste… y ésta que está aquí lo ve todos los días… Y Mamá… Mamá no deja de hablar de Ricardo y de ti, pero sobre todo de ti.

—A veces me siento tan culpable…

—Después de que me contaste lo de Robertico comprendo por qué no has ido, pero ya ha pasado mucho tiempo y no debes dejar que te manipule desde la tumba.

—Tú sabes, Menchu, que en los últimos años me he dado cuenta de que yo viví la primera etapa del exilio en estado de shock, como anestesiada, como un robot casi… Creo que fue mi manera, y quizás la de muchos, de poder lidiar con el vuelco tan grande que dieron nuestras vidas. Pero tienes razón… Estoy decidida. Voy a ir a ver a Mamá… voy a ir a Cuba.

—Oye, piénsalo bien… no quiero que después…

—Te juro que voy a ir, aunque nada más lo pienso y se me aflojan las piernas…

—Te entiendo, yo también tenía miedo de venir.

—¿Tenías miedo de mí?

—Bueno, tú sabes...

—¡Ajá! Canalla... —y le comencé a hacer cosquillas como cuando éramos niñas.

—Lauri, por favor... —me suplicaba Menchu— por favor...

Reíamos para aliviar la tensión. Ambas intuíamos que por mucho que nos doliera había cosas que teníamos que decirnos.

—Ay, Menchu, ¿qué pasó? ¿Cómo fue posible que nos separáramos tanto?

—La vida, Lauri, la vida...

—La vida no, Fidel Castro... ese hombre no paga...

—Vamos a dejar eso...

—Yo no entiendo, Menchu, que todavía a estas alturas ustedes no quieran reconocer que se equivocaron...

—Lauri, no ganamos nada con esta discusión.

—No estamos discutiendo, Menchu...

—Bueno, ¿qué quieres que te diga? Que no debí enamorarme de Lázaro porque era marxista, que todas las horas que me pasé alfabetizando, que toda la caña que corté, que las escuelas que he diseñado, que el único lugar adonde he viajado, la Unión Soviética, que toda la miseria que he pasado, y que todos los sacrificios que hemos hecho, no valen nada... que mi vida no vale nada, que la vida de doce millones en la Isla no vale nada, que debemos agachar la cabeza ante el exilio, humillarnos, o sea, decir nos equivocamos, señores hermanos, ustedes lo saben todo, vengan, sálvennos... vengan con sus mercados abarrotados de comida, vengan con sus discursos decimonónicos a darnos lecciones, a nosotros, de patriotismo...

Mi primera reacción fue de enojo, pero después traté de colocarme en su pellejo, y acabé pidiéndole que me perdonara.

—No, Lauri, no es cuestión de perdonar sino de tratar de entendernos. Además, no lo digo tanto por ti, sino por las cosas que he oído desde que estoy aquí... ¿No se dan cuenta, mi hermana, de que para bien o para mal, ésa fue mi vida, de que ésa es Cuba, y no la que ustedes se han inventado?

—Eso... eso precisamente es lo peor de todo. Hemos vivido casi cuarenta años suspirando por Cuba, llenando nuestras casas de fotos de Cuba, de pinturas de flamboyanes de Cuba, escribiendo poesías de Cuba , componiendo canciones de Cuba, hablándoles a los hijos de Cuba, negándonos a que este país nos trague, pensando en Cuba día y noche, al tanto de las noticias de Cuba, fundando una Casa Cuba donde quiera que hay una colonia cubana, sintiéndonos extranjeros en todas partes, ¡y ahora tú me vas a salir con que tampoco en Cuba vamos a tener derecho ni a opinar! En ninguna parte contamos ni vamos a contar. Ni aquí ni allá. Somos... somos... ¡escoria!

—Ahora eres tú la que estás exagerando... Si ustedes han triunfado... mira qué casa más linda tienes...

—Menchu, no me jeringues. Esta casa es una mierda. ¿Qué coño es una casa para el que no tiene país? Yo no tengo Patria, ¿entiendes? Yo quiero a Cuba pero Cuba no me quiere a mí... ¡Oh! Y el mundo... para que te enteres... ¿tú sabes quiénes son los exiliados a quienes el mundo acoge? A los últimos, a los que ya vienen con un nombre de Cuba, a los que han sido parte del gobierno hasta antes de ayer, a los que escriben regodeándose en la miseria de allá... porque, oye, la miseria vende, el sexo vende, el meneo de los fondillos en los escenarios vende... el toque de tambores vende... pero ¿y los muertos, Lauri, y los presos, y los ahogados, y los fracasados como Robertico, y los exiliados anónimos de todos los días... y mis hijos que son americanos y no lo son... de apellido Fernández y pelo negro? En ellos nadie quiere pensar. Ellos no cuentan.

—Óyete hablar. Son cosas que si te las hubiera dicho Robertico se las hubieras rebatido.

—Sí, pero en parte tenía razón.

—Sí, todos tenemos parte de razón y ninguno tiene toda la razón.

—Si yo tuviera un sólo deseo para Cuba ¿sabes cuál sería? Que ningún cubano tuviera que vivir exiliado. Nunca más, Menchu, nunca más.

—Y yo prohibiría los adioses... Pero no llores así, mi hermana, por la memoria de Papá te lo pido. Mira, si parece un sueño, boba, aquí estamos, juntas, recordando tantas cosas.

—Un sueño... ¡Una pesadilla ha sido nuestra vida! Cuando la vivíamos no nos dábamos cuenta, pero la retórica de la Guerra Fría fue... fue muy fuerte. Yo estaba en Washington...

—Sí, esa fue mi etapa moscovita... Pero ya no pienses en eso. Lo importante es que hoy sabemos que es mucho más lo que nos une que lo que nos separa.

—Sí, a nosotras sí, pero, ¿y se hubieran entendido Robertico y Lázaro?

—No sé... no sé siquiera si nos hubiéramos entendido tú y yo si ellos vivieran.

—Es que las mujeres somos distintas... Y con Pedritín, ¿llegaré a entenderme?

—Si tratas...

—Y si trata él ¿...no?

—El gesto de mandarte el collar ya es una buena señal... Mira, yo también tengo mis dudas de cómo me llevaré con Ricardo.

—Muy bien... ya verás... se van a llevar muy bien, si Ricardo es un pedazo de pan con ojos...

—También Pedritín... Ése es el drama, tanta gente buena a quienes les han repartido los papeles de malos de la película.

—Lauri, eso me ha hecho pensar en las películas de vaqueros...

—¿Te acuerdas cómo adorábamos a Roy Rogers?

—Todavía aquí, en el exilio, a mi suegro le encantaba ver los episodios de Wyat Earp y a Pedro Pablo también.

—No me has dicho más nada de él...

—Hace poco murió...

—¿Tu suegro?

—No, Roy Rogers. Roberto ahí anda... con sus ochenta y pico de años... Está bien... bueno, con sus achaques... Olga lo cuida mucho. El problema de las personas mayores aquí es muy serio.

—No será peor que allá... Fíjate, uno de mis antiguos compañeros de trabajo acaba de operarse de una hernia, porque cada vez que tenía que llevar a su abuela al médico había que cargarla para bajar y subir las escaleras. Era una mujer alta y más bien gorda... te imaginas... Menos mal que la pobre vieja ya se murió... esa gente ha pasado tanto...

—Oye, Mechita... ¿te acuerdas cuando te decíamos así porque explotabas por cualquier cosa...?

—Alguna ventaja tienen los años... a mí me han dado paciencia.

—Y a mí, confianza en mí misma... ¡Si uno supiera de joven lo que sabe de mayor!

—También he aprendido a estar sola.

—¿Sufriste mucho con lo de Lázaro?

—Sí, todavía lo extraño. Y a mi hija. Ahora sólo tengo a Mamá. Pero es como si los papeles se hubieran invertido, y ella fuera mi hija y yo la madre. Si supieras que estando allá a veces me quejo, sobre todo por las obligaciones constantes, pero ahora que llevo unos días fuera, la extraño como loca...

—Mañana mismo vamos a ir a la agencia a llenar los papeles para mi viaje... y... después te voy a llevar a comer al Versalles. Caballero, parece mentira que lleves aquí dos semanas y no hayamos ido...

—Bueno, y allá yo te voy a llevar al Palenque... es como un bohío grande, yendo por la Quinta Avenida, pasado el Yacht Club...

—Nada más pensarlo y me entran escalofríos por dentro... y me da un salto en el estómago.

—No se lo voy a decir a Mamá hasta última hora o no va a haber quien la aguante...

—Oye, toda esta ansiedad me ha dado hambre... ¿Tú crees que ya es hora de una visita a la cocina?

A las dos nos encantaba el chocolate y nos dábamos tremendos atracones de helado todas las noches. A veces Menchu me decía con tono nostálgico:

—Allá son muy buenos los helados...

Yo me burlaba de ella:

—Sí, y tienen más sabores que en Baskin Robbins.

—No, ya no hay muchos sabores, pero son riquísimos.

Todas las conversaciones abrían la puerta de un nuevo recuerdo:

—Oye, ¿te acuerdas del Tropicream que había en la Calle Doce…?

—Claro…

—Íbamos mucho cuando pepillas.

—Y a las matinés en el Cine Miramar…

—Si ahí fue que conocí a Robertico… Tú no habías ido ese día… ¿Has pensado alguna vez qué hubiera pasado si Robertico se hubiera enamorado de ti en vez de mí?

—No, no lo he pensado… pero me imagino que yo hubiera tenido tu vida y tú la mía.

—Sí, son vidas intercambiables… que por un accidente del destino, como que no fuiste al cine una tarde…

A veces, de lo trivial, surgían preguntas que quizás antes ni nos habíamos atrevido a hacernos a nosotras mismas.

—Tú no has sido feliz, ¿verdad, Lauri?

—No, y no sólo por Robertico, sino porque siempre he vivido con la idea de que se trataba de una etapa transitoria, de que mi vida estaba en Cuba. Y ya ves, se me ha ido la vida… Pero tampoco la cambiaría por la tuya. No tendría los hijos que tengo… y… tú tampoco has sido feliz.

—Quizás la felicidad no exista.

—Quizás sólo haya instantes felices y ésos los hemos tenido.

—Mira… éste es uno de ellos…

—Sí… Otra cosa que he aprendido con los años es que nadie hace feliz a nadie. Uno se hace su propia felicidad y viene de muchas partes. ¿Me entiendes? Me casé tan enamorada de Robertico, creía que él era responsable de mi dicha, que las cosas que no compartía con él no contaban… y después me he ido dando cuenta de que no es así…

—Yo tenía un amigo que decía que a la vida había que amarla desinteresadamente, por sí misma…

—Qué frase más cierta.

—¿Tú sabes qué es lo peor de ir envejeciendo?

—…que se te caen las tetas…

—Lauri, en serio… lo peor para mí son los muertos. Me acuerdo que cuando éramos niñas y nos llevaban a la Parroquia el Día de los Santos Difuntos, yo rezaba por Tío Nel y por aquella compañerita que murió de leucemia cuando estábamos en quinto grado… y por el abuelo que no llegamos a conocer… ésos eran entonces nuestros muertos, pero ahora…

—Sí… Mama Luya… Papá… Robertico… Lázaro… Julio Eduardo… Adela…

—Gilda… Camilito…

—Vidal…

—¿Murió el tío de Robertico?

—Sí, bastante joven.

—¿De cáncer también?

—No sé. Yo creo que de SIDA. No me di cuenta hasta muchos años después, pero era homosexual y al principio de la epidemia se fue en unos meses.

—Pobre hombre. Y hasta gente de nuestra edad se empieza a morir.

—El año pasado tres amigos míos…

—No puedo pensar en el día que me falte Mamá.

—Y Tía Flor…

—También nacen otros. No puedo creer que ya seas abuela… Es la vida… Pero mejor cambiamos el tema.

En algunos momentos compartíamos aspectos tan íntimos de nuestras vidas que ninguna de las dos nos habíamos siquiera atrevido a dejarlos por escrito en nuestros respectivos diarios.

—A ver, además de Gastón ¿no has tenido otros amores?

—Bueno, nada serio… ¿y tú?

—Tampoco nada serio, pero sí…

—Qué calladito te lo tenías… cuéntame.

—Bueno, es un español que viaja a Cuba por negocios de vez en cuando.

—Mi hermana, a lo mejor te casas y más adelante te vas a España, ya tienes allá a Tania.

—Y hasta Ernestico está ahora en Madrid… pero no, Lauri.

—¿Por qué no?

—Porque es un hombre encantador, bien parecido, culto, que ha viajado... con plata...

—Pero es casado...

—No... aunque algo debe tener por allá...

—¿Entonces?

—Parte de mi atractivo para él es mi ambiente. Ese hombre está enamorado de Cuba, no de mí. Si me llevara a su mundo, yo estaría fuera de lugar. Romperíamos la magia de lo que tenemos ahora y ninguno de los dos seríamos felices.

—Es cierto que los años dan madurez.

—Bueno, ahora cuéntame tú.

—Prométeme que no te vas a escandalizar.

—¿Escandalizarme yo? ¡Con las cosas que he visto en la vida!

—Me da pena...

—Mi hermana... no seas boba.

—Bueno, tengo una relación con un muchacho más joven que yo.

—Me parece muy bien.

—Es sólo un poco mayor que Pedro Pablo... pero es muy maduro.

—¿Y?

—Y un amante maravilloso. Olvídate, chica, que en la cama no es lo mismo un hombre a los 50 y pico que a los 30 y pico. Ya se me había olvidado.

—¿Y estás enamorada de él?

—No, ni él de mí, pero nos gustamos y nos queremos. No te lo puedo explicar. Es parte de crecer, de darse cuenta de que las cosas en la vida no son todas de acuerdo al libreto que nos dieron. ¿Me entiendes?

—Claro... Y me parece muy bien. ¿Tus hijos lo saben?

—No... por Dios. Lo bueno es que ninguno de los dos hemos tratado de complicar las cosas. Tampoco me sentiría cómoda saliendo con él. ¡Se creerían que es mi hijo!

Cada día que pasaba valoraba más el grado de compenetración que habíamos logrado mi hermana y yo. Nos habíamos separado en la adolescencia y nos reencontrábamos como dos mujeres ya maduras, pero era como si el tiempo no hubiera pasado.

—Ay, Menchu, yo creo que no he hablado con nadie así desde que me fui de Cuba...

—Yo tampoco, Lauri.

—Prométeme que nunca más estaremos tan separadas.

—Las cosas van a ser distintas de ahora en adelante.

—Si hubiera cambios en Cuba.

—Los habrá algún día... Lo que yo no quiero es que le hagan daño a Cuba... que humillen a los cubanos.

—Yo tampoco quiero eso. Pero es tan largo el proceso... ¿Qué hacemos mientras...?

—¡Si yo tuviera la respuesta!

—Por lo pronto hay que irse a dormir que deben ser como las 3 y pico de la madrugada.

—¡Por Dios... el tiempo vuela! Si está a punto de amanecernos...

Ya habíamos apagado las luces, cuando oí que me preguntaba:

—Oye, Lauri, ¿te acuerdas de cuando Mamá nos vestía iguales? —y me dormí con la imagen de dos niñas, con idénticas batas de organza, correteando alegres en un jardín de La Habana bajo la sombra generosa de un almendro.

A la mañana siguiente, mientras desayunábamos, observé a mi hermana. En unas pocas semanas había cambiado. De pronto me parecía como si estuviera contemplando mi propia imagen.

—Oye, tú has engordado desde que llegaste... o como diría Mamá, estás más repuestica... Pero ¡ese pelo! Ahora mismo nos vamos las dos a pelar y a teñir —y enseguida llamé para pedir turno.

De la peluquería salimos para las tiendas.

—Escoge lo que quieras, Menchu... y deja de fijarte en los precios.

Entramos juntas al probador con el mismo pantalón blanco y la misma blusa de cuadritos blancos y negros.

—Me recordó un ajuar que teníamos de jovencitas.

—A mí también.

De pronto, vestidas y peinadas iguales, nos miramos al espejo, y nos quedamos mudas. Era como si estuviéramos viendo doble. Éramos otra vez idénticas.

—¿Tú crees que Mamá nos podrá distinguir todavía? —le pregunté.

—Pronto sabremos… ¿No?

CAPÍTULO TRECE
Juntas de nuevo

CUANDO MENCHU REGRESÓ A CUBA, sentí un vacío tan grande que temí caer en un estado depresivo. La extrañaba inmensamente. Al principio me costó trabajo hablar de lo que había significado para mí el reencuentro con mi hermana. Temía que nadie me entendiera. Pero en cuanto me decidí a compartir con otros mi experiencia, comencé a enterarme de historias muy similares. A pesar de todo, los valores de familia habían sobrevivido por encima de las diferencias ideológicas. Me conmovió el entusiasmo de mis hijos cuando les confié que por fin había decidido volver a Cuba. También mi suegro me animó:

—Haces muy bien, mijita. Han pasado muchos años y debes ir a ver a tu madre. Además, es bueno que la gente vaya a Cuba…

Antes de irse Menchu, habíamos ido a la agencia de viaje y yo había llenado todos los papeles. Ahora esperaba con ansias las cuatro semanas que a veces demora el permiso de entrada a Cuba. Me daba rabia tener que pedir una visa para ir a mi país, pero después de todo, me decía, voy a ir con pasaporte americano.

Me sentía muy nerviosa. Era como si una bandada de pájaros me revoloteara dentro, desde la garganta hasta el estómago. Así que trataba de pensar en otra cosa. Me refugiaba en los recuerdos del tiempo compartido con Menchu, del viaje tan maravilloso que habíamos hecho juntas a Nueva York a ver a Ricardo y a Tía Flor, de tantos momentos felices que habíamos compartido en Miami.

Por fin me llamaron de la agencia. Me habían negado el permiso. No lo podía creer. Había estado casi cuarenta años sin querer ir a Cuba, pero nunca se me había ocurrido que no me dejaran entrar a mi propio país. Sentía tanta rabia, tanto dolor, tanta impotencia… No sabía qué hacer. Por fin llamé a Menchu.

—Cálmate… Estas cosas pasan. Déjame ver qué averiguo…

Fue un largo mes de espera hasta que oí de nuevo su voz:

—Lauri, te van a dar el permiso…

La verdad es que no sabía que viajar a Cuba pudiera ser tan complicado. Finalmente me dieron el pasaje para el viernes 2, apenas unos días antes de que se cumplieran cuarenta años de aquel 13 de julio en que me había marchado. Por primera vez en tanto tiempo Menchu y yo podríamos celebrar juntas nuestro cumpleaños.

Cuando empecé a decir que iba a Cuba, descubrí cuánta gente había ido ya. Personas que nunca me hubiera imaginado. Todo el mundo me daba consejos:

—Compra una maleta de lona… un gusano… son las que pesan menos.

—Lleva de regalo café, sobrecitos de sazón, algunos jabones… champú no, que pesa mucho…

—Es preferible comprarles cosas allá que pagar $2 por libra de exceso de equipaje.

—Pesa la maleta antes en el Publix para que no te pases de las 44 libras…

—Pon *kleenex* siempre en la cartera porque en ningún lado hay papel de inodoro… y *wipes,* por si se va el agua…

—No se te olviden las aspirinas… y antiácidos, antiestamínicos, curitas… todo lo que creas que puedas necesitar… allí no hay nada… Si no lo usas, se lo dejas a la familia.

Luego comenzaron los encargos:

—¿Puedes llevarle esta carta a mi hermana y este pomo de vitaminas?

—Si no te importa, es para mi madrina… son unos filtros de agua…

—Unos espejuelos para mi tío… por favor.

Por el día me mantenía serena, escogiendo con cuidado la ropa que quería llevar para no llamar mucho lo atención, haciendo los preparativos normales de todos los viajes —suspender los periódicos, pedirle a la vecina que me recogiera el correo y me regara las matas…— pero por las noches no podía dormir. Cerraba los ojos y veía imágenes de La Habana… una calle… un tejado… una ventana… un rostro… el mar… siempre el mar, y mucha luz, una luz tan fuerte que me despertaba. Imágenes que creía ya olvidadas desfilaban por mi mente. La ciudad de mi infancia, dormida en el subconsciente, tomaba otra vez vida. A los recuerdos se sobreponían las imágenes de esa Habana en ruinas que tantas veces había visto en los documentales. En ocasiones, justo cuando creía conciliar el sueño, tenía la sensación de que me caía en un vacío, y me despertaba sobresaltada. Otras noches contemplaba como en un trance las caras de mi hermano y de mis primos... los veía niños, como cuando me había ido, pero luego sus rostros iban cambiando, haciéndose adolescentes, hombres... En mis sueños, sin embargo, no podía distinguir a mi madre, aunque sentía su presencia, aspiraba su aroma... Cuando pasaban las horas y no lograba dormir, me ponía a estudiar un mapa de La Habana que había conseguido. Trazaba con el dedo sobre el papel el camino de mi casa a mi escuela, al conservatorio de piano, a la playa, a la casa de mi abuela, todo por las calles tantas veces recorridas... Otras veces buscaba en el internet información sobre Cuba. Era increíble la cantidad de ofertas turísticas que había.

Cuando regresé de Miami, no hacía más que pensar en mi hermana. Tenía muchas ganas de volverla a ver, pero su visita me asustaba. Lauri tenía una visión idealizada de Cuba. ¿Le decepcionaría la realidad? ¿Podría ver, entre tanta miseria, el alma verdadera de la Isla y de su gente? Estaba tan acostumbrada a vivir bien, ¿cómo se adaptaría, aunque fuera sólo por unos días, a las condiciones tan difíciles que para nosotros se habían hecho ya naturales? ¿Cómo sería el encuentro con la vieja? A veces pensaba en la historia del hijo pródigo. ¿Sentiría celos de mi hermana? ¿Cómo le afectaría la visita a Mamá? ¿Sería demasiado la emoción para su corazón? ¿Cómo se llevaría Lauri con Pedritín? ¿Y con Maruja? Me asustaba que mi hermana fuera a decir algo que hiriera a mi amiga. O viceversa.

Cuando Lauri llamó con la noticia de que le habían negado el permiso, me fui enseguida a ver a un amigo de Lázaro que tenía conexiones en las altas esferas del gobierno. Me enteré entonces de que mi hermana hacía años tenía prohibida la entrada al país.

—Tú sabes que Laura no es terrorista ni va a venir a perjudicar a nadie.

—Ahora, no; pero antes, quién sabe...

—¡Si mi hermana es incapaz de matar una cucaracha!

—Pero su marido...

—Su marido ya está muerto y enterrado.

—Sí, pero el suegro...

—El suegro es un viejo de más de ochenta años.

—Bueno, chica, déjame ver qué puedo hacer.

Afortunadamente todo se resolvió y pude comenzar los preparativos para la llegada de Lauri. Hubiera querido arreglar un poco la casa, pero me fue imposible conseguir pintura. Eso sí, encontré quien me ayudara y le di una buena limpieza. En un clóset donde Mamá y yo aún teníamos cosas guardadas en la casa de El Vedado, busqué la sobrecama que le habían regalado a Lauri por su boda y que nunca había estrenado. También me llevé las fotos de cuando cumplimos quince años, y una vieja muñeca de trapo que habíamos bautizado con el nombre de Leonor, por el cuento de Martí. Y claro, las *madonnas* de Rafael que habían adornado las cabeceras de nuestras camas cuando niñas. Con eso le preparé lo mejor posible el antiguo cuarto de Tía Flor.

¿Sospechará algo Mamá? A veces temo que una emoción tan grande de pronto pueda hacerle daño, que debo prepararla. Pero si pasa algo y Lauri no viene, será peor la desilusión.

Ya sé que nos llevamos bien, que nos entendemos, pero una cosa es allá y otra es acá... Mi ansiedad aumenta a medida que se acerca el día.

⁓

No quise molestar a nadie y fui al aeropuerto sola en un taxi. Tenía que estar a las 7 de la mañana. ¡Para un vuelo tan corto que salía a la una del día! Sentí una mezcla de tristeza y rabia cuando vi a tantos cubanos con sus maletas de lona. Algunos llevaban ruedas de bicicleta. Otros, flores plásticas para las tumbas de sus muertos. Era obvio que muchos habían hecho el viaje con anterioridad. Unos pocos, como yo, regresaban por primera vez en años.

Antes de las diez de la mañana ya todo el equipaje estaba despachado. Desayuné, compré el periódico y llamé a mis hijos por teléfono.

—Mami, todo te va a salir muy bien. Dale un beso a Tía —me animó Pedro Pablo.

—Tráeme un poco de arena de alguna playa —me pidió Bobby Junior.

También hablé con mi suegro.

—Mijita, no vas a tener ningún problema, tú verás...

Debió haberme leído el pensamiento porque la verdad es que tenía bastante miedo. A nadie se lo había confesado, pero cuando pensaba que Bobby había peleado en Bahía de Cochinos, cuando recordaba mis años en Washington de activista en favor de los derechos humanos, y que algunas veces había participado en programas de Radio Martí, me inquietaba. Incluso me veía encerrada en una celda, con unos hombres vestidos de milicianos que me ponían grabaciones en mi propia voz criticando al régimen, me mostraban fotos, recortes de periódicos, y me acosaban a preguntas. Me decía a mí misma que ya las cosas no eran así, que gente más comprometida que yo había regresado y no les había pasado nada, que yo no era una persona prominente... De todas formas, por si acaso, había dejado mi testamento y una carta para los muchachos encima de la cómoda. Al regreso me reiré de todo esto... pensaba.

Menos mal que Menchu pudo venir a Miami, pues antes de haber puesto un pie de regreso en la Isla, me ha servido de puente. A través de mi hermana he aprendido mucho de la vida en Cuba, he podido darme cuenta de que somos iguales ella y yo. Y no sólo por el parecido físico. Menchu es el espejo de la que no fui y pude haber sido.

En verdad, mi mayor miedo no es que me pase algo. Tantos años buscando cosas que me unieran a la realidad cubana, luchando porque no se me convirtiera en una imagen distorsionada, de foto amarillenta, por no vivir divorciada de la gente en la Isla, bebiendo en las pupilas de los recién llegados las imágenes de mi tierra, tendiendo la mano a pesar de tantas y tan diversas distancias... ¿Lo habré conseguido? Acaso, pese a tantas precauciones, lleve exceso de equipaje. ¿En qué maleta pongo mi dolor de exiliada, la nostalgia acumulada, el desarraigo sufrido? En definitiva, lo que más temo es que me vaya a sentir extranjera en mi patria. Entonces no tendría ya sitio en el mundo. Aquí, en Estados Unidos, nunca me sentiré que pertenezco. ¿Será cierto que regreso, al fin, a casa?

✺

Pedritín se ofreció para llevarme a buscar a Lauri. Hubiera preferido ir sola, pero no tengo carro y no me parece bien ir en taxi. Además, aunque él me lo dijo como si fuera por hacerme el favor, quizás en el fondo también quiera ir a recibirla. Mamá luce de lo más tranquila, pero no puedo creer que no sospeche algo. Ella siempre se las lleva en el aire.

✺

Por fin despega el avión. Miami se aleja. Siento el corazón latiéndome con fuerza. Nos sirven una merienda, pero no puedo probar bocado. Apenas han pasado unos minutos, cuando oigo a alguien que dice:

—Ya se ve.

Aprieto el rostro contra el cristal. Esta vez no es como cuando el viaje a la base de Guantánamo que hubo que tomar una ruta más larga porque no se podía volar sobre la Isla, y demoramos muchísimo. Ahora, apenas dejamos de ver los Everglades, cuando, entre nubes, se divisa ya la costa norte. Dios mío, es como una máquina del tiempo. Cuarenta años salvados en cuarenta minutos. Cuatro décadas en que mi tierra ha estado tan lejos cuando en realidad está tan cerca. El avión va dando la vuelta, y, de pronto, diviso La Habana, la forma inconfundible de su bahía, la cúpula del Capitolio que brillaba bajo el sol, y, como el centinela que en los cuentos de hadas custodia los viejos castillos, el Morro, fiel guardián de la ciudad y de mis recuerdos de niña.

Los pasajeros comenzaron a cantar el Himno Nacional. No pude unirme al coro porque no me salía la voz. Para mis adentros, muy bajito, le di gracias a la Virgen porque Cuba y mi madre me hubieran esperado tantos años.

Reconocí en seguida el viejo aeropuerto, pero el avión siguió de largo hasta detenerse en una terminal nueva, más pequeña. "Aeropuerto José Martí" decía en grandes letras azules. Me temblaban las piernas cuando pisé por primera vez mi suelo. Sentí que las palmas me daban la bienvenida. Las palmas novias de Martí, las palmas que opacaban la majestuosidad del Niágara ante los ojos melancólicos del Heredia. Tuve un extraño deseo de inclinarme a besar la tierra. Pero olvídate, con el poco ejercicio que hago, va y no me puedo levantar después... ¿Caballero, cómo lo hará el Papa, tan viejecito...? Mira que uno piensa cosas absurdas en los momentos más graves. Ya estaba frente a la caseta de Inmigración cuando me asaltaron las dudas otra vez. ¿Y si no me dejan entrar? El oficial me pareció tan jovencito...

—No me pierda este papel que lo tiene que presentar a la salida... —me dijo en tono amable, casi cariñoso.

—Puede pasar... Y... bienvenida a su país... —oí sus palabras mientras sonaba un timbre y empujaba la puerta hacia el salón de aduana.

Primero vi a Pedritín. No se parecía a las fotos que me habían mandado sino a la imagen que veía en mis sueños. Tenía la misma carita de niño. Nos dimos un abrazo apretado. Sentí que todo el rencor acumulado se disolvía en lágrimas, que había recuperado de golpe a mi hermano menor y me invadía de nuevo aquella alegría sin límite que había experimentado cuando nació.

—Bueno, ¿y para mí no hay nada...? —me reclamaba Menchu. La abracé.

—Oye... ni que nos hubiéramos puesto de acuerdo...

Entonces me di cuenta de que estábamos vestidas iguales, con el pantalón y la blusa que habíamos comprado juntas en Miami.

Montamos en el Lada de Pedritín. La primera impresión no fue buena. Cuba me pareció un país subdesarrollado, tan distinto a como yo lo recordaba. Las llegadas a las ciudades no suelen ser bonitas, pensé para animarme. Tampoco reconocía muchas cosas. Hasta que, de pronto, Menchu me dijo:

—Mira, Lauri… —y me indicaba a mano derecha.

—¡Pero si es Río Cristal…! ¿Te acuerdas cuando íbamos los domingos con Tía Flor y sus amigos escritores?

—Claro… si estaba siempre Rómulo Gallegos.

—Y Andrés Eloy Blanco.

Cuando llegamos al Palacio de los Deportes brotaron nuevos recuerdos.

—Papá nos traía aquí todos los años al circo.

—¡Y Mamá luego nos desinfectaba con alcohol!

—¿Cómo está Mamá, Menchu?

—Bien… cada día se parece más a Mamá Luya. Como duerme en el cuarto que era de ella y ahora también se acuesta a la siesta, te juro que a veces me parece que es Mama Luya. Con las vitaminas que tú mandas ha recuperado algo la vista, pero no del todo. Eso sí, la mente la tiene bien clara.

—Me voy a desviar un momento para llevar unos papeles al correo. Así le damos un paseíto a Lauri antes de llegar a casa… —dijo Pedritín.

—Mejor… así ya Mamá estará levantada cuando lleguemos —comentó Lauri.

Pasamos por la Plaza de la Revolución, con su gran monumento a Martí y el mural del Che Guevara… Bajamos por la Calle G, o Avenida de los Presidentes…

—¿Ésa no era la consulta de nuestro médico? —pregunté, pues a cada paso iba reconociendo más y más lugares.

Cuando al final de la calle divisé el Malecón, tuve que sacar un kleenex de la cartera.

—Tranquila, mi hermana… que aún te quedan muchas emociones.

Pedritín entró al tunel. Apareció del otro lado la fuente donde comienza la Quinta Avenida.

—¿Aquí no estaba Kasalta…? Nos traían en los cumpleañoss y nos encantaba comer bisté empanizado con espaguetis.

—No... no estaba Kasalta... está... lo están arreglando...

—No lo puedo creer...

—¿Y por aquí no estaba el reloj...?

—Sí, míralo...

—¡Qué memoria, mi hermanita!

—Pedritín... Yo... yo nunca he olvidado esto... y la Iglesia de Santa Rita... ¡Ay, Menchu!, si por aquí vivía Gracielita y montábamos bicicleta en ese parque...

—Ahora se llama Emiliano Zapata.

—Mira... mira, la casa de Grau... si todavía tiene los tinajones...

En la calle de La Copa, Pedritín dobló a la derecha.

—Es que han puesto un correo aquí... —me explicó Menchu.

—Pero si ésta es la casa de Lucrecia y Anita...

—Bueno... ahora es la Embajada de Serbia.

Pedritín parqueó y me tiré de la máquina.

—Menchu, ¡las veces que veníamos aquí a jugar con ellas! Cómo me acuerdo de Tío Ernesto... En esta casa murió... Y allí estaba el Centro Comercial y el Lisboa.

—Están... ahí están todavía...

—Es como si el tiempo se hubiera detenido. —Yo pasaba del llanto, a la risa, al asombro.

Mientras Pedritín despachaba las cartas, Menchu y yo caminamos por la cuadra recordando el antiguo barrio de nuestras primas.

—Aquí vivían los Moreno, ¿te acuerdas?

—Y aquí estaba la bodega de Luis...

—Y allá la Quincalla de Fuentes...

—Estos edificios de apartamentos sí que están deteriorados...

Pedritín nos había alcanzado en el carro y nos tocaba el fotuto. Enseguida me monté.

—Vamos, Menchu, apúrate, que ya no aguanto las ganas de ver a Mamá.

A veces me parecía que era niña otra vez y que íbamos a casa de mi abuela. De pronto todo me era tan familiar como si nunca me hubiera ido. Cuando llegamos y vi la casita tan despintada sentí un latigazo de dolor y de vergüenza.

La reja del jardincito del frente, las lozetas verdinegras que llegaban hasta los tres escalones de entrada, el farolito de la luz, todo estaba idéntico. Nunca antes había sentido una emoción mayor, pero, al mismo tiempo, me encontraba serena.

—Déjame entrar sola. Como estoy vestida igual que tú y no ve bien, y como no me espera, me confundirá contigo.

—Entra diciéndole "¿Qué hay, viejita, dormiste bien el mediodía?," y dale un beso.

Seguí las instrucciones de mi hermana.

—Bien... mijita, dormí bien y tuve un sueño muy lindo. Enseguida te lo cuento, pero primero alcánzame un vaso de agua.

Entré derecho a la cocina. Se me llenaron de lágrimas los ojos cuando vi los mismos vasos de aluminio que teníamos cuando me fui, cada uno de un color distinto. Nunca más había pensado en ellos, y ahora recordaba perfectamente que el de Mamá era el verde. Pero no estaba allí. Entonces se me ocurrió abrir el refrigerador y lo encontré dentro.

—Toma, Mamá.

—Gracias, mija.

Me senté en la butaca al lado de mi madre. Tenía unas ganas locas de abrazarla, de echarme en su regazo llorando, pero me contuve.

—Bueno, ¿no me vas a contar el sueño?

—No lo recuerdo bien... tú sabes como son los sueños... pero era algo de un hombre que tenía dos hijos, uno que se va por muchos años y el otro se queda...

Me quedé sin respiración. ¿Me habría reconocido?

—¿Y...?

—No... son boberías mías... luego te lo cuento... ven... acércate, que ahí estás a contra luz y casi no te veo...

Me senté en el suelo, a los pies de mi madre, como cuando de niña lo hacía a los de mi abuela. Me acarició el pelo.

—Tú sabes que con este problema de la vista, a veces ando bizca...

—¿Sí?

—Fíjate que raro, tú estás aquí conmigo y a mí me parece como si te viera por ahí por un pasillo... ¿No será tu hermana...?

∽

Cuando Mamá la reconoció, Lauri comenzó a llorar tan fuerte que Pedritín le tuvo que traer un vaso de agua.

En seguida salí de mi escondite, y traté de quitarle un poco de dramatismo a la situación por temor a que el impacto de las emociones le hiciera daño a Mamá:

—¡No te pudimos engañar, vieja! Y eso que no ves bien...

—El corazón de una madre es difícil de engañar... Además, ¿para quién si no para Lauri iban a ser todos esos preparativos? No creas que porque no haya preguntado no me había dado cuenta...

Nos pasamos la tarde entre risas, lágrimas, recuerdos y planes de lo que haríamos en los próximos días.

Lauri no podía separarse de Mamá. De continuo se le acercaba y la abrazaba:

—Me parece mentira... me parece mentira.

—A mí también, mija, a mí también.

Lejos de ponerme celosa, como había temido, sentía una inmensa alegría y un profundo alivio, como si ese raro vacío, esa especie de frío interno que me había herido el pecho todos estos años, se fuera convirtiendo poco a poco en una tibia llama, en un cálido bálsamo.

∽

Lo primero que hicimos a la mañana siguiente fue ir al cementerio. Cuando esperábamos en la Calle 12, casi esquina a Zapata, a que nos prepararan dos jarrones de flores, sentí que las imágenes se me sobreponían, que el tiempo pasado invadía el presente. Veía a mi madre joven. Ricardo era de nuevo un muchachón. Menchu y yo íbamos de la mano de Papá a poner flores a Tío Nel.

Cuando llegamos al panteón, me sorprendió como el paso del tiempo le había robado al mármol negro todo su brillo y su color, y sentí que ese punto de dolor y vacío que me dejó para siempre en el alma el fallecimiento de mi padre, comenzaba a sangrar de nuevo. Y lloré, lloré esas lágrimas que no había podido derramar el día que había recibido la noticia de su muerte. Me alivió colocarle las flores y rezar junto a mi hermana bajo el cálido sol patrio.

Visitamos después la tumba de los abuelos. Evoqué con claridad la imagen de Mama Luya en el descanso de las escaleras, su mirada gris acero sosteniendo la mía, tal y como la había visto por última vez hacía cuarenta años cuando salí de Cuba aquel 13 de julio. Y me eché a llorar otra vez.

—Vamos, Lauri… no te pongas así…

En los días sucesivos recorrimos nuestra antigua escuela, la iglesia donde hicimos la primera comunión, la playa donde aprendimos a nadar. La vieja casona de El Vedado, donde transcurrió nuestra infancia y adolescencia, estaba como suspendida en el tiempo. Los mismos canteros en el portal, el mismo vitral de tonos azules en el medio punto de la puerta de entrada, las mismas lozas verdes y negras… No sé por qué los pisos me impresionaron mucho. Quizás el universo del niño está muy cerca del suelo. Sobre él nos sentábamos a jugar a los yaquis, a hacer la tarea, a pintar. Y apostábamos a ver quién podía caminar más sin tocar las rayas…

Es increíble cómo Lauri se acuerda de todo. Cuando pasamos por la Casa de la Cultura, enseguida comentó:

—Ese edificio era antes el Liceo…

Cuando vio la Giraldilla, el monumento a los estudiantes, el Templete, se emocionó como si se hubiera encontrado con viejos amigos. Pedritín estaba boquiabierto de que supiera más de la historia de La Habana que él mismo.

—Aquí se dio la primera misa...

—A este hotel venía mucho Hemingway... —Sacaba foto tras foto y repetía, como nosotros aquí:

—No es fácil... no es fácil...

Frente a la Catedral, el Palacio de los Capitanes Generales, la Iglesia de San Francisco, la Plaza Vieja, parecía un peregrino que llegaba a Tierra Santa.

—Menchu, la Habana Vieja es preciosa...

—Sí, y la están restaurando muy bien... antes de jubilarme yo ayudé con algunos planes de reconstrucción...

Lauri todo lo elogiaba. Una tarde tomando helados de coco con "limonadas cubanas" en un café en la Plaza de Armas, exclamó feliz:

—Oye, Menchu... tú tienes razón, los helados aquí son riquísimos.

—Debe ser el azúcar...

En la Bodeguita del Medio nos sucedió algo inaudito. Lauri insistió en invitarnos a tomar un mojito. De pronto se levantó de la barra como si tuviera un resorte en el fondillo y fue directa a unas viejas fotos detrás de un cristal.

—Miren... miren... aquí está Tía Flor en esa foto...

Y en efecto, allí estaba, en medio de un grupo de personas, entre las que me pareció reconocer al poeta Guillén.

—Todos estos años nunca nos habíamos dado cuenta de que esa foto estaba ahí, y Lauri acaba de llegar y la encuentra en un momento... —Pedritín se sorprendió de nuevo.

—Ay, mi hermanito, es que yo en realidad nunca me he ido.

La Patria me acogía, me abrazaban las ramas, me acariciaba la brisa, me sonreían las calles, me guiñaban los ojos los marpacíficos, bailaban para mí los crotos. Las olas se rompían contra el Malecón bañando mi piel y el salitre sobre mi rostro se me confundía con las lágrimas. En cada calle aparecía un recuerdo: la casa de alguna amiguita, la consulta de un médico, un cine muchas veces frecuentado. Hasta se me antojaba que los venados a la entrada del zoológico saltaban a darme la bienvenida.

La Habana —es cierto— está deteriorada. Me hace pensar en una gran dama venida a menos, avejentada, mal pintada, mal vestida, que muestra al descubierto sus heridas y arrugas, pero que conserva intacta su elegancia y su dignidad. Quizás el mayor consuelo lo hallé en los árboles: en esos almendros frente a mi casa cuyas sombras cobijaron mis sueños infantiles, en los altos pinos en Playa Veneciana, en las uvas caletas, en las esbeltas palmas, en los gruesos tronco en el Parque del Ahorcado, donde jugamos tantas tardes de nuestra infancia.

A cada rato Lauri nos decía lo mismo:

—No ha sido nostalgia de exiliados. Es verdad. Nuestro cielo es más azul, nuestras playas son más bellas, nuestro aire es más límpido.

Con tantos halagos a Cuba, en seguida se ganó a Pedritín que de inmediato olvidó toda la basura que había hablado y se deshizo en atenciones con ella.

Yo también me sentía feliz. Mis inquietudes habían sido infundadas. Lauri se comportaba distinto en La Habana que en Miami. De verdad parecía que nunca se había ido. Fue generosa con todos, pero siempre con mucho tacto, para no herir a nadie.

—Menchu, ¿tú crees que Maruja se ofenda si le hago algún regalo? Tú sabes... además de los jabones que le traje... si le dejo algún dinerito... ella fue tan buena en quedarse con Mamá cuando tú fuiste a verme...

El reencuentro con los primos también fue maravilloso. Nos pudimos reunir todos en la casa de El Vedado el día de nuestro cumpleaños. Lauri congenió muy bien con Magaly, y con Armandito, ni se diga, como si hubieran dejado de verse el día anterior. Se pasaron la noche hablando de pelota. Hasta con la mujer de Pedritín se llevó bien.

Lamenté que no estuviera Tania con nosotros.

—Ni Ernestico... —añadió Mamá.

∽

Los veintiún días que pasé en Cuba, los viví intensamente, como queriendo recuperar el tiempo perdido. Caía en la cama exhausta. Y dormía como un lirón. Nunca me había pasado algo así; no extrañaba a Miami, ni siquiera a mis hijos, aunque en ocasiones pensaba cómo me gustaría regresar con ellos.

No sé que disfruté más, si los paseos con mis hermanos, o los ratos que compartí con Mamá, a quien le fui contando mi vida, pero de forma distinta que a Menchu, tratando de suavizar los momentos difíciles y de enfatizar los aspectos positivos. Sobre todo, le hablé mucho de mis hijos y de Tyler. Hice todo lo posible por atenderla y aliviar un poco a mi hermana. A los pocos comenzó a cambiarnos los nombres:

—Menchu… no, Lauri…

—Mira eso, tú que eras antes la única que podías distinguirnos, vieja… —la choteábamos.

—Se me confunden en el corazón, porque las quiero a las dos por igual.

Me sorprendió lo generoso que son los cubanos en su pobreza. En todas las casas a las que fuimos nos ofrecían café, un jugo, hasta un flan. Y eso que viven tan mal. Es lo que más me parte el alma. Quisiera poder ayudar a todo el mundo… Pude hacer algunos regalitos, pero naturalmente, Mamá y Menchu eran las que más me preocupaban. Al menos les compré un buen ventilador y comieron mejor en esos días. También les dejé la despensa con bastantes cosas para que vayan resolviendo hasta que les pueda mandar otra vez dinero. Me parecía que todo lo que hiciera por ellas era poco.

La gente se quejaba constantemente del régimen. Sólo una vez me atreví a hacerle un comentario a Menchu:

—No entiendo si todos están en contra, por qué no hacen nada…

—Menchu, porque es difícil… Además, no te fíes… hay mucha gente todavía que está con esto…

—Serán los beneficiados…

—Y los que le temen al cambio.

Una semana antes de la fecha de partida, Lauri me dijo que quería que fuéramos un par de días a Varadero. Traté de darle largas al asunto. Pero insistía:

—¿Tú crees que Mamá quiera venir? ¿O que a Maruja pueda quedarse a acompañándola? Sería sólo dos días...

—No es eso...

—¿Entonces...?

—Tú quieres dormir allá una noche, ¿no?

—Sí, porque ir y volver en un mismo día es demasiado, ¿no? Podemos ir a un hotel...

No tuve más remedio que decirle la verdad.

—Mira, Lauri, es que yo no puedo ir a los mismos hoteles.

—Menchu... no puedo creerlo...

—A veces cuando ha venido Alfredo, mi amigo español, hemos tenido problemas... por eso ahora siempre alquila una casa... prefiero no pasar el mal rato...

—Pues no te preocupes. No vamos.

—Tú puedes ir si quieres...

—No, mi hermana, de ninguna manera. Ya en otra ocasión será.

Más que no ir a Varadero, me irritó que los cubanos aceptaran tan mansamente la humillación de no poder frecuentar los lugares destinados a los turistas. Pero no dije nada.

No fue lo único que me molestó. Una noche Armandito y Magaly nos invitaron a una función de gala del Ballet Nacional en el Gran Teatro de La Habana, el antiguo Teatro Nacional.

—Ay, Menchu, pero sí aquí veníamos mucho de niñas...

En seguida me di cuenta de que la gente iba muy bien vestida, como no había visto a nadie en La Habana hasta entonces. También noté que cuando nos íbamos, Armandito le dio unas monedas a unos muchachos que andaban revoloteando cerca del automóvil, y que le decían:

—Mire que le cuidé el carro bien, compañero.

Magaly debió darse cuenta de mi mal humor.

—¿Qué te pasa que estás tan callada, Lauri? ¿No te gustó el ballet?

—No, todo lo contrario, les agradezco mucho que me trajeran.

Cuando nos dejaron en casa y nos quedamos solas Menchu y yo, no pude más:

—Mi hermana, yo no entiendo… Cuarenta años de Revolución y tantos sacrificios de tanta gente, ¡y total! Hoy en día hay una nueva clase alta… Esa gente iba muy bien vestida, calzada y perfumada… muy distinto a Maruja, a las amigas que me has presentado… a ti y a mí, que parecíamos las parientas pobres de Magaly.

—Bueno, como Armandito estaba en la FAR y ahora en una empresa mixta…

—Mira, me alegra mucho que estén bien, pero así es muy fácil ser revolucionario. ¿Tú sabes en quienes he pensado? Te vas a reír…

—No sé…

—En mis suegros… Si lo que les quitaron a ellos, y no hablo de dinero, Menchu, sino que les quitaron la vida… la vida que vivían, sus carreras, sus casas, sus barrios… si hubiera sido para que Cuba estuviera mejor, quizás hubiera valido la pena, pero ¡mira, mira bien este desastre! ¡Coño, chica, no sabes cómo me duele…!

—Lauri, tienes que comprender que las diferencias sociales que ves son características de la coyuntura actual, pero que incluso muchos de los que no pueden calzar ni vestir bien han recibido educación, atención médica, seguro social y unas posibilidades de ascenso cultural y social que no estaban a su alcance hace 50 años. Te podría mencionar nombres de hijos de criadas que hoy tienen un doctorado… o hijos de campesinos analfabetos que han llegado a dirigir centros de investigaciones.

—Menchu, no me vengas con ésa… Sí, está bien, no te niego nada de lo que me dices, ¿pero a qué precio? En los Estados Unidos también la gente más humilde puede llegar hasta a ser Presidente del país pero no al costo de tanta represión ni de quitarles a unos para darles a otros ni de acabar con las libertades individuales.

—Mi hermana, por favor, vamos a no pelear...

—De veras que yo tampoco quiero discutir... si también en este viaje he comprendido otras cosas... como por qué te aturdías tanto en el supermercado... a veces me parecías hasta... no sé... malagradecida, porque hice tantos esfuerzos porque lo pasaras bien, porque no te faltara nada... y, no te lo digo por sacártelo en cara ni mucho menos, pero allá todo cuesta dinero, y el dinero viene de lo que uno trabaja, no se da silvestre en el monte... pero ahora me doy cuenta... los cubanos son muy... no sé si decir tercos... o quizás orgullositos...

—Tal vez... pero no podemos perder la dignidad... si no...

—Otra cosa que he entendido es que nos es cierto el cliché repetido tantas veces de que han aniquilado el pasado... al contrario, si lo que no hay es nada nuevo...

—Tienes razón. Aquí lo más incierto es el futuro.

—Ay, Menchu, ¡qué desgracia la de los cubanos!

Y en la madrugada habanera, en la saleta de la casa de Mamá Luya, donde tanto habíamos correteado juntas de niñas, sentí un gran dolor por Cuba que me punzaba el corazón.

Se acercaba la fecha de la partida. Menos mal que con la casa llena de tanta gente que venían a despedirse de Lauri y a traer cartas y encargos para Miami, no habíamos tenido ni tiempo para entristecernos.

—Regresaré en cuanto pueda... —Lauri le prometía de continuo a Mamá—. Y te traeré a tus nietos.

—Ya me puedo morir tranquila.

—No digas eso, vieja, por Dios... ahora que me haces tanta falta. Además, voy a convencer a Ricardo para que venga.

∽

La tarde antes de marcharme, Menchu quiso llevarme a Casablanca. Cruzamos la bahía en la lanchita. Llegamos hasta el parador. La Habana se veía preciosa del otro lado de las aguas.

—Ven, te invito a un helado… mi último helado en Cuba…

—Bueno, en este viaje…

Sentí la necesidad de decirle algo a mi hermana:

—Menchu, yo entiendo que tú no te quieras ir. Antes no lo comprendía, pero ahora sí… y aunque me entristece que vivan con tantas dificultades y los ayudaré en lo que pueda, me alegra que ustedes estén aquí.

—Yo también sé que tú no te puedas quedar…

—Al menos, no por ahora… lo entiendes… ¿verdad?

—Sí, una cosa es unos días… pero es difícil…

—Y no es por la comida ni por la falta de agua…

—Yo lo sé. Yo también comprendí muchas cosas cuando fui a Miami.

—¿Sí?

—Pienso que muchos aquí no han sido justos con los primeros exiliados… tantas veces que se ha dicho que son traidores, vendidos a los americanos, etc., y es conmovedor ver cómo han luchado para mantener vivo el recuerdo de Cuba y trasmitirlo a los hijos. Yo sé que tú quieres a Cuba.

—Si yo digo que ser cubano es una enfermedad incurable… que se trasmite en la sangre… y a veces hasta se contagia.

—Es que Cuba tiene una especie de magia… por eso los extranjeros se enamoran de nuestro país.

—¡No sabes cuánto ha significado este viaje para mí!

—Y para todos nosotros…

—No, Menchu, no lo puedes entender. Claro que lo más importante ha sido verlos. Pero es más que eso. El regreso a mi Patria ha puesto en perspectiva toda mi vida. No lo creerás, hasta me ha hecho comprender y perdonar a Robertico, algo que no había logrado antes.

—Cuánto me alegro, mi hermana.

—Además, ahora no tengo dudas de quien soy. Ni tampoco pienso ya que mi Patria no me quiere. Aunque me muriera mañana, aunque no pudiera regresar nunca más…

—Chica, no hables así…

—Ménchu, atiéndeme… Lo que quiero decirte es que esa herida tan inmensa que llevaba dentro ha comenzado al fin a cicatrizar. Tantas veces que había pensado que la Revolución nos lo había quitado todo a los exiliados, pero no lo consiguieron… No se dieron cuenta de que llevábamos el paraíso dentro. Todos mis temores eran infundados. Me he sentido en casa, pese a todo lo demás que ni vamos a mencionar… Es una victoria, muy íntima y chiquitica, pero para mí es suficiente.

—Me alegro, Lauri… si entre los cubanos no puede haber rencores…

Habíamos ya terminado el helado. Contemplamos una vez más el perfil de la ciudad y las cambiantes luces del crepúsculo reflejándose en las agua de la bahía. Antes de irnos nos acercamos al Cristo.

Alcé los ojos ante la blanca figura que me pareció inmensamente grande.

—Ven, vamos a rezar un Padre Nuestro.

Luego nos quedamos largo rato, tomadas de la mano, en silencio.

⁓

La noche antes de irse Lauri, nos acostamos temprano. No hablamos mucho. Estábamos cansadas y sentíamos quizás que ya no hacían falta palabras para entendernos.

Me di cuenta de que Lauri trató de no dramatizar mucho la despedida para evitarle emociones a la vieja. Tal vez ella misma sintiera que ya no podía más.

⁓

Aunque esperaba volver en cuanto pudiera, en el momento de abrazar a mi madre, temí que fuera por última vez. Ahora que la había recuperado no quería perderla de nuevo. Como si me adivinara el pensamiento, me dijo en tono sereno:

—Lauri, vete tranquila, mijita. Vuelve cuando puedas… Yo siempre te estaré esperando.

∽

Pedritín había dicho que iba a mandarnos a un amigo para llevarnos al aeropuerto porque a esa hora le era imposible venir. Pero se apareció a tiempo.

—No podía dejar que te fueras sin despedirnos… Vamos, yo las llevo a Rancho Boyeros.

A todos nos pereció que el reloj caminaba con demasiada prisa. No queríamos separarnos otra vez. Sentíamos el mismo dolor en el medio del pecho como si se nos partiera de nuevo el corazón en dos.

∽

Cuando el avión despegó, estuve mirando por la ventanilla hasta que las lágrimas y la distancia no me dejaban ver más el contorno de la Isla, y todo se convirtió en azul de cielo y mar.

∽

Vi el avión despegar, lo seguí con la mirada mientras levantaba el vuelo. Cuando que se perdió entre las nubes, aún yo agitaba la mano para decirle adiós a mi hermana.

En casa, Mamá me esperaba para comer.

—Vamos, vieja, tienes que alimentarte y estar fuerte para cuando regrese Lauri.

—Sí, Lauri con sus hijos, y Ricardo y los suyos, y Tania, y Ernestico… para cuando estemos por fin reunidos todos.

—A lo mejor las próximas Navidades…

—A lo mejor...

Comíamos en silencio mientras en el noticiero hablaban de los preparativos para la próxima cumbre de los presidentes iberoamericanos que se celebraría en La Habana a fines de año. De pronto, la vieja me dijo:

—Ay, mija, apaga eso. Es siempre la misma cantaleta.

Lloro hasta que me vence el cansancio. Cierro los ojos. Pero no puedo dormir. No hago más que ver la luz cegadora de La Habana. La llevo prendida en la retina. Todavía me hiere los ojos.

BILINGUAL GLOSSARY OF CUBAN TERMS
AND IDIOMATIC EXPRESSIONS

alfabetización La campaña de alfabetización de 1961, en la cual participaba un gran número de los jóvenes, aumentó el porcentaje de los alfabetizados cubanos, según cifras oficiales, de aproximadamente 80% a 96%. (The national literacy campain started in 1961, in which large numbers of youth participated, raised the proportion of Cubans who could read and write to 96%.)

altoparlantes altavoces (speakers)

ANAP Asociación Nacional de Agricultores Pequeños (National Association of Small Farmers)

auto coche (car, automobile)

bienes raíces venta de inmuebles (real estate)

bijol una especie común en Cuba usada para sustituir el azafrán (Cuban culinary spice used instead of saffron)

bisneando haciendo negocios, vendiendo algo, a veces ilegalmente (doing business, sometimes in the black market)

bitongos privilegiados (of the privileged class)

blúmer pantalón interior femenino (panties)

bolsa negra la compraventa e intercambio extraoficial de productos y servicios, muchas veces a base de divisa (ahora llamada CUC), la moneda reservada para turistas (a cambio del peso cubano, la moneda en que se pagan los salarios). (black market)

bombillos (tubes)

cake torta, tarta, pastel (cake)

cartera licencia para manejar (driver's license)

cassettes casetes (cassettes)

CDR Comités de la Defensa de la Revolución (Committees in Defense of the Revolution, neighborhood watch groups)

chotear bromear, hacer un chiste (joke, tease, to make fun of)

contén bordillo (curb)

croto Codiaeum es un género de planta de la familia Euphorbiaceae (croton)

deshabillé negligé (negligee)

diplotiendas tiendas originalmente reservadas para vender productos de lujo a precios elevados a los diplomáticos que residían en la isla. En las diplotiendas todo se pagaba con divisa (ahora llamada CUC), un sistema monetario a base de dinero extranjero, originalmente el dólar EEUU, que se implementaba para ingresar capital al país. (diplomatic stores)

escarpines medias (Bobby socks)

FAR Fuerzas Armadas Revolucionarias (Revolutionary Armed Forces)

fiñe niño (kid)

FMC/FCW Federación de Mujeres Cubanas (Federation of Cuban Women)

fondillo trasero, nalgas (butt, ass)

formarse la piñacera armarse una pelea (start a ruckus)

fotuto bocina (car horn)

fritas hamburguesas y otros sándwiches (sandwich with meat fried on the flat grill)

guagua autobús (city bus)

guajiro campesino, residente del interior (peasant, hillbilly, hick)

gusano palabra despectiva para los cubanos que huyeron de la isla después de la revolución (worm, deserter)

jaba bolsa para hacer las compras (bag, sack)

jeringar (de jeringa) expresión idiomática para molestar, importunar (mess with, as in "don't mess with me")

jimaguas gemelas (twins)

jineteando prostituyéndose (working as a prostitute)

llevárselas en el aire darse cuenta de todo (pick up on things)

mañanita bata ligera de encaje (lacy robe)

marpacíficos flor tropical de la familia Malvaceae, de colores vibrantes (hibiscus)

Materva refresco cubano hecho a base de mate (Cuban soda made with yerba mate, a tea popular in Latin America)

mechón vela (candle)

microfracción término oficialista durante los años 60 para el sector de la izquierda cubana en contra de la revolución, pretende minimizar la extensión e impacto del mismo (official term during the 60s that minimizes the political sector of the Cuban left opposed to the Revolution (micro-fraction)

MINFAR Ministerio de las Fuerzas Armadas Revolucionarias (Ministry of the Revolutionary Armed Forces)

MINIT Ministerio del Interior (Ministry of the Interior)

MINTRAB Ministerio del Trabajo (Ministry of Labor)

mochas machete (machete)

mogotes colinas peculiares de algunas zonas de Cuba, singulares por sus topes planos (hills, flat-topped hillocks)

OEA Organización de Estados Americanos (Organization of American States)

ONU Organización de Naciones Unidas (United Nations)

paladares pequeños restaurantes en casas privadas, un tipo de cuentapropismo autorizado por el gobierno cubano (small restaurants in private homes, a type of authorized free enterprise)

papitas a la juliana Papas finitas fritas (Julienned potates, thin cut french fries)

pisicorre camioneta (station wagon)

pitusa pantalón de mezclilla (blue jeans)

refugio un programa para ayudar a los refugiados cubanos (Cuban Refugee Program at Freedom Tower)

ropón camisón para dormir (nightgown)

sayitas faldas (skirts)

sayuelas (underskirt, petticoats)

subir la parada raise the stakes

timón volante (steering wheel)

UJC Unión de Jóvenes Comunistas (Young Communist Union)

Vicarias Vicaria Catharanthus, planta con pequeñas flores (Madagascar rosy periwinkle) *vocero* persona designada para hablar por los demás (spokesperson)

yaquis cantillos, un juego de niños (jacks)

zafras cosechas de caña (sugar cane harvest)

WORKS CITED

Bohemia. 51:3 (August 2, 1959). Print.

—. *51:49* (September 20, 1959). Print.

—. *51:38* (September, 20, 1959). Print.

—. *52:2* (January 10, 1960). Print.

—. *53:34* (August 20, 1961). Print.

—. *58:12* (April 1, 1966). Print.

—. *59:39* (September 29, 1967). Print.

—. *59:13* (April 1, 1966). Print.

—. *56:50* (September 11, 1964). Print.

—. *56:35* (August 22, 1964). Print.

—. *60:38* (September 20, 1968). Print.

—. *62:18* (May 1, 1970). Print.

—. *62:18* (May 2, 1970). Print.

—. *50:35* (September 1, 1967). Print.

—. *65:52* (December 28, 1973). Print.

—. *72:15* (April 11, 1980). Print.

—. *72:17* (April 25, 1980). Print.

—. *72:18* (May 2, 1980). Print.

—. *79:2* (January 9, 1987). Print.

—. *83:5* (February 1, 1991). Print.

—. *83:7* (February 15, 1991). Print.

—. *84:31* (July 31, 1992). Print.

—. *85:23* (June 4, 1993). Print.

Castro, Fidel. Discurso pronunciado en el acto de presentación del Comité Central del Partido Comunista, en el Teatro Chaplin. (Speech delivered at the "Chaplin" Theater for the opening ceremony of the Central Committee of the Cuban Communist Party.) 3 October 1965. Web. <http://www.cuba.cu/gobierno/discursos/1965/esp/f031065e.html>.

—. Discurso pronunciado en el desfile militar con motivo de la conmemoración del VIII Aniversario de la Revolución, en la Plaza de la Revolución. (Speech delivered at the military parade and review for the commemoration of the 8th anniversary of the Revolution. Plaza of the Revolution). 2 January 1967. Web. <http://www.cuba.cu/gobierno/discursos/1967/esp/f020167e.html>.

—. Discurso pronunciado en el acto de inauguración de la presa "Vietnam Heroico" que tuvo lugar en la Isla de Pinos. (Speech delivered at the groundbreaking ceremony for the "Heroic Vietnam Dam". Isle of Pines.) 12 August 1967. Web. <http://www.cuba.cu/gobierno/discursos/1967/esp/f120867e.html>.

—. Discurso pronunciado en la inauguración del seminternado de la primaria "Juan Manuel Márquez, en Boca de Jaruco. (Speech delivered at the inauguration for the "Juan Manuel Marquez" Elementary School. Boca de Jaruco.) 15 March 1968. Web. http://www.cuba.cu/gobierno/discursos/1968/esp/f150368e.html.

—. Discurso pronunciado en la clausura del Primer Congreso Nacional de Educación y Cultura, teatro de la Central de los Trabajadores de Cuba. (Speech delivered at the closing ceremony of the 1st National Conference on Education and Culture, held at the CTC Theater.) 30 April 1971. Web. <http://www.cuba.cu/gobierno/discursos/1971/esp/f300471e.html>.

—. Discurso pronunciado en el acto conmemorativo del Primero de Mayo, Plaza de la Revolución José Martí. (Speech delivered at the ceremony to commemorate the 1st of May. Plaza of the Revolution.) 1 May 1980. Web. <http://www.cuba.cu/gobierno/discursos/1980/esp/f010580e.html>.

—. Discurso pronunciado con motivo del XXVII Aniversario del asalto al Cuartel Moncada, Las Tunas, durante el vigésimo aniversario de Playa Girón. (Speech delivered for the 28th anniversary of the attack on the Moncada Barracks, celebrated in Las Tunas during the 20 Year Anniversary of the Bay of Pigs.) 26 July 1981. Web. <http://www.cuba.cu/gobierno/discursos/1981/esp/f260781e.html>.

—. Discurso pronunciado en la clausura del VIII Congreso de la Federación de Estudiantes de la Enseñanza Media, Palacio de Convenciones. (Speech delivered at the closing ceremony for the 8th Conference of the FEEM at the Palacio de las Convenciones.) 6 December 1991. Web. <http://www.cuba.cu/gobierno/discursos/1991/esp/f061291e.html>.

Del Prado, Pura. "Monólogo de una exiliada." *La otra orilla.* Madrid, Plaza Mayor Ediciones, 1972. Print.

Facts on File Worlds News Digest. New York: Facts on File, Inc. 19.978 (July 23–29, 1959): 237–244. Print.

—. New York: Facts on File, Inc. 20.1049 (1–7 December 1960): 433–444. Print.

—. New York: Facts on File, Inc. 20.1051 (15–21 December 1960): 453–464. Print.

—. New York: Facts on File, Inc. 21.1069 (20–26 April 1961): 145–152. Print.

—. New York: Facts on File, Inc. 22.1147 (18–24 October 1962): 361–372. Print.

—. New York: Facts on File, Inc. 23.1191 (22–28 August 1963): 297–304. Print.

—. New York: Facts on File, Inc. 23.1204 (21–27 November 1963): 409–420. Print.

—. New York: Facts on File, Inc. 26.1362 (1–7 December 1966): 457–472. Print.

—. New York: Facts on File, Inc. 27.1394 (13–19 July 1967): 265–280. Print.

—. New York: Facts on File, Inc. 28.1431 (28 March–3 April 1968): 121–136. Print.

—. New York: Facts on File, Inc. 28.1432 (4–10 April 1968): 137–144. Print.

—. New York: Facts on File, Inc. 28.1441 (6–12 June 1968): 225–240. Print.

—. New York: Facts on File, Inc. 29.1502 (7–13 August 1969): 501–516. Print.

Greve, Frank and Miguel Pérez. "Castro´s Jails: Still Bulging 17 Years Later." *Miami Herald* 23 May 1976: A1. Print

Granma. Reproduced in *Bohemia,* 72:15 (11 April 1980). Print.

Guillén, Nicolás. "Fusilamiento" in *Cantos para soldados y sones para turistas,* 1937; rpt. Buenos Aires: Editorial Losada, 1961. Print.

El Miami Herald 13 October 1979. Print.

En sus proprias palabras (In Their Own Words). Dir. Jorge Ulla and and Lawrence Ott, Jr. U.S. Information Agency. 1980. Film

Miami Herald 9 April 1980: 20A. Print.

El Nuevo Herald 6 October 1979. Print.

El Nuevo Herald 11 November 1989: A1. Print.

El Nuevo Herald 8–15 June 1990. Print.

El Nuevo Herald 6 August 1994. Print.

El Nuevo Herald 12 September 1994: A1. Print.

El Nuevo Herald 13 September 1994: A1 and A6 Print.

Rivero, Raúl. *Papel de Hombre.* Havana, Unión de Escritores y Artistas de Cuba, 1970. Print.

Torres, Omar. "Impromtu." *Tiempo robado.* New York: Contra Viento y Marea, 1978. Print

Washington Post 9 August 1974: A1. Print.

Washington Post 30 April 1975: A1. Print.

Wilkinson, Mary Louise. "Unified Exile Group Claims Cash Backing." *Miami News* 2 June 1963: A1. Print.

AUTHOR'S BIO

Uva de Aragón (Havana, 1944) has published a dozen books of essays, poetry, short stories, and the novel *Memoria del Silencio* (2002), which now is offered in its first translation into English. An adaptation of the novel into a play, produced under the direction of Virginia Aponte by Ago Teatro in Caracas in the spring and summer of 2014, and in Miami in the fall of the same year, was acclaimed by audiences and critics alike. Some of her short stories and a play have also been translated and appear in textbooks and anthologies such as *The Voice of the Turtle, Cuba: A Traveler's Literary Companion, Cubana* and *Cuban-American Theater.* She writes a column for El Nuevo Herald, which can also be read in her blog *Habanera Soy* http://uvadearagon.wordpress. com. De Aragón has merited several literary awards in the United States, Europe and her native Cuba. Until her retirement in 2011, she was Associate Director of the Cuban Research Institute at Florida International University, where she also taught. Dr. de Aragón served for six years as Associate Editor of *Cuban Studies,* the most important academic journal focusing on Cuba. She is a graduate of the University of Miami, where she obtained a Ph.D. in Latin American and Spanish Literature. Uva has lived in the United States since 1959; She returned to Cuba in 1999 and now visits the Island frequently, where her work has also been included in anthologies and literary magazines. She comes from a family of writers, has two daughters and four grandsons.

TRANSLATOR'S BIO

Jeffrey C. Barnett is Professor of Romance Languages and serves as the Latin American and Caribbean Studies Program Head at Washington and Lee University. Since 1989 he has taught classes on language, culture, and literature both domestically and abroad, including courses on the Spanish-American novel of the Boom, Caribbean literature, and literary translation. His articles on Spanish-American narrative and comparative literary studies have appeared in journals in Spain, Latin America, and the U.S. He has translated a diverse selection of Latin American authors, ranging from the short stories of Carlos Fuentes to the epic poetry of Martín del Barco Centenera. Currently he is translating *Rebaños* (2010), a volume of poetry by Cuban author Zurelys López Amaya. Uva de Aragón's *The Memory of Silence* marks his first book length translation. He has lived in Honduras, Mexico, and Spain. When not in the classroom or translating, he spends his time riding cross country on his motorcycle to find inspiration for his blog "From the Road: The Moto-Odysseys of the Big Papi."